# Sabrina & Kate

OTHER BOOKS AND BOOKS ON CASSETTE
BY CHERI J. CRANE:

*Kate's Turn*

*Kate's Return*

*Forever Kate*

*Following Kate*

# Sabrina & Kate

*a novel*

## Cheri J. Crane

Covenant Communications, Inc.

Cover photograph by "Picture This . . . by Sara Staker"

Cover design copyrighted 2000 by Covenant Communications, Inc.

Published by Covenant Communications, Inc.
American Fork, Utah

Printed in the United States of America
First Printing: May 2000

07 06 05 04 03 02 01 00    10 9 8 7 6 5 4 3 2 1

ISBN 1-57734-660-2

*For my sons, Kris, Derek, and Devin,*
*who have also grown up in Kate's shadow.*

# Acknowledgments

Once again I must tip my hat to those who toiled beside me. A big thank you goes out to my husband and our three sons for their continued support and encouragement. To those friends who keep me going—*je vous aime tous!*

I would also like to express my gratitude to the people who work behind the scenes at Covenant. You play an important role in the production of these books. Thanks for all you do.

One last note. It should be mentioned that there really was a play entitled *The Adventure of a Lifetime*, written and directed by Shelley Burdick and myself in 1994 for a group of talented Mia Maids. To quote Charles Dickens, "It was the best of times, it was the worst of times." As with the characters in this book, we often questioned our sanity during that production, but the end result was very much worth the effort. Lives changed and talents were developed, including our own. It was truly the adventure of a lifetime.

# Prologue

Fifteen-year-old Sabrina Erickson anxiously paced the living room floor of her new home as she waited for her friends to arrive. She walked by the large front window, glanced out, then retreated to the couch across the room. Picking up a copy of the latest issue of the *New Era* magazine, she thumbed unseeing through the pages, her gaze riveted on the front room window. She twirled a strand of long blonde hair around one finger as her blue eyes strayed continually from the magazine in her lap.

Across the hall in the dining room, Sabrina's mother reorganized the china cabinet. Another unpacked box had surfaced, one that contained several delicate china cups with matching plates. One by one, Sue Erickson removed the treasured items from the cardboard box, carefully unwrapping the set of china she had inherited from her grandmother. When she heard Sabrina sigh, Sue glanced up, amused by her daughter's impatience. She understood Sabrina's eagerness—the Blaketown County fair was in full swing, something that promised entertainment and the chance to spend time with a group of new friends.

Sabrina and her parents had moved to Blaketown, Idaho, from Bozeman, Montana, during the summer, a transition that had been a welcome change for the entire family. Sabrina's older sister, Kate, and Kate's husband, Mike Jeffries, had moved to this community over a year ago. Both had found employment in the small Idaho town; Kate taught history and drama at the high school, while Mike supervised the local forest service office. Impressed by the friendly atmosphere, Sabrina's parents had decided to relocate to Blaketown, hoping it would give Sabrina a fresh start after a disastrous freshman year at Bozeman High. They also wanted to be closer to Kate and Mike who were now expecting their first child.

As Sue continued to muse over the events of the summer, a loud horn startled her, causing her to jump. She fumbled with the cup in her hand, but managed to catch it before it fell to the floor. When the horn sounded, Sabrina dropped the magazine on the couch and glanced out the front room window at the Jeep Cherokee now sitting in the driveway. Grabbing the jacket her mother had insisted that she take, Sabrina hurried to the front door. "Bye, Mom."

Sue, a beautiful redhead, walked out of the dining room into the entry way. Her green eyes settled on her youngest child. "You remembered your jacket?"

Sabrina smiled at her mother, holding out the jacket in question. "Yes."

"Okay . . . well . . . you girls have fun. We'll probably see you later at the rodeo tonight."

"Sounds good," Sabrina said as her friend Bev honked the horn again. "I'd better go."

"Do you have enough change?" Sue pressed.

Sabrina tried very hard not to roll her eyes. Because she was the youngest in the family, her parents had always been overprotective of her, something that had been a continued source of irritation. "Dad gave me twenty dollars this morning before he left for work," Sabrina said, opening the front door.

"Be sure to eat something before the rodeo," Sue persisted.

"We'll probably grab a hamburger at one of the food booths," Sabrina promised as she stepped out onto the porch.

"Have fun," Sue said, unaware that she had repeated herself.

Sabrina smiled. "I plan to," she said, closing the screen door behind her.

* * *

Fifteen-year-old Mandy Hopkins glanced sullenly around the crowded fairground. The thin brunette had no wish to be here, stuck in a town so small that it wasn't listed on most maps. The county fair was the biggest thing to happen in Blaketown, Idaho, since she had come to live with her aunt and uncle, Betty and Lyle Sandler, earlier that summer. Judging from the reaction of the local residents, most thought the fair was a tremendous highlight in their lives. Not Mandy—she couldn't remember a time when she had been more bored.

There had been plenty of exciting options in Salt Lake City before her parents had decided to send her to Blaketown to regain what they called a "healthy" perspective. Remembering the fun she'd had in the past, Mandy's scowl deepened. She was convinced her parents had overreacted, ruining her life because they didn't understand who she was. For years, Eric and Lorena Hopkins had tried to mold their daughter into their interpretation of a stalwart, LDS youth. Mandy was convinced there was more to life than adhering to old-fashioned beliefs. Exciting television shows and movies had introduced an appealing, uninhibited lifestyle. Lyrics that had blasted constantly on the stereo in Mandy's bedroom had enticed her to try things that were forbidden in her household. Colorful books and magazines had assured her that the life her parents wanted her to lead was not only sheltered, but stifling.

Drawn to friends who shared her outlook on life, Mandy had spent as much time with them as possible, turning her back on her parents and their "precious" standards. She had quickly realized there were several ways to get around her parents' rules. When her mother refused to let her go to school dressed in the immodest attire that her friends all sported, Mandy had learned to begin the day wearing something her mother liked. Later at school, she had changed into the offensive clothes that had been carefully tucked into her backpack the night before.

Mandy had also discovered that if she waited until her parents were both asleep, she could sneak out her bedroom window at night and rendezvous with friends. She had often hurried down the street to a waiting car that had whisked her away to the excitement she craved. Other nights she had simply caught a bus, or walked, depending on the distance.

Given little choice about attending church each Sunday, Mandy had endured countless sacrament meetings, only to slip outside to the parking lot during Sunday School to spend time with one or two teachers or priests who were also sluffing class that hour. Occasionally, they had all piled in a car to head for the nearest convenience store to pick out doughnuts or candy to munch on. Other Sundays, they had simply sat on the curb in front of the church house, discussing provocative subjects that were more interesting than scripture study. As her reputation as a "fun girl" had spread, Mandy found that she had gained a certain amount of what she thought was respect from the older boys, and as she wished, her popularity among them had soared.

Mandy had assumed that as long as she was back in time for Young Women, no one would miss her during Sunday School, including her parents. She had always made it a point to sit quietly during her Mia Maid class, certain that Sister Munson was blind to her so-called "inappropriate conduct." Mandy had never realized how that leader had agonized over her, just as she had never known about the numerous talks Sister Munson had had with her mother. Although the two women were unaware of most of Mandy's activities, they had discerned that things were far from good. The glow that radiated from other, more valiant young women, was gone. The life Mandy was choosing to lead showed in her face—in the harsh glare emanating from her defiant brown eyes.

Thinking back on all of this, Mandy knew the real trouble had started two years ago, when her parents had first complained about her "churlish" attitude, emphasizing that on a good day she was unpleasant to be around. Mandy knew this wasn't true—none of her friends had felt that way at all. Her friends had always told her to "cheer down," that she was too lighthearted when it came to something as serious as life.

In her parents' opinion, Mandy had also been spending far too much time with an undesirable young man known as Blade, an individual who took pride in wearing a nose ring, and flaunting tatoos and a bizarre, bleached hair style that defied the law of gravity. Mandy's parents hadn't given him a chance, certain he was corrupting their daughter. They had rejected the feelings Mandy had developed for Blade, unwilling to share their daughter's belief that Blade was a very sensitive, caring individual.

Recently, her parents had also worried over how Mandy and her friends had elected to dress in black attire, which was actually more modest than what they had worn in the past. Mandy had tried to explain that wearing black clothes and makeup didn't mean that they were part of an occult movement, but again, her parents hadn't listened. Instead, they had said rude things about her friends, exclaiming that these were horrible girls who thought shoplifting was a daily exercise.

Stealing was wrong and Mandy knew that; she hadn't participated the few times her friends had decided to try this challenging pastime, acting as a lookout instead. She had reasoned that her friends were only taking small items that wouldn't be missed: lipstick, mascara, candy, and gum. Unfortunately, this conduct had led to the arrest of the six girls, herself included. Their target that day had been a small convenience store managed by a man in Mandy's ward. He had dropped the charges with the understanding that Mandy and her friends would perform several hours of community service to atone for their misdeed.

It was after this incident that Mandy's parents had decided to take further action to prevent this from happening again. Rumors had been trickling their way for quite some time concerning other negative behavior that had involved their daughter, stories that had included wild parties and immoral behavior. Fearing their daughter *was* capable of such things, Eric and Lorena had agreed it was time to take a drastic stand. Nothing else they had tried had worked: the lectures, the groundings, the increased restrictions—none of it had fazed Mandy. They hoped that after spending time in a smaller community, Mandy would revert to the smiling girl they had once known and loved. They prayed that putting distance between herself and her wild friends would close this turbulent chapter in their oldest daughter's life.

"Small towns are wonderful. You'll see . . . you'll make new friends," Eric Hopkins had encouraged before leaving Mandy to his sister's care. "We brought you here during the summer so you can get acquainted with some of the kids your age before school starts. If you'll get involved and give this a chance, you'll grow to love Blaketown." Pausing, he had struggled for a way to break through the indifferent wall his daughter had erected between them. "I enjoyed growing up in this community," he had said finally. "It's a wonderful place. The people here are . . . well, you'll see." He had then given her an intense squeeze, something that was repeated by her mother, who showered her embrace with tears.

"This is so hard," Lorena had exclaimed, drawing back from the one-sided hug. "But it's for the best. Someday you'll understand why we made this decision." With that her parents had driven away, taking her younger sister and two small brothers home—a place where she was no longer welcome.

Miserably homesick, something she would never admit, Mandy sealed off these troubling thoughts and wandered into an exhibit building, glowering at anyone who happened to look her way. This fair was about the lamest excuse for entertainment she had ever seen! One Ferris wheel, a merry-go-round, a giant pillow for the younger kids to bounce around on, and some sort of goofy ride that twirled people upside down. Other attractions included assorted animals in smelly sheds, and a handful of booths and carnival games to waste money on—money she didn't have. Mandy hadn't found a summer job, not that she had spent much time looking. For the most part she had moped around, convinced her life was over. As she continued to explore the fairgrounds, she knew that it was. No friends, no fun, no life, at least, not for her. She impatiently pushed her way through the crowded exhibit building, pulling a face when several annoying comments assailed her protesting ears.

"Did you see the colors Martha used in her quilt? It's gorgeous!"

"Well, would you look at that? I got a blue ribbon!"

"I can't believe she beat me with her jam again . . . my berries are just as good—"

"This is like living in Mayberry," Mandy muttered, thinking of the old sitcom reruns she had watched several years ago on a cable channel in her Salt Lake home. The television show had highlighted the lives of the citizens of the make-believe small town during the 1950s. Mandy was convinced several Blaketown residents resembled the cast members of Mayberry. "Aunt Bee," Mandy proclaimed snidely, her gaze settling on an older, heavyset woman. "Opie," she continued, spying a small, red-haired boy who was chasing a puppy through the building. Earlier that afternoon, she had noticed the puppies he was trying to give away. One must have escaped. "This is a job for Barney Fife," she jeered. Turning around, she bumped into a small, wiry man who seemed intent on chasing the red-haired boy.

"Sorry . . . I mean . . . watch where you're going, young lady," the man said, hurrying on his way.

Mandy almost grinned, replaying the man's high-pitched voice in her head. He was a dead-ringer for Barney, the overzealous deputy of Mayberry fame. "I wonder where Otis is?" she mumbled, thinking of the town drunk from the TV show. Suddenly eager to exit the building to search, Mandy pushed past a group of kids. She grimaced when a young boy spilled a cup of root beer down one leg of her new, wide-legged jeans. "Look what you did, you moronic twerp!"

"Hey, you bumped into him," a younger voice accused as Mandy found herself immersed in a heated verbal battle with a group of small boys.

"Well, guess what—you're not supposed to have drinks in here! Didn't you see the sign out front?!" Mandy retorted, secretly enjoying this chance to throw rules in someone else's face.

At that moment, Bev Henderson, a tall, striking young woman walked into the building, followed by two teenage girls. The three friends were laughing over the way one of the carnival workers had flirted with them.

"I can't believe that guy. He really thought we were impressed by him," Sabrina Erickson said, following behind Bev. She adjusted the colorful tie in her long blonde hair, sensing it was coming loose.

"He thinks he's a gift to the world," seventeen-year-old Karen Beyer agreed, referring to the flirting carnival worker. She glanced longingly at Sabrina's hair. A month ago, Karen had decided to have her own blonde hair cut shorter in an attractive new style that feathered around her face. Everyone said it made her look older—Karen also liked the time she saved on styling her hair, but there were moments when she missed its former length. She returned Sabrina's smile, her brown eyes sparkling with amusement. "I think he really liked Bev."

"Not funny, Karen," Bev replied, pulling her medium-length, black hair up against her neck. She released it, gazing with interest at the scene taking place in front of them. "How cool is that?!" she exclaimed, her blue eyes flashing dangerously.

"What?" Karen asked, spotting the cause for concern.

"Why is that girl ripping on my brother?" Bev replied, moving forward.

Karen smiled; so much had changed this year. A few months ago, Bev had rarely acknowledged her younger half-brothers—now she was willing to stand up for the four-year-old twins. Things had been better since Bev had decided to accept her stepmother, a tiny miracle that had been a long time coming.

"I wonder where Mom is?" Bev asked, referring to her step-mother, Gina. Her own mother had passed away several years ago with ovarian cancer. Her father had eventually remarried, giving Bev a new mother and two half-brothers, something she had resented until recently. Earlier that spring, a life-changing experience had helped Bev realize how important her family was.

This adventure had occurred when Sabrina had come with her parents to visit Kate and Mike one weekend in April. During that time, Kate had introduced Sabrina to Bev and Karen, two of her high school students. While sharing a meal at a local teen hangout, Bev, Karen, and Sabrina had commiserated about the unfairness of life; each girl had faced a separate challenge. Still grieving for her own mother, Bev had severely strained the relationship between herself and her stepmother. Karen's mother, a recovering alcoholic, had recently been released from prison, an event Karen had been dreading. That left Sabrina, who had decided her life in Bozeman was about as miser-able as it could possibly get, thanks to a group of former friends who had decided popularity held priority over Church standards. In an attempt to boost their spirits, the three girls had traveled through a local canyon to a forest sanctuary not far from Blaketown. Followed by a curious young lady named Terri Jeppson, the four young women had disappeared for several hours before causing alarm in the town below.

That night, as these girls had sung the blues over their combined misfortune, Bev had pulled out a bottle of her father's best wine, revealing her solution to heartache. The campfire pity party had then transformed into a nightmare as Karen's father, someone she hadn't seen in years, made a surprise appearance early the next morning, intent on kidnapping his daughter. Suffering from an acute hangover and giving chase in unfamiliar territory, Bev had fallen, fracturing her leg in two places. Sabrina and Terri had managed to crudely splint Bev's leg utilizing skills learned at girls' camp. Working together to survive, the four girls had eventually been rescued, thanks to the valiant effort made by state police officers, and the local Forest Service. Sabrina's brother-in-law, Mike, and his coworker, Brett Randall, had tracked the girls down using their forestry expertise and the talents of specially trained dogs.

This traumatic incident had drawn these young women together in a tight bond of friendship; the difference in their ages didn't matter. Bev, Karen, and Terri were older than Sabrina; Bev and Karen would be seniors this fall, Terri would be a junior, while Sabrina would be a sophomore. They still struggled with varied problems, but were making positive strides in their individual quests to turn weaknesses into strengths.

"Jake and Drake were supposed to be with Gina," Bev said now, glancing around the exhibit building for her stepmother.

"She was talking to my mom a few minutes ago," Karen offered. "Your brothers were with her then."

"They probably wandered off," Bev assumed. "They're notorious for that," she said, hurrying to Jake's side. "Whatzzup?" she asked, confronting the girl who had been lecturing her brother.

"She's not nice," Jake Henderson said, hiding behind Bev's leg.

"Are you his keeper?" Mandy demanded angrily.

Bev's blue eyes darkened as she returned the stranger's abrasive gaze. "I don't think he's the only one who needs one!"

Infuriated by the insult, Mandy shoved Bev, knocking her into the young boys.

"What is your problem?!" Bev exclaimed, regaining her balance.

"Like you care!" Mandy returned. Whirling around, she stomped out of the building.

"What was that all about?" Karen asked, moving closer to Bev.

"I don't know, but she'll regret it if she ever messes with me again!" Bev placed a protective arm around her younger brother and glanced over her shoulder, but didn't see any sign of the girl who had been shoving Jake around. Deciding to let it go, Bev returned her brothers to her stepmother's care, then explored the exhibit building with her friends, determined to enjoy the rest of the afternoon.

\* \* \*

"Slow down . . . remember to breathe—we have plenty of time before the rodeo starts," Bev said, teasing Sabrina.

Sabrina grinned, then continued to wolf down the cheeseburger in her hands. "Sorry, I'm just so starved," she said between bites.

"How can you be that hungry?" Karen asked, marveling at the food their friend had consumed since they had arrived at the fair. "First a candied apple, then cotton candy, two huge pops, now a cheeseburger with fries!" She shook her head. "Where do you put it all?"

Shrugging, Sabrina reached for the can of root beer that was sitting in front of her on a wooden picnic table. For several weeks her appetite had steadily increased, something she had attributed to the intense workout she had been getting with the high school volleyball team each morning in preparation for the fall season. With Kate's encouragement, Sabrina had gone out for high school volleyball and had made the final cut on the junior varsity team.

"If I ate that much, my body would start resembling that giant pillow over there," Bev said, pointing to the inflated carnival pillow that several young children were bouncing on. "Do you know how lucky you are? You can eat like this and walk around looking like a toothpick with eyes!"

"I guess I take after my mom. She's never had a weight problem— unlike Dad. He's always fought his weight."

"Your dad looks great," Karen countered. "Compared to most men his age, he's done very well."

"He'd appreciate hearing that," Sabrina said as she reached for more fries. "Mom's always on his case, trying to get him to watch what he eats," she said before cramming the fries into her mouth.

Amused by Sabrina's behavior, Karen and Bev nibbled demurely at the corn dogs they had purchased at a nearby food booth, waving as they spotted several kids their age. They smiled a few minutes later when Terri approached.

"Here you are finally," Bev sang out, sliding over on the wooden bench to make room for the slender brunette. "How did the babysitting adventure go?"

Terri crossed her heavily lashed brown eyes, drawing a laugh from the other girls. "I'd rather babysit anyone but my little brothers and sisters. They act like they've never been taught anything, they won't mind, and the pay is lousy." She pulled out a wad of dollar bills. "At least I earned enough to go to the rodeo tonight."

"Good! We were just grabbing a quick bite before we head over to buy the tickets," Karen replied. "Want something to eat?"

Terri glanced at the corn dog in Karen's hand, then turned to look at the line forming at the food booth. "How much time do we have?"

"The rodeo doesn't start until seven. We have over an hour—go for it," Karen encouraged.

"Okay," Terri agreed, her brown hair bobbing under her chin as she moved to stand in line.

Bev glanced at Sabrina. "Want Terri to pick something up for you? Maybe another hamburger, another order of fries?"

Laughing, Sabrina nearly choked on the fries she had stuffed into her mouth. When she could breathe again, she shot Bev a dirty look. "That was mean!"

"Just thought I'd check," Bev replied, smiling. "We'd hate for you to waste away during the rodeo."

"I'll be fine," Sabrina assured the older girl. "Besides, I can always buy something from one of the vendors inside the arena if I get desperate."

Bev glanced at Karen. "What are we going to do with this girl?"

"I say, as long as she's buying, it's not a problem," Karen replied, stealing a couple of Sabrina's fries.

"I saw that," Sabrina warned.

"Karen! How dare you take food from this future volleyball star! She has to keep her strength up." Turning, Bev hollered at Terri. "Hey, Terri, pick up another order of fries. I'll pay you back when you get over here." Terri nodded in agreement.

"That's okay," Sabrina countered. "I'm starting to feel full."

"Slight miracle, but who said these fries were for you?" Bev answered. "I'll split them with Karen. That'll keep her out of your supply."

"You're too kind," Karen said dryly.

"That's what friends are for," Bev replied, grinning at Karen and Sabrina.

Karen lifted an eyebrow. "Thanks for the reminder."

Bev shrugged, then reached for a couple of Sabrina's fries herself, enjoying the outraged expressions on the other girls' faces.

# Chapter 1

*People think I have a talent for writing. They read my papers, themes, and the articles I write for our high school newspaper, and gush with compliments. What really bothers me—they assume that they know me—that what I write reflects who I am. They don't realize I make a lot of things up. Scrambled images crowd inside of my head. I write them down to clear some space, to make room for what is really important—at least, to me.*

*Everyone thinks I'm funny, a rebel at heart, a leader. They don't see the other side of me—the girl who constantly doubts herself. They never realize there are moments when I don't know what I'm doing—even though I pretend that I do.*

*There are times when I hurt so much inside—times when I miss my mother. I cry alone, bitter tears that don't begin to ease the heart wounds I carry. I scream in silence, protesting the unfairness that surrounds me. And when it gets to be too much, I write things no one will ever see. After it spills out, the paper is crumpled and discarded—no one sees the scarring crack I carry inside.*

Bev scowled at her notebook. Shaking her head, she quietly ripped out the page, wadded it into a ball, and set it on her desk. Stifling a yawn, the tall girl stretched. In her opinion, the summer had passed too quickly. Here it was, the middle of the first week of school and already she was feeling burnt out. This wasn't good considering it was her senior year—a year she wanted to savor.

Her blue eyes twinkling with mischief, Bev glanced around. She wasn't the only one struggling on this gorgeous September day. The classroom was filled with teenagers who were striving to complete the challenging assignment, one made by Doris Kelsey, a veteran English teacher—a popular faculty member of Blaketown High. The soft strains of Chopin encouraged as students filled the empty lines of their notebooks with what they hoped were insightful sentences.

Shifting her gaze to the front of the room, Bev met the wondering look of one of her favorite teachers. Bev returned Mrs. Kelsey's smile, picked up her pencil, and tried again. How hard could it be to write something that revealed a secret part of yourself? Forcing herself to concentrate, she stared at her notebook until the words finally came.

Across the room, Bev's best friend, Karen, wrestled with the same assignment. The attractive blonde normally thrived on composing themes; Karen and Bev were the co-editors of *The Blaketown Buzz*, the high school newspaper that had started up last year. Karen had been writing anonymous editorials, articles that often inflamed the residents of this small Idaho town. Her editorials had stirred fiery debates as she tackled the issues of the day: alcoholism, broken homes, child abuse, teen pregnancy, and judgmental thinking. Karen's controversial editorials had generated *The Blaketown Buzz* into a popular publication. This year they were printing twice as many copies to keep up with the demand. Local businesses bought ads to finance the cost. Doris Kelsey and the new history teacher, Kate Jeffries, continued to supervise the entire operation, meeting with their journalism students after school three nights a week.

Karen had decided to heed Mrs. Kelsey's advice and planned to major in journalism at college next year. Things would be tight financially, but the school counselor had assured her that with her grade-point average, she would be eligible for scholarships. Her mother, Edie, had been putting in long hours at the local hospital as she worked to earn her LPN degree, promising that by next year, she would be in a position to help fund her daughter's education. Karen knew her mother was trying very hard to make up for the years she hadn't been there, and she appreciated the effort Edie was making on her behalf. It saddened her to think of the time that had been wasted, but Karen was grateful she finally had the chance to know and love the woman who had brought her into this world.

An alcoholic, Edie—short for Eden—had a history of getting involved with undesirable men. Divorced from Karen's father, Edie had eventually landed herself in prison for helping a boyfriend flee the scene of a crime, a botched armed robbery, something she had no clue about until her arrest. Charged with being an accessory, she had served three long years in prison, years that had sobered her, helping her to realize the mistakes she had made in her life. After her release last year, Edie had promised Karen that she would never drink again, a pledge she vowed to keep.

Reflecting on all of this, Karen reread the paragraph she had written for today's creative writing assignment. She shifted back on her chair, annoyed that the words wouldn't come as easily as she had expected.

*My heart is a cavern, filled with winding passageways. Some are easily explored, lit with brilliant flames, filled with colored beauty. Others lie hidden in murky darkness. Unexplored, most fear to tread the uncertain path. Beyond one passageway lies a steel door. I alone possess the key to this silent chamber; the only one permitted entry. Within its icy walls, I tremble, for here I am naked . . . here I am revealed . . .*

Karen chewed on her pencil as she searched for a description that would convey the imagery she desired.

Terri was sitting behind Karen, contending with the same assignment. The sixteen-year-old pondered her current life, well aware that she had changed drastically during the past year, maturing in a way that had surprised most in Blaketown. The oldest child in her family, Terri had been babied her entire life by a doting mother. Spoiled, used to having her own way, she had gone the rounds with Bev and Karen repeatedly since her arrival in high school. Taking advantage of her tenacious nature, Cleo Partridge, the high school principal, had used Terri to try to destroy the high school newspaper last year, something Cleo had detested, certain it portrayed her school in a bad light.

Terri had been spying on Bev and Karen during their "canyon adventure," eager to sniff out anything that would lead to the downfall of the editors of *The Blaketown Buzz*. When things had gone horribly wrong, Terri had tapped into a hidden strength to courageously guide Sabrina and Bev to safety. Fast friends now with Bev, Karen, and Sabrina, Terri would be forever grateful for the inner growth that had propelled her past her former self. Her mind stirring with a sudden flash of creativity, Terri continued to write.

*I cringe over the girl I used to be: petty, selfish, eager for attention. Sometimes we can't see who we really are until life holds up a mirror. If I looked into that mirror today, the reflection would be smiling . . .*

In an upper corner of the classroom, Sabrina set her pencil down, trying to collect her thoughts. Her mind wandered as she relived several colorful scenes from the past year, including the "canyon adventure," as they now called it. Coming up empty, she considered each member of her family, searching for something that could be transformed into an essay.

She thought about her father, Greg Erickson. Tall and slightly pudgy, his hair thin and greying, Greg had bravely opened a computer store in an empty building on Blaketown's main street. After a slow start, business had gradually improved as the residents of this isolated community began to enjoy the advantages of the computer world, several hooking up to the Internet under Greg's expert tutelage.

Sue, Sabrina's mother, was a beautiful, vibrant woman who kept herself busy helping out with her husband's new store, as well as crocheting and sewing baby clothes in anticipation of her first grandchild. Overjoyed at the thought of becoming a grandmother, Sue was especially glad that their family had moved to Blaketown. She looked forward to the arrival of their newest family member, eager to help Kate with the challenges a baby would bring.

Tyler, Sabrina's older brother, was serving a mission in California. He would return home before Christmas, another family event the Ericksons were anticipating with great excitement. Kate's baby and Tyler would appear at approximately the same time in December, two precious gifts the entire family would enjoy.

Kate and her husband, Mike, were so busy with their respective careers, Sabrina wondered how they would work in being parents. Kate loved teaching high school, almost as much as Mike enjoyed supervising the local Forest Service. In Sabrina's opinion, something would have to give when their baby was born—maybe Kate would take a hiatus from teaching. She doubted Kate would mind too much; it had taken her older sister so long to get pregnant, the entire family had been convinced that something was wrong. Last spring, it had been a welcome relief to learn that Kate was expecting.

Sabrina traced the rough edge of her desk. Several images had come to mind, but nothing that would reveal a secret part of herself. She smiled, knowing her life had improved over last year; she had grown to love Blaketown and the wonderful friends she had made. The only concern she had at the moment was enduring this creative writing class. She wasn't sure she liked writing, but Kate had talked her into taking this class. Sabrina was more interested in science, math, and volleyball, things she excelled in. For her, writing could be a drudging chore. But her new friends all worked on the high school newspaper, something else that had influenced her to try this class.

"Doris is a wonderful teacher," Kate had enthused a few weeks ago. "Everyone loves her."

That part was true—Doris could make learning proper grammar fun. Her witty humor kept the class entertaining. Writing was a skill Sabrina wanted to improve, hoping to become a reporter for the high school newspaper. She was almost jealous of the relationship Bev, Karen, and Terri shared with Doris and Kate, and longed for the closeness she had observed between her friends and these two teachers.

Things were better now between Sabrina and Kate. Several years ago, Kate had struggled through high school, making undesirable choices that had nearly ruined her life. Involved in a car accident that had caused her to slip into a coma, a vivid dream had changed Kate's life forever—a dream that had given Kate the chance to journey across the plains with pioneer ancestors. When she had regained consciousness, Kate had turned her life around, an arduous task thanks to a few people in the Bozeman community who had been unwilling to let go of who she had been before. Finally succeeding, Kate had graduated from high school with honor, then had gone onto college—eventually serving an LDS mission in Scotland, touching numerous lives with her fervent testimony. Upon her return, she had married her high school sweetheart, Mike Jeffries, in the Idaho Falls temple.

Despite Kate's achievements, as Sabrina had approached her teenage years, the young woman had found herself being constantly compared to her older sister. Every decision had been scrutinized by family members, church leaders, and local residents who had tried to fit Sabrina into Kate's broken mold. Fearing Sabrina would repeat the mistakes Kate had made at her age, their parents had been overly cautious, causing a deep rift between the two sisters.

Finally catching onto the problem, Greg and Sue had granted their youngest daughter more freedom. In time, Sabrina's angry resentment had dissolved as comparisons between herself and Kate had ceased. It had helped to move to Blaketown, where Sabrina could establish who she was without the criticism that had flourished in Bozeman; she no longer felt like she was living in Kate's shadow.

Suddenly feeling inspired, Sabrina picked up her pencil and tried again.

*I like living in Blaketown. It has given me a chance to show the world who I really am. Here, people don't think I'm Kate—the sequel. Here, I am Sabrina.*

Sitting two desks ahead of Sabrina, fifteen-year-old Mandy Hopkins continued to doodle inappropriate pictures on her notebook. She glanced at her watch, wishing this class would end; her stomach had been upset most of the day. She had turned down the hearty breakfast her aunt had cooked—again—settling for a piece of toast.

"Oh, man," she exclaimed silently. "I've probably caught the flu! Great! Perfect! Just what I need . . . on top of everything else." The queasiness increased until she finally raised her hand, then dashed out of the room.

Lifting an eyebrow, Doris Kelsey watched Mandy leave. She had noticed how pale this newest student of hers had been today. Hoping it was nothing serious, she decided to check on Mandy and wandered out of the classroom.

# Chapter 2

"Mandy, do you feel like you could drink some chicken broth?" Betty Sandler asked, stepping inside Mandy's bedroom. Mandy was lying on her bed, staring at the ceiling.

Repulsed by her aunt's suggestion, Mandy shook her head. Rolling onto her side, she turned her back to the woman.

Betty gazed sadly at her defiant niece. The past three months had been difficult as she and her husband had tried to establish a loving bond with Mandy. So far, their attempts had failed; Mandy was more troubled that her parents had guessed.

"I'm fine, okay! I just need some sleep," Mandy grumbled, hoping her aunt would take the hint and leave her alone. This wasn't a big deal; she had been fighting nausea off and on for several weeks, convinced it was because her parents had dragged her to Blaketown against her will. She missed her friends and she missed Blade. There were times when she ached for him, when she wished he was here to make this nightmare tolerable. She had tried to call him several times since her arrival in Blaketown. Each time, his mother had bluntly informed her that Blade was busy, or gone for the evening. Tears now pricked at Mandy's eyes as she wondered if Blade had found someone else. She held her breath, trying not to cry as she continued to worry over her relationship with Blade.

She had blown her chance to return to Salt Lake. Her parents had come to see her last month, willing to take her home if she would agree to a new, stricter set of rules. Furious, Mandy had told them what they could do with their demands; angry pride had prevented her from listening to what they had thought were credible requests.

She had finally run upstairs to her room in the Sandler house, slamming the door in response. Secretly, she had hoped her mother would follow, that her parents would give in and let her come home without the strict rules. Instead, they had climbed in the car and driven back to Utah to wait for a time when Mandy would be more reasonable. *Like they were?* Why were they so controlling? What had happened to the precious gift of agency that her parents were always spouting off about? Didn't she have a right to live her life the way she wanted?

As Mandy contended with inner turmoil, Betty prayed for guidance; she had no idea how to help her niece. It had been different with her own children. Raising four boys and three girls hadn't always been easy—they had each fought their own battles, but love had cemented their family together. Together they had worked on the farm, raising steers, hay, and grain. The boys had learned to operate the tractor, harrow bed, and grain combine at an early age. The girls had been responsible for keeping the house clean, taking care of the chickens that provided them with eggs, and had helped their mother with the large garden they raised every summer. As the Sandler children had matured, heading in different directions, the lessons they had absorbed had shaped them into responsible adults. Their youngest was the only one still home—eighteen-year-old Sara. A senior this year, Sara resented Mandy's intrusion during her final year at home.

Betty glanced at her hands. Calloused and rough from years of hard labor, they weren't soft or manicured like Mandy's mother's hands. Betty wasn't comfortable in fancy dresses—with her tall, big-boned frame, she preferred jeans and a baggy sweatshirt. Well aware that she lacked the sophistication Mandy had grown up with, Betty was at a loss when it came to figuring out how to reach her niece. She knew Mandy thought of her as a country hick; the lack of respect already shown had conveyed that message. Despite her misgivings, Betty knew she would keep trying. Eric, Mandy's father, was Betty's youngest brother, someone she had always tried to help. Somewhere in Mandy had to be the goodness found in her parents. Determined to root it out, Betty prayed for the patience this challenge would require.

"Would you like some Seven-up?" she offered.

"NO! Leave me alone!"

Wincing over the sharpness in her niece's voice, Betty left the room, pulling the door shut behind her. Mandy waited until she could no longer hear her aunt's footsteps on the stairs, then gave in to the tears that had threatened most of the day, sobbing into the feather pillow on her bed.

* * *

"Hi Grandma, I'm home," Karen announced, the aroma of chocolate chip cookies drawing her into the kitchen of the small house she and her mother shared with Edie's mother, Adele Hadley. Entering the kitchen, Karen selected a cookie. Savoring the warm, sweet flavor, she closed her eyes.

"Hello, Karen," Adele said as she pulled a hot cookie sheet from the oven.

"These are so good," Karen exclaimed, reaching for another plump cookie.

"Thank you. Try to save some room for dinner," Adele added, as she removed the newest batch of cookies from the cookie sheet.

"I always have room for your cooking," Karen countered, grabbing another cookie before she hurried from the kitchen to start on her homework.

"Karen!" Adele scolded lightly, smiling at the girl she had practically raised by herself. Even before Karen's mother had gone to prison, Edie's parenting skills had been lacking. Karen had spent most of her seventeen years living with Adele, a grandmother who loved her dearly. Adele had tried to avoid the mistakes she had made with her daughter, Edie, and had maintained a loving, but firm rein on her headstrong granddaughter. She suspected she had been too lenient with Edie after her father had died years ago, years that had beckoned Edie on a path of self-destruction. Grateful that they all had a second chance, Adele vowed to make the most of the opportunity life had given them to become a family.

After slipping the freshly baked cookies from the cookie sheet, Adele began spooning out another batch of dough to bake. Placing the cookies in the oven, she glanced at the clock. It was nearly four o'clock; Edie was late getting home. This week, Edie's shift as a nurse's aide at the local hospital had been from 7:00 a.m. till 3:00 p.m. Deciding her daughter must be running a few errands, Adele concentrated on fixing dinner. Tonight they would have spaghetti and meatballs, one of Edie's favorites.

Adele did most of the cooking in this household, something she didn't mind. Karen was always busy with homework and school activities—Edie was usually exhausted by the time she came home from work. Her shifts at the hospital varied from days, to afternoons, to a few midnights each month. When Edie was home, she studied for the LPN course she was taking, something she would hopefully complete next spring. The spare time Edie had was split between her daughter, Karen, and Brett Randall, a man who was rapidly becoming part of the family.

Brett and Edie had started dating before Karen's "canyon adventure" last spring. That experience had strengthened their relationship as it had blossomed into romance. Adele was convinced Brett would pop "the question" in the near future, something she eagerly anticipated. Edie had endured too many bad relationships in her life— Brett was just the kind of man Adele wanted her daughter to marry.

Brett worked as a ranger for the local forest service. A quiet, humble man, he had been content to live his life alone—something that had changed after he had met Edie. In the past, a noticeable limp from a birth defect had made Brett extremely self-conscious around women. Now he hardly limped at all, buoyed by the love he possessed for Edie. A kindhearted man, Brett hadn't been discouraged by her colorful past. Instead he had assured her that in his eyes, she was an amazing woman, someone he wanted to share his life with. The only thing holding him back was the LDS Church.

Since Edie's reformation, her testimony had grown drastically, and unlike her past relationships, this time she desired a temple wedding. Brett had been going to church with her for several weeks, but was hesitant to commit to the LDS ordinance. He longed to spend an eternity with Edie, but wasn't sure the Church was all she believed it to be. Still bitter over the way members had treated him in the past, Brett was convinced that a genuine church of Christ would be filled with Christ-like people, not those who belittled and gossiped.

Anxious to help, Adele had stressed that the Church was perfect, but its members were not. Unfortunately, Brett had been deeply wounded by the snide remarks made by members of his home ward in northern Idaho. Criticized by the boys his age because of his lack of coordination, Brett had retreated into a shell, something that had encouraged his quiet love of nature. Years later, after his move to Blaketown, Brett had been ignored, in his opinion, avoided, until he had started attending church this summer. Convinced the people in Edie's home ward were now friendly because he was "convert material," Brett was wary of the attempts that were being made to fellowship him.

Realizing what was at stake, whenever Adele had the chance, she journeyed three hours to the Idaho Falls Temple and after going through a session, submitted both Edie's and Brett's names to be prayed over. On fast Sundays, she fasted and prayed that Brett would feel the Spirit, that the ashes of his testimony would flare into a glowing ember. She had become very fond of Brett and wanted nothing but happiness for him, and for Edie.

As she thought of her daughter's future wedding, Adele smiled. Brett would be coming over for dinner tonight, another reason she was putting so much effort into this meal. After dinner, Edie and Brett planned to attend a special fireside their stake was sponsoring for single adults.

Brett wasn't the only missionary effort being made by their family. Lately Karen had been bringing Bev to church on Sundays, and Young Women on Tuesday nights. A nonmember, Bev was intrigued by the idea that her family could be sealed together forever and had asked numerous questions about where her mother was, desiring her own personal witness that she would have the chance to see her mother again after this life. The budding testimony Bev was gaining had been crucial as she waged a personal war against alcoholism.

Since junior high, Bev had secretly turned to liquor to soothe the pain of losing her mother. As close as Karen had been to Bev, this information had come as a shock during their "canyon adventure." After their dramatic rescue, Karen had tried to help her friend kick a habit that threatened to destroy her life. Pointing to the heartache alcohol had brought into her own life, compliments of Edie, Karen was finally succeeding with Bev where counselors had lost hope. The treatment program Bev had tried during the summer had been less than successful; the urge to drink had been too strong, stronger than her will to quit. Faking her way through the program, she had been released to another bout with the liquid affliction. Bev had now gone nearly six weeks without a drink, leaning heavily on Karen for supporting encouragement. As Karen had tried to teach basic gospel principles, she had helped Bev learn how to pray, certain her friend could find the courage to overcome her drinking problem with the Lord's help.

Proudly reflecting on the positive impact her granddaughter was having on everyone around her, Adele didn't hear the front door open and jumped, startled, when Edie entered the kitchen.

"Hi, Mom," Edie said, setting her purse on the table. Like Karen, she loved chocolate chip cookies and quickly sampled one. "These are wonderful! If I could cook half as good as you, I'd have it made."

"You'll get there," Adele replied, beaming at her beautiful daughter. "How was your day?"

Edie pulled a face, her brown eyes reflecting the exhaustion she felt. Grabbing at the clip that held her long blonde hair in place, she released it and shook her hair down around her shoulders.

"That bad, huh?"

Nodding, Edie walked to the fridge, opened it, and reached for the milk. She grabbed a glass out of the cupboard, poured it full, then returned the gallon container to the fridge. "That's why I'm so late," she said, selecting two more cookies before sitting down at the table.

Adele sat across from Edie, waiting patiently for her daughter to unwind.

"It was awful—just before the shift changed, a little boy was brought into ER. He had broken a glass vase—he was covered with lacerations. Three of the cuts were so deep—it took several stitches . . . and guess who got to hold him down!"

"You," Adele supplied sympathetically. Edie's compassionate nature always took over in crisis situations. As a result, she was becoming a favored nurse; the doctors appreciated her ability to calm patients, especially children.

"Yep. Me—we had no choice. His mother nearly passed out during the first stitch."

"I'm sure you handled it just fine," Adele said, rising to stir the spaghetti sauce.

"I survived, but that boy's screams really got to me today. He wasn't old enough to understand we were trying to help him. Halfway through the ordeal, he bit me."

"What?!"

Edie held up her arm, pointing to a Band-aid.

"Why the little scamp," Adele replied.

"I almost called him worse than that," Edie informed her mother.

"Is it very deep?" Adele asked, focusing on her daughter's arm.

"No, but it did break the skin," she sighed. "He had a gash along one cheek we were trying to repair—I suppose I got too close to his face." Edie gazed at her mother. "I don't know . . . maybe I'm making a mistake . . . maybe I'm not nurse material."

"Why would you say that?"

"I didn't handle this afternoon very well. When that boy bit me . . . I wanted to wring his neck!"

"A normal reaction under the circumstances," Adele offered. "Don't let it throw you. You're a wonderful nurse! I've seen you in action," she reminded Edie, remembering how her daughter had tenderly cared for her last spring after Edie's ex-husband had assaulted her, shoving her into the kitchen stove during an argument. Roger Beyer had an ugly temper, one of the reasons Edie had divorced him. After Edie's release from prison, Roger had hoped for a reconciliation. When Roger had stopped by Adele's house looking for Edie, he had erupted over the news that Edie was dating someone else. He had hurt his former mother-in-law when she had refused to tell him where Edie had gone on her date with Brett that night.

Seeking revenge, Roger had then tried getting Edie's attention by taking their daughter, Karen. How grateful Adele was that Brett had been able to locate Karen and her friends before things had spiraled out of control.

Roger was currently in jail, a place he would call home for several years. His list of public offenses had been long, including the assault and battery charge brought against him by Edie for what he had done to her mother. Suffering from a concussion, Adele had spent a few days in the hospital to recover. Edie had taken it upon herself to personally care for her mother, exhibiting a natural tendency that had impressed Adele, and her doctor. "You're just tired, overworked, and underpaid," Adele now stated, trying to get Edie to smile.

"True," Edie sighed.

Karen bounced into the kitchen and moved behind her mother, draping her arms around Edie. "Hi, Mom. I thought I heard you two talking in here."

"Hi," Edie replied, leaning back into her daughter's hug.

"Tough day?" Karen asked.

"The worst," Edie responded. "I even have a few battle scars," she said, holding up her arm for sympathy.

"What happened?" Karen sat down between her mother and grandmother, staring at her mother's arm.

While Edie recounted her day, Adele checked on the spaghetti noodles, glad she had cooked up one of Edie's favorites. It might help soothe over what had happened earlier that day, taking Edie's mind off a situation that had been out of her control.

* * *

"So, what did you think?" Edie asked as she walked out of the stake center with Brett.

Tugging at his tie to loosen its tight hold, Brett stalled. The speaker tonight had been quite good—he was struggling with the subject matter—being spiritually prepared in the latter days. As he had looked around the chapel, he had been disturbed by the complacent expressions of the people in that room. Why did these Latter-day Saints think they were the only ones who were going to make it in these troubled times? He knew several people who weren't LDS who were actually living more Christlike lives than others he could mention who were classified as Mormons. A couple of men sitting in the audience tonight had been divorced because of their inability to be faithful to their wives. He knew of others who were rumored to be involved with shady business practices. Yet, because they attended church every Sunday, they were spiritually prepared?! Bothered by the inconsistencies he had observed among LDS Church members most of his life, Brett wondered how this church could possibly claim to have all of the answers.

"Brett?" Edie prompted, her delicate mouth curving into a worried frown.

Brett smiled and reached for Edie's hand, giving it a light squeeze. "Sorry, I'm a little preoccupied tonight." With his free hand, he self-consciously smoothed his brown hair to the side.

"About what?" Edie asked, her hopes rising. Tonight the Spirit had touched her heart as the speaker had listed several things that would help promote spiritual strength. Personal scripture study and prayer had been encouraged, as well as adhering to the values taught by the Church. She had seen firsthand what could happen when those standards were disregarded. Her own life had nearly been ruined because of the choices she had made in the past. Glancing at Brett, she wondered if he had absorbed as much as she had tonight from the inspiring fireside.

Knowing his continued skepticism would only hurt Edie, Brett decided to steer the conversation away from the fireside. "I'm always preoccupied with you," he said, pulling her close for a brief kiss.

When they pulled apart, Edie smiled at the extraordinary man she loved. Brett had done so much for her the past few months, rebuilding her self-esteem in a way no other man had done before. That alone would have drawn her to him; but when he had brought her daughter safely down from the mountain last spring, Brett had permanently wedged himself inside of her heart. "I love you, Brett Randall," she whispered now.

His own emotions running high, Brett reached for her hand, brought it to his mouth and tenderly kissed the back of it. "There's no way I can possibly tell you how much you mean to me," he said, holding her hand as they walked back to his car.

"Brett, where do you see us in five years?" Edie asked, leaning against his Suzuki Samurai.

Brett dug the keys out of his pocket as he considered the question. Deciding he would be better off to keep the answer light, he grinned. "I see us living blissfully in that beautiful log home I've been building outside of town, raising a herd of kids—"

"A herd?" Edie stammered, blushing. She wanted more children; it tore at her heart to know that Karen would be off to college in a year. She had missed so much of her daughter's life, she craved a chance to try again, to be a better mother.

"Yes. I'd say twelve, thirteen . . ."

Catching on to Brett's teasing mood, Edie smiled. "That's all, huh?"

"Well, if you'd like more, I'm sure that could be arranged," Brett replied, leaning close for another kiss.

"Brett, I do want something more," Edie said softly when he drew back.

"I know," Brett replied, wishing he could give Edie her heart's desire. Right now a temple marriage seemed so far away.

"Promise me one thing."

Brett braced himself, fearing it would be an ultimatum.

"Promise that you'll start praying about us . . . about what is really important in life." She smiled sadly. "I know people in our church have hurt you . . . no one understands that more than I do."

Nodding, Brett knew that was true. Edie had been stung repeatedly by gossip, by those who had been unwilling to let go of her flamboyant past.

"I didn't start feeling better inside until I forgave those who had hurt me most." Edie gazed steadily at Brett. "You have to let go of the bitterness, Brett. It's eating you up inside. It keeps you from feeling the Spirit. That Spirit was here tonight . . . but you have to open your heart to feel it."

Brett looked down at the ground, awkwardly shuffling his feet.

"You are such a wonderful man—I don't want to be with anyone else . . . but I want to do things right this time. I want our relationship to be sealed for eternity. I want to know that Karen, and any children we may have together, will be ours, forever." Edie paused, wishing Brett could understand how important it was to start their life together in a manner that was pleasing to God. She had learned for herself that if a marriage wasn't based on mutual respect, if fundamental values weren't shared, it was a disaster waiting to happen.

Brett met Edie's searching gaze. "I can't think of anything I'd like more than spending an eternity with you." His tanned face revealed the worry in his heart. "Give me time, Edie. I think you're right—I need to sort some things out." He smiled. "I know this much . . . I can't live without you."

Blinking back tears, Edie knew the same was true for her about him. Later that night as she knelt beside her bed to pray, she pleaded for a change of heart for Brett. As a quiet peace calmed her, she rose to her feet and sat for several minutes on the side of her bed. It would be all right, Brett would find his way. Together they would start a new life, one she could hardly wait to begin.

* * *

Too wound up to sleep, Bev wandered around her bedroom, scowling at the black sky she could see from the small bay window. Dressed only in a thin nightshirt, she shivered. Why did tonight seem so dark? Troubled, she reached for the Book of Mormon Karen had given her a few weeks ago. Seeking answers, she opened it up to Ether and the following scripture seemed to jump out at her:

". . . if men come unto me I will show unto them their weakness. I give unto men weakness that they may be humble; and my grace is sufficient for all men that humble themselves before me; for if they humble themselves before me, and have faith in me, then will I make weak things become strong unto them."

"Man, do I ever have a weakness," Bev mumbled as she continued to fight the urge to drink. Closing the Book of Mormon, she knelt by the side of her bed and begged for strength. Tears splashed down the sides of her face as she struggled with a raging inner battle. Just when she felt like she was losing ground, the bedroom door opened.

"Bev, are you all right?" Gina Henderson asked. The thirty-two-year-old had been downstairs folding clothes when a feeling that she should check on her stepdaughter had overwhelmed her.

Shaking her head, Bev continued to sob into the mattress.

Entering the room, Gina pulled Bev up into her arms and murmured consoling words as the teenager continued to cry. When the torrential storm passed, Bev retreated to her bed. Gina sat down beside her stepdaughter as Bev stretched out, staring up at the ceiling.

"Is it ever going to get any better?" Bev asked. "Tonight I want a drink so bad—"

"It takes time, Bev. Be patient with yourself. I think you've done really well lately." A wisp of brown hair had fallen across Gina's forehead in an annoying fashion and she brushed it away. "You'll get through this."

"But tonight—"

"Try focusing on something else," Gina suggested.

"I can't," Bev said, tears reappearing.

Fearing the answer, Gina gathered her courage. "What's bothering you? Why do you crave a drink tonight?"

Bev closed her eyes. How could she explain what she didn't understand herself?

"Is this about your mother?" Gina asked, inner pain flickering from her dark eyes. For nearly seven years, Gina had attempted to fill those maternal shoes. As Bev had continuously opposed her efforts, Gina had decided that her feet were much too small. She had tried to be Bev's friend, had imagined herself as an older sister, but neither role had fit comfortably. Bev had resented Gina's intrusion into her life, clinging stubbornly to the superior image of her biological mother. Bev's father had been blind to the continued conflict between his second wife and his daughter. The few times Gina had approached him, James had laughed it off as a phase Bev was going through, citing Gina's inexperience as a parent as a possible cause for the recurrent problem.

Convinced she would always be considered beneath contempt by the young woman, Gina had been elated over Bev's acceptance of her last spring. After Karen's kidnapping, Bev had turned to Gina for comfort. Following the dramatic rescue, Gina had been the one to wade in after her stepdaughter when Bev's drinking problem had been revealed. James would have preferred looking the other way, but Gina had insisted on getting to the heart of the problem. From this action, Bev had finally understood how much her stepmother cared. The image of Bev's mother, someone Bev bore an uncanny resemblance to, would continue to waver invisibly between the two, but the distance had narrowed, bridged by love.

"Bev?" Gina prompted again.

Bev slowly opened her eyes. "Today in Creative Writing we had to share a hidden part of ourselves. I went too deep. I tried to explain what it felt like losing Mom," she explained. "It was a mistake. I thought I could handle it—is it ever going to quit hurting?" she asked, softly crying.

Grabbing tissue out of a colorful cardboard box on the nightstand, Gina handed it to Bev. "You will always miss loved ones when they die. Time makes it hurt less, but there will be days when that pain will hit hard."

"It's been eleven years!" Bev sniffed. "What's wrong with me?! Am I dwelling on it like Dad says?" she asked, wiping at her eyes and nose with the soft white tissue.

"There's nothing wrong with you. Maybe if you'd been allowed to grieve for your mother after her death . . . to express what you were feeling years ago, it wouldn't have built up inside of you like this," Gina said with a touch of anger. She was convinced James had handled his first wife's death poorly, forcing Bev to internalize her heartache. Bev had always idolized her father and had taken to heart his philosophy that tears were a useless waste of time.

"He kept saying that we had to go on—that we couldn't look back."

"Your father meant well, but he didn't know how to deal with your mother's death. He had no idea how to help you. You were never given a chance for closure after losing your mother," Gina continued.

"Have you ever lost anyone?"

Gina glanced down at the quilted bedspread. This was something she had never thought she would disclose, but sensed now that it might be what Bev needed to hear. "When I was ten, my oldest brother was killed in a freak accident."

Bev's eyes widened with surprise. "Serious?"

"Yes," Gina confirmed. "At the time, I thought my world had come to an end. I loved Danny so much."

"How did he die?"

"He drowned," Gina revealed as she nervously played with her medium-length hair. "He was on a camping trip with a group of friends. They had all gone swimming in a mountain lake they had discovered on this trip. Danny was a great swimmer, but he was a show-off. He swam out past the others to a large rock that stood out in the middle of the lake. His friends said that he climbed up on the rock and tried to do a fancy dive. When he disappeared from sight . . . his friends thought he was clowning around—they didn't realize he was in trouble until it was too late." She paused, the memory releasing a hidden sorrow. "He had dived into a group of rocks that were hidden beneath the surface of the lake. The impact knocked him unconscious. By the time his friends found him, he was already gone."

"That must've been awful," Bev breathed.

Nodding, Gina picked up one of the tissues Bev hadn't used and wiped at her own eyes.

"How did you get through it?"

"It wasn't easy—heartache never is," Gina said, glancing at Bev. "But my family handled it differently than you and your dad. We cried together, shared memories—"

"Dad never wants to talk about Mom," Bev interjected.

"I know," Gina sympathized. "But if you ever want to talk about her, I'm here."

Sitting up, Bev reached for Gina as the tears continued to flow. Exhausted, she finally pulled away from her stepmother, lying down on the cushioned bed. Emotionally drained, she closed her eyes as Gina hummed a lullaby she usually reserved for the twins. When Bev started to doze, Gina stood and covered her with a blanket that had been folded on the end of the bed.

"Here you are," a bass voice interrupted as James Henderson poked his head inside the bedroom. He had just arrived home from a school board meeting and had spent the past five minutes searching the house for his pretty wife.

Gina nodded tiredly at her tall husband.

"Again?!" James demanded.

Holding a finger to her lips, Gina left the room, motioning for James to follow.

"What are we going to do with that girl?" James sputtered angrily as he and Gina moved downstairs into the living room.

"She's doing remarkably well," Gina replied, wishing James would understand how hard Bev was trying to conquer her penchant for alcohol.

"Maybe we need to send her somewhere else—there has to be a place that can help her."

"There is . . . it's called home," Gina responded, her own temper flaring. "We tried a treatment center. I know they help other people, but it didn't work for Bev. She needs us—you and me, and her friends, to get through this."

James snorted in disgust. "Her *friends*—the ones who think prayer makes it all better?!"

"Bev was praying tonight. I was down here in the living room folding clothes . . . I sensed she was in trouble . . . I don't know how to explain it . . . I just knew."

"It's silly nonsense!" James thundered, disconcerted by his own inability to reach his daughter. The past few months had been frustrating as he had watched Bev repeatedly turn to Gina for comfort and guidance. Hurt by this, he had sensed that both Gina and Bev blamed him for Bev's alcoholism. It also bothered him that Bev was interested in a religion that went against everything he believed.

"Please keep your voice down. I finally got Bev to sleep—"

"That girl is eighteen years old! She doesn't need to be babied! She needs a good dose of reality, not some warped version of religion!"

"Bev's prayer was answered tonight," Gina continued bravely. "She is being watched over whether you want to believe it or not!" In the past, Gina hadn't stood up to James, something she feared had contributed to Bev's problem.

"Call it what you want, my daughter has a condition that we can't fix! I say we find a place that can, and get her away from all of these brain-washing Mormons!"

"*Your* daughter? I love that girl like my own, James! I should have some say in how we handle this!"

Storming across the room, James unlocked a small cupboard above a polished, wooden counter and pulled out a bottle of whiskey. He couldn't take much more of this—first Bev, now Gina. Why were women so difficult?! He opened an insulated container and selected a couple of ice cubes, dropping them into a small glass. Reaching for the whiskey, he filled the glass with the amber-colored liquid.

"Would it be so bad if Bev turns to prayer instead of alcohol?" Gina asked, gazing at the shot glass in her husband's hand.

Ignoring his wife's subtle inference, James downed the small glass of whiskey. He had given prayer a chance once, years ago. Bev's mother had still died. To his way of thinking, prayer was a waste of time, something weak people clung to when disaster struck.

"Mommy?" a small voice ventured.

Gina turned, forcing a smile at her four-year-old son. "What is it, Drake? You're supposed to be in bed asleep."

"I was sleepin'. I heard Daddy yell and now Bev's cryin'," Drake said, pointing up the stairs. "Why is Bev so sad?"

Giving James a livid look, Gina moved Drake toward the stairs, hurrying up with him. Why couldn't James see what he was doing to their family? Why couldn't he understand that he was the biggest reason Bev had turned to alcohol? Furious, Gina tamped down what she was feeling, knowing anger was the last thing Bev needed. She sent Drake back to bed, then reentered her stepdaughter's room, hoping she could undo the damage already done.

# Chapter 3

Sue glanced at the kitchen clock, then at Sabrina who was hungrily devouring the French toast on her plate.

"I know . . . I'm going to be late, again," Sabrina said as she reached for her glass of milk.

"Your sister may teach your first class, but Kate will still mark you tardy," Sue replied, running a hand through her short, red hair.

"Trust me, I know," Sabrina said, jamming another bite of breakfast inside her mouth.

"Why is it so hard for you to wake up when the alarm goes off?"

Sabrina tried very hard not to pull a face. They had been going through this same routine for nearly two weeks. She couldn't explain why she felt so tired. When the alarm went off, it barely registered. At first, she had wondered if it was because of the demanding volleyball practices she had been enduring after school each day. It was frustrating to see that her teammates' stamina was increasing while hers appeared to be dwindling.

At a game earlier this week, Sabrina had been part of the starting lineup. She had played the first set with a fierce intensity, helping her team slip ahead to victory. The second set had been a different story. A strange exhaustion had sapped her strength, causing her to miss easy returns and to blow her usually dynamic serve. Embarrassed when her coach had pulled her out of the game, Sabrina had been close to tears. She didn't know what was going on, but hated how it was affecting every aspect of her life.

"And the way you eat . . . why are you losing so much weight?" Sue quizzed. She couldn't figure out what was going on with her youngest daughter. Sabrina was usually so full of life, eager to start each day. During recent weeks, she had become sluggish and had lost interest in what was going on around her. Concerned, Sue had asked Kate about Sabrina's strange behavior. Kate had assured that to the best of her knowledge, Sabrina wasn't messing around with alcohol or drugs, but had noticed that her younger sister had been fighting to stay awake in class.

"Does she sleep at night?" Kate had asked during their last visit.

"In between trips to the bathroom. She's up and down all night," Sue had responded.

"Why?"

Sue had shrugged. "It's probably all of the water that girl drinks before going to bed. Honestly, I don't know where she puts everything she eats and drinks. She must have a hollow leg."

"Or a camel bladder," Kate had teased. "Maybe she inherited that from you."

"Not funny," Sue had chided. "I'd rather be that way than like you, Tyler, and your father. Every time we go anywhere, we have to allow so much time for potty runs for you three it takes us twice as long to travel!"

"Sabrina's never been that way," Kate had commented.

"Until now. Now, she's running to the bathroom every five minutes."

Kate's green eyes had sparkled impishly. "Well, if she's drinking as much water as you say she is, that's probably why." She had patted her bulging stomach. "Myself, I have a good excuse for running to the bathroom every five minutes," she had said, wincing as her baby kicked in protest.

As she continued to reflect on her conversation with Kate, Sue searched Sabrina's face for clues. What was wrong with her youngest daughter? This morning, Sabrina looked slightly flushed. Concerned, Sue crossed the kitchen and felt her daughter's forehead.

"Mom!" Sabrina complained. "I'm fine—just a little tired."

"Okay," Sue replied, "but tonight, why don't you slow down. It's Friday—after volleyball practice, come home, relax, and spend the weekend catching up on your rest. You have two important games next week."

"But Terri's throwing a party! All the videos, popcorn, and pop we can handle."

Sue gazed thoughtfully at her daughter. "Another all-nighter?"

Smiling sheepishly, Sabrina continued to attack the French toast on her plate. She had never eaten this much breakfast before. Now, even after finishing a huge meal, she was often so famished by ten o'clock if she didn't snack on something between classes it felt like she was starving. Her head ached continuously, growing worse after she ate. She wondered if she was coming down with a weird flu bug. "There, I'm done," Sabrina said, rising from the table. "Could you please drive me to school this morning? That would save me some time."

Glancing down at her robe, Sue sighed. "Give me five minutes."

"Thanks, Mom, you're the greatest," Sabrina said, moving to kiss her mother's cheek before she hurried from the kitchen.

Sue winced; Sabrina's breath had definitely taken a turn for the worse. A sickening sweet, fruity odor. Of course, the girl had just consumed a plateful of French toast, dripping with maple syrup—that had to be the culprit. Setting Sabrina's plate in the sink, Sue ran to change into jeans and a sweatshirt. Ten minutes later, she dragged Sabrina out to the car and headed to the high school.

\* \* \*

"Why don't you stay home from school today?" Betty Sandler encouraged her niece.

"Yeah . . . great . . . whatever," Mandy replied, too sick to care. She had spent the morning losing the contents of her stomach—again. This was getting old fast. She had never enjoyed being sick and was now convinced that she was dying—there was no other explanation. She was dying of a broken heart, and no one was concerned, least of all her parents. Her mother had called this morning to talk to her, a conversation that had offered little comfort.

"Mandy, your aunt Betty tells me you've been sick. What's wrong?" Lorena had asked.

"Do you really care?" Mandy had thrown back in her mother's face.

There had been a slight pause, then Lorena had spoken in a strained voice. "Someday, you'll understand how much I do care. Do you think it's easy, having you this far away, especially when you're sick?"

"Then let me come home," Mandy had pleaded.

Lorena had paused again for several seconds. "We would love for you to be here . . . with us . . . to have our family together again. But it has to be on the terms we've already discussed. Your father and I have agreed, we can't go back to the way it was before. That was no way for any of us to live. The fighting . . . the yelling . . . the lies, not to mention the poor example you were setting for your younger sister and brothers. Our bishop thinks this is a good way to—"

"The bishop?! You don't care about me . . . you only care about what other people think! What other people might say . . . just like Blade told me!"

"I would hardly call that young man a reliable source," Lorena had countered.

"You and Dad are ruining my life! Don't you know how much I love Blade?! He's the only one who understands me! He's the only one I want to be with!" Mandy had wailed before shoving the phone at her aunt. From the one-sided conversation she could overhear, Mandy had gathered that her mother had alternated between tears and angry outbursts of her own. Aunt Betty had tried to soothe the woman, but Mandy suspected her mother was probably still blowing steam, too upset to realize that her daughter was very likely lying on her death bed. Maybe if she died, her parents would see how miserable they had made her.

"Maybe later you can try some toast," Betty said now, interrupting Mandy's morbid train of thought.

Groaning at her aunt's suggestion, Mandy pulled the quilt over her head.

"Mandy, I am not the enemy!" Betty said, tiring of her niece's insolent behavior. "I'm trying to help you."

"You can help me most by leaving me alone!" Mandy exclaimed.

Enraged, Betty stomped out of the bedroom. The disrespect Mandy had shown during Lorena's phone call had been eating at her all morning. Marching downstairs, Betty promised to give Mandy the space she desired. She threw on a jacket and went out to help her husband repair the line of fence he wanted to finish that day.

* * *

Doris Kelsey glanced around the classroom. Creative Writing was one of her favorite classes to teach. It was in this relaxed environment that she could encourage budding talent and get better acquainted with some of the students she barely knew in her formal English classes. Doris loved working with young people and it showed in the way that she taught. She had influenced countless lives with her infectious love of life, literature, and writing. Using humor and a quick wit to reach some of her more challenging students, she rarely had to resort to less subtle means to control her classes.

Surprisingly, the assignment she had made yesterday had been a challenge for this class, so Doris had agreed to let the students continue working on the essay today. "Write something that will reveal a secret part of yourselves," she had asked, trying to get these students to reach beyond the normal scope of writing.

To enhance the creative atmosphere, she popped in a tape of *Enya*. As the Gaelic strains filtered softly throughout the room, Doris glanced around, her gaze settling on Bev Henderson. Very aware of the challenges Bev was facing, it tore at Doris' heart to see the tired strain in the senior's face. Hoping Bev could alleviate some of the stress she was feeling through her writing, Doris offered an encouraging smile. Relieved to see Bev return the smile, Doris shifted her gaze to Karen, Bev's best friend. These two young women had been through so much together. Karen had been there for Bev when Bev's father had remarried. Bev had been there for Karen when Karen's mother had been sent to prison. As their trials had continued, the two girls had helped each other survive. Their friendship was solid enough to make room for others, including Terri Jeppson, a formerly annoying young lady, and Sabrina Erickson, Kate's younger sister. Doris studied the four girls; each were so different, and yet similar traits were continually surfacing. Their challenges were shaping them into strong leaders, trend-setters— girls that most people respected.

With that thought in mind, Doris focused on the empty desk Mandy Hopkins usually claimed. Mandy had been extremely sick yesterday and Doris wasn't surprised by her absence today. She knew very little about the new student, only that Mandy had moved to Blaketown during the summer and was living with her relatives, the Sandlers. Mandy was a marked contrast to her cousin, Sara Sandler. A senior, Sara was as polite and gracious as Mandy was obstinate. Sara wasn't the most beautiful girl in the school, but was easily one of the most popular. Currently serving as the high school student body president, Sara didn't lack for friends, something Mandy certainly did. Mandy seemed content to remain a loner; her brusque attitude had successfully squelched the efforts that had been made to welcome her to Blaketown. Doris had tried to talk Bev and Karen into befriending Mandy, but both girls, Bev especially, had refused to cooperate. Surprised by their response, she had insisted on knowing why.

"Mandy is trouble we don't need!" Bev had exclaimed, leaving the classroom in a huff.

Pushing for more information, Doris had eventually learned from Karen that Bev had had a run-in with Mandy just before school had started.

"Mandy's lucky Bev didn't knock the smirk off her face that day at the fair," Karen had stressed. "With everything Bev's dealing with right now, being around Mandy isn't a good idea. Ask someone else to be her friend—it is not going to happen with me or Bev."

Doris had asked several other students to make an effort with Mandy, but the new girl seemed determined to push everyone away— no one had been able to reach her. Taking an added interest in this troubled girl, Doris was certain that Mandy's anger masked pain and fear. She had seen this before with other students—Karen Beyer for one. Last year, Karen had been so upset with her mother, she had written poetry filled with raging despair. Alarmed, Doris had made it a point to take the brooding young woman under her wing, encouraging Karen's efforts as the anonymous editor of *The Blaketown Buzz*. It had given Karen a much-needed release for the anger she had been carrying inside. As time had passed, Karen had softened, establishing a close relationship with her mother, Edie. Her turbulent life was finally settling into a comfortable routine, one that encouraged positive growth.

Doris would be the first one to admit that being a teenager in today's world was a difficult thing. It often broke her heart to see the challenges in her students' lives. She had decided that one of her responsibilities was to point out the positive things in existence, to hold out the hope of a brighter tomorrow. She wasn't always as successful as she had been with Karen, but had promised herself that she would always try to reach out to those who struggled.

As Doris continued to evaluate her students, Sabrina shifted in her chair, trying her best to stay awake. She wondered if she was catching the same flu bug Mandy had gone home with yesterday. Extremely nauseated—Sabrina also ached everywhere, felt extremely cold, and had a horrible headache. If it got any worse, she might follow Mandy's example and go home. But then she would miss volleyball practice after school and Terri's party tonight. Doing her best to ignore the unpleasant signals her body was sending, Sabrina continued to work on her essay.

By the time class ended, Sabrina had managed to finish the assignment, something she hoped made sense. Her head pounding, she found it difficult to follow what Bev and Karen were saying as they left the classroom together. Terri sprinted far ahead, hurrying to a P.E. class on the other side of the school.

"Hey, Sabrina, are you feeling okay?" Karen asked, glancing back at the sophomore. "You're awfully pale."

Bev turned to gaze at the younger girl. "Karen's right, you look terrible. Maybe we'd better feed you again," she teased. "After all, lunch is an entire hour away."

"No food right now," Sabrina said, offering a small smile. "I don't feel very good," she admitted. Her aching head seemed to make everything spin.

"Maybe you'd better go home," Karen sympathized.

"Yeah, before you give it to the rest of us," Bev added. When Sabrina didn't smile, Bev moved to the younger girl's side. "Hey, I was kidding, okay?! We'll help you get to Kate's room. She has prep period this hour. She can take you home."

Vaguely aware that she was being escorted to her sister's class-room, Sabrina allowed herself to be led along, grateful that her friends were propelling her in the right direction. She lacked the energy to move very far by herself.

"Hey, Kate," Bev called out as she and Karen tried to steady Sabrina, "your little sis is really sick."

"What?" Kate asked, turning from the file cabinet in her class-room. One look at Sabrina confirmed Bev's diagnosis. "Sit her down," Kate advised, hurrying across the room. Karen and Bev managed to lower Sabrina into a nearby desk, then held onto their friend to keep her from slipping out of the plastic chair.

"Sabrina, can you hear me?" Kate worriedly asked.

Sabrina nodded weakly, her blue eyes glazed.

"What's wrong?" Kate asked her younger sister.

"I don't know," Sabrina mumbled. She slumped down, resting her head on the desk. Groaning, she tried very hard to control the tears that felt close at hand. Why would she be crying? It was just the flu. This was silly. Embarrassed, she kept her face hidden as everything faded to a fuzzy black.

"Sabrina! Great, she's passed out! Okay, here's the deal, I'll get some help . . . we'll load her in my car and I'll take her up to the hospital. Can you two stay with her for a couple of minutes?" Kate asked as the tardy bell rang. Ignoring it, Bev and Karen agreed to remain with Sabrina.

Feeling awkward, Kate hurried as fast as her pregnant frame would allow. Six months along, Kate was heavier than she had ever been in her entire life. Although thrilled by the prospects of becoming a mother, Kate wasn't used to the extra demands made on her body during recent months. Before school started, she had succumbed to having her long auburn hair cut. It now hung under her chin in a becoming fashion in preparation for the hectic months ahead, a style that would be easier to maintain with her limited time.

Picking up her pace, Kate made her way to the office, called her mother, then handed her keys to the school secretary, instructing the good-natured woman to pull the red, Dodge Neon up to the front steps of the high school. Next Kate rounded up Gary Barnes, a biology teacher who did double-duty as Sabrina's volleyball coach. The muscular man carried Sabrina out of the classroom and down the hall of the school. Bev and Karen insisted on helping and between the four of them, they were able to get Sabrina out to the car. Kate pushed down the front bucket seat on the right-hand side of the car, and they laid Sabrina on it. Ignoring the coach's admonition to return to the Biology II class he taught that hour, Bev and Karen dashed to the car Bev had driven to school that day. Anxious to find out what was going on with Sabrina, they followed Kate to the hospital.

\* \* \*

"There, that's better," Betty said, relieved that Mandy had been able to keep a piece of toast down. "Do you want to try some Sprite?"

Nodding, Mandy continued to chew on the second piece of toast her aunt had brought up to her room. As the day had progressed, the nausea had eased. Maybe this rotten flu was finally going away.

"There's a liter of Sprite in the fridge downstairs. Why don't you come down with me and I'll pour you a glass. You could lay on the couch and watch TV for a bit," Betty offered, hoping to entice Mandy out of her room. As far as she was concerned, this girl had spent far too much time cooped up in the guest room that had been converted to Mandy's bedroom.

"Okay," Mandy agreed, ready for a change of scenery. Anything had to be better than lying up here, staring at the cracked ceiling.

Encouraged, Betty led the way down the stairs. Maybe in time, Mandy would come to see that all of this was for her benefit. Only then could they begin to help her find her way back.

\* \* \*

"I'm sorry things are so crazy with your dad right now," Karen commented, smiling sympathetically at Bev.

Bev glanced around the hospital waiting room, then at Karen who was sitting beside her. "I can't believe Dad wants to send me away again. It didn't work last time, what makes him think it will now?!"

"But you're doing better! It's been six weeks since your last drink, right?"

"Yeah," Bev supplied. "Last night I thought I was going to cave in again—I wanted a drink so bad." Ashamed, she searched her friend's face for understanding. "It's tough to explain."

"I know how hard it's been for my mom. Would it help to talk to her? She's stayed away from that stuff for nearly four years."

A glimmer of hope danced in Bev's blue eyes. "Has it been that long?"

"Yes," Karen answered. "She nearly blew it last year, thanks to me. I was pretty hard on her when she first got out of prison."

"She's put you through quite a bit most of your life. How were you to know she was serious about getting her act together?" Bev reminded Karen. Rising, she moved to the window and stared at the line of cars in the hospital parking lot.

"Bev, I know you're serious this time too," Karen encouraged, moving to stand beside her friend. "You can do this!"

"Where were you last night?" Bev groaned. "I could've used some cheerleading." She paused, pondering the night's events. "Actually, I think I had extra help last night."

"Really?" Karen asked. "What happened?"

"Promise you won't laugh?"

"Bev," Karen complained, "I never laugh when something means this much to you."

"I know, I'm just not very comfortable talking about stuff like this."

"Stuff like what?" Karen pried.

"Like having a prayer answered." Embarrassed, Bev blushed.

Smiling warmly, Karen waited for Bev to continue.

"I was so desperate last night, I picked up that book you gave me."

"The Book of Mormon?" Karen questioned.

"That's the one . . . I read this scripture about dealing with weaknesses—something about turning them to strengths." Bev tried to ignore the exultant look on Karen's face. "I felt like I should pray for help, so I did."

"And?"

"And later, Gina told me that she felt like she should check on me. I might've messed up if she hadn't been there last night."

Karen gazed steadily at Bev. "If no one had been there, what would you have done?"

"I'm not sure."

"That's when you call me," Karen insisted.

"Even if it's late at night?"

"Anytime you need me, I'm here for you," Karen said, drawing Bev into a hug.

Unable to respond, Bev squeezed Karen back. At that moment, Greg Erickson hurried through the front door of the hospital, startling the girls who quickly pulled apart.

"Where's Sabrina?" he asked, glancing at his daughter's friends. It wasn't very reassuring to see that both girls had been crying.

"She's in the ER," Karen stammered. "They're running tests. Kate and your wife are with her."

"Let us know if you hear anything," Bev requested, wiping at her eyes.

Nodding, Greg hurried down the hall, turning a corner to head for the ER.

"He probably thinks we're both a couple of wimps," Bev said.

"We are," Karen teased, getting a smile, and a light smack on the arm from Bev.

# Chapter 4

"Diabetes?" Sue stammered, falling back into the chair she had been sitting in. She stared at her daughter's still form in the hospital bed. After Sabrina had regained consciousness in the ER, the exhausted young woman had slept through most of the afternoon.

Doctor Davis looked up from the chart in his hand to confirm the diagnosis. In the forty years he had served as a local doctor, he had found that sharing this kind of news didn't get any easier. There was no easy way to tell a family that a loved one was facing a serious, chronic illness.

"Are you sure?" Greg questioned, slipping an arm around Sue's trembling shoulders.

Mike reached for Kate, placing a supportive arm around his wife's bulging waist. His dark eyes reflected the concern he felt for his wife and her family.

"Yes—her blood sugar level was in the seven hundred range when she was first brought in. We've rechecked it four times since then. Even with the insulin we're giving her, she's still in the high four hundreds."

"What's normal?" Greg asked.

"The normal range is eighty to one hundred and twenty," the doctor explained. Then, noticing that Sabrina was stirring, he motioned for everyone to follow him out into the hall. He shut the door to Sabrina's hospital room before facing her family. "In my experience, your reaction to this news will affect how well Sabrina will respond." He glanced gravely from face to worried face. "I know you have a million questions—I'll try to answer them as best I can, but let me start by assuring you that your daughter can still lead a normal life."

"Giving shots is normal?!" Greg exclaimed, as a feeling of helpless rage surged through his system. He had seen the negative impact diabetes had had on his father during the final years of his life. Complications from this disease had eventually led to his death three years ago.

"For some diabetics it is," Doctor Davis replied calmly. He motioned for the family to follow him to the cafeteria, desiring privacy, and a chance to move these people away from Sabrina until the shock of what he had to tell them began to wear off.

"All right," he began again when everyone was seated around a table, "let me start by stressing that none of you are responsible for what Sabrina has developed." The doctor focused on Sue Erickson, Sabrina's mother. He knew most parents blamed themselves when their children were diagnosed with a serious illness. "It wasn't anything you did or didn't do. Sabrina has what we call Type 1 diabetes. Her immune system went haywire and instead of fighting off disease or an infection, the antibodies destroyed the beta cells in her pancreas, causing her to develop diabetes. Without the beta cells, insulin can't be produced and her body can't use the food she eats."

"It wasn't anything she ate that brought this on? Too much candy or pop?" Sue asked tearfully.

Doctor Davis shook his head. "No. She may have a genetic tendency toward this disease but—"

"My father was a diabetic," Greg exclaimed, crushed by this news. It was his fault—his family line.

"That may or may not have had anything to do with Sabrina," the doctor replied. "I'm assuming your father developed this disease later in his life?"

Greg nodded slowly.

"He was a Type 2 diabetic."

"What's the difference?" Kate asked numbly.

"Type 2 diabetics usually develop the disease when they're much older than Sabrina. With this form of the disease, the pancreas still produces insulin, but for some reason, it has become lazy. A healthy diet and exercise can encourage it to work more efficiently.

Sometimes Type 2s take oral medications that stimulate the pancreas to produce more insulin. If that fails, we prescribe shots of insulin." He took a deep breath then asked, "Was your father overweight?"

"Yes," Greg revealed.

"He fits the typical pattern for Type 2s. The heavier you are, the harder your pancreas has to work. Sometimes after years of being overworked, it quits, or barely functions."

"And Type 1s?" Sue pressed.

"Your daughter is actually underweight. Type 1s always have to go on insulin because their pancreas no longer works. With the shots of insulin, Sabrina's body will be able to utilize the food she eats. It's the insulin that breaks food down into particles the body can use."

"That's why she was losing so much weight!" Sue exclaimed. "She was starving to death and I didn't even realize it!"

"You had no way of knowing what was going on. Sabrina had classic symptoms, the weight loss, extreme thirst, frequent urination, fatigue, unusual hunger, nausea . . . but if you don't know what you're looking for, you pass it off as the flu. You reason that this person is continuously running to the bathroom because of the amount of water they drink. It's a vicious cycle."

"Will she be all right?" Sue asked, voicing her main concern.

"Yes. We caught her before she slipped into a coma. We've been pumping IV fluids through her system. She was understandably dehydrated. We'll continue to give her insulin to combat the high blood sugar level . . . eventually, things will balance out. When we get Sabrina stabilized, I would suggest taking her to see a specialist."

"Do you know of one?" Greg asked.

"I do. He runs a clinic for diabetics in Idaho Falls. I can help you set up an appointment."

"Idaho Falls?" Sue repeated. "That's nearly three hours away."

"We can handle emergencies that may occur with Sabrina here in Blaketown, but for long-term care, I would recommend a specialist who's on top of the latest research." He gazed at Greg. "I assume you have insurance?"

Greg nodded. "I'm self-employed, but we do have a policy. I'm not sure how good it is . . . there's some clause about getting pre-approval for the doctors we see. If they're part of the insurance plan, then they'll cover a goodly portion of the expense. If not, we're on our own." He sighed deeply. "I had wonderful insurance benefits with a computer company in Bozeman, Montana." His head slipped to his hands. "Maybe we shouldn't have moved."

"Things will work out," the doctor replied. "I'm sure there will be more questions, but for now, I think you could use some time to absorb what I've already told you. Sabrina will need all of you to be as supportive as possible. Her lifestyle is about to change on a permanent basis. Again, how well she does will depend a great deal on you." He smiled, hoping to ease their heavy hearts. "I don't know Sabrina well yet, but I'm guessing she's a special young lady. She'll get through this, especially if she knows you're in her corner."

"How do we tell her?" Overwhelmed by the magnitude of this newest challenge, Sue burst into tears.

"Sabrina will take her cues from you. If she senses you're scared, she will be too. If she thinks you're okay about this, then she'll react accordingly. There will be an adjustment period, but she'll adapt. You all will." He offered a smile to the despondent family. "When you're ready, I'll come in with you to answer any questions Sabrina may have." Turning, he left the cafeteria.

* * *

Opening her eyes, Sabrina glanced around the small room, then at her hospital bed. "Where am I?" she asked, confused.

"You're in the hospital . . . Blaketown Memorial," a soft voice replied.

Sabrina turned her head, relieved to see Karen's mom, Edie, at her side. "The hospital?"

"Yes. You were very sick when they brought you in earlier today."

"Where's my mom?" Sabrina murmured, her mouth feeling unusually dry.

"She was here with you most of the afternoon. She just stepped out in the hall for minute with the doctor," Edie said, smiling as she checked Sabrina's blood pressure. A new monitor purchased for the hospital by the local Lion's Club automatically revealed Sabrina's vital signs from a lighted probe connected to the young woman's index finger. Edie was pleased to note that her young patient's blood pressure was closer to the normal range.

"Could I have some water?" Sabrina asked, licking her dry lips.

"Sure. I filled a pitcher of ice water for you a few minutes ago. I'll pour a glass for you." Edie slid a small, portable table closer to Sabrina's bed and reached for the pitcher of water. This would make Doctor Davis happy. He wanted fluids pushed as they tried to adjust Sabrina's blood sugar level. After filling a glass with water, Edie raised the head of Sabrina's bed, then helped the trembling teen take a drink.

"Why am I so shaky?"

"You're weak from being so sick," Edie answered as she lowered Sabrina against the pillow. She wished the young woman's family would reappear to handle the battery of questions Sabrina was sure to ask.

"This must be some flu bug," Sabrina muttered, glancing at the IV lines that surrounded her. "How many IVs am I hooked to?"

"Three," Edie said, her guard up.

"Why so many?" Sabrina pondered, noting that an IV seemed to sprout from each arm, as well as one leg.

"You were very dehydrated," Edie replied, praying Sabrina wouldn't push the issue. "Your body needs fluids. Earlier, the veins in your wrists and hands collapsed because you were so dehydrated. That's why the IVs are in your arms and leg."

"I'm dehydrated? That's weird—especially the way I've been drinking water." Glancing away from the slender tubing connected to her body, she looked up at Edie. "What time is it?"

"Nearly four o'clock," Edie said, examining her watch.

"Wow! The last thing I remember is sitting in Kate's classroom. That was around eleven. Everything seems fuzzy after that."

"It's because of this illness," Edie responded. She patted Sabrina's arm reassuringly. "You'll be fine, though. We're right on top of things."

Sabrina offered a small smile. "I'm glad you're my nurse."

"You're among friends. It's our job to take good care of you." Edie gave Sabrina's shoulder a light squeeze. "Now, is there anything I can do to make you more comfortable?"

"Could you find my mom?"

"Sure. She'll be glad to know you're awake." Moving to the door, Edie opened it and looked down the hall. There was no sign of Doctor Davis or Sabrina's family. Reluctant to leave Sabrina alone, she left the door open, hoping someone would notice. Turning, she walked back to the hospital bed.

"Is she in the hall?" Sabrina probed.

Before Edie could respond, Doctor Davis poked his head in. He smiled at Edie, then at Sabrina. "Well, you've finally decided to join us! It's about time, Sleeping Beauty—I'd like to get in a round of golf this afternoon," he teased. "I'll go tell your family you're awake. They were grabbing a snack at the cafeteria, doctor's orders. I don't think any of them had eaten lunch today. I know they'll want to come see you."

Sabrina visibly relaxed at this news.

"Edie will stay with you until your family returns to your room. If you need anything, just let her know," the doctor continued. He wiggled his eyebrows, then disappeared into the hall.

"Is he for real?" Sabrina asked, looking at Edie.

Edie laughed. "He tries to be funny, emphasis on 'tries.' He's a good man, though, and an excellent doctor."

"I'll take your word for it."

"Good girl. Karen tells me you're thinking about joining the high school newspaper staff," Edie said, hoping to sway the conversation from Sabrina's current condition.

"Yeah, I'm thinking about it." She frowned slightly. "I'm not sure I have what it takes to be a reporter. I'd rather play volleyball."

"Oh," Edie said, trying to keep her voice light. Could Sabrina still participate in school sports? She was just starting to study the treatment of diabetes and was unsure what Sabrina's limitations would be with this disease.

"I hope my coach will understand why I wasn't to practice this afternoon."

"He'll understand," Edie reassured.

"He's probably wondering what my problem is. Lately, I haven't had much energy." She gazed again at the IVs flowing into her body. "This will take care of that, right?"

"It will," Edie replied brightly. She wasn't sure how much longer she could keep up this act with Sabrina. She had grown quite fond of

Karen's new friend over the summer and knew the diagnosis of diabetes would upset Sabrina. She also knew how this would affect Karen and wasn't looking forward to divulging this news to her daughter.

"Sabrina, you're awake," Sue said, entering the room. She shared an apprehensive look with Edie, then moved to her daughter's side, reaching down to caress Sabrina's hand. "I just left for a few minutes."

"I know," Sabrina replied, noticing her mother's reddened, puffy eyes. "Mom . . ." she started to say as her father walked into the room.

"How's my girl?" Greg asked a little too cheerfully.

"What's going on?" Sabrina responded, sensing that something was wrong.

"It's okay, sweetheart," Sue tried to console. She leaned down to kiss Sabrina's forehead.

"I'm dying, right?!" Sabrina exclaimed.

"NO!" Sue said emphatically. "You're going to be just fine!"

Sabrina gazed into her mother's face and saw concerned love. "I will?"

"Sabrina, I've never lied to you before, and I won't start now. You do have a serious illness, but you will recover—"

"What's wrong with me?" Sabrina asked, trying not to cry when she saw the look of fear in her father's face.

"You've developed diabetes," Sue said, aching for her daughter.

Sabrina stared at her mother, then at her father, then at Edie. "What? Like Grandpa Erickson?"

"No, your diabetes is different! It has nothing to do with what you saw Grandpa go through! He didn't control his blood sugar, mostly because he didn't want to. You'll learn to control yours and live a normal life!" Sue emphasized.

"But . . . how? I don't understand . . . why?" Sabrina asked, as tears made an appearance.

"We're not sure, honey. It wasn't anything you did—it just happened, and now we have to make the best of it." Sue carefully moved the IV tubing out of the way, leaned down and hugged Sabrina. "It's going to be all right. We have a lot to learn, but we're in this together."

Too weak to return her mother's hug, Sabrina continued to cry. She envisioned giving herself shots like her grandfather had done and the image terrified her.

"Your father and Mike would like to give you a priesthood blessing," Sue said, releasing her hold on Sabrina. The fifteen-year-old gazed tearfully up at her mother, reaching for Sue's hand. Sue held it inside of her own, grateful the IVs were connected to the veins in Sabrina's arms. She continued to squeeze her youngest daughter's hand as Greg and Mike prepared to give Sabrina a much needed blessing.

\* \* \*

A few minutes past five o'clock, Edie walked down the hall of the small county hospital. Normally the day shift ran until 3:00 p.m. She had volunteered to stay later today to help with Sabrina. Wearily, she turned a corner, heading for the waiting room to see if Karen and her friends were still there.

"What's going on?" Karen asked as her mother moved into view. "All we've heard is that Sabrina's stabilized. Do they know what's wrong with her?"

Edie glanced at the three young women. She had known that Karen and Bev had come in with Sabrina and assumed Terri had arrived after school.

"Is it bad?" Karen prodded.

"Sit down girls. Sabrina's family asked me to talk to you three. We might as well do it here."

Bev exchanged a worried look with Karen, then returned to her chair. Karen and Terri sat on each side of her, the three girls bracing themselves for what they assumed was bad news.

"Sabrina has diabetes," Edie began.

"What?" Terri exclaimed. "But she's too young! Only old people get that, right?"

Edie shook her head. "Even young children can become diabetics."

"Will she have to give herself shots?" Bev asked, appalled.

"Yes. Her pancreas doesn't work, so she'll have to give herself shots to get the insulin she'll need to live."

Absorbing this news, the three girls sat in shocked silence.

"Sabrina will be all right, but she's going to need you three now more than ever," Edie began.

"What can we do to help?" Karen responded.

"She'll need to know that you don't mind the changes that will take place in her life. Most teenagers try very hard to fit in with everyone else. This will be difficult for Sabrina . . . she's dealing with something most people her age have no clue about."

"Anything else?" Bev asked.

"Learn all you can about diabetes. Be there for her when she has a bad day. It would also be a good idea to learn to recognize the signs that indicate she's in trouble. If her blood sugar runs too high, or too low, she may need your help." Edie smiled warmly at the girls. "Sabrina will get through this. She was given quite a blessing by her father and brother-in-law."

"Oh?" Karen prompted, curious.

Taking a deep breath, Edie recalled the phrase that had touched her most. "Sabrina was promised that she would learn and grow from this experience. That because of what she'll learn, she'll be able to help others around her." Still remembering what she had felt during Sabrina's blessing, Edie saw a silent plea in Bev's face and promised herself she would find the time to talk privately with her daughter's closest friend. Anxious to prevent Bev from the heartache she had experienced as a result of alcoholism, Edie felt a certain amount of responsibility shift to her shoulders. Rising, she invited the three girls to join her for a hamburger at a local drive-in.

"But what about Sabrina?" Terri asked, her brown hair bobbing under her chin as she stood.

"Sabrina needs to spend some time with her family. Later tonight, before visiting hours are over, would be a good time for you girls to see her," Edie suggested.

Agreeing, the teenagers followed Edie out of the hospital, still stunned over their friend's diagnosis.

# Chapter 5

"So, how's our little Mandy doin'?" the robust farmer asked as he swaggered into the large living room. Plopping down in his favorite recliner, Lyle Sandler offered his niece a teasing smile. Before Mandy could roll her eyes in disgust, her uncle began singing a song that was driving her crazy, something he sang at least a couple of times every day. "Ohhhh Mandy, you came and you gave without taking . . ."

Refusing to look at her uncle, Mandy shifted around on the couch, staring dismally out the large picture window into the night.

"Dad!" eighteen-year-old Sara groaned. "Please! I can't take Barely-Man-Enough tonight. I have a headache." Lowering her book, she silently pleaded with her father to ease up on Mandy.

"I'll have you know Barry Manilow is a national shrine. A musical gift to the world." In his deepest voice he sang out, "Barry writes the songs that make the whole world cry . . ."

*You can say that again,* Mandy thought to herself.

"Dad, I said please!"

Lyle grinned at his youngest child. "Your li'l ol' head be achin'?" he asked, patting his balding head.

"Yes, thanks to you," Sara returned, trying to refocus on *The Odyssey,* by Homer, the book she had to read this weekend for accelerated English.

"You're studyin' too hard," Lyle exclaimed. "You're wearin' out your brain cells. Pretty soon, they'll go on strike. Then where will you be?"

Despite herself, Sara smiled. She loved her father dearly, and most times, enjoyed his teasing nature. If only Mandy wasn't here. Mandy always exploded whenever Sara's father tried to have a little fun. Sara couldn't stand Mandy's unwelcome outbursts; her younger cousin always caused an ugly scene, upsetting the entire family.

Returning his daughter's smile, Lyle tried again with Mandy. He was certain that eventually, his niece would start responding to his unique sense of humor. It had always worked with his own children. Whenever they had been out of sorts, he had always been able to get a smile out of them. Mandy was a supreme challenge. "So, your tender tummy is on the mend, Mandy? Say, that's quite a tongue twister. Tender tummy on the mend Mandy," he repeated.

Still refusing to answer, Mandy continued to stare out the window. She had learned that the more she railed against him, the worse Uncle Lyle got. It was best to ignore him until he selected another victim.

"Sabrina Erickson was really sick at school today . . . right around lunch hour. I think they had to take her up to the hospital," Sara said, trying to draw her father's attention away from her cousin.

"What's the matter with that school? What are they feedin' you kids at the trough these days? First Mandy, now Sabrina . . ."

Giving up, Sara set her book down on the small end table beside the loveseat. "I ate at the cafeteria today and I didn't get sick," she pointed out.

"That's 'cuz you're used to your mother's cooking," Lyle returned, laughing.

"I heard that," Betty replied from the kitchen where she was sweeping the floor.

Lyle's hazel-colored eyes crinkled with merriment. His wife was one of the best cooks in the county. He felt it was his duty to keep her humble with constructive criticism once in a while. "Well, if it ain't the trough, there must be something else makin' all of you kids sick. Maybe one of those mysterious new diseases is plaguing our fair city."

Mandy silently protested—Blaketown was hardly a city.

"Let's see, we got the E-bowl-a, that disease where if you bowl too much, your arm falls off."

"Ebola is a deadly virus that was discovered in Africa, Dad," Sara corrected. "I did a research paper on it last year. It's a horrible disease."

"Then there's HIVE, which comes from standin' too close to

where the bees live," Lyle continued, ignoring his daughter's protests.

"HIV isn't caused . . ." Sara tried to interrupt, starting to enjoy this battle of wits with her father.

"Or maybe one of those ADES diseases. Let's see, there's lemonade, orangeade, Band-aid, First-aid—"

"Would you just shut up!" Mandy exclaimed, rising from the couch. "Some things aren't funny!" Hurrying from the room, she ran upstairs and slammed her bedroom door.

"What is wrong with that girl?" Lyle asked, standing.

"You need to quit provoking her, Lyle," Betty advised, stepping into the living room.

"I was only kidding around, like I always do. Why should I change who I am for that ungrateful thing we've got livin' with us?"

"Does she have to stay here?" Sara added to the chorus. "It's so embarrassing when people learn she's my cousin. The other day she tripped and dropped her books. You should've heard what came out of her mouth!"

"Trust me, I've probably heard that and more the past couple of days," Betty informed her daughter. "Where Mandy learned to swear like that I'll never know!"

"Let's call her parents and tell them this isn't working out," Sara continued, hoping to sway her mother.

"And where does Mandy go from here?" Betty asked.

"Who cares! She's ruining my senior year! Does that matter to either of you?" Sara returned, glancing from her mother to her dad. "It's like living with a Tasmanian devil, and that's putting it mildly."

"Taz . . . it has a certain charm," Lyle said, savoring this newest idea. "Thanks, Sara, I've been tryin' to come up with a nickname for our newest family member."

"You call her that and you'll really see some fireworks," Sara warned. "Mandy has no sense of humor, no patience, no personality—"

"Items you excel in," Lyle interrupted. "Maybe she could learn from you, Miss Student Body President!"

"So you're saying we're stuck with her?" Disappointed, Sara could see the answer in her mother's face.

"If we can somehow turn her around—she's family, Sara. She's in trouble and we've been asked to help. I'm not saying it will be easy—heaven knows it would be easier to send her back, but how are we all going to feel someday when we leave this life and discover that we were supposed to help Mandy? Maybe we're the only ones who can reach her right now."

"We're doing such a good job of that!" Sara snapped.

"I'm the one who comes up with the one-liners around here, young lady," Lyle chided. "Tell you what, I'll try to control myself around Mandy. She's a bit touchy right now, so I won't go out of my way to . . . what was it you said, dear, 'provoke' her?"

Betty nodded. "Remember, they say that those who deserve love the least need it the most."

"There's not enough love in the world . . ." Sara began, then paused when she saw the look on her mother's face.

"What the girl needs now, is love, sweet love," Lyle sang loudly, trying to bail his daughter out of a lecture.

"Let's give it another try," Betty encouraged. "Maybe if we pray for her, love her, show her kindness whenever she messes up, we'll finally get through to her." She gazed solemnly at her husband and daughter. "If we give up on her, I fear this family will lose her forever. Now, will you two help me with this or not?"

Sara nodded glumly.

"You bet!" Lyle responded, pulling his wife into an intense hug. "We'll star in our own version of, 'Honey, I Shrunk the Attitude!'"

"Lyle!" Betty scolded.

"I'll be good, you'll see," he said, leaning down to give his wife a kiss. "Don't I always make everything better?"

Blushing, Sara turned away from her parents as they shared another kiss. As far as she was concerned, if there wasn't enough love in this household to touch Mandy's heart, Mandy was a lost cause.

* * *

Bev, Karen, and Terri walked down the hall of the hospital to Sabrina's room. They paused outside of the partially opened door, trying to "psych up." Edie had cautioned them earlier, instructing them to be optimistic—Sabrina's sagging spirits needed a cheering lift.

Summoning her courage, Bev strode in first, dragging in the helium-filled balloons they had brought with them. One was made of mylar—it sported a cute mouse with a large sign that said, "Get Well Soon!" something they had purchased at the new large grocery store down the street from the hospital.

"Hey, there, Sabrina," Bev said, smiling at the younger girl as she tied the balloons to the IV stand at the head of Sabrina's bed. Karen and Terri entered the room, standing at the foot of the hospital bed.

"Hey, guys," Sabrina replied. "Thanks for the balloons."

"You're welcome," Karen said.

Rising from a chair near Sabrina's bed, Sue smiled gratefully at Sabrina's friends, girls who meant so much in her daughter's life right now. "Sabrina, I need to slip out for a minute. Visit with your friends and I'll be back to check on you."

A panicked look crossed Sabrina's face as Sue moved toward the door. Doing her best to ignore it, Sue walked out of the room. She knew Sabrina was worried about how her friends would react to her new condition. Hoping the four girls could work through this on their own, Sue headed for the waiting room to find the rest of her family.

"This is the same room they put me in last spring with my broken leg," Bev observed, glancing around Sabrina's hospital room. "Same lovely green color."

"It's the second room I've been in today. I woke up in intensive care," Sabrina shared.

"Mom says you're doing great," Karen said. "That's why they moved you."

"She's a wonderful nurse," Sabrina responded. "I hope she's working tomorrow."

"She is," Karen replied. "I think she'll request having you as one of her patients."

"Good," Sabrina said, relieved. "Most of these nurses are okay, but your mom is the best."

"That's what I hear." Karen smiled. "I'm proud of her, but I'll be glad when she finally passes this LPN course. When she's not up here at the hospital, she's home studying. It's getting to be a drag."

"How are you feeling tonight?" Terri asked, leaning against the wall by the side of Sabrina's bed.

Shrugging, Sabrina found she couldn't reply. She closed her eyes to stymie the tears that had been making a frequent appearance all afternoon.

"Hey, it's us, remember, we're here for you, Breeny," Bev said, using the nickname they had learned from Kate, a nickname Sabrina no longer minded. Reaching down, Bev patted Sabrina's shoulder.

"I know," Sabrina said, opening her eyes. She held her breath, still fighting to remain in control. "It's just so—"

"Crappy. Go ahead, say it," Bev encouraged.

"Nice vocabulary, future English major," Karen teased.

"I was trying to tone it down for you morons."

"Mormons," Terri corrected.

"Yeah, whatever, same diff," Bev retorted. "Bottom line, Sabrina feels like . . . help me out here, what's a Mormon word for . . . surely you have words that you use when life is a bummer. Stuff like, darn, flip, shoot—"

"Don't even go there," Karen warned good-naturedly.

"Shoot is good. I wish someone would do that and put me out of my misery," Sabrina commented.

Unsure of Sabrina's mood, Terri, Karen, and Bev exchanged a concerned glance.

"Instead, I get to shoot up . . . it's even legal. I'll have needle tracks and no one will even care."

"Now I'll know where to get my supplies," Bev returned, deciding to go for humor. "Next time I need a few good drugs, I'll hit you up for some syringes. That's what friends are for, right?"

"Yeah, sure," Sabrina replied, trying to smile. The vision of giving herself shots the rest of her life didn't appeal to her. She was already convinced her future would be constantly filled with pain. All day they had drawn blood from her arm every two hours to check her blood sugar level. Two of the IV sites had started to swell. Deciding Sabrina was sufficiently hydrated, those IVs had been removed, leaving one in her left arm. If that site swelled up like the others had, they would have to start another IV, something Sabrina hoped to avoid. Making a monumental effort to rise above the depression she felt, Sabrina struggled for something to say. "It's some party we're having tonight."

"Trust me, this is more fun than watching the videos Terri picked out for tonight. *Barney's Great Adventure, The Teletubbies Rebel,* and what was the other one?" Bev asked.

Terri lifted an eyebrow, then smiled. "*The Revenge of Pokéman,*" she offered.

Bev grinned her appreciation for Terri's contribution. "That's the one. That's when I said, girls, we have to get a life. Let's go see Sabrina."

"I used to have a life," Sabrina replied, then wished she hadn't. She hated the looks of pity on her friends' faces. "Kate said that I got you guys out of a Biology II test today," she said, trying to salvage the moment.

Bev brightened immediately. "Hey, that's right! Cool! Now we won't have to worry about it until Monday."

Hoping to make Sabrina laugh, Karen decided to ham things up. She held a hand to her forehead and exclaimed dramatically, "And I was so ready for that test! The hours I spent studying . . . now I'll have it hanging over my head all weekend. How will I survive?"

"Oh, give it a rest," Bev returned, "you weren't any more ready for that test than I was."

"Shhh, not in front of the lower classmen," Karen cautioned, "think of the example we should be setting."

"Since when has that ever been a consideration?" Terri asked, pleased that she had successfully slammed the older girls.

"Ooooh, she got us where it hurts," Bev responded, clasping her hands over her heart. She was delighted to see a smile tugging at the corners of Sabrina's mouth.

"It's about time," Terri continued, figuring she was on a roll. "How often have you nailed me to the wall?"

"Not often enough," Bev threatened. "Sabrina, mind if we borrow a few of your syringes? We have a smart aleck junior we need to take care of here."

Sabrina glanced around, but the only item she could find was a tiny lancet that was lying on the small table beside her bed. "Will this do?"

"Maybe to tack up one earlobe," Karen said, grinning.

Terri tried her best to look indignant. "My ears are already pierced."

"Okay, we'll go for the nose," Bev threatened. "We could glue a nice sparkly rhinestone in it later on." The four friends continued to share lighthearted banter for several minutes until a lab tech entered the hospital room. Bev glanced at the handsome young man, then at Sabrina. "Sabrina, you've been holding out on us. If I'd known men like this existed, I'd've passed out at school a long time ago."

"He's all mine," Sabrina responded, winking at the man in the white lab coat.

"Sorry girls, I'm spoken for," he said, grinning as he pointed to his wedding ring.

"Isn't that the way," Bev sighed. "The good ones are always taken."

"Speaking of taking, I need to get a blood sample from this young lady," the lab tech said, smiling at Sabrina.

"Is that our cue to leave?" Terri asked.

"If you can handle a little blood, you can stay," the lab tech replied. He snapped on a pair of fresh, rubber gloves, then prepared a syringe.

Sabrina forced a smile at the young man she had met a couple of hours ago. At least this guy was gentler than the one who had drawn blood earlier that day. Still, this wasn't her idea of a fun time.

At the sight of the syringe, Terri turned a shade paler. Noticing, Bev got Karen's attention, nudging her toward the junior.

"Terri, let's go see if there are any new babies," Karen invited, catching onto the problem. She grabbed Terri's arm and guided the younger girl from the room before she fainted.

"Couldn't hack it, eh?" Sabrina guessed, glancing at Bev.

"Terri's made of weaker stuff," Bev replied.

"Yeah, right. I saw how weak she was last spring," Sabrina reminded the senior, remembering that Terri was the one who had taken charge when Bev had broken her leg during their canyon adventure.

"Some people can't take the sight of blood," the lab tech offered. "Myself, I think it's a pretty color. Red, the color of love."

"You're spoken for, remember," Bev teased.

"Sorry, I'm a romantic at heart," he replied, checking an abused vein in Sabrina's right arm. "We'll have to pick on this vein again," he apologized, tightening a plastic strip around Sabrina's right arm. He waited a few seconds, then reached for the syringe.

Bev moved around to the other side of the bed. Reaching down, she gripped Sabrina's left hand. "Look at me, Breeny," she encouraged, drawing Sabrina's attention away from the syringe.

Wincing as the needle entered her bruised arm, Sabrina clung to Bev's hand. She held her breath as two small vials of blood were drawn from her arm.

"There, we're done," the lab tech announced as he capped the second vial. He labeled the vials, then gathered up his supplies in a handy plastic tote and left the room. "See you later," he called back.

"That's what I'm afraid of," Sabrina breathed, relaxing her grip on Bev's hand.

"You're not in this alone," Bev said softly.

Unable to reply, Sabrina nodded as tiny tears slipped from the corner of each eye.

"Sometimes life just—" Bev searched for a word that wouldn't offend.

"Stinks!" Karen suggested, stepping back into the room.

"Reeks!" Terri added, appearing behind Karen.

"There you are, you brave thing," Bev teased, grinning at Terri.

"So, I'm not cut out to be a nurse," Terri admitted.

"Or a doctor," Karen supplied. She gazed at Bev. "You might be, though."

"Maybe. Doctor Bev Henderson! I like the sound of that."

"Maybe you could find a cure for this rotten disease," Sabrina suggested, trying to regain her sense of humor.

"Maybe. Maybe I could find a cure for everything that plagues this crazy world, including stupidity. I'd start with high school freshmen everywhere."

"You're nice," Terri chided.

"Do you like freshmen?" Bev questioned.

"I was one last year," Sabrina reminded the older girls.

"I rest my case," Bev teased. As the girls continued to give each other a bad time, laughing over several outrageous comments, most compliments of Bev, Sue stepped into the room. Hiding behind the door, she was thrilled things were going this well between the four friends. Slipping out into the hall, Sue was relieved that Sabrina's friends were making her laugh, something her family had been unable to do all day.

# Chapter 6

When she was certain everyone had gone to bed, Mandy crept downstairs. Her stomach growled as she made her way to the kitchen. Opening the fridge, she assessed its contents, looking for something that would satisfy the hunger she felt. She was about to give up when she spied a piece of leftover fried chicken. Deciding that would do, she took it out of the fridge and set it on the counter. She then pulled out a liter of Sprite and poured herself a small glass. When she had returned the pop to the fridge and shut the door, she moved her small meal to the kitchen table, sitting in the spot her Aunt Betty usually claimed.

Mandy scowled, thinking of her aunt, a woman she considered coarse and pitiful. There were times when she almost missed her mother, a loving, petite woman who always smelled like vanilla. Aunt Betty's hands were calloused, her mannerisms unpolished, and her clothes made her look like a common farmhand. Taking a bite of the cold chicken, Mandy chewed slowly, surprised by how good it tasted. That was one thing her aunt could do well—cook. She guessed that through having all of those children, Aunt Betty had become an expert in that department.

Mandy consumed the small piece of chicken, then drank the Sprite. As she set the glass down, she was relieved that the pain in her stomach had diminished. She was tiring of this rotten flu bug, of the way it was controlling her life. Frowning, Mandy knew she couldn't lie to herself anymore. That was why she had been on edge earlier—Uncle Lyle's attempt at being funny had opened a door she had been trying to barricade for several weeks.

How long had she been warned about avoiding certain situations? "Don't date until you're sixteen," had been shoved in her face for years. "Never date a nonmember, or someone who doesn't have the same standards," was another piece of advice Mandy had chosen to ignore. "Group date, and don't allow yourself to date one person repeatedly." That was laughable. Blade was the only boy she had ever cared about, the only boy who had ever made her feel like a woman, even though she was only fifteen. "Don't stay out past midnight, no necking or petting, and don't allow yourself to spend time alone with a member of the opposite sex in a situation that would compromise your standards." Her standards had been compromised all right, under the very noses of her parents, teachers, and leaders!

Why had she given in to Blade that night? She had finally succumbed to his pleading caresses, allowing him to go further than she had ever intended. Little by little he had eased past former barriers, leading her into a moment of intense passion that had disappointed. It hadn't been as wonderful as she had always imagined it would be. A fleeting moment of physical pleasure that had filled her with guilt and made her susceptible to a wide range of afflictions, things her parents, teachers at school, and even her Young Women leaders had warned her about in past rebuking sermons.

Judging from Blade's expertise, Mandy was certain she hadn't been the first girl he had been with. They hadn't used any form of protection. If Blade had been carrying a venereal disease, he could have easily passed it to her that night. AIDS was another shadowy nightmare she tried to dismiss. She didn't know much about the dreaded disease, only that it could be transmitted sexually, and that it could kill a person. Was she now going to die because she had made one mistake? Her friends had lost their virginity long before she had; none of them had had any apparent problems. Instead, they had often made fun of her for trying to wait—why was she the only one being punished?

She grimaced, imagining her parents' reaction to what she had done. They had been so upset over the shoplifting incident, they had no idea what she had really been tampering with in May. If they couldn't tolerate a little stealing, they certainly wouldn't handle the news that she had been immoral. Alternating between worry and disdain, she had found it easier to pretend that nothing had happened, but could only fool herself for so long. Blade had hounded her constantly for what he now believed he was entitled to whenever they were together. She had been able to stall him off with plausible excuses, but each time he had put his arms around her, she had been filled with a desperate longing that had conflicted with a sense of self-loathing.

When the nausea had first started, she had thought it was the result of the sick, guilty feeling that had gnawed at her since that night with Blade. After moving to Blaketown, she had attributed it to homesickness. Now she was trying to convince herself it was the flu, but an uneasy feeling tormented as she considered how long she had been afflicted—nearly four months. Suddenly panicking, she stood away from her aunt's kitchen table and glanced down at her abdomen. There was no sign of any swelling. She hadn't gained weight—lately she had been losing it. She couldn't be pregnant, not after just one time. Her gaze shifted to a calendar hanging under the kitchen clock. Her monthly cycle had always been irregular, but she had never skipped four months before, usually only one or two.

Returning to the chair, she sank down and laid her head on the table. This was so unfair—other people did whatever they wanted and it never caught up to them. Shedding tears of frustration, Mandy was unaware that her aunt was standing in the doorway behind her.

Feeling helpless, Betty watched Mandy cry. She sensed that whatever was bothering her niece would have to wait for another time, when the young woman was ready to talk. Turning, Betty retraced her steps down the hall to the master bedroom. She knelt by her bed for the second time that night and petitioned for a way to help Mandy, a request she made at least twice a day.

\* \* \*

"Insert the needle inside of the rubber top of the insulin bottle," a heavy-set, registered nurse named Greta advised Sabrina as Sue and Edie watched from the other side of the hospital bed. "Okay, now slowly draw the plunger back on your syringe."

Concentrating, Sabrina followed the RN's instructions.

"Only fill it with five units of NPH," Greta instructed. "That's all your doctor wants you to have this morning."

"That's not very much," Sabrina commented, pulling the needle out of the insulin bottle after withdrawing the correct amount of insulin.

"Until we get you regulated, you won't be giving yourself a lot of insulin. We're still trying to get everything balanced. Your blood sugar level, your diet, the amount of exercise you'll need . . . and there's a chance your pancreas may still be putting out some insulin on its own. Most Type 1 diabetics go through what we call the honeymoon period for a while."

Blushing, Sabrina glanced at Edie, then at her mother. Both women tried to smile reassuringly at the struggling teen.

"You'll get bursts of insulin from your pancreas before it finally quits," the RN explained.

"How long will that happen?" Sue asked, concerned.

"It varies—usually six months to a year."

"And after that?" Sabrina wondered.

"You're on your own, so to speak. It's actually easier then to know how much insulin you're going to require. For now, we'll take it safe and slow, and gradually increase the amount as needed." The large woman grinned at her patient. "Trust me, before long, you'll be adjusting it by yourself—soon you'll know as much about your condition as your doctor does."

Trying to maintain a brave face for her mother, Sabrina held up the syringe. "Is that why I have to learn how to give my own shots?"

"Yes. We'll show your mom too, that way she can help you out once in a while. Some spots are harder to reach by yourself."

Sue paled at the thought of giving her youngest daughter shots, but vowed to react as courageously as Sabrina had to this news.

"So . . . do I give this shot to myself this morning?" Sabrina asked nervously.

"If you'd like to—or I can give it, if you'd rather, or your mother can. We would like to see you try it yourself a couple of times before you leave the hospital," Greta replied.

"How long will I be here?"

"It depends on how long it takes to get you regulated. You keep improving like you are and I would guess in a couple of days," Greta informed her.

Sabrina shared a pained look with her mother. She was hoping to get out sooner than that.

"So, young lady, what will it be this morning? Do you want me to give that shot for you, or are you going to try it yourself?" Greta prompted.

"I'll try it. I have to learn anyway, right?" Sabrina challenged. "I might as well start now."

"You're a trooper," the RN encouraged. "It's better if you learn how to give these shots yourself right off the bat."

"Where do I give it?"

Greta considered Sabrina's question. The easiest place to give a shot like this was in the stomach, but she wasn't sure how Sabrina would react to that news. Deciding to go with a place that didn't sound as tender, she patted Sabrina's leg. "Let's start with your upper thigh. Most of us have fatty tissue there."

Insulted, Sabrina tried not to glare at the nurse.

Unaware that she had offended her patient, the RN pointed to the tiny needle Sabrina was about to inject herself with. "The needles we use today are so much sharper and smaller than they've ever been. They go in slick as a whistle. It's a subcutaneous shot, that means it barely goes under the skin. It's not bad at all."

Certain the nurse was lying, Sabrina slowly drew her leg out from under the covers. "Upper thigh?"

"Yep. Pull up your gown a bit. Don't be shy!"

Feeling the blush in her face, Sabrina obediently bared her thigh. She was rapidly learning there was no pride in the hospital.

"Now take this alcohol swab and wipe it over where you think you'll give the shot. Then remember where you gave it so you can rotate sites. That way you won't build up scar tissue."

"Where am I supposed to rotate my shots?" Sabrina asked, glancing at the syringe in her hand. Yesterday, she was convinced she was becoming a human pin cushion. Her adventures today were reinforcing that image.

"Today we'll start with your right leg. That thigh of yours offers quite a large area, so you can give several shots in that location,"

Greta instructed, oblivious once again to the dirty look Sabrina sent her direction. "Then in a couple of days, you can rotate to the top of your left leg. After that, I'd suggest the stomach."

Her eyes widening, Sabrina glanced down at her abdomen. "What?!"

"It sounds worse than it is," the RN promised. "Again, there's usually fatty tissue in that area—"

"I am not fat!"

"I'll say," Greta laughed. "If a good wind came up you'd blow right away . . . now where was I?"

"Rotation sites," Edie sighed, wishing Greta could be more discreet. This was hard enough on Sabrina; enduring Greta's tactless bedside manner was making it more difficult.

"Oh, yes—you'll find quite a few locations around your stomach, hips, and the back of your arms," Greta enthused.

Wilting noticeably, Sabrina was tempted to throw the syringe in the garbage container near her bed. For the hundredth time, she wondered what she could have possibly done in her life to deserve this.

"Well, time's a-wastin'. Let's get to it!" Greta exclaimed, gesturing to the syringe in Sabrina's trembling hand. "Pick a spot on that leg of yours."

"Does it matter where?" Sabrina asked, trying to remain calm.

"Not really. I would suggest in the middle. Push up a tiny bit of skin . . . good, like that. Now lower your syringe and push the needle in."

Holding her breath, Sabrina tried to force the needle through her skin. With the first prick, she shuddered. "I don't know if I can do this," she stammered, pulling the needle away from her leg.

"It's like anything else, practice makes perfect," the RN encouraged. "Stick it in quick and get it over with."

The look on Sue's face melted Edie's heart. The future LPN knew how she would feel if the roles were reversed, if Karen was the one learning to give shots instead of Sabrina. Sue had held up remarkably well, but it was evident from the strained expression on her face that this woman couldn't take much more.

"C'mon honey, you can do it," Sue said, concealing the heartache she felt.

Holding her breath, this time Sabrina succeeded and forced the needle through her skin. Wincing, she pushed in the plunger. "OW!" she exclaimed as she forced the insulin into her leg.

"It'll sometimes sting for minute, but that wasn't too bad for your first time," Greta praised. "Pretty soon, you'll be able to slip that needle in there without even feeling it."

"I doubt that," Sabrina murmured as she recapped her syringe.

"You did great," Sue complimented, her smile not reaching her eyes. "Better than I could do."

"You'll get your chance to learn too, Mom," the RN promised, much to Sue's dismay. "You've done well this morning, Sabrina. You gave your own shot and earlier you did your fasting blood sugar test all by yourself."

"Yes, I'm such a big girl," Sabrina grumbled quietly as she examined the tiny hole in the top of her middle finger. Before learning to give her morning shot, she had been shown how to operate her own blood sugar monitor. She had learned how to insert a slender strip inside of a small computerized machine that would keep track of her blood sugar level. After the strip was in place, she had then pricked her finger, placing a drop of blood on a special section of the strip. The lancet had stung as it had entered her finger, but it was better than enduring the *lab tech vampires*, as she had started to call them. "When do I get breakfast?" she asked, feeling hungry.

"In about forty minutes. It takes time for the insulin to do its job. Later, when you can use Humalog insulin, you can eat ten minutes after you give your shot. The NPH insulin you gave yourself this morning is slower and in your system longer." Greta explained.

"Humalog?" Sue asked before Sabrina could voice the same question.

"It's the newest insulin—fast-acting insulin that is. Several diabetics in this town have switched from regular insulin to it. That way there's not such a time span between when you give the shot and when you can eat. In my opinion, it makes life simpler for diabetics."

Sabrina gazed up at the RN. "How many people have diabetes in Blaketown?"

"There's around ten to fifteen Type 2s."

Looking disappointed, Sabrina covered her leg with the blanket on her hospital bed. She now knew that most Type 2s were much older than she was.

"There's a Type 1 at the middle school, a girl, and it seems like there's a senior boy. What is his name? I can see his face . . . dark hair, wears glasses. A real smart kid." The RN grinned. "I can't think of his name right now, but I'll bet he'd be a good one to talk to when you get the chance. He takes pretty good care of himself. We've only seen him in here a couple of times. Once was when the flu knocked the tar out of him."

Her interest perking, Sabrina made herself a mental note to ask Bev and Karen about the senior. In a town this small, they would know if he was anyone she would be interested in meeting.

"How do illnesses affect diabetics?" Sue pressed.

"Colds, flu, infections, and injuries have an impact on the blood sugar level. Some things raise it, others lower it. It varies from diabetic to diabetic. That's why it's so crucial to check the blood sugar level at least three or four times a day. More when you're sick. Then you can tell how much insulin you'll need during that time."

Sue sank down in the uncomfortable chair she had slept in last night. How would they ever learn everything they would need to know about this horrid disease?

"Well Sabrina, now that we've got you all set for breakfast, why don't we get you into the shower," Greta suggested. "It'll make you feel a lot better."

Sabrina cringed. The last thing she wanted to do was take a shower with everyone watching, especially this RN.

"Greta, you have so much to do this morning," Edie said, coming to the rescue, "Sue and I can handle Sabrina's shower."

"There is a woman down the hall that I need to check on. She might be having a baby today. I hope so, I love babies," Greta said, moving to the door. "You get cleaned up, Sabrina, and we'll have your breakfast here shortly," she added. Grinning at everyone, the RN left the room.

"Thanks, Edie," Sabrina breathed. "I'm not sure I could've handled much more of her."

"Greta's a good nurse," Edie reproved gently. "She comes on a little strong sometimes, but—"

"A little?!" Sabrina returned.

"Sabrina," Sue warned, giving her daughter's shoulder a reassuring squeeze. "Let's get you into the shower. Then you can eat."

"Good, I'm starved," Sabrina replied, swinging her legs around to the other side of the bed. She waited until Edie had closed the door, then with her mother's help, slipped down to the floor. Weak and extremely shaky, she was glad her mother was hanging onto her. Edie came around the other side and offered added support. With their help, she was able to move across the room into the small bathroom. Walking with the IV took some practice, but she was already getting around more easily than she had last night. She tried not to let it bother her when Edie started to unfasten her gown for her. She knew both women were keeping a close eye on her because of her continued dizziness, and tried to make the best of it. It was better than falling, something that had almost taken place last night when she had tried to use the bathroom by herself.

When Edie pulled the hospital gown away, Sabrina moved into the shower, her mother remaining in the tiny room to keep track of her. Stepping back into Sabrina's room, Edie set the gown on a nearby chair and began remaking the hospital bed, something that posed a challenge because of the flowers and balloons that filled the small room. After straightening the bed, she moved some of the flowers from the small table by Sabrina's bed to make room for the breakfast tray she would bring in later. When she finished, Edie picked up the clean gown she had brought in earlier and handed it to Sue.

"How are you doing, hon?" Sue asked, draping the gown over the metal bar near the toilet.

"I'm okay," Sabrina said, enjoying the shower. The warm water felt wonderful after everything she had been subjected to since yesterday, a welcome treat she was reluctant to end. The only time she needed her mother's assistance was when she attempted to wash her long hair. Finally rinsing off the last of the shampoo, Sabrina stepped out of the shower, shivering. Sue helped dry her off, then reached for the clean gown, quickly snapping it into place.

"You're getting pretty good at that," Sabrina commented.

"Thanks," Sue replied, wrapping her daughter's blonde hair in a thick, white towel. "I should've had your father bring your blow dryer in last night."

"It'll air dry. That's actually better for my hair," Sabrina said, allowing her mother to guide her across the room. As Sue and Edie worked together to help her climb into the freshly made bed, Sabrina wished the dizziness would ease. At least the nausea was fading.

"Feel any better?" Edie asked, gathering the soiled gown and wet towels for the hospital laundry.

"Yeah. That shower helped. I don't feel so scruffy," Sabrina answered, lifting her head to remove the towel. She rubbed it over her hair, then handed it to her mother to give to Edie.

"I'll drop this stuff off, then I'll see if your breakfast is ready," Edie said as she walked out of the room.

"Mom, is there a pick or a comb handy that I can use to untangle this mop?"

Sue reached for her purse and pulled out a pink plastic pick. "Will this do?"

Nodding, Sabrina took the pick from her mother and began running it through her hair. She had nearly finished when Edie reappeared with a tray of hot food.

"Breakfast is served," Edie said, setting the tray on the table beside Sabrina's bed. She moved the small portable table across the bed, adjusting it and the bed until it was comfortable for Sabrina to eat.

"There you go," Edie said, lifting the cover from the plate on the tray.

Sabrina glanced at the plate of food. Two poached eggs, two pieces of toast with a small container of sugar-free jelly, a small serving of hash browns, and a glass of orange juice.

"How does it look?" Edie asked.

"Wonderful," Sabrina replied. It was the first meal offered since her arrival the day before.

"You enjoy it and I'll take your mom down to the cafeteria so she can get something to eat too." Edie motioned for Sue to follow her from the room.

"But Sabrina . . . shouldn't I—" Sue whispered.

"She'll be all right," Edie said, leading Sue out into the hall. "I'm more concerned about you right now. I heard that you barely picked at the tray they brought you for dinner last night, and I doubt you got much sleep in that chair by your daughter's bed. You need a good breakfast."

"But—"

"Sue, I know you're worried, but she'll be fine. Sabrina does need you, but you'll be no good to her if you get sick." Edie smiled at Sue. "Let's go see what we can round up for you to eat this morning."

Giving in, Sue followed Edie down the hall.

# Chapter 7

While Sabrina took a much-needed nap, Sue slipped out of the hospital room to stretch her legs. As she wandered down the hall, she tried to focus on the progress that was being made. Sabrina's blood sugar had come down considerably. Although it was still in the two hundred range, it hadn't spiked above that level today, something that had pleased everyone involved. After lunch, Sue and Edie had helped Sabrina take a short walk down the hall to help the young woman regain her strength. When they had returned to her room, Sabrina had fallen into a deep sleep, drained by the exertion made that day. As Sabrina had silently slumbered, Sue had watched for several minutes, relieved that her daughter's coloring had improved—a healthy pink flush was now apparent in Sabrina's cheeks.

On the whole, Sabrina was doing remarkably well, but the ache inside Sue's heart was almost more than she could bear. For nearly two days she had tucked it away with counterfeit smiles, trying to be strong for everyone around her, Sabrina most of all. The effort was taking its toll. Slowly she made her way toward the waiting room on the chance that her husband was there.

"Mom, are you all right?"

Glancing up, Sue's eyes filled with tears. Wordlessly, she moved into Kate's arms and quietly wept through her frustration. When Sue regained her composure, she was embarrassed to learn that Kate wasn't alone—Doris Kelsey had come with her daughter to check on Sabrina. "Sorry . . . I guess it all just hit," Sue stammered, drawing back from Kate.

"Don't apologize," Doris chided. She handed a white paper bag to Kate, then gave Sue an intense hug. When she released Kate's mother, she smiled. "How's Sabrina doing this afternoon?"

"Pretty good. We had her up walking after lunch. Right now she's asleep. That's why I wandered out here—I was trying to clear my head," Sue explained, as she self-consciously brushed at her eyes. She accepted the small package of tissue Kate had found in her purse, drew out a couple of tissues, and wiped at her face.

Concerned by her mother's emotional state, Kate forced a smile. "Where's Dad?"

"I was hoping he'd be here in the waiting room, but he must be back down at the store," Sue replied. "He can only stand to be up here for a short time."

"He's taking this pretty hard," Doris guessed.

"It's killing him to see Sabrina go through this. It's hard on both of us, but for Greg it's worse. He's blaming himself."

"Why?" Kate said, concerned.

"Because of your grandfather. Your dad still thinks there's a connection between your grandfather's diabetes and Sabrina's."

Kate rubbed at her aching back, wincing as the baby kicked hard against her rib cage. "I thought Dad understood that Grandpa's diabetes and Sabrina's are two separate conditions."

"Most fathers are protective of their daughters," Doris offered. "I'm sure my husband would be reacting just like Greg if this was one of our girls." She pointed to the white paper sack in Kate's hand. "By the way, we brought you and Greg a sandwich. Kate mentioned that you haven't been able to eat much since this all started. She also shared that you love chicken sandwiches. We thought we'd bring one up and see if we could entice you to eat."

Sue glanced at Doris, then Kate. "You brought me a chicken sandwich?"

Kate handed her mother the white bag from a local drive-in. "We brought you two chicken sandwiches, one is for Dad. We thought you might prefer them over hospital cuisine."

"Thank you," Sue said, taking the bag. She opened the top and breathed deeply. "They smell wonderful."

"They taste good too. Let's go down to the cafeteria and get a pop to go with your sandwich," Kate suggested. "Maybe I'll give Dad a quick call and tell him to come up here to join you."

"No need, I'm right behind you," Greg answered, moving from the front foyer into the small waiting room. "I thought I'd better come check on my girls."

"Good idea," Kate said, giving her father a meaningful look.

Greg glanced from Kate to Sue, frowning when he saw the strained look on his wife's face.

"We brought you a sandwich," Doris said, gesturing to the sack in Sue's hand. "Why don't you and Sue go to the cafeteria and relax for a bit? Kate and I can keep an eye on Sabrina while you eat," she offered, sensing Kate's parents needed some time alone.

"Sounds like a plan," Greg said. He had skipped breakfast that morning and had only nibbled at a small bag of chips for lunch. He hadn't felt hungry until now; the smell of chicken sandwiches beckoned.

"Okay, let's go eat," Sue agreed. "You know where we'll be if you need us."

Nodding, Kate was relieved to see her parents walk toward the cafeteria. A visit she had made to the hospital earlier that day had revealed how little her mother had eaten or slept since yesterday. She hoped both parents would start eating again before they took up residence in the hospital beside Sabrina.

* * *

"Kate, are you sure about this?"

"Mom, you're exhausted! I'm amazed you're still standing," Kate replied. "You need to start taking care of yourself. Go home and get some rest."

Sue gazed at her stubborn daughter. "You're the one who needs to get plenty of sleep."

"I'll be fine. Besides, in my condition, the hospital is a safe place to be," Kate pointed out. "Now go home, take a long bath, get a good night's sleep, and come back tomorrow when Sabrina really needs you."

Sue's moist eyes expressed the gratitude in her heart.

"I can't begin to replace you, but tonight, let me be Sabrina's comfy object," Kate pleaded.

"But Kate—"

"Mom, you know I can be just as headstrong as you are," Kate continued. "If you refuse to go, I'll simply stay here with you. Then we'll both look wonderful tomorrow. Only in your case, they'll admit you in the morning . . . put you in a hospital bed beside Sabrina. You'll be a lot of help to her then."

Sue almost smiled at Kate's tenacity. She glanced down the hall again. If something went wrong, if Sabrina's blood sugar dropped in the night, she wanted to be here to make sure everything was all right.

"If you had behaved and gone home earlier today for a nap like we suggested, I might be more lenient, but as it stands, you're dead on your feet. When Sabrina was a baby, you could maybe get by with two or three hours of sleep at night, but you're older now, your body needs more rest," Kate joked.

"Okay, I give up. I'll go home," Sue sighed wearily. She knew Kate was right—she felt terrible. Maybe tomorrow, after a good night's rest, things would look better. "Let me talk to Sabrina first," she said, ignoring the jubilant expression on her oldest daughter's face.

\* \* \*

"Anything else exciting and new in your life?" Sabrina asked, enjoying this chance to spend time with Kate. Everyone's schedules were so crazy right now, she didn't see as much of her sister as she had thought she would after their move to Blaketown.

"Sandi called last night," Kate replied.

"Sandi?"

"Sandi Kearns Campbell—my friend from high school."

"Oh, yeah, the one who married that man in the wheelchair."

Kate lifted an eyebrow. "His name is Ian."

Sabrina blushed slightly. "Ian," she repeated. "He seemed like an okay guy at their reception."

"He is. He'd better be, he's married to one of my best friends," Kate informed her.

"How are they doing?"

"Good—busy. Ian started his own accounting business a couple of years ago and now has so many clients it's a challenge for him to keep up."

"Didn't they have a little girl?"

"Yes, Kaitlin, she's five years old now."

"Kaitlin . . . that's right, they named her after you," Sabrina exclaimed.

"Well, I was the one who introduced Ian to Sandi," Kate replied.

Sabrina wiggled her eyebrows. "Are you ready to introduce me to someone . . . say a handsome stud who won't care that I have a decrepit body?"

Sabrina's tone was cheery, but Kate could tell this was a valid concern for her sister. "Sabrina, someday you'll meet a guy who'll knock you off your feet. When it's right, he won't mind that you have diabetes, just like Sandi didn't mind that Ian was in a wheelchair."

Sabrina was quiet for several seconds, then asked, "Are you sure Sandi didn't mind?"

"Sandi loves Ian. She knew there would be challenges, and there have been—"

"Like what?"

Taking a deep breath, Kate silently begged for inspiration. What did Sabrina need to hear?

"Kate?"

"Sorry, I was thinking about something Sandi told me last night. She'd really like another baby—but she knows they were lucky to have Kaitlin. She understood from the beginning that the chances of having a family with Ian would be slim." From Sabrina's alarmed expression, Kate knew her sister was struggling with similar fears. "Sandi told me last night that things have a way of working out. She hasn't been able to get pregnant since she had Kaitlin, so they signed up for an adoption waiting list a couple of years ago. If they can't adopt a baby, they'll request an older child, maybe one with special needs. Those two have so much love to share that any child who is lucky enough to come into their home will have a wonderful life." She smiled encouragingly at Sabrina, but still saw a trace of doubt in her sister's face. "I'm not saying that you'll have to adopt. Mom asked

Doctor Davis yesterday if you would be able to have children someday, and he said that if you took care of yourself, you could. So don't worry about things like that right now. Worry about learning all you can about your condition so it won't stop you from accomplishing what you want to do in this life."

"Okay," Sabrina said grudgingly.

"Now, let's concentrate on the positive things that are going on with you."

"Like what?"

"Like—you're starting to feel better. And from all of the flowers and balloons in this room, it's obvious you have family and friends who love you. The best part is that tonight, you get to spend quality time with me," Kate teased.

Sabrina groaned. "Anything else?"

Giving her sister a dirty look, Kate then glanced at her watch, seeing that it was almost 10:20 p.m. "Yes, it's getting late. We should probably call it a day."

"I'm not sure I can sleep tonight," Sabrina sighed.

"How about a bedtime story—or a lullaby?" Kate joked.

Sabrina grinned at her sister. "Definitely a story. I've heard you sing."

Pretending to be hurt, Kate positioned herself comfortably in the reclining chair that would serve as her bed for the evening. "All right. Let me think. I know, how about the story of *Sabrina, the Teenage Witch?!*"

"Not funny," Sabrina replied. "That has to be the lamest show—"

"Remember, we're going to be positive tonight," Kate reminded her sister.

"Oh, that's right. Okay, I am positive that is the lamest show!" Erupting in giggles, Sabrina ducked when Kate threw a pillow at her. It landed on the floor in front of the RN who had come down to see what all of the noise was about.

"Ahem," Greta said, looking indignant. Working a double-shift to fill in for an ill nurse, she had lost her sense of humor. "What is this pillow doing on the floor?"

"It's a detective. It's looking for a case—a pillow case," Kate said, trying to keep a straight face. She lost it when Sabrina burst out laughing.

"Do you two realize where you are?" Greta persevered, stooping to pick up the pillow. She dusted off imaginary dirt and placed it on the foot of Sabrina's bed.

"No, but I'm sure you'll tell us," Sabrina said just loud enough for Kate to overhear.

Kate maintained a somber look and motioned for her sister to cool it. She didn't want to get kicked out of the hospital for rowdy behavior; their mother would never forgive her. "We're very sorry," she said politely. "It won't happen again."

"Well, see that it doesn't. We have some very sick individuals in this hospital." Turning, Greta marched indignantly out of the room.

"And she's the sickest," Sabrina breathed, trying to stifle her laughter with a pillow.

Kate began snickering, but managed to control the volume. When she thought she was under better control, she awkwardly stood, walked across the room, and closed the door. "There, now maybe we can breathe without appearing before a firing squad in the morning." She stretched, trying to alleviate the pressure her baby was putting on her rib cage.

"At least a firing squad would put us out of our misery," Sabrina said, her mood sobering.

"Hey, what happened to keeping a positive outlook?" Kate asked, returning to her chair-bed.

"I'm trying." Sabrina glanced sheepishly at her sister. "How would you like to give yourself shots the rest of your life?"

Kate considered the question. "I'd probably hate it at first," she answered truthfully.

"See, I have a good reason to feel sorry for myself."

"You didn't let me finish. I'd hate it at first, but when I realized I didn't have a choice, I would try to make the best of it."

Sabrina gazed steadily at her older sister for several long seconds. "Knowing you, you probably would." She was convinced Kate had a way of coming out on top of most situations.

"I'm sure I'd have my bad days, but when it came right down to it, I think I would look at it like a test."

"A test? I've had a lot of those lately. Mostly blood sugar tests. They're a real kick."

"I was talking about life tests," Kate replied, spreading her mother's quilt over her body. She slid back in the recliner, making herself as comfortable as possible. "Our grandmother used to say that this world is a giant classroom. We're here to learn and grow as much as we can. We never know when we're going to get hit with a pop quiz, so we always have to try to be prepared."

"How can you be prepared for something like this?" Sabrina asked, her eyes bright with tears.

"By knowing who you are and why you're here," Kate replied. "You're a daughter of God, Breeny. That makes you pretty special. You've been sent here to learn. You knew before coming that you would be tested. I'm not sure what you're supposed to learn from this trial, but I'm guessing it will help you grow into the woman your Heavenly Father desires, if you'll let it."

"Am I being punished for something?"

Kate stared at her younger sister.

"I mean . . . I did mess up a few months ago—that night I got drunk with Bev—"

"We all make mistakes, Breeny. That's why we have the gift of repentance. You straightened everything out, right?"

Sabrina nodded.

"And you've done well since then—what's happening now has nothing to do with what took place that night," Kate emphasized.

"Are you sure?" Sabrina pressed, troubled.

"I'm positive. Again—we were sent here to be tested. Those tests come even when you're doing everything you're supposed to do. Sabrina, you're a wonderful young woman. You're not being punished. Do you believe me—or do I need to drag our bishop in here to talk to you?"

Sabrina shook her head, relieved by Kate's answer.

"Is anything else bothering you?"

"I'm scared," Sabrina admitted, revealing something she had kept to herself for two days.

"I know, and I wish I could make this one go away, we all wish that, but none of us can make it disappear. Someday there might be a cure. Until then, we have to learn all we can to deal with this so that you don't end up in trouble."

"But what if I can't do it . . . what if it's too hard?"

Kate reached up to give Sabrina's hand a soft squeeze. "I'll share one of my favorite sayings with you. It goes something like this—no one would have crossed the ocean if he could've gotten off the ship in a storm. I thought about that one a lot after I was in that coma. I had a lot of healing and growing up to do. Sometimes it was really tough."

Sabrina mulled the phrase over in her mind. "Can I get off this ship if I have a life preserver? I'd be content to float in the ocean."

"Think of the wonderful things that have happened because people were brave enough to stay on board during those storms," Kate challenged.

"Let's see—now we have holidays like Columbus Day and Thanksgiving!" Sabrina said sarcastically.

"I was thinking more along the lines of . . . oh, I don't know, the establishment of our country. The United States exists because of brave people like Columbus and the pilgrims."

"Okay, I get your point, Ms. History Teacher. I should consider myself a brave voyager."

"That's more like it," Kate said, ignoring the caustic edge to Sabrina's response. "I'll tell you something that I always think about whenever I remember that saying," she said, climbing out of the chair.

"What?" Sabrina asked.

"You get comfy and we'll call this your bedtime story tonight. Then whenever you get scared, when you think you can't cross this ocean, I want you to remember some people who did."

Agreeing, Sabrina allowed her sister to officially tuck her in bed. Leaning down, Kate planted a soft kiss on Sabrina's forehead, then reached to dim the lights before climbing back into her chair. "Here's one of my favorite stories," Kate said, snuggling under her mother's quilt. "You'll find it in the Book of Mormon."

Groaning, Sabrina pretended to be asleep.

"Give this a chance, or I'll get Greta the Terrible back in here," Kate threatened.

"I'm listening," Sabrina responded.

"Good . . . now where was I? Oh, yes, my favorite Book of Mormon story. You'll find this in Ether, in case you want to read it yourself sometime."

Sabrina muttered something under her breath.

"What was that?"

"I said, oh, goody. I'll remember that."

"Good girl," Kate said, smiling at Sabrina's lack of enthusiasm. She prayed the Spirit would touch her sister's heart as she recounted a scripture passage she felt prompted to share. "Ether contains the history of the Jaredite people. As you'll recall, these people lived back in the days when they tried to build the tower of Babel, a tower that was supposed to reach heaven. Anyway, to make a long story short, Jared and his brother were very righteous men. When Heavenly Father caused the languages to be mixed up because of the wicked way people had worked together to build the tower, Jared's family, Jared's brother's family, and some of their friends were permitted to speak the same language."

"What does that have to do with—"

"Patience—I'm getting to the good stuff."

"Thanks for telling me; I'd hate to miss it."

Kate gave Sabrina a pained look, then continued with the story. "Jared's brother was a spiritual giant. He prayed that they would be guided to a land choice above all other lands. This request was granted. They were instructed to gather their flocks, seeds of every kind, and their families to a certain place by the sea. They traveled a long way and were told through Jared's brother that they were being led to a land of promise. When they reached this great sea, the brother of Jared—"

"Doesn't he have a name?" Sabrina interrupted.

"Who?"

"The brother of Jared. If he was so important, why doesn't he have his own name? I mean, I didn't exactly enjoy being called the sister of Kate in Bozeman."

"I see," Kate replied, amused. At least Sabrina was listening. "It seems like I read what his name was somewhere . . . I believe his name was Mahonri Moriancumer."

Sabrina wrinkled her nose. "Let's stick to the brother of Jared."

"If you insist. Anyway, as I was saying, before I was rudely interrupted," Kate said, enjoying Sabrina's disgusted gasp, "when these people finally reached the big sea that divided the other lands, the brother of Jared was instructed to build special barges. These barges were unlike anything they'd ever seen before."

"Like the ship Nephi was asked to build?"

"No, actually, these barges were very different. I like to think of them as the forerunner of the submarine."

"You're kidding?! Are you sure this story is in the Book of Mormon?"

"Obviously you've never read the entire book," Kate guessed.

"I've read most of it," Sabrina said. "Maybe I missed this story."

*And maybe you weren't paying attention*, Kate guessed silently. *I hope you'll listen now.* Aloud she said, "These barges were designed like dishes, fastened together. A few years ago, a Sunday School teacher of mine held up two small bowls to demonstrate what they looked like. He set one over the other so their tops were linked together like a primitive submarine."

"That sounds cool."

"I'm sure it was," Kate agreed. "When they were finished, the brother of Jared had a few concerns. He prayed to the Lord and mentioned that those barges were very dark inside. There was no light and no air because they were designed to be airtight. He also pointed out that they had no way to steer these things. Jared's brother was told to make a hole in the top and bottom of each barge, holes that could let air in, or be stopped up, depending on which end happened to be right side up in the ocean."

"That's a good idea."

"The brother of Jared thought so too. The holes were cut and he knew that they would be able to get enough air to breathe. He was still concerned about the light. He suspected this would be a long journey and wondered how they would survive it in the dark."

"That would be pretty scary to cross the ocean in something like that. What if they had claustrophobia?" Sabrina commented.

"Exactly. But when Jared's brother prayed about this, the Lord told him that they couldn't make windows in these barges—windows would be dashed to pieces by the force of the water. They couldn't light a fire inside of the barges for obvious reasons. Then the Lord explained that these barges were designed to bob about in the water like a whale, that at times, they would be in the midst of the sea.

They would be guided along by the wind He promised to send. Then He said something to the brother of Jared that has always stayed with me. It's one of my favorite scriptures. Want to hear it?"

"Sure," Sabrina said, subdued by the seriousness of her older sister's voice.

"I memorized this scripture when I was in the MTC, preparing for my mission. I hope I can remember it. Anyway, here goes: 'Behold, I prepare you against these things; for ye cannot cross this great deep save I prepare you against the waves of the sea, and the winds which have gone forth, and the floods which shall come.'"

"Could you repeat that?" Sabrina asked, wondering at the way her heart seemed to burn.

Kate repeated the verse, then continued with the story. "The Lord asked Jared's brother to find something that could contain the light He longed to give them on their frightening journey. The brother of Jared was able to form sixteen white, clear stones that were transparent as glass. He took these to the top of a mountain and prayed again, desiring that the Lord would touch those stones with His finger, filling them with light. Jared's brother had such faith, that he saw the Lord's finger as each stone was touched. Because of his great faith, he was also permitted to see the spirit body of Jesus Christ."

Overwhelmed by emotion, Kate paused for a few seconds.

"That would be so awesome," Sabrina said. "I can't even imagine what Jared's brother must've felt."

"I can't either," Kate agreed, "but what a comfort it must've been to have sure knowledge, to know where life's light truly comes from." She waited for a few seconds, giving Sabrina a chance to absorb what she was trying to teach her. "Later, the brother of Jared took those precious stones with him down the mountain and placed them in the barges. Then they prepared for their journey and entered the barges, trusting in the Lord, knowing that He would direct them safely toward the promised land. They faced frightening storms, but the light within shone brightly and eventually they reached their destination."

Her heart touched in a way she couldn't describe, Sabrina quietly cried. After a few minutes, she asked Kate to repeat what had become for her a favorite scripture:

" . . . Behold, I prepare you against these things; for ye cannot cross this great deep save I prepare you against the waves of the sea, and the winds which have gone forth, and the floods which shall come . . . "

"Whenever I'm facing a difficult challenge, I think about that scripture," Kate commented. "We all face journeys that test us. If we have the light of Christ within, we can withstand any storm that comes our way. We may not always understand where it is we're supposed to be heading on those journeys, but we've been promised that we'll never be alone, that we can be worthy of an eternal promised land if we'll keep the commandments and endure to the end." Kate reached up until she found Sabrina's hand and gave it a gentle squeeze. "You're on a journey right now, Breeny. One that will take every ounce of courage and faith you can muster. Just remember you're not in this alone. You have quite a crew aboard your ship."

"Don't you mean barge?" Sabrina said, a new hope dancing in her eyes.

"One equipped with a glowing light," Kate replied. An hour later when Greta stepped into the room to check on things, Kate and Sabrina were both sound asleep, their hands still locked together. Frowning her disapproval, Greta left the room.

# Chapter 8

"Where've you been, Bev?" James Henderson asked, glancing up at his daughter when she walked into the living room. He shifted his gaze to his watch.

"Up at the hospital visiting Sabrina. I asked Gina earlier—"

"I know, she told me. That was quite a while ago. I doubt they'd let you visit Sabrina until this late hour. It's nearly 11:00 p.m."

"We left the hospital around nine, dropped Terri off at her house, and then I spent some time with Karen and her mom at their house. Edie wanted to talk to me," Bev said, reviewing in her mind the advice Edie had given her concerning their mutual alcoholic weakness. Counseling Bev to avoid being around those who drank and places where alcohol was served, Bev studied her father. He failed on both counts. From the belligerent way he was acting, she guessed he had been indulging in one of his favorite alcoholic beverages that evening.

"Why did Edie want to talk to you?" James asked, skeptical of Bev's excuse.

Deciding it was best to avoid the issue of alcoholism, Bev shared the other item Edie had discussed with Bev, Terri, and Karen the day before. "Edie was teaching us what to watch for if Sabrina gets into trouble with her diabetes," Bev explained as she sat down on the forest green couch across the room from her father.

"I wish someone could teach me what to watch for when you're in trouble."

"Dad! What's that supposed to mean?"

"It means I'm fed up with your inability to cope with life. This drinking problem of yours has got to stop!"

"I'm trying! What—you think I was off drinking tonight?"

James met his daughter's challenging gaze with a look of disdain. "Isn't that how you solve your problems? Whenever you're upset, you turn to alcohol. You're upset about this Mormon friend of yours becoming a diabetic . . . I have a right to be concerned!" he exclaimed, rising to glare at her.

Stung by his reply, Bev stood up. "For your information, I haven't had a drink in six weeks, but it's tempting, especially when you treat me like I'm some sort of low-life!" Angrily brushing past her father, she stomped upstairs to her room and slammed the door.

"Was that really necessary?" Gina asked, stepping into the living room. "She's been upset enough as it is. This thing about Sabrina has her stomach twisted in knots. Then you jump her case because she's a few minutes late getting home."

"I'm her father! I have a right to know where she is and what she's doing!"

Gina took a deep breath, trying to control her temper. "Maybe if you'd been more concerned a few years ago—"

"It's not my fault my daughter is a drunkard!" Furious, James stormed to the front door.

"Let me guess, you're heading for a local bar, the place you go when you have problems to solve! That's how you cope!" When James remained silent, Gina continued to fume as he opened the door to leave. "Bev has tried so hard to be like you! When you're upset, where do you go? What do you turn to? What kind of example have you been setting for her?"

Still refusing to answer, James slammed the front door and marched angrily to his Jeep.

Bursting into tears, Gina retreated to their bedroom, too distraught to comfort Bev. Closing her bedroom door, she threw herself onto the king-sized bed and sobbed into a pillow.

* * *

Stifling a yawn, Brett Randall glanced around the crowded chapel, unimpressed with the subject the high counselor was addressing that day, the importance of paying tithing. He had tried paying it during his youth, but had never seen any benefits directed his way. If blessings had been showered upon him, he hadn't noticed. The best thing that had ever happened to him hadn't been the result of paying tithing, something he hadn't done in years. Edie was the greatest thing to come into his life, someone he loved with all of his heart, which was why he was enduring this dry session of Church.

There were times when he still couldn't believe that someone as beautiful, as wonderful as Edie, would want to be seen with him. Almost shyly, Brett reached to hold her hand. Something as simple as that sent chills racing up and down his spine and made his heart beat as though it would work its way out of his chest. It filled him with such exhilaration, he was certain he had found heaven on earth.

Edie turned her head, dazzling him with her warming smile. She looked elegant today in the powder blue dress she had recently bought for herself. Brett returned her smile, then noticed the way Karen was grinning at them. His face colored slightly. He was well aware of Karen's approval of this relationship and knew that Karen and her grandmother, Adele, were hoping he would ask Edie to marry him in the near future. It was something Brett longed to do—he had even purchased the ring—if only the Church hadn't intruded. He had promised Edie that he would pray about the Church and their relationship. He had even started reading the Book of Mormon again, but hadn't received any major revelations. Maybe Edie was right, he had to let go of the bitterness in his heart before he could feel the promptings of the Spirit. Silently renewing his pledge, he focused on the pulpit, making a valiant effort to listen as the high counselor continued to speak.

Edie shifted closer to Brett, enjoying the security of his warm handclasp. As she felt Karen move around on the other side of her, Edie glanced at her daughter. Karen was looking over her shoulder, scanning the padded benches behind them.

"Looking for someone?" Edie whispered.

"I'm watching for Bev," Karen replied. Bev didn't always make it to church in time for sacrament meeting, the first meeting in their ward, but she had faithfully attended Sunday School and Young Women. Sometimes Bev came in late to sacrament meeting and slipped in toward the back of the chapel, but there was no sign of her today.

"She'll be here," Edie said confidently. "She told you last night that she would come."

"I know," Karen whispered back. "But I can't help worrying about her. I think she really needs the gospel in her life right now." Turning back around, Karen faced the front of the chapel.

Edie slipped her free arm around Karen's shoulders. "She's lucky to have a good friend like you."

"She's always been there for me," Karen replied. Leaning against her mother's shoulder, she relaxed, hoping Bev would show up soon.

\* \* \*

Gina woke with a start. She was lying on top of her bed, fully dressed, still wearing her clothes from yesterday. Sitting up, she groaned. Her neck felt kinked and she tried to pop it. When that failed, she rubbed it and slid off the bed to the floor. Her mind clearing, she stared at her reflection in the large mirror above the dresser. Her forlorn expression revealed the fear in her heart. James hadn't come home last night. Or if he had, he hadn't spent the night in their room. Panicking, she opened the bedroom door and hurried down the hall. She found the twins in the living room watching cartoons, but there was no sign of her husband. The view from the front window confirmed that James hadn't returned; his Jeep Cherokee was still missing from the driveway.

"Mommy, what's wrong?" Jake asked, his tousled brown hair sticking out in varied directions.

"Nothing. I was checking to see if your father had left yet this morning," Gina responded as she replaced the drapes behind the TV.

Drake frowned at his mother.

"What is it, honey?"

"I didn't see Daddy leave. Is he sleepin'?"

Gina grimaced—her concern was valid. She assumed the twins had been up for quite some time. If the four-year-olds hadn't seen their father, James must've spent the night somewhere else. Sick at heart, Gina moved away from the window. She wandered across the room to the fancy home bar, James' pride and joy, and discovered more "good" news. Someone had been into the locked cabinet and had smashed the glass front to get what they wanted. Closing her eyes, Gina willed herself to remain in control. She would not run out of the house and down the street screaming, she would calmly face the mess this day was becoming.

Taking a deep breath, she opened her eyes and began a careful evaluation of the cabinet. Every bottle of liquor was missing. There must've been five or six bottles in there last night. Surely Bev hadn't tried to drink all of it. Her heart sinking lower than before, Gina walked toward the stairs, each step filled with dread. "Why, Bev?" she muttered under her breath as she started to climb upstairs to Bev's bedroom. "I know things aren't great right now, but this will just make it worse. When your father does come home . . . if he decides to come home . . . and sees what you've done—"

"Hi Gina . . . uh, Mom," Bev sang out, appearing at the top of the stairs.

Gina blinked. For someone who should be totally inebriated, Bev looked great. The young woman was dressed in one of her best dresses and was busy fastening in a pair of matching green earrings.

"Bev?"

"I have an excellent idea. Why don't you get a quick bite to eat—the boys and I already had a bowl of cereal—then get dressed? I'll get the twins ready and we'll all go to church this morning . . . except for Dad, of course. He's still off pouting somewhere," she said breathlessly.

Her mouth falling open, Gina stared as Bev made her way down the stairs. "You look wonderful," she stammered as the teenager moved past.

"Thanks. That's what I was going for. There's this cute boy in Karen's ward—he's a member of the football team. Anyway, I was hoping he'd notice."

"Bev . . . the liquor cabinet . . . " Gina said, following the young woman into the dining room.

"Don't worry, I'll pay to have it fixed," Bev offered. "I was ticked off last night. Dad had no business acting that way—toward either of us. I decided if he was so determined to keep me from drinking again, we'd start by cleaning up his inventory."

"What did you do?"

"Broke into his supply and got rid of it."

"What?" Gina asked. "How?"

"I dumped it all down the kitchen sink," Bev grinned. "I enjoyed every minute of it. I imagined Dad's reaction as I poured his precious booze down the drain."

Gina stared at her stepdaughter. Bev had done the very thing she had wanted to do last night, but hadn't dared. "Bev, I understand why you did it, but when your father—"

"Is *he* being nice or fair?"

Gina answered with her silence.

"He's always telling me to be a woman of action, to quit moping around. I'm finally living up to one of his standards."

"Bev, I know you're upset—"

"Not anymore!" Bev bubbled with delight. "It felt so good when the last drop was dumped out last night. And I think I'm onto something. I'll make a deal with Dad. I'll stay away from the booze if he will."

"He's going to be furious."

Bev gazed steadily at her stepmother. "If he wants me to change, don't you think he owes it to me to not flaunt alcohol in my face every time I turn around?"

Gina rubbed at her throbbing neck. "Don't get me wrong, I agree with what you did. I've been tempted to do it myself. We'll face this one together."

"YES!" Bev said excitedly, holding out her hand, palm up.

Puzzled, Gina stared at it.

"Give me five—we're a team now, right?"

"Right," Gina said, giving Bev a firm slap on the hand.

Growing more serious, Bev frowned. "I did a lot of thinking last night. I heard most of what you two said to each other before Dad left—that part about me following his example. I'm not saying that what I did was right . . . the drinking . . . but maybe I wouldn't have tried drinking if that liquor cabinet hadn't been so easy to get into. Dad never locked that cabinet until he found out I had a problem. Now he keeps it locked, but we all know what's in there. What if Jake or Drake gets curious one day, like I did? What if they decide to try Daddy's favorite beverage?"

Disturbed by that image, Gina nodded. "I've thought about that one myself. It scares me."

"Karen's always telling me that you don't need to get drunk to have fun . . . to enjoy life. I'm starting to believe her. I want my life back—I want to put this behind me and move on."

Her heart swelling with pride, Gina embraced Bev. "I am so impressed with you today."

"Does that mean you'll go to church with me?"

Drawing back, Gina searched Bev's face. "If it means that much to you, we'll go."

Thrilled, Bev hurried into the living room to round up her brothers. Getting them ready for church would take some time and enthusiastic pleading. Gina watched Bev hustle the twins
upstairs, then stepped into the kitchen to look for something to eat.

# Chapter 9

As sunlight filtered into his office, James slowly lifted his head off his desk. Moving his head took a great deal of effort; he was certain it had doubled in size since last night. He waited until the room quit spinning, then tried to stand. Uncertain of how he had found his way to his car dealership last night, he glanced around the office, scowling at the mess he had made of his desk. Folders had been thrown around the room. Loose papers littered the floor. An empty bottle of Seagram's 7 lay tipped on its side on top of the desk, a few drops had spilled onto the large desk calendar.

James licked his dry lips and wished the bottle held more than a few drops. Disgusted with himself, he shook his head, then wished he hadn't as the pounding increased. Swearing, he pushed his way out of the office and headed for the small restroom. There he splashed water onto his face and stared at himself in the mirror. Vague images of the past night came to mind. He remembered fighting with Beverly, then with Gina before storming out of the house. He had driven to a local bar and had talked the bartender into selling him a bottle of whiskey. He had decided to spend some time alone, thinking things over. He remembered going to the city park where he had polished off most of the bottle he had brought with him. From there, the images were distorted, hazy. He had no memory of coming here, something that frightened him; he had never allowed himself to get this far out of control before.

As a sickening thought crossed his mind, he ignored his pain-filled head and ran out of the restroom. He hurried out the side door of the building, running to his Jeep. The dented fender revealed what he had suspected. He had driven while intoxicated. What had he done? Who or what had he hit? Consumed with guilty anguish, he replayed the night's events through his mind, and came up blank.

"NO! Please," he pleaded, sinking to his knees on the blacktop. "Please God, if there is a God . . . help me . . . help me remember. Please tell me I didn't hurt anyone. I'll never drink again . . . just please let everything be all right!" He remained on his knees until the pinched circulation inspired him to move. Rising, he staggered across the car lot, tormenting himself with what he might have done. As he moved forward, he bumped into one of the newest cars on his lot, a white Chevy Malibu. Glancing down, his eyes widened at the sight of the smashed fender. He carefully examined the damage, then fled back to his Jeep. The white paint of the Malibu matched the white flecks on the Jeep Cherokee's chrome bumper. He did a quick survey of the other cars and found that the Malibu was the only one that had sustained damage. Sweet relief swept through him as he concluded that he had only inflicted harm to a stationary, inanimate object. The park was just down the street from his car dealership. He had probably driven down here, pulled into the lot, smashed into the Malibu, backed up the Jeep, shut it off, and stumbled into his office.

He tallied what it would cost to repair the damage. The Malibu could be fixed—his Jeep could be fixed. There was a slim chance he had inflicted harm elsewhere, but not likely. He had thoroughly inspected the Jeep. The only dent was the one that matched the dent in the Malibu. As he continued to estimate what it would take to restore both cars to their original condition, he pondered the additional consequences he would be facing. Fixing the Malibu would be easier than repairing broken hearts.

He thought of Gina, then Bev. What had he been thinking? Both would be worried sick, wondering where he was, especially Gina. James cringed at what he had put his wife through. He loved her so much; without her, his life would be a shambles, as it had been after Gayle had died. Gina had brought purpose back into his existence, had given him two wonderful sons. She had tried so hard to mother Bev—without his support.

Suddenly, he could see things with such clarity. Bev *had been* emulating him. It *was* his fault Bev had turned to alcohol. He had always bragged that he was just a social drinker. If that was true, then why did he drink alone, usually at home after work? A beer here and there—a shot of whiskey to top things off. Add it all up and where did it lead? He knew the answer. It led to a daughter who drank to cope with pain, as he had done so often through the years.

Sinking down to the blacktop, he broke one of his most stringent rules and cried, something he hadn't done since the day Gayle had passed away.

* * *

"Do you think that handsome hunk of a football player noticed me?" Bev asked Karen in a hushed voice as the two girls wandered down the carpeted hallway to the Young Women room of the church house.

"How could he miss you?" Karen teased. "The way you kept offering your opinion in Sunday School, everyone noticed you."

"Hey, someone had to liven things up in there. Talk about boring!"

Karen lifted an eyebrow. "Our Sunday School teacher doesn't usually read the lesson out of the manual. He usually puts a lot of time in on his lessons."

"He did seem better prepared last week," Bev conceded. Changing the subject she asked, "Do you think Gina's all right?"

"My mom and grandma will take good care of her," Karen promised. "They'll be in Relief Society by now. I think Gina will really like it."

Bev pursed her lips. "I hope so. Gina told me once that she was a Lutheran. She hasn't been to church in years, though, not since she met Dad. Dad doesn't do the church thing." She winced. "My father is going to have an absolute fit when he gets home."

"Why?"

Bev pulled a face. "Well, besides the fact that we all came to a church he thinks is 'silly nonsense' this morning, I sort of smashed his liquor cabinet last night."

"How do you 'sort of' do something like that?" Karen probed.

"I was mad. Dad said some pretty rotten things last night." Bev swallowed the lump in her throat. "He thinks I'm such a loser."

"No, he doesn't. He's just worried about you."

"If he's so worried about me, then why does he jump all over me for nothing, threaten to send me away, and parade his freedom to drink whatever he wants whenever he wants?"

Karen smiled. "That's why you smashed his liquor cabinet."

"I didn't totally smash it—it was locked. I had to break the glass out of the front to get to the bottles he had stashed in there."

"And did what with them?" Karen asked, alarmed.

"Relax, I dumped them down the kitchen sink."

Karen grinned. "Good for you!"

"It seemed like a brilliant idea at the time but now I don't know. Things got pretty crazy last night. After I left your house, I went home and got the third degree from Dad, something I didn't appreciate or deserve. When I finally ran upstairs, he got into a horrible fight with Gina—she tried to stick up for me again. Dad threw a fit, stormed out of the house, and drove off. After he left, Gina locked herself in their bedroom to cry and I decided to make something very clear to my father." The two girls paused outside of the Young Women room. "I want him to realize that he's part of the problem, that he is making this harder for me."

"Your dad seems like a reasonable guy."

"Not when he's had a few too many. I could smell the liquor on him last night during our argument, which probably explains why he was so ornery. If he doesn't sober up before coming home today, there could be a major eruption at my house this afternoon."

Karen smiled wistfully. "I don't suppose you'll be able to go up with me to see Sabrina later?"

"Probably not. At least, not until I know where things stand. The liquor cabinet is bad enough, but this . . . bringing Gina and my brothers to church . . . to an LDS church . . . if I come up missing, you'll know what happened."

"I'll start praying for you," Karen replied.

"Somebody better," Bev groaned as they walked into the Young Women room. "And hopefully, Someone is listening."

\* \* \*

After a careful inspection of the city park, James drove home. He could see no other signs of damage from his escapade last night and breathed a sigh of relief. He had been lucky—this time. It made him sick to think about what could have happened. A few minutes later as he drove down the street to his house, he wondered how he would find things at home. Gina would be worried, probably furious. A fleeting smile curved his lips. Gina had more spunk than he ever would have guessed. His second wife had an easygoing disposition, but he was learning that she would only be pushed so far. His first wife, Gayle, had been a regular spitfire, someone who knew what she wanted out of life and would stop at nothing to achieve it. Gayle never would've put up with his drinking, something he had avoided through most of their marriage. He had turned to alcohol the nights death had hovered too close. The cancer had caused so much pain, Gayle had been in a medicated coma the final days of her life. James had found a separate cure for his misery, a prescription that now presented too many side effects.

"Well, Gayle, I've certainly made a mess of things," James sighed. "If you are still aware of us, of how I've let Bev down, please know that I'm sorry." He shuddered, thinking again of how close he had come to ruining his life last night. Numerous deaths had resulted from stunts like the one he had pulled. Flinching at the thought, he pulled into the driveway and shut off the Jeep. He took a deep breath in anticipation of the battle ahead and wondered if Gina would question his fidelity. If the tables were turned—if she had been the one to stay out all night, he would certainly voice a few suspicions. James knew it would take time to rebuild the trust he had shared with his second wife. He hoped she would forgive him, that somehow, he could prove to both Gina and Bev he was truly sorry for his actions, for the hurtful things he had said and done last night.

Anxious to get the impending confrontation over with, he opened the door on his side of the Jeep and lowered himself to the paved driveway. He entered the house through the front door and walked into the living room. "Hello? I'm home." When there was no reply, he glanced toward the bar, something he had insisted be built into this house, a beautiful new home he had bought the same year he and Gina had married. Moving closer to the bar, James stared at the smashed glass door. Bev or Gina? Regret pierced his heart. He hoped Gina had been the culprit, that her anger had propelled her to break the door and remove the liquor he had stashed behind its transparent boundary. If Bev was the guilty party—he had goaded her into drinking again. His heart on the floor, he noticed a piece of paper lying on the counter. Picking it up, he began to read.

> *Hi Dad,*
> *I hope you're all right. We've been pretty worried about you. Sorry about your liquor cabinet. I lost my head a little last night . . .*

His vision blurring, James imagined the worse possible scenario. Blaming himself, he gripped Bev's letter in his hand and moved to a nearby chair to finish reading.

> *. . . I was so angry, so hurt by what you said last night, I decided to get rid of your stash of whiskey and wine. Maybe I shouldn't have done it, but I've decided that if I'm going to lick my so-called "problem," there can't be any alcohol in the house. It makes it too hard . . .*

James began breathing easier. Smiling at his daughter's nerve, he continued reading.

> *. . . so I dumped out everything you had. I need your help, Dad. I can't do this alone. And I don't ever want Jake or Drake to have to fight this same battle. Please understand why I did this. I will pay to have your cabinet fixed, but can't we fill it with something else? I'll make you a deal, I'll stay away from the alcohol if you will. I know this will probably make you really mad, but I think you have a problem too. There, I've said it. I've wanted to for a long time, but I haven't dared. Maybe we can beat this thing together.*
> *Something else I want to mention, I wish you'd treat Gina better. I know you're probably shocked I said that,*

*but I'd hate to lose her from the family. You and I have both pushed her too far. She's taken a lot of abuse, but I think she's reached the breaking point. We both need her, Dad! She's helped me so much the past few months. I know I haven't always treated her very nice either, but I do love her. She's my mom for now. I think Mom (Gayle) would like her. Please can't we pull together and be more like a real family?*

*There's something else I have to tell you, you're probably not going to like this either, but it's too late now. You weren't here to stop us. We all went to church this morning . . .*

James shook his head. Bev was exactly like her mother! His daughter had always resembled Gayle physically, but when it came to her personality, he had assumed that Bev had taken after him. He realized that she had tried to fit that mold, but after reading this letter it was clear that Bev was the image of her mother. Gayle had always believed that he was something special. She had pushed him to try harder, to be more considerate of others. Gayle had never been afraid to voice her opinion, something he had loved about her. He stared at the letter in his hand. He sensed Gayle would be very proud of their daughter, of the courageous statement she was finally making. Bev would be bullied no longer, and from what he gathered, neither would Gina.

*. . . Dad, I think there's something pretty special about this church. You've known Karen for years. You know what she's been through. The testimony she has of the gospel of Jesus Christ as taught by the people you lovingly call "those *@#!! Mormons," has given her the strength she has needed to survive it. Now that her mother is active in this church again, Edie is doing so well. There's really something to this religion; it seems to change lives for the better!*

*You may not believe this, but I **am** doing better too. What the LDS church teaches about life makes sense. The* *standards they teach **are good**. I want to find out for myself if this church teaches the truth about our purpose in this world. The feeling I have when I attend their meetings tells me it does. I'm not saying you ever have to believe in it, but please respect my beliefs.*

*Gina was so upset over everything last night, I thought maybe she'd feel better if she went to church with me this morning. We took the twins with us. They have something called Primary for them. I'll think they'll like it.*

*We'll be home soon. Karen's ward gets out at 12:00 p.m. I hope you'll be there when we get back. I know we have some things to discuss, but try to understand where I'm coming from.*

*Love ya, Bev*

James reread the letter, then set it down on the end table. His daughter was right, they had a lot to discuss when everyone finally came home.

\* \* \*

Karen followed Bev to the foyer. She sensed how nervous her friend was and wished she could do something to help. Instead, all she could do is offer support from the sidelines, something Bev had done repeatedly for her.

"As soon as Mom comes with the twins, I guess we'll head home. Could be interesting."

"Call me later," Karen requested. "Let me know how it's going."

"Plan on it," Bev replied. "Tell Sabrina I'm thinking about her," she added. "I'm glad they asked us to make a poster for her today in Young Women. That ought to cheer her up."

Karen nodded. "I'm sure Sabrina will like it."

"It sounds like she'll be getting out of the hospital soon."

"Either tomorrow or Tuesday."

"It won't be easy for her . . . the shots, the diet," Bev mused. "Still, right now, I'd trade her places in a heartbeat."

Karen gazed sympathetically at Bev. "Maybe it won't be as bad as you think."

"It'll probably be worse, but at least I won't have to face Dad alone. Gina will be there. She told me this morning that we're in this one together."

"It'll be two against one."

"Keep praying for us; we can use all the help we can get." Bev shifted her gaze as her stepmother and brothers made a sudden appearance.

"Slow down boys," Gina called out as she was dragged forward by the twins. "Remember we're in a church house," she admonished.

"I'm starved!" Jake hollered, releasing his mother to bolt for the door.

"Me too!" Drake agreed, following his brother.

"We might as well head home," Gina said. "Your brothers think it's time for lunch."

"How did you like Relief Society?" Karen asked.

Gina searched for a way to tell Karen about her experience. She was still hugging it to herself, the feeling of peace that had filled her heart as a lesson about the Savior had been taught. Her eyes glistening, she simply said, "I enjoyed it very much."

Karen exchanged an elated smile with Bev. Both girls could tell that Gina's heart had been touched by the Spirit, the same Spirit that had softened Bev's outlook on life.

"Think you'll come next week?" Karen asked, unable to resist the question.

The desire was there, but Gina wasn't sure how James would react to any of this. "We'll have to see," she murmured. "Well, Bev, should we go?"

"Yeah. Might as well get this over with." Bev turned to Karen. "Remember, if I come up missing, you'll find what's left of me stuffed inside of Dad's liquor cabinet." She winked at Karen, then followed her stepmother out of the church.

On the way home, the twins chattered excitedly about the video they had watched in Primary.

"It's called staring time," Jake explained. "Today we stared at a movie."

"It was about Jesus," Drake said, picking up the storyline. "He helped people."

"And we sang songs, but we didn't know the words, so we hummed," Jake said.

"I had to sit by a girl," Drake complained. "She smelled funny."

Trying to keep a straight face," Bev glanced back at the four-year-olds. "Why did she smell funny?"

"She smelled like you do when you like boys," Drake replied.

Gina glanced away from the road to smile at Bev. "She must've been wearing perfume."

"I see," Bev said dryly. "So, Drake, you think I smell funny?"

"Yeah. 'Specially when guys come to pick you up at the house." Drake and Jake both cracked up, snickering at their older sister. "You smell funny today. Do you like another boy?"

Giving up, Bev turned her back to her brothers. "Men! They're all alike. They frustrate the he—"

"Bev!" Gina warned.

"I was going to say heck. Trust me, I've reformed. I'm learning there are some things you don't say if you want to be a good Mormon."

"What's a Mormon?" Jake asked.

"Those are the people we went to church with today," Gina explained, turning onto their street.

"They prefer to be called Latter-day Saints," Bev added.

"Ladder-day cents?" Drake repeated. "I don't get it!"

"Ladders and pennies," Jake said, giggling.

Gina rolled her eyes. They had so much to learn about this church Bev was investigating. Personally, she had several questions she longed to ask, issues that would have to wait for another time. As she glanced down the road toward their home, she was relieved to see that James was there. Apprehensive of his current mood, she pulled in beside the Jeep and pressing the button under the dash, waited until the garage door had opened before driving the Pontiac Grand Prix inside.

James saw his family pull in the driveway and hustled around putting the finishing touches on the luncheon he had prepared. It wasn't as fancy as he would have liked, but he had managed to fix meatloaf, mashed potatoes, and had heated up two jars of bottled gravy he had found in the cupboard. He had thrown a couple of cans of corn on to boil a few minutes ago. Turning down the heat, he grabbed the napkins he had located and bustled through the kitchen into the dining room where he had painstakingly set the table. He had just set the napkins in their proper place when his family trooped into the kitchen.

"Somethin' smells good!" Jake exclaimed, his mouth watering. The cold cereal he had eaten for breakfast hadn't stayed with him very long.

"Yeah! Let's eat!" Drake suggested.

Gina glanced around her kitchen, stunned. She wondered if her husband had hired someone to cook lunch. James had never cooked anything since their marriage, leaving most of the domestic duties to her. Was this his way of making up for last night?

Bev was as shocked as her stepmother. "Dad did this?" she said, opening the oven to gape at the meatloaf. "He used to cook quite a bit after Mom died. But that was—"

"Before he married me, six years ago," Gina finished.

"Seven next month," James interrupted, poking his head into the kitchen. "I'd say it's about time I took my turn—periodically."

"Go Dad!" Bev said, taking in the bright green apron he was wearing.

Unable to speak, Gina stared at her husband. This was the last thing she had expected. A warm feeling entered her heart until it collided with a horrible thought. What had James done last night? Was this his way of making up for something she didn't want to know about?

James saw Gina's mixed reaction and told Bev to take her brothers upstairs to change their clothes for dinner. Bev obediently removed herself and her brothers from the tension that was building in the kitchen. Pulling Drake away from the stove and gathering Jake from the dining room, Bev led the two complaining boys out of sight.

"James—" Gina started, but couldn't finish. She was heartsick over what she feared had happened.

"Honey, I am so sorry," James began.

Closing her eyes, Gina tried to block out the pain that threatened to overwhelm.

"It isn't what you think," he continued, waiting until she had opened her eyes to look at him.

"I spent the night at my office . . . by myself."

Gina gazed sadly into her husband's eyes and saw that he was being honest with her. "Why didn't you come home, then?" she asked, relieved.

"I was stone drunk," he admitted. "I don't even remember driving to the car lot."

"What?! James!"

"I'm not proud of what I did . . . and you can't tell me anything I haven't already hit myself over the head with. It was stupid; I did everything I've been telling Bev not to do. I went to the bar, bought a bottle of whiskey, drove to the park, and proceeded to get drunk. That's the last thing I remember until this morning. Evidently, I drove down the street to my car lot, plowed into the front of a new car, smashed up its fender and my Jeep's front bumper."

"Oh, James," Gina groaned.

"Again, I was an idiot—I'll say it freely. You should see my office. It looks like it was hit by a tornado. Files are dumped out everywhere. Papers are mixed up all over the floor. I fell asleep at my desk on top of the bottle of whiskey—it wasn't a very comfortable pillow."

Absorbing his confession, Gina remained silent.

"When I woke up this morning, I was a mess. My head still feels like it's inside of a vise," he said, hoping for sympathy. Judging by the look on his wife's face, sympathy was the last thing Gina would offer. "When I realized I had no memory of how I had arrived at my office, I ran outside, checked my Jeep, and saw the dent. I was so afraid I'd done some real damage, maybe even hurt someone. What a relief it was to discover that I had only hit one of my cars."

At first, Gina thought she was imagining the sorrowful expression on his face; it was the first time she had ever seen James show emotion of this nature. Unsure of how to handle any of this, she was startled when James moved close, selecting one of her soft hands to hold inside of his own.

"Gina, that was enough for me to wake up, to see what I was doing to myself, to you, and to our kids, especially Bev. I'd had a couple of drinks before she got home last night. Everything seemed out of focus, I couldn't think clearly. I took it out on her, then you. I'm not in control when I drink . . . something you've been trying to get me to see. I know now that I have a problem, like *our* daughter. That's probably why I was so hard on her. I was seeing myself in her—I was blaming Bev for my mistake." A repentant look on his face, James smiled sheepishly. "Can you ever forgive me?"

Gina nodded, melting into her husband's loving embrace.

# Chapter 10

Sabrina stepped into her bedroom, taking in every detail. Mormonad posters still hung on three of the four bedroom walls, posters that had inspired her in the past. She focused on one that bore a picture of the Savior. Its message, "YOU ARE NEVER ALONE," caught her attention. Her gaze shifted to the oak dresser she had inherited from Kate. The top still contained her scripture quad and a picture of her family, one taken before her older brother, Tyler, had left on his mission. A small ring tree beckoned from one corner of the dresser. On it were the two rings that had been removed during her stay in the hospital. One ring contained her birthstone, the other was a gift from Kate, a silver CTR ring.

Crossing to her dresser, Sabrina reached for the CTR ring, replacing it on the ring finger of her right hand. Symbolic, it held special meaning for her now. She turned and looked at her white canopied bed. The pillows and stuffed animals were in their proper place, something she was certain her mother had done recently. Sabrina knew she had lacked the energy to keep this room clean for quite some time. Her bed looked so inviting, she decided to lie down for a brief rest.

Moving the stuffed animals, Sabrina adjusted the pillows behind her head and relaxed. It felt wonderful to be home, in the sanctuary her bedroom offered. She loved this room, including the feeling of peace that it inspired. She might not have appreciated it as much before, but now it was her refuge, a place where she could be alone to sort things out. Privacy was something she had come to cherish since her stay in the hospital. Here she could unwind, enjoy the calming quiet, and make sense of what had happened.

In less than a week, her entire life had been turned upside down. Through no fault of her own, her existence had been altered permanently. Classified as a diabetic, she knew this title would shadow who she was until a cure for diabetes became available. Doctor Davis had emphasized the new developments that had occurred with this disease. With the new tools and insulin now on the market, life for a diabetic was easier than it had ever been. Despite that, Sabrina wondered how long she would have to wait before a cure was in sight. Would it happen in her lifetime?

Smiling, Sabrina wondered if she would live to see the millennium. She had learned in seminary that people who lived after the second coming of Christ would never suffer from health problems. That was something to look forward to. No more shots or pain—no more nausea or fatigue. It would be a wonderful time to live.

There had been a lot of talk as the year 2000 had drawn close. So many people had been convinced that it would trigger cataclysmic events, that the end of the world was in sight. Even in the LDS Church, some members had panicked, overreacting to rampant rumors. Sabrina liked what her father had said a few weeks ago, that no one but Heavenly Father and Jesus Christ knew when the Savior would return. That day could come now, next year, maybe a hundred years or more from now. Her father had then stated that there was no need to fear the future, and he had reminded his family that they lived in a wonderful time. Positive things were happening, despite the crime, the corruption, and chaos. He had counseled them to heed the advice given by church leaders, to get prepared for the days ahead, quoting the scripture found in Doctrine & Covenants 38:30: " . . . if ye are prepared ye shall not fear."

It was a scripture that brought her great comfort, especially now. When she had first heard her father quote it from memory, she had thought that it meant it was important to have adequate food storage on hand, something her parents had both been working toward for a long time. Her father also believed in keeping money in savings to handle emergencies and had stressed how crucial it was to stay out of debt. All of these things were essential, but Sabrina was starting to realize that it was also important to build up spiritual strength as well.

This newest challenge in her life had overwhelmed her with fear. The night she had spent at the hospital with Kate, her older sister had gently reminded her to nourish her testimony, stressing that the strength needed to overcome tests could be found in the gospel of Jesus Christ. Sabrina desired the light of Christ to guide her on this unknown, and at times, frightening journey. She knew that was how she would survive this ordeal that had descended without warning. Determination was rapidly replacing the doubts, the numerous fears that plagued her. Daily she would do those things her sister had suggested to nurture the testimony of her heart.

During personal prayers, she would beg for guidance, for courage, and for comfort on the days when it seemed to be too much. She would study the scriptures, learning for herself the stories that would inspire, that would promote a sense of well-being. Always she would remind herself that she was a daughter of God, someone who had been sent here to learn and grow. She anticipated there would be tough days ahead, but a glimmer of hope had been handed to her, compliments of Kate.

Sabrina knew her parents' hearts had been broken. Though both pretended that everything was fine, they were struggling. They had tried to be strong for her; now it was her turn. She was confident she could live up to the blessing given to her in the hospital, one that had promised she would be able to help others, perhaps as Kate had helped her.

Closing her eyes, Sabrina drifted off to sleep and dreamt of sailing a ship across a darkened ocean. A light reflecting from her heart eased the way, helping her to stay on course. As the dream continued, a smile appeared on Sabrina's face, one her mother wondered at when she slipped into the room to check on her youngest daughter.

\* \* \*

"Tyler?!" Sabrina squealed into the phone. "Mom said you called earlier when I was asleep."

The twenty-one-year-old elder grinned. "Hey, tone it down, I might need my ears here in the mission field. Periodically people call me names. It would be rude not to hear them."

"I can't believe you called again. I was afraid they'd only let you try once."

"It wasn't easy, but with my suave looks and charm I was able to talk the mission president into letting me check on you. How's it goin'?"

"I'm fine, Ty, don't worry about me," Sabrina insisted, picturing her older brother. His hair had darkened as he had grown older, becoming an attractive shade of brown. He had inherited their mother's green eyes, eyes that reflected his playful personality. "How's California?"

"With this haircut and the clothes they make a person wear, I'm not having much of a social life, considering I'm in the babe capital of the world."

"You'd better never let Mom hear you talk like that," Sabrina teased. "Girls should be the last thing on your mind, Elder!"

Tyler grinned with relief, grateful that his younger sister still possessed a sense of humor. After hearing how downhearted his mother had been earlier that day, he wasn't sure what to expect from Sabrina. "Not to worry. I will never bring shame to the family name, at least, not intentionally." He paused, enjoying Sabrina's laugh. "So, squirt, how are you really doing?"

"Like I said, I'm okay," she responded.

"Promise?"

"Promise," Sabrina replied. "How about you, Ty?"

"I've decided to go with my full name out here—Elder Tyler Erickson. You can't believe the smart alecks who think it's funny that an Elder Ty is wearing a tie."

Sitting down on a padded stool, Sabrina shook her head. "You haven't changed a bit!"

"Oh, yeah? Dad told me going on a mission would put hair on my chest. Guess what?! I sprouted my first one day before yesterday."

"Seriously, how are things going in the mission field?"

"It's a challenge, people in this district aren't very receptive, but we have another baptism next week. An entire family this time! We've been working with them for about three months. They dragged their feet so much at first, I was ready to give up. Now they want us to start teaching extended family members. It's an awesome thing sharing the gospel. Now I know what Kate was trying to say in her letters when she served her mission in Scotland," he said excitedly.

"Maybe someday I'll serve a mission of my own," Sabrina replied.

"I wouldn't be at all surprised," Tyler said, feeling more than he could ever say over the phone. "Remember, we Ericksons tend to accomplish wondrous things when pressure is applied."

"Then I should be a great success," Sabrina responded. "The pressure is definitely building."

"It is?"

Sabrina glanced around, making sure her parents were nowhere in sight. "You know how Mom and Dad are naturally a little overprotective when it comes to their children?"

"Especially when it concerns the baby of the family," Tyler interjected.

"Thanks," Sabrina said dryly. "This is my first day home from the hospital and I'm already going crazy. I can't even go to the bathroom by myself. "

"I thought you were trained long ago," Tyler teased.

"You know what I mean," Sabrina sighed. "Mom and Dad are hovering over me."

"Breeny, remember, it's because they love you so much. You'll probably never know how hard this has hit them," he said, his own chest feeling tight. "Be patient with them, they'll adjust, maybe not as well as you seem to be doing, but they'll get there." *We all will*, he added to himself. "Well, I'd better not ring up too big of a bill. The mission president is already giving me the high sign, but I just wanted to make sure you were all right."

"I'm fine, Tyler," Sabrina stressed. "I love you, and I can't wait for you to come home."

"Love you too, sis," Tyler managed to say before his emotions got the best of him. "'Bye. Tell everyone I called, again." Hanging up the phone, he took a deep breath, then glanced at his companion.

"Everything all right with Sabrina?"

"She's doing great!"

"Ready to leave?"

"Yeah, let me grab my quad," Tyler said, moving across the room.

* * *

"I'm so happy for you," Karen said, smiling across the small table at Bev. "See, life can be pretty great!" She picked up the chocolate malt she had ordered at the drive-in and took a sip.

"Something I never thought possible," Bev replied, setting a long plastic spoon inside of her root beer float. "I keep waiting for Dad to backslide, but so far, he's done really well." She laughed, reaching for her purse. "I have to show you something he wanted us both to sign last night. I think he's serious about this." She pulled out an envelope and handed it to Karen.

Karen set her malt on the table and opened the envelope. Inside was a contract Bev's father had drawn up, one that stated alcohol was no longer allowed in the Henderson household. Two paragraphs drew her attention. The first declared James Henderson's determination to never drink again—his signature emphasizing the serious nature of his pledge. The second paragraph was the agreement Bev had signed, one that mimicked her father's promise. "You guys are official."

"You bet! Read the bottom, the part that says Gina can punish us severely if we mess up."

It was Karen's turn to laugh.

"What's so funny?"

"I can't see Gina hurting either one of you."

Bev grimaced. "You're probably right. Her heart's too soft."

"I'll volunteer for the job. I know how to hurt you good."

"Oh?" Bev challenged.

"I would make you walk everywhere for an entire year."

"No car?" Bev asked, pretending to be scared.

"No car! No Jeep, no motorcycle. Nothing, nada! Your own two legs would become your permanent mode of transportation."

"Remind me to keep you away from Gina," Bev teased.

"Dream on," Karen returned. "I say a little teamwork is in order. I'm sure your stepmother can figure out ways to keep your father humble. I'll take on that responsibility for you."

"You would, wouldn't you?"

"What are friends for?" Karen quipped, using the line Bev usually threw out.

* * *

Alarmed, Mandy stepped off the weight scale in her aunt's private bathroom. In one week, she had gained five pounds. Five pounds?! That had never happened before. The nausea she had been experiencing had eased, allowing her to eat, but she hadn't consumed more than she usually did. She had noticed other changes with her body, changes that scared her. Two days ago, she had browsed through the local community library and had found a book that contained details about pregnancy. Most of her symptoms had been listed at the beginning of the book. Appalled, she had closed it and returned the book to the shelf.

Remembering what she had read, Mandy cautiously made her way out of her aunt's bathroom and upstairs to her own room to think. Confused, she was also terribly frightened. Who could she talk to? Blade—the person responsible for the mess she was in? Blade—who wouldn't return any of her phone calls? Her mother—who freaked out over stolen gum? Or her aunt Betty—who watched her with those huge cow eyes, longing for a closeness that would never happen? Then there was Sara, her *beloved* cousin—*Miss Perfect* who had made sure that Mandy would never be accepted at Blaketown High. Everywhere Mandy went in that school, she could hear the whispers, the laughter behind her back. She was branded, just as thoroughly as Uncle Lyle's prize heifers.

Now that was scary—she was starting to think like a farmer. She had to get out of this place before she went crazy! Vowing to do just that, Mandy stretched out on her bed and tried to envision a way to escape this ordeal.

* * *

"You want me to quit the volleyball team?!" Sabrina gaped at her parents, then at Coach Barnes. She had wondered why her coach had come by the house this afternoon. His visit was becoming an unwelcome surprise. This couldn't be happening; she loved sports—especially volleyball. A few weeks ago, the coach had told her that she was varsity material—now this?! Shock gave way to anger as the unfairness of the situation descended. "I've worked so hard . . . spent hours at practice and just because I've been a little sick—"

Sue faced her daughter's fury head on. "Sabrina, your father and I have discussed this with Coach Barnes and we feel that it's in your best interest—"

"Doesn't my opinion count for anything?!" Sabrina asked, banging her fist on the arm of the couch.

"Honey, you know that it does," Greg replied. "You have to admit, right now, your blood sugar levels are everywhere but where they're supposed to be."

"The specialist said that would happen," Sabrina reminded her parents. "He explained that at first it would be a challenge to regulate my levels because my pancreas is still putting out some insulin on its own. It's not my fault my blood sugar keeps bouncing. I'm doing the best that I can," she tearfully rebutted.

Her luminous green eyes tinged with a deep sadness, Sue placed a hand on Sabrina's shoulder. "You're trying harder than I think most people would. But your doctor stressed that our first priority is to give you a chance to get back on your feet."

"I'm supposed to exercise—exercise is good for a diabetic!"

Sue shook her head. She had known this would be a difficult conversation. "Walking, or riding your bike a short distance is one thing, but Sabrina, none of us think you're ready to play in a challenging, physical game. What if you have a reaction during the middle of a heated set? What if you don't realize that that's the problem? Do you think any of us want to see you sprawled on the gym floor unconscious?"

"Trust me, I'm learning what an insulin reaction feels like," Sabrina protested. "I had one this morning, remember?"

"I know," Sue replied. "You had one last night, too. And three the day before," she said, hoping to reason with Sabrina.

"Before my blood sugar drops, I feel shaky, dizzy, and I break out in a cold sweat. If that happens during a game, I'll know it's time to eat something. I'll check my level before each game and if it's low, I'll eat an extra snack, like the specialist said to do."

"Sabrina, in the past twenty-four hours, you have bounced from 45 to 322. Every day this past week we've fought an uphill battle to keep your blood sugar where it's supposed to be. We're still trying to figure out how much insulin you're going to need. Until you're under better control, we have to take a few precautions. We didn't make this decision lightly. I called your specialist this morning and he agreed that we needed to start you out with something more mellow, then when you're under better control, you can try more vigorous activities."

"Oh, like needlepoint?!" Her eyes misting, Sabrina shared a betrayed look with her father, then her coach. She still couldn't believe they were doing this to her.

"Sabrina, it won't be forever," Coach Barnes said, smiling kindly. "You have a lot of talent . . . talent that we need. I agree with your parents though, right now; you have to take care of yourself. Maybe in a few weeks, you'll be ready to join the team."

"In a few weeks the season will be over!" Sabrina protested hotly.

Coach Barnes tried to suppress the grin that threatened to surface. This girl was extremely spirited, something that made her an outstanding player. "Right now, we need someone to help take stats at the games. You can still travel with the team." He glanced at her parents, hoping they would agree, certain it was a compromise Sabrina could live with.

"Like I'm sure my parents will let me go," Sabrina said glumly.

Sue glanced at Greg and could see that he was as troubled by this suggestion as she was. She wished Coach Barnes had mentioned this possibility earlier—now, she felt trapped. Truthfully, it worried her sick to think of Sabrina traveling, there were so many things that could go wrong. But they had also been cautioned by Sabrina's diabetic specialist not to overreact.

*"In time, you'll come to accept diabetes as a routine part of Sabrina's life. She will too, especially if you don't hover. There are a few restrictions, but it's crucial to combine those rules with the knowledge that she can lead a fairly normal life. Stress the guidelines, then encourage her to take responsibility for her diabetes. If we can get her motivated enough, I think she'll do exceptionally well."*

"A pretty tall order," Sue thought silently as she agonized over the predicament the coach had placed them in. "Sabrina, if you'd like to take stats for a while, I don't see a problem with it," she extended bravely. Greg looked worried, but nodded his agreement.

"From a setter to a statistician?" Sabrina grumbled.

"Hey, it's my final offer . . . for now," Coach Barnes informed her. "At least you'd still be part of the team. You're sidelined, but not for the entire season. Unless I miss my guess, I look for you to be playing in some of our final key games."

Sabrina glanced at her parents. She read the concern in their eyes and lowered her gaze.

"Honey, your coach is right. We'll all work together on this. As soon as we're in agreement that you're ready, we'll let you give volleyball another try," Greg promised.

"After things settle down, we'll see how you do at practice a time or two," the coach challenged. "If you can handle that, then we'll pull you off the bench."

"Really?" Sabrina asked, glancing around the living room.

"Get yourself under good control, then we'll talk," Sue affirmed.

Agreeing, Sabrina silently vowed that she would try even harder to adhere to her new diet and schedule; so much was riding on how well she did, including her future health.

# Chapter 11

James lay staring at the ceiling in the large master bedroom as his wife slept quietly beside him. Glancing at the clock, he knew sleep wouldn't come as easily for him that night. Beads of perspiration collected on his forehead as the compulsion to drink grew stronger. Restless, he rose from the bed and slipped out into the hall. Walking into the living room, he stared at the bar. The damaged glass had been replaced, but the bottles of liquor had not. Instead, the cabinets were filled with containers of nuts, microwavable popcorn, and other favorite TV snack foods. Breathing in deeply, James turned and wandered into the kitchen. He looked through the fridge, but discovered that milk was the strongest drink in its possession. Scowling, he moved to the sink, turned on the faucet, and splashed cold water on his face.

If Bev could beat this, he could too; after all, he was much stronger—physically. As he glared at the shadowed image of himself in the kitchen window, he acknowledged that there was a strength Bev was drawing on that he could not fathom. She claimed it was her growing testimony of the true gospel of Jesus Christ. Discouraged, James turned his back to the window and leaned against the counter. Religion had never played an important role in his life, even after Gayle had died. He had reasoned that a merciful God would not have allowed her to die—to develop a disease that had taken her from him bit by bit until there was nothing left but a pain-riddled shell.

Guilt nagged, reminding him of the promise he had made at the car lot after he had discovered the dent in his Jeep. *Please God, if there is a God . . . help me . . . help me remember. Please tell me I didn't hurt*

*anyone. I'll never drink again . . . just please let everything be all right.*
As the pledge echoed inside his head, James whirled around to glower
out the kitchen window. "All right! I made a promise. You kept your
end of the deal . . . I'll try to keep mine. Just let me get some sleep!"
Turning back around, he winced as the urge to drink grew stronger.
One little drink, that's all it would take. Something to soothe his
nerves, to quiet the buzzing in his head. Repulsed by the temptation,
he stormed into the living room and flopped on the couch. Grabbing
a sofa pillow, he pulled it over his head, trying to drown out the inner
voice that screamed for relief.

* * *

"James, you look terrible this morning."

James glanced up from his desk at the man who had stepped into
his office—Ray Jasper, a longtime friend and business associate.
"Thanks for the vote of confidence. How's life treating you?"

"Obviously better than it is you. What's wrong?"

James rubbed at the back of his neck. "I haven't been sleeping well
lately."

"Why?" Ray asked, sitting down on a cushioned chair in front of
the desk. "Don't tell me you and Gina are having problems?"

"No, nothing like that," James hurriedly assured him.

"Then what? Is your business going down the tubes?"

"Hardly," James replied. "I'm just not feeling my best right now."

Ray flashed a perfect white smile. "Health—that would've been
my next guess. Sometimes these aging bodies have a mind of their
own," he said, laughing.

"What are you up to today?" James asked, changing the subject.

"I came by to see if I could talk you into a round of golf this
morning. Things are slow at the bank. I thought maybe we could slip
away for a couple of hours."

"I don't know," James hesitated.

"Come on. It'll make you feel better. Maybe that's what you need,
some fresh air. A little exercise. It'll make a world of difference—help
you sleep tonight."

"Maybe you're right. I know I'm not accomplishing much here

today. My new salesman can cover any car deals that might be made in my absence. Let's do it. Let's go."

Grinning, Ray nodded. "I'm with you. Let's get out of here."

* * *

"Watch where you're going!" Mandy snarled when Karen accidentally bumped into her at school in a crowded hallway later that same day.

"Sorry!" Karen returned, reaching down to pick up a book Mandy had dropped. "Here you go, oh friendliest of sophomores."

Seething, Mandy refused to reply. She snatched the book out of Karen's hand and stomped down the hall toward her locker, glaring at anyone who happened to look her way.

Disgusted, Karen shook her head, then moved on toward her own locker. She smiled when Bev approached.

"I see you survived another unpleasant encounter with the sophomore from Hades," Bev teased.

"True story," Karen said, stuffing her books inside of her locker. "I swear that girl's attitude is getting worse, not better. What is up with her?"

Bev shrugged. "Who knows? Her cousin, Sara, thinks that girl is hopeless. Sara told me the other day that living with Mandy is like living with a wounded mountain lion."

"Why do you suppose she's so angry all of the time?"

"I don't think Mandy has to have a reason—I think it's just her natural, charming disposition. No wonder her parents got rid of her." Bev opened her own locker and threw her book bag inside. "Enough about the Salt Lake she-devil. Let's go grab a quick bite of lunch," she suggested, closing her locker.

"Cafeteria or downtown?"

"They're serving shepherd's pie today—is there any doubt?! Let's head downtown. I'll drive," Bev offered, motioning across the hall to Sabrina and Terri. "Come girls, it's time to feed our resident diabetic."

Sabrina gave Bev a dirty look. "Resident diabetic?" she asked, moving closer to the older girls.

Bev reached to pinch Sabrina's cheek. "Yes, you cute little thing, you." She hurried away before Sabrina could retaliate, leading the way out of the school.

* * *

Observing that Mandy was once again sitting alone in the bustling high school cafeteria, Doris turned down an invitation to sit by a group of teachers and carried her tray to Mandy's table.

"Mind if I sit down?"

"It's a free country," Mandy mumbled, picking at the food on her tray. Still a bit queasy, she was having a difficult time eating the conglomeration that had been prepared that day. Shepherd's pie had never been one of her favorites, but she was learning that if she didn't keep something in her stomach, the nausea grew worse.

"How are you doing today?" Doris asked brightly, sitting down across from the sophomore.

Refusing to answer, Mandy shoved a spoonful of cheese-covered potatoes into her mouth. She forced herself to swallow, then reached for the small carton of milk on her tray to help wash it down.

Silently searching for a way to ease into a conversation with the young woman, Doris glanced at the necklace Mandy was wearing. She had noticed that lately, Mandy wore this necklace on a regular basis—a small heart-shaped locket supported by a delicate gold chain. "That's a beautiful necklace," she complimented.

Startled by the comment, Mandy briefly dropped her guard. "Uh . . . thanks . . . it was a gift."

Doris smiled warmly. "A gift?" she repeated, inviting Mandy to elaborate.

Nodding, Mandy averted her eyes. "Yeah, Mom gave it to me for my birthday last year," she explained, her voice thickening.

Recognizing the signs, Doris knew this girl was on an emotional roller coaster. As she had suspected, the angry wall Mandy kept between herself and everyone else was more fragile than it appeared. "You must miss your mother very much," she said sympathetically.

"Yeah, right! She can't even stand the sight of me!" Mandy exclaimed.

"I doubt that," Doris countered. "Sometimes mothers and daughters drive each other crazy, but the love between them rarely dies."

Using anger to avoid the onslaught of tears that threatened, Mandy rose from the table and scowled at Doris. "I'm out of here!"

she exclaimed, turning her back on the tray of food and the English teacher. Sighing, Doris began picking at the food on her own tray, so caught up in her thoughts that she didn't notice when Kate approached.

"Need a shoulder?" Kate asked, carefully placing her tray of food on the table beside Doris.

"Not as much as a young lady I could mention," Doris answered as she watched Mandy storm out of the cafeteria.

* * *

"Tough luck," Ray called out when James missed his final shot.

Annoyed, James shook his head. The noticeable tremor in his hands had made this game a losing battle.

"To celebrate my victory, something that doesn't happen very often when we play golf, I'll buy you lunch."

"You're on," James replied, setting his golf club back in the bag. "Where?"

"Why not here? They have a nice restaurant in the lodge."

"Sounds good." The two friends loaded their bags into the golf cart, then Ray drove them back to the lodge. A few minutes later, they followed a young waitress to a small table near a window that overlooked the golf course.

"Feeling any better?" Ray asked.

James nodded. "I think the fresh air did me some good."

"I know something else that will too," Ray said, motioning for the waitress. "We'll take a round of beer."

"Uh . . . Ray . . . I believe I'll pass. I'm trying to cut down."

Ray glanced at James in disbelief. "It's just a beer, James. What's the harm?"

James considered the question. What was the harm of one beer? It wasn't like he would be downing a bottle of whiskey, just a beer—a simple beer. His mouth watered at the prospect.

"Well?" Ray pressed as the waitress shifted her gaze to James.

* * *

After enjoying a lengthy lunch with Ray, James swung by his car dealership for an hour, then headed home. Whistling, he opened the front door and walked into the living room. "Hi, everyone, I'm home."

"In here," Gina called from the kitchen. "I'm starting dinner."

Still whistling, James headed into the kitchen. He moved behind Gina, grabbed her around the waist, and gave her a big squeeze.

"You're home early, what's the occasion?" Gina asked, relieved that her husband was in a good mood. He had been on edge most of the week, losing his temper repeatedly over trivial matters, most that had involved their children. She had tried to be understanding, explaining to Bev and the twins that they shouldn't take their father's angry outbursts to heart while he tried to adjust to his new, non-alcoholic existence. Facing James, Gina smiled, thrilled that he was finally in a pleasant frame of mind.

"It's been a good day," James exclaimed, giving her another hug. He was startled when Gina pushed away from him. "What's wrong?"

Her eyes filling with tears, Gina gripped the handle of the oven for support.

"Gina?!"

"James . . . how could you?! You promised! You signed a pledge with Bev—I really thought you were serious about this."

"About what?"

Gina glared accusingly at her husband. "I can smell it on you—you've been drinking!"

Moving to the cupboard, James slapped his hands against the counter. "One lousy beer and she acts like I've committed murder!"

"One, James?" Gina pushed.

"Okay, two! It's not like I came home loaded!" he exclaimed, whirling around. "If I can get by with a beer now and then, what's the harm?" he replied, using his friend's argument.

"What *is* the harm, James? When beer isn't enough anymore . . . then what? Back to the whiskey . . . back to what you claimed you never wanted again?!" With that statement, the tears ran freely down both sides of her face and she bolted from the room.

Pulling the keys out of his pocket, James left the house through the kitchen door. He climbed inside of his Jeep and roared out of the driveway, not caring that he nearly backed into a neighbor's car as it passed by.

\* \* \*

"Mom, it'll be okay," Bev said as she patted her stepmother's back. Disappointment pierced her own heart, but she knew it was nothing compared to what Gina was experiencing.

Gina continued to sob into a pillow on her bed, shattered by James' betrayal.

"I messed up a few times before I got my act together," Bev reminded her. "You didn't give up on me. Remember when you found me totally sloshed in the garage, after I left the treatment program this summer?"

Calming, Gina pictured Bev on her hands and knees in the garage, too wasted to find her way back inside of the house. Gina had managed to drag Bev inside and down the hall to the bathroom where a lukewarm shower had penetrated her stepdaughter's drunken stupor. Afterwards, Gina had guided Bev up to her room where she had put the young woman to bed. A stern but loving lecture had been delivered the next morning as Gina had done her best to give Bev the courage to keep trying.

"Dad's had this problem longer. It's probably going to take more time . . . maybe some counseling."

"Your father will never agree to counseling!" Gina replied, rolling over to face Bev. "He's too proud—he'll never ask for help. He'll just keep running his life . . . our lives into the ground! I don't want this for you . . . for the boys . . . or for me."

"So, what do we do?"

Gina pulled herself up into a sitting position. "I don't know, Bev. I honestly don't know."

"Do you still love Dad?" Bev asked, fearing the answer.

Gina wiped at her eyes, then met Bev's pleading gaze. "You know I do. I'm just not very happy with him right now."

"I learned at the treatment center that alcoholism is an illness. An alcoholic can't always see what they're doing to themselves, or to their family or friends. Edie told me the same thing. She also said that it took something pretty traumatic to get her attention. Her wake-up call was landing in prison. My wake-up call came twice, first during our *canyon adventure*—I can't believe I talked Sabrina into getting drunk that night. She'll probably never know how much I'll always regret that. Then later, I couldn't help Karen because of the shape I was in. My best friend could've been seriously hurt and all I could do was stagger around until I broke my leg. I've never felt so helpless in my entire life."

"What was your second wake-up call?" Gina asked, curious.

A blush crept into Bev's face. "I got homesick at the rehab center—I missed you all so much—I was ready to do anything to come home." She smiled shyly. "I'll bet you never thought I'd struggle with that."

"Actually, I suspected you would," Gina answered, surprising her stepdaughter. "It was the first time you'd ever been away from home, at least, by yourself. I wondered how you'd handle it."

"Not very well. And when I came back—I decided I had to figure out what this life is all about. I had so many questions. That's why I started going to church with Karen. She told me how excited she is to be sealed to her mother someday—that families are meant to be together forever—it touched something deep inside of me."

"You want to be with your mother forever," Gina guessed.

Bev smiled at her stepmother. "I want *all* of us to be a forever family. That includes you."

Gina affectionately brushed Bev's cheek with her hand. "I don't know, Bev, sometimes I wonder where I fit in all of this. I just think I'm making headway, first with you, then your father—then everything falls apart. I'm not sure I'm up to much more. What will Drake and Jake be like in a few years? If they follow this family's trend—I don't know what I'll do. They don't really understand what has been going on with you or your father, but someday they will. How will I handle it?"

"Edie and I had a long talk a couple of weeks ago," Bev replied, tracing the pattern on the quilted bedspread with her finger. "She said that part of her problem was that she never learned from her mother's example. Adele's been through a lot, but she still smiles—she doesn't give up. She doesn't need a crutch like alcohol to help her through. That's what we need to teach Jake and Drake—that with the right attitude, you can handle difficult things. Adele's husband died in a horrible tractor accident, but she was able to go on because she knew there was a purpose to this life—she knew that someday she would be with her husband again."

"Karen's family has been a good influence on you," Gina observed. "And I like the LDS belief that families are meant to be together—even after this life is through. If you really knew that was possible, it could make a big difference in how you look at things."

"It made a difference for Adele," Bev replied. "She survived Edie going to prison and raised Karen by herself, because she loved both of them so much. She never gave up on Edie, even when Karen did—the woman is amazing. Adele bore her testimony in church last month. The whole time she was speaking, I felt goose-bumps up and down my arms. I knew she believed every word that she said. People talk about becoming more Christ-like—Adele's there. She's always doing things for other people, always going the extra mile—she's one of my heroes."

"I can see why," Gina replied, picturing Edie's sweet mother.

Bev gazed steadily at her stepmother. "Another hero is sitting beside me on this bed."

Surprised, Gina stared at the teenager.

"You've put up with so much from me—but you kept trying. Even when I made things horrible for you." Bev lowered her head contritely. "I am so sorry for how I treated you, and for what you're going through now. You don't deserve any of this."

With one hand, Gina lifted Bev's chin, locking her troubled gaze with her own. "I forgave you a long time ago," she stressed. "As for this mess with your father, we'll survive somehow."

Relieved by that assurance, Bev nodded. "You always manage to think of something."

"Right now I don't feel too inspired," Gina replied. "I'm not sure what to do." The two of them mulled things over as several seconds passed in silence.

"Why don't we talk to Edie?" Bev finally offered. "She might have some suggestions."

Sighing heavily, Gina ran a hand through her tousled brown hair. "That might be a start. I wonder if she's home?"

Bev glanced at her watch. "When I talked to Karen earlier, she said her mother was working the morning shift at the hospital. She's probably home now . . . unless she's with Brett."

"What will we do with the twins?"

"Call Dad's sister. I'm sure she wouldn't mind watching them for a while," Bev suggested.

Nodding, Gina reached across the bed and grabbed for the phone. "What's Karen's number?" She pushed in the numbers as Bev rattled them off from memory. "Thanks," she said as she waited for someone to answer. "Hello, Adele? Is Edie there?" Gina nervously gripped the phone. "Edie—would you mind if Bev and I came over? We need your help."

# Chapter 12

Karen watched as Bev and Gina climbed into their car and drove away. She stared after them for several long seconds before closing the front door.

Edie stepped into the living room and gazed at Karen, wondering at the way her daughter was lingering near the door. "Is everything all right?"

"Yeah," Karen lied. She kept her back to her mother, unwilling to reveal the tears that were threatening to spill down her face.

Sensing her daughter's struggle, Edie didn't push. Instead, she gathered the rest of the dessert plates from the living room and took them into the kitchen where Adele was insisting on rinsing them off for the dishwasher.

"Karen's really upset," Edie said in a hushed voice as she scraped cake crumbs from the small plates into the garbage.

"I know," Adele replied, meeting her daughter's worried gaze. "Bev has been like a sister to her . . . when Bev hurts, Karen hurts."

"Maybe you'd better talk to her . . . you always know what to say," Edie suggested, handing the plates to her mother.

Adele shook her head. "You're the one Karen needs."

"But—"

"Go on. I'll finish up in here. You finish up in there—go talk to Karen."

Edie lifted an eyebrow. "But Mom—"

"You don't need me to fill in for you anymore," Adele said softly. "You can do this."

Edie glanced toward the living room. "Do you think I shared too much with Gina and Bev? I pretty much told them everything. Karen was so quiet through it all . . . did I embarrass her?"

"I'm glad you can use what you've been through to help others. I'm sure Karen feels the same way," Adele replied. Impulsively, she reached for Edie and gave her a loving squeeze. "I'm so proud of you," she said, drawing back. "You've become a remarkable woman and a wonderful mother." She smiled warmly at her teary-eyed daughter. "Now, go talk to Karen."

Unable to reply, Edie left the room. Taking a deep breath, she walked into the living room, but Karen was nowhere in sight. She moved down the hall to the bedroom she shared with her daughter and found Karen sitting on a chair near the window. Before she could say anything, Karen stood, pretending to stare out the window.

Sighing, Edie closed the door and crossing to the twin bed closest to the window, sat down, unsure of what to say. "Karen . . . about tonight . . . I'm sorry if—"

"Do you think things will work out for Bev's family?" Karen asked, trying to sway the conversation from fears that were tearing her apart.

"I don't know. I hope so," Edie replied, troubled by the tears that were slipping down her daughter's face.

"Bev was so happy a few days ago—I thought things were turning around."

"Don't give up yet, this is far from over," Edie replied. "At the moment, I'm more concerned about you," she added.

Karen held her breath, but tears continued to make an awkward appearance.

"Sit down, we need to talk," Edie invited.

Wiping at her eyes, Karen obediently turned from the window and sat on a chair, facing her mother.

"Did I upset you tonight when I told Gina and Bev about my past?" Edie probed.

"Mom, I know why you shared those things . . . but it brings back so much," Karen replied. "It hurts . . . and sometimes I still . . ." she paused, reluctant to confide her concerns.

"Go on," Edie prompted. After several seconds passed in silence, she decided to force the issue. "You still wonder if I'll drink again?" When the only reply was Karen's quiet sob, Edie knew she had found the problem. "Karen . . . I promised you months ago that I would never touch alcohol again," she said, a trifle hurt.

"I know," Karen responded.

"You have to trust me . . . I didn't say this to you before . . . you'd already been through so much when your dad tried to run off with you last spring—I didn't want to say anything that would upset you . . . but do you realize that none of that would have happened if you had trusted me? You thought I was drinking that night . . . then you headed up that canyon with your friends—it was a disaster waiting to happen!"

"When I saw you walk into a bar . . . what was I supposed to think?" Karen asked.

Frustrated, Edie clenched her fists, then relaxed the tight hold, sensing this had to be settled calmly—anger would only make it worse. "I went into the bar that night to try to talk sense to your father, not to get drunk. He was threatening to push for custody of you."

"I know . . . I'm sorry . . . I should've given you more credit than I did. And I know what I'm saying is hurting you now . . . I'm not explaining any of this very well. Earlier, Bev looked so down—I knew exactly how she felt. How it feels to get your hopes up . . . and then have them crushed."

Ashamed, Edie stared down at her hands. "I've let you down most of your life. I wish I could erase all of that . . . but I can't. All I can promise is that the future will be better . . . for both of us."

"Will it, Mom? I know you've done well for a long time . . . but when you told Gina that there are still days when you fight the urge to drink—"

"I said that to help Gina understand that it's a continuous battle. Karen, I'll never drink again . . . you have to believe me!"

But you still get that urge?" Karen pressed.

"Once in a while . . . when I've had a bad day—"

"Can you understand how that makes me feel? What if things don't work out between you and Brett? Or you lose your job . . . or something else happens? How are you going to cope with it?"

Edie gazed tearfully at her daughter. "You didn't let me finish. When I have a bad day . . . when that urge comes . . . I've learned to block it out. I pray for strength and it's granted. I think about you . . . about how disappointed you would be . . . I think about Mom and all

she's been through because of me. I think about what I want out of
life now." A deep pain reflected from her moist blue eyes. "If things
don't work out with Brett, I'll deal with it. I'm not saying it would be
easy . . . but for the first time in my life, all of the pieces are starting
to come together. Do you think I would do anything to jeopardize
that? I have you back in my life . . . that alone means so much! I'm
working toward a career I enjoy . . . and I really think Brett and I will
be fine. We're starting a temple prep class this Sunday, did you know
that?"

"Serious?"

Edie nodded. "It was Brett's idea. He's come a long way the past
few weeks. I suspect I'll be showing off a ring in the near future."

For the first time that night, Karen smiled. "That would be so
great!"

"You'll be the first to know when it happens," Edie promised.
"Now—back to you—I want this cleared up once and for all. I can't
replace the years that were wasted between us, but I am trying my
best to give you everything I can now."

"I know, but sometimes I feel so cheated," Karen sniffed. "After
this year . . . I'll be off to college. You're finally part of my life, but it's
only for a few short months."

"I feel the same way," Edie informed her daughter. Rising to her
feet, she drew Karen into an intense hug. "But I will always be a part
of your life, no matter where you are," she said in a strained voice.

Karen responded by squeezing her mother tight.

* * *

Still immersed in a dank reservoir of self-pity, James returned
home later that night. Propelled by anger, he had headed up one of
the local canyons earlier to think things through. To his credit, he
hadn't taken along a six-pack of beer to alleviate his distress. Instead,
he had driven to Bev's forest retreat empty-handed. Making his way
to her beloved camping spot, he had wandered to the creek, gazing at
the gurgling water as it had moved past. How many wine bottles had
this stream hidden for his daughter? Probably more than he wanted
to know about.

Withdrawing to the secluded thicket, he had sat near a tall pine tree, and for the first time in several years, listened to the sounds Gayle had always loved. His first wife had always enjoyed coming here, proclaiming it was a healing sanctuary. Closing his eyes, he had tried to recapture the peaceful magic of the past. Birds had serenaded, blissfully unaware of his presence, crickets had chirped, and an occasional insect had buzzed near his ear. Despite their soothing orchestration, his attempts at meditation failed, blocked by inner turmoil.

He had spent the rest of the evening debating with himself. Was his desire to drink stronger than the love he felt for his family? He didn't think so. Could he handle drinking a couple of beers periodically, or did he possess a serious problem, one that Bev had inherited from him? Round and round his thoughts had spiraled, until he had given up, heading home to an uncertain welcome. There were no easy answers, just as there was no quick fix to this dilemma.

Now, as he entered the house through the kitchen door, he hesitated in the silent room, idly wondering if Gina had been able to finish dinner. His growling stomach reminded him that he hadn't eaten a thing since lunch. Lunch! That's where all of this trouble had started—this afternoon with Ray! Frowning, he knew it had actually started with himself; he was the one who had made a poor choice. He could have refused the beer this afternoon, avoiding all of this. Instead, he had added fuel to a fire that threatened to burn out of control.

Gathering his courage, he walked out of the kitchen, crossed the dining room, and entered the living room. As he had anticipated, Gina was waiting up for him. Relief that she was still there converted to dread as he prepared himself for a heated argument.

"Gina . . . I'm sorry."

Gina glanced at her husband, then closed the health magazine she had been reading and set it on the couch beside her. Edie had loaned it to her, explaining that it contained an informative article on alcoholism. Standing, Gina pushed down the anger as she remembered what Edie had advised.

*"The best thing you can do right now is love him, but be firm. He has to know how you feel, but neither of you will be able to come to terms with this until James admits he has a problem. The desire to change has*

*to come from him. Even then, it's so hard. I nearly blew it myself a time or two last year . . . and that was after going three years without a drink. You learn that you can never let your guard down."*

"Gina . . . please forgive me—I wasn't out drinking tonight, I promise," James said in a rush. "I needed some time to think. I went for a drive." He searched Gina's face for understanding. "I want to make this right between us."

"There's only one thing I want to hear from you," she replied, choosing her words carefully.

"That I'm sorry? I already said it. I'll say it again—"

"No, and no excuses . . . please."

James looked perplexed. "Then what?"

"I need to hear what you truly think about this situation, and then I'll tell you what my feelings are."

Puzzled, James studied the swirled pattern in the grey carpeted floor. What did Gina want him to say? "I made a mistake this afternoon. Maybe you haven't noticed, but giving up alcohol cold turkey isn't the easiest thing I've ever done."

"I *have* noticed, we all have. Why do you think we've been walking around on eggshells all week? It's like living with a grumpy bear." When James started to protest, she held up a hand. "Just remember something—it wasn't easy for Bev either."

James scowled at his wife. "But this is different—"

"Is it? You expected her to quit overnight. When she didn't, you made her life miserable."

"Are you saying paybacks are bad?"

"I'm saying your daughter was the first one to stick up for you this afternoon. She knows what you're going through."

Chagrined, James focused on the carpet again.

"James, look at me," Gina pleaded. She waited until their eyes were linked. "I was as hard on you this afternoon as you were on Bev. I expected a miracle . . . but I can see now that this will be a continuous process. That doesn't mean I approve of what you did today, but I am trying to understand."

"I want to beat this thing, you have to believe that," James replied. "I'm not sure what the next step is, but I'll do whatever it takes to keep this family together. I don't want to lose you or our kids." His jaw tightened with unspoken emotion.

"As long as I know you're trying, you'll never lose me," Gina assured, reaching for him.

# Chapter 13

"This is so great!" Sabrina exclaimed, thrilled that she was heading out of town on an adventure that didn't include doctors or tests. "After the past couple of weeks, I really need a break," she added, reflecting on the challenge her life had become. She felt suffocated by her parents who were hounding her constantly about her blood sugar levels; isolated from her friends on the volleyball team who thought it was gross to poke your finger several times a day; and discouraged by the way her blood sugar continued to bounce as she waged her private war against diabetes.

"We all need a break," Karen said, turning to look over the seat at the younger girl. She smiled at Sabrina, then at Terri. "It's the weekend! Party on!"

"Something that is definitely overdue," Bev said, glancing away from the road as she struggled to keep a smile on her face. The turmoil in her own household had intensified. Her father was striving to do better, but he had slipped twice in the past week. His last round of drinking had taken place the night before. He had had a terrible fight with Gina over a six-pack of beer she had discovered in a small fridge at the car dealership. When she had confronted him with it, he had stormed out of the building, returning home later in a drunken daze. Gina had spent most of the night crying.

"Hey, keep those baby blues glued to the road," Karen said, adjusting her seat belt. She had seen the melancholy look on Bev's face and knew her friend was suffering. Aching for her, Karen wished she could soften what Bev was going through.

Bev refocused on the road, slowing the Jeep to the speed limit. "Better, Mom?" she said, trying to keep her voice light.

"Much," Karen replied. "And don't give me credit for being your mother. That's a thankless job if there ever was one."

"You're full of compliments today," Bev answered, trying to grin. "Maybe I don't want to be your roommate at college after all."

"Promise?" Karen joked, trying to lighten the mood.

"I still can't believe you guys will be graduating this year," Terri said. "What's Blaketown going to do without you?"

"You two will have to pick up the slack," Bev said, smiling in the rearview mirror. "I have great faith in both of you. You'll carry the torch and make us proud."

"We'll try, but those are some big shoes to fill," Sabrina said.

"Especially Bev's," Karen teased. "My feet are much smaller."

"So, I have a solid foundation to stand on," Bev challenged.

"Yes, you do," Karen said, giving Bev a meaningful look. Earlier this morning, before Bev had picked up Sabrina and Terri, the two of them had spent several minutes discussing Bev's situation at home. Karen had reminded Bev that her growing testimony would help her through this trying time. "Your testimony can be an anchor, no matter how bad it gets," Karen had consoled. "Mine was for me while Mom was in prison. Plus I had Grandma in my corner, just like you have Gina. Don't give up on your dad. Pray for him. Love him. Someday it will click for him. Just like it did for my mother."

Remembering the conversation, Bev smiled sadly at Karen, indicating that she hadn't forgotten her friend's advice.

"How many apartments are we checking out today?" Terri asked, jarring Karen and Bev back to the current topic.

"We've already called on several. Today we'll try to see about six or seven of the best deals and hopefully come up with one we like that's in the right price range," Karen replied.

"I think it's neat you'll both be going to ISU," Sabrina commented. "It'll be less scary with two of you there."

"Less scary?" Bev said, deciding to enjoy today despite the unpleasantness at home. "ISU won't know what hit it when we arrive on campus!" she exclaimed, her blue eyes twinkling.

"Why did you both decide on ISU?" Terri asked, curious.

"The school counselor has all but promised me a major scholarship at ISU. That was my biggest influence," Karen replied. "I had considered going to BYU, but money will be tight. Getting a scholarship to ISU will be an answer to prayers."

"Mine included," Bev said, her eyes linking with Karen's. She had planned on attending ISU for a long time, honoring her father's wishes to attend his alma mater. It had saddened her to think she would be separated from Karen.

"Why are you already looking for housing?" Terri asked, glancing out the window on her side of the Jeep. "It's almost a year away."

"If we wait till the last minute, we won't have much of a selection," Karen informed her. "Besides, you know how winters are in Blaketown. I'd rather get things locked in now while the weather's warm."

"I don't blame you," Sabrina replied, her heart lighter than it had been in days. She glanced out the window on her side of the Jeep. It was a beautiful October morning with hardly a cloud in the sky. Physically, she felt good and was eager to spend this day with her friends. She knew that after looking at the apartments, they would head to the mall to do some shopping, one of her favorite pastimes.

Bev cranked up the radio as a recent hit by Celine Dion played over the airwaves:

*". . . when you want it the most, there's no easy way out. When you're ready to go and your heart's left in doubt, don't give up on your faith, love comes to those who believe it . . . ."*

\* \* \*

Aggravated by the embarrassment she felt, Mandy forced herself to enter the small drugstore. Unable to sleep the night before, she had concluded that this was the only way she could get a pregnancy test. No one really knew her in this town. They probably wouldn't even notice what she was buying. She had come early enough in the morning—few people would be in the store. If she had her driver's license, she would drive to a larger town, maybe Pocatello. Grimacing, Mandy knew that if she had her license, she wouldn't stay in this poor excuse for a town, she'd go somewhere far away from everyone who had ever known or hurt her. As it was, she had to bide her time, hating every second of her life in Blaketown.

Mandy spent several minutes walking around the small store until she found what she was looking for. She gazed at the boxes on the shelf; there were three different brands to choose from. Unsure which would be the best, Mandy selected the one called *Precise*. Every time she reached for the box, someone walked by. Disgusted with herself, she picked up the offending box and walked to the front of the store, dismayed when she saw Doris Kelsey standing in line ahead of her. Quickly hiding the pregnancy kit behind her back, she ducked behind a rack of books.

"I'm glad the doctor was good enough to call in this antibiotic for my husband," Doris chirped. "Hopefully this prescription will make that man of mine feel better," she added, handing her check to the clerk. "I have to head out of town later this morning. I'm counting on this to revive him in my absence."

"There's a lot of mean bugs going around right now," the clerk sympathized.

"I know. Several of my students have been sick too." Doris picked up the small white bag that contained her husband's prescription and turned to leave. Spotting Mandy, she smiled. Since their encounter in the lunchroom, Doris had consistently tried to make headway with this young woman. Mandy had refused to cooperate, choosing to keep to herself. Refusing to give up, Doris was convinced that eventually, she would be able to break through Mandy's defenses. "Hello, Mandy. How are you this morning?" she bubbled, moving near the rack of LDS books.

Staring down at the tiled floor, Mandy mumbled an incoherent greeting.

"You're a little pale—are you feeling all right?"

"I'm fine," was the terse reply.

"You've sure had a time with the flu."

"Yeah," was the constrained reply.

"You must've caught that nasty virus going around," Doris sympathized. "For some reason, it keeps coming back on people. One minute they feel better, then it hits them again." As Doris continued to visit with Mandy, an older woman from Doris' LDS ward walked around the corner. She didn't see Mandy until it was too late and ran into the back of the young woman, causing Mandy to drop what she had been hiding. Her face crimson, Mandy scrambled to pick up the box as Doris helped the older woman to her feet.

"Are you all right?" Doris asked the woman.

"Yes, I think so. I am so sorry, young lady. I didn't even see you standing there."

"I'm okay," Mandy said gruffly, figuring the damage was done; Doris had to have seen what she was holding.

Mandy was correct in that assumption. Doris had seen the box before Mandy had picked it up. Unsure of what to say, Doris was distracted momentarily by the woman from her ward.

"It's my husband's birthday tomorrow. I never know what to get him. He has everything. He usually hates the clothes I pick out. I thought maybe I'd get him some of that cologne he likes. I'll have this clerk help me find it." Muttering under her breath, the older woman moved to the counter.

"Mandy?" Doris said, glancing at the box in the young woman's hands.

"Oh, this. I had to come pick this kit up for . . ." She was tempted to say Sara, but knew Doris would never believe her. "For my aunt."

Doris studied Mandy's face. "Your aunt? She's expecting again? After all this time?"

Slipping comfortably into the lie, Mandy nodded. "At least, she thinks so. She doesn't want anyone to know about it yet, so if you could keep it quiet—"

"That's why you were hiding the box," Doris replied, not fooled for a minute by Mandy's act. This girl was quick on her feet, but Doris had years of experience behind her when it came to discerning truth from fiction, especially from her students. Mandy's lie was apparent in her face, in the nervous gestures she was using. Her heart ached for the teenager; no wonder Mandy had been acting like a moody shrew. "Mandy, if you ever need to talk, my door is always open."

"Uh . . . yeah . . . thanks," Mandy stammered, turning away. Where was that stupid clerk? She wanted to get out of here now before other prying eyes assaulted her privacy.

"Sometimes when the world seems crazy, when you feel like everything is crashing down on top of you, it helps to know that you have a friend. I can be that friend, Mandy, if you'll let me."

Great! Mrs. Kelsey had guessed who the kit was for. This teacher wasn't as easy to deceive as most adults she knew. "I'm okay," Mandy said, relieved when the clerk returned to her post behind the cash register. She moved past Doris and handed the box to the clerk who gave her an appraising look. Steaming, Mandy could hardly wait to get out of this place. She handed over the money she had begged out of her aunt, claiming she needed to purchase an item for school. Accepting the change, Mandy grabbed the white sack and hurried out of the store.

The clerk turned to Doris, a questioning look on her face.

"Let's keep this one quiet," Doris suggested to the young woman behind the counter.

"I don't even know who she is," the clerk returned, "but my heart goes out to her if she's in that kind of trouble."

Agreeing, Doris left the store, sorrowing over the young sophomore with the sad, lonely eyes.

\* \* \*

"No checkmark. Please don't let there be a checkmark," Mandy murmured as she waited for the longest minute of her life to pass. When it was time, she picked up the test indicator and frowned. A blue checkmark was showing. There was no question about the color or shape. Swearing under her breath, Mandy sank down on the side of the tub and cried.

\* \* \*

"Have you seen Mandy?" Betty asked Sara.

Sara glanced up from the kitchen table where she had been working on a calculus assignment. "Not since dinner, why?"

"She's not upstairs in her room—I've looked all over the house. Where could that girl be?"

"Who knows," Sara replied, concentrating on a difficult problem.

"Maybe she wandered outside. It is a nice, warm night. Maybe she went for another walk," Betty said. "I wish she'd get in the habit of letting me know where she is. She took off early this morning, walked three miles into town, weak as a kitten. I would have given her a ride if she had told me she wanted to go."

"Mandy does what Mandy wants whenever Mandy wants to," Sara responded.

Betty frowned at her youngest daughter. "You're not helping matters. I thought you were going to start being nicer to her."

"I'm staying out of her way, that ought to make her happy," Sara defended herself. "She hates me. Hates who I am and what I stand for. I'm better off to steer clear of her."

Muttering to herself, Betty walked out of the kitchen. She moved to the closet in the hall, opened it, and reached for her jacket. Mandy had barely picked at her dinner, something Betty was getting used to, but tonight it was as though the girl had the weight of the world on her shoulders. Deciding to get to the bottom of this, Betty threw on a blue, fleece jacket and walked outside.

* * *

Sitting on a stump, staring at the rippling pond, Mandy rested her chin in her hands. Her secret, the one she had kept from everyone but her friends in Salt Lake, would soon be known. Everyone, her mother, her father, her sister, her little brothers . . . Aunt Betty, Uncle Lyle . . . Sara, soon they would all know what she had done with Blade. She hated for Sara to know most of all—Sara the self-righteous goody-goody that everyone loved. Her cousin made her sick, the way Sara was so nice to everyone else, but treated her like she was a piece of garbage. Sara had no right to judge her, no right to make sure everyone at this lousy school knew how terrible she was. Mandy didn't stand a chance in this town, the barriers were already in place, compliments of her own cousin.

Groaning, Mandy was too numb for tears. After seeing the results of the pregnancy test, she had tried to convince herself it was wrong, but knew better. She was pregnant—with Blade's child—sicker and more afraid than she had ever been in her life. All afternoon she had wanted to call Blade, to share this predicament, but pride had held her back. He hadn't answered or returned any of her other phone calls. What made her think he would agree to talk to her this time?

She considered her options. In a town this small, she was certain an abortion was out of the question—not that she could ever bring herself to do it. There was a living person inside of her. If she aborted it, she would be guilty of murder, breaking another commandment, adding it to her growing list of sins.

If she told Aunt Betty, the woman would have a raging fit. Her reaction would be nothing compared to the one her parents would have.

Mandy wanted to die. Death would solve all of her problems. Maybe then everyone would realize what they had done to her—maybe then they would see how they had hurt her, Blade included. She suspected Blade would want nothing to do with this baby. He had told her several times that he hated kids, that he would never have any of his own. Wouldn't he be surprised to learn that he was responsible for the life growing inside of her?

If she had the baby, maybe she could give it to someone else to raise—but who? She was certain her parents wouldn't want this child, she wasn't sure she wanted this child. How could she take care of an infant when she could barely take care of herself?

Mandy stood and walked down to the pond. Leaning, she stuck her finger in the water. Shivering, she shook the water from it. She wondered how deep the pond was. If she kept her face under the water, it wouldn't matter how shallow it was, it would suffice.

In the distance, she heard her aunt call her name. Panicking, she bolted away from the pond. She didn't want to talk to anyone, not now, not until she had figured out what to do. She ran down the dirt road, heading back to town, unwilling to submit herself to her aunt's scrutiny.

# Chapter 14

Around five o'clock, after spending time and money together, Bev, Karen, Terri, and Sabrina reluctantly decided to head for home. They loaded their treasures from the Pine Ridge Mall in the back of the Jeep Cherokee, then climbed in, reclaiming their original seats. Karen sat up front with Bev, while Sabrina and Terri sat on the bench seat in back.

Bev picked up the cell phone Gina had insisted that she bring and dialed her home phone number, praying someone would answer. All day an uneasy feeling had tormented her—she hoped a quick call home would alleviate the dread in her heart.

"Hello?" Gina said, glancing at the caller ID. *Unknown name, unknown number* indicated that it was either a salesman, or Bev on the cellular phone. She was relieved to hear Bev's voice.

"Hi, Mom. We're leaving Pocatello now."

"Okay, we'll be expecting you in a couple of hours. Did you find an apartment?"

"Yeah, it's great, it's that one I told you about last night . . . a one-bedroom apartment in the basement of a house near campus. They're looking for two tenants for next year. It would be perfect, if they'll accept us."

"Is there any doubt?" Gina asked, trying to keep her voice light. She didn't want Bev to know she had spent most of the afternoon in tears.

"It's hard to say. The landlady said she's already received several applications. Karen gave her one of those pitiful looks she specializes in, so we might stand a chance," Bev said, enjoying the indignant expression on her friend's face. "Anyway, I'll tell you all about it when I get home."

"Okay. Be careful. It'll probably be dark before you get here," Gina cautioned.

"We'll be fine," Bev assured. "How are things looking on the home front?"

"Uh . . . well . . . your father and I have been talking."

"And?"

"And . . . I'll fill you in when you get home."

"Everything's okay, right?" Bev asked, glancing around at her friends. She was relieved to see that the three girls were preoccupied, watching in fascination as Sabrina checked her blood sugar.

"I think your father is starting to realize that he needs help. He told me today that he might check out a local AA organization."

Bev grinned. "He might? That's great!"

"It is," Gina agreed. "Come home and we'll talk about it."

Catching the strain in her stepmother's voice, Bev closed her eyes. "You're not telling me everything, are you?"

"Bev, it'll be all right. Concentrate on getting home in one piece—that's the important thing right now."

"This doesn't sound good. You'll still be there when I get home, right?"

Gina swallowed past the lump in her throat. Why was her stepdaughter always so perceptive? Earlier this afternoon, she had given James an ultimatum she wasn't sure he could live with. He had offered to attend Alcoholics Anonymous, but had said it with such sarcasm, she had known he wasn't serious. Her threat to leave if things didn't change had prompted him to walk out of the house. The truth was, Gina didn't know how this would all end. Her marriage was in trouble, but that was the last thing Bev needed to hear, especially before driving home from Pocatello.

"Mom?" Bev prompted.

"Honey, I will always be here for you," Gina said with more strength than she felt. "Now be careful, come home, and we'll talk. I love you."

"I love you too, Mom," Bev said. Clicking off the phone, she set it down on the seat beside her, a strange look on her face. She opened the door on her side of the Jeep and slipped down to the paved parking lot, closing the door behind her.

"What's wrong?" Karen asked, climbing out of the Jeep. She shut the door on her side and motioned for the others to remain in the car.

"It just felt strange when I hung up . . . I don't know. This feeling like something bad is about to happen."

"Is this about your dad?" Karen pressed.

Bev gazed at her friend. "Yeah . . . Mom wouldn't tell me what was going on, but they must've had another major blowout today. The thing is, there was so much pain in her voice—I know it's serious." She moved away from the Jeep, unwilling to let her friends see her cry. Karen followed, making it clear that she knew what friends were really for as she embraced the taller girl.

\* \* \*

"Any sign of Mandy yet?" Lyle asked his wife.

Betty shook her head as she climbed down from the wooden fence where she had sat, gazing into the distance. "Something doesn't feel right. I'm worried."

"Something's got the animals spooked too," Lyle responded. "They're acting skittish." He gazed up at the sky. "There's no sign of a storm coming in. I'm not sure what their problem is."

"Maybe they sense a coyote nearby," Betty suggested.

"Maybe," Lyle agreed. "I'll keep a sharp eye on things tonight." He glanced at his wife, noting the furrowed brow. "First, though, I think I'll change into something a little less fragrant and then drive into town to look for our wayward stray. I'll probably find Mandy drowning her sorrows in a malt at one of the drive-ins."

"I hope that's all we find," Betty breathed. She walked with Lyle to the house, anxious to help him search for their niece.

\* \* \*

Adele Hadley glanced at the kitchen clock. Time was moving painfully slow; it promised to be a long, lonely evening. Edie was at the hospital working an afternoon shift, and Karen hadn't returned from Pocatello—both had told her to not worry about fixing dinner. Instead, she had heated a meat pie for herself in the microwave, eating it in the living room as she watched TV.

Discarding the empty cardboard container in the garbage, Adele glanced outside. Restless, she leaned against the sink, staring out the kitchen window. "Karen's cat," she said suddenly, moving away from the sink. "Karen won't be here in time to feed it." Adele walked to the kitchen counter and opened a cabinet door, pulling out a small metal tin of cat food. Locating a can opener in a nearby drawer, she opened the can, then headed out the side door. She glanced around, looking for the cat, then walked down the small porch to the driveway.

"Here kitty, kitty," she called out, scraping the moist cat food into a small metal dish near the side of the house. She continued to look, but there was no sign of the large calico. "Must be out hunting mice. She'll come home when she's hungry," Adele said, walking to the plastic garbage container near the side of her house. She unfastened the lid, threw in the empty tin can, then heard a rustling sound behind her in the log shed out back. "That must be where that cat is hiding," she said, making sure the garbage lid was secured in place. "Here kitty, kitty," she tried again, walking to the shed.

\* \* \*

Kicking at a rock, Mandy wandered into Blaketown. A slight breeze played with her hair as she started down Main Street. She had no idea where she was going or what she would do. Confused fear dominated every thought as she trudged down the sidewalk. Pausing outside of a variety store, she glanced in and saw a rack of baby clothes. A scream swelled inside of her. It was released a few seconds later when she heard a thunderous roar.

\* \* \*

"Did you hear that?" Sue asked her husband as she stepped away from the kitchen sink. "Hear what?" Greg asked, glancing up from the newspaper in his hands. He set the paper down on the dining room table and listened intently. "What did you hear?" he asked as the house began to vibrate. "What the heck?!" He tried to stand, but the force of the quake pushed against him. "Sue, crawl in the dining room, quick!"

Sue had already lost her balance, falling to the floor, bruising her shoulder. "I'll try," she stammered, inching her way to the table as dishes, items stacked on the counter, and wall hangings began to fall around her.

Greg managed to roll off the chair and scooted toward his wife, reaching for her, adrenaline lending him added strength as the floor beneath them continued to sway. In the seconds that seemed like hours, he was able to drag Sue under the sturdy oak table. They huddled together as the motion intensified around them.

* * *

"Lyle, what are you doing?" Betty Sandler demanded as the car began careening wildly.

"It's not me. The ground is shaking," Lyle exclaimed, doing his best to control the old Plymouth sedan. "Hang on, we're goin' for a ride," he said, driving off the road. The car plunged through a fence and into a recently plowed field.

"Where are you going?" Betty asked.

"I'm getting us away from the power lines," Lyle shouted back as he tried to force the car toward the center of the field. As it bogged down in the loose soil, he gave up and shut off the engine.

"Now what do we do?" Betty hollered.

"Hold on tight and pray this quake ends soon."

Her thoughts centering on Sara and Mandy, Betty tearfully prayed for their safety as Lyle pushed the seat back, easing his bulging stomach away from the steering wheel.

* * *

"Bev, this isn't funny," Terri cried out as the Jeep swerved again, nearly colliding with a truck heading the opposite direction.

"Am I laughing?" Bev shot back, gripping the steering wheel as she avoided the car behind the truck and tried to maneuver the Jeep into the proper lane.

"It's an earthquake!" Karen exclaimed, watching as a large crack appeared in the road ahead of them.

"DUH!" Bev replied, seeing the same crack. "Oh, man, what do we do now?!" she asked as Terri screamed.

Sabrina shut her eyes, pleading for protection for herself and her friends as the Jeep spun off the road and down into the barrow pit approximately seven miles outside of Blaketown.

\* \* \*

"Is it over?" a feeble voice asked when the violent shaking finally ceased.

"I don't know," Edie replied as she slowly stood. When the earthquake had started, she had been checking this patient's vital signs. Fearing for the safety of the older woman, Edie had spread herself valiantly over her patient, trying to protect her from falling debris. A painting hung above the bed had fallen onto Edie's back, then had bounced off, the glass from the frame shattering on the tiled floor.

"Are you all right?" Edie asked, wincing as she straightened. Blinking in the darkness, she was relieved when the emergency generator started up, providing minimum lighting.

"I'm fine. Are you? What was that crashing sound?" the woman asked.

"A painting on the wall fell down," Edie replied, rubbing at her back. She stepped gingerly around the shards of glass. "I think I'll see how everyone else is doing," she added, stepping out of the room as another tremor threw her to the floor.

\* \* \*

"Is everyone all right?" Karen asked as she unfastened her seatbelt. When Bev moaned, Karen slid close to her friend. "You really smacked your head—you're bleeding all over the place," she said as Bev sat back from the steering wheel.

"Trust me, I know," Bev said, reaching a hand to the gash in her forehead. "Gina tried to tell Dad to have air-bags installed in this thing. Man, I wish he had listened! He never listens to anything either one of us says!"

In a state of shock, Terri fumbled with her seatbelt as she tried to unbuckle the metal clasp. "Why aren't there any air-bags?" she heard herself ask.

"This Jeep is one of Dad's treasures. It's older than the hills, but he loves it. He tries very hard to keep it as it was when he bought it several years ago, before air-bags were a popular item."

Karen glanced over the seat. "Terri, are you okay?"

"Yeah, I think so. That was scary," Terri replied.

"It was," Karen agreed as she reached for her purse. She searched it, then Bev's, but was unable to find anything to stop the bleeding. "Don't you have a first-aid kit in here somewhere?"

"I wish," Bev replied. "There's one in Gina's Grand Prix, but that doesn't help us now." She peered over the seat at the younger girls. "You're awfully quiet back there, Sabrina. Are you all right?"

Terri glanced at Sabrina. "Uh, oh," she said, moving for a closer look.

"I don't like the sound of that," Karen said. As she leaned over to check on Sabrina, an aftershock rumbled through, propelling Karen over the seat into Terri.

\* \* \*

"Here we go again," Sue exclaimed, tightening her hold on Greg.

"It's not as strong at the first one. That's a good sign. It's probably an aftershock," Greg guessed as the tremor continued.

"How many more of these will we feel?"

"I don't know. I've only experienced one other earthquake before, and that was on my mission."

"How bad was it?" Sue asked as things settled down, a silent calm descending.

"About like this one. Things shaking everywhere, a lot of structural damage was done."

"Was anyone hurt?" Sue ventured, thinking of Kate, Mike, and Sabrina, as well as their neighbors and friends.

"A few people," Greg replied as he surveyed the damage to their house that he could already see. "Guess we'll find out how sturdy this home is," he mused as the small chandelier above the wooden table continued to swing through the air.

\* \* \*

Severely rattled, Sara drew herself up on her knees. She gripped the carpeted floor of the living room for support. The quake had prevented her from moving very far from the couch she had been sitting on. She waited several minutes, then stood, taking small, hesitant steps, hoping the earthquake was over. Terrified, she wondered if her parents had survived and wished fervently that they had remained at home. Mandy's face came to mind. It was Mandy's fault her parents had left! Where were they all now? Another aftershock vibrated the house, throwing Sara toward a recliner. She held onto the arms of the chair as the geological spasm continued, her sobs drowned out by the crashing sounds that filled the house.

\* \* \*

"She's coming around," Greta said, motioning to Dr. Davis.

The aging doctor approached Edie, his face creased with worry. "She'll have one doozy of a headache," he said, examining the growing bump on Edie's forehead.

Edie forced her eyes open, then wished she hadn't as a bright light assaulted her vision.

"Edie, can you hear me?" Greta asked.

"I'll handle this," Dr. Davis said gruffly, gesturing for the RN to move out of the way. "You hold the flashlight for me while I see if she's okay." He ignored the sour look on Greta's face and tenderly touched Edie's cheek. "Edie, can you hear me?" he asked, repeating Greta's question.

Greta rolled her eyes, but obediently held up the large flashlight at the angle the doctor had requested.

"What happened?" Edie asked, closing her eyes against the bright light.

"You fell and bumped your head," Greta replied.

Doctor Davis cleared his throat, shot Greta a dirty look, then said, "You bumped your head. We found you on the floor near a patient's room."

Her memory returning, Edie frowned. "The earthquake!"

Greta grinned, relieved that Edie could remember what had happened.

"Do you hurt anywhere else?" the doctor probed.

"My back," Edie said, more aware of her surroundings. She saw that she was in CCU near the nurses' station, lying on top of the hospital bed. "What am I doing in here?" she asked.

"It was the closest room I could find," Greta responded.

"Greta was the one who found you. She dragged you in here . . . without waiting to see if you'd damaged your neck, or back," he added, giving Greta another disgruntled look.

"I'll be fine," Edie said, trying to smile, the slight movement triggering a stinging sensation across her face.

"You'll have a few bruises; you fell face down," the doctor explained, noticing Edie's discomfort. "The good news is that you didn't break any facial bones. Now what's this about your back?"

"A painting fell . . . it caught me in the back," Edie said.

"Let's have a look," the doctor said, motioning for Greta to assist. They gently rolled Edie onto her side. Greta pulled up the white cotton blouse Edie had tucked inside of a white skirt, revealing an ugly contusion across the middle of the younger woman's slender back.

"How heavy was that painting?" Doctor Davis asked as he assessed the damage.

"I don't know," Edie breathed as he touched a very tender area.

"It doesn't look like you've broken anything. Probably bruised a couple of ribs, and you have a nasty-looking welt forming across there," he said, smoothing Edie's blouse back into place. "Do you think you can move? Maybe you'd better go home and take it easy," he suggested.

With Greta's help, Edie stood, momentarily dizzy. She waited until her head quit swimming, then took a couple of steps. Her entire rib cage hurt with every breath.

"Think you can manage?" the doctor asked, concerned.

"Yeah," Edie said, her face pinched with pain. "Do you think there will be a lot of injuries from this quake?"

"Hopefully not, but you never know. You're our first casualty. I pray that's as serious as it gets."

Just then a young man ran to the nurses' station. "Is anyone here?"

Greta stepped out of CCU. "What's wrong?" she asked, recognizing Mike Jeffries.

"It's my wife. She's hurt . . . she's bleeding," he said, motioning down the hall.

"We'll be right there," Greta said, moving behind him.

"Will you be all right by yourself?" Doctor Davis asked Edie.

"Yes! Go! They need you worse than I do," she replied, leaning against the portable table for support.

Nodding, the doctor left the room.

\* \* \*

"Well, we're about as stuck as a person can get," Lyle said, shutting off the engine. He turned and gazed at his wife. "Why don't you stay put . . . who knows how many more tremors there will be . . . you'll be safer here. I'll walk back to the ranch and check on Sara. Then I'll see if my truck will fire up and I'll come back for you."

Betty answered by opening the door on her side of the car.

"What do you think you're doing?"

"Going with you. Do you honestly think I'd be better off worryin' myself sick while my family may be in trouble?"

Lyle grinned at his stubborn wife. "We'll have to walk about three miles, unless we can hitch a ride. We were nearly to Blaketown."

"Then we'd best get started," Betty replied, closing the car door on her side.

\* \* \*

"I just thought I had a headache before," Terri complained, untangling herself from Karen.

"I'm the one who should be whining," Karen replied, rubbing her head. "Bev always said you were hard-headed, but I didn't believe her until now." She glanced at Sabrina. "Sabrina's out cold—she has to be. We haven't heard one peep out of her since we ran off the road." Karen moved next to Sabrina and felt for a pulse. "Good news,

Sabrina's still with us," she said, turning to look at Bev. She gaped at her friend. "What are you pressing against your forehead?"

"I found it in your purse," Bev said, bravely holding a mini-pad against the gash in her head.

Karen glanced at Terri, both girls striving to keep a straight face.

"Hey, it works," Bev said, embarrassed. "It's the only thing I could find. I'd say under the circumstances, I did great."

"You did, future medical whiz," Karen replied, sobering as she refocused on Sabrina. "Why is she unconscious?"

"Did she bang her head against the window?" Bev asked.

"It's a possibility," Karen said as she unfastened the younger girl's seatbelt. She carefully turned Sabrina's head for a better look. "Bev, can you flip on a light in here—it's getting pretty dark, I can't see what I'm doing." She waited until Bev had turned on the light, then examined Sabrina for injuries. "There's our problem. Look at that bump." Karen frowned, realizing how close it was to Sabrina's temple. "I don't like this at all."

"What?" Terri asked, moving for a better look.

"Mom was studying head trauma a few weeks ago. She said that if you get hit hard enough in that area," Karen said, pointing to the side of Sabrina's head, "it can be serious, even fatal."

"Oh, that's just great! Now what do we do?" Terri asked, panic-stricken. "I can't believe this! We almost run into that truck, then we plunge off the road because of this stupid earthquake . . . now you tell me Sabrina might die?"

Bev's eyes widened as she saw how close Terri was to becoming hysterical. "Hey, chill, okay? We've been through worse."

Karen grabbed Terri's arm. "Bev's right. We've got to stay calm if we're going to survive this. We have to think straight. Sabrina's life may depend on us right now."

Terri gulped the air repeatedly in an attempt to control herself.

"Terri, you're going to hyperventilate. Quit freaking out on us. We don't need you passing out, too," Karen said, tightening her hold on the younger girl. "Slow it down; don't breathe so fast."

Bursting into tears, Terri pulled away from Karen, holding her head in her hands. Karen glanced at Bev, her eyes communicating the concern she felt for both of the younger girls.

"Terri, we need you to help us. I can't do much right now until I get this bleeding stopped. Karen needs you to help with Sabrina," Bev said, her voice softening. "I need you to be okay, like you were last spring . . . after I broke my leg. You were so awesome. You kept your head when the rest of us lost it." Bev paused to see if she was having an impact on the younger girl. Terri was still holding her head, but the sobbing had ceased.

"It'll be okay," Karen soothed, patting the junior's shoulder. "The worst of it is over. Now we need to work together to get out of this mess."

"We're not that far from Blaketown," Bev added, relieved when Terri lifted her head to gaze at her. "If I can get this Jeep to run, we'll take Sabrina straight to the hospital."

Terri turned her tear-streaked face to look at Sabrina. Ashamed of her outburst, she hoped to redeem herself by coming to Sabrina's aid. Wiping at her eyes, she moved closer to the unconscious girl. She glanced at Karen. "What if it's her blood sugar?" she sniffed. She turned to look at Bev. "Remember what Edie told us about that? If it's low, we have to do something immediately."

Closing her eyes, Karen tried to recall the symptoms her mother had described.

"If her blood sugar is too low, it could make her pass out," Terri stressed.

"If it's too high, she can slip into a coma," Bev added.

Karen touched Sabrina's skin. It felt cold and clammy. "Sabrina checked her blood sugar before we left Pocatello. What was it?"

"Ninety something," Terri offered. "I promised Sue I'd keep an eye on Sabrina. That's why I was watching every time she checked her blood sugar today. It hasn't been very high—mostly in the low to normal range."

Karen studied Sabrina's face. "She's awfully pale. I'll bet it's too low."

"Her blood sugar could've been on its way down before we left Pocatello and she didn't catch on that she was in trouble," Bev suggested.

Terri gazed thoughtfully at the younger girl. "If she's in pain, maybe it dropped her level."

"How do we do find out where she's at?" Karen asked.

"Let's run a check." Bev pointed to Sabrina's purse on the floor beneath Karen's feet. "Sabrina showed me how to use her machine last week."

Bending down, Terri reached for Sabrina's purse. Opening the leather bag, she rummaged around until she found the small black case. "Here you go."

"You guys will have to help me with this. I've got to use one hand to hold this pad against my head," Bev said, frustrated. "I wish we could find some tape to stick it in place!"

As Terri began to search for tape of any kind, Karen unzipped the case around Sabrina's glucose monitor. "What do I do first?"

# Chapter 15

When severe pain heralded another contraction, Kate gritted her teeth. She clutched Mike's hand, squeezing it with a fierce intensity.

"It'll be okay," he said, trying to cover for how scared he really was.

"Breathe out slowly, Kate," Edie encouraged, standing on the other side of the young woman. "Take a deep breath, then breathe out again," she said, trying to calm her.

"It's too soon. I can't have this baby now," Kate said, gripping Mike's hand tighter than before. "I'm not due till December."

"I don't think we have a choice," Dr. Davis said as he examined Kate. "How did you fall again?"

"Down the porch steps," Mike disclosed. "We were going to get a hamburger when the earthquake hit," he added, still trying to make sense of what had happened.

"When I felt myself fall, I tried to turn so the baby wouldn't be hurt," Kate moaned. "I tried to protect her."

"It'll be all right," Edie soothed.

"It *has* to be! We've waited so long for this baby," Kate said, tears rolling down the sides of her face. She held her breath when another sharp pain gripped her abdomen.

"Where is that anesthesiologist?" the doctor complained. "He should know that he'll be needed up here at the hospital!"

"Maybe he can't get here," Edie offered. "I'm sure he'd come if he could." She peeked around the white curtain at the crowded ER and the hallway beyond. Earlier, she had decided to stay when she saw how many injured people were gathering at the hospital. A younger doctor and three other nurses had voluntarily made an appearance, easing the load, but it was still chaotic. From the look of things, it was just the beginning.

"I could give you something for the pain," Dr. Davis said to Kate, hating the amount of misery she was in.

"No, not if it'll hurt the baby," she said through clenched teeth.

"Those contractions are coming pretty close together," the doctor observed. He motioned for Edie to step around the curtain with him. "We are in serious trouble here," he said in a hushed voice. "I'm certain the placenta has torn loose. That means we have no choice—this baby will be born about nine weeks early. Have they been able to get that radio at the nurses' station to work yet?"

"I don't know," Edie replied.

"If they haven't, round up someone with a cellular phone. We need to contact Life Flight out of Pocatello. Let them know we have a preemie that's about to be born."

Nodding, Edie made her way out of the room. As she started down the hall, she heard someone call her name. She turned, seeing Gina Henderson. "Are you all right?"

Gina shook her head. "James is missing—Jake's okay, but they're working on Drake in ER. The bunk beds collapsed. He was playing in the bottom bunk when it happened." Her eyes traveled fearfully to ER. "Do you know what they're doing in there with Drake? They're making me wait out here."

"I don't know, I was helping with another patient," Edie replied sympathetically, well aware that if Drake was in ER, his condition was serious. They were treating people according to the gravity of their situation. Those with major injuries were taking precedence over those with minor wounds. "Has there been any word from the girls?"

"Bev called before they left Pocatello," Gina replied, sharing a worried look with Edie. "They were on their way home when this happened." Closing her eyes, Gina looked as rough as she felt.

Edie leaned down and gave her friend a hug, ignoring the pain still radiating from her back and ribs. "Gina, I wish I could stay here with you, but I have to get a message out to Life Flight. We have a woman who is about to deliver prematurely," she said, pulling back. "I won't be gone long, then I'll check on Drake for you." Her stomach churning over her own daughter, Edie hurried as fast as she could to the nurses' station.

* * *

Sara made her way carefully down the wooden stairs to the basement, grateful her mother had had the foresight to keep a flashlight in the hall closet; it had made her task easier. She found the electrical box on the wall midway down the stairs and made sure the power was turned off to the house. Even though it appeared the earthquake had taken care of it, she wanted be sure the electricity was shut off.

Water was running through the unfinished basement. She shined the flashlight around until she located the broken pipe. Trying very hard to remember what her father had told her to do in an emergency, she walked down the rest of the stairs and waded through the ankle-deep water until she found the valve she was looking for. She was grateful she had shoes on as the glass from several shattered canning jars crunched underfoot as she moved. Upon reaching the valve, she tried to turn it with one hand and failed. Spying a nearby set of shelves, she positioned the flashlight on it so that she could see what she was doing. She moved back to the water valve, using both hands to try to break it free. Just when she was about to give up and start looking for a wrench, it turned and she shut off the water. She was unsure how to get rid of the water already in the basement, but felt certain she had done what she could to prevent further damage.

Retrieving the flashlight, she walked back up to the main level of the house. Several of her father's heifers were bawling in a nearby corral. Sara decided that was her next responsibility and prepared to check on the animals closest to the house. Shivering, her legs chilled from the water in the basement, she hurried upstairs to her bedroom to change into something dry before venturing outside.

* * *

"How many aftershocks were there?" Sue asked as she stood. Her bruised shoulder throbbed, reminding her of the fall the initial quake had triggered.

"I counted three," Greg replied, shining a flashlight around the jumbled kitchen.

"At least they've stopped."

"For now," he replied.

Sue stared at her husband. "For now?"

"They can continue on through the night and into tomorrow, even the rest of the week," Greg responded. "There could be after-shocks months from now."

"That's something to look forward to," she said, dismayed by this news. "Let's get out of here and check on our kids. I'm worried about Mike and Kate. And when were Sabrina and her friends getting back from Pocatello?"

"I thought you knew?"

Sue shook her head. "Sabrina was so excited to finally spend a day with her friends, I didn't insist on a curfew." She tried to look at her watch, but darkness had cloaked the interior of the house.

"Let me check on a couple of things here, then we'll head over to the duplex," Greg said, referring to the place Kate and Mike were renting. He lit the oil lamp Sue had kept stored in a kitchen cupboard, setting it in the middle of the wooden table in the dining room.

"Is that a good idea? What if we get another aftershock? That's all we'd need is a fire."

"Good point," Greg replied. "Sorry, I'm not thinking too clearly." He flipped the flashlight back on. "Do we have another flashlight stashed somewhere? I hate to leave you sitting here in the dark."

"There's one in the utility room, on a shelf above the washer . . . at least, that's where it was before this started. Who knows where it is now."

"Found it," Greg called back to her a few seconds later. "It had rolled onto the floor, but it still works. Blow out that lamp, set it somewhere safe, if there is such a place, and use this instead," he said, walking through the kitchen to hand her the flashlight. "When things are more stable, we can use the lamp. Who knows how long we'll be without power? That oil lamp might come in handy later on."

Fearing her husband was right, Sue found a secure corner to store the lamp, then cleared a path to the front door as she waited for Greg to shut off the water and gas lines to their house.

* * *

"Are you sure you know what you're doing?" Terri asked as Bev prepared the glucagon shot Sabrina kept in her purse for emergencies.

"I followed the instructions Karen read." Bev carefully shook up the small vial, mixing the solution that would snap Sabrina out of insulin shock. "I'm just glad Sabrina told me about this last week. This shot of glucose should raise her blood sugar up to where it needs to be."

"I still think hitting her head knocked her cold," Karen said, jumping when someone tapped on the Jeep window. "Great! Now what?"

"I think we're safe, it looks like a woman," Bev said. She scooted over to the door, rolling down the window.

"Are you girls all right?" the woman asked.

"Mrs. Kelsey?" Bev stammered, recognizing the English teacher. "What are you doing out here?"

"It was my grandson's birthday—I drove up to Blackfoot this morning. It gave me an excuse to visit with my daughter and her family." Doris frowned, noticing the shape Sabrina was in. Karen and Terri were on each side of the unconscious girl. "I saw your Jeep was off the road and wondered if you were okay."

"Are you alone?" Bev asked.

"Yes. My husband caught that rotten flu going around. I wasn't sure I dared leave him, but he insisted that I go." Worry reflected from her eyes as she thought about her husband. "Back to you girls— how is everyone doing?"

"Most of us are all right," Terri replied, hoping her friends wouldn't mention her moment of panic.

"If you can call surviving an earthquake all right," Karen added.

"I thought I felt something strange several minutes ago—my car was shaking like it had a flat tire. Then it quit. The radio station I was listening to announced that an earthquake had hit near Blaketown. I was hoping they were wrong."

"They're not," Bev assured the teacher. "It was pretty wild for a few minutes. I've never felt anything like it before. How does it look out there? We haven't stepped out of the Jeep."

"In the dark, it's hard to tell what kind of damage has been done." Doris said, glancing again at Sabrina. "How bad is she?"

"Her blood sugar is in the 30s," Karen replied. "We just ran a test." She leaned over the front seat to open the door for the teacher. "Climb in, we can use some help."

Grabbing the door for support, Doris pulled herself up into the Jeep. She gazed at Bev's forehead and lifted an eyebrow.

"It's all I could find," Bev said, her face flushing as she fingered the mini-pad taped to her forehead.

"In this instance, whatever works," Doris said. "What did you use to tape it in place?"

"Some black electrical tape we found under the seat," Terri supplied.

"You girls are pretty resourceful," Doris complimented. She gazed at the syringe in Bev's hand. "I assume that's for Sabrina?"

Bev nodded. "According to the instructions, it should contain enough glucose to snap her out of insulin shock."

"Let's give it to her, then," Doris encouraged. "Who's going to do the honors?"

"Will you?" Bev asked, her head aching. She held out the syringe to Doris.

Doris accepted the syringe and slipped out of the Jeep. "Karen, you and Terri hold tight to Sabrina, I don't want her falling out of the car while I'm giving her this shot. Especially if there's another after-shock like I felt a few minutes ago."

The two girls sprang into action, holding Sabrina tight as Doris opened the door.

\* \* \*

"Dad, we need your cell phone," Mike panted, out of breath. "Is it charged up?"

"Yes, if I can find it in this mess," Greg answered. "Where's Kate?" he asked as Sue moved into view.

Still gasping for air, Mike shook his head. "She fell—the baby's coming, we've got to reach Pocatello . . . Life Flight. The power's down. The radio won't work at the hospital. Something fell on top of it. We need your cell phone."

"Where's Kate?" Sue asked, panicking.

"At the hospital. We have to hurry."

"Did you run all the way down here?" Greg asked as they moved to the front door.

"No. The streets are torn up pretty bad in places. Trees are down. I had to park a block away to get here."

"Let's go," Greg said, remembering he had left the cell phone in his car.

Sue was already out the door running down what was left of their sidewalk.

\* \* \*

"James!" Gina exclaimed, rushing to her husband when she spotted him walking down the hall of the hospital.

Unable to speak, James enfolded her in his arms, grateful that he had finally found his wife. He had been at the city park when the quake had hit. Sitting on a park bench feeling sorry for himself, he had finished the second can in a six-pack of beer when everything had started shaking around him. At first, he had thought his drinking was the culprit. Eventually he had caught on to what was really taking place and had panicked, thinking of his family. Fear had sobered him immediately. Making his way home, he had narrowly avoided being crushed under a falling tree. An adrenaline rush had given him the strength to run the rest of the way home. He had continued to run as he had explored their house, his trepidation increasing when he had spied the collapsed bunk beds and the spots of blood on the bedding and carpet in the twins' room. That image fresh in his mind, he pulled back from Gina. "Where are the boys?"

"Jake is with your sister. He's a little shaken, but okay. Your brother-in-law helped me bring Drake to the hospital."

"Drake was hurt?" James prompted.

"He was playing on the bottom bunk when the quake hit . . . it collapsed on top of him," Gina said, large tears rolling down her face. "He has a broken leg, cracked ribs, and a concussion."

James embraced his wife a second time, hoping to calm her.

Glancing around, he was stunned by how many people were waiting to be seen. "Where is Drake now?"

"They're casting his leg down the hall," Gina said, her voice muffled against his chest.

"Why aren't you with him?"

"There isn't room. They were casting two others at the same time. I was told to wait here. Edie's with him—he likes her—I know he's in good hands." Pulling away, she looked accusingly at her husband, the relief she had initially felt giving way to intense anger. "Where have you been?"she asked, repulsed by the smell of beer on his breath.

"Not where I was supposed to be," James admitted. "Gina, I'd say I'm sorry, but I'm not sure you'd believe me. What can I do—"

"Not now, James, I can't take it. Right now, I need to know that my children are all right. I know where Jake is, I think Drake will be fine, but no one has any idea where Bev or her friends are," Gina said, pained rage flashing from her eyes.

"Bev is missing?" James asked, feeling like the wind had just been knocked out of him. "Where is she?"

"She was on her way home from Pocatello when the quake hit," Gina replied. "She's probably not too far from here. If you want to do something to help—find our daughter, bring her to me, and then we'll talk! Until then, I don't want to hear anything you have to say!" Whirling around, she fled down the hall to check on Drake. James gaped after her, stung by her reaction.

\* \* \*

"Please let Sara be all right," Betty Sandler pleaded under her breath as she headed toward the farmhouse to search for her daughter. As they had walked up the long driveway, Lyle had heard a major commotion in the barn and had decided to check on things there first. Betty had resented his choice, even when he had mentioned the strong prompting that had urged him to hurry into the barn.

"Sara?" Betty yelled as she entered the darkened house alone. Feeling her way to a drawer near the kitchen sink, she found the flashlight kept there, flipped it on, and brandished it around the room."Sara, can you hear me?" She moved from room to room, dismayed by the damage. Furniture was overturned; pictures and other items that hadn't been securely fastened lay scattered across the floor. Fearing what Sara's condition would be, Betty tested the stairs. When they appeared to be sturdy, she headed up to check in the bedrooms. "Sara?!"

As Betty continued to frantically search, Lyle entered the house with their daughter, whom he had found in the barn. Taking Sara's flashlight, he shined it around, wincing at the mess he could see. "Your mama is probably running crazy through this house looking for you." He gave her another hug. "I'm proud of you. Your quick thinking saved that horse," he said, grateful that his youngest daughter had been able to free one of his prize mares from a roll of wire meshing before the horse went berserk. Lyle looked around at the darkened house. "Betty? We're down here. Sara's fine!"

Her pulse rate slowing, Betty expressed the gratitude in her heart. *Thank you, Father. Thank you! Now please help us find Mandy. Please let her be all right too.*

\* \* \*

"Kate, do you feel an urge to push?" the young doctor asked.

Kate nodded, clinging to Edie's hand. Perspiration glistened from her face, an indication of the effort she was making to give birth without the aid of painkillers. She glanced around the dimly lit delivery room, grateful they had transferred her in here for privacy. Dr. Davis had left her to the care of a new doctor she had never met before, someone Dr. Davis had assured was a skilled physician.

"Don't push yet—I'll tell you when. It won't be long now. You've dilated pretty fast," the new doctor commented as he continued to track Kate's progress.

"Tell me about it," Kate said as another contraction took her breath away. Closing her eyes, she prayed Mike would come—that he would bring her parents. They had to be all right. She wouldn't believe otherwise.

Greta's loud voice could be heard above the commotion in the hall. "They're down in the delivery room!" the RN boomed.

Kate watched the doorway, crying with relief when she saw Mike appear with her mother.

"We're here, Kate," Sue said, crossing the room to her daughter. "We're here," she soothed, kissing Kate's damp forehead. She moved to the other side to make room for Mike as Edie slipped back by the doctor.

"Your dad's down the hall with Dr. Davis. They've already made the call. Life Flight will be here soon," Mike revealed, gripping Kate's hand in his own.

"That's good news!" the young doctor said as another contraction caused Kate to cry out.

"Breathe, Kate," Sue advised, "breathe." Her face grim, she did her best to help Mike calm his frightened wife.

* * *

"There, that's better," Doris said, studying her handiwork.

"It feels better too," Bev replied, looking in the rearview mirror at the steri-strips Doris had neatly affixed across the gash in her forehead. "I'm glad you had that first-aid kit with you. I would've felt stupid going into town looking like I did."

"I never travel anywhere without it," the teacher replied as she closed the kit in her hands. "Too many things can happen."

"I'll say," Bev replied, glancing over the seat at the other girls. "Any change with Sabrina?"

"Her blood sugar is up to 97. That's good, right?" Terri asked.

"It's normal," Bev said.

"She's still out. I told you it was this bump on her head," Karen stated. "We need to get her to the hospital."

"Agreed," Doris said. "Bev try your engine. I'm thinking we'll have an easier time getting around in this Jeep than we will in my Lumina. That is quite a crack in the road ahead."

"It's a good thing you set out those road flares as a warning," Terri said.

"They came with the emergency road kit I keep in my car."

"You are one prepared lady," Bev marveled.

Doris smiled at the young woman. "Not always. I'm just glad I was this time. Now, let's see if this jalopy will run."

Nodding, Bev tried the engine. It sputtered, then slowly sprang into life. "This Jeep may have its drawbacks, but it does have one heck of an engine." She turned to Doris. "Would you mind driving? I'm not sure I'm up to it."

"I'm not sure I am either, but I'll give it a try," Doris said, slipping out of her side of the Jeep. "Trade me places," she said before shutting the door.

Bev slid over, fastening her seatbelt. "You guys buckle up back there, too. There's three seatbelts back there. Dad did see to that. He never takes us anywhere unless we're all buckled in."

With Terri's help, Karen moved Sabrina to the middle of the seat, then fastened her in with a seatbelt. Once their friend was settled, they buckled themselves in, each girl bracing Sabrina up on their side of the car.

"Ready back there?" Doris asked.

"As ready as we'll ever be," Karen replied.

"If you girls wouldn't mind, I'd feel better if we had a word of prayer before we begin this adventure."

Nodding in agreement, the three girls closed their eyes.

"I gather you'd like me to offer the prayer?" Doris asked, slightly amused.

"Please," Bev said, opening her eyes to plead with the teacher. It had been such a relief to let Doris take charge of their situation. As the oldest girl, and the driver, she had felt overwhelmed by responsibility. Having Doris with them had alleviated immense pressure.

"Okay, here goes," Doris said as she began the prayer. Expressing gratitude that their lives had been spared, she asked humbly for added protection as they made their way toward Blaketown. After petitioning for Sabrina's well-being, and for the safety of their families, she ended the prayer and glanced around. "Well, let's give this a try," she said. Shifting into reverse, she edged away from the wooden fence Bev had hit earlier. It took some tricky maneuvering, but eventually she was able to ease the Jeep back onto the road. She smiled when the girls clapped to show their admiration.

"All right Doris!" Bev exclaimed. "I mean, Mrs. Kelsey."

"Under these circumstances, call me Doris. We'll revert to Mrs. Kelsey when things get back to normal."

"Do you think they ever will?" Karen asked, worried about what they would find at home.

Crossing her fingers, Doris held them up for the girls to see. "On we go," she said, driving carefully through the fissure in the road.

\* \* \*

Edie found she couldn't speak when Brett Randall made an appearance at the hospital. She hurried into his arms, burying her face in his shoulder. Unsure of what to say, Brett held her, grateful she was alive. Already a rumored casualty report was gaining momentum around town. He wasn't sure how much truth there was to the rumor, but with a quake this strong, it was a possibility.

"I'm sorry I'm such a mess," Edie said, pulling back to wipe at her eyes. "There's still no word about Karen or her friends. We don't know where they're at. And it's been so crazy here, so many people are hurt, people that I know and I care about." She gazed somberly at Brett. "Mike and Kate might lose their baby."

"No," Brett groaned, knowing how much this baby meant to the Jeffries. He and Mike had become close friends working together at the Forest Service. He was well aware how excited Mike and Kate had been about becoming parents.

"Kate took a nasty fall during the earthquake. She went into labor. I've been in delivery with them for over an hour. In fact, I really should head back to check on things. I was asked to call to see how close Life Flight is. The way Kate's hemorrhaging, they'll send both her and the baby out when Life Flight gets here."

"Has she had the baby yet?"

"No, but I'm sure she'll have it before the helicopter arrives."

"I'm sorry this has been so rough for you," Brett said sympathetically. "I would've come by earlier, but they've had me out helping the police play search and rescue. Is there anything I can do to help you now?"

Edie thought for a second, then said, "I haven't heard anything from Mom yet. I know the phone lines are down and she probably doesn't dare walk up here, but I'd feel better if I knew she was all right."

"Consider it done," Brett replied. "I'll head over to your house right now to check on her. Then maybe I'll see what I can find out about Karen and her friends."

Smiling, Edie kissed his cheek. "You're always coming to my rescue."

"Count on it," he promised, pulling her close for a brief, but tender kiss.

* * *

Disgusted, Dr. Davis shook his head at the obstinate patient sitting in front of him. "Now, look, young lady, we don't have time for this. Didn't you see all of the people out waiting in the hall? We brought you in here because of the way your arm's bleeding. Sit still and let me stitch up that gash or I'll—"

"Or you'll what?" Mandy Hopkins asked defiantly.

The doctor gestured to the nurse standing beside Mandy. "I'll let Greta here give you an enema to drain some of the meanness out of you!" he threatened.

Mandy glowered at the man in front of her. She had been dragged to the hospital against her will by one of the local police officers. They had found her wandering around in a daze, covered with glass, blood seeping from a deep cut in her arm, an injury that had taken place when the glass front of the variety store had shattered during the quake.

"We'll probably be picking glass out of you for days," the doctor thundered. "Now you sit there and behave or we'll do things the hard way!"

Giving in, Mandy tried to maintain a brave front as the doctor began numbing her arm with a shot. She cried out when he applied pressure to thwart the bleeding.

"I haven't even started stitching yet!"

"My arm really hurts," Mandy said, the pain humbling her. "That's why I didn't want you to touch it."

Taking in her pallid color, Dr. Davis looked more closely at her arm. "Did you fall on this arm . . . maybe catch yourself with it?"

Mandy nodded.

Swearing under his breath, the doctor turned to Greta. "I'll bet she has a fracture. I should've thought of that. It might be just a crack, but we'll need x-rays to verify what we're dealing with." He gazed at Mandy. "Who are your parents?"

"Why?"

Certain his blood pressure was on the rise, Dr. Davis tried very hard to remain in control. "We'll need to get word to them. I'm sure they'll be worried."

Mandy mumbled her parents' names.

"Hopkins?" Greta repeated, recording the information. "I haven't heard that name in years. There used to be a Hopkins family that lived just outside of town on a big farm. Are you related to them? I used to go to school with a Betty Hopkins. I can't remember her married name."

Mandy shrugged. When she saw the livid look on the doctor's face, she gave in. "I'm living with my aunt and uncle, Betty and Lyle Sandler."

"Lucky them," Dr. Davis muttered as he prepared to stitch up her arm.

"Sandler—Betty Hopkins Sandler. I remember now, she married that farmer from Firth. You must be Betty's niece," Greta guessed, writing down the information.

"See if you can locate Betty," Dr. Davis said to Greta. He then gazed steadily at Mandy. "I'll take care of this gash, then x-ray your arm to see if it's broken. I promise I'll be as gentle as I can," he added, ignoring the incredulous look on the young woman's face.

* * *

Kate cried out again. The misery she was enduring affected Sue as deeply as it did Mike.

"Oh, honey," Sue breathed, aching for her daughter. "I am so sorry it's happening this way." Picking up Kate's hand, she held it tightly in her own.

"It's all right, Kate," Mike said, putting his arm around Kate's shoulders. "We're just about there."

"Don't push, not yet," the doctor admonished. "I want to make sure this baby is turned the way we want him—"

"Her!" Kate insisted. "It's a girl!"

"Her," the doctor repeated, glancing at Mike who shrugged. Kate had been convinced for weeks that this baby was a girl. "We want her to come out as smoothly as possible." He gently prodded, feeling the baby's tiny shoulder. "Okay, go ahead and push," he said, motioning for Edie to move beside him. "How close is Life Flight?" he whispered.

"They'll be here in about five minutes," Edie replied in a hushed voice.

"Good. This baby will need to be ventilated with oxygen. The lungs will not be mature enough for her to breathe on her own yet," he said just loud enough for the nurse's aide to hear. He then smiled encouragingly at Kate. "Here we go, you're doing great, Kate. A few more minutes and this part of it will be over."

# Chapter 16

"Recorded as one of the largest earthquakes in southeastern Idaho, the eyes of the entire state are focused on the isolated community of Blaketown. According to our latest report, the epicenter was located two miles north of the small Idaho town. Seismic waves have been measured with a 6.5 magnitude on the Richter Scale, which is equivalent to approximately 50 kilotons of TNT being detonated. Tremors were felt as far away as Salt Lake City. With an intensity rating of eight on the Mercali Scale, the devastation will be slight in specially designed structures, but considerable damage can take place in ordinary buildings. We've been told that the rocky soil conditions prevalent in that area could have been a stabilizing factor, which might have kept destruction to a minimum, although early reports indicate that considerable damage has taken place. We have yet to hear if there were any casualties . . ."

Hearing more than she wanted, Bev shut off the radio. Doris tried to smile encouragingly at the young woman, but felt as scared as Bev looked.

"They could be wrong," Terri said, clinging to hope. "It might not be as bad as they're making it sound. Like I'm sure a news team could get through! We barely made it through. You saw all of the cars that were abandoned along the way."

"It'll be all right," Karen said, trying to convince herself.

As they approached the outskirts of Blaketown, a heavy silence descended. No one spoke as they stared at the small fires lighting the night sky. Doris slowed the Jeep, doing her best to avoid the tree limbs and rubble that covered the road. It had taken nearly an hour to drive six miles. Several times they had moved off the road to avoid gaping cracks, or fallen trees. Twice they had stopped to move rocks and branches from blocking their path. As they had traveled, they had come across several motorists who were stranded and had promised to send help as soon as they arrived in Blaketown. Their progress had been slow, but steady. The four-wheel-drive utility vehicle had successfully handled the challenges that had been encountered. Now, unsure of what they would find ahead, they almost wished they had remained where they were.

"What are all of those fires?" Terri ventured.

"Probably gas lines," Doris replied. "I hope my husband thought to shut ours off." As they crested a small hill, Doris braked to a stop. For several seconds, they stared at the town below. Gathering her courage, the English teacher pushed the gas pedal, guiding the Jeep toward their hometown.

* * *

"I'm glad I finally found you," Betty said, slipping an arm around Mandy's waist. It had taken a great deal of persuasion, but she had convinced Lyle that she could drive into Blaketown by herself to search for their niece. He had planned to come with her to look for Mandy, but she had declined his offer when they had learned that a neighbor was pinned under a portion of the ceiling in his house. Betty had encouraged him to go help, assuring that she could find Mandy on her own. Concerned, Sara had volunteered to come with her, but again, Betty had refused the extra help. Sara had been asked to watch the neighbor's children as their father was removed from the fragments of wood and debris in their home. Betty had insisted that Sara stay with their neighbor's children, reminding her daughter that the aftershocks had ceased for the time being. On their hike from the Plymouth sedan, Betty and Lyle had learned that most of the road from Blaketown to their house was intact. She had encountered only minor obstacles on her return to Blaketown. What a relief it had been to learn that Mandy had been found and was being treated for minor injuries at the hospital.

"We've been so worried!" Betty now exclaimed, squeezing her niece against her.

"I'm fine," Mandy lied.

"I can see how fine you are," Betty retorted, releasing her hold on Mandy. "And what's this about you being a difficult patient?"

Mandy's scowl deepened. "This is a nightmare," she grumbled.

"One we're all living," Betty said, giving Mandy a stern look. "Later, we'll discuss why you wandered off. You had us worried sick," she said, pacing around the x-ray room.

"Sorry," Mandy mumbled as the x-ray technician walked into the room.

"Hello, there. I understand we're looking for a fractured arm," he said, glancing at the order in his hands.

"You can still take x-rays?" Betty asked. "The power's out all over town."

"We have emergency backup generators to keep some things going here at the hospital. That's why we still have lights available. One generator is rigged to handle the portable x-ray machine we've been using tonight." He smiled at Mandy. "Now legally I have to ask this question, so don't feel insulted—is there a chance you might be pregnant?"

Turning a shade paler, Mandy stared at the technician.

* * *

"There goes Life Flight," Bev said, pointing out her side of the window. Doris and the other girls saw the blinking lights of the emergency helicopter as it prepared to leave Blaketown. Praying it was carrying strangers, they looked the other way, taking in the damage that surrounded them. Blaketown resembled a war zone.

"I'll drive around back to the ER," Doris said. "Then we'll get someone to help us unload Sabrina. I don't want to move her too much until we know for sure what's going on with her." Driving the Jeep as close to the emergency ramp as possible, she shut off the engine and handed the keys to Bev. "Wait here, I'll hurry."

"Doris," Bev said, reaching for a hug. "Thanks. I don't know what we would've done if you hadn't been there."

Returning the hug, Doris drew back to smile encouragingly at the three girls. "I'm glad I was there too." Struggling for composure, she opened the door on her side and lowered herself to the ground.

As Doris walked through the emergency room exit, a small truck pulled in beside the Jeep. Exultant, James leaped down from the truck and hollered Bev's name. Her eyes widening, Bev opened the door of the Jeep and ran to her father, only too glad to be gathered in his strong arms.

"I was driving around looking for you—I spotted the Jeep, but couldn't get to where you were until now, these streets are such a mess," James exclaimed. "Are you all right?" He drew back to examine his daughter, wincing over the gash in her forehead. "A memory dent, eh?" he said softly, touching her face.

"It's nothing. Sabrina's the one who's really hurt."

James glanced toward the Jeep. "How bad?"

"I don't know. We tried to get her here as quickly as we could, but like you said, the streets . . . and the highway to Blaketown . . . it's all a mess. It took us forever."

"Well, I know someone who is going to be thrilled to see you."

"Gina?" Bev guessed.

James nodded. He could only hope that eventually Bev's step-mother would be glad to see him as well. He knew what he had to do to insure that and hoped he could find the strength to succeed. One thing was for certain—now that his family was back together, he would do whatever it took to keep it that way.

* * *

"Edie, we need your help again," Greta said excitedly, motioning for the nurse's aide to follow her from Drake Henderson's hospital room. She knew Edie would want to see what had just come through the door into ER. "Gina, you'd better come with us too," the RN added, pointing to Drake's mother.

"More injuries?" Edie asked.

Refusing to answer, Greta led the way down the hall.

Exhausted, Edie felt dead on her feet, but forced herself to follow the RN. In this one night she had seen more emergencies than she had in an entire year. Preparing herself for whatever was ahead, she turned the corner behind Greta. She looked up to see Karen and her friends with Doris Kelsey and James Henderson. Paralyzed by relief, she froze in place, then began to cry.

Karen found her legs before Edie did and raced forward, throwing herself into her mother's arms. They hugged each other tight, unspoken gratitude streaming down their faces.

Coming into the hall behind Edie, Gina stood transfixed, staring at James, then at Bev. Covering her mouth with one hand, she began to cry in earnest, only too glad to accept a combined embrace from her husband and daughter.

\* \* \*

"What would happen if I was pregnant?" Mandy stammered, surprising herself by how protective she suddenly felt of her unborn child.

"We'd take added precautions. Use a couple of heavy lead shields to protect the baby," the x-ray tech replied.

Mandy swallowed past the lump in her throat, unable to meet her aunt's questioning stare. "I'll need a shield," she said.

Betty continued to stare at her niece, the missing pieces falling into place in the puzzle Mandy had become.

\* \* \*

"Are you sure you want me to go with Mike?" Greg asked, glancing from Sabrina's unconscious form to Sue.

Sue nodded. "As far as we can tell, Sabrina is in no immediate danger. Her vital signs are good and her blood sugar is normal. You heard the doctor. She's suffering from a concussion thanks to that blow to her head. She should regain consciousness soon."

Greg frowned, remembering another time when a daughter had received a traumatic blow to the head. Kate had been in a coma for nearly five weeks. "They weren't sure how long Kate would be unconscious after her accident a few years ago," he pointed out. "It turned out to be more serious than they thought."

"This can't be like it was for Kate," Sue said firmly. "Sabrina will snap out of this. In the meantime, Mike needs to be there for Kate and for little Susan Colleen," she said, still seeing the tiny grand-

daughter who had arrived an hour ago. Kate had insisted on naming
her baby before leaving the Blaketown hospital, desiring to name this
daughter after her mother, Susan Mahoney Erickson, and her fourth
great-grandmother, Colleen Mahoney. Mike had graciously accepted
the name, declaring that the tiny infant would possess the strength of
both grandmothers. Colleen, as they would call her, had weighed in
at three pounds, four ounces. As anticipated, her tiny lungs weren't
mature and the neonatal Life Flight team had immediately intubated
Colleen, giving her the oxygen she would need to survive.

Because Kate had lost so much blood during Colleen's birth, they
had taken her with the baby to Bannock Regional Medical Center in
Pocatello. Mike was determined to follow in his Chevy Blazer,
anxious to be with his wife and small daughter.

"I'll feel better if you go with Mike," Sue stated calmly. "He's
upset and I don't think he should be alone."

"I don't want to leave you here alone either," Greg replied.

"I'll be all right here with Sabrina."

Torn between a sense of duty to both daughters, Greg hesitated.

"There is one thing you and Mike could do before you leave."
Sue gazed steadily at her husband. "Give Sabrina a priesthood
blessing before you go."

Agreeing, Greg left Sabrina's hospital room to search for his son-
in-law.

* * *

"Hey, little bro," Bev said, sitting down on the side of Drake's
hospital bed. "How are you doin'?"

"My leg hurts," Drake said, trying not to cry.

"I know how you feel," Bev replied. "My leg hurt just like that
last spring."

"Did you cry?"

Feeling Gina's hands on her shoulders, Bev shared a watery smile
with her little brother. "There's nothing wrong with tears, big guy.
Sometimes it makes you feel better."

* * *

"'Bye, Doris. Thanks again for everything you did," Terri said.

Exhausted, Doris nodded. Her face lined with worry, she wondered how well her husband had fared during the quake.

Terri smiled shyly at Bev's father. "And thanks for giving me a ride home."

"You're welcome," James replied, watching as the young woman climbed out of the Jeep to run toward her house. "I haven't heard anything about Terri's family. I hope they're all okay," he said, concerned.

Doris watched as Terri's mother opened the door, squealing her delight over Terri's surprise appearance. "I'd say that was a pretty good indication," she replied.

"I'd still feel better if we knew for sure," James persisted.

"Let me ask," Doris offered, rolling down the window on her side of the Jeep. "Margo?" she called to Terri's mother.

Margo released Terri from a smothering embrace and gazed at the Jeep.

"Is everyone okay in your family?"

"As good as can be expected," Margo replied. "Much better now that we know Terri's safe. Thank you for bringing her home."

Nodding, Doris rolled up the window, anxious to see how things were at her own house.

"I'd like to add my thanks to Margo's. You worked a miracle getting those girls home, through those road conditions," James said as he pulled out into the street.

"It wasn't me, James, I was merely an instrument. Our Father in Heaven was the one calling the shots."

Reflecting on this, he drove the English teacher across town to her home where she was relieved to learn that her husband was alive and as feisty as ever.

# Chapter 17

Flipping off his flashlight, Brett stepped onto the front porch of Adele's house. He had carefully searched every room, including the small basement. Adele was nowhere to be seen. A sudden thought came to mind. Adele was always helping others—she was probably down the street at a neighbor's house doing what she could to assist during this crisis. He walked across the lawn and into the street, wondering if he should go door to door, asking if anyone had seen her. As he wandered down the street, he felt prompted to return to Adele's house. He retraced his steps, this time noticing the collapsed log shed behind the older home. Feeling sick inside, he walked back to investigate.

Shining his flashlight across the jumbled heap, he prayed Adele wasn't underneath. He moved closer, and after testing one of the rotting logs, was able to ease it out of the pile. He removed two more logs, then knelt, using his flashlight to search in the small space he had cleared. "Adele?" When there was no response, he continued to probe through the rubble. After several minutes he was about to give up when he spotted a patch of color buried under a toppled wall of logs. Throwing off his jacket, he frantically removed logs as fast as he could, his heart pounding in his ears.

* * *

"There, you're all set," Dr. Davis said, trying to get a smile out of Mandy as he finished with her cast. When the old joke failed, he glanced at Mandy's aunt. Embarrassed by her niece's condition, Betty avoided his attentive gaze. He understood her discomfiture; the x-ray technician had already shared Mandy's predicament, concerned that her fall had endangered the baby. A quick examination had revealed that the most serious injury was Mandy's arm. As far as the doctor could tell, Mandy's baby was fine.

Picking up on Betty's need to spend some private time with her niece, the doctor rose from the padded stool. "Well, I'd stay and chat, but there are still several customers waiting for service."

"Are we free to leave?" Betty asked.

"Yes," the doctor replied as he moved out of the tension-filled room.

Mandy stared dismally at the pink cast. When Dr. Davis had asked for a color preference, she had let him decide, not caring how her arm looked. Nothing seemed to matter anymore. Betty spent several uncomfortable seconds examining her hands. "How are you feeling?"she finally asked, unsure of what to say now that she was alone with her niece.

"I'm fine," Mandy mumbled, fighting tears.

"Are you? Mandy, why didn't you say anything before? How long have you known?"

"Go ahead and tell me how disgusting I am! I'm sure you won't be the first or last person to feel that way." Mandy chewed her bottom lip to keep from crying.

Sensing Mandy's vulnerability, Betty's heart softened toward her niece. Mandy had made a terrible mistake, but she was still a young woman in need of comfort. Moving across the small room, Betty startled her niece with a loving embrace. Trembling, the defiant teen crumbled in her aunt's arms, tears replacing the anger that had consumed her for weeks.

\* \* \*

Out of breath, Brett Randall entered the hospital through the emergency doors. When he spotted Dr. Davis, he motioned for him to approach.

"What's up, Brett? Don't tell me you've brought me more business? I can't keep up as it is," the doctor quipped.

Pensive, Brett waited until the doctor was beside him, then whispered into his ear. Blanching at what he had to say, the doctor stared at the man he knew Edie planned to marry. He wordlessly followed Brett out of the emergency doors to the Suzuki Samurai that waited near the emergency ramp.

* * *

Betty leaned tiredly against the wall of the waiting room as Mandy stepped into the women's restroom to freshen up before they headed back to the ranch. "How in the world are we going to deal with this?" Betty murmured. She was so preoccupied, she didn't notice when Edie entered the small room.

"There's a phone call for you," Edie said, her soft voice causing Betty to jump slightly.

"A phone call?" Betty repeated, puzzled by this news. "Aren't the phone lines down?"

"We're using a cellular phone," Edie explained.

"Who would know to call me here?"

"They said it was a relative," Edie replied. "We're not sure how long the battery charge will hold up on this phone, so if you could make this quick, we'd appreciate it," she added. "We're trying to save it for emergency purposes."

Understanding, Betty nodded and gripped the phone. "Hello?"

"Betty?" Lorena Hopkins said. "Oh, good, I wasn't sure I could get through."

"Where are you?" Betty asked, picturing Mandy's mother.

"In Pocatello. As soon as we heard about the earthquake, we drove up from Salt Lake. Is everyone all right?"

Betty paused. How could she possibly answer that question?

"Betty? Is someone hurt—is Mandy safe?"

At the mention of her name, Mandy walked out of the rest room, her reddened eyes puffy from crying.

"Mandy hurt her arm . . . it's a simple fracture . . . they had to cast it after they stitched up a gash. Everyone else in our family is all right."

"Mandy broke her arm? That's why you're at the hospital," Lorena said, relieved. "We're here at Bannock Regional in Pocatello. We heard they had access to the hospital there in Blaketown. The only reason they let us call is because of Mandy—because we're her parents. We knew it would be a long shot, we weren't sure anyone would know where you were, but we had to try."

"I'm glad you called. I wondered how we would get word to you. I knew you would be worried."

Mandy gawked at the phone. "My parents?" she mouthed to her aunt.

Betty nodded. "Do you want to talk to your mom?" she mouthed back to Mandy.

Shaking her head, Mandy sat in a nearby chair and began to cry again.

"Is Mandy there, could I talk to her?"

"Lorena, they need this phone back at the nurses' station. They're trying to save it for emergency calls."

"Okay. Tell Mandy we love her and we'll be there as soon as they reopen the road."

"I will," Betty promised. "Be careful when you come." Turning the phone off, she handed it to Edie.

* * *

A few minutes later, Edie returned to the nurses' station and gave the cell phone to one of the LPNs standing behind the white counter.

"Edie?"

Turning, Edie smiled at Gina. "How's Drake?"

"He's feeling a little better." Gina tried to smile, but her lips refused to curve. She ached for her friend, knowing that what they had to tell her would be devastating. Brett and Dr. Davis had asked her to locate Edie and bring her to a secluded room down the hall. "Edie, could you come with me for a minute?"

"Sure," Edie replied, following Gina to a room where Dr. Davis stood waiting with Brett. "Brett!" she exclaimed excitedly. Her excitement faded when she saw the look on his face. "Where's Mom?"

"Edie, there's no easy way to tell you this," Dr. Davis began as Brett stood protectively near, his heart breaking for the woman he loved.

"What is it . . . what's wrong?" Edie searched Brett's face for answers.

"Honey, it's your mother," Brett said.

"Did you find her? Is she hurt?"

Hating what he had to say, Brett's voice broke. "Edie . . . she's gone . . . she didn't survive."

Grappling with the enormity of that statement, Edie was unaware that Gina had gripped her from behind, fearing her trembling friend would faint.

"If it's any comfort, she didn't suffer," Doctor Davis emphasized. "She was taken in an instant."

Numb, the voices around her seemed to roar as a muffled ocean as Edie fell back against Gina. Her mother's sweet face came to mind, her affectionate smile, the security she had always provided. Blinking rapidly, Edie sank down inside of herself, silently screaming her pain.

\* \* \*

"They'll leave the steri-strips in place?" Karen asked Bev as the two girls wandered out of Drake's hospital room.

Bev fingered the gash in her forehead. "Yeah. They said Doris did a great job and they'd be better off to leave it alone. They don't even think I'll have much of a scar."

"You could always cover it with bangs," Karen suggested.

"True. I'll call it my memory dent."

"Your what?"

"My memory dent. That's what Dad called the first dent I put in his Jeep. He never had it fixed so I'd always remember what happened."

"I see," Karen laughed. "I wonder what my memory dent will be from this adventure?"

"I don't know, but at least one good thing has come from all of this—my parents are speaking to each other again. The way Dad's talking, I think there's hope; he's finally caught on to what Edie and I both learned the hard way."

"What's that?"

Bev smiled. "Family is worth any sacrifice."

"I agree," Karen replied.

Discussing the earthquake, the two girls continued walking down the hall of the hospital. As they passed by a small room, Bev glanced in, startled when she saw Karen's mother sobbing in Gina's arms. Bev pointed toward the room and slipped inside, Karen right behind her.

"Mom! What is it?" Karen exclaimed.

Tensing against Gina, Edie closed her eyes. How could she possibly tell Karen that her grandmother was dead?

"Karen . . ." Brett started.

"No, I need to talk to her . . . I need to be the one to tell her," Edie exclaimed, pulling away from Gina. "I know you're all concerned . . . I appreciate you being here with me, but please, give me a few minutes alone with Karen," she pleaded.

Respecting Edie's wishes, everyone but Karen left the small room, though Gina had to forcefully drag a protesting Bev out into the hall. When they all left, Edie crossed to the door, pulling it shut.

"Mom, you're really scaring me here, what's going on?"

Edie wiped at her eyes, but the tears continued to flow. Silently praying for strength she didn't have, she faced her daughter. "Karen, not long ago we talked about challenges, about things that could possibly go wrong . . . I never dreamed we'd be facing something like this so soon—"

"What's happened?!" Karen asked, a growing sense of dread knotting in her stomach. "Is it Sabrina? Is it more serious than we thought?"

"No, honey, Sabrina will be fine. She's already starting to stir. She'll probably regain consciousness later tonight."

"Then who . . . Grandma?" Karen guessed, seeing the answer in her mother's anguished face. "NO!" She bolted for the door, but Edie stopped her.

"Karen—"

"No, I don't want to hear this!" Karen pulled away from her mother. "Grandma's okay, I know she is! I had a calm feeling when we drove into Blaketown. I know Grandma's all right!"

"She *is* all right, but she's no longer with us," Edie stressed. "Brett found her . . . she was killed instantly when the quake hit. She was out in that wooden shed—"

"NO!" Karen sank down on the floor and hugged herself. "NO!"

Edie knelt beside her wailing daughter, ignoring Karen's attempts to push her away. Forcing the young woman against her, she held Karen tight until the tears finally came. A few minutes later, Brett opened the door to check on them. Karen was clinging to Edie, her young heart shattered beyond anything she had every known. Unobserved, Brett quietly pulled the door shut, giving Edie and Karen the privacy they desired as they mourned the loss of the mother they had shared.

# Chapter 18

The news reporter searched for an appropriate backdrop as he prepared to convey the dramatic events that had occurred during the past two days in Blaketown, Idaho. Settling for an uprooted tree, he stood in front of it, waiting for the signal from his cameraman.

"We're going live in four, three, two, one—" the man pointed a finger at the reporter who assumed a sober expression as he reported news the entire state craved.

"Good afternoon. As you can see, I'm reporting live from Blaketown, Idaho, a town Mother Nature tried to uproot," he said, gesturing to the tree behind him. "Unlike this tree, Blaketown has prevailed, its 3,000 residents uniting together to repair the damage caused by the earthquake Saturday night. It is now Tuesday afternoon. In this short length of time, Blaketown citizens have already cleared a great deal of the debris from its ravaged streets. In this isolated community, they have drawn on the strength of each other to survive this catastrophe.

"We have witnessed loving sacrifice, courage, and determination as the citizens in this small Idaho community attempt to rebuild their town. In a day when neighbor rarely thinks of neighbor, we are seeing unselfishness that is unsurpassed as most Blaketown residents have freely shared food and supplies regardless of religion, race, or creed. All are as one as houses are restored and families reunited.

"As was expected, there were several injuries, some serious enough to be transferred to larger hospitals. Sadly, there were three fatalities. Sixty-eight-year-old Hank Davies, who suffered a heart attack; fifty-six-year-old Adele Hadley, who was found beneath a collapsed shed;

and five-year-old Ryan Benson, who fell into his family's new private well when the loose soil crumbled beneath his feet." Pausing, the reporter glanced through his notes. "This morning, the entire community turned out in full force for little Ryan's funeral. The line for the viewing extended into the street as this town came to show its support for the Benson family. That was repeated at the viewing held for Hank Davies earlier this afternoon. There is little doubt the same compassion will be exhibited at the funeral for Adele Hadley tomorrow morning.

"We have footage of today's activities which we'll show at this time." The reporter took a deep breath as the tape they had recorded earlier was transmitted into homes throughout the state and parts of the nation. Allowing a few seconds for the television audience to absorb several poignant scenes, the reporter continued to speak, narrating what was passing before their eyes.

" . . . an outpouring of loving concern, of peaceful calm has filled this valley. Never has this reporter experienced anything like what we have felt this day." He waited as the live feed was refocused on himself. "Why is it that we see the best part of ourselves in action when tragedy strikes? Why can't we strive for this unity when all is well?" He paused again, giving his words the impact he desired. "Live from Blaketown, this is Allen Gordon."

* * *

Mandy sat in the living room of her aunt's house and wished again that she had died in the earthquake. She was convinced that would've been easier than facing her parents who were now on their way to Blaketown. The roads had finally been opened to general traffic, allowing passage to relatives, friends, and those eager to offer added assistance and support.

Support was something Mandy hadn't lacked since Saturday night. She had been stunned by her aunt's gentle acceptance of her predicament. Even Uncle Lyle had been surprisingly sensitive. Giving her a hug that morning, he hadn't said anything; for once, he was at a loss for words. His hug had said enough, indicating his sorrow for what she was going through.

Sara didn't know yet. For that, Mandy was grateful. This morning, Sara had gone to Adele Hadley's funeral to represent their family, oblivious of Mandy's dilemma. Betty had simply told Sara that Mandy's parents were on their way from Pocatello and that she and Lyle needed to stay at home to talk to them about Mandy's future plans. After the funeral, Sara was heading a project her ward's youth had taken on to organize the food that had been sent into their community from varied organizations outside of the valley. During her absence, Mandy's parents would arrive and the impending scene would hopefully be over before Sara returned home.

Throughout the morning, Betty had tried to bolster Mandy's spirits, but nothing could alleviate the anxiety that filled the young woman's heart. Mandy knew her parents would be furious. Her mother would not be as understanding as Aunt Betty had been. Her father wouldn't hug her as tenderly as Uncle Lyle.

Ashamed, Mandy regretted how poorly she had treated her aunt and uncle since her arrival that summer. Convinced she was unworthy of their sympathetic kindness, Mandy felt she deserved the harsh treatment she suspected her parents would supply. A few months ago, she could have handled their anger with defiance. Now she felt defeated, beaten into a corner. Remorse tormented her, but there was no way to repair the damage already done; the choices she had made in May had ruined her life. She was convinced it would never get better.

\* \* \*

Eric and Lorena Hopkins followed Lyle into the Sandler home, eager to see their daughter.

"I haven't been able to sleep since Saturday," Lorena shared. "All I've been able to think about is Mandy and what all of you must be going through." She smiled at her brother-in-law. "I hope you won't mind, we loaded up on groceries for you. They're still in the car. We figured you could probably use a few things that won't be available here for a while."

"Thanks . . . that's pretty thoughtful of you," Lyle replied.

"I can't believe how good things are already looking," Eric commented, describing what they had seen as they had driven through Blaketown. "Your community is really organized."

"We've just learned how to work together," Lyle said. He gave Eric a meaningful look. "Calamities can bring people together, or tear them apart. It's a personal choice."

Wondering at Lyle's meaning, Eric moved with his wife into the living room. Lorena beamed when she saw Mandy and quickly crossed the room toward her daughter. As she drew closer, she was confused by the stricken expression on her oldest daughter's face. "Mandy?"

Mandy slowly stood, her right arm in a sling. "Hi, Mom," she mumbled, avoiding her mother's searching gaze.

Deciding Mandy was getting a hug whether she wanted one or not, Lorena carefully embraced the young woman, mindful of the broken arm. Instead of the expected aloofness, Mandy buried her face against her mother and began to cry. "Oh, Mandy, I know . . . I've missed you so much too," Lorena soothed, kissing the top of her daughter's head. When Mandy's tears were the only response, Lorena cast a wondering look at her sister-in-law.

Betty longed to take the lead, to shoulder this difficult task for her niece, but knew it was Mandy's responsibility to inform her parents. Silently she urged Mandy to tell Lorena the truth.

As Mandy continued to cry, Lorena wondered if this was a good sign. Had her daughter finally come to her senses as she had hoped? "Mandy, why are you so upset? Are you ready to come home?" she asked softly. The question made Mandy cry harder. Concerned, Lorena ventured another glance at Betty, but couldn't read the other woman's expression.

"Is it the earthquake? I know you've been through so much. But you're all right now. It's over—you're safe."

Unable to speak, Mandy retreated to the recliner, curling up in a ball.

Perplexed, Eric shook his head. "What is it, Mandy?"

Her breath coming in gulping sobs, Mandy shook her head. She couldn't do this. It was too hard.

"Mandy?" Kneeling down by the recliner, Lorena smoothed the hair away from her daughter's face. "What's wrong?"

"Mama . . ." Mandy stammered, reverting to the name she had called her mother years ago. Her dark eyes glistened with unshed tears. "I'm in trouble."

"What kind of trouble?" Lorena asked, still stroking Mandy's hair in an attempt to calm her. "Have you done something wrong?"

"No, Mom, you don't get it . . . I'm **in trouble**," Mandy said, unable to say the word that had haunted her for weeks.

Eric glowered around the room. Why was Mandy hedging Lorena's questions? What had she done this time? Drugs? Alcohol? More shoplifting? The worry he had felt over his daughter during the earthquake transformed to anger and he was tempted to shake Mandy until she told them what was going on.

"In trouble?" Lorena stammered as she suddenly caught the meaning. "No! You can't be! You've been up here since June. You haven't been with Blade in weeks! Are you telling me you're pregnant?" Shame consumed Mandy and she couldn't look her mother in the eye. "Oh, Mandy, no!" Lorena exclaimed, her worst fears confirmed by Mandy's reaction.

* * *

Bev glanced nervously around the church house. She hadn't been to a funeral since her mother had died. The small service held then had only been for immediate family members. Yesterday, she had volunteered to stay with Drake while her parents attended the funerals for Ryan Benson and Hank Davies. Knowing she needed to come today, she had pushed aside a personal aversion in order to be here for Karen and Edie.

She was amazed by how many people were standing in line at Adele's viewing that morning, waiting to express their concern, to show their support for Karen and her mother. It seemed as though the entire valley had come to pay their final respects to a woman most had loved. As Bev continued to stand in line behind her father and Gina, she wondered what she would say to Karen.

Saturday night, Gina had insisted on taking Karen and Edie to their house, knowing that under the circumstances, it would have been too hard that first night to face the home they had shared with Adele. Leaving Drake to James' care at the hospital, Gina had driven Edie, Brett, Karen, and Bev across town to the slightly damaged Henderson abode. Brett and Gina had spent a long time in the kitchen with Edie. Bev had tried to talk to Karen in the living room, but had struggled for words as Karen had continued to cry. Bev understood Karen's pain; Adele had been more of a mother than a grandmother to Karen. Karen's heart wound went very deep and Bev had wondered how her friend would handle this tremendous loss in her life.

Surprisingly, as Karen and Edie had continued to grieve Saturday night, a sweet, peaceful feeling had filled the Henderson house, calming the Beyers in a way nothing else had. Bev and Gina had been unable to discuss what they had felt that night without choking up.

Reflecting on this, Bev moved with her parents through the line and into the Relief Society room of the LDS church house. She was impressed by the beautiful arrangement of flowers that decorated the casket. Due to the quake, flowers were hard to come by right now. Adele had always loved flowers; Bev felt certain Brett was responsible for their appearance here today. In her opinion, there wasn't much that man wouldn't do for Edie or Karen.

Looking away, Bev was unwilling to view Adele's body, instead she focused on Karen and the small line of family members that had gathered. An only child, Edie stood between Brett and Karen for support. On the other side of Brett were a couple of older women Bev assumed were Adele's sisters; both resembled Adele greatly. There were also a couple of men around Edie's age, hovering near Adele's sisters, possibly cousins, Bev decided.

James Henderson led the way through the line for his family. He embraced Karen, then reached for Edie. Straightening, the tall man shook Brett's hand, murmuring awkward words of condolence. Gina followed her husband's lead, lingering with Edie before maneuvering through the rest of the line.

Bev reached for Karen, pressing her friend against her as a shared pain bonded them closer than before. Giving Karen an intense squeeze, Bev pulled back.

Karen wiped at her eyes, her gaze shifting to the still form in the cushioned casket. "This doesn't seem real. I keep thinking Grandma will wake up."

"Remember what you've been telling me about my mom," Bev replied.

Karen smiled tearfully at her friend. "It's true, Bev. Your mom . . . my grandmother . . . they *do* live on. We will see them again. Off and on today, I keep feeling like Grandma's close—that she knows how hard this is."

"It can't be very easy for her to leave you two behind," Bev said, referring to Edie and Karen. "She loved you both so much."

"She'll always be a part of our lives," Karen replied. "I'll carry her love in here," she said, pointing to her heart.

Bev reached for another hug, then moved on to Edie.

"Thanks for coming," Edie said, holding Bev close. "I'm so glad Karen has you for a friend."

Stepping back, Bev smiled. "I'm the one who's grateful—for both of you—and for your mother. She always made me feel better about things . . . whenever I was down about something. And those choco-late chip cookies of hers—"

"Mom had a special way about her," Edie said, pulling a piece of tissue out of a pocket in her green dress.

Bev glanced behind her toward the casket—it wasn't as bad as she had thought it would be. Adele looked peaceful, dressed in white. "Your mother was an awesome lady."

"She always will be," Edie replied.

Nodding, Bev moved forward, sensing the impatience of the line behind her. "Hi, guy," she said to Brett as the two of them shook hands. She was surprised when Brett pulled her close for a hug.

"Thanks for being such a good friend to the women in my life."

"Sure," Bev said as he released her. "They've been there for me." She glanced at Edie and Karen, then at Brett. "Take good care of them," she admonished.

"I plan to," Brett replied in a hushed voice. "The other day, Adele and I were talking." He paused, the memory now tender. "I wonder if she knew . . . she said the same thing to me then. 'Take care of my girls, Brett. They're going to need you.'" He looked toward the casket. "I'll keep my promise, Adele," he whispered.

Bev squeezed his hand, then continued through the line.

\* \* \*

After exiting the Relief Society room, Terri walked back down the hall of the church house, pausing briefly to talk to Sabrina who was still standing in line with her parents. It had been a relief to learn that Sabrina's concussion hadn't been as serious as they had first thought.

"I'm glad you're feeling better," Terri said.

"Me too. Thanks again for all you guys did for me that night . . . it would've been a lot worse if you hadn't kept track of my blood sugar."

Terri smiled sadly at the younger girl. "It's a good thing Edie taught us what to watch for."

"I know. I feel so bad about what happened to her mother. Edie did so much for me, and for Kate that night—"

"How is Kate?"

Sabrina glanced at her parents who were visiting quietly with the people in line behind them. "She'll be okay; it's her baby we're worried about. Colleen has been losing weight, one lung collapsed . . . it's still pretty scary. That's why they transferred her to McKay-Dee hospital down in Ogden, Utah."

"We'll keep praying for her."

Sabrina nodded. "One thing is in our favor. The neonatologist told Kate and Mike that Colleen has a ninety-five percent chance of making it."

"That's great! It's a lot better than I thought."

"There's so much more they can do for preemies now. Hopefully they'll get to bring Colleen home in a few weeks."

"I'm sorry your family has been hit with so much."

"We're not the only ones," Sabrina said quietly, thinking of Karen. "Where's the rest of your family?"

"My little brother woke up with a fever this morning. Mom decided to stay home with him. Dad's here somewhere . . . he'll be one of the pallbearers."

"So will my dad," Sabrina revealed. She glanced at the small, white program in her hands. "Bev's dad is listed too . . . and Brett. These other two must be relatives."

Terri nodded. "I just met them. They're Edie's cousins."

"Are you staying for the funeral?"

"Yes," Terri replied.

"Would you mind saving a place for us?" Sabrina asked, pointing to herself and her mother. "We may be stuck in this line for a while."

Consenting to Sabrina's request, Terri walked down the hall to enter the chapel. She glanced around, wondering where to sit among the crowd that had already gathered.

"Hello, Terri, how are you doing?"

Startled, Terri looked up, then spotted Doris and her husband seated together on the padded bench to the right of where she was standing. "Okay," she said despondently.

"Have a seat," Doris invited, picking up on the young woman's somber mood.

"I told Sabrina I'd save room for her and Sue."

"What about her dad?"

He'll be sitting with the pallbearers," Terri replied.

"That's right. Well, there's plenty of room on this bench for all of us," Doris assured the young woman.

Nodding her appreciation, Terri sat down beside the teacher.

"You seem pretty upset this morning," Doris commented.

"I keep going over everything that happened Saturday night," Terri responded. "Sometimes it seems like a bad dream. Then there are times like today when it's too real." Closing her eyes, she tried to block the pain in her heart. Though she didn't know Adele as well as she would've liked, she had always appreciated the kindness Karen's grandmother had freely exhibited. It hurt to know Adele was gone; she couldn't imagine what Karen was going through.

"I can't believe Karen's grandmother is really dead," Terri murmured, opening her eyes.

Doris silently agreed as she looked around the chapel that was steadily filling with those who had loved Adele Hadley. "The past few days have been very difficult," she said, glancing at Terri.

Troubled by what her friends were going through, Terri began to open up to the teacher, expressing the fears in her heart. "This whole year has been hard! It makes me wonder what's next? I mean, first Bev had to go through that treatment center . . . she has struggled so much with this alcohol problem—and with her parents. Then Sabrina gets sick with something that won't ever go away. She has to give herself shots the rest of her life! She has to poke her finger several times a day to check her blood sugar. I'm not sure I could do it . . . I can't stand the sight of blood," she said, shuddering.

"It's amazing what you can get used to when you don't have a choice," Doris observed.

Terri frowned. "I've been reading about diabetes—"

"That's really good of you. I'm sure Sabrina will appreciate your thoughtfulness," the teacher complimented, proud of the way Terri had changed. No longer self-centered, this young woman had become extremely compassionate. Unlike Bev and Karen, Terri had at least tried to befriend Mandy since September. Mandy had ignored every effort Terri had made on her behalf, but at least Terri had tried.

"There are so many things that can go wrong for diabetics," Terri said, still focused on Sabrina.

"Not if Sabrina will take care of herself," Doris explained calmly.

"That's just it!" Terri burst out. "Why should she have to deal with that? Why has Bev been through so much? Why did Karen's grandmother die? Why did we have an earthquake? I don't get it— nothing makes sense anymore! Why are all of these things happening? Are we being punished?" she asked, her brown eyes filled with tears. She gratefully accepted a handful of tissue from Doris, something she hadn't thought to bring in her rush to get ready that morning. Using a portion to wipe at her face, she stored the rest in the pocket of the denim dress she was wearing.

"Terri, it's true that some choices lead to difficult consequences," Doris said gently. "That's why we have the commandments, the standards, even the Word of Wisdom to guide us. They can help us find true happiness in today's troubled world. Take the Word of Wisdom, for example. How often have scientists come out with warnings in recent years that go right along with what we've been counseled to do since Joseph Smith revealed back in 1833 how important it is to take care of our bodies?"

"I know," Terri replied. "Now there's warning labels on cigarettes and a ton of stuff about avoiding alcohol and what it can do to you. And last year when I did a research paper on caffeine, it made me want to never drink cola again," she said, disgusted.

"Exactly," Doris replied. "Consider all of the immorality that is taking place in today's world. Can people be truly happy when they turn their backs on important values?" she asked, thinking of Mandy Hopkins.

"Well, no. I mean . . . if you mess around with stuff like that you can ruin your life. My mom told me about the different diseases people can get . . . and that some girls get pregnant when they're not even old enough to date," Terri said, blushing.

"Can you see that sometimes we bring hardships on ourselves?"

Still looking confused, Terri nodded, her brown hair bobbing under her chin. "Yeah, but what did Blaketown do to deserve all of the destruction that happened Saturday night?"

"We aren't being punished, we're being tested, something we agreed to experience when we were in the premortal world. When we're facing trials, we shouldn't try to place blame on ourselves or others. Instead, we should do our best to accept whatever has happened. Life wasn't meant to be a free ride—we have to earn our way to the celestial kingdom."

"I think I want off this merry-go-round!"

"You don't mean that," Doris replied.

"Maybe. I used to think life was terrible if I had to do the dishes at home or if I didn't get straight A's at school. Now those things seem so trivial." Terri glared down at her hands. "It makes me sick to think about how shallow I used to be."

Doris smiled kindly at the young woman sitting beside her. "We all go through a refining process in this life. Afflictions can help us grow and become better people. Sometimes we need to change—we need to be shaken out of the ruts we sometimes fall into."

"Maybe Bev needed to change a little, but she's doing great now. Sabrina and Karen have always had their act together—"

"Not always," Doris replied. "They're not perfect."

Terri shook her head. "*I'm* the one who needs refining."

"We *all* have room for improvement. We need challenges to grow and learn. That's part of why we're here."

"But why are so many things happening now, all at once? It's like everywhere you turn, things are such a mess!"

Doris thought of the recent scandal in the White House and of the economic distress many were experiencing in this troubled era. Images of tragic news stories from the past couple of years surfaced. "It has been predicted that in our day there will be many calamities. It's one of the signs of our times. In fact, I have a scripture to show you," she said, reaching for her scripture bag. During the funerals held yesterday, Doris had wished she had brought her scriptures to mark the verses of comfort that had been read over the pulpit by Church leaders. She had brought them with her today, better prepared for what she assumed would be another spiritual boost. Quickly thumbing through the index, she located the desired scripture and looked it up. "There it is," she murmured, handing her triple combination to Terri. Read verse 3 of Helaman 12."

Terri obediently read the scripture Doris wanted her to see:

"And thus we see that except the Lord doth chasten his people with many afflictions, yea, except he doth visit them with death and with terror, and with famine and with all manner of pestilence, they will not remember him."

Unsettled by the verse, Terri turned to Doris. "That doesn't make me feel better."

"Don't be upset, I thought it might help explain part of what is taking place in the world today. Here, let me show you another scripture, one that was shared from this pulpit yesterday during Ryan's funeral." She took the book from Terri and thumbed through the pages, stopping at D&C 42:46. Handing the book of scripture to Terri, Doris silently read the verse with her student:

"And it shall come to pass that those that die in me shall not taste of death, for it shall be sweet unto them."

"Terri, these three people who were taken from our community over the weekend were righteous individuals. Little Ryan was completely innocent. They weren't being punished; it was simply their time to leave this mortal world. Time for them to take on other responsibilities in the Spirit World where the gospel of Jesus Christ is being preached to those who didn't hear it before or understand it while on this earth." She smiled at Terri. "As for the rest of us, we have to continue on with faith. We're given quite a promise—if we'll live up to what we know is right." Retrieving her scriptures, she searched for a verse that she felt certain would ease Terri's heart. "There, that's the one."

Looking where Doris had pointed in 1 Nephi 22:17, Terri read the following verse:

"Wherefore, he will preserve the righteous by his power, even if it so be that the fulness of his wrath must come . . ."

"Okay, one more verse should sum things up."

Terri shook her head in amazement. "You really know your scriptures."

"That comes with time and study. I've often found answers to problems in the scriptures. They're especially comforting now." She skimmed through several pages, stopping in the Doctrine & Covenants. "There, read this."

Once again focusing on where Doris had instructed her to read, Terri scanned the following scripture:

" . . . fear not, let your hearts be comforted; yea, rejoice evermore, and in everything give thanks . . . all things wherewith you have been afflicted shall work together for your good, and to my name's glory saith the Lord."

"Terri, we're living in a wonderful time. We have advantages no other generation has ever seen. True, there are numerous trials and life seems to pick up pace every year. We're surrounded by chaos, but on the other hand, there have always been challenges. I can't think of one time in history when people weren't tested. Remember—that was the purpose of this world. Think about what the Mormon pioneers endured or what the Israelites suffered before Moses led them out of Egypt. It couldn't have been easy for Nephi and his family to leave their comfortable home in Jerusalem, to turn their backs to worldly wealth to live in the wilderness. They were being prepared for the journey they would face, for a chance to dwell in a promised land, just as we're being prepared now for what lies ahead. These tests and trials will help us become better people, if we'll let them. Think about what you learned about yourself during what you girls call your *canyon adventure*. You'll never be the same, will you?"

Blushing, Terri shook her head.

"Because of what you girls experienced then, you were able to cope extremely well with what took place Saturday night."

"But you were there to help us."

"If I hadn't shown up, you girls would've been fine. You were already handling the most serious problems when I arrived." She smiled kindly at Terri. "Down through the ages, people have been tried in various ways. Some have succeeded in rising above whatever obstacles come their way. They're the ones who will make it straight to the top. How can we possibly feel comfortable with these celestial candidates if we don't bravely face challenges of our own—if we don't allow ourselves to be spiritually stretched?"

"I hadn't thought about it that way," Terri replied. "Sometimes it seems like we're being picked on, but like you said, maybe we're being stretched." She speculated on this for a few seconds, then asked, "But what happens if we break?"

"Do you think anyone has ever suffered as much as the Savior did in this mortal world?"

Reflecting on the life of Jesus Christ, Terri shook her head again.

"He alone lived a perfect life, then willingly suffered for all of us, enduring the pain we would all feel. I can't even imagine what He withstood as He paid the price for our mistakes in the Garden of Gethsemane. He did that to help us. He understands the heartache we feel as well as the discomfort our physical bodies sometimes plague us with. He was ridiculed and persecuted more than any of us will ever face. There isn't anything He doesn't understand. That is why He gave us the precious gift of the Comforter, the Holy Ghost, to ease our hearts. Did you notice anything a few minutes ago when you were in the Relief Society room?"

Unsure of what Doris was getting at, Terri shrugged.

"Didn't you feel the sense of peace that is surrounding Karen's family today?"

Pondering this, Terri nodded. It had surprised her how calm Karen and her mother had seemed as they comforted those who had come to offer solace.

"Think about how strong Bev has become through her challenges. Kate was telling me the other day that Bev has been asking a lot of questions about our church. Who knows when that seed of a testimony will take root, but it's already making a difference in Bev, in the way she looks at life. Her themes in Creative Writing reflect the growth that is taking place." Doris glanced across the chapel at Bev who was sitting quietly beside Gina.

Terri followed the teacher's gaze and knew Doris was right. Bev had been changing steadily since last spring.

"Have you seen a change with Sabrina?" Doris asked.

Terri reflected on how positive Sabrina's attitude was, most of the time. "She isn't flipping out anymore about being a diabetic—she seems okay about it."

Doris nodded. "Sabrina is another young lady who is becoming very strong because of the challenges she faces every day."

"She doesn't even wince when she checks her blood sugar. She acts like it doesn't hurt."

"Special comfort is available to those who sincerely seek spiritual guidance, another part of the test. I've known people who have faced smaller trials, things that have totally overwhelmed them because they were too proud to pray for help. There are so many blessings our Father in Heaven longs to give us, but we have to ask for His guidance. Then we have to be willing to listen. We may not always like the answer when it comes, but someday when we look back over our lives, we'll understand that those things that stretched us the most, shaped us into who our Father in Heaven knew we could be."

"I've got a long way to go," Terri sighed.

Doris smiled at the young woman. "Actually, I think you're well on your way."

Unconvinced, Terri shook her head. "I'm still a little concerned here. What's my test going to be? I mean, out of the four of us, I'm the only one not dealing with a major crisis. The earthquake was scary, but my family was watched over. No one was hurt and we're already repairing the damage to our house."

"Maybe right now your challenge is being a good friend to Bev, Karen, and Sabrina," Doris pointed out. "They need your strength and compassion. That might be your test for now. That's another reason we're here, to learn the importance of helping each other. Remember what the Savior taught—He wants us to love and serve each other, as He loves and helps us all."

"I'll do my best," Terri promised, her voice sounding husky. A warming glow began pushing the doubting fears aside as she sensed the truth of what Doris had taught her.

Before Doris could reply, Sabrina walked in with her parents, and they took a place on the bench beside Terri. From the determined look on her face, Doris knew Terri would keep the pledge she had just made.

# Chapter 19

Later that same afternoon, Lorena made her way up the stairs to her daughter's current bedroom. Betty and Lyle were still in the kitchen trying to console Eric. For Lorena, there was no consolation—she felt as though the word, **FAILURE,** was permanently imbedded in her forehead. Waves of angry grief threatened to engulf her. There was so much going on inside of her, she didn't know how to react. During the three days she had spent in Pocatello, she had agonized over Mandy, fearing the danger the earthquake had presented. Now she was facing an emotional shockwave of similar magnitude, one that threatened the well-being of her family.

Mandy had retreated upstairs, away from the commotion after the initial outburst in the living room. Deciding she had better check on her, Lorena paused outside of the bedroom door. The sounds were muffled, but she could tell Mandy was still crying. She had never seen her daughter this distraught, not even when she and Eric had taken her to court for the shoplifting incident. Why had it taken something this painful to pierce their daughter's heart? Why hadn't they been able to reach her before?

Knocking once on the door, Lorena opened it. She moved into the room and closed the door behind her. "Mandy, I know you're upset—we're all upset, but we need to start making decisions." She crossed the room and sat on the bed as Mandy tried to stifle her tears. Carefully rolling onto her back, Mandy sat up to face her mother. As Lorena gazed at her daughter's tear-streaked face, she felt torn by the desire to punish *and* comfort her daughter. Nothing in her life had prepared her for this crossroads. "For now, we—your father and I—

we think it's best if you come home with us," she stammered, "at least until we figure out what we're going to do."

Large tears rolled down Mandy's face. She had convinced herself she would never be welcome home again. "I can come home?" she sniffed.

Nodding, her own eyes brimming with tears, Lorena drew her daughter into a hug.

"What about Dad?" Mandy managed to ask a few minutes later.

Lorena closed her eyes. Eric was so furious. She hoped Betty and Lyle could calm him down before they headed home in the morning. It was probably a good thing they were a state away from Blade; there was little doubt what her husband would try to do if they were in Salt Lake right now. She prayed Eric would eventually listen to reason. Raging on about the mistake that had been made wouldn't make it go away—it would only drive the wedge deeper between themselves and Mandy.

"Mom?" Mandy pressed, her ears still ringing with the bitter accusations her father had hurled at her an hour ago. She drew back from her mother, searching for an answer.

"Give him time. This is not the kind of news any parent wants to hear. We're all going to have our moments. Myself—I want to scream," Lorena said, rising to pace the floor. "I want Blade to answer for this!" she continued, her voice trembling. "And I want to know why you didn't listen when we talked about this very thing!"

The pain reflecting from her mother's eyes tore at Mandy's heart. Ashamed, she looked away. Her mother was right, she had been taught—it was no one's fault but her own. She could've told Blade "No." She could've stopped seeing him when things first started getting out of hand. For that matter, if she had heeded her parents and leaders, she never would've dated Blade.

"Most of all, I want us to be a family again," Lorena exclaimed as she continued to pace around the room. "I'm not sure it will ever be like it was before all of this happened, but someday . . . I pray that we will feel like a family again!"

Mandy wasn't sure that was possible, but she knew now that she needed her family's support. Repeating a phrase she had already uttered several times that day, she murmured how sorry she was.

"I'm sorry too, Mandy," Lorena agreed. "But this time, sorry won't make it better." She watched as Mandy contritely lowered her head. "Admitting you're sorry is a start, though," Lorena added, relenting. Returning to Mandy's bed, Lorena sat down and had a long, overdue talk with her daughter.

\* \* \*

After the funeral dinner, when everyone else headed home, Brett heeded Edie's request to drive both her and Karen back up to the cemetery. He parked close to the flower-covered mound where Adele's body had been laid to rest. Slipping down from the Suzuki Samurai, he hurried around to help Edie out of the small four-wheel-drive, then pushed the front bucket seat out of the way and helped Karen climb to the ground. Sensing their desire to be alone, he remained by the Samurai, his blue eyes tinged with a deep sadness.

In silence, Edie and Karen trudged toward Adele's grave. Edie stared down at the arrangement of flowers Brett had provided for her mother that day. Kneeling beside the mound, she pulled two white roses loose. Rising, she handed one to Karen. Earlier they had discussed pressing flowers from this arrangement, a tender reminder of what this day had been.

The Comforter had descended upon the two of them in a major fashion since Saturday night. Heartache came in small bursts, releasing the pain they now carried. Surprisingly, Edie had been able to get through this traumatic time without craving alcohol. Drawing strength from the calming peace in her heart, she knew that the best way to honor her mother's memory was to emulate her life. The responsibility she felt toward Karen would never allow her to backtrack.

Edie glanced around the small cemetery. It was a beautiful place. Lined with trees, there was a reverence here she had never observed before. Silently promising that she would come often with bright bouquets of flowers, she could almost feel her mother's approving love.

Caught up in her thoughts, she was unaware that Karen was crying. When she heard her daughter sniff, Edie snapped out of the trance-like daze to pull her daughter close.

"I'm sorry, Mom," Karen mumbled, apologizing for her tears.

"I'm not," Edie countered, pressing Karen against her. "Let it go," she encouraged. "Don't you dare keep it all inside."

* * *

"We're going to miss you," Betty said the next morning, dabbing at her eyes with a wad of tissue. Moving across the living room to hug her niece goodbye, she thought her heart would burst.

Mandy allowed her aunt to cry over her for a few minutes before pulling away. Dry-eyed, the young woman nodded briefly at her Uncle Lyle, then at Sara, then slowly followed her parents out to the car.

"I still can't believe this is happening!" Sara exclaimed as her mother shut the front door.

"I know. That poor little thing—"

"If anyone finds out—I'll never live it down," Sara continued.

Certain she hadn't heard right, Betty gazed steadily at her youngest daughter. "*You'll* never live this down?"

"It was bad enough when she was swearing and upsetting everyone with her foul mouth. Now this! People are going to think—"

"Since when does it matter more what other people think, than what your own family is going through?"

Sensing a major storm was brewing, Lyle walked outside. This time Sara deserved the lecture he knew was coming. Betty would straighten their daughter out. In the meantime, there were chores he needed to attend to, animals to feed and water, repairs to make that would keep him occupied while Sara and Betty had a meeting of the minds.

In the living room of the Sandler house, the tension between mother and daughter grew. Sara glared at her mother, convinced she was in the right. "Mom, you have to admit, Mandy has been nothing but trouble since she came here to live."

"Sara Elizabeth Sandler! What kind of compassion is that? After everything this community has been through, how can you still be so self-centered?"

Surprised by her mother's anger, Sara blinked rapidly. What had she done? Mandy was the one who was pregnant.

"Your cousin is going through a horrible time right now. No matter what they decide to do, Mandy will suffer."

Remaining silent, Sara felt certain Mandy deserved every bit of what was coming. You do the deed, you pay the price, as far as she was concerned. Why did her mother think Mandy had any redeeming qualitites? "Mom, I'm sorry she's hurting—I'm sorry she's pregnant. It's not my fault, okay? All I've ever tried to do is the right thing. Why should I be punished because my cousin messed up her life? This is my last year at home. Next year I'll go to college. Is it so wrong for me to want my senior year to be special? All Mandy has done is cause trouble!"

"I know it's your senior year; that's all we've heard since June. Would it have been so terrible for you to have shared this year with Mandy?"

Refusing to answer, Sara glanced at her watch. "I promised Sister Harrop I'd help clean up some of the houses that were hit hard in our ward. I'd better go," she said, changing the subject. "Is it all right if I take the truck?"

Betty gazed long and hard at Sara. "Sure, take the truck. That's all you care about, your own little world. Nothing else matters!"

"Mom!" Sara complained.

"You'd better leave for a bit—that'll give me time to cool down. Just don't make any plans tonight; you and I are going to spend it together. Obviously I've neglected to teach you what it means to be Christlike." Turning, Betty left the living room, her daughter's stunned gape following her from the room.

* * *

"Are you doing okay, Sabrina?" Sue asked, glancing over the front seat of the Dodge Durango.

"I'm fine, Mom," came the weary reply.

Sue realized she was crowding Sabrina, but couldn't resist keeping a close eye on her youngest child. They had been through too much lately to take anything for granted. "We're almost to Ogden. This close to noon, why don't we stop somewhere to eat?"

"I'd rather see Kate and my new niece first," Sabrina said stubbornly.

"Honey, you know with these shots of insulin, you're on a tight schedule. Let's eat lunch first."

"Your mother's right," Greg sided as he skillfully drove down the freeway. It was a welcome change to drive on roads that were for the most part smooth and intact. "We'll grab a quick bite. That way we won't have to worry about your blood sugar level or my empty stomach."

Sue turned from Sabrina and smiled at her husband. "It's settled then. To keep your father in a friendly mood, we'll feed him. Besides, once we get to the McKay-Dee Hospital, I'll want to stay for as long as they'll let us. I can't wait to hold Colleen."

"They may not let you," Greg cautioned. "You heard what Mike said this morning. To control the risk of infectious disease, Colleen's visitors are limited to immediate family."

"Well, I'm her grandmother!"

"They wouldn't let Mike's mother hold her the other day."

Sue smiled. "But I'm Kate's mother."

Greg shared a dubious look with Sabrina in the rearview mirror. Father and daughter were in agreement that this could be an interesting visit.

* * *

Kate hummed a lullaby as she gently rubbed Colleen's tiny stomach. Following the nurse's instructions, Kate made sure the oxygen tubes hooked to Colleen were secure, smiling when she felt her daughter squirm, convinced that Colleen was responding to her soft touch. In the past couple of days, Colleen had started breathing more evenly, her heart rate and blood oxygen levels steadying after a session of what Kate called "mother-daughter bonding." Kate loved the semi-private time she could spend with her daughter, even if it was only for a short while. She continued to stroke the feather-soft skin on Colleen's stomach, longing for a time when she could cuddle her baby to her heart's content. "I love you so much," she said in a hushed voice. "Keep growing. I want to take you home with me soon."

* * *

"This is so unfair!" Sue exclaimed. "I've waited so long for this grandchild, and now I can't even hold her!"

Mike tried to keep a straight face as Greg dramatically pantomimed Sue's distress behind her back. "Colleen wasn't even supposed to be born until December. Right now, we have to keep her isolated, protected like she would've been inside of Kate."

"You get to hold her," Sue protested.

"Not for very long and it seems like every nurse in the neonatal nursery is watching me when I do. You'll get to hold her too, eventually. We're lucky they've consented to let you in to see her. Even then, you'll have to scrub up and wear a special gown and mask," Mike explained.

"Can I see her?" Sabrina asked hopefully.

"They'll only let two in at a time," Mike replied.

Greg sighed heavily. He had looked forward to seeing his grand-daughter, but knew how excited Sue and Sabrina had been to come today. "Let these two go," he said.

"Maybe later today, they'll let you in," Mike consoled his father-in-law. "Too much stimulation isn't good for Colleen right now. We have to space things out." He glanced at his watch. "Kate's been with her for quite a while. She should be coming out soon."

As if on cue, an exhausted Kate walked down the hall. Recently released from the hospital, she was dressed in a pair of loose-fitting jeans and a comfortable sweatshirt. She accepted a hug from her parents, then focused on Sabrina. "I'm glad you're all right," she said, embracing her younger sister.

"Same here," Sabrina returned when Kate pulled away. "How's that niece of mine doing?"

"She's a fighter," Kate laughed. "She already has quite the person-ality. I suspect Colleen will be a very independent young lady."

"Oh?" Sue said, enjoying this tidbit of information. For a long time she had wished for Kate to have a child like herself—stubborn, independent, and extremely impatient.

"Colleen hates bright lights and loud noises." Kate frowned. "She especially hates being poked for all of the tests they've had to run on her. I hate that part too."

"It won't be forever," Sue reminded her daughter.

"No, it just seems like it now," Kate replied. "I'm grateful she's alive, but it's so hard, knowing it'll be weeks before we can take her home." She attempted a smile. "The good news is, she's having a better time of it today, but she needs to rest for a while. We can come back in a couple of hours for your visit with her. While she's sleeping, let's get something to eat. I'm starved," she suggested.

Sabrina shared an indignant look with her parents. "I told you we should've waited."

Shaking her head, Sue motioned for Kate and Mike to follow them to the elevator.

# Chapter 20

"You think I should consider giving this baby up for adoption?" Mandy asked her mother.

"Mandy, it breaks my heart to even suggest it, but we've got to be realistic. We have to think about what is best for this baby," Lorena replied.

Her stomach churning, Mandy moved to her bedroom window and stared outside. She focused on an old tree in the yard, one whose leaves had already fallen. It looked as empty as she felt inside.

"Our church teaches that when an unmarried young woman like yourself gets pregnant, it is usually in the best interest of the baby and the unwed mother to give that baby up for adoption. I've already talked to our bishop and he recommended that we set up an appointment with the local LDS Social Services. That way your baby can be adopted by an LDS couple and raised in the Church."

"You talked to the bishop?" Mandy asked, whirling around to face her mother. "Why? This isn't any of his business!"

"Mandy, whether you realize it or not, our bishop is entitled to know what is going on. In fact, he wants to meet with you in the near future."

"So he can call me to repentance?" Mandy said bitterly. "Like that's going to change anything!"

"I think talking to him will make you feel better. He can help you—"

"I know—why don't we get a t-shirt printed up, one that says, 'Yo, I'm a pregnant teenager'?! I'll wear it everyday, and that way everyone can know what a horrible person I am!"

Lorena bit her lip, struggling for control. The only thing holding her back was the pain in her daughter's voice. "You are not a horrible person, and we aren't trying to let the whole world know what's going on! You said you wanted our help, now give us a chance," she pleaded.

"Well, what if I want to keep my baby? What if Blade decides he wants to marry me?"

Shuddering at the thought, Lorena sat in the wooden chair next to the desk in Mandy's bedroom.

"It could happen, you know. Whatever we decide, Blade has a right to know . . . it is his baby, too."

"Mandy, do you honestly think Blade wants to be a father? He isn't the type of man to take care of anyone but himself."

Angered by that accusation, Mandy turned her back to her mother and glared at the tree in the yard. "You've never been willing to give him a chance. You only see what you want to see."

"I don't think I'm the only one guilty of that," Lorena replied. Rising, she gazed longingly at Mandy's back. She had thought this crisis was bringing them closer together, but the decisions that had to be made were tearing them apart. "Think about what I've said, you know in your heart what the right choice is. Realize this isn't easy for any of us," she said, leaving the room before Mandy could see the tears streaming down her face.

\* \* \*

"She wants to talk to that degenerate?!" Eric exclaimed, outraged at the thought of his daughter having anything else to do with Blade.

"Eric, legally we have to let him know Mandy's pregnant. Then when he expresses a total lack of interest, which we both know will happen, he has no further claim to Mandy's baby. It's part of the Utah code, I checked it out." Lorena sat down on their bed and watched as her husband paced the carpeted floor of the master bedroom. "I wish there was another way to handle this. Mandy will be so devastated when Blade reacts the way we know he will."

"What if I deal with Blade?! That way I can get a few points across that he has coming and we leave Mandy out of it!"

Lorena prayed for patience; Eric was not making any of this easy. "Mandy wants to talk to him herself. I know Blade will hurt her—more than he already has—but I think Mandy needs to see his reaction for herself. Now that the shock of her pregnancy is wearing off, she's entertaining fantasies of marrying Blade and raising her baby."

"It'll never happen!" Eric fumed. "Mandy will never marry that thing with the hair . . . with the earrings . . . if I have to—"

"If you have to what?" Lorena interrupted. "Eric, if you touch that boy, you'll make an unbearable situation worse."

Muttering under his breath, Eric stormed into the bathroom connected to their bedroom and closed the door firmly behind him.

Lorena held her aching head in her hands. She wasn't sure how much more of this she could take. Unfortunately, it would probably get worse before it got better. Eric was a walking time bomb, Mandy alternated between tears and angry outbursts, and as for herself, she felt like she was on the verge of an emotional collapse. Mandy's younger sister already knew something was very wrong. The twelve-year-old had been asking far too many questions since they had brought Mandy home. Lorena knew she would have to level with her soon, but wanted a chance to absorb the grief in her heart first. Her sons were young enough to miss the fireworks observed by their twelve-year-old sister. At six and four, they were content to throw their toys all over the place, making a shambles out of their normally clean house.

Currently, Lorena couldn't cope with housework, her job as a bank teller, or anything that vaguely resembled normal life. Every time she bumped into a friend or an acquaintance, she felt certain they could see the stress she was under as the pain in her heart echoed in her face. Eventually her friends, co-workers, and neighbors would catch on that something was amiss in the Hopkins household. Soon the entire ward would be buzzing with the scandal. She was certain she would be blamed, condemned for not teaching Mandy the hazards of immorality. These people would never realize that she had talked to Mandy several times concerning that very subject. She had prayed over her oldest daughter continuously since Mandy had started hanging around with a rough crowd. Leaving Mandy in Idaho was the hardest thing she had ever done, but she had gone through with it in an effort to keep her daughter from what they were now facing. She had tried everything she could think of to prevent this from happening, but knew people would give her full credit for what had taken place.

As she contemplated the reaction of the people around them to Mandy's plight, Lorena stared at the door her husband had closed between them. Feeling betrayed by Eric's behavior, needing his strength instead of his anger, Lorena retreated to her knees and poured her heart out to her Father in Heaven. Several minutes later when Eric had cooled down enough to exit the bathroom, that is how he found her, beside the bed on her knees, her face buried in her hands. His wife's quiet sobs cracked through the rage in his heart. Penitent, he moved across the carpeted floor to gather Lorena up in his arms when she finished her prayer.

* * *

Mandy was apprehensive about meeting with Blade, something she would never reveal to either parent. It had surprised her when they had granted permission to arrange a rendezvous with her former boyfriend. She was uncertain how Blade would react but felt strongly that he had to be told about his potential fatherhood. She had called Blade last night, setting up a time when she could talk to him. He had seemed distant on the phone, but had agreed to see her, curious to see what she wanted. Deciding it would be best to deliver this news in person, she had refused to tell him over the phone. Now here she was, on her way to his house, with her parents as an escort.

Earlier, her parents had agreed to wait in the car while Mandy shared her news with Blade. Both had offered to come in with her, but honoring Mandy's wishes, they had decided to give her the space she desired. They expected Blade to break their daughter's heart, but they could see no other way to handle the situation.

"Well, here we are," Eric announced as he parked the sedan against the curb in front of the small house Blade shared with his mother. "Are you sure you don't want us to go in with you?"

"No, I'll take care of this myself," Mandy said, opening the car door on her side.

"We'll be right here if you need anything," Lorena offered.

Nodding, Mandy climbed out of the car and walked up the broken sidewalk to the front porch. As she stepped up to the door, a cat hiding in the shadows hissed and brushed past her feet. A shudder went through her and she wondered if her reception from Blade would be any better. Gathering her courage, she pushed the doorbell. Then, remembering it didn't work, she knocked loudly on the peeling wooden door.

"Yeah? What do you want?" Blade's mother asked, opening the door.

Mandy had never been overly fond of Blade's mother. Divorced three times that Mandy knew of, the slender blonde was a chain-smoker who spent most of her time drunk. With a cigarette in hand, Blade's mother looked amused when Mandy averted her face from a puff of rancid smoke. Thinking of her baby and certain she had heard somewhere that secondhand smoke could be harmful to unborn children, Mandy tried to avoid breathing the exhaled smoke and asked to see Blade.

"Blade, you got company," his mother called out, moving away from the door.

After what seemed like forever, Blade made an appearance at the door. He was dressed in tight jeans and a torn tank top; the smell of smoke hung heavily about him. Despite his ragged look, Mandy's heart leaped with excitement. "Oh, yeah, I forgot you were coming," he said, stepping out onto the porch. He gazed at her broken arm and laughed. "Did your parents do that to you for misbehaving?"

"No. I fell during that earthquake in Idaho."

"Oh, yeah. I forgot about that. What was it like?"

"Scary—kind of like now," she added.

Blade scowled at her. "What's up?"

"We need to talk," Mandy began.

"We need to do more than that," he returned, leering at her.

"Blade, I'm serious. This is important."

"Are you back for good? Is that what you came to tell me?"

"Can we go somewhere private?"

"Sure," Blade said eagerly, pulling the door shut behind him. "Let's go for a ride on my bike," he offered, pointing to his motorcycle in the driveway.

"No, Blade. My parents are waiting in the car . . . could we just go into your backyard?"

Blade glanced up, glaring at the sedan parked in front of his house. Why had Mandy brought her parents, or was it the other way around? Certain he didn't like what he was seeing, he pointed around the side of the house. "The backyard it is. That way they can't see anything," he added, grinning wickedly. He jumped off the porch and led the way behind the dilapidated house. As they walked into the backyard, Blade laughed. "Well, here we are. I'd offer you a seat, but as you can see, we don't have much in the way of yard furniture."

Mandy glanced around, appalled by the cans, beer bottles, and trash that littered the browning grass. Her gaze settled on a weathered picnic table near a fruit tree. "Let's sit over there," she suggested.

"Okay, but we might both end up with splinters," he teased. "The grass would be softer for our . . . reunion."

Ignoring Blade's less than subtle hint, Mandy carefully made her way to the wooden table and after brushing off a pile of dirty leaves, sat down. Blade sat across from her, not caring that he was resting on a similar pile of dirty leaves.

"What's goin' on?"

"Blade . . . this is so hard," she stammered.

"Did you miss me?"

"Of course I missed you," she returned. "I tried to call you several times but you were never home and you never returned—"

"You don't act excited to see me," Blade said, changing the subject. "You haven't even given me a kiss yet!"

"A kiss is what started all of this," Mandy replied, shaking her head. "Blade, I'm pregnant!" she blurted out.

Blade stared at her, then laughed. "You found yourself a boyfriend in Idaho," he guessed.

"It's yours!"

"What?"

"*We're* going to have a baby."

"Are you sure?" he asked, his mood sobering.

"Positive."

Rising, Blade ran a hand through his wild hair. "I can't believe this! How do you know it's mine?"

"You're the only one I've been with," she replied, bursting into tears.

"Man!" he said kicking at several bottles, shattering two of them into sharp shards of glass. "Way to make my day!"

Mandy took a deep breath, trying to calm down.

Walking back to the table, Blade glowered at her. "Obviously your parents know. That's why they brought you, right?! I mean before you left for Idaho, they wouldn't give you permission to breathe the same air that I do! They think I'm some sort of freak! Now—let me guess . . . they want me to make this right?!"

Discouraged by his reaction, Mandy lowered her head.

"What am I supposed to do? I mean, one time, that's all. One lousy time . . . you wouldn't even let me near you after that." Blade slapped the table hard, then went back to kicking cans and bottles around the yard. After several minutes, he stopped and approached the table again. "Why didn't you tell me first . . . before you told your parents? We could've worked this out."

Mandy smiled with relief. Blade had been shocked by the news, but he would come through. She knew they could be happy together.

"You could've aborted it before anyone even knew there was a problem!" he accused.

Her hopes dashing against the bitterness in Blade's voice, Mandy stared at him. "You would've asked me to have an abortion?"

"It's the only smart thing to do!" he responded.

"Blade, I'm four months along!" she said tearfully.

"It's not too late. I've known of other girls who've had it done then."

Disgusted, Mandy looked away, wondering if Blade had fathered other children who would never have a chance to live. The thought made her sick inside.

"I'll pay for it. Tell your parents it's your life and they can't stop you from—"

Tears giving way to rage, Mandy stood defiantly. "I will never have an abortion! There is a living person growing inside of me— you're asking me to murder our child!"

"Well, what do you expect me to do about this mess you've gotten me into?!"

"My parents were right," Mandy exclaimed.

"Oh?" he challenged.

"The most important person in the world to you is you! You used me . . . I didn't mean anything to you . . . just like our baby means nothing to you!" Turning, she walked away.

"Mandy . . . look . . . I've saved up some money. I'll pay for an abortion, but I won't pay for that kid! You bring it into this world, you're on your own! I want nothing to do with it!"

Whirling around, her eyes blazing, Mandy faced Blade. "Don't worry, I'll never ask you for anything again!" With that she walked out of the yard and out of Blade's life.

# Chapter 21

In the two weeks that had passed since the earthquake, most of the power, gas, and phone lines had been restored in Blaketown. Several houses were still being repaired and it would take time for the damaged streets to be fixed, but improvements were being made at a faster rate than most had thought possible. A few restaurants and stores were opening for business again, while others continued to reconstruct their buildings. School was scheduled to start again the coming Monday, signaling that life was slowly returning to normal.

That Saturday, Bev, Karen, Terri, and Sabrina got together to catch each other up-to-date on the latest happenings in their lives. Meeting at Bev's house, they spent the afternoon organizing the large video library in the family room, something Gina had been unable to tackle because of Drake's injuries. Drake was improving, but required a large share of his mother's time now that he was out of the hospital.

When they had restored the family room to its former state, the four girls cooked up a batch of cookies and popcorn, then watched a video that had caught Bev's eye, *The Princess Bride*. After the movie, Karen drove Sabrina and Terri home, then headed to the house she now shared with her mother—her grandmother's home. Parking the car in the driveway, she shunned the empty space where the log shed had once stood and entered the house through the back door.

"Hi, Mom," she said walking into the kitchen.

Edie turned from the casserole she was making for dinner. "You're home early. I thought you'd be spending most of the evening with your friends."

Karen moved beside her mother and eyed the tuna casserole. It didn't look as enticing as Grandma's, but it would suffice for supper. "Sabrina had to get home—she and her family are heading back down to Ogden tonight. It's her father's birthday tomorrow and he wanted to go see his granddaughter. It sounded like they'll spend the rest of the weekend in Ogden. Bev has to babysit for her parents tonight, and Terri promised her mom she'd help her get caught up on laundry." Karen didn't add the fourth reason she was home; she didn't want her mother spending tonight alone. Brett was out of town visiting his parents for the weekend. Edie had been invited to go with him, but at the last minute, had decided on a quiet weekend at home.

"No date for the evening?" Edie teased as she cut several pieces of cheese to spread over the top of the casserole.

Choosing to remain silent, Karen retreated to the fridge for a glass of water. A boiling order was still in effect for the community. Keeping the boiled water cold was the only way Karen or Edie could tolerate the bland-tasting liquid.

"Karen?" Edie pressed.

"A date in this town?!" Karen asked, filling her glass full of water. "Get real!"

"There are several young men who would love to ask you out, if you'd give them a chance," Edie replied, adding a final piece of cheese. Reaching for the tinfoil, she covered the top of the casserole.

"Like who?" Karen asked, moving to the sink.

"Like Bill Proctor," Edie responded as she placed the casserole dish inside the oven.

Karen nearly choked on the water she had just swallowed. Coughing into the sink, she scowled at her mother. "Bill?" she repeated when she could speak.

"What's wrong with Bill?"

"He's so neanderthal!"

Edie adjusted the oven heat, then turned to look at her daughter. "Neanderthal?"

"He's about as smart as a fence post and he has those thick, bushy eyebrows that cover most of his forehead."

"Okay, I get the point. What about Gerald Reynolds? He called again this afternoon."

"I don't believe you," Karen interrupted. "I could've spent the weekend with Bev. You don't have to stay here and babysit me. Why didn't you go home with Brett? He seemed so disappointed."

"I know. Maybe I should've gone . . . it's hard to explain."

"Try. I'm not going anywhere tonight," Karen coaxed.

Turning, Edie gave her daughter a pained look.

"Why are you dragging your feet? Brett finished the temple prep class with you. You said yourself his testimony is growing by leaps and bounds. You guys are crazy about each other. What's holding you back?"

"Karen—his parents will want to know all about me."

"So?"

"Everything . . . do you really think they'll welcome me with open arms when they learn I was in prison? I can't keep something like that from them."

Karen returned her mother's troubled stare. "Mom, you're not the same person you were then. You were dating such a loser . . . you didn't know he had planned to rob that convenience store. As far as I'm concerned, you should never have gone to prison."

"If I hadn't—maybe I wouldn't have gotten my act together. Maybe the time I spent there opened my eyes to how I was wasting my life."

"Mom, we've already agreed that we can't change the past. You said yourself that we need to focus on the future. Your future is with Brett. He loves you so much. I'm sure his parents will too—if you'll give them that chance."

The oven timer signaled that dinner was ready. "Should we go see if it's edible?" Edie invited, relieved to change the subject.

"If it's not, we can always order pizza. They deliver now, you know," Karen said, rising to her feet. "We almost ordered one today at Bev's house to try it out."

"Your faith in me is overwhelming," Edie said, standing. "I think from now on we'll take turns. You'll make fun of my cooking tonight—tomorrow I'll make fun of yours."

"And whenever it gets too bad, we order out."

"Agreed," Edie said, moving back into the kitchen to turn off the timer. Sniffing the acrid odor radiating from the oven, she quickly grabbed two potholders and removed the casserole dish from the oven. Dismayed by the blackened color, she set it on the stove.

"That looks interesting," Karen commented. "What did you set the temperature on?"

"Broil," Edie moaned. "I meant to set it on bake. Now what?"

"Pepperoni or Canadian bacon?" Karen giggled.

Edie gave her daughter an indignant look. "Sausage," she requested.

Nodding, Karen grabbed the phone book and reached for the phone. After she placed the order, the doorbell rang. "That was quick," she joked, hurrying to the front door. She opened it, staring at Brett and a couple she guessed had to be his parents. "Brett?"

"Hi, Karen. I'd like you to meet my parents. Mom, Dad, this is your future granddaughter."

Lifting an eyebrow, Karen glanced back at her mother who looked as stunned as she felt.

* * *

Diane Randall handed Edie the final plate to be placed into the dishwasher, then watched as the slender blonde latched the front of the machine. Diane had to admit, her son had fallen in love with a lovely woman. "There, they can wash while we visit," Diane said brightly.

"Yeah," Edie replied, still very self-conscious around Brett's mother. After Brett's surprise appearance, another pizza had been ordered. Edie had invited everyone into the living room where an awkward conversation had taken place as they had waited for the pizza to be delivered. When it finally arrived, it had been consumed in silence as they had all searched for a way to ease the discomfort everyone was feeling. Gathering the plates, Brett had slipped into the kitchen with Edie to apologize for what he felt had been an intrusion.

"I'm sorry, Edie. My parents wanted to meet you. I've told them so much about you—"

"That's what worries me," Edie had retorted.

"It was all good," he had stressed. "When I told them you weren't up to the trip right now, they decided to fly down. I picked them up at the Pocatello airport this morning. They're here because they care and they want to get better acquainted with you."

"Do they know about my past?"

Finally comprehending Edie's discomfort, Brett had pulled her close. "Edie, none of that matters. It doesn't matter to me—why should it matter to them?"

"You haven't told them," she had guessed.

"Do you want me to?"

Shaking her head, Edie had pulled away. "No, it should come from me."

"Edie, you don't have to—"

"I don't want them hearing it from some other source. If I'm going to be part of this family, they need to know the truth about me."

Brett had smiled warmly. "The truth about you is that you are a gorgeous woman with a heart of pure gold." He had kissed her soundly before leading her back into the living room.

After a few more minutes of polite conversation, Brett's father had asked for a tour of Blaketown. Karen had eagerly left with Brett and his father, leaving Edie alone with Diane. Edie would never know that it had been Karen's idea, that her daughter had conspired with Brett's father to give Edie a chance to spend some time alone with her future mother-in-law.

Diane had been aware of the scheme, but had welcomed the chance to put Edie more at ease. Now that the dishes were loaded, she wondered how to break the ice with her son's intended wife. "Edie, Brett tells me that you've been learning how to crochet."

Edie nodded. "Mom was teaching me . . . she was so gifted with that sort of thing." She frowned as a sharp inner pain pierced through her heart.

Sensing Edie's distress, Diane mentally kicked herself for touching on a sensitive subject. She tried to atone by offering words of consolation. "You must miss your mother very much. Brett said she was a wonderful woman."

Unable to reply, Edie sat down at the kitchen table.

Following her lead, Diane sat down beside her. "My mother passed away when I was in college," she shared, smiling sadly. "I don't think it's ever an easy thing."

"You were quite young when she died," Edie commented. She gazed at Brett's mother. She now knew where he had inherited his warm, blue eyes. Brett's personality was more like his father's—reserved, quiet, just the opposite of Diane's. Edie had already learned that Diane was very outgoing, and that she possessed a fun sense of humor. Earlier Diane had made several valiant attempts to make everyone laugh, failing only because of the awkwardness of the situation.

"I was—young and foolish. Before my mother died, I had started running around with the wrong crowd—after her death, I slipped even further down that trail. I did things I'm not very proud of. Don't tell Brett, but I almost landed in jail one night."

Edie stared at the woman sitting beside her.

Blushing, Diane had no idea why she was sharing this story from her past with a young woman she was trying to impress. "You probably think I'm terrible," she sputtered, embarrassed.

"No, I don't," Edie said, relaxing. "If you don't mind me asking, how did you almost end up in jail?"

"I was at a bar with a group of rowdy friends. We got into a fight with some other drunks . . . it got pretty wild before the police arrived. Most of my friends were arrested. I happened to sneak out the back before they blocked the door." She shook her head. "The things we do when we're not thinking clearly."

"I can relate," Edie said. In a rush, she shared some of her own experiences with Diane. When she finished, it felt like a tremendous weight had been lifted from her shoulders. "Now you must think I'm terrible," she said, echoing Diane's earlier fear.

Diane gazed steadily at Edie. "Far from it. I think you're one of the most courageous young women I've ever met. You've overcome tremendous odds—that says a lot for what kind of person you really are." She smiled. "And I'll never be able to thank you enough for helping Brett find his way back into the Church." Tearing up, she patted Edie's arm. "You're just the kind of woman I hoped he'd find. You two complement each other. I noticed that tonight. You belong together."

"Then you're okay if Brett and I decide to get married?" Edie asked.

"Better than okay. I say, let's set a date and get things planned!"

Edie flushed a deep red color. "Brett hasn't asked me yet."

"Well, if he doesn't, I will!" Diane quipped, laughing. "If he lets you get away, I'll never forgive him."

\* \* \*

It was late when James and Gina returned home. They entered the darkened house through the side door and carefully made their way through the kitchen. Upon entering the living room, they discovered that Bev had fallen asleep on the couch with her younger brothers, one tucked under each arm, the TV still blaring away.

"Where's your camera?" James whispered.

"On the dresser in our bedroom," Gina replied. Amused, she watched as James tiptoed down the hall to retrieve the camera. She couldn't believe the difference in him the past couple of weeks. Since the earthquake, he had faithfully adhered to his promise to stay sober. To prove his sincerity, he had joined a local AA organization, something that had strengthened his resolve. Now whenever the urge to drink afflicted, he called one of the new friends he had made at Alcoholics Anonymous. So far, they had been able to talk him through those difficult times. Eventually, he hoped to shake off the tight grip of alcoholism. The effort he was making had convinced Gina that he was serious about regaining control of his life and she was doing all that she could to encourage him.

It had astonished her last week when Bev had asked James if she could invite the LDS missionaries to visit their home. Bev had emphasized that no one else had to listen to the discussions, but that she was determined to learn more about this church before she became a member. Instead of the anticipated scene, James had calmly given permission, stating that he might sit in on some of the discussions himself. Since Adele's funeral, James had softened toward the LDS Church. The emphasis placed on families appealed to him and he wanted to learn more. He was especially intrigued by the concept of eternal families, an interest Gina shared with him. She knew she could live this way forever, surrounded by James and their children.

"Found it," James whispered as he walked into the living room with the camera. "I can't miss this shot. It's priceless. I think I'll have it enlarged and hang it right over the couch." Concentrating, he aimed the camera and pushed a button to release the shutter. Bev's eyes opened when the flash went off. Startled, she jumped. Her brothers were too sound asleep to notice and continued to snooze.

"What the heck?" Bev exclaimed, relaxing when she saw that it was her parents. "What are you guys doing?" she asked, untangling herself from her brothers.

"Capturing a Kodak moment," James replied.

"Oh, that's great. I'll bet I look beautiful."

James handed the camera to Gina and gave his daughter a hug. "You are beautiful! Always remember that!" He pulled back from Bev, lifted Drake up into his arms, then carried his sleeping son upstairs.

Bev continued to stare after him. "What did you do with my real father?"

Gina set the camera on the TV. "That is your real father, Bev," she said, shutting off the television set. "And the man I fell in love with." Turning she carried Jake up the stairs, leaving Bev to speculate about the changes that were taking place in their family.

# Chapter 22

"Sandi! It's so good to hear from you!" Kate exclaimed, gripping the phone. "How's Salt Lake these days? How are you and Ian doing?" she asked, picturing her petite friend, Sandi Kearns Campbell. Close friends since high school, Kate and Sandi still kept in touch, especially when something exciting happened in their lives.

"Great!" Sandi replied. "Never better!"

"You sound like you have news to share," Kate encouraged.

"I do, but first I want to let you know how sorry I am about everything that's happened with you and your family! I didn't know you had been hurt in that earthquake until last night. Mom called and told me. I guess our former mutual leader got a letter from your mother. She shared the news with my mother."

Kate sighed. She hadn't even thought about letting people know that Colleen had been born.

"How are you doing?"

"Better. Colleen is starting to gain a little weight back. It was touch and go right at first, but she's holding her own now. It'll be several weeks before we can take her home, but she's improving."

"That's great," Sandi replied.

"Now tell me your good news," Kate encouraged.

"We're getting a baby too!"

Kate grinned. "That's wonderful!"

"We've been on a waiting list for so long, we'd almost given up hope. Now Kaitlin will have a little brother or sister."

"I'll bet she's excited," Kate replied, picturing the five-year-old girl Sandi had named after her. Kate had introduced Sandi to Ian, something the couple would always be grateful for.

"She's not the only one," Sandi informed her. "I can hardly wait, and you should hear Ian."

"Yeah, let her hear Ian," Kate overheard Ian say in the background.

"Kate, this husband of mine wants to talk to you," Sandi bubbled.

"Put him on," Kate replied.

Ian pushed his wheelchair closer to his wife and reached for the phone. "Kate, can you believe it?! We're getting a baby!"

"That's great!" Kate enthused.

"We were so lucky to have Kaitlin—Sandi's pregnancy was a definite miracle! Now this! I feel strongly that Kaitlin will be getting a little sister."

Tears pricked at the back of Kate's eyes. Ian had been in a car accident several years ago and was paralyzed from the waist down. He had been told that the chances of becoming a father were remote. It hadn't mattered to Sandi who had made it clear that she loved Ian regardless of the challenges he faced. Married in the Provo temple, they had both been so happy when they had beaten the odds and little Kaitlin had been born. Since that time, Sandi had been unable to conceive and they had decided to adopt, desiring a younger sibling for their daughter to grow up with.

". . . we met the girl . . . our baby's mother . . . two days ago," Ian shared, drawing Kate back to their conversation. He paused, fighting the thickness in his throat. "She'll never know how much this precious gift means to us." He handed the phone back to his wife.

Tears racing down her own face, Sandi struggled for control. "Kate—there are no words to describe what we're feeling. Gratitude, joy, and heartache for that sweet girl. She looked so scared when we met. My heart went out to her. I can't imagine how difficult this is for her."

Her own eyes misting, Kate understood Sandi's excited joy. She and Mike had discussed adoption before she had found out that she was expecting last spring. "I'm sure she must know that you and Ian will give that baby a wonderful home."

"I still can't believe she picked us," Sandi replied.

"I can," Kate stated, knowing what a wonderful mother Sandi was, not to mention the way Ian lovingly spoiled Kaitlin.

"It breaks my heart when I think about the abortions that destroy precious lives. There are so many couples like us who would love to give these babies a wonderful home."

Silently agreeing, Kate shifted around in the chair in the waiting room of the hospital.

"But enough about me, how are you feeling?"

"Truth?" Kate asked, smiling.

"You bet! I want to hear it all."

"It's been interesting," Kate admitted. "I don't even want to think about how awful it was the night Colleen was born. Nothing could have prepared me for that experience." She told Sandi about Colleen's delivery and their emergency flight to Pocatello.

"I didn't realize how blessed I was when Kaitlin was born. They gave me an epidural—I didn't feel much of anything."

"I guess the important thing is we did both get through it."

"I'll bet Colleen is cute," Sandi replied.

"She is. She doesn't have much hair yet, but it looks like it will be dark."

Sandi grinned. "She'll have her daddy's thick brown hair. I know it's too early to tell, but if she has your beautiful green eyes, she'll be a knock-out. You guys will have your hands full keeping the boys away from her."

"We'll cross that bridge when we come to it," Kate responded.

"How's Colleen doing?"

"She's holding her own right now. We have to take it on a day-to-day basis. One day she improves. Then one or two minor complications set in and we're back to square one."

"She will be all right, though, in time?" Sandi pressed.

"Yeah, things could be a lot worse. I've seen other preemies since our stay here. Colleen is doing remarkably well compared to some of them."

"You'll get through this. I've seen you survive other things with flying colors."

Kate smiled. "Yes, you have," she said, relaxing as the two friends reminisced about past adventures they had shared.

\* \* \*

Doris handed Kate the tiny pink dress and small, pink fuzzy teddy bear she had purchased for baby Colleen on her way to Ogden.

"These are so cute," Kate exclaimed, looking them over. "I can't wait until we can start dressing Colleen in some of the outfits people have been giving her.

"It's a lot of fun," Doris replied, sitting down in a comfortable chair in the hospital waiting room. "You've told me all about Colleen. How are you doing?"

Struggling, Kate bit her bottom lip.

"That well, huh?" Doris said, giving Kate a compassionate look.

"Sorry, usually I'm okay. This is just so hard. No one understands."

"They probably won't unless they've been there," Doris said, offering a warm smile. "You're under a lot of stress. You don't know from one minute until the next what's going to happen and you're practically living here at the hospital. That has to be difficult."

Kate nodded. "Mike, Mom, Mike's mother, our fathers—everyone's been great. But they don't know how this is tearing my heart out. Every day I get to watch other couples take their healthy babies home—it drives me crazy. Colleen keeps improving, but we've had a few setbacks. Her bilirubin shot up—she's jaundiced. Yesterday she started running a fever." Teary-eyed, she gazed at Doris. "Why did it have to happen like this?"

Doris shrugged. "Sometimes there are no easy answers. I do have a temporary solution—why don't you come with me for a bite of lunch? I think you could use a break from this place, from all of the buzzers, alarms, and commotion." Reaching for Kate's jacket, she refused to take "no" for an answer and guided the young woman down the hall toward the elevator.

* * *

"The first time Colleen spit up all over Mike, I thought he was going to turn inside out," Kate laughed.

Doris smiled, relieved. "It's so good to finally hear you laugh. You had me worried back at the hospital."

"I'm sorry I sounded so down."

"You have nothing to be sorry about. I'm just glad I came up to see you today."

Kate ate another bite of her taco salad, then asked, "Wasn't school supposed to start today?"

"It was, but they're still working on the furnace at the high school. The other Blaketown schools are up and running, just not ours. They're hoping to have things fixed by tonight." Doris took a sip of buttermilk, then set her glass down on the table. "That reminds me, what have you decided to do about teaching?"

"I'm through—for this year, anyway. We'll see how things look next fall. Mike said he already talked to Cleo about it for me; he knew I was worried."

Doris pictured the tall, skinny principal and shuddered.

"Cleo was actually pretty good about the whole thing. I think she's mellowing."

"She must be," Doris replied. "What will she do with your classes?"

Kate finished chewing another bite of salad, then drank a sip of ice water to finish washing it down. "It sounded like she was pulling in a substitute full-time. The woman Cleo has in mind actually has a teaching degree—her youngest started school this year, so she'd like to start teaching again."

"See, things have a way of working out," Doris said brightly.

"Sometimes," Kate agreed.

"That reminds me, I never had the chance to tell you that one of our students has been going through quite an ordeal."

"Who?" Kate asked as several of her former students came to mind.

"Mandy Hopkins."

Kate pictured the girl who had moved to Blaketown from Salt Lake. "She's been awfully sick. Is it something serious?"

"You might say that. She's pregnant."

Staring at Doris, Kate set her glass down on the table. "You're kidding?!"

"I wish I was. I stumbled onto her secret that infamous Saturday when Blaketown got whammied."

"That's a day—I should say—night, none of us will forget," Kate commented.

"True," Doris said. She told Kate what she had seen that day in the drugstore when Mandy had purchased the pregnancy kit.

"She told you it was for her aunt?"

"Yes. I knew that was a long shot—Betty is older than I am."

"That poor girl," Kate said quietly. "It's hard enough when it's something you want, when you have all of the support in the world. She must be so scared."

"From what her aunt tells me, she's terrified."

"You talked to Betty Sandler?"

Doris nodded. "A couple of days ago. I ran into her at the grocery store and asked how Mandy was doing. She told me they were working things out. Her parents were understandably shocked and upset, but now they're trying to be supportive."

"What will Mandy do with her baby?" Kate asked, curious.

"She's giving it up for adoption. Betty said that Mandy's already met with the couple who will be adopting her baby. LDS Social Services is handling the arrangement."

"So her baby will be going to an LDS home. That's good."

"Yes, it is. Betty told me there's quite a story behind that. Naturally, Mandy was struggling with the concept of giving up her baby. The baby's father didn't want anything to do with Mandy or her baby, and Mandy's parents felt it would be best to give the child up for adoption. Betty said that Mandy finally prayed about it; probably the first prayer that girl has offered in years. That night she had a dream—she saw a couple she knew would love her child as much as she did. Then a few days later, she saw that same couple's picture in a file she was shown."

"This is quite a story," Kate said.

"There's more," Doris continued. "It seems that in Mandy's dream, the couple she saw—the husband was in a wheelchair."

Kate stared at Doris.

"When she saw the actual picture, the husband was indeed in a wheelchair. I'd say Mandy received some guidance there, what do you think?"

To stall, Kate took another sip of water. Was it just a coincidence? Were Sandi and Ian adopting Mandy's baby? Deciding it would be best to keep this one to herself, Kate swallowed more water.

"Kate?" Doris prompted.

"I hope things will work out for everyone involved," Kate replied. "It does sound like Mandy received some extra help."

"This trial is far from over, but at least now she has a game plan. I wish more young people would open their eyes to the misfortune they can bring on themselves when they ignore the standards taught by our church," Doris said. "I hate to see kids become a statistic."

"I was almost one of those. I was playing with fire in high school, dating a total jerk who wanted to use me like Mandy was used by her boyfriend," Kate admitted. "I was so lucky! If it hadn't been for that car accident, and the dream I had during the coma, I might've followed a path just like Mandy's."

"We all have the gift of agency," Doris sighed. "The path we select to follow in this life is our choice."

# Chapter 23

As things continued to stabilize in Blaketown, Doris and her husband were called into the stake president's office. Hoping neither of them were up for a stake calling, Doris soon learned that her fears were right on target.

"Brother and Sister Kelsey," President Emerson said, welcoming the couple into his cramped office. "I'm so glad you came to see me."

"Did we have a choice?" Doris teased.

"Actually no," the stake president returned. He smiled warmly at Doris' husband. "Brother Kelsey, would it be all right if we borrowed your wife for a temporary stake calling?"

Phil Kelsey glanced at his wife, then at the stake president. "What exactly did you have in mind?" he ventured.

"We need Doris and her talents. We know how respected she is among the teenagers in our stake."

Doris sank down in the chair in front of the wooden desk. "Not Stake Young Women," she groaned to herself.

"Which is why we felt so strongly that this calling is inspired. Sister Kelsey, I'm sure you're aware of how upset our young people have been since this earthquake."

Doris nodded. What was President Emerson getting at?

"Several have come into this office, scared about the future." He rested his hands on his desk. "Now we all know that isn't good," he said, smiling at Phil, then Doris. "These young people need to dream dreams, establish goals . . . we don't want them to allow fear to dictate their actions." He focused on Doris. "I have it on good authority that you recently calmed a young lady who was convinced that she and her friends were being picked on."

If Doris had dared, she would've slapped her forehead. Terri's father was a counselor to President Emerson. She had brought this on herself.

"We know that you have a way of using teaching moments to ease your students' hearts. Which brings me to the reason we've asked you and your husband to come in tonight."

Bracing herself, Doris held her breath.

"We've put considerable prayer into this and we've decided that it would be a good thing to involve our youth in a positive, wholesome activity that will help rebuild their confidence. Something that might boost their sagging testimonies and refocus them on developing their talents. In short, we'd like to invite you to write, and then direct a play."

Doris sank even lower in her chair, barely feeling her husband's arm as it slipped around her slumped shoulders.

"A play that will teach them, as they have fun. Something you excel in."

Remaining silent, Doris blinked rapidly.

"We'll give you any assistance that you might need to pull this together. Draw on the youth from all of the wards in our stake for this production. Involve anyone who wants to participate. Not all of them will feel comfortable on stage, but I'm sure you could use them behind the scenes, with costumes, make-up, lighting, sound, and so forth." He gazed steadily at the wilting woman in front of him. "I know it seems like an ambitious task, but I've never seen you back down from a challenge yet."

"A play?" Doris stammered.

The stake president smiled, revealing his even, white teeth. "Yes! Kids love that sort of thing. I know you have quite a talent for writing—what do you think? Phil?"

"I think if Doris decides she's up to this, she can do just about anything."

"My thoughts exactly. Doris?"

"How long do I have to pull this off?" Doris asked.

"Take as much time as you need. I realize a production of this nature will involve a great deal of effort. That's the beauty of the thing. It'll keep our kids busy during a time when they're starting to question their purpose in life."

Doris froze in place as an idea began to take shape. "Repeat what you just said."

"This will take a great deal of effort—"

"No," Doris interrupted. "After that . . . what was it you said . . . something about helping them remember their purpose in life."

The stake president beamed. "I knew you were the one to tackle this. You've already got an idea . . . am I right?"

Doris gave him a pained look. "I hate it when this happens. I probably won't be able to sleep at all tonight. I can see it in my head . . . it'll work, but I've got to get this down before it's gone. Greg Erickson has been repairing my computer for me—it was damaged during the quake. I'll tell him to put a rush on it."

"Paper and pencil will work until it's fixed," the stake president enticed.

"Paper and pencil it will be for a while," Doris replied. "Now tell me again, do I have the freedom to call upon anyone I want or need to help with this little assignment?"

"Yes, including nonmembers if you feel so inclined."

"And if they refuse to cooperate?"

"You just send them my way if they give you any hassle."

Liking the sound of that, Doris accepted the calling, her excitement growing as ideas continued to pop into her head.

\* \* \*

"You want me to write the songs for this play?" Terri asked, her eyes wide with surprise.

Doris nodded, handing Terri a copy of the script she had slaved over for a couple of weeks. Knowing Terri was partially responsible for her new responsibility, the English teacher took great delight in involving this young lady. "If you need help with the lyrics, I know a couple of talented young women who could assist you."

Terri offered a rueful smile. "Karen and Bev?"

"The very two that came to mind. Well, what do you think?"

Terri glanced up at Doris. "You really want me to do this?"

Doris smiled at the junior. "You'll do a great job. I've heard you play the piano and I've also seen some of the poetry you've written this year. You have a gift," she encouraged.

"Thanks—I think. When do rehearsals start?"

"Next week," Doris said. "This Friday night is the audition. We'll meet with those interested in performing, cast it, and start rehearsing next Wednesday night."

"There's no way I can have these songs written by then!"

"We'll start by helping these kids get a feel for the roles they're playing. That will give you time to come up with the songs," Doris promised. "Besides, the way things have already fallen into place, I'm sure you'll have extra help with this assignment. The message of this play is important."

"What's it about?" Terri asked, thumbing through the script.

"The basic theme is the plan of salvation," Doris revealed.

"Oh?" Terri asked, trying to be polite. This sounded like a dry subject.

"It starts with a group of young people in the premortal world, all excited about the chance they'll have to come down to this earth to learn and grow. They've been saved for the latter days, which makes them impatient, but they're convinced that they will be valiant sons and daughters of their Father in Heaven when they are finally born. In the next scene, we're introduced to these same characters again, only in the flesh . . . so to speak. We'll see that each one has challenges that will help them grow and learn. They won't remember the noble promises they made to each other when the veil is drawn—and there are a couple of scenes where some of them aren't very nice. As the play continues, some make good choices, others drift away from the straight and narrow path. By the end of the play, it's obvious how important it is to stay in tune to receive the guidance we need on this earth."

"Wow!" Terri said, impressed. "This sounds great! I'm already getting some ideas. In fact, is it okay if I get started?"

"That's better than okay," Doris exclaimed as the young woman hurried out of her classroom. "She'll do a great job," she said to herself.

\* \* \*

"Now in this scene, Sabrina, you're the ultimate nerd," Doris instructed.

Sabrina shook her head as the other cast members laughed. "But I was such a great leader in the premortal scene."

"Exactly," Doris said. "Have any of you kids ever wondered what kind of person you were in the premortal world?" Without waiting for an answer, the English teacher excitedly continued. "We know you were valiant . . . you were saved for this time for a reason. When you were born, the memory of who you were before is gone. It's quite a test, but it will show what you're made of."

"I'm a nerd?" Sabrina protested.

Doris laughed. "Sometimes we don't believe in ourselves as much as we should in this life. That's one of the points I'm trying to make with this production. Sabrina, your character will also help people understand that we need to treat each other better than we do. Most times, we're too quick to judge. As you'll see with your character, you'll overcome several obstacles that will shape you into a strong individual. You'll relearn who you really are."

Bev raised her hand. "I have a question . . . was this thing type-cast, or what?" She grinned when everyone laughed.

"I take it you're referring to the character you're playing," Doris assumed. "We know you're investigating our church right now. We thought you could bring a lot of depth to this role. Your character is a nonmember, trying to figure out what's important in life. I think you'll do a great job with it."

"I'll try," Bev promised. "Now, about this solo part I sing with Sabrina—"

"You both have beautiful voices," Doris replied. "You're an alto, Sabrina's a soprano. You'll blend well in two-part harmony."

"Where's the music?" Bev asked.

"Being written even as we speak," Doris enthused. "Karen and Terri have promised to have it ready for us in a few days."

"I have a question," Gerald Reynolds said, stepping forward. "My character is a real jerk!"

"That's a question? Like I said, typecasting," Bev teased.

"Did Karen have anything to do with me getting this part?" Gerald asked, ignoring Bev.

"No. She's strictly in charge of the music," Doris replied, trying to keep a straight face. She was all too aware of the friction that existed between Gerald and Karen. "Karen and Terri will be directing that portion of this production." Doris smiled around at the young people sitting on the stage of the stake center. "You'll all do a terrific job. I want you to have fun and get to know each other better. You might even surprise yourselves and actually learn something from this experience. Now, let's get started. First, we'll block the opening scene." As the cast milled around, Doris began figuring out where each character would stand on the stage.

# Chapter 24

"These songs are perfect," Doris said, her gaze settling on Terri and Karen. She gave both girls a hug, then handed her assistant director a copy of the lyrics.

In the beginning, Sue Erickson had reluctantly agreed to help Doris direct the play. She was finding herself getting more involved with it as time and the play progressed. On a positive note, it gave her something else to think about besides Kate and little Colleen. Colleen had taken a turn for the worst in recent days, developing a case of pneumonia. Back on the respirators they were all beginning to hate, Colleen was fighting for her life—again.

"Terri, play through this first song, the one for the opening scene. I'd like Sue to hear it."

Terri walked across the stake gym floor and sat down at the piano. As she played, Sue followed along with the set of lyrics in her hand.

> It's not my time!
> I have to wait at the end of the line!
> Sit here and wait while I focus and contemplate—
> All the things I'll do,
> All the places I'll go,
> When I'm finally on Earth, below.
> But now is not my time,
> 'Cuz I'm stuck at the end of the line.
> So I'll sit here and wait,
> Try to meditate,
> And not stagnate—

While I plan my fate,
Stuck at the end of the line!
'Cuz it's not my time,
Not my time,
Not my time.

"It's wonderful!" Sue exclaimed, rereading the lyrics. "Doris is right, you two did a great job with this assignment."

"Thanks," Terri and Karen said in unison.

"You make quite the team," Doris added. "Do me another favor?"

"What?" Karen asked suspiciously.

"Karen, sing the theme song you two wrote—Terri, accompany her. You've got to hear this one, Sue!"

"You want me to sing it?"

Doris nodded. "Karen, you have a beautiful voice . . . you should use it more often."

"You can do it," Terri encouraged. "You were singing these songs the whole time we were writing them."

"But that's different. I didn't have an audience."

Doris glanced around the gym. "Newsflash, you still don't. It's just me and Sister Erickson. Now sing!"

Giving in, Karen moved beside the piano. "I'll try," she said, glancing at the music in her hands.

"Which one is she doing?" Sue asked.

"*The Adventure of a Lifetime*, the song based on the title of our production," Doris replied.

Sue quickly thumbed through the music Doris had handed her and located the song.

"Hit it, Terri," Doris said.

Grinning, Terri began playing a lively tune, nodding when it was time for Karen to start singing:

It's the adventure of a lifetime, a lifetime of adventure,
A time when we'll discover who we are and what we'll be.
The adventure of a lifetime, a lifetime of adventure,
And the journey I will take is up to me.

I'll be a valiant warrior in the battle down on Earth,
I'll be a source of inspiration from my birth.
The world is out there waiting
And I'm through with contemplating;
I'm ready to prove to all my worth.

It's the adventure of a lifetime, a lifetime of adventure,
A time when we'll discover who we are and what we'll be.
The adventure of a lifetime, a lifetime of adventure,
And the journey I will take is up to me!

I will stand for righteousness and truth,
I will be a leader in my youth,
I will learn and grow from all I see,
My progress will be up to me,
And I will never drink vermouth!

It's the adventure of a lifetime, a lifetime of adventure,
A time when we'll discover who we are and what we'll be.
The adventure of a lifetime, a lifetime of adventure,
And the journey I will take is up to me!
The adventure of a lifetime, a lifetime of adventure,
And the journey I will take is up to me!
To me!
To me!

"To me!" Karen repeated, yelling it the final time as Terri played a vigorous ending.

"That is so good!" Sue enthused. "The play itself is wonderful, but this music—it makes it come alive."

Doris laughed. "I don't know whether to be insulted or tell you I knew this play was meant to be a musical!"

"Don't be insulted," Sue advised. "I'm just saying this music will add so much. And Doris is right, you have a beautiful voice, Karen." Smiling at Karen's blush, Sue turned to Doris. "We have to use her voice somewhere in this production."

"I plan to. I was thinking there might be a couple of places where we could have her sing while the cast is acting out some of those silent scenes."

"Now, wait a minute," Karen sputtered.

"That is a great idea!" Sue replied.

"I think so too," Terri echoed.

"And Terri, you've done an outstanding job with the music. It's so upbeat. I can still hear that tune in my head," Sue exclaimed.

Now it was Terri's turn to be embarrassed, but pleased by the compliments.

"I know what you're saying," Doris said. "This number is so snappy, can't you just see our cast each singing solo lines, putting emphasis on those great lyrics."

"That is an inspired idea," Sue responded.

"I have another idea. Karen that was a great play on words, using 'vermouth' to rhyme with 'youth.'"

"Thanks," Karen replied.

"Not everyone will catch on to what it means," Doris continued.

"What is vermouth?" Sue asked sheepishly. "I thought it was a color."

"It's another word for wine," Karen explained.

"I see. That *is* clever," Sue said, rereading the verse.

"After that verse, why don't we have one of our characters yell out, 'What?' and another cast member will reply, 'It's wine,' or something like that? I think there's room for that before the chorus is sung again. It would clarify things for the audience."

"That'd work," Karen answered Doris. "I was worried no one would catch that phrase."

"It's important enough, I want everyone to understand what is being said," Doris replied. "Now girls, why don't you play through the other songs you came up with."

"How many songs are there?" Sue asked.

"Six," Doris said.

"You girls are amazing!" Sue replied.

"Remember that," Karen said, grinning.

* * *

Eighteen-year-old Garrett Hughes walked down off the stage and reached for his backpack. He unzipped it and removed a small black case. Intrigued, Sabrina watched as he opened the case, revealing a blood sugar monitor similar to hers. She slipped down off the stage and approached him.

"You have diabetes," she guessed. She had forgotten that someone else at the high school was living with this disease.

"Yep," Garrett replied, pricking the middle finger of his right hand. "I heard you do, too."

Sabrina nodded, watching as he expertly covered a small square of the strip in his blood sugar monitor with a drop of blood.

"I feel a little funny. I thought I'd better check this out before we started rehearsing that dance."

"Maybe I'd better see where mine is at," Sabrina replied, walking to where she had left her purse on the gym floor. She opened her purse and reached for her blood sugar monitor. Sitting on the floor, she started running a test.

"How is it?" Garrett asked a few seconds later, walking over to where Sabrina was sitting.

"What was yours?" she countered.

"Ninety-five."

"That's great!"

"It's actually low for me. If I don't eat something now, they'll have to pick me up off the floor in a few minutes."

Sabrina's machine beeped, announcing that it had finished the test.

Garrett adjusted his glasses. "And the magic number is?"

"Two hundred and eleven."

"A little high, but you'll knock it right back down with all of this running around we do during rehearsal."

"Probably," Sabrina sighed, slipping her glucose machine back inside of its case.

Garrett opened a granola bar and began eating it. "I'd offer you a bite," he said between mouthfuls, "but I don't think it would help you. How many shots do you give a day?"

"Two. They're still waiting to see how long my pancreas will put out insulin on its own."

"It took me about a year to get past that milestone," Garrett sympathized.

"How many shots do you give now?"

"I used to give four," he replied, grinning when Sabrina gasped. "I was on the tight control method. I still am; they've proven there's fewer complications that way. Now, I count carbohydrates and use an insulin pump."

"You have an insulin pump?" Sabrina asked, curious. "The specialist I'm seeing now said that might be an option for me eventually."

"It's a great way to go. I have more freedom with it."

"How does it work?" she asked.

Garrett unclipped his pump from the belt under his t-shirt and showed her the small computer. "It's a mini IV site. You use a needle to insert the cannula under your skin, then draw out the needle when the cannula is in place. I change sites about every 3 days. It's so comfortable—most of the time, I don't even feel it."

"Where's the insulin?"

"Stored in the back of the pump inside of a syringe." He showed her where the syringe was, then flipped the grey square around and revealed the buttons on the front. "I can program basal rates that drip in day and night, whatever amount my doctor and I decide that I need. When it's time to eat, I punch in a bolus of insulin, again, figuring out how much insulin I'll need to cover whatever it is I'm eating."

"That looks so cool," Sabrina said longingly.

"The best part is, I'm not on a set schedule anymore. You know how the insulin you're giving now peaks at different times so you have to eat at certain times?"

Sabrina nodded.

"With this, I'm only giving regular, fast-acting insulin, so it does its job, then lets the basal rates pick up the slack. I punch in a bolus and I can eat whenever I want." He lifted up his shirt and reattached the insulin pump to his belt.

"I had no idea that was even there."

"Most people don't. I don't mind if they do. It's part of me, part of who I am."

"How long have you had diabetes?"

"Since I was six years old," Garrett replied.

"You were so young!" Sabrina sympathized.

"I almost think it's better that way. It was part of my life nearly from the beginning. I think for me, it was easier to accept. I know there's a girl at the junior high who is having a horrible time adjusting. She doesn't want to deal with it. She doesn't realize how much is riding on how well she takes care of herself. Myself, I intend to live a long, full life, and the diabetes won't stop me! I participate in sports, I'm a member of our school's Aca-Deca team, and I enjoy starring in productions like this musical."

"Like my specialist told me, learn to control it so it doesn't control you," Sabrina said, referring to the diabetes. "I had to quit volleyball for a while, but after I got my blood sugar under better control, I was able to play in the district tournament."

"That's great," Garrett replied. "I heard your team did quite well."

"We did. If we'd won our final game, we would've gone to state, but maybe next year. The best part was, I was able to play most of the time without any problem. I had one small reaction after an intense set, but I drank some Gatorade and went back out to play in the next set."

"Hey, you two, are you ready to join the rest of the cast?" Sue asked, hating to interrupt, but knowing they needed to make the most of the rehearsal time left that night.

"Sure," Garrett said. "Race you," he added, beating Sabrina back on stage.

\* \* \*

"Let me get this straight . . . you're a nonmember playing a nonmember?" James asked his daughter.

"Uh huh," Bev replied. "It works, don't you think? Now, give me my cue, please."

Grinning, James thumbed through the script, finding the scene Bev wanted to practice. "Okay, I play the part of an idiot who is giving you a bad time, right?"

"Gerald's part, yeah!" Bev grinned.

"Here goes," he said, clearing his throat. "Hey, Zack, check out Brenda . . . Brenda?"

"That's my name in the play, Dad."

"Brenda it is," James replied. "Hey, Zack, check out Brenda. Can you believe what she's wearing? She must think she's really hot." He lowered the script again. "What are you wearing in this scene?"

"A short mini-skirt with a halter-top."

"What?!"

"It's all implied. No one will ever see me in it. I'll be offstage wearing very modest attire."

"Then how—"

"Gerald's character tells the audience what I'm supposedly wearing."

"I see. If you're offstage, then why do you have to memorize any lines?"

"The lines you're reading are my cue. I have another scene right after this one. In that scene, I'm home crying because of how people are treating me. I need to hear these lines so that I can get into character."

"And what are you wearing then?"

"A robe. I'll be sitting on a bed, writing in my journal."

James glanced at his daughter. "I think this was cast very well," he teased. "You love wearing your robe around the house—you'd wear it all day if you could."

"Just read the part, okay," Bev said dryly.

Still grinning, James reread the lines.

\* \* \*

"All right, listen up. During this scene, Bev will be on this side of the stage, sitting on her bed, writing in her journal. We've decided to pre-record her part. She'll act it out while we play her lines over the speakers. The audience will be hearing her thoughts. After her journal entry is read, Bev will freeze in place. Sue thought that would add a dramatic flare and I think she's right," Doris said, glancing through her notes.

The cast clowned around, cheering for Sue.

"On the other side of the stage, we'll have Sabrina who is sitting by herself at a stake dance. Gerald and Garrett will be dancing with their dates. They'll do their dance, then freeze in place. While they're frozen, we'll hear Sabrina's thoughts over the speaker. Then she'll freeze in place. In the center of the stage, we'll have Karen walk out, dressed in white. Karen's character is still in the premortal world, waiting for her chance to come to this earth. In the meantime, she sees what her former brothers and sisters are doing, the good choices, and the mistakes they're making. That's when she sings 'No Matter How Dark the Storm.' Now, let's have everyone slip into their places. We'll pretend the tape is playing over the sound system. Freeze, Bev—good. Those of you who are involved with that part of the scene, pretend that you've already danced and freeze in place. Again the tape plays over the speakers. Freeze in place Sabrina. Terri, start the song."

"Do you want us to perform it now?" Terri asked, glancing at Karen who was pacing nervously on stage.

"Yes. I'd like the cast to hear this song, then we'll run through the entire scene again," Doris replied.

Terri adjusted her sheets of music, then began to play through the introduction. Karen walked out center stage and started to sing, quietly at first, then stronger as she became part of the song:

> There are times when the world seems an awful place to be,
> When the sky is full of thunder and the sun is hard to see.
> Sometimes fear and inner pain make you want to run and hide,
> And you cry all alone, in a world filled with pride.
> But no matter how dark the storm,
> There's a harbor, safe and warm—
> Where the Savior holds forth His hand,
> See His footprints in the sand.
> Though life is hard, you're not alone,
> The Savior's love will guide you home.
> Through the darkness, He shines a light,
> An endless glow through the blackest night,
> And life's shadows will fade from sight—
> Through the gospel's light.

Close your heart to empty voices that seek to cause you pain,
The sun will always shine, after a chilling rain.
Lift your eyes to the heavens, there is hope shining there,
A silver lining lies hidden in every cloud of despair.

But no matter how dark the storm,
There's a harbor, safe and warm—
Where the Savior holds forth His hand,
See His footprints in the sand.
Though life is hard, you're not alone,
The Savior's love will guide you home.
Through the darkness, He shines a light,
An endless glow through the blackest night,
And life's shadows will fade from sight—
Through the gospel's light.

At the end of the song, Karen's eyes were so blurred with tears, she couldn't see that everyone else was in the same condition.

A few minutes later, Doris motioned for Sue to come close. "Sue, I was thinking—what if we showed slides of the Savior on a large screen behind Karen while she sings? It would add so much to the powerful message of that beautiful song."

Sue envisioned the impact the slide would have on the audience. "Let's do it!"

Nodding, Doris walked to the front of the stage to announce their decision.

# Chapter 25

"I look huge!" Mandy complained as she studied herself in the mirror. Her mother had brought her to pick out a few maternity tops, something she dreaded wearing.

"You look fine," Lorena replied. "Do you like the color?"

"Does the color matter? I feel like I'm wearing a tent."

"Trust me, you'll want something that fits loose. I wish I'd kept my maternity clothes—I had some cute tops—but I gave them all away after your youngest brother was born. We knew he was our last one."

Mandy's eyes clouded with pain. "Were you excited when you found out you were expecting me?" she asked, focusing on the mirror. She could see her mother's face reflected in it.

Lorena smiled. "At first I was scared. I didn't know what to expect, but a few days later I wanted the entire world to know I was pregnant." Realizing how her answer had affected Mandy, she tried to change the subject. "Why don't you try this other blouse? You might like it better."

"Mom, I wish it could be different . . . this would be so exciting. Instead, I see so many cute things for babies and a part of me dies."

"There will be another time, Mandy. In a few years, when you're ready for this responsibility, you'll have another baby."

Willing herself not to cry, Mandy nodded, grabbed the other blouse and moved into a stall to change.

\* \* \*

"Well, what do you think?" Sandi asked breathlessly.

Ian glanced around the nursery Sandi had been working on for several weeks. Painted mint green, it would work for either a boy or a girl. The room was filled with colorful wall hangings and stuffed animals. Over the sturdy oak crib hung a mobile with colored shapes. "It looks fantastic. This is going to be one spoiled baby."

"I'll do my best," Sandi replied.

"So will I," Ian promised, pushing his wheelchair closer to his wife. He drew her down for a kiss. "Have you thought of any names yet?" he asked, releasing her.

"A couple. How about you?"

"I was thinking, if it was a boy, we should name him Soup."

"That's not even funny, Mr. Campbell!"

Ian laughed. "Okay, what's your contribution?"

"If it's a girl, I was thinking of something like Julia."

"Julia," Ian repeated, trying it out. "As in Roberts?" he asked, wiggling his eyebrows.

"As in my great-grandmother," Sandi informed him.

"And if it's a boy?"

"Dale Ian Campbell?" Sandi revealed.

"It has a certain charm," Ian replied. "My dad's name, combined with mine. I like it."

"I'm glad." Sandi gazed intently at the crib. "Oh, Ian, I can hardly wait. Already, my arms are aching to hold that baby!"

"My arms are aching too," Ian teased, holding them out to his wife. Sighing contentedly, Sandi sat on her husband's lap for a lengthy embrace.

\* \* \*

"Mom, are you busy?" Sara Sandler asked, walking into the kitchen where her mother was punching down bread dough.

"Usually. What do you need?" Betty replied, her hands covered with dough.

"To apologize."

"Oh?" Betty asked, giving the dough a final workout.

"For being such an imbecile."

Startled by Sara's declaration, Betty moved to the kitchen sink to wash her hands. After drying them on a towel, she selected a clean towel to cover the bread dough. "Would this have something to do with Mandy?" she guessed.

Sara nodded. "It has everything to do with Mandy. I am so sorry for how I treated her."

"What brought on this change of heart?" Betty asked, curious.

"This play I'm in . . . the one Sister Kelsey and Sister Erickson are directing."

"I see."

"Sabrina and Bev play two characters that the rest of us tease and make fun of because they're different. But in the opening scene, we're all in the premortal world, brothers and sisters looking out for each other—helping each other. It made me think about how I had treated Mandy. What if I knew her before we were born? What if I had promised to help her here on this earth if she ever messed up? While she was here, I thought Mandy was such a disgusting person, but I'm the one who was disgusting. I judged her. Instead of trying to make things easier for her, I made it harder."

Betty gazed silently at her daughter.

"Go ahead and say it—you tried to tell me that, even before Mandy left. I didn't . . . I wouldn't let myself understand what you were saying until we started working on this musical."

"This play sounds like it's something pretty special."

"It is. I can't explain what it's like being part of it. There are times while we're rehearsing when the Spirit is so strong in that room. I know this play can help people. It's already helped me." Sara gazed intently at her mother. "What can I do to make things up to Mandy?"

"I'm not sure, hon," Betty replied. "Think about it. Pray about it. Something will come to mind, I'm sure."

Hoping her mother was right, Sara retreated to her bedroom.

\* \* \*

"You made it through all of that traffic," Lorena said as Betty, Lyle, and Sara Sandler entered her brick home in Salt Lake City.

"It was nigh onto causing me stress, but I persevered," Lyle quipped. "I just imagined those semis were ornery old bulls and stayed out of their way."

"Whatever works," Eric Hopkins said, reaching to shake Lyle's hand. "I'm glad you were able to come down for the weekend. We'll enjoy having you."

"Well, we don't want to be any bother," Betty replied. "We don't get down this way very often—"

"Not at all," Sara interrupted her mother.

"True. But we wanted to see how everyone was doing," Betty continued. "How's Mandy?"

"It's been tough, but she's hanging in there," Lorena answered. "It'll mean a lot that you're here." Turning, she led the way into the large family room for a visit.

"Where's Mandy?" Sara asked, glancing around.

"Down the hall in her bedroom, where she stays most of the time," Lorena replied.

"Would it be all right if I talked to her?"

Lorena smiled at her niece. "Sure, I think Mandy would like that. Her room is the second door on the right."

"Thanks," Sara said, moving down the hall. "Mandy?" she called out a few seconds later, timidly knocking on her cousin's bedroom door.

"Come in," Mandy invited.

Taking a deep breath, Sara opened the door and stepped inside the room.

Expecting her aunt Betty, Mandy was resentful of Sara's appearance. "Oh, it's you."

"I deserved that," Sara admitted, moving closer to Mandy's bed. She tried to avoid looking at Mandy's bulging stomach, but her eyes wandered that direction anyway. "Mandy, I'm not sure what to say to you—I can't take back how I treated you—or what I said to some of my friends about you—but I want you to know that I'm sorry."

Surprised by her cousin's confession, Mandy slid back on the bed and motioned for Sara to sit down. Sara sat on the end of Mandy's soft bed and glanced around her cousin's room. It looked a lot like her own bedroom in Blaketown, with posters and stuffed animals. The resemblance tugged at her heart—Mandy was too young to be facing what was ahead of her.

"Why are you telling me this?" Mandy asked.

"Because I was wrong to act like I did toward you," Sara replied.

Mandy studied her cousin's face, but there was no trace of the insincerity she had expected. Sara was being candid, something she decided to risk as well. "I didn't exactly go out of my way to be friendly to you."

"But you were dealing with a lot—I should've been more caring. Mom kept telling me to be understanding, but I didn't listen."

"I didn't listen to my mom either," Mandy mused. "I think your mistake is easier to fix."

Ashamed, Sara swallowed past the lump in her throat. "Can you ever forgive me for being such an idiot?"

"I'm not in a position to judge anyone else," Mandy replied. "Don't worry about it. It's okay."

"It's not okay, Mandy. I wish there was something I could do to make it up to you."

"Maybe there is," Mandy said.

"Name it," Sara said eagerly.

"Don't go around Blaketown broadcasting that I'm pregnant—"

"I haven't said a word to anyone but Mom," Sara pledged.

"And take me somewhere for ice cream. It sounds so good right now and I hate to bother my parents." She smiled shyly at her older cousin.

"I'll take you anywhere you say," Sara promised.

"There's a Baskin-Robbins about four blocks from here," Mandy suggested.

"I'll ask Mom if I can take the car, but it shouldn't be a problem. In fact, it would probably be good for me to learn how to drive in a larger area. I'll go to school in Provo next fall."

"You don't have a problem being seen with me?" Mandy asked.

"Not anymore."

"Even if we were in Blaketown?"

Rising, Sara smiled down at her cousin. "Even if we were in Blaketown. Come back with us for a few days; I'd like to have a chance to make things up to you."

"Not necessary," Mandy said, carefully standing. "I know you mean it. That's all that matters."

# Epilogue

The weeks passed quickly for everyone but Mike, Kate, and Colleen. For them the days dragged on as Colleen slowly recovered, finally growing as they had hoped. December arrived, heralding Tyler Erickson's homecoming. On the appointed day, a large crowd of family and friends gathered at the Salt Lake City airport to greet the returning elder. It was an emotional time for the Erickson family as Kate and Mike brought their daughter home for Christmas a few days after Tyler's arrival.

Karen and Edie made it through the holidays, thanks to friends who rallied around them, easing the heartache they still endured over losing Adele. Brett's parents invited them to come up to Coeur d'Alene for Christmas, which helped bolster their spirits. Doing his part, Brett proposed to Edie on Christmas Eve. He excitedly placed a beautiful diamond ring on her finger as his parents and Karen squealed with delight. The rest of the visit flew by as wedding plans were discussed with joyful enthusiasm.

During the second weekend in January, another remarkable event took place at the local stake center as the Henderson family invited friends and neighbors to gather for their baptism. Refusing to attend, James' sister's family kept their distance, certain their relatives were joining a bizarre religion. Their rejection hurt, but was anticipated. James assured Gina and Bev that someday, they would comprehend the happiness the true gospel could bring. In the meantime, the Hendersons were determined to reciprocate their negative reaction with love.

The day of the baptism, the entire family prepared themselves for what would be an unforgettable day.

"Do I look all right?" Bev asked Karen that afternoon, feeling awkward in the white jumpsuit she was wearing.

"You've never looked more beautiful," Karen replied, drawing Bev into an emotional hug.

"Are you ready, Bev?" Gina interrupted, walking into the women's rest room. Wearing a long, beautiful white dress she had sewn for this occasion, one she hoped to wear in the temple someday, she looked as radiant as Bev.

"I've been ready for this for quite a while," Bev replied.

Gina smiled warmly at her daughter. "It took the rest of us a little longer to come around."

"Mostly Dad," Bev replied, laughing. "He had quite a time conquering his problem with the Word of Wisdom. We were all praying for him—the missionaries gave him at least two priesthood blessings that I know of. Sometimes I still can't believe it all came together. He struggled so much with paying tithing, but now he claims his business is better than ever."

"A lot of things are," Gina said, slipping an arm around Bev's waist. "Shall we go? They're waiting for us in the chapel. They'd like to start this meeting on time."

"Let's head out," Bev said, moving out of the restroom with Gina. "Coming, Karen?"

"I'll be right there," Karen replied, walking into one of the stalls to grab a handful of tissue. The way she was already tearing up, tissue would be a needful thing.

* * *

As January progressed, several frantic rehearsals kept Doris and Sue busy as they put the finishing touches on the production they knew was *The Adventure of a Lifetime.* Exhausted by the pace they were keeping, both women were pleased by the effect the play had already had on several cast members.

Karen had concentrated on developing her talents, something that had given her a much- needed boost after losing her grandmother. In a surprising twist, Karen had also agreed to a date with Gerald Reynolds a few weeks into the rehearsals. As Edie had anticipated, her daughter thoroughly enjoyed herself, discovering that Gerald was actually a sensitive, caring individual.

Bev's growing ability to discern the Spirit in varied settings had led her to believe that this was indeed the true church of Jesus Christ, her testimony blooming as she had enjoyed lively discussions with the LDS missionaries, two humble elders who had taught her family the gospel.

Because the songs Karen and Terri had written had been so popular, Terri was determined to compose more music after this musical was performed. She had always wanted to discover something special about herself and had finally tapped into an area of strength her parents and leaders had assured was there.

As the weeks had passed, a special friendship had flourished between Sabrina and Garrett; the two diabetics kidded each other continuously about the challenge they shared. Comparing blood sugar levels, they egged each other on to better, tighter control. Sue had noticed the way Garrett looked at Sabrina and suspected that when her daughter turned 16 in the spring, Sabrina would have a date for the Senior Prom.

There were others involved with the production whose lives and hearts were touched in ways Doris, Sue, and the stake president hadn't planned on. A new unity seemed to exist between this cast of talented teens. Doris had seen that attitude spread to the high school as the influence of the cast members had a ripple-effect on those around them. Contention didn't cease, but there wasn't as much of it. Some of the students were more respectful toward each other and the teachers. As the stake president had hoped, most were once again planning for their future lives, excited by the numerous possibilities. Thrilled by what was taking place, and praying it wasn't a temporary fix, Doris was grateful for this chance to serve in a positive way. She knew she would be relieved when it was over, but she would always treasure the memories and friendships that had formed as a result.

\* \* \*

The first week of February, *The Adventure of a Lifetime* was so well-received, it was performed three nights in a row. The third and final night the stake center was filled to capacity by those who had already seen it, and by those who had heard rave reviews of the previous performances. Sitting in the audience that final night were several non-members, including James' sister's family, something Bev wouldn't learn until the final curtain call when the lights were turned up.

Edie and Brett had come three nights in a row, impressed with the talented daughter who would be sealed to them in the near future. Brett's parents had driven down for the occasion and had been only too happy to accompany Edie and Brett to all three performances.

Sue had requested seats near the front of the stage for her family that night. Tyler had come early and was obediently saving seats for the other members of their family. He too had attended all three nights, still absorbing the changes that had taken place in his baby sister, someone who had blossomed into a stunning young woman.

A few days ago as his gaze had followed Sabrina across the stage during dress rehearsal, Tyler had been unaware that someone else had been observing him just as intently. Bev had seen pictures of Sabrina's older brother, but now knew those pictures had not done this handsome elder justice. Her heart fluttering in her chest, Bev did her best to keep her cool; only Karen guessed the cause of her friend's discomfort.

As the directors and cast scurried around to get ready, Mike and Kate walked into the stake center, followed by Greg who was proudly holding his first grandchild in his arms.

"How's Grandpa's girl?" he asked, cuddling his granddaughter, thrilled when Colleen giggled. "Did you hear that? She definitely takes after Grandpa," he said, grinning broadly. "We Ericksons enjoy life to the fullest!" Exchanging a delighted smile, Mike drew Kate close, thrilled that life was taking a turn for the better.

As the audience continued to arrive, Doris and Sue made last-minute adjustments to the scenery and lights. Just before the curtain was drawn, the cast gathered together.

"Sister Kelsey," Terri said, requesting the English teacher's attention.

"Yes, Terri, what is it?" Doris gazed at the cast of teens she had grown to love.

"We need you and Sister Erickson to come out front for a minute," Terri replied.

Before Doris or Sue could argue, the cast grouped around them, forcing them through the curtains and onto the stage out front. Bev moved to one of the microphones and pulled it from the stand.

"Ladies and gentlemen, before we begin tonight, we'd like to pay a special tribute to two women who have made so much possible . . ." Unprepared for the wave of sentiment that hit her, Bev paused, struggling for control. She tried to speak, but the words wouldn't come.

Karen walked up behind her and took the mike from Bev's hand, smiling first at her friend, then at the audience. "This has been a year we will always remember. So much has happened. Wonderful things," she said, her eyes straying to where she knew her mother and Brett were sitting together. "Others that were heartbreaking. Part of what has made it tolerable for me is this play that you're about to see tonight," she paused as Bev's affliction also gripped her. Sensing Karen's dilemma, Terri stepped forward next.

"What my friends are trying to say is that we owe so much to these two ladies who've had to put up with us the past couple of months. We'll never fully understand the time and effort that went into this production, but it was something we all needed. I know I learned so much . . ." Now it was Terri's turn to cry.

Sabrina accepted the mike Terri held out to her. "It's been interesting having my mother as a director, but I survived." She paused as the audience laughed. A bright spotlight prevented her from seeing those who sat below. She blinked, then smiled. "If we think about it, we're all cast members on this earth. We all have a part to play. Sometimes we forget our lines, we don't remember what our focus should be, but with the proper guidance, we can find our way. If we'll heed the Greatest Director of All, we'll never go wrong." She turned to tearfully smile at Doris, then at her mother. "This is our way of saying thanks. And the way things are going, we'd better wrap this up or we'll all sit down and have a good cry instead of pulling this production together tonight." She handed the microphone to Garrett to hold as two beautiful rose corsages were given to Doris and Sue. The two women pinned them on as the audience stood to give them a standing ovation. Taking a bow, the directors retreated backstage to compose themselves during the opening prayer.

* * *

That same night, another drama was unfolding at a hospital in Salt Lake County as fifteen-year-old Mandy Hopkins went into labor. Her parents rushed her to the hospital in a panic when it became evident that the time they had been dreading had arrived. After she had endured five hours of hard labor, it was determined that the baby couldn't turn from the semi-breech position; Mandy's small frame didn't offer enough room. Deciding a C-section was in order, Mandy was rushed into surgery and a baby girl was born, the future daughter of Ian and Sandi Campbell. Shedding tears of her own when she heard her baby wail, Mandy prayed for strength, the kind that would see her through the difficult days ahead.

* * *

Midway through the musical as the stage lights were dimmed and Karen began to sing her final solo, the audience was mesmerized by the contrast of the black backdrop and Karen's white dress. Karen's angelic voice captivated as she continued to sing, "No Matter How Dark the Storm."

During the final chorus as the slide of the Savior appeared behind her, a sweet spirit filled the large room:

> But no matter how dark the storm,
> There's a harbor, safe and warm—
> Where the Savior holds forth His hand,
> See His footprints in the sand.
> Though life is hard, you're not alone,
> The Savior's love will guide you home.
> Through the darkness, He shines a light,
> An endless glow through the blackest night,
> And life's shadows will fade from sight—
> Through the gospel's light.

Kate Jeffries glanced around when the song was finished, noting that there were few dry eyes in the surrounding audience. Tears racing down her own cheeks, she was amazed by what Doris and her mother had been able to do with these kids. She had had minor success working with some of these same students in the drama class she had taught, but had never seen them impact an audience like they were doing tonight.

In the final scene as everyone linked arms to perform the closing number, the house lights were turned up before the last chorus, and the audience was invited to join in singing the theme of the production, a song most would carry in their hearts:

> It's the adventure of a lifetime, a lifetime of adventure,
> A time when we'll discover who we are and what we'll be.
> The adventure of a lifetime, a lifetime of adventure,
> And the journey I will take is up to me,
> To me!
> To me!
> TO ME!

# Author's Note

Nearly two years ago, as the initial concept came to mind for this book, I felt that it needed to address some key issues: teen pregnancy, diabetes, and alcoholism. Why did I choose to focus on so many topics? In today's world, life has picked up pace and it seems that everywhere we turn, there are trials, challenges, and disasters happening on a continual basis. Offhand, I can't think of anyone who isn't dealing with adversity of some form. People around the world are receiving a wake-up call—these are indeed the days of tribulation seen by past prophets and recorded in the scriptures (see Doctrine & Covenants 29:8 and 54:10; Moses 7:61).

Although it is a perilous time, it is also a wonderful time. No other generation has been blessed with the technology we enjoy. Hope, faith, and charity thrive. It is my prayer that this book might in some small way, point toward these three keys of endurance (see Moroni 7:42-47).

If we truly understand the plan of salvation, we know that these tests are part of why we are here. Combine these trials with the gift of individual choice, and it makes for lives that are filled with adventures of every kind—both positive and negative. Some choices lead to heartache, others to joy—we have the freedom to decide that for ourselves.

That is the main theme of this book—the importance of the choices we make, the consequences that result, and the reminder that we can grow from the challenging mountains that often lie in our path. I'd like to share a poem I wrote a few years ago, words that came during a time when I attempted to climb an emotional mountain that seemed insurmountable:

## Alpiniste

Darkness overwhelms—
It is too much,
I cannot climb the sheer rock
That slices 'til I bleed—
There is no strength to face this challenge.

But I have come this far—
To give up now makes a mockery of all that
has passed before.
Closing my eyes, I am led by an inner peace
that beckons,
Reminding me of a presence that has been
there all along.
Slowly, I make my way, clutching at
handholds that guide—
Sustain.
The Sun shines bright upon my face as I make
the final stretch,
Reaching for what most would deem beyond
my grasp.

It is finished.
I have learned to face the wind—
The clouds,
The rain.
I have conquered the fear that held me back.
At the summit is a beauty that was
always there—
Beyond my limited sight.

I turn and see another mountain—
But I have learned to climb.

Incidentally, for those who might be interested, *alpiniste* is French for mountain climber. It is my own personal opinion that at some point in our lives we all slip into that role. I've tried to illustrate that with the characters in this book.

One of the mountains examined in this book is the problem of teen pregnancy. Currently this sensitive issue is being addressed by the LDS Church. A special video is being shown throughout the stakes of Zion in an attempt to combat what is becoming a national crisis. Statistics show an increase in its occurrence. Abortions are on the rise; babies are abandoned and left to die by girls who are too immature to fully understand the implications of that choice. Numerous young mothers are opting to keep their babies, raising them in single-parent situations that aren't always in the best interest of the child.

The Church of Jesus Christ of Latter-day Saints has taken a stand on this issue. In a letter that was sent to Church leaders in 1994, it states:

> . . . We note with alarm the continued decline of moral values in society and the resultant number of children being reared by unwed parents. A child needs both a mother *and* a father who provide love, support, and all the blessings of the gospel. Every effort should be made in helping those who conceive out of wedlock to establish an eternal family relationship. When the unwed parents are unable or unwilling to marry, they should be encouraged to place the child for adoption, preferably through LDS Social Services. Placing the infant for adoption through LDS Social Services helps ensure that the baby will be reared in a faithful Latter-day Saint family and will receive the blessings of the sacred sealing covenant. Unwed parents who do not marry should not be counseled to keep the infant as a condition of repentance or out of obligation to care for ones own. . . . The interests of the child should be the paramount consideration. Such a decision enables the unwed parent to do what is best for the child and enhances the prospect for the blessings of the gospel in the lives of all concerned. (First Presidency Letter, 1 February 1994; *Ensign,* June 1994, p. 76)

Four months after I submitted my manuscript to Covenant, an article appeared in the July 1998 issue of the *Ensign* magazine, "But What Was Best for the Baby?" As I read it, I was stunned—the name selected to protect the identity of the girl in this article was the same name I had chosen for the pregnant teenager in my book, Mandy. The *Ensign* article shared one girl's true experience with this particular trial, supporting the viewpoint I had taken with my manuscript. Later

I came across other Church articles that also support this. (See Monte J. Brough, "Guidance for Unwed Parents," *Ensign,* September 1994, pp.19-23; Gordon B. Hinckley, "Save the Children," *Ensign,* November 1994, pp. 52-54; Gordon B. Hinckley, "What Are People Asking About Us?" *Ensign,* November 1998, p. 71.)

As for the other topics dealt with in this book, they are timely concerns. I read an article in a newspaper a few months ago that declared diabetes is becoming an epidemic. Current diets and lack of exercise are often blamed; fingers are also pointed at factors such as heredity and high stress levels. These may all play a part, but for those of us who live with Type 1 diabetes, the cause is still a mystery. Our immune systems go haywire, triggering the destruction of fragile islet cells in the pancreas.

Regardless of its cause, diabetes is a challenging chronic illness that has to be dealt with on a daily basis. It shadows every aspect of our lives, but it doesn't have to dominate our attitudes. There is no reason to live in fear or depression. So many new and wonderful discoveries are being made with this disease that I fully believe that there will be a cure in the not too distant future.

In the March 2000 issue of the *Diabetic Forecast,* an American Diabetes Association publication, it excitedly reveals how close we are to islet cell transplantation, something that could cure Type 1 diabetes. Healthy pancreatic islet cells taken from pigs are encapsulated inside membranes that prevent the body's immune system from destroying them. These cells then produce the insulin needed for proper digestion. Although this technique is far from polished, it offers hope.

This year, a new computerized watch is being considered for release by the FDA. Called the GlucoWatch Monitor, it absorbs fluid from the skin to read blood sugar levels—no more finger pokes, something my fingers would appreciate.

In the nineteen years that I have lived with this disease, I have seen numerous advances. I'm currently wearing my third insulin pump—each pump improves with easier features that enhance blood sugar control. I now use an insulin called Humalog that works within ten minutes of its release into my system. Diabetic friends of mine who give shots have assured me that the new syringes are so sharp and the needles so tiny, you hardly feel the injections. Diabetes is still a challenge, but as I've tried to point out in this book, you can live a full, productive life as a diabetic, if you learn to take care of yourself. There are numerous support groups and resources available for diabetics. Most cities provide listings for local organizations. You can also contact the American Diabetes Association at 1-800-DIABETES (1-800-342-2383) or check out their web site (www.diabetes.org).

Alcoholism is another subject tackled in the pages of this book. Some may think that I chose the Mary Poppins approach. I realize that unfortunately there are alcoholic situations without happy endings—families and individual lives can be destroyed. I have seen the toll this disease has taken in the lives of people I have loved. I chose to take a positive stance in this book. Sometimes hope makes all the difference when dealing with destructive forces. Support groups like Alcoholics Anonymous offer positive incentives and a nonjudgmental setting. Alcoholism is an illness that consumes lives. How crucial it is to provide education to prevent it from taking root and support to help those who are fighting this battle.

This book also contains a major natural disaster. These catastrophes have been taking place since humanity was placed on this mortal sphere. In our day, I believe they are happening on a more frequent basis to wake us up to what is really important. Periodically the news reports share uplifting stories of courage, love, and faith when tragedies strike. Hearts are touched when we see communities working together to survive these ordeals that often assail us without warning. Selfishness is forgotten as people reach out to help those around them. What a wonderful world it would be if we could render Christlike acts of service without disaster as a catalyst.

Challenging trials will continue to be a part of our lives. I suspect that is why we are constantly counseled in the scriptures to endure till the end. This life wasn't meant to be easy. I'll admit, there are times when I've longed for a permanent Calgon moment, but in my heart I know that I have learned the most from those things that have literally brought me to my knees. The trials never end. There will always be some new challenge to face, another round of stretching as we endure the Refiner's Fire.

We all face mountains in life. They challenge and beckon us forward, promising a view that is unsurpassed if we'll endure the climb.

I love what President Gordon B. Hinckley had to say on this very subject in his new book, *Standing for Something*. In a chapter that discusses the importance of keeping a positive outlook on life, he states:

> We all tend to worry about the future. . . . There
> will doubtless be challenges of all varieties. No one
> can avoid them. But we must not despair or give up.
> We must look for the sunlight through the clouds. (p. 103)

It is my fervent prayer that we will all find the strength to do so throughout our "adventure of a lifetime." To borrow once again from the song I wrote that bears that same title:

> *It's the adventure of a lifetime, a lifetime of adventure,*
> *A time when we'll discover who we are and what we'll be.*
> *The adventure of a lifetime, a lifetime of adventure,*
> *And the journey I will take is up to me!*

## ABOUT THE AUTHOR

A former resident of Ashton, Idaho, Cheri J. Crane graduated from Ricks College with plans to teach high school English, French, and drama. Instead of completing her degree at Brigham Young University, she married a sharp-looking returned missionary named Kennon. They made their home in Bennington, Idaho, where they now live with their three sons—Kris, Derek, and Devin.

Cheri enjoys numerous hobbies that include cooking, gardening, composing music, and participating in sports. She also heads a local chapter of the ADA (American Diabetes Association). She has spent most of her married life serving in the Primary and in the Young Women. She currently serves as the ward teacher improvement coordinator.

Cheri is the author of four best-selling young adult novels—*Kate's Turn, Kate's Return, Forever Kate,* and *Following Kate.* She can be reached at the following e-mail address: **cj38@lds.net**.

*Dr. Lisa Krivickas is my dear friend, colleague, and teacher. She has been dedicating herself to caring for patients with amyotrophic lateral sclerosis for many years at Harvard University. Now, as a patient of ALS, she learns more about the disease from a different perspective. She returns this knowledge to her patients and the ALS Community.*

# Contents

**Living With the Reality of Amyotrophic Lateral Sclerosis**

**Managing Advanced Disease and End-of-Life Issues**

**Where You Can Turn to For Help**

# Foreword

Amyotrophic lateral sclerosis (ALS) commands public attention these days. *Tuesdays With Morrie,* a book about the last year of the life of a patient with ALS, was at the top of best-seller lists for more than 4 years, and the noted actor Jack Lemmon starred in the film version. Newspapers and magazines actively publish the poignant stories of individual patients in the grip of a cruel disease, and they actively describe scientific advances in attempts to find a cure. It is difficult to account for this public interest for a rare disease except that ALS is a clear reminder of human mortality. And ALS is one of few diseases where drug therapy has not altered the inexorable progression of symptoms, at least not in any way visible to the patient or family.

ALS cannot be cured, but it can be treated. Research efforts have expanded in the past decade, and progress in the basic science of ALS has been phenomenal. It has become the focus of discussions of end-of-life issues and palliative care. An effective treatment must be coming soon.

What to do in the meantime? There has been a profusion of books about ALS for physicians and scientists, but until this book first appeared there had not yet been one specifically designed for patients and their families. This handbook fills a major void.

Patients and families now usually know about "Lou Gehrig's disease." At least they have heard of it, and they know the prognosis is ominous. At the start, however, they know nothing about coping because they do not know what, specifically, to expect. And physicians are not all equally skilled in transmitting the information, in part because there is no single correct way to do it. Physicians differ in personality and so do patients; each encounter involves different people. Few patients seem to want a detailed preview of the future, but some do.

Therein lies a paradox. The principle of patient autonomy requires freedom of choice for the person. But true freedom of choice requires detailed information about what lies ahead. Maintaining hope is a major goal and is not aided by too much information given too soon. How much to tell and when to tell are challenges for the health care workers.

Regardless of their views about long-range events, almost all patients and families want to know what to do at the moment. Almost all patients and families want to participate in therapeutic trials. Patients are sometimes given contradictory advice about rehabilitation exercises. Patients need guidance about the only Food and Drug Administration–approved drug for the treatment of ALS, riluzole (Rilutek), as well as new experimental preparations and drugs like lithium carbonate, drugs that have been approved for some other diseases and are therefore known to be safe and are being used for patients with ALS. They have to be properly informed about new research advances, including stem cell therapy. They need to know about different sites of neurologic care. Patients and families also need help to deal with the maze of alternative remedies: antioxidants, creatine, anabolic steroids, vitamins, and dietary supplements. They need help emotionally; many physicians believe erroneously that any patient with ALS must be depressed and therefore needs antidepressant medication. Patients need help in learning about the use of therapeutic drugs to control symptoms of salivation, difficulty sleeping, aches and pains, trouble voiding, and sexual activity. Options for relieving difficulty swallowing range from dietary adjustment to a simple operation. Speech therapy or computerized voice synthesizers can ameliorate difficulty speaking. Wheelchairs and other devices require choices. Patients need direction in choosing the site of their care—single physician or multidisciplinary clinical center. Patients desire help in dealing with end-of-life issues and, confronted with major options, they differ in their ultimate choices about mechanical ventilation. Patients and their families want to know about financial issues for their personal situation. Many want to learn how they can support biomedical research, by raising money or by giving permission for postmortem examination.

That recitation is quite a list of serious considerations, but in this book experienced contributors provide the essential information. Readers will recognize that the writers are not all neurologists or even physicians in other specialties. Some are nurses, or clergy, or have some other background that helps all of us—patients, families, caregivers—meet the challenges of ALS.

Dr. Mitsumoto is to be congratulated and thanked for this update of a handbook that has been so helpful in the past. This new version is especially welcome now.

*Lewis P. Rowland, MD*

# Preface

The first edition of this book, edited with the late Forbes H. Norris, MD, and published in 1992, was intended for health care professionals. However, patients and their families were frequent readers of the book because no comprehensive book on amyotrophic lateral sclerosis (ALS) management was available for them. For that reason the second edition was extensively revised and rewritten to address the concerns of everyone living with the disease in an accessible, straightforward way. This edition was edited with Theodore L. Munsat, MD.

Since publication of the last edition, our understanding and treatment of ALS have changed dramatically. The many puzzles of this disease are being steadily solved. A number of causes of familial ALS have been identified, and the mechanisms of motor neuron cell death are much better understood. The FDA approved riluzole in 1996 as the first drug ever approved for the treatment of ALS. Although expected for the past dozen years, it is frustrating to say that additional drugs have not been developed. Yet, new drugs continue to be tested and others are on the horizon.

The American Academy of Neurology's ALS Practice Parameter Task Force published the recommendations for the care and treatment of patients with ALS in 1999, which were developed by using an evidence-based approach, an approach that uses detailed and uniform analysis of the medical literature. They are now in the process of producing new recommendations based on new data. ALS Clinical Assessment Research and Education (ALS CARE.) provided extensive invaluable information about the current status of patient care and management, including the medical, psychosocial, and financial issues of both patients and caregivers. Since the last edition of this book, significant advancement has been seen in the care and management for patients with ALS and their families. In particular, respiratory care, care in approaching the end of life, and other symptomatic treatments have been truly eye opening. Finally, nonprofit voluntary organizations, not only the Muscular Dystrophy Association (MDA, ALS Division) and the ALS Association, but also a number of ALS research organizations, have become instrumental in supporting research for a cure and have increased their efforts to improve public awareness of this disease. ALS Research Group, a national group of those who study ALS consisting of more than 70 ALS centers or clinics, made a monumental accomplishment in collecting DNA from a large number of patients and healthy controls. It was only possible through a huge collaborative effort from the National Institute of Neurological Diseases and Stroke, the MDA, and the ALS Association. In the past, medical management has been the sole domain of health care professionals. Recently, however, patients and families have taken a much more active role in disseminating medical and related information. Although the Internet provides information in an unprecedented manner, much of this information is fragmented and of uncertain validity. We felt strongly that a carefully and critically edited book written by experts in the field is the best resource for patients and their families. This was the main thrust in the second edition. Theodore L. Munsat, the coeditor of the second edition, who is now concentrating his time on the World Federation of Neurology and still consulting for Northeastern ALS Study Group, has decided to step down from the editing of this book but contributed an excellent chapter. It is always an honor and we are very fortunate to have a Foreword from Lewis P. Rowland, MD, who probably has seen the largest number of patients with ALS and is a teacher for many of us.

It is an honor and delight when patients and their families mention this book and give positive comments. This has been a driving force to renew the edition, because there is enough new information and knowledge to make a new edition worthwhile. We have several new authors who have contributed chapters. We also have updated all chapters to reflect new information and expanded the chapters dealing with quality of life for both patients with ALS and their caregivers. We trust that readers will find those chapters discussing less-often-addressed topics, such as mourning and bereavement, informative and useful.

# Acknowledgments

I express my deepest feelings for patients and families who live with this difficult disease. Many of them have been benevolent and kind enough to help us in the various research projects that we have been conducting. They have been the greatest teachers for us. My executive assistant, Olena Jennings, MA, MFA, helped a great deal in administrative matters and offered some editorial assistance, besides contributing a chapter about resources available. Noreen Henson, acquisitions editor, also encouraged us to do this new edition and kept us moving forward. Last, but not least, I thank all the authors and coauthors who put their enormous expertise and knowledge into their chapters and also have been patient enough to get through the book-making effort.

# Contributors

**Lisa Adams, MA**
Speech Language Pathologist
Department of Rehabilitation
Silvercrest Center for Nursing
  and Rehabilitation
Jamaica, New York

**Steven M. Albert, PhD**
Professor and Associate Chair
Department of Behavioral
  and Community Health
  Sciences
Graduate School of Public Health
University of Pittsburgh
Pittsburgh, Pennsylvania

**Frederick A. Anderson, Jr., PhD**
Professor
Department of Surgery
University of Massachusetts
Medical School
Worcester, Massachusetts

**Jinsy A. Andrews, MD**
Assistant Professor
  of Neurology
Department of Neurology
Columbia University
The Neurological Institute
New York, New York

**Nazem Atassi, MD**
Fellow
Department of Neurology
MGH Neurology Associates
Boston, Massachusetts

**Robert C. Basner, MD**
Associate Professor of
  Clinical Medicine
Department of Medicine
Columbia University
College of Physicians and Surgeons
New York, New York

**Richard S. Bedlack, MD PhD MSc**
Associate Professor
Department of Medicine/Neurology
Duke University Medical Center
Durham VA Medical Center
Durham, North Carolina

**Vanina Dal Bello-Haas, PT, PhD**
Associate Professor
School of Physical Therapy
University of Saskatchewan
Saskatoon, Saskatchewan, Canada

**Gian Domenico Borasio, MD**
Chair in Palliative Medicine
Interdisciplinary Center
  for Palliative Medicine
Head, Motor Neuron Disease
  Research Group
Department of Neurology
Munich University Hospital
  Grosshadern
Munich, Germany

**Mark B. Bromberg, MD, PhD**
Professor of Neurology
Department of Neurology
University of Utah
Salt Lake City, Utah

**Lucie Bruijn, BPharm, MSc, PhD**
Senior VP, Research and
   Development
Department of Research
The ALS Association
Palm Harbor, Florida

**John T. Calcavecchia,
   BS, PTA, MBA**
Assistive Technology Supplier
ATG Rehab
Newington, Connecticut

**Patricia Casey**
Les Turner ALS Foundation
Skokie, Illinois

**David A. Chad, MD**
Staff Neurologist
Director, Professor of Neurology
   and Pathology
Department of Neurology
Massachusetts General Hospital
Umass Memorial Health Care
Boston, Massachusetts

**Stacey M. Champion, BA**
Clinical Research Coordinator
Department of Forbes Norris
   MDA/ALS Research Center
California Pacific Medical Center
San Francisco, California

**Winston T. Cheng, MS, CCC-SLP**
Speech-Language Pathology
   Section Chief
Department of Speech and Hearing
Columbia University Medical Center
New York, New York

**Marlene A. Ciechoski**
ALS Hope Foundation
Philadelphia, Pennsylvania

**Valerie A. Cwik, MD**
Medical Director
Muscular Dystrophy Association
Tucson, Arizona

**Kate E. Dalton, MS, RD**
Registered Dietitian
The Eleanor and
   Lou Gehrig MDA/ALS
   Research Center
Columbia University Medical
   Center
New York, New York

**Dallas A. Forshew, RN, BSN**
Manager, Clinical Research
Forbes Norris ALS Research
   Center
California Pacific Medical
   Center
San Francisco, California

**Steve Gibson, BA**
Vice President
Government Relations and
   Public Affairs
Department of Advocacy
The ALS Association
Washington, DC

**Michael C. Graves, MD**
Professor of Neurology
Department of Neurology
University of California
Los Angeles, California

**Laurie Gutmann, MD**
Professor
Department of Neurology
West Virginia University
Morgantown, West Virginia

**Gabriela Harrington-Moroney, RN, BSN**
Clinical Research Nurse
Department of Neurology
The Neurological Institute
Columbia University
New York, New York

**Estelle S. Harris, MD**
Associate Professor
Department of Medicine
Division of Respiratory,
    Critical Care, and Occupational
    Pulmonary Medicine
University of Utah
Salt Lake City, Utah

**Terri Heiman-Patterson, MD**
Professor
Department of Neurology
Drexel University
Philadelphia, Pennsylvania

**Nada El Husseini, MD**
Resident
Department of Medicine/Neurology
Duke University Medical Center
Durham, North Carolina

**Carlayne Elizabeth Jackson, MD**
Professor of Neurology
    and Otolaryngology
Department of Neurology
University of Texas Health Science
    Center San Antonio
San Antonio, Texas

**Olena Jennings, MA, MFA**
Administrative Coordinator
Department of Neurology
Columbia University Medical Center
New York, New York

**Petra Kaufmann, MD, MSc**
Assistant Professor of Neurology
Department of Neurology
The Neurological Institute
Columbia University
New York, New York

**Marta Kazandjian, MA, CCC-SLP, BRS-S**
Director
Department of Speech Pathology
Center for Digestive
    Diseases and Swallowing
    Disorders
Silvercrest Center for Nursing
    and Rehabilitation
Queens, New York

**Lisa S. Krivickas, MD**
Associate Professor
Associate Chair of
    Academic Affairs
Department of Physical Medicine
    and Rehabilitation
Harvard Medical School
Boston, Massachusetts

**Bushra Malik, MD**
Fellow
Department of Neurology
Center for Headache and Pain
Cleveland Clinic Foundation
Cleveland, Ohio

**Sharon Matland, RN, BSN, MBA**
Vice President, Patient Services
Department of Patient Services
The ALS Association
Calabasas Hills, California

**Justin Mhoon, MD**
Resident
Department of Medicine/
Neurology
Duke University Medical Center
Durham, North Carolina

**Robert G. Miller, MD**
Director
Department of Neurology
Forbes Norris MDA/ALS Research
  Center
California Pacific Medical Center
San Francisco, California

**Hiroshi Mitsumoto, MD, DSc**
Wesley J. Mowe Professor of
  Neurology
Director, Department of Neurology
Columbia University
  Medical Center
New York, New York

**Jacqueline Montes, PT, MA, NCS**
Department of Neurology
Spinal Muscular Atrophy Clinical
  Research Center
Columbia University
New York, New York

**Theodore L. Munsat, MD**
Professor Emeritus of Neurology
Department of Neurology
Tufts University
Boston, Massachusetts

**N. Michael Murphy, MD**
Clinical Professor
Department of Psychiatry
Albany Medical College
Albany, New York

**Bob Osborne, RN**
Case Manager
Sutter Health
San Francisco, California

**Judith Godwin Rabkin,
  PhD, MPH**
Professor of Clinical Psychology
  in Psychiatry
Department of Psychiatry
College of Physicians and Surgeons
Columbia University
Research Scientist
Department of Psychiatry
New York State Psychiatric Institute
New York, New York

**Stacy Rudnicki, MD**
Professor
Department of Neurology
University of Arkansas
  Medical Center
Little Rock, Arkansas

**Linda I. Boynton De Sepulveda,
  ADN, BSN, MN, DNSc**
Chief Executive Officer
ALS Haven
Montecito, California

**Jeremy Shefner, MD, PhD**
Professor and Chair
Department of Neurology
State University of New York
Syracuse, New York

**Mark J. Stillman, MD**
Director
Department of Neurology
Center for Headache and Pain
Cleveland Clinic Foundation
Cleveland, Ohio

**Ronit Sukenick, DPT, BS**
Physical Therapist
Department of Rehabilitation Medicine
Eleanor and Lou Gehrig MDA/ALS
    Research Center
Columbia University Medical Center
New York, New York

**Barbara Ellen Thompson,**
    **OTD, MSW, BSOT**
Associate Professor
Department of Occupational Therapy
The Sage Colleges
Troy, New York

**Mary Eleanor Toms, MD**
Medical Director
Department of Palliative Care
Beacon Hospice and Palliative
    Care Services
East Providence,
    Rhode Island

**Margaret Wahl, RN, BSN**
Medical and Science Editor
Department of Publications
Muscular Dystrophy
    Association
Tucson, Arizona

# Amyotrophic Lateral Sclerosis: An Overview

# 1

# What Is Amyotrophic Lateral Sclerosis?

## Valerie A. Cwik

*Fans, for the past two weeks you have been reading about the bad break I got. Yet today I consider myself the luckiest man on the face of the earth . . . I may have had a tough break, but I have an awful lot to live for. (1)*

With those words, Lou Gehrig announced his retirement from the New York Yankees on July 4, 1939, at the age of 36, ending one of the most remarkable careers in the game of baseball. During his 17 years with the Yankees, Gehrig played in 2,164 regular season games, hitting 493 home runs. His consecutive game record of 2,130, which earned him the nickname "Iron Horse," stood until 1995, when it was broken by Baltimore Orioles shortstop Cal Ripken Jr. Most Americans had probably never heard of amyotrophic lateral sclerosis (ALS) before Lou Gehrig, and even now, most people are not aware of what a diagnosis of ALS truly means until an individual or family member is affected.

ALS belongs to a family of inherited and acquired disorders that, together, constitute the motor neuron diseases. Motor neurons are those cells in the brain, brain stem, and spinal cord that control the voluntary movements of muscles, and in motor neuron diseases, damage to these cells causes weakness and, sometimes, total paralysis and death. The family of motor neuron diseases includes such diverse disorders as botulism, tetanus, poliomyelitis, and spinal muscular atrophy, as well as ALS. In most cases of ALS, called sporadic ALS (SALS), motor neurons degenerate and die prematurely of unknown causes. However, in roughly 10% of ALS, the disease is inherited and is called familial ALS (FALS); for some with

FALS the causative genetic mutation can be identified, but for others the genetic defects remain unknown.

## Historical Perspective

Motor neuron disorders, including ALS, were starting to be recognized nearly a century before Lou Gehrig developed his first symptoms. Case reports describing the clinical motor neuron syndromes of progressive muscular atrophy, primary lateral sclerosis, progressive bulbar palsy, and "classic" ALS began to appear in the French and British medical literature in the 1830s, authored by such renowned physicians as Sir Charles Bell, Francois Aran, and Amand Duchenne (2–4). One of the earliest cases of ALS was reported in considerable detail in 1853 (5). The patient, Prosper Lecomte, was an unfortunate 30-year-old circus proprietor whose problems began in September 1848 with weakness of the right hand. By the following July he had weakness of both legs; walking became difficult and he tripped over small objects. This was followed two months later by weakness of the left hand and slurred speech. He had to give up working by the end of 1849. Over the next 3 years his symptoms progressed steadily, so that by February 1853 he was bedridden and unable to speak or swallow. On February 12, 1853, Lecomte died at the age of 35, 4.5 years after the onset of his first symptom. In that early paper many features of classic ALS were clearly described, including progressive wasting, weakness and spasticity of the limbs, speech and swallowing difficulty, and death within five years of symptom onset.

In 1874 a French physician, Jean Martin Charcot, who is regarded as the founder of modern neurology and perhaps the most successful teacher of clinical medicine, established the clinical and pathologic characteristics of ALS (6). Charcot stressed the importance of meticulous observation to his students. To that end, Charcot is reported to have employed a housemaid with ALS and therefore was able to systematically observe the clinical manifestations of her disease (7). She was later admitted to the Salpêtrière infirmary so that Charcot could obtain an autopsy and define the pathologic features of the disease. His descriptions of ALS remain amazingly accurate to this day, and as a result ALS is referred to as Charcot's disease in some parts of the world (8). In the United Kingdom it is known as motor neurone disease. Americans are familiar with the terms *Lou Gehrig's disease* and *ALS* and know that it is a devastating, uniformly fatal disorder.

## Research

The number of yearly publications in professional journals loosely reflects the amount of active research about a given disease. In searching *Cumulated Index Medicus*, *Current List of Medical Literature*, MEDLINE, and PubMed by the key words *amyotrophic lateral sclerosis,* one finds nearly 10,000 scientific papers for the years 1920–2008; more than half have been published in the past 15 years alone (Figure 1.1). For the year 1920, there were no publications about ALS listed in *Index*

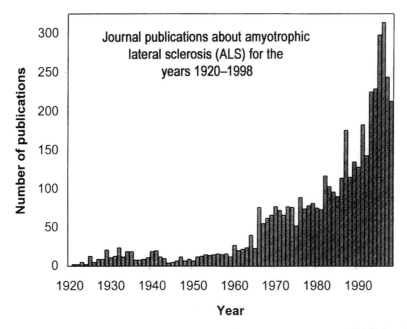

**Figure 1.1** Journal publications about amyotrophic lateral sclerosis (ALS) for the years 1920–1998. The number of publications about ALS in scientific and medical journals has increased substantially over the past 40 years. (The number of publications for 2008 includes January through July.)

*Medicus.* From 1921 through the mid-1960s, the number of yearly publications about ALS was generally less than 25; this number essentially tripled for the years 1966–1981. By 1993–1998, there were more than 200 annual publications about ALS, and over the past decade the number of publications about ALS has averaged approximately 500 annually. These numbers reflect only the papers published in referenced journals. They do not include oral and poster presentations at scientific and professional meetings, nor do they include other publications, such as books about ALS.

From 1920 through the 1940s, most publications about ALS were single-case reports or small series describing the clinical features and course of the disease, descriptions of the pathologic findings in the various ALS syndromes, or reports about putative causative factors. There also were sporadic reports about treatments, particularly vitamin therapies. The 1950s and 1960s saw increasing interest in the epidemiology of ALS, particularly with regard to ALS on Guam and in the western Pacific. Since 1970 there has been a substantial increase in the number of papers about the possible etiologies and pathogeneses of ALS, and about therapeutic trials. In recent years, the focus of research has shifted from strictly clinical observations and patient-based research to include the development of animal models for ALS; investigation of the cellular, biochemical, molecular, and genetic bases for motor neuron diseases; and drug screening and development.

## Epidemiology

With few exceptions, ALS has had a uniform distribution worldwide over the past 50 to 60 years, despite differences in climate, geography, race, cultures, and diet. ALS strikes approximately 1 to 2 in every 100,000 adults annually worldwide, and it has long been apparent that men are at somewhat higher risk for developing the disease than are women, although this gender difference disappears at older ages. The prevalence of the disease—the number of persons who will have the disease at any given time—is estimated to be 1 to 7 per 100,000 population.

For the first half of the 20th century exceptional clusters of ALS, 50 to 100 times higher than worldwide rates, were reported in the residents of 3 islands in the western Pacific: the Japanese villagers of the Kii peninsula of Honshu Island, Japan; the Chamorro people on the islands of Guam and Rota of the Marianas chain of Micronesia; and the Auyu and Jakai people of West New Guinea, Indonesia (9–11). For the past 50 years, new cases of ALS have declined steadily in these regions to rates closer to those in the rest of the world. Although the cause(s) of these clusters is not known, environmental factors, such as exposure to neurotoxins in the diet and mineral imbalances in drinking water, have been postulated (12,13).

There have been a number of reports of smaller ALS concentrations. The occurrence of ALS in both (unrelated) partners of a married couple (conjugal ALS) has been reported in the United States and Italy (14–16). Conjugal ALS also affected 2 couples in southern France (17). One person developed the disease in 1977; the other 3 became symptomatic in 1990 and 1991. The question of genetic susceptibility or an environmental etiologic factor was raised because all 4 individuals were from the same geographic region (Languedoc-Roussillon). In the case of nonidentical twin brothers developing ALS within 2 years of one another, an intrauterine toxic or infectious exposure was postulated as a causative factor (18).

Small geographic clusters of ALS have also been reported. Between 1975 and 1983 ALS was diagnosed in 6 residents of Two Rivers, Wisconsin. Physical trauma, consumption of fish from Lake Michigan, and a family history of cancer occurred more frequently in these patients than in non-ALS subjects from the same community (19). Additional small clusters include 3 patients, all Ashkenazi Jews, in a single apartment building in Montreal, who developed ALS within an 18-month period, and 3 unrelated men living within a block of one another in Burlington, North Carolina (20,21). In the North Carolina cluster, all 3 men had speech and swallowing difficulty at the onset of their disease, and ALS was diagnosed in 2 of the men within a 2-month period. Kilnes and Hochberg reported that 4 patients in rural South Dakota, 3 of whom had lived within a 3-km radius for all of their lives, developed ALS within a 10-year period. High selenium content in the regional soil was noted (22).

Recent epidemiologic studies have demonstrated an increased risk for ALS among Italian soccer players (23,24). Although the cause remains unknown, hypotheses that have been proposed to explain the higher-than-expected risk include vigorous physical activity, trauma, use of performance-enhancing drugs or dietary supplements, and exposure to pesticides on the playing field.

An elevated risk for ALS has also been reported among veterans of the U.S. military, particularly those who served in the 1991 Gulf War (25–27). In the Gulf-deployed personnel, new cases of ALS increased steadily between 1994 and 1996, about 4 to 6 years after deployment, peaking in 1996 (28). By 2001, the risk had dropped to the same level as nondeployed military. As in other outbreaks, environmental factors or events, along with genetic factors, are thought to have led to the temporary increase in ALS cases. Although this theory remains unproven, that the increased risk correlated with deployment to certain geographic locations lends support to that argument (29). In response to the concern for ALS in the U.S. military population, the Department of Veterans Affairs has established a registry to identify and track living veterans with ALS (30).

Although these and other clusters continue to raise the specter of a toxic basis for ALS, to date, no definite cause-and-effect relationship between any environmental toxin or transmissible and/or infectious agent and the development of ALS has been firmly established.

A few countries, including Mexico, Poland, and Italy, actually report lower than average rates of ALS (31–34). The reason for the apparent lower risk is not known, but if areas of low risk do indeed exist, explanations for this lower risk should be sought.

## Etiology and Pathogenesis of ALS

Despite all that we have learned about ALS over the past 150 or so years, some of the questions that were raised by our neurologic forefathers about the cause of ALS have only recently been resolved, and others remain unanswered.

Charcot in 1875 may have been the first to question the relationship between remote poliomyelitis infection and the subsequent development of ALS (35). Although there is little evidence to implicate the poliovirus or any other virus as a cause of ALS, this question remains open at this time (36–38).

Interest in heavy metal intoxication as a cause of ALS has been high for more than a century. Wilson, in 1907, is credited as being the first to question whether lead poisoning causes ALS (39). Further support for a heavy metal hypothesis came from a variety of sources, such as the finding of increased levels of aluminum and manganese and diminished levels of calcium and magnesium in the soil and drinking water of the regions of the western Pacific, where the incidence of ALS was particularly high, and the reports of increased lead and heavy metal exposure in people with ALS compared with controls (13,40,41). We now know that lead and mercury intoxication may cause reversible ALS-like syndromes (42,43). Although the relationship between toxic environmental factors and the development of ALS remains unsettled, it is likely that heavy metals play only a marginal role, if any, in the development of this disease.

In the mid-20th century, ALS was thought, by some, to be not a single disease entity but a syndrome of varying causes (44). Suspected causes included dietary deficiency and gastrointestinal dysfunction; infectious or inflammatory disorders, such as syphilis, remote poliomyelitis, or a severe upper respiratory tract infection at onset; and vascular disorders such as generalized atherosclerosis and coronary artery disease (at the time, the authors did not recognize the coincidence of a rare disease, ALS, with very common vascular diseases).

The deficiency syndrome hypothesis persisted for many years, championed by a Swedish physician, Dr. Ask-Upmark, who observed the development of ALS in several patients who had undergone gastric resection (45). He theorized that the common nutritional problems that followed surgical resection of the stomach led to a "certain malnutrition" and the subsequent development of ALS. He also acknowledged, however, that some cases of ALS might have resulted from system atrophy or abiotrophy (premature aging) (46).

## Genes and Proteins

Over the past several decades, a multitude of putative causes have been suggested, investigated, and often refuted or discarded (Table 1.1). And although the cause, or causes, of most cases of ALS remains unknown, significant insights into the pathogenic mechanisms of familial and sporadic ALS have developed in recent years. For example, for those with FALS, approximately 20% will have a mutation, or defect, in the superoxide dismutase (SOD1) gene on chromosome 21 (47,48). The enzyme SOD1 normally functions as an antioxidant, helping to eliminate potentially damaging free radicals in cells throughout the body. Defects in the SOD1 gene lead to the production of a toxic SOD1 protein that damages motor neurons and surrounding cells in the nervous system, causing ALS. To date, more than 100 unique mutations in this gene have been associated with the development of FALS. Rarely, mutations in the genes for other proteins, such as alsin, spastin, senataxin, dynactin, and vesicle-associated membrane protein B, have also been reported to cause FALS (49–53). For others with FALS, the underlying genetic causes remain to be elucidated

Finding the cause of sporadic ALS remains a considerable challenge to researchers. Many suspect that ALS is a multifactorial disease, and that there may be genetic, environmental, and other unknown risk factors that combine to trigger the onset of the disease. Over the past several years, reports of genetic alterations that may predispose individuals to the development of ALS have appeared in the literature. Although these genetic alterations, called single-nucleotide polymorphisms (SNPs), in and of themselves may not cause SALS, their presence may increase the risk for developing the disease. Such alterations have been reported in paraoxanase genes, which are involved in the detoxification of certain pesticides and chemical nerve agents, and, in the European population, in the gene for the protein DPP6, which is a component of neuronal potassium channels (54–57).

Another interesting finding has been a possible link between the risk for SALS and the number of copies one has of the survival motor neuron, or SMN1, gene

**Table 1.1** Putative Causes and Etiologic Factors for Amyotrophic Lateral Sclerosis

| | |
|---|---|
| **Altered immunity** | **Heavy metals and trace minerals** |
| Antibodies to calcium channels | Aluminum |
| Antineuronal antibodies | Copper |
| Antisprouting antibodies | Lead |
| **Disordered neuronal metabolism or function** | Manganese |
| | Mercury |
| Abnormal neurotransmitter function | Selenium |
| Abnormal thyrotropin-releasing hormone | **Infectious or inflammatory factors** |
| Altered axonal transport | Activated astrocytes |
| Defects in neuronal membrane structure or function | Activated microglia |
| Defects in the urea cycle | Severe upper respiratory infection |
| Disordered calcium, phosphate, and bone metabolism | Syphylis |
| | Viruses, especially poliovirus |
| Hyperparathyroidism | **Nutritional disorders** |
| Loss of cholinergic receptors | Dietary deficiencies |
| Loss/dysfunction of androgen receptors | Gastrointestinal dysfunction |
| **Excitotoxicity** | Vitamin deficiencies |
| Alterations in serum and spinal fluid amino acids | **Physical injury** |
| | Pneumatic tools |
| Glutamate transporter protein deficiency | Prior surgery |
| Seed of *Cycas circinalis* | Prior trauma |
| **Genetic disorders and abnormalities** | **Toxic agents or exposures** |
| | Animal carcasses and hides |
| Defects in alsin gene | Endogenous "toxins" |
| Defects in dynactin gene | Gasoline |
| Defects in senataxin gene | Household pets |
| Defects in superoxide dismutase gene | Spinal anesthesia |
| Defects in VAPB gene | **Other** |
| DNA and RNA abnormalities | Abiotrophy (premature aging) |
| Genetic markers/HLA antigen | Malignancy |
| Hexosaminidase deficiency | Neurotrophic factor deficiencies |
| Single-nucleotide polymorphisms (SNPs) | Paraproteinemia |
| | Vascular disorders |

(58,59). Mutations in that gene cause another type of motor neuron disease called spinal muscular atrophy (or SMA).

Other studies have focused on the role of the protein TDP43 and its association with ALS, particularly ALS with frontotemporal dementia. Abnormal TDP-43 protein is a common finding in SALS, ALS with frontotemporal dementia, and some cases of FALS (60). Interestingly, abnormal TDP-43 protein is *not* found in FALS because of SOD1 mutations, suggesting different mechanisms for the cause of these diseases.

### Animal Models

Identification of the SOD1 mutation and other gene defects has led to the development of several animal models of motor neuron disease. Study of the cellular, biochemical, and molecular changes that occur over the course of the disease in animals is providing insights into the changes that likely are occurring in the nervous system of humans with ALS. Such mechanisms include excitotoxicity from glutamate mishandling, free radical damage, mitochondrial dysfunction, protein aggregation, and neurofilament tangling. In addition, there is substantial evidence that cells other than motor neurons, such as astrocytes and microglia—the immune cells of the central nervous system—can impact the course of ALS.

These studies, and others that will be discussed in later chapters, confirm what has been long suspected, that ALS is a very complex, multifactorial disease and we have probably only scratched the surface in our understanding of it.

## Treatment of ALS

The comprehensive treatment of ALS is the main theme of this book. Although, currently, there is no drug or therapy that effectively stops or slows the progression of ALS, this should not be interpreted to mean that there is no treatment for ALS. In fact, there is a tremendous amount that can be done to maintain independence and quality of life for people with the disease. The multitude of therapies and resources available—drug and nondrug, medical and nonmedical—are reviewed in substantial detail in subsequent chapters. Only a few background comments are made here.

### Drug Therapies

The failure to find an effective drug therapy for ALS has not been for lack of trying. To date, nearly 100 different medications (and a few nondrug therapies) have been anecdotally reported or tested in therapeutic trials and most were found to be ineffective in halting or significantly slowing the course of this disorder (Table 1.2). Over the past several decades the treatments tested have covered the gamut from antiviral agents and antibiotics to chemotherapies, from immunomodulating agents to neurotrophic factors.

**Table 1.2** Therapies Tried for Amyotrophic Lateral Sclerosis

**Antiglutamate/antiexcitotoxic agents**

Branched-chain amino acids

Dextromethorphan

Gabapentin

Glycine

Lamotrigine

L-Threonine

Naloxone

Riluzole

Topiramate

**Anti-inflammatories/immune system modulators**

Azathioprine

Celecoxib

Cyclophosphamide

Cyclosporine A

Glatiramer acetate

Hydrocortisone (oral and intrathecal)

Interferon (subcutaneous and intrathecal)

Intravenous immune globulin

Levamisole

Plasma exchange

Prednisolone

Thalidomide

Whole-body lymphoid irradiation

Zenvia

**Agents that may act on neuronal metabolism/ antiapoptotic agents**

Arimoclomol

Buspirone

Creatine

Eldepryl

Growth hormone

Lecithin

Minocycline

Pentoxyfilline

Pramipexole

TCH346

Testosterone

Thyrotropin releasing hormone (intravenous, intrathecal, intramuscular, oral)

**Antioxidants**

Beta-carotene

Centrophenoxine

Coenzyme Q10

Cytochrome C

Edavarone

Glutathione

L-cysteine

Lipoic acid

Melatonin

N-acetylcysteine

Selegeline

Selenium

Superoxide dismutase 1 (SOD1)

Vitamin C

Vitamin E (oral, intravenous, and intramuscular)

**Cholinergic agents**

Neostigmine

Physostigmine

Priscoline

3,4-diaminopyridine

THA

*(Continued)*

**Table 1.2** Therapies Tried for Amyotrophic Lateral
Sclerosis  (*Continued*)

**Neurotrophic agents**

Brain-derived neurotrophic factor (BDNF)

Ciliary neurotrophic factor (CNTF)

Insulin-like growth factor (IGF-1, myotrophin)

Xaliproden

**Antimicrobial agents**

Ceftriaxone

Tilerone hydrochloride

Trypan blue

Trypan red

**Antiviral agents**

Amantadine

Indinavir

Isoprinosine

Transfer factor

Zidovudine

**Nutritional supplements and vitamins**

Crude liver extract

Intravenous amino acids

Octacosanol

Vitamin B1 (thiamine)

Vitamin B6 (pyridoxine)

Vitamin B12

"Vitamin B" in yeast preparation

**Calcium channel blockers and chelating agents**

Calcium disodium edetate

Dantrolene

Nimodipine

Penicillamine

Verapamil

**Other**

Adrenal cortex

Antihistaminic agents

Balneotherapy (natural mineral water baths)

Bovine gangliosides

Bromocriptine

Cervico-dorsal electroshock therapy

Guanidine

5-hydroxytrytophan

Hyperbaric oxygen

Olfactory cells

Phthalazinol

Snake venom (modified neuro-toxin)

Stem cells

Toluloxy propanediol

Probably the most ubiquitous treatment for ALS over the past century has been the antioxidant vitamin E (tocopherol). Anecdotal reports of the use of this vitamin appear in the literature as early as the 1920s, and daily injections of vitamin E were given to Lou Gehrig for treatment of his disease (61). At that time vitamin E was used not for its antioxidant properties but in part because ALS was thought to be the result of a deficiency state. In 1940 Wechsler reported remarkable beneficial responses to vitamin E therapy in 14 of 20 patients (62). Unfortunately, several subsequent series failed to obtain any good results with vitamins E or B6 (63–65). Despite such discouraging results, many neurologists continue to recommend vitamins for the treatment of ALS, particularly those with antioxidant properties. Although it is no longer believed that ALS is caused by a nutritional deficiency, the rationale for such therapy is based on the discoveries that (a) a mutation in the gene for copper/zinc superoxide dismutase, an endogenous antioxidant, is one cause of familial ALS; and (b) vitamin E appears to delay the onset and slow the progression of clinical symptomatology in a mouse model of familial ALS (48,66). A recent retrospective study in humans also suggests that vitamin E ingestion may protect against the development of ALS (67).

In 1995, after years of negative results from multiple clinical trials testing a wide variety of therapies, a significant breakthrough for the treatment of ALS occurred when riluzole was shown to have a modest effect on prolonging survival in ALS (68). Currently riluzole is the only medication approved by the U.S. Food and Drug Administration for the treatment of ALS. But riluzole is not the last word in ALS treatment. More effective therapies are necessary, and every suggestion for a potential treatment is considered seriously. The ease of electronic communication is impacting ALS treatment. Online forums and chat rooms permit rapid sharing of information and data, much of it anecdotal, about both drug and nondrug therapies. A clinical trial of gabapentin, which was developed as an antiepileptic agent, was initiated in part because of a patient's report of beneficial response to this medication on an electronic bulletin board (69). Gabapentin was eventually shown not to be effective for the treatment of ALS, emphasizing the importance of following up on anecdotal reports with randomized clinical trials.

## Nondrug Therapies

In 1955 Schwarz and King reported that "present treatment is basically a matter of supportive treatment and good medical art" (70). Good medical care remains the cornerstone of ALS treatment and includes attention to both the physical and the emotional effects of this disorder. Recognition of the importance of quality of life and end-of-life issues is also increasing. Over the past decade there have been some attempts at systematic investigation of nondrug therapies in an effort to better define what "good medical art" means for ALS. Clinical studies are now under way to assess therapies such as the utility of early feeding tube placements, the optimization of noninvasive ventilatory support, and the use of diaphragm pacemakers in ALS.

## Classification of ALS

One can approach the classification of ALS in several ways, based on (a) clinical syndromes, (b) mode of acquisition, and (c) degree of diagnostic certainty.

## Clinical ALS Syndromes

The various ALS syndromes differ according to clinical signs and symptoms, as well as prognosis. To better understand the classification schemes for ALS, one must have a rudimentary understanding of neuroanatomy. As mentioned previously, motor neurons are those cells in the brain, brain stem, and spinal cord that control voluntary movements of muscles. There are two types of motor neurons: upper motor neurons and lower motor neurons (also called anterior horn cells). Both sets of motor neurons are required for optimal control of skeletal muscles. Upper motor neurons reside in the brain in a region called the motor cortex. The upper motor neurons send out processes, called axons, that connect (synapse) with lower motor neurons in the brain stem and spinal cord. In turn, the lower motor neurons send out axons that synapse on muscles in the face, pharynx, chest, and limbs, exerting direct control over muscle contraction. Upper motor neurons are involved in the initiation of voluntary movements and the maintenance of appropriate muscle tone. When upper motor neurons are damaged, the limbs become spastic and the reflexes are exaggerated. When lower motor neurons are lost, the muscles become weak and wasted, or atrophic, and the reflexes may disappear. The combination of symptoms and signs of damage to both upper and lower motor neurons in several body regions allows the neurologist to make a diagnosis of definite ALS. Classic ALS is marked by exaggerated reflexes, or spasticity, along with weakness and wasting of the facial, limb, and respiratory muscles.

Sometimes, however, there may be signs of either upper motor neuron or lower motor neuron loss, but not both. At other times the symptoms and signs of disease may be present in only one region, such as the speech and swallowing, or bulbar, apparatus. This leads to some confusion about the diagnosis for patients, as physicians may use other terms to describe the clinical syndrome: primary lateral sclerosis, progressive muscular atrophy, or progressive bulbar palsy.

In *primary lateral sclerosis* only the upper motor neurons degenerate, leaving the lower motor neurons intact. The limbs become stiff and spastic, without the development of significant weakness or atrophy. This is a rare syndrome and should be considered an entity distinct from ALS. In some instances, patients with pure upper motor neuron findings initially will later develop features more typical of ALS. This is called upper motor neuron onset ALS, or the primary lateral sclerosis form of ALS.

When only the lower motor neurons are affected, leading to severe wasting and weakness in the muscles with loss of reflexes, the disorder is known as *progressive muscular atrophy*. The signs of upper motor neuron dysfunction are not noted. This is called lower motor neuron onset ALS, or the progressive muscular atrophy form of ALS.

With *progressive bulbar palsy,* the disorder starts in the muscles of speech and swallowing, causing slurred speech and choking. Patients eventually lose all ability to speak and swallow. Pure progressive bulbar palsy is also extremely rare; most patients later develop classic ALS.

## Mode of Acquisition

As discussed previously, individuals acquire ALS in one of two ways, sporadically or genetically, with the vast majority having the sporadic form of the disease. In familial forms, ALS may be inherited as a dominant or recessive disease. In dominantly inherited ALS, such as occurs with the SOD1 mutation, each child of an affected parent has a 50% chance of inheriting the mutation and, thus, of developing the disease. In the rare recessive forms of ALS, both parents are carriers of a genetic mutation although they do not have the disease. Their children each have a 25% chance of getting defective genes from both parents, and thus developing the disease.

For the most part ALS is a disease of adults. There are exceedingly rare reports of childhood onset of ALS. In such cases, the disease is usually recessively inherited.

## Certainty of Diagnosis

Perhaps most confusing and frustrating for patients is the classification of ALS based on degree of diagnostic certainty. Although researchers are looking for biomarkers (blood tests, imaging studies, or other tests) that will allow for more precise and earlier diagnosis, at the present time there is no single laboratory test that allows one to make a diagnosis of ALS with 100% certainty, particularly in its early stages. The diagnosis is based on a constellation of physical symptoms and signs and laboratory data that are consistent with ALS and the exclusion of other diagnostic entities that may mimic ALS. In the very earliest stages of the disease, when its signs and symptoms are limited to a single body region, the clinical features may suggest another neurologic disorder. It is the progression of disease to involve multiple body regions that allows for a diagnosis of definite ALS.

The following diagnostic categories have been identified by the World Federation of Neurology Research Group on Motor Neuron Diseases: Clinically Possible ALS, Clinically Probable ALS–Laboratory-supported, Clinically Probable ALS, and Clinically Definite ALS (Table 1.3) (71). Diagnostic criteria for each category have been established and refined to increase the degree of likelihood that the disease is really ALS and serve to alert the physician to search for disorders that may mimic ALS, particularly in its early stages. Although the use of these terms is sometimes distressing to patients because they are uncertain of the diagnosis when told they have "possible" or "probable" ALS, the criteria are in place to protect the patient from an improper diagnosis.

## Conclusions

Researchers are intently focused on finding the causes of and developing truly effective therapies for ALS by using a combination of established methods, such as epidemiology studies; and cutting-edge, state-of-the-art science, such as whole

**Table 1.3** Diagnostic Categories for Amyotrophic Lateral Sclerosis (ALS) (UMN = Upper Motor Neuron; LMN = Lower Motor Neuron) (54)

1. **Clinically Definite ALS** is defined, based on clinical evidence alone, by the presence of UMN as well as LMN signs in the bulbar region and at least 2 spinal regions, or by the presence of UMN and LMN signs in 3 spinal regions.

2. **Clinically Probable ALS** is defined, based on clinical evidence alone, by UMN and LMN signs in at least 2 regions with some UMN necessarily rostral to (above) the LMN signs.

3. **Clinically Probable ALS–Laboratory-supported** is defined when clinical signs of UMN and LMN dysfunction are in only 1 region, or when UMN signs alone are present in 1 region, and LMN signs defined by electromyography criteria are present in at least 2 regions, with proper application of neuroimaging and clinical laboratory protocols to exclude other causes.

4. **Clinically Possible ALS** is defined when clinical signs of UMN and LMN dysfunction are found together in only 1 region or UMN signs are found alone in 2 or more regions; or LMN signs are found rostral to UMN signs and the diagnosis of Clinically Probable ALS–Laboratory-supported cannot be proven by evidence based on clinical grounds in conjunction with electrodiagnostic, neurophysiologic, neuroimaging, or clinical laboratory studies. Other diagnoses must have been excluded to accept a diagnosis of Clinically Possible ALS.

genome analysis and proteomic studies. At the same time, clinicians are focused on optimizing medical management to extend both quantity and quality of life. The following chapters will expand on some of the information introduced in this chapter and discuss the many treatment options available to manage the different aspects of ALS.

## References

1. Bak R. *Lou Gehrig: An American Classic.* Dallas: Taylor Publishing Co.; 1995:160–161.
2. Bell C. *The Nervous System of the Human Body.* London: Longman; 1830:132–136, 160–161.
3. Aran FA. Recherches sur une maladie non encore decrite du systeme musculaire (atrophie musculaire progressive). *Arch Gen Med.* 1850;24:15–35.
4. Duchenne G. Paralysie musculaire progressive de la langue, du voile du palais et des levres. *Arch Gen Med.* 1860;16:283–296, 431–445.
5. Veltema AN. The case of the saltimbanque Prosper Lecomte. A contribution to the study of the history of progressive muscular atrophy (Aran-Duchenne) and amyotrophic lateral sclerosis (Charcot). *Clin Neurol Neurosurg.* 1975;78:204–209.
6. Charcot J-M. De la sclerose laterale amyotrophique: Symptomatologie. *Prog Med.* 1874;2:453–455.
7. Jean M. Charcot. In: Beighton P, Beighton G, eds. *The Man Behind the Syndrome.* Heidelberg: Springer-Verlag; 1998:27.

8. Guillain G. Amyotrophic lateral sclerosis. In: Bailey P, trans-ed. *J.-M. Charcot. 1825–1893 His Life—His Work.* New York, NY: Paul B. Hoeber, Inc.; 1959:106–108.

9. Kimura K, Yase Y, Higashi Y, et al. Epidemiological and geomedical studies on amyotrophic lateral sclerosis. *Dis Nerv Syst.* 1963;24:155–159.

10. Reed DM, Brody JA. Amyotrophic lateral sclerosis and parkinsonism—dementia on Guam, 1945–1972. *Am J Epidemiol.* 1975;101:287–301.

11. Gajdusek DC. Motor-neuron disease in natives of New Guinea. *N Engl J Med.* 1963;268:474–476.

12. Kurland LT. Amyotrophic lateral sclerosis and Parkinson's disease complex on Guam linked to an environmental neurotoxin. *Trends Neurosci.* 1988;11:51–54.

13. Yase Y. The pathogenesis of amyotrophic lateral sclerosis. *Lancet.* 1972;2:292–296.

14. Chad D, Mitsumoto H, Adelman LS, et al. Conjugal motor neuron disease. *Neurology.* 1982;32:306–307.

15. Cornblath DR, Kurland LT, Boylan KB, et al. Conjugal amyotrophic lateral sclerosis: Report of a young married couple. *Neurology.* 1993;43:2378–2380.

16. Paolino E, Granieri E, Tola MR, et al. Conjugal amyotrophic lateral sclerosis [letter]. *Ann Neurol.* 1983;14:699.

17. Camu W, Cadilhac J, Billiard M. Amyotrophic lateral sclerosis: a report on two couples from southern France. *Neurology.* 1994;44:547–548.

18. Estrin WJ. Amyotrophic lateral sclerosis in dizygotic twins. *Neurology.* 1977;27:692–694.

19. Sienko DG, Davis JP, Taylor JA, et al. Amyotrophic lateral sclerosis: a case-control study following detection of a cluster in a small Wisconsin community. *Arch Neurol.* 1990;47:38–41.

20. Melmed C, Krieger C. A cluster of amyotrophic lateral sclerosis. *Arch Neurol.* 1982;39:595–596.

21. Hochberg FH, Bryan JA, Whelan MA. Clustering of amyotrophic lateral sclerosis. *Lancet.* 1974;1:34.

22. Kilnes AW, Hochberg FH. Amyotrophic lateral sclerosis in a high selenium environment. *JAMA.* 1977;237:2843–2844.

23. Chiò A, Benzi G, Dossena M, et al. Severely increased risk of amyotrophic lateral sclerosis among Italian professional football players. *Brain.* 2005;128:472–476.

24. Belli S, Vanacore N. Proportionate mortality of Italian soccer players: is amyotrophic lateral sclerosis an occupational disease? *Eur J Epidemiol.* 2005;20:237–342.

25. Weisskopf MG, O'Reilly EJ, McCullough ML, et al. Prospective study of military service and mortality from ALS. *Neurology.* 2005;64:32–37.

26. Horner RD, Kamins KG, Feussner JR, et al. Occurrence of amyotrophic lateral sclerosis among Gulf War veterans. *Neurology.* 2003;61:742–749.

27. Haley RW. Excess incidence of ALS in young Gulf War veterans. *Neurology.* 2003;61:750–756.

28. Horner RD, Grambow SC, Coffman CJ, et al. Amyotrophic lateral sclerosis among 1991 Gulf War veterans: evidence for a time-limited outbreak. *Neuroepidemiology.* 2008;31:28–32.

29. Miranda ML, Galeano MAO, Tassone E, et al. Spatial analysis of the etiology of amyotrophic lateral sclerosis among 1991 Gulf War veterans. *Neurotoxicology.* In press.

30. Kasarkis EJ, Dominic K, Oddone EZ. The National Registry of Veterans with Amyotrophic Lateral Sclerosis: Department of Veterans Affairs Cooperative Studies Program (CSP) #500a. *Amyotroph Lateral Scler Other Motor Neuron Disord.* 2004;1:129–132.

31. Olivares L, Esteban ES, Alter M. Mexican "resistance" to amyotrophic lateral sclerosis. *Arch Neurol.* 1972;27:397–402.

32. Cendrowski W, Wender W, Owsianowski M. Analyse epidemiologique de la sclerose laterale amyotrophique sur le territoire de la Grand-Pologne. *Acta Neurol Scand.* 1970;46:609–617.

33. Rosati G, Pinna L, Granieri E, et al. Studies on epidemiological, clinical and etiological aspects of ALS disease in Sardinia, Southern Italy. *Acta Neurol Scand.* 1977;55:231–244.
34. Salemi G, Fierro B, Arcara A, et al. Amyotrophic lateral sclerosis in Palermo, Italy: an epidemiologic study. *Ital J Neurol Sci.* 1989;10:505–509.
35. Charcot JM. Observation communique en 1875. a la Societe de Biologie par M. Raymond. Paralysie essentielle de l'Enfance: Atrophie musculaire consecutive. *Gaz Med (Paris).* 1875:225–226.
36. Cremer NE, Oshiro LS, Norris FH, et al. Cultures of tissues from patients with amyotrophic lateral sclerosis. *Arch Neurol.* 1973;29:331–333.
37. Roos RP, Viola MV, Wollmann R, et al. Amyotrophic lateral sclerosis with antecedent poliomyelitis. *Arch Neurol.* 1980;37:312–313.
38. Weiner LP, Stohlman SA, Davis RL. Attempts to demonstrate virus in amyotrophic lateral sclerosis. *Neurology.* 1980;30:1319–1322.
39. Wilson SAK. The amyotrophy of chronic lead poisoning: amyotrophic lateral sclerosis of toxic origin. *Rev Neurol Psychiatr.* 1907;5:441–445.
40. Currier RD, Haerer AF. Amyotrophic lateral sclerosis and metallic toxins. *Arch Environ Health.* 1968;17:712–719.
41. Roelofs-Iverson RA, Mulder DW, Elveback LR, et al. ALS and heavy metals: a pilot case-control study. *Neurology.* 1984;34:393–395.
42. Boothby JA, deJesus PV, Rowland LP. Reversible forms of motor neuron disease. *Arch Neurol.* 1974;31:18–23.
43. Adams CR, Ziegler DK, Lin JT. Mercury intoxication simulating amyotrophic lateral sclerosis. *JAMA.* 1983;250:642–643.
44. Wechsler IS, Sapirstein MR, Stein A. Primary and symptomatic amyotrophic lateral sclerosis: a clinical study of 81 cases. *Am J Med Sci.* 1944;208:70–71.
45. Ask-Upmark E. Amyotrophic lateral sclerosis observed in 5 persons after gastric resection. *Gastroenterology.* 1950;15:257–259.
46. Ask-Upmark E. Precipitating factors in the pathogenesis of amyotrophic lateral sclerosis. *Acta Med Scand.* 1961;170:717–723.
47. Siddique T, Figlewicz DA, Pericak-Vance MA, et al. Linkage of a gene causing familial amyotrophic lateral sclerosis to chromosome 21 and evidence of genetic-locus heterogeneity. *N Engl J Med.* 1991;324:1381–1384.
48. Rosen DR, Siddique T, Patterson D, et al. Mutations in Cu/Zn superoxide dismutase gene are associated with familial amyotrophic lateral sclerosis. *Nature.* 1993;362:59–62.
49. Yang Y, Hentati A, Deng HX, et al. The gene encoding alsin, a protein with three guanine-nucleotide exchange factor domains, is mutated in a form of recessive amyotrophic lateral sclerosis. *Nat Genet.* 2001;29:160–165.
50. Meyer T, Schwan A, Dullinger JS, et al. Early-onset ALS with long-term survival associated with spastin gene mutation. *Neurology.* 2005;65:141–143.
51. Chen YZ, Bennett CL, Huynh HM, et al. DNA/RNA helicase gene mutations in a form of juvenile amyotrophic lateral sclerosis (ALS4). *Am J Hum Genet.* 2004;74:1128–1135.
52. Münch C, Sedlmeier R, Meyer T, et al. Point mutations of the p150 subunit of dynactin (DCTN1) gene in ALS. *Neurology.* 2004;63:724–726.
53. Nishimura AL, Mitne-Neto M, Silva HC, et al. A mutation in the vesicle-trafficking protein VAPB causes late-onset spinal muscular atrophy and amyotrophic lateral sclerosis. *Am J Hum Genet.* 2004;75:822–831.
54. Slowik A, Tomik B, Wolkow PP, et al. Paraoxonase gene polymorphisms and sporadic ALS. *Neurology.* 2006;67:766–770.
55. Saeed M, Siddique N, Hung WY, et al. Paraoxonase cluster polymorphisms are associated with sporadic ALS. *Neurology.* 2006;67:771–776.

56. van Es MA, van Vught PW, Blauw HM, et al. Genetic variation in DPP6 is associated with susceptibility to amyotrophic lateral sclerosis. *Nat Genet.* 2008;40:29–31.
57. Cronin S, Berger S, Ding J, et al. A genome-wide association study of sporadic ALS in a homogenous Irish population. *Hum Mol Genet.* 2008;17:768–774.
58. Corcia P, Mayeux-Portas V, Khoris J, et al. Abnormal SMN1 gene copy number is a susceptibility factor for amyotrophic lateral sclerosis. *Ann Neurology.* 2002;51:243–246.
59. Corcia P, Camu W, Halimi JM, et al. SMN1 gene, but not SMN2, is a risk factor for sporadic ALS. *Neurology.* 2006;67:1147–1150.
60. Mackenzie IR, Bigio EH, Ince PG, et al. Pathological TDP-43 distinguishes sporadic amyotrophic lateral sclerosis from amyotrophic lateral sclerosis with SOD1 mutations. *Ann Neurol.* 2007;61:427–434.
61. Bak R. *Lou Gehrig: An American Classic.* Dallas, TX: Taylor Publishing Co.; 1995:164.
62. Wechsler IS. The treatment of amyotrophic lateral sclerosis with vitamin E (tocopherols). *Am J Med Sci.* 1940;200:765–778.
63. Eaton LM, Woltman HW, Butt HR. Vitamins E and B6 in the treatment of neuromuscular diseases. *Mayo Clin Proc* 1941;16:523–527.
64. Denker PG, Scheinman L. Treatment of amyotrophic lateral sclerosis with vitamin E (alpha-tocopherol). *JAMA.* 1941;116:1895.
65. Ferrebee JW, Klingman WO, Frantz AM. Vitamin E and vitamin B6. Clinical experience in the treatment of muscular dystrophy and amyotrophic lateral sclerosis. *JAMA.* 1941;116:1895.
66. Gurney ME, Cutting FB, Zhai P, et al. Benefit of vitamin E, riluzole, and gabapentin in a transgenic model of familial amyotrophic lateral sclerosis. *Ann Neurol.* 1996;39:147–157.
67. Ascherio A, Weisskopf MG, O'Reilly EJ, et al. Vitamin E intake and risk of amyotrophic lateral sclerosis. *Ann Neurol.* 2005;57:104–110.
68. Bensimon G, Lacomblez L, Meininger V. A controlled trial of riluzole in amyotrophic lateral sclerosis. ALS/Riluzole Study Group. *N Engl J Med.* 1994;330:585–591.
69. Miller RG, Moore D, Young LA, et al. Placebo-controlled trial of gabapentin in patients with amyotrophic lateral sclerosis. *Neurology.* 1996;47:1383–1388.
70. Schwarz GA, King G. Neuromuscular diseases of later maturity. Part 1. *Geriatrics.* 1955;10:197–207.
71. Brooks BR, Miller RG, Swash M, et al. El Escorial revisited: revised criteria for the diagnosis of amyotrophic lateral sclerosis. *ALS Other Motor Neuron Disord.* 2000;1:293–299.

# 2

# The Clinical Features and Prognosis of Amyotrophic Lateral Sclerosis

## Hiroshi Mitsumoto

The human brain has billions of nerve cells, or neurons. There are more than 80 different types of these nerve cells, and some are highly specialized. Diseases that cause neuron loss or impair neuron function, such as Alzheimer's disease, Parkinson disease, and amyotrophic lateral sclerosis (ALS), are a group of disorders that cause specific types of neurons to degenerate; hence, the term neurodegeneration is used to describe these diseases. For example, Alzheimer's disease affects neurons that control memory and intelligence, whereas in Parkinson disease the neurons that control complex movements are diseased. ALS is familiar to many people as Lou Gehrig's disease, named for the baseball legend who suffered from it. It is a disorder of the motor neurons, which are responsible for contracting the skeletal muscles. To varying degrees, it affects two groups of motor neurons, the upper and lower motor neurons. In ALS the motor neurons gradually lose their ability to function, and the symptoms that are characteristic of ALS eventually appear. This chapter discusses the clinical signs and symptoms of ALS, their neuroanatomic and physiologic bases, the initial symptoms, and the prognosis of the disease.

### The Preclinical Stages of ALS

The important question as to when ALS really begins remains unanswered. In general, it is agreed that the disease is probably already well along in its course when patients first notice muscle weakness. A well-documented record of this preclinical course in ALS is Lou Gehrig's batting average—his batting average

21

and number of home runs started deteriorating one year before he noticed the signs of the disease that forced him to retire from baseball. In an important long-term investigation, people were studied who were known to have a mutation in the SOD1 gene. These mutations are found in patients who have familial ALS, which is ALS that appears to run in families. The subjects were all healthy and were evaluated for changes in muscle function during the study by using a test called the motor unit number estimate (MUNE). The results of this test remained normal until about 3 to 16 months before the subjects developed muscle weakness. This finding suggests that something happens to the motor neuron system within this time period. An extensive autopsy study done many years ago in patients who died of acute poliomyelitis (rapid paralysis caused by poliovirus infection) showed that as many as 50% of the motor neurons in the spinal cord had become nonfunctional even when the muscles controlled by those neurons had normal strength. In a similar study in patients with ALS, as many as 80% of these cells had been lost before muscle weakness was detected. These studies suggest that by the time motor neuron disease is diagnosed, a significant proportion of motor neurons may already be lost.

To understand how the disease progresses so insidiously during the preclinical stage and how normal muscle strength is maintained while motor neurons are progressively lost, some knowledge is needed about the anatomic and physiologic relationship between the motor neuron and the muscle fibers (Figure 2.1). Each skeletal muscle is composed of numerous muscle fibers, and each motor neuron in the spinal cord controls a number of muscle fibers. In large muscles, such as those of the trunk, buttock, or calf, one motor neuron controls (innervates) more than 1,000 muscle fibers, whereas in the much smaller hand muscles, one motor neuron controls only about 100 muscle fibers, which permits the fine control that is needed to perform small, delicate movements. The nerve fiber, or axon, that emerges from the motor neuron branches extensively after it enters the muscle so that each small nerve branch innervates only a single muscle fiber. The entire group of muscle fibers innervated by one motor neuron is called the *motor unit*. The muscle fibers in one motor unit are not grouped together in the muscle. Instead, they are scattered widely and intermixed with other muscle fibers that belong to many other motor units.

When a motor neuron is diseased, it no longer can control its motor unit (Figure 2.2). This process is called *denervation*. Muscle fibers that are denervated lose their ability to contract and thus waste and shrink, a process called *denervation atrophy*. Once the muscle fibers are denervated, nerve fibers that belong to healthy motor neurons develop "sprouts" and take over the neural control of denervated muscle fibers. In this way, healthy motor neurons reinnervate the denervated muscle fibers so that muscle contraction is maintained. On the other hand, this means that the healthy motor neurons are expanding the size of their motor units, which eventually leads to coarser movement. In general, as long as the balance between denervation and reinnervation is maintained, muscle weakness may not become clinically apparent. However, as the disease progresses, the speed of neuronal degeneration exceeds that of reinnervation; moreover, once-healthy motor neurons may be affected. The process seems to be initially undetectable because patients

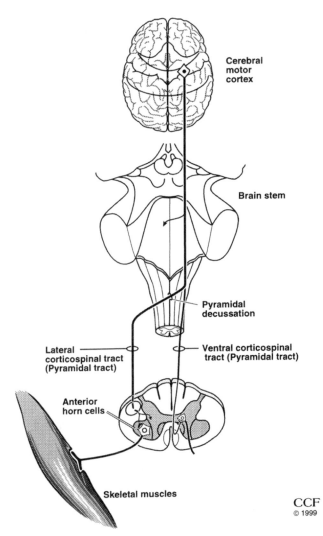

**Figure 2.1** As described in the text, two types of motor neurons control muscle contraction. One is the upper motor neuron system. The upper motor neurons are found mainly in the cerebral motor cortex and exert control over the lower motor neurons, which are often called anterior horn cells. Nerve fibers arising from the upper motor neurons descend from the cerebral cortex to the lower brain stem, where the majority of nerve fibers cross over to the opposite side and then further descend through the spinal cord finally to reach lower motor neurons. These main descending bundles of fibers are called the *corticospinal* or *pyramidal tracts*. The tracts transmit the muscle contraction signal that arises from the upper motor neurons. When this signal reaches and stimulates the lower motor neurons, a new signal is generated in the lower motor neurons, which transmit the signal beyond the spinal cord to ultimately reach individual muscle fibers and directly contract these fibers.

have no symptoms that they or their physician notice. It is not known how long this preclinical stage lasts before muscle weakness becomes clinically apparent. It depends on the rate of motor neuron degeneration and reinnervation. When detailed electrodiagnostic tests that measure the electrical activity of nerves and muscles are performed, neurologists may find evidence of extensive reinnervation, even when ALS is in a very early stage. The 2001 Aggarwal & Nicholson study from Australia mentioned above provides an important clue. Although the study concerns familial ALS, it is possible that a similar phenomenon may occur in sporadic ALS.

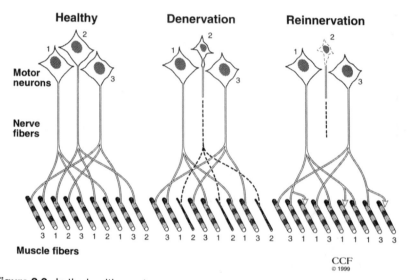

**Figure 2.2** In the healthy motor neuron system, each lower motor neuron (anterior horn cell) controls (innervates) a number of muscle fibers (the motor unit). This relationship is depicted in the left panel. The center panel shows the events that occur in motor neuron disease. When a motor neuron (neuron 2) is diseased, it no longer can control the muscle fibers it innervates, and the fibers undergo denervation (dotted lines in the center panel). Denervated muscle fibers shrink and become unable to contract (muscle fiber 2 in the center panel). If surrounding lower motor neurons (neurons 1 and 3) are still healthy, these motor neurons can activate regeneration of nerve fibers to take over the control of the denervated muscle fibers. When this takeover process, called *reinnervation,* is completed, the denervated muscle fibers are controlled by different motor neurons. As shown in the right panel, the end result is that neurons 1 and 3 expand their motor unit territory—motor neuron 1 now controls 5 muscle fibers instead of 3 and motor neuron 3 now controls 4 muscle fibers. As long as this process is maintained, normal muscle strength can be sustained while the number of motor neurons is slowly reduced.

## Presenting Symptoms

ALS is one of several progressive wasting and weakening diseases of the skeletal muscles. Approximately 60% of patients notice weakness as the first symptom. Typically the weakness occurs in the arm or leg muscles or in the muscles that control speech and swallowing (the *bulbar* muscles). In general, in one third of patients the weakness begins in the arm; in another one third it begins in the leg. Approximately one fourth of patients first develop weakness in the bulbar muscles. The few remaining patients experience a generalized onset, with simultaneous involvement of the arms, legs, and bulbar muscles. On rare occasions weakness affects only one side of the body in the initial stages, or it resembles a nerve palsy ( paralysis) that occurs in nerves of the forearm (the radial or ulnar nerves) or a nerve at the shin called the peroneal nerve. Other unusual initial symptoms include weakness that first involves muscles at the back of the neck or respiratory difficulty because muscles that assist in breathing have been affected. When the initial symptoms begin in such unusual locations, the diagnosis of ALS is difficult to make and is often delayed for some time.

Other initial symptoms that lead patients to consult a physician are muscle pain or cramps. In our experience, pain and cramps are relatively rare as initial symptoms. However, muscle cramping is one of the most common symptoms in the early stages of the disease and occurs in 80% to 90% of patients. Muscle twitching (fasciculations) and weight loss may be the first symptoms in a small percentage of patients. Muscle stiffness, difficulty walking, or excessive fatigue may be presenting symptoms in other patients. Muscle twitches and cramps occur in completely healthy people, so it is important to understand that there is absolutely no reason to suspect ALS when these symptoms occur alone.

## Neuroanatomic and Physiologic Bases of the Clinical Symptoms

Motor neurons are located in the brain, brain stem (a structure at the base of the brain that is inside the skull and connects the brain to the spinal cord), and spinal cord as shown in Figure 2.1. The hallmark of ALS is muscle weakness that is caused by abnormal function of the lower motor neurons. ALS also affects the upper motor neurons, and the involvement of these two motor neuron groups produces the features that are characteristic of ALS. A brief overview of the upper and lower motor neuron anatomy is helpful to understand how the specific signs and symptoms develop in ALS.

### Upper Motor Neurons

The upper motor neurons control the lower motor neurons. Anatomically, the upper motor neurons reside in the brain and brain stem, whereas the lower motor neurons are in the spinal cord. The brain's outer layer, or cerebral cortex, is divided into individual areas that specialize in particular functions. The cerebral motor cortex is specialized in motor control and consists of the *primary motor cortex,* the *supplementary motor cortex,* and the *premotor area.* These areas work together to execute the most complex human body movements. Upper motor neurons that are in the primary motor cortex can directly contract individual muscles. For example, the principle motor neurons in the primary motor cortex, called *giant pyramidal neurons* or *Betz cells,* work with a greater number of surrounding smaller motor neurons to contract individual skeletal muscles.

Nerve fibers extend from the motor neurons in the motor cortex to form large nerve fiber groups that descend from the brain to the spinal cord. These large descending fiber groups are called the *corticospinal* and *corticobulbar tracts.* Nerve fibers arising from neurons in the primary motor cortex constitute approximately one third of the fibers in these tracts. Another one third are derived from the motor areas that plan and program motor performance. The remaining one third is derived from an area called the somatic sensory cortex and the adjacent temporal lobe region. This arrangement indicates that lower motor neurons receive broad control from the cerebral cortex, including the frontal lobes (the primary and supplementary motor cortices, and premotor areas), parietal lobe (the primary somatic sensory cortex), and the temporal lobe.

The corticobulbar tracts descend initially with the corticospinal tracts but then branch away in the brain stem. Through the corticobulbar tracts, the upper motor neurons control the brain stem lower motor neurons that belong to cranial nerves V (jaw movement), VII (face and lip movements), IX and X (throat and vocal cord movements), and XII (tongue movements).

The main corticospinal tracts (called the pyramidal tracts) descend to the spinal cord from the brain through the brain stem. In the brain stem, however, most of these corticospinal fibers (75% to 90%) cross to the opposite side and form the lateral corticospinal tracts in the spinal cord. The fibers that do not cross continue to descend on the same side and form the ventral, or anterior, corticospinal tracts. The lateral corticospinal tracts send fibers to lower motor neurons that control arm and leg muscles that require independent, unilateral control. For example, these motor neurons allow the right hand to move independently of the left hand. In contrast, the anterior corticospinal tracts (which are located close to the center of the spinal cord) send fibers to motor neurons, both right and left sides, that control postural muscles near the center of the trunk, which must have bilateral control so they can act together to hold the body upright and straight.

## Brain Stem Motor Control

The motor neurons of the spinal cord are also controlled by special neurons in the brain stem (such as the vestibular nuclei and reticular formation). These neurons regulate the sensitivity of muscle reflexes, muscle tone, and the balance between the flexor and extensor muscle groups of the upper (arms) and lower (legs) extremities, trunk, and neck. When one stands, sits, or positions one's body in virtually any way, one has continuous automatic, or involuntary, control of muscle tone; otherwise, the body could not maintain its posture. This system is complex, controlling many reflexes and involuntary body postures. These particular brain stem neurons are considered upper motor neurons in a broad sense because they strongly influence skeletal muscle tone. Groups of nerve fibers from these brain stem neurons extend in several descending tracts to the lower motor neurons in the spinal cord.

## Limbic Motor Control

The limbic system consists of a number of brain structures that together are closely involved in emotional experience and expression. The system also is associated with a wide variety of autonomic, visceral, and endocrine functions. (*Autonomic function* refers to functions regulated by the autonomic nervous system, such as sweating or heart rate; they may also be affected by one's emotional state. *Visceral* pertains to the gastrointestinal organs.) Recent studies clearly indicate that the limbic system strongly influences lower motor neurons in the brain stem and spinal cord. Thus, the emotional state and experience of an individual affects the overall spinal cord motor neuron activity. Of particular importance, several groups of brain stem neurons belonging to the limbic system influence basic behaviors, such as respiration, vomiting, swallowing, chewing, and licking, as well as emotional expression, including crying and laughing.

## Lower Motor Neurons

The lower motor neurons are located in the brain stem and spinal cord and send out nerve fibers to directly innervate skeletal muscle fibers. These motor neurons are lowest in the hierarchy of motor control. They are clustered in pools, and form columns that extend down the spinal cord. Because lower motor neurons are located in the anterior gray matter, or anterior horn, of the spinal cord, they are also known as *anterior horn cells.* The anterior horn contains neurons associated with the motor system, whereas the posterior horn contains neurons associated with the sensory system. Anterior horn cells vary in size. Large motor neurons are the most common and often are called *alpha-motoneurons;* they are the principal motor neurons that innervate muscle fibers.

The alpha-motoneuron is among the largest neurons of the nervous system. It has a single nerve fiber (axon) that extends to innervate a muscle, and it has a number of large extensions called *dendrites,* which branch like a tree and receive signals extensively from other neurons, including upper motor neurons and the sensory feedback system. One alpha-motoneuron innervates one group of muscle fibers, or motor unit, as discussed above.

## Interneurons

Interneurons are small neurons in the anterior gray matter or in the brain stem motor neuron groups. They are of paramount importance in determining how the lower motor neurons control muscle contraction. The interneurons receive extensive upper motor neuron control from the brain stem descending tracts, corticospinal tracts, and limbic system. They also receive sensory feedback information from the skeletal muscles. Interneurons form intricate neuronal circuits to program numerous basic leg, arm, and body movements. For example, the quick reflex to a sudden sting to your arm is programmed in the interneurons. These circuits also are a fundamental component of complex, fine motor movements.

## Signs and Symptoms of Upper Motor Neuron Dysfunction

Slowly progressive dysfunction and impairment of upper motor neurons cause the characteristic clinical signs and symptoms discussed here.

### Loss of Dexterity

Voluntary movements that require fine dexterity are the product of the integrated activation of the complex lower motor neuron and interneuron circuits of the spinal cord that control fine muscle movement; however, by exerting control via the corticospinal tracts, the upper motor neurons ultimately control such actions. Thus, a prominent and early sign of upper motor neuron dysfunction is a loss of dexterity. When dexterity is impaired, voluntary and even reflex motions become awkward. Patients may initially experience stiffness, slowness, and clumsiness when performing any motion that requires fine movement, such as any rapid repetitive motion of the fingers, feet, and even the lips or tongue.

### Loss of Muscle Strength (Weakness)

Another sign of upper motor neuron dysfunction is a loss of muscle strength. Because the upper motor neurons are affected but lower motor units are normally preserved, muscle weakness resulting from upper motor neuron dysfunction generally is mild and not as severe as that seen in lower motor neuron involvement. In patients with severe upper motor neuron disease, accurately assessing the muscle strength becomes difficult because muscle spasticity and loss of dexterity prevent effective activation of the motor units.

### Spasticity

Spasticity is an abnormal state in which muscle tension is increased and sustained when the muscle is lengthened (stretched). When spasticity exists, passively stretching or actively shortening a muscle spontaneously elicits a reflex that increases muscle tension. This reflex occurs because the motor neurons are more excitable. Thus, muscle relaxation is delayed, making smooth contraction difficult because the antagonist muscles—the opposite muscles that normally relax and elongate when the other muscles contract—also increase their muscle tone.

Passive movement becomes nearly impossible when muscles are severely spastic. Sometimes spastic muscles lose their normal smooth action during passive movement, suddenly increase their resistance, and then resist further passive movement. This particular type of muscle resistance is referred to as a "catch." However, if a sustained passive stretch is applied to spastic muscles in this circumstance, they quickly release the tension and relax, an event often described as the "clasp-knife phenomenon."

Although spasticity is the central feature of upper motor neuron dysfunction, how this dysfunction leads to spasticity is not fully understood. Several explanations are likely. Upper motor neurons in the cerebral cortex control some upper motor neurons in the brain stem that control muscle tone. When this control is lost, the brain stem upper motor neurons become overactive and signal to increase muscle tone in the leg and arm muscles; upper motor neuron dysfunction also increases the sensitivity of tension-sensing structures in the muscles called muscle fiber spindles, so muscles also become more sensitive to passive stretching. Moreover, upper motor neuron dysfunction reduces the availability of a chemical called glutamate that sends excitatory messages to neurons. Lower motor neurons and interneurons become hypersensitive to glutamate, so even a very small amount of glutamate can easily and forcefully contract muscles.

## Pathologic Hyperreflexia

Pathologic hyperreflexia (exaggerated muscle stretch reflexes) is another crucial manifestation of upper motor neuron dysfunction in ALS. When the muscle tendon is tapped, the muscle spindle stretches and sends an excitatory impulse. In healthy people this impulse produces a typical reflex with quick muscle contraction called a *monosynaptic muscle stretch reflex*. When upper motor neuron control is disrupted, stretch reflexes become abnormally exaggerated because the inhibition exerted by the upper motor neurons is impaired. In pathologic hyperreflexia, only a slight or distant stimulus is needed to elicit the reflex response. For example, an ordinary tendon tap elicits reflexes in neighboring muscles (an event called *spreading*), and manual stretching of the muscle induces repeated, rhythmic muscle contractions called *clonus*. Such responses indicate that upper motor neurons are disrupted or dysfunctional.

## Pathologic Reflexes

A pathologic reflex is a reflex whose presence is abnormal; in healthy individuals these reflexes are inhibited and thus do not occur. These reflexes are primitive; that is, they normally are present early in development but then disappear. When upper motor neurons and their tracts are dysfunctional, these reflexes are no longer inhibited and can be easily elicited. The *Babinski sign* is one of the most important signs in clinical neurology. It is characterized by an upward extension of the great toe, often accompanied by fanning of the other toes that occurs when one strokes the outer edge of the sole with a blunt object from the heel toward the toes. In healthy adults the big toe flexes (curls down) in response to this stimulation. If present, the Babinski sign is a definitive sign of upper motor neuron dysfunction. Other pathologic reflexes also may be present, most of which are variations of the Babinski sign.

In the upper extremities, the *Hoffmann sign* may indicate abnormality. This reflex is triggered by the quick release that occurs after the joint at the tip of the middle finger is forcefully flexed. A reflex inward curling of the thumb on the same hand is a positive response. Tapping the belly of the middle finger tip can also elicit a similar thumb flexion (the *Trömner sign*). When these reflexes appear only on one side, they are always abnormal. However, in healthy young people bilateral positive reflexes may not be abnormal because they are not unusual in these individuals.

## Spastic Bulbar Palsy

When upper motor neurons and the corticobulbar fibers that control speaking, chewing, and swallowing are affected, a unique upper motor neuron syndrome appears, called *spastic bulbar palsy.* The term *spastic* indicates that the dysfunction is located in the upper motor neurons. The actual weakness in the bulbar muscles (see below) is milder than that found in *paretic* or *flaccid bulbar palsy,* terms that are used to describe the effects of lower motor neuron dysfunction in these muscles. The voice may sound forced because much effort is needed to force air through the upper airway. Repetitive movements of the lips, tongue, and pharynx become particularly slow because of reduced dexterity. The term *pseudobulbar palsy* is often used to distinguish spastic palsy from paretic bulbar palsy, which occurs when the lower motor neurons of the brain stem are affected.

Symptoms include difficulties in speaking, chewing, and swallowing because the highly coordinated bulbar muscles produce slow, stiff movements. Patients with spastic bulbar palsy also appear to have poor emotional control that is characterized by spontaneous or unmotivated crying and laughter. Ordinary discussions or questions about subjects with emotional content often abruptly trigger crying or laughter, sometimes without any clear reason, which is embarrassing to patients. The underlying mechanism may be caused by rhythmic contractions of muscles involved in speech and respiration. It usually lasts up to a few minutes. This phenomenon occurs because the limbic motor neurons, which control muscles producing primitive vocalization (crying and laughing), no longer inhibit such a phenomenon. This phenomenon, called pseudobulbar affect, can be properly managed (see "Treating the Symptoms of Amyotrophic Lateral Sclerosis" chapter).

## Signs and Symptoms of Lower Motor Neuron Dysfunction

### Loss of Muscle Strength (Weakness)

The loss of a motor neuron means that its motor unit is also lost. In contrast, impaired motor neuron function leads to abnormal or impaired activation of the motor unit. In either case, as the number of functional motor units progressively decreases, so does muscle strength. In ALS, the weakness caused by lower motor neuron dysfunction is much greater than that caused by upper motor neuron dysfunction.

Muscle weakness is the cardinal sign and symptom of ALS. It almost always occurs in isolated muscle areas at onset and is followed by progressive weakness. Weakness in ALS usually is not associated with pain.

Muscle weakness in the hand muscles causes difficulty in performing fine movements with the fingers, such as pinching, turning keys, buttoning, using a zipper, or writing. When it occurs in the arms, people may be unable to carry an object, throw a ball, or raise an object above shoulder level. When weakness develops in the foot, the foot commonly slaps the floor. Such *footdrop* makes climbing stairs difficult, and patients may trip and fall.

## Muscle Atrophy

The muscle fiber volume decreases markedly when muscle fibers are denervated. This process is called *denervation atrophy*. Motor neuron death leads to atrophy of all muscle fibers belonging to the motor unit; partial damage to a motor unit causes atrophy in a limited number of its muscle fibers. In ALS the progressive loss of motor neurons results in an atrophy in which the affected skeletal muscles are wasted. Atrophy of the hand muscles, one of most common sites of muscle atrophy in ALS, is easily recognized by patients and physicians, even in the early stages of the disease. Muscle atrophy can affect any skeletal muscles, but the muscles in the forearms or hands and lower leg and foot muscles (the *distal* muscles) generally atrophy more often than muscles near the body trunk (the *proximal* muscles).

## Hyporeflexia

If the disease involves only the lower motor neurons, reflexes that occur when a muscle is stretched are decreased or even absent. This condition is referred to as *hyporeflexia* and is in contrast to the *hyperreflexia* that occurs in upper motor neuron dysfunction. Hyporeflexia results from the loss of active motor units and insufficient muscle contraction. When muscles become totally paralyzed or atrophied, hyperreflexia that developed earlier in the course of the disease may disappear. In some situations, a pathologic hyperreflexia may occur in wasted muscles, a unique paradox in ALS.

## Muscle Hypotonicity or Flaccidity

*Hypotonicity* or *flaccidity* refers to the decrease or complete loss of normal muscle resistance to passive movements. In contrast to spasticity, the muscle lies inert and floppy when passively manipulated.

## Fasciculations

*Fasciculations* are fine, rapid, flickering, and sometimes vermicular (worm-like) twitching of a portion of the muscle. They occur irregularly and repeatedly, but not necessarily in the same location. Fasciculations are believed to be produced by spontaneous electrical discharges of the motor neuron nerve fiber. The cause is not known. In general, the larger the muscle, the greater the size of the fasciculations. In tongue muscles, for example, the fasciculations are small movements on the tongue surface. Fasciculations are found in almost all patients with ALS, but rarely are they an initial symptom. When their presence cannot be confirmed by clinical examination, an examination called needle electromyography may be helpful to identify them. It is important to remember that fasciculations are common and occur in healthy persons, a condition that is termed *benign fasciculation;* in the absence of neurologic findings, such as weakness or atrophy, benign fasciculations usually have no serious clinical implications.

## Muscle Cramps

Muscle cramps (i.e., a charley horse) are another common symptom of lower motor neuron dysfunction. A muscle cramp is a sudden, involuntary, sustained muscle contraction with severe pain that interrupts activity or sleep. In a true cramp, this shortening of the muscle is accompanied by visible or palpable knotting and often shifts the affected joint into an abnormal position; stretching or massaging relieves it. Sudden muscle pains often described as "muscle spasms" are not associated with severe muscle contraction, so they are not true muscle cramps. The cause of muscle cramps is poorly understood, although cramps and fasciculations are likely to share a similar mechanism that is referred to as *hyperexcitability* of motor axons. In hyperexcitability, the electrical discharge from the nerve cell is continuous, which results in an involuntary sustained contraction.

As with fasciculations, muscle cramps (especially in the calves) are common in healthy people. In ALS, however, muscle cramps occur not only in the usual sites, such as the calf, but also in the thighs, arms, hands, abdomen, neck, jaw, and even the tongue. They are one of the most frequently encountered symptoms in ALS.

## Muscle Weakness in the Trunk

Weakness in cervical and thoracic extensor muscles, which keep the body and head erect and straight, often occur in ALS. Such weakness allows the head to fall forward, so the head is in a position known as head droop. In advanced stages the neck becomes completely flexed so that the head drops forward and patients cannot see farther than several feet away. Consequently, walking, eating, and even breathing are seriously impaired. Muscle pain in the overstretched neck extensors is common. To compensate, patients may bend the body backward in an attempt to maintain a distant view while walking.

## Bulbar Signs and Symptoms

Muscles controlling speaking, chewing, and swallowing are innervated by cranial nerves VII (facial), IX (glossopharyngeal), X (vagus), and XII (hypoglossal). The neurons that control these muscles are located in the brain stem, which is also called the *medulla.* Because the medulla also is known as the "bulb," neurologic signs and symptoms resulting from the loss of medullary neurons and their axons are referred to as *bulbar palsy.* Although not controlled in the medulla, cranial nerve V (the trigeminal nerve) usually is also implicated because it controls jaw movement. When the lower motor neurons of the medulla are primarily affected, the condition is called *flaccid* or *paretic bulbar palsy.* In contrast, when upper motor neurons and their descending tracts (the corticobulbar tracts) are affected, *spastic bulbar palsy* develops ("spastic" indicating the upper motor neuron dysfunction), as discussed in the section on upper motor neuron dysfunction. When bulbar palsy is present in ALS, it usually is a mixed palsy that consists of a varying mixture of flaccid and spastic components.

When the bulbar muscles are affected, examination may reveal weakness in the facial muscles. Patients may not be able to close their eyes tightly or may have difficulty opening and closing their mouth. Puckering the lips and puffing the cheeks out while holding air in the mouth also is difficult, as is smiling broadly or naturally. The tongue surface may be wavy and irregular because the tongue muscle is weakened and wasted. Fasciculations can be observed only when the tongue is in a resting position. Tongue movement may be impaired and moving the tongue to either side may be difficult, indicating weakness. When a healthy person speaks, the soft palate rises, but in ALS this elevation may be limited if the palate muscle has weakened.

## Dysarthria

Difficulty in speaking, or *dysarthria,* occurs in ALS because the muscles involved in producing sound and speech are impaired. Initial problems include an inability to shout or sing, a weakened voice, and difficulty with enunciation. Speech sometimes becomes slurred and slowed. When paralysis of the vocal cords begins, the voice takes on either a hoarse or a whispering quality. When the muscles acting as a valve between mouth and nasal cavity become weak, air may leak from the mouth into the nose during enunciation, which results in a nasal tone. In either case, enunciation becomes progressively more difficult, and in the advanced stages of ALS speech becomes hard to understand and finally nonexistent (*anarthria*).

## Dysphagia

*Dysphagia* means that chewing and swallowing are impaired; dysarthria usually accompanies it. When the bulbar muscles are weakened, manipulating food inside the mouth is difficult, and food can become trapped between the gum and the cheek. Patients may be unable to form a small ball of food or move food down into the throat, and they may experience weak or uncoordinated movements when swallowing. Small pieces of dry, crumbly food are more difficult to handle than food with a soft, smooth consistency. Patients with dysphagia caused by neural dysfunction generally also have more difficulty swallowing liquids than solids because liquids move quickly into the throat before the epiglottis—the valve that closes the airway to the lungs—can fully close. Liquids sometimes regurgitate into the nose if a similar valve between the mouth and nose does not close properly. As the disease progresses, swallowing may trigger reflex coughing, a warning that dysphagia is serious and has led to food or liquid entering the airway, an event called *aspiration*. At this stage of the disease, patients require increasingly more time to finish a meal, and eating becomes a great chore. Talking while eating, a bulbar function that requires skillful coordination, eventually becomes impossible. The risk of aspiration becomes significant when the cough reflex is weakened because vocal, swallowing, and respiratory muscles have become paralyzed. Speech pathologists should be consulted to evaluate swallowing dysfunction in depth; a modified barium swallowing test may be useful to analyze dysphagia and to assist in teaching the patient suitable swallowing techniques (see Chapter 10).

## Sialorrhea

Patients with ALS frequently report sialorrhea (drooling) that is both disabling and embarrassing. It occurs because the spontaneous automatic swallowing that normally clears excessive saliva is reduced and the lower facial muscles have become too weak to close both lips tightly to prevent leakage. It is aggravated by the drooping head posture discussed above.

## Aspiration and Laryngospasm

In healthy individuals, the epiglottis closes automatically upon swallowing. Incomplete or uncoordinated closure may allow liquid, saliva, or food to pass into the larynx. This aspiration usually triggers the cough reflex or choking. Aspiration can be a life-threatening event and may result in aspiration pneumonia. However, no signs of aspiration may be apparent when the amount aspirated is small. A modified barium swallowing test, which should be attended by an experienced speech pathologist, is required to investigate possible aspiration.

Cough attacks, an exaggerated gag reflex, or aspiration to the larynx may trigger a sudden narrowing of the upper airway (laryngospasm), which is characterized by loud breathing during inhalation. Laryngospasm is generally not considered to be life threatening.

## Respiratory Symptoms

Weakness in the respiratory muscles causes the respiratory symptoms seen in ALS. Three sets of muscles are used during respiration: the diaphragm, which is the sole respiratory muscle used actively during inhalation; the muscles between the ribs (intercostal muscles); and the abdominal muscles, which function during exhala-

joints. Because of the pain, patients tend to not move the affected joints, which further aggravates the contracture. Aggressive physical therapy and range-of-motion exercise are crucial to prevent painful contracture.

## "Rare" Manifestations of ALS

Clinically, ALS is a "pure" motor neuron syndrome; however, other systems, such as the sensory and autonomic systems, the external ocular (eye) muscles, or higher brain cortical function (memory and intelligence), are not completely spared. Instead, these systems appear to be affected in the late stages of the disease or the impairment is evident only if highly sophisticated techniques are used. Generally, however, when impairment of the sensory system, ocular muscles, or higher cortical function is identified, neurologists must be cautious in their diagnosis of ALS.

### Sensory Impairment

A small proportion of patients with ALS report "numbness" or ill-defined pain in the lower legs or arms. The use of the word numbness does not necessarily imply sensory impairment; patients may even be describing muscle weakness. Sensory impairment has not been found in ALS patients, but sensory complaints are not unusual. In our studies nearly 20% of patients with motor neuron disease (180 with ALS and 36 with progressive muscular atrophy) had ill-defined sensory symptoms of paresthesia (a burning or prickling sensation) or focal pain. However, sensory examination showed no abnormalities except a decreased sensitivity to vibration in the toes, which is not an unusual neurologic change, because it also occurs in healthy elderly people.

Although a routine neurologic examination reveals no sensory abnormalities in most patients with ALS, more sophisticated quantitative sensory testing may reveal clear abnormalities. These patients are more sensitive to some types of sensory stimuli, particularly to vibratory stimuli, but sensitivity to touch and changes in temperature are normal. Electrophysiologic tests, including somatosensory evoked potentials, are abnormal in some patients with typical ALS. Pathologic studies reveal that the number of myelinated fibers in the peripheral sensory nerves is lower in these individuals. These findings support the opinion that ALS is not a pure motor neuron syndrome but rather a generalized neuronal disease that primarily involves the motor neurons.

### Dementia

Although rare, dementia may occur in patients who have otherwise typical ALS. Epidemiologic data on dementia in ALS are scarce, but its frequency is reported as less than 5%. Mild dementia may not be detected, particularly in patients with bulbar palsy whose impaired ability to speak makes assessing mental function particularly difficult. In addition, the dementia in ALS seems to be more common in patients with bulbar palsy than in those with predominant extremity involvement; consequently, dementia may not have been detected in some of these latter patients.

In the past several years, a condition called frontotemporal dementia or cognitive impairment has come to be recognized as occurring more frequently in ALS than previously thought. Neuroimaging tests indicate that the size of the frontal and temporal areas of the brain is diminished as are the metabolism and blood circulation to these areas. Patients may develop personality changes, some paranoid ideas, and childish behavior; become withdrawn and less talkative; and have difficulty making decisions. Memory is not significantly affected. When very sophisticated neuropsychological tests are performed, they reveal subtle but clear abnormalities in as many as 50% of patients with ALS. This finding is rather surprising. Because it is now recognized that this condition occurs fairly frequently, neurologists should obtain a careful and thorough patient history, and if it indicates any hint of cognitive impairment, detailed neuropsychological tests should be ordered. Frontotemporal dementia can also occur by itself or in association with other neurodegenerative diseases. That frontotemporal dementia occurs more commonly than previously believed suggests that ALS is not a pure motor neuron disease and may affect other parts of the brain. However, it is important to remember that severe dementia is still generally rare, as discussed at the beginning of this section. Importantly, the prevalence of frontotemporal dementia has provided scientists with a new direction for investigating the causes of ALS.

For neurologists who evaluate patients with ALS, a careful and thorough mental status examination is essential in identifying any underlying dementing disease or frontotemporal cognitive impairment. Depression is one of the most common psychological processes in patients with ALS, and it may mimic dementia. Therefore, neurologists must be careful to distinguish depression from dementia.

The cause of dementia in ALS is complex and may have several explanations. We assume that frontotemporal dementia is the most common cause if dementia is present in patients with ALS. However, Alzheimer's disease can be present independently of the ALS. Although the dementia in Alzheimer's disease affects more memory functions, it can look very similar and be difficult to distinguish from frontotemporal dementia. Again, neuropsychological testing is crucial. A very unusual dementia occurs in the western Pacific. It is part of a condition called ALS parkinsonism-dementia complex. Patients with this condition have symptoms of Parkinson disease plus dementia. Clinically, about 5% of the patients in the western Pacific who have parkinsonism-dementia develop ALS, but 38% of patients with ALS in this region develop parkinsonism-dementia. However, detailed autopsy studies of the brain in these patients have revealed that ALS and the parkinsonism-dementia complex of the western Pacific are the same disease process. Although the combination of ALS and parkinsonism-dementia almost exclusively occurs in the western Pacific as an endemic form, both familial and rare sporadic cases of a clinically identical syndrome have been reported outside this region. In patients with ALS and dementia, further investigation, including molecular and autopsy studies, is crucial to understanding the mechanisms of dementia in ALS.

## Extrapyramidal (Parkinsonian) Signs

Parkinsonism is a key feature of the parkinsonism-dementia complex seen in the western Pacific. Although parkinsonian signs are rare in patients with classic ALS outside this region, some cases have been reported in the United States and other countries. Parkinsonian features include slow body movements, increased muscle tone, diminished facial expression, stooped posture, and postural instability. In ALS, however, these features may be masked by marked spasticity and dominated or replaced by progressive lower motor neuron signs, such as muscle atrophy and weakness.

## Ocular Palsy

The eye muscles typically are spared in ALS. When ocular motility is tested in depth, however, the velocity of smooth pursuit movement (how fast both eyes move simultaneously) is lower in approximately 50% of patients with typical ALS. Such ocular abnormalities are thought to be caused by dysfunction in the upper motor neurons, which control motor performance and planning. Patients who have been on a ventilator for long periods may have a high frequency of ocular abnormalities, such as the inability to voluntarily close their eyes or complete ocular paralysis (ophthalmoplegia). Therefore, ocular motor control may be affected in the later stages of ALS.

## Bladder and Bowel Dysfunction

A group of motor neurons located near the end of the spinal cord is called the *Onufrowicz nucleus*. The Onufrowicz nucleus controls the pelvic floor muscles and the muscles involved in emptying urine from the bladder and emptying stool at the anus. Patients usually do not note any significant impairment concerning urination or defecation. However, a detailed analysis of bladder function in 38 patients with ALS revealed that almost one third had abnormal bladder function. Because bladder and bowel control involves not only skeletal muscles but also the involuntary autonomic neurons, these data suggest that control over sympathetic, parasympathetic, and somatic neurons may be abnormal in ALS. It is not unusual for patients with ALS to have urinary urgency. However, before attributing such urgency to ALS, it is essential to determine that the bladder itself or the reproductive organs are not causing the urgency. Although bowel function in ALS has not been systematically studied, in our experience, abnormal bowel function is very rare.

## Bed Sores

Sensory perception and cutaneous autonomic function remain normal in people with ALS. This may help prevent bedsores (decubiti). However, bed sores occasionally do occur, particularly in patients who require prolonged ventilatory support.

## Prognosis in ALS

It is important to understand that the prognosis of ALS varies greatly from patient to patient. Rarely, patients may die within several months after onset, whereas others may live more than 30 years. A slowing in progression and even improvement have been reported, and we have personally seen such patients, but these situations are rare. The prognosis is usually expressed in terms of the duration of the disease. The duration of disease in ALS is defined as the interval between the onset of symptoms and death. Recent studies indicate that the average duration of disease in ALS ranges from 27 to 43 months. However, the median duration ranges from 23 to 52 months. The median is important to consider because it is a measure that eliminates the extreme cases—those with a very short duration such as several months or a very long duration of 20 or more years. Compared with the duration of disease, the survival rate may be a better indicator of prognosis because it gives the probability of survival at the time a research study is initiated or at the time of diagnosis. In ALS, the 5-year survival rate ranges from 9% to 40%, with an average of 25%; the 10-year survival rate ranges from 8% to 16%.

### Factors That Influence Prognosis

Epidemiologic studies suggest some factors that are related to prognosis. Age probably has the strongest relationship to prognosis: usually the younger the patients, the longer the duration of the disease. In general, severe clinical involvement at diagnosis reliably predicts a rapidly progressive clinical course. A short interval between symptom onset and diagnosis is also associated with increased disability and poor prognosis, whereas a longer delay from onset of symptoms to diagnosis is associated with less disability and longer survival. However, this factor should be viewed cautiously because ALS is now diagnosed much earlier since public awareness and medical diagnostic approaches have improved in recent years.

One of the most intriguing and important studies in recent years indicates that the better the patient's psychological well-being, the longer the survival. Other factors associated with better prognosis include the presence of either a purely upper motor neuron or a purely lower motor neuron form, and onset in the extremity muscles rather than in the bulbar muscles. A poorer prognosis has been linked to bulbar onset, impaired respiratory function at diagnosis, or respiratory failure at the onset of disease. However, the need for a noninvasive positive air ventilator in these patients does not always predict a poor prognosis. Low serum chloride levels are associated with poorer prognosis, but this is only applicable at the advanced stages of the disease.

Some studies indicate survival is prolonged more than a year in people who take riluzole, but these studies are all retrospective studies, that is, the investigators analyzed data from their own patients, which may cause some bias. An intriguing association between weight loss and prognosis has been reported. It appears severe weight loss may result in a short disease course. It has also been suggested that hyperlipidemia (high cholesterol levels) may be associated with better prognosis. Any of these claims must be studied further and confirmed, but patients undoubtedly have a better prognosis if they maintain a good caloric intake and their weight.

## Patients With a Prolonged Course

It is well known to ALS experts that occasionally, in patients who appear to have typical ALS, the disease may either cease to progress or progress very slowly. A good proportion of patients with ALS are long survivors, living beyond 5 years after diagnosis, and 8% to 16% of patients live up to 10 years. The duration of illness alone does not distinguish between typical and protracted forms of ALS. In fact, people who survive for more than 10 years may not be all that rare. We have monitored patients who had a protracted course, but we were not certain about the diagnosis of ALS; we designated their condition "atypical" ALS. Such patients require further investigation to characterize this aspect of ALS.

The two longest documented durations of ALS are 32 and 39 years. In fact, one of the leading ALS experts (the late Forbes H. Norris, MD) even used the term "benign" ALS because the course of ALS in such cases was not the typical progressive course. In these patients, the annual decline in function is minimal. Although the disease progresses very slowly, overall functional impairment is still severe. In 28 male patients of 613 patients with sporadic ALS, progression ceased for at least 5 years. Others have suggested that a patient's disease "resistance" might influence the course of ALS. Determining whether patients with a more benign course have more reinnervation activity or experience other moderating influences is particularly important to improving our understanding of prognosis in ALS.

## "Reversible" ALS

Patients have been described who presented with ALS-like features and subsequently improved. In one such patient, ALS developed but progressed minimally for 6 years; however, the patient then suddenly grew worse, developed generalized fasciculations, and died within 2 years. Mulder and Howard described a 49-year-old surgeon who developed weakness in the left arm followed by weakness in the left leg along with fasciculations. Examination showed features typical of ALS. The muscle strength in his extremities gradually improved over several months, and reexamination after 6 years showed nearly normal muscle strength.

Similar cases of recovery or improvement from other motor neuron diseases also have been reported. It is interesting that all cases reported to date are characterized by predominantly lower motor neuron signs, although in some patients, reflexes are abnormal but not pathologic. No patient had spasticity or bulbar symptoms. Based on the El Escorial World Federation of Neurology diagnostic criteria, these cases probably are not classic ALS. Identifying and understanding similar cases of this "reversible" ALS syndrome is an important task for neurologists.

## Acknowledgment

I thank the many patients with ALS and their families who visited our ALS clinic and candidly discussed many issues with us. We are indebted to our patients for teaching us about this difficult disease. I also thank the health care team at the Eleanor and Lou Gehrig MDA/ALS Research Center, Columbia University Medical Center, for providing support, dedication, and excellent work. Cassandra Talerico-Kaplin, PhD, Cleveland Clinic, provided substantive editing.

## Further Reading

Aggarwal A, Nicholson G. Detection of preclinical motor neurone loss in SOD1 mutation carriers using motor unit number estimation, *J Neurol Neurosurg Psychiatry,* 73: 199–201.

Mitsumoto H, Chad DA, Pioro EP. *Amyotrophic Lateral Sclerosis.* New York, NY: Oxford University Press; 1997.

Mitsumoto H, Przedborski S, Gordon P, eds. *Amyotrophic Lateral Sclerosis. Current Science and Approaches to Therapy.* New York, NY: Taylor & Francis; 2006.

Radunovic A, Mitsumoto H, Leigh PN. Clinical care of patients with amyotrophic lateral sclerosis. *Lancet Neurol.* 2007;6:913–925.

The spectrum of motor neuron disorders. In: Brown RH Jr, Swash M, Pasinelli P, eds. *Amyotrophic Lateral Sclerosis.* London: Informa; 2006:3–24.

# 3

# The Diagnosis
# of Amyotrophic
# Lateral Sclerosis

## David A. Chad

You—or a loved one—probably were first referred to a neurologist for assistance in establishing a diagnosis because of an unexplained weakness or clumsiness in the hand or foot, muscle cramping associated with weakness, or difficulties speaking or swallowing. The neurologist's task was to review all prior records, take a careful history, and perform a detailed and meticulous physical examination. He or she was then in a position to arrive at the most likely *clinical diagnosis* (a diagnosis grounded in clinical evidence) and *differential diagnoses* (possible alternative considerations). Laboratory studies probably were recommended, including radiologic or imaging studies of the brain and spinal cord, electrodiagnostic testing (nerve conduction studies and electromyographic needle examination), and a variety of blood tests. When this testing—a process that may take a couple of weeks—was complete, the neurologist probably met with you to discuss the clinical and laboratory findings and to present his or her diagnostic impression.

## History of the Illness: Listening to Your Concerns

As an important first step in the diagnostic process, the neurologist should listen to what the patient and family say about new symptoms experienced by the patient. After the patient and family relate their observations and describe changes in how the patient feels and how he or she has been functioning, the neurologist generally asks specific questions in an effort to understand the nature of the problem

43

as fully as possible. Although the complaint may appear to involve only one or two regions of the body, the neurologist's questions typically will be designed to evaluate neurologic regions literally from head to toe. The neurologist asks about speaking, chewing, swallowing; the facility with which the patient feels he or she can maintain the head erect; strength and dexterity in the arms; and the ease of rising from a seated position, walking a distance, or climbing a flight of stairs. Patients are asked about the ease of breathing, in particular at night and during exercise, and about the state of their muscles—if there has been loss of muscle bulk, twitching, or cramping.

The neurologist also asks about neurologic functions controlled by nervous system structures outside the motor system (recall that amyotrophic lateral sclerosis [ALS] is almost always strictly a disease of motor function), although such functions generally are not affected by ALS per se. The reason for asking these questions is to look for clues that suggest that the motor complaints are a part of a neurologic disorder other than ALS. For example, the neurologist asks about memory loss; visual changes; and the presence of numbness, tingling, or prickling. There also will be inquiries about the presence of pain, in particular, in the neck spreading into the arms or in the back spreading into the legs, and about any difficulties controlling the bladder or bowel. Questions such as these are asked because some nervous system disorders involve the motor system and one or more of the following systems: cognitive, visual, sensory, and autonomic. Unless the answers to these questions are sought, a disease masquerading as ALS could be missed or its diagnosis delayed. The neurologist typically also asks about the patient's general health. Although certain changes are expected in ALS, such as fatigue, difficulty sleeping, weight loss, and depression (the latter often as a reaction to the presence of unexplained symptoms), other symptoms might indicate an unexpected medical condition that might be associated with features of ALS. For example, the neurologist will probe the patient's history for signs of an infectious disease, thyroid abnormalities, an underlying tumor, or exposure to toxic agents, each of which could cause at least some of the motor changes found in ALS.

The neurologist also asks questions about family history. Up to 10% of all people with ALS will have at least one affected family member and are therefore classified as having familial ALS. Patients with familial ALS carry a genetic mutation that may be passed on to their children. In 20% of these familial cases, the mutation involves the gene coding for the protein copper/zinc superoxide dismutase (SOD1), which is an enzyme whose normal function is to limit the production of potentially toxic intracellular free radicals. More than 100 different mutations in the SOD1 gene have now been identified. The precise mechanism by which the mutated SOD1 enzyme causes the motor neuron loss in ALS is not certain, but it is likely that the mutation confers on the enzyme an unwanted neurotoxic property that causes damage to, and subsequently loss of, motor neurons. In most instances, the familial disease is clinically similar to the more common *sporadic* (arising spontaneously) form.

When the history taking is completed, the patient, family, and neurologist should feel that the neurologist has heard an up-to-date and complete account of the patient's medical and neurologic history.

## The Neurologic Examination

The neurologist approaches the examination in an orderly fashion, beginning with the evaluation of behavior, mood, language, and memory. Most people with ALS have a normal mental status examination, and another diagnosis is considered if major abnormalities are detected in one or more areas of mental or cognitive function. In the past few years, however, clinical and basic science research has revealed that some patients may experience changes in personality, judgment, planning, and social functioning. These changes in personality and in mental processes, which are sometimes quite subtle, represent a form of dementia called frontotemporal dementia and appear to be a part of the ALS disease process. Researchers are finding that this dementia appears to accompany ALS and may even precede it in some cases.

The next part of the neurologic examination focuses on the function of the cranial nerves, especially those nerves supplying the muscles of the head and neck, which are commonly affected in ALS. These nerves are responsible for the normal appearance and function of facial, tongue, jaw, pharyngeal, and laryngeal (throat) muscles. The neurologist inspects these muscles looking for signs of muscle atrophy and spontaneous twitching (fasciculations) and tests their strength. Other functions controlled by the cranial nerves are assessed, including vision, eye movements, and hearing, but these typically are preserved in ALS; if they are affected, the involvement may be a clue to the presence of another disease.

In the third portion of the neurologic examination, muscle bulk and strength are assessed in the upper extremities, chest, and abdomen, and in the lower extremities. The neurologist examines the muscles for evidence of atrophy; scans the facial muscles, tongue, limb, and trunk musculature for tremors; and evaluates muscle strength. Muscle strength typically is graded on a scale (called the Medical Research Council [MRC] scale ranging from 5 [*normal*] to 0 [*complete paralysis*]). A grade of MRC 4 indicates mild to moderate muscle weakness; a grade of MRC 3 indicates that a muscle is so weak it can only oppose the effects of gravity; and a muscle graded MRC 2 is weaker still, active only if gravity can be eliminated. A muscle graded MRC 1 has sufficient strength to generate only a flicker of movement and does not quite move around a joint. Although a person may be complaining of weakness in only one area, such as an arm or a leg, the neurologist typically explores all areas, even those that are not symptomatic, and often finds abnormalities of which the patient has perhaps not yet become aware.

The next step during the course of the examination is to assess muscle tone and reflexes. Normally there is no notable resistance to movement when a portion of a limb is flexed or extended around a joint. Because of the degeneration of the upper motor neurons (UMNs) that occurs in ALS, there is mild to moderate resistance to passive extension of a limb around its joint, followed by a sudden giving way during extension, a deviation from normal tone called *spasticity*. Because of this increased muscle tone, repetitive motions such as finger and foot tapping cannot be performed quickly; instead, they are done in a slow and effortful fashion. In ALS the activity of reflexes is increased; tapping the tendon of one joint often leads to activation not only of the expected reflex but also of adjacent reflexes, a phenomenon known as spread of reflex activity, which is indicative of UMN loss. Tendon reflexes are expected to be active or hyperactive in ALS. It is not uncommon for reflexes to be normal in the early stages of the illness and increase in activity as the disease progresses. If reflexes are persistently reduced or absent, an alternative diagnosis might be explored.

Ambulation or gait is the next function to be tested. If the disease has affected the lumbosacral region, leg muscles may be weakened or spastic, and walking will accordingly be abnormal. A common initial manifestation of ALS is weakness of the foot and toe dorsiflexor muscles, leading to footdrop. The wide-based, staggering gait characteristic of diseases that involve the cerebellum or sensory loss is not a part of ALS unless an additional disease complicates it.

Sensation—the ability to detect pin prick, cold, light touch, tuning fork vibration, and movements of a joint up or down—usually is evaluated last. Sensory function is typically normal in ALS. Elderly people may have some reduction in the acuity of their sensation, but more pronounced degrees of sensory loss raise the possibility of an alternative diagnosis.

## Clinical Diagnosis

Two major categories of neurologic findings are required to establish the clinical diagnosis of ALS: (a) evidence on clinical examination of muscle weakness, atrophy, and fasciculation (tremor). These are known as lower motor neuron (LMN) signs and are caused by the degeneration or loss of motor nerve cells in the brain stem or spinal cord; and (b) increased muscle tone with slow and difficult movements associated with heightened reflexes (hyperreflexia) and the spread of reflex activity; these are UMN signs caused by degeneration or loss of motor nerve cells in the brain (motor cortex).

Because a variety of neurologic disorders produce LMN signs, UMNs signs, or both, criteria have been proposed to increase the level of certainty about the diagnosis of ALS. Neurologists experienced in the diagnosis, management, and care of ALS patients met in April 1998 at Airlie House for the World Federation of Neurology ALS Conference to revise the diagnostic criteria for ALS. The group stated that the diagnosis of ALS be considered probable on clinical grounds when the combination of UMN and LMN signs are found in at least 2 regions, with some UMN signs being found above some LMN signs. The diagnosis of clinically definite ALS is made when there is evidence on clinical grounds of the presence of combined UMN and LMN signs in the bulbar region and at least 2 spinal regions, or when UMN signs are present in 2 spinal regions and LMN signs are present in 3 spinal regions.

The four defined regions for these signs are the bulbar region of the brain and three spinal regions: cervical, thoracic, and lumbosacral. Each region encompasses specific muscle groups. The designation *bulbar* refers to the jaw, face, palate, tongue, and laryngeal muscles. The cervical region includes the neck, arm, hand, and diaphragm muscles. The thoracic region includes the back and abdominal muscles. The lumbosacral region refers to the back, abdominal, leg, and foot muscles.

The clinical findings of UMN or LMN signs or both often are restricted to a single region, or the findings may be in multiple regions but are only UMN or only LMN in type. In these cases the diagnosis of ALS cannot be established with certainty, and the neurologist will want to repeat the examination in several months to determine whether there has been progressive spread of signs to other regions or the development of UMN and LMN signs combined. Only in these instances is it possible to make the diagnosis of ALS clinically with a greater degree of certainty.

## Differential Diagnosis

In our experience, if the clinical evidence points to either probable or definite ALS, the diagnosis is most often correct. Because a variety of neurologic disorders present with features similar to those of ALS, however, we need to ask whether our patient might have a more benign disorder. This is termed a differential diagnosis because we must distinguish the disease from other diseases whose symptoms may be similar.

Diseases that affect the brain stem may produce combined UMN and LMN signs in muscles supplied by the cranial nerves (the bulbar region). These conditions include neoplasms of the brain stem, most commonly brain stem glioma; multiple small strokes of the brain stem; and multiple sclerosis. They usually can be readily identified on a magnetic resonance imaging (MRI) scan of the brain that includes brain stem structures. In all three conditions, the MRI results would be abnormal. In contrast, the MRI results usually are normal in ALS.

Another group of conditions whose symptoms can mimic ALS involves the spinal cord. Perhaps the most common condition is osteoarthritis of the cervical spine (spondylotic myelopathy) that leads to compression of the cervical spinal cord and nerve roots. Its symptoms include LMN signs in the arms (sometimes with coexisting UMN signs) and UMN signs in the legs, features that certainly are consistent with ALS. However, spondylotic myelopathy is often painful, and, in addition to the motor abnormalities, sensory symptoms and signs are usually quite prominent, and there may be a disturbance in the control of urination and bowel function. The latter are usually not seen in ALS, although in some patients with pronounced UMN signs (a great deal of leg stiffness or spasticity), urinary urgency may occur. Magnetic resonance imaging of the cervical spine can determine whether there is a significant degree of spondylotic myelopathy. Although arthritic changes of the cervical spine are common in the age group of patients who develop ALS, clinically significant spondylotic myelopathy rarely occurs without an accompanying radiologic picture of advanced disease. In ALS cervical cord and adjacent nerve roots are typically normal or, at the most, only mildly compromised by arthritic change; hence, spondylotic myelopathy can usually be excluded by the combination of clinical and radiologic features.

Another disease that affects the cervical spinal cord is syringomyelia, a condition in which a fluid-filled cavity develops in the central portion of the cord and gradually expands to cause injury to both lower motor neurons and descending corticospinal tracts, as well as the ascending sensory pathways that convey sensations of pain and temperature. The clinical result is a combination of LMN signs in the arms and sometimes UMN signs in the legs, which alone suggests ALS, except that there also is typically a pronounced loss of feeling to pain and temperature in the hands. The disease is recognized radiologically by MRI studies that disclose the central cord cavity.

Some diseases of the peripheral nerves may produce fairly widespread LMN signs and hence simulate at least LMN involvement of ALS. Specific electrodiagnostic testing (see next section), however, can assess the function of the peripheral nerves. Focal regions of demyelination (loss of the thick, lipid-rich insulation that surrounds motor axons) along upper extremity motor nerve fibers underlie a condition called multifocal motor neuropathy, with a block in nerve conduction that simulates ALS. This condition can almost always be recognized with careful electrodiagnostic testing. Apart from mild to moderate reduction in motor amplitudes because of a loss of motor neurons, people with ALS per se are expected to have essentially normal results in nerve conduction studies.

Some diseases of muscle may suggest ALS, especially those that involve muscle wasting and weakness. Electromyography is a powerful diagnostic tool in distinguishing these conditions from ALS.

## Laboratory Investigations

We recommend a variety of investigations to confirm or disprove a diagnosis of ALS, including electromyography, neuroimaging of the brain and spinal cord, and clinical laboratory (blood test) studies. Testing is needed to confirm the diagnosis. In addition, because a variety of neurologic disorders present with features similar to those of ALS, it is important to search for test abnormalities that are characteristic of these conditions.

Electrophysiologic testing, known as electromyography or EMG, is done to confirm the loss of LMNs in clinically affected regions and to detect the earliest electrophysiologic signs of LMN loss in areas that do not yet appear to be involved clinically. The EMG examination has two parts. The first involves the evaluation of peripheral nerve function—determining whether motor and sensory nerve conduction velocities and motor and sensory elicited responses are normal. In ALS the nerve conduction velocity should be within the normal range or only mildly reduced. Slowed velocities suggest that the patient's problem might stem from a peripheral neuropathy. We look for a difference between the amplitudes of the motor responses when the nerve is stimulated at different sites. Only minor differences should be found in ALS, so the detection of major differences points to an alternative diagnosis.

In the second part of the study a needle electrode is inserted into various muscles from different anatomic regions. There is no unexpected spontaneous electrical activity when the needle is inserted into healthy muscle. As the normal muscle begins to contract, the electrical signatures of motor unit potentials can be observed, and they have expected, normal firing rates. In contrast, when the electrode is inserted into a muscle affected by ALS, there is abnormal spontaneous activity that indicates loss of the lower motor neurons that had supported the individual muscle fibers of that muscle; the loss of nerve supply by a muscle because of degeneration of an LMN is called acute denervation. During the voluntary muscle contraction portion of the test, fewer units than normal fire, and the surviving motor unit potentials fire at rapid rates. Additionally, instead of the normal waveform, higher-amplitude waveforms of longer duration than normal are seen. If the results of the needle EMG examination are normal, it suggests that either the disease process has not yet involved the area being studied or that the diagnosis of ALS is mistaken and the clinical problem should be carefully reevaluated.

Although the EMG is sometimes associated with transitory discomfort, we strongly believe that it is an essential component of the diagnostic process and should be performed by an experienced practitioner on every patient who is evaluated for ALS.

Neuroimaging studies (MRI) are done to confirm normal anatomy and examine for motor pathway abnormalities occasionally seen in ALS. Another major purpose of the test is to look for structural pathology in the brain, brain stem, or cervical spinal cord that may cause UMN and/or LMN signs and may simulate ALS. In ALS itself, brain and spinal cord MRI studies are expected to be normal or show only mild abnormalities without definite evidence of other brain stem, spinal cord, or nerve root pathology.

Blood testing is done primarily to confirm that results are normal. In most patients with ALS, we do not expect to find abnormalities in blood count or in the various blood chemistry tests used to indirectly assess the function of the bone marrow, liver, kidney, and other major organ systems. In some patients with ALS, the muscle enzyme known as creatine kinase or CK is moderately elevated, probably because of changes that occur in muscles after they have lost their nerve supply. Although no blood test abnormalities are specifically diagnostic of ALS, we are looking for evidence of treatable or reversible disorders of an autoimmune, metabolic, endocrine, neoplastic, infectious, or toxic nature that may, on occasion, alter the nervous system in such a way as to produce UMN and LMN signs, thereby simulating ALS.

In addition to blood test studies, we examine the cerebrospinal fluid (CSF) in some patients when features of the clinical presentation are atypical. This includes people with clinical evidence of ALS who are younger than the age range typically encountered for the disease (usually <40 years), when there is evidence of a systemic or nervous system infection, or when we suspect an underlying systemic malignancy. Tests performed on the CSF include measurement and analysis of protein, glucose, and total number of white blood cells.

In a few cases, we recommend bone marrow evaluation, a procedure that is indicated to look for an underlying neoplasm (usually a lymphoma or Hodgkin disease), which is on rare occasion associated with clinical features of ALS.

Other special tests include evaluation for the presence of an antibody called anti-Hu. A neurologist might be prompted to test for anti-Hu when abnormal signs in nonmotor areas, such as cognitive functioning, coordination, and sensation, accompany clinical features of ALS. Such a constellation of findings suggests a more diffuse central nervous system (CNS) disorder—possibly a paraneoplastic syndrome in which neurologic findings are immune-mediated and triggered by the presence of a tumor (typically small-cell lung carcinoma). Another test that may be ordered is the leukocyte hexosaminodase-A assay. Patients recommended for this test typically are much younger than the usual age range of onset of ALS and have associated mental changes, incoordination, and sensory abnormalities.

For individuals with at least one affected family member with a confirmed diagnosis of ALS, testing for the presence of a mutation in the SOD1 gene is indicated. As previously noted, approximately 20% of patients with familial ALS will be found to have a mutation in the SOD1 gene. If a mutation is identified, then the cause of the ALS has been established. As mentioned, although there are well-described distinctive clinical patterns associated with some of the SOD1 mutations that differ from the most common form of sporadic ALS, the clinical features of familial ALS are broadly similar to sporadic ALS. Testing for at-risk and asymptomatic individuals (siblings and children of an affected individual) can be provided, but because of the potential significant impact on the person undergoing testing, we recommend pretest consultation with a certified genetic counselor and a clinical psychologist, as well as a neurologist.

We recommend the DNA test for the cytosine-adenosine-guanidine (CAG) expanded trinucleotide repeat in the androgen receptor gene on the X chromosome in men who are younger than the usual age of onset for ALS (<40 years) and have associated enlargement of breast tissue (gynecomastia), sensory changes, and abnormalities of coordination. Patients who test positive have the disease known as bulbospinal neuronopathy, or Kennedy syndrome, which unlike most cases of ALS, is a disease that is slowly progressive over decades.

## Presentation of the Diagnosis

The diagnosis of ALS requires a process of clinical evaluation, neuroimaging, electrodiagnostic testing, and laboratory studies. Because of the varied nature and complexity of testing procedures, it simply takes time for the full investigation to be completed, usually 2 to 3 weeks. During that time, you and your family will understandably be anxious for the neurologist to share his or her thoughts on the nature of the ailment. Before coming to the neurologist, you probably were concerned that the underlying problem was serious and may have already considered ALS as a possibility. Even before all laboratory data are gathered together, therefore, you will want at least some preliminary opinion from the neurologist. In these circumstances many of us share our thoughts with our patients. Although the laboratory tests may not yet have been completed, if we discover strong clinical evidence of ALS and the patient suspects the diagnosis, we would indicate that findings detected on the examination are indeed compatible with ALS but that further testing is needed for confirmation. We also point out that we will explore the laboratory tests carefully and leave no stone unturned as we search for clues that might reveal remediable or treatable conditions.

Neurologists experienced in ALS diagnosis and care present the diagnosis frankly, with honesty and hope and only after careful evaluation and testing. We prefer to provide information to you and your family gradually so that you will have time to adjust. Facts should not be thrust on you until you are ready for them. Patients report that disclosure is best when they are not overwhelmed with too much information too soon. We strive to set aside plenty of time, a minimum of 45 minutes, to speak directly with a patient and his or her family members, in comfortable physical surroundings, in a quiet room, free of distractions. We feel strongly that a patient should not hear the news of the diagnosis alone. We suggest that, if at all possible, a relative, friend, or some representative of the patient's support network be in attendance. Written materials that discuss the multifaceted aspects of ALS symptoms and symptom management—those published by the Muscular Dystrophy Association and the ALS Association are especially appropriate—are useful, because they can be read at your own pace after the initial shock of the diagnosis has lessened. We also contact patients weekly for a period of several weeks immediately after diagnosis to provide support and information and to schedule a near-term revisit for further discussion.

At the time of diagnosis we attempt to provide hope in several ways.

- We emphasize that you will not face the disease alone and will never be ignored or abandoned. A team of health professionals will provide multidisciplinary care every step along the journey, helping you to cope with new physical and psychosocial realities and adapt to the ongoing changes and challenges of the disease. We encourage our patients to seek comprehensive care at specialized ALS centers, which have been designated by the Muscular Dystrophy Association and the ALS Association. In these centers, the neurologist joins subspecialists in other disciplines to do all that is possible to ensure patient well being, and that your wishes related to how you are cared for and whether certain interventions are utilized or not will be respected at all times.

- We point out that, although ALS is a progressive disease, the conventional wisdom of rapid deterioration does not necessarily apply to everyone and that slower progression is well documented, with some patients having 5, 10, 15, or more years ahead of them after diagnosis.

- Although the course of ALS is one of progressive weakness, it is important to emphasize that cognitive clarity and psychic energy are usually preserved and they may compensate for loss of strength and movement by maintaining social interactions.

- We present the current state of knowledge of the pathogenesis of ALS to our patients, because many of them find this knowledge helpful. We inform our patients that no one yet fully understands ALS, that we are uncertain about the cause and pathogenesis, but that we are entering a new era of therapies based on evidence from research in the basic sciences. We repeat Dr. Lewis Rowland's "fifth level of hope," which, to paraphrase, is that one day, a very bright scientist or researcher is going to get lucky and unravel the mysterious biology of ALS so that we have an effective treatment. Along these lines, we inform our patients about any clinical trials that are actively recruiting in our region and strive to enroll those who are interested and who fulfill eligibility criteria.

- We indicate that, although there is at present one Food and Drug Administration (FDA)-approved drug for ALS called riluzole with a modest positive effect on the course of the disease, other drugs with promise are being evaluated in clinical trials.

- After presenting the diagnosis, we typically suggest a second opinion and are very willing to facilitate the visit, providing a list of names of ALS specialists and making office notes and reports of all test results readily available. Our colleague, Professor Walter G. Bradley, points out that "the availability of the second opinion helps the patient and family members feel that the door is always left open, and that the initial physician's mind is not closed to other possibilities."

# 4

# Treating the Symptoms of Amyotrophic Lateral Sclerosis

## Carlayne Elizabeth Jackson

Amyotrophic lateral sclerosis (ALS) results in a large constellation of symptoms for which there *is* effective therapy. Unfortunately, few randomized controlled trials of medications or interventions have addressed symptom management. As a result, physicians caring for people with ALS base their selection of specific therapies on personal experience and reports from colleagues and patients (1–3). The lack of scientific data to guide therapy decisions has led to a wide variety of management practices. This chapter will review many of the challenging symptoms you may experience and explain the treatment options that are available. Clearly, not all of the symptoms included in this review are experienced by every person with ALS.

It is important for you to discuss the symptoms you are experiencing with your physician and health care team and to become familiar with what can be done to manage these symptoms effectively. Ultimately, each decision about treatment interventions is yours to make.

## Disease-Related Symptoms

### Excess Saliva/Drooling

Excess saliva is a common symptom of ALS and can result in coughing, choking, or drooling (2). These symptoms are caused by swallowing difficulties that result from tongue and throat muscle weakness rather than by increased saliva

**Table 4.1** Medications for Drooling

| Medication | Dose |
|---|---|
| Amitriptyline | 25–50 mg at bedtime |
| Atropine | 0.4 mg every 4–6 h<br>1–2 ophthalmic drops under the tongue every 4–6 h |
| Glycopyrrolate | 1–2 mg every 8 h |
| Hyoscyamine sulfate | 0.125–0.25 mg every 4–6 h (available as oral tablets, elixir, or sublingual tablets) |
| Diphenydramine | 25–50 mg every 8 h |
| Scopolamine transdermal patch | 0.5 mg applied behind ear every 3 d |

production. The American Academy of Neurology practice parameter for the care of ALS patients recommends both treatment with medications (Table 4.1) and the use of a suction machine, if necessary (4). Side effects associated with these therapies may include constipation, fatigue, impotence, bladder retention, blurred vision, rapid heart beat, and dizziness. In addition, these medications should not be taken if you have a history of glaucoma, an enlarged prostate, or cardiac conduction disorders. Selection of a particular medication often depends on the severity and frequency of your drooling. Drooling associated with meal-times or a particular time of day may be treated with as-needed administration of hyoscyamine due to its short-term benefit. Scopolomine patches or amitriptyline provide a more continuous effect.

If you have difficulty swallowing medications, you may prefer a medication that can be given under your tongue or through a patch on your skin, or is available in a liquid form that can be administered directly through a percutaneous endoscopic gastrostomy (PEG) tube. In general, all of these medications may cause or aggravate existing problems with constipation, and therefore it is recommended that a stool softener be started at the same time the medication for drooling is prescribed.

If your drooling cannot be treated effectively with medications, you should discuss with your doctor the option of receiving botulinum toxin injections (5–10). Botulinum toxin paralyzes the nerves that stimulate the salivary glands to make saliva. These injections are given with a very small needle directly into the sali-vary glands and generally have to be repeated every 8–12 weeks. A recent study showed that this treatment resulted in improvement in 90% of the patients who received it and had no serious side effects (11).

## Thick Phlegm

People with ALS frequently report the sensation of something being stuck in the back of their throat and the inability to clear their phlegm because of an ineffective cough. The symptoms are frequently misinterpreted as being related to allergies but generally do not respond to antihistamines or decongestants. Thick phlegm may occur as a result of inadequate fluid intake or mouth breathing, or as a side effect from the medications used to treat drooling. Medications that have shown some benefit include high-dose guafenesin (1,800–2,400 mg/day), β-blockers (propranolol), or inhalation breathing treatments with saline or acetylcysteine using a device called a nebulizer. An uncontrolled survey of other alternative measures includes dark grape juice, papaya tablets, sugar-free citrus lozenges, and grape seed oil (12). Dietary changes that may help include decreasing alcohol and caffeine use, increasing fluid intake, and eliminating dairy products. Using a cool mist humidifier while you sleep can also be helpful. If these strategies are not helpful, you should discuss with your doctor the use of a mechanical insufflator-exsufflator (CoughAssist, Respironics) (13). This device acts like a vacuum to help pull out thick, sticky secretions from your upper airway.

## Laryngospasm

Laryngospasm is a sudden sensation of being unable to breath or a feeling that your throat is constricting. Laryngospasm is caused by an abrupt, prolonged closure of the vocal cords which may be triggered by smoke, strong smells, alcohol, spicy foods, liquids or saliva swallowed "down the wrong way," and/or acid reflux. Laryngospasm usually ends on its own within several seconds and you can help resolve the episode by repeatedly swallowing while breathing through your nose. Liquid lorazepam in a concentrated formulation applied as a few drops under the tongue, in general, will quickly stop the spasm. If you also have symptoms suggestive of gastroesophageal reflux disease (GERD), such as heartburn, acid taste, bad breath, cough, nausea, throat irritation, or hoarseness, discuss medical treatment for these symptoms with your physician. Because GERD may be worsened by breathing muscle weakness and overeating, people with ALS who use a PEG tube for feedings should consider therapy with medications to help digestion (metochlorpropamide 10 mg, 30 min before meals and at bedtime) as well as either antacids or proton pump inhibitors (omeprazole, ranitidine, or famotidine).

## Jaw Quivering/Clenching

Some people with ALS may experience quivering or clenching of their jaw when they are cold, anxious, yawning, or even speaking. If this condition becomes bothersome, your doctor may recommend treatment with either clonazepam or lorazepam. If the jaw clenching limits your ability to open your mouth to brush your teeth, injections of botulinum toxin into the jaw muscle (masseter) may also be helpful.

## Anxiety/Depression

Symptoms of depression and anxiety are certainly understandable after receiving a diagnosis of ALS and may manifest in a variety of ways: loss of interest in hobbies, social isolation, poor appetite, sleep disturbances, denial, irritability,

**Table 4.2** Medications for Depression and Uncontrolled
Laughter/Crying

| Medication | Dose | Common Side Effects |
|---|---|---|
| SSRI antidepressants: | | Sexual dysfunction |
| • Paroxetine | 10–50 mg daily | Sleep disturbance |
| • Fluoxetine | 10–30 mg daily | Anxiety |
| • Fluvoxamine | 50 mg 1–2 times/d | |
| • Sertraline | 50–100 1–2 times/d | |
| • Citalopram | 20–60 mg daily | |
| Tricyclic antidepressants: | | Dry mouth |
| • Amitryptiline | 25–75 mg at bedtime | Fatigue |
| • Nortriptyline | | Dizziness |
| • Desipramine | | Urinary retention |
| | | Constipation |
| Mirtazapine | 15 mg at bedtime | Abnormal dreams |
| | | Confusion |
| | | Constipation |
| Ventafaxine | 37.5–75 mg 2–3 times/d | Poor appetite |
| | | Constipation |
| | | Weight loss |
| | | Impotence |
| | | Anxiety |
| | | Dizziness |

SSRI = selective serotonin reuptake inhibitor.

or anger. These symptoms should be discussed with your physician and treated aggressively. A referral to a psychiatrist, psychologist, social worker, or support group can help you cope with the emotional issues you might experience.

The most common medications used to treat symptoms of anxiety and depression are included in Table 4.2. Most of these medications take at least one month to become effective, so you must give them an adequate trial to see if they will be helpful. If you develop any side effects from the treatment, be sure to discuss these with your physician so that another medication can be chosen. In general, the medications are started at a low dose but may need adjustments depending on your response.

## Uncontrollable Laughter or Crying (Pseudobulbar Affect)

People with ALS sometimes experience sudden, involuntary outbursts of uncontrolled laughter or crying that are inappropriate in the context of the situation and occur with minimal or no provocation. This phenomenon is thought to be caused by the loss of nerve cell inhibition over the brain centers involved with producing emotion and is felt to be unrelated to symptoms of depression (14–15). Currently, there is no FDA-approved therapy available for pseudobulbar affect, but medications used to treat depression are usually helpful (Table 4.2). The benefits of a combination of dextromethorphan and quinidine in a controlled study have been reported (16). More than 50% of patients treated with this medication combination were free of symptoms after 15 days of treatment. A further study to determine the best dose and safety of these medications is underway.

## Pain, Cramps, and Spasms

Pain affecting people with ALS is often due to a combination of different factors. Many treatments exist to prevent and effectively treat these multiple sources of pain, and you should discuss these with your physician if you experience them (Table 4.3).

One cause of pain is muscle cramps, which are sudden, involuntary muscle contractions that may be triggered by exertion of any muscle group in your legs, arms, abdomen, back, jaw, or throat. These muscle contractions may vary considerably in terms of their severity and frequency. Mild cramps are generally relieved by doing stretching exercises and by staying well-hydrated.

People with ALS can also experience stiffness (spasticity) in their muscles that can cause further difficulty walking or coordinating movements. If you are experiencing muscle stiffness and/or cramps that interfere with your activities or awaken you from sleep, your doctor may consider treatment with a prescription medication such as baclofen, dantrolene sodium, tizanidine, or gabapentin (17). Side effects from these medications may include weakness, fatigue, and

**Table 4.3** Causes and Treatment of Pain

| Cause | Treatments | Medications |
|---|---|---|
| Spasms/cramping/ stiffness | Stretching, range-of-motion exercises | Baclofen (oral or intrathecal), dantrium, tizanidine, gabapentin, clonazepam |
| Immobility | Stationary peddler, standing frame, aquatic therapy, range-of-motion exercises, collar for neck support, alternating-pressure mattress | Non-steroidal anti-inflammatory, joint injections |
| Edema | Massage, elastic support hose, elevation | Diuretic |

sleepiness. Starting these medications at low doses and then increasing the dose slowly can minimize these effects. You should never abruptly stop any of these medications.

If you experience stiffness that cannot be adequately controlled with oral medications, you should discuss with your physician the option of an *intrathecal* baclofen pump that is surgically implanted in your abdomen and delivers medication directly into the spinal fluid through a small tube (18–19). One significant advantage of intrathecal administration is the ability to vary the dose throughout the day depending on when you are experiencing the most severe symptoms. Additional bolus doses early in the morning or later in the evening can be programmed as well. Prior to consideration of intrathecal dosing, a test dose should be administered via lumbar puncture to assess your response to the medication.

Immobility can result in the development of joint contractures that can also be painful. Adhesive capsilitis (frozen shoulder) is a very common source of pain secondary to shoulder weakness. A daily home exercise program consisting of stretching and range-of-motion exercises has been reported to lessen or eliminate muscle stiffness and cramping as well as reduce the risk of developing joint contractures. Manuals on appropriate therapeutic exercises for people with ALS are available through both the Muscular Dystrophy Association and the ALS Association.

Mild pain can be treated with nonsteroidal anti-inflammatory medications such as ibuprofen or naproxen sodium. Narcotic medications are generally not recommended because they may cause suppression of the respiratory muscles, constipation, and nausea. Transdermal patches for pain should be avoided because drug absorption can be very erratic and unpredictable.

## Urinary Urgency

Some people with ALS, especially those with significant lower extremity stiffness, may have difficulty holding their urine and "making it to the bathroom in time." You may need to urinate as often as every 1 to 2 hours, even though each time you are only able to urinate a small amount.

It is important to discuss these symptoms with your doctor and be sure that they are not related to a bladder infection or enlargement of the prostate gland. If no other cause is identified, your doctor may prescribe oxybutynin (Ditropan) or tolterodine tartrate (Detrol). Oxybutynin is usually taken in a dose of 5 mg 2 to 3 times per day, and can be crushed and put through a PEG tube. Oxybutynin is also available in doses of 5 mg, 10 mg, and 15 mg as an extended release tablet that can be taken once a day, although it cannot be crushed. Tolterodine tartrate is longer acting and can be taken in a dose of 1 to 2 mg twice a day. If your symptoms are mild, medications and unscheduled accidents can sometimes be avoided by using a voiding schedule in which you attempt to urinate every 2 to 3 hours regardless of whether you have an urge.

## Constipation

Constipation is a frequent symptom in people with ALS, particularly when they become less mobile. Constipation can be aggravated by the use of medications for drooling or by the use of narcotic medications for pain or air hunger. If you develop constipation after starting a new medication, you should discuss this with your physician. Inadequate fluid intake because of swallowing difficulties, arm weakness, or a desire to minimize trips to the bathroom may also contribute to the problem. In later stages of the disease, your abdominal wall muscles may weaken to the point that you may have difficulty pushing the stool out, even if it is soft.

Initial management of constipation should include over-the-counter stool softeners such as Surfak 240 mg twice daily, Colace 50 to 300 mg daily, or Senokot 2 to 4 tablets daily. If these are ineffective, milk of magnesia, Miralax, or Dulcolax tablets can be added to the regimen. In patients with a PEG tube, lactulose (1–2 tablespoons 1–2 times daily) can be put through the tube as long as they are not impacted. There are a variety of different enemas, as well as magnesium citrate, that can be used in urgent situations. A creative recipe for constipation that has been recommended is "power pudding," which consists of equal parts of prunes, prune juice, apple sauce, and bran. Two tablespoons with each meal and at bedtime, along with adequate fluid intake and fruits and vegetables in the diet, can be as effective as medications for constipation in many cases.

## Swelling of Hands and Feet

Swelling of the hands and feet is a common complication of immobility. This is because the muscles are not able to help pump blood back to the heart. The consequences of chronic swelling can include pain, deep vein thrombosis (DVT), sensory nerve damage, and impaired range of motion. Conservative management can be very effective in treating edema, but diligent compliance is essential for optimal benefit. Elevation of the legs is probably the simplest and most effective early treatment. Putting a pillow under your calves when you are reclining or laying flat can additionally help the drainage of fluid from your legs. When you are purchasing a motorized wheelchair, be sure that your physician has ordered elevating leg rests. Motorized scooters do not offer this option and therefore are not recommended in patients who are wheelchair dependent more than 2 hours per day.

When periodic elevation of the arms and legs is not effective in reducing edema, specialized elastic stockings may be effective. Many brands and variations of specialized support hose are available; however, custom-fit prescription elasticized support stockings are the most beneficial. You should use people who are specially trained for fitting compression hose.

If the swelling in your feet or hands becomes painful or does not improve overnight with elevation, you should see your physician immediately to rule out the possibility of a blood clot or DVT. If a blood clot is not treated urgently, it can break away and travel to the lungs (pulmonary embolus), causing severe shortness of breath and/or death. DVTs can be diagnosed with a Doppler study and treated successfully with medications to thin your blood. You should discuss DVT prophylaxis with your doctor before any period of prolonged inactivity such as airline or car travel.

## Sleep Disturbances

Many factors may contribute to sleep disturbances in people with ALS, including respiratory muscle weakness, difficulty repositioning in bed, anxiety, depression, and pain. The consequences of impaired sleep include daytime fatigue, difficulty concentrating, and worsening depression. Available solutions to address impaired sleep are as varied as the diverse problems causing it. Addressing the underlying cause of your sleep disturbance is the preferred method of treatment rather than simply masking the symptoms with medications.

One of the most common causes of sleep disruption is respiratory muscle weakness. When your muscles are not strong enough to keep your oxygen levels normal, your brain will wake you up to take a deeper breath. To determine whether your sleep disruption is related to your breathing, your doctor will monitor your pulmonary function tests (forced vital capacity [FVC]) periodically. In addition, your doctor may recommend a nocturnal oximetry study during which you have to wear a probe on your finger that will measure your oxygen saturation and pulse while you sleep. Depending on the results of your breathing tests and nocturnal oximetry study, recommendations may be made to use a noninvasive positive pressure ventilator at night to help support your weak respiratory muscles and improve sleep quality.

Periodic leg movements can be another factor leading to disrupted sleep or insomnia. These movements are involuntary spasms or kicks of the legs that are severe enough to awaken you and/or your bed partner throughout the night. Periodic leg movements can be treated effectively with medications such as clonazepam, pramapexole (Mirapex), ropinirole (Requip), or carbidopa/levodopa (Sinemet).

Another factor leading to sleep disruption can be related to your inability to turn over easily and reposition yourself. A power, hospital-type bed can be extremely helpful to enhance movement and positioning. Many people with ALS find that sleeping with their head elevated at least 30° makes it easier to breath and control their saliva. An alternating pressure air pad or gel overlay mattress can also lessen the discomfort from limited mobility in bed. The use of satin sheets or nightwear may also make it easier for you to reposition yourself.

Anxiety and depression can also cause insomnia, especially shortly after your diagnosis, and your doctor may recommend treatment with a medication to help relieve these symptoms. In that regard, mirtazapine, amitriptyline, and trazodone can be especially effective because of their sedative side effects. Medications to treat anxiety, such as benzodiazepines, can be helpful but should be avoided at bedtime because of their potential to suppress the breathing muscles.

If treatment of the underlying cause of your sleep disturbance is not effective, you should discuss with your physician the possibility of taking a sleeping aid such as benadryl, zolpidem tartrate (Ambien CR), or erzopiclone (Lunesta). These medications have a low potential for addiction, are safe for long-term use, and are preferred because of their low risk of respiratory depression. Alternative pharmacologic agents, such as melatonin, passionflower, lavender, and hops, have been effective for individual patients; however, their benefits are quite variable and untested.

## Fatigue

Fatigue and decreased endurance are among the most common complaints in people with ALS, particularly early in course of the disease. The initial challenge in treating fatigue is in the identification of the cause (Table 4.4).

Conserving your energy by pacing your activities and taking frequent rest periods is perhaps the simplest and most effective method for treating fatigue. Deconditioning from the lack of exercise can be more disabling and fatigue inducing than controlled activity and exercise. In general, you should avoid activities that cause your muscles to ache or burn afterward and focus on low-impact aerobic activities such as swimming, walking, or riding a stationary bicycle.

Mild to moderate breathing-muscle weakness resulting in disrupted sleep is significantly underrecognized as a cause of daytime fatigue (20–23). Standard measures of pulmonary health (FVC, maximal inspiratory pressure, and nocturnal oximetry studies) are helpful in deciding whether you might benefit from nighttime use of noninvasive ventilation (BiPAP).

**Table 4.4** Causes of Fatigue in ALS

| Cause | Treatment |
| --- | --- |
| Physical fatigue | Rest, energy conservation, exercise as tolerated, adaptive equipment, medications (Table 4.5) |
| Lack of interest in activities, difficulty concentrating, anxiety | Consider antidepressant medication (Table 4.2) |
| Failure to feel rested after sleep | Consider noninvasive positive pressure ventilation at night |
| Pain or physical discomfort | See "Pains, Cramps, and Spasms" section, consider antidepressant medication, stretching and range-of-motion exercises |
| Medications | Identify sedating medications (Table 4.6) and discuss alternative treatments with your physician |

Medications to treat your fatigue may be considered if it is severe enough to affect your ability to perform your daily activities (Table 4.5) (24). Before considering any of these medications, however, it is important to be sure that your fatigue is not being caused by medications you might be taking to treat other symptoms (Table 4.6).

**Table 4.5** Medications Used to Treat Fatigue

| Drug | Dose | Side effects |
|------|------|-------------|
| Amantadine (Symmetrel) | 100 mg 1–3 times/d | Insomnia, vivid dreams |
| Modafinil (Provigil) | 200 mg/d in the morning or 100 mg in the morning and 100 mg at lunchtime | Headache, insomnia |
| Pemoline (Cylert) | 18.75–56.25 mg/d | Irritability, restlessness, insomnia, potential liver problems |
| Bupropion, sustained release (Wellbutrin-XL) | 150–300 mg/d | Agitation, anxiety, insomnia |
| Fluoxetine (Prozac) | 20–80 mg/d | Weakness, nausea, insomnia |
| Venlafaxine (Effexor-XR) | 75–225 mg/d | Weakness, nausea, dizziness |

**Table 4.6** Commonly Used Medications That May Cause Fatigue

| Drug Class | Indication | Examples |
|-----------|-----------|----------|
| Analgesics | Pain | Butalbital, oxycodone, tramadol |
| Antispasticity | Spasms, spasticity | Baclofen, dantrium, tizanidine, clonazepam |
| Anticonvulsants | Pain, cramps, fasciculations | Gabapentin, carbamazepine, divaloprex |
| Antidepressants | Depression | Tricyclics (amitryptiline), SSRI (sertraline, paroxetine, others in this class) |
| Antihistamines | Congestion | Diphenhydramine, loratadine, fexofenadine |
| Anticholinergics | Drooling | Hyocyanime, glycopyrrolate, scopalamine |

SSRI = selective serotonin reuptake inhibitor.

## Slurred Speech

Slurred, slow, or strangulated speech is caused by weakness and incoordination of the tongue, lips, and throat muscles. Simple techniques such as speaking slowly, overexaggerating like a "bad Shakespearean actor," and spelling out words can be early strategies to improving your ability to be understood. If you are having difficulty communicating effectively because of changes in your speech, you should be evaluated by a speech therapist who has experience in augmentative communication. A large variety of speech devices can be used to help you communicate effectively; these range from simple letter boards to elaborate computer systems that can be operated with a head mouse.

## Swallowing Difficulties

Weakness of the tongue and throat muscles can also result in progressive swallowing difficulties. For mild swallowing problems, simple strategies to avoid choking can include tucking your chin down while swallowing, swallowing 2 to 3 times for every mouthful of food, taking sips of fluid between swallows, and avoiding foods that cause the most difficulty. A swallowing evaluation by a speech therapist can be helpful in determining which foods to eliminate and to be sure that you are not swallowing foods into your airway (aspiration). If your swallowing difficulties result in weight loss, or it begins to take a long time to complete your meals, you should discuss the option of a PEG tube with your doctor. Ideally, the PEG tube should be placed before you develop significant breathing muscle weakness or have any problems with aspiration. Once the PEG tube is in place, you can continue to eat for pleasure and then use the PEG tube to supplement your oral intake with a formula that your doctor can prescribe. Formulas that are high in fiber and protein are generally preferred. If you develop symptoms of bloating, cramping, or diarrhea after your tube feedings, medicines such as metoclopramide can be taken before each feeding to aid in emptying your stomach. In addition, sometimes administering the formula more slowly by using a "kangaroo pump" can eliminate stomach discomfort. You can also release gas from your stomach by opening the PEG tube and placing pressure over your stomach to "burp the tube."

## Shortness of Breath

Breathing problems are a common result of progressive respiratory muscle weakness (see Chapter 12), and it is important to be evaluated by a pulmonologist who is familiar with ALS. When shortness of breath is due to progression of ALS, symptoms usually occur during sleep and may include difficulty laying flat, frequent awakenings, bad dreams, and attacks of anxiety. Severe respiratory muscle weakness may lead to an accumulation of carbon dioxide in your blood that may cause headaches, confusion, hallucinations, or severe drowsiness. Weakness of breathing muscles may be treated successfully with a noninvasive ventilatior (NIV or BiPAP machine), which initially is used only at night but can eventually be used as often as necessary during the day to control symptoms of shortness of breath. The use of noninvasive ventilation has been shown to improve both survival and quality of life (25). If you develop acute breathing difficulties, you should be evaluated by a physician immediately to rule out the possibility of an underlying infection (pneumonia) or a pulmonary embolism. If you are advanced in your disease and have decided not to use noninvasive ventilation, your doctor or hospice may recommend the use of lorazepam, morphine, or oxygen to relieve any "air hunger."

## Summary

It is important to emphasize that ALS is not "untreatable," and many available interventions can markedly enhance your quality of life. It is essential that you communicate your symptoms and concerns with your team of health care providers so that these issues can be managed aggressively. Becoming familiar with treatments that are potentially available to treat your symptoms is an important step in being able to join your team in making the best choices for your care.

## References

1. Forshew DA, Bromberg MB. A survey of clinicians' practice in the symptomatic treatment of ALS. *Amyotroph Lateral Scler Other Motor Neuron Disord.* 2003;4:258–263.
2. Sufit R, Miller R, Mitsumoto H, et al. Prevalence and treatment outcomes of sialorrhea in amyotrophic lateral sclerosis patients as assessed by the ALS Patient Care Database. *Ann Neurol.* 1999;46:506.
3. Miller RG, Anderson FA Jr, Bradley WG, et al. The ALS patient care database: goals, design, and early results. ALS CARE Study Group. *Neurology.* 2000;54:53–57.
4. Bradley WG, Anderson F, Bromberg M, et al. Current management of ALS: comparison of the ALS CARE Database and the AAN Practice Parameter. The American Academy of Neurology. *Neurology.* 2001;57:500–504.
5. Portis M, Gamba M, Bertaccji G, Vaj P. Treatment of sialorrhea with ultrasound guided botulinum toxin type A injection in patients with neurological disorders. *J Neurol Neurosurg Psychiatry.* 2001;70(4):538–540.
6. Giess R, Naumann M, Werner E, et al. Injections of botulinum toxin A into the salivary glands improve sialorrhoea in amyotrophic lateral sclerosis [comment]. *J Neurol Neurosurg Psychiatry.* 2000;69:121–123.
7. Rowe D, Erjavec S. An open-label pilot study of intra-parotid botulinum toxin A injections in the treatment of sialorrhea in motor neuron disease. *Amyotroph Lateral Scler Other Motor Neuron Disord.* 2003;4:53–54.
8. Winterholler MG, Erbguth FJ, Wolf S, et al. Botulinum toxin for the treatment of sialorrhoea in ALS: serious side effects of a transductal approach [comment]. *J Neurol Neurosurg Psychiatry.* 2001;70:417–418.
9. Bhatia KP, Munchau A, Brown P. Botulinum toxin is a useful treatment in excessive drooling in saliva. *J Neurol Neurosurg Psychiatry.* 1999;67(5):697.
10. Tan EK, Lo YL, Seah A, Auchus AP. Recurrent jaw dislocation after botulinum toxin treatment for sialorrhoea in amyotrophic lateral sclerosis. *J Neurol Sci.* 2001;190:95–97.

11. Jackson CE, Rosenfeld J, Gronseth G, et al. A randomized, double-blind study of botulinum toxin type B for sialorrhea in patients with ALS. Accepted to *Muscle & Nerve.*
12. Gelinas D. Treating the symptoms of ALS. In: Mitsumoto H, Munsat TL, eds. *Amyotrophic Lateral Sclerosis: A Guide for Patients and Families.* New York, NY: Demos; 2001:47–62.
13. Bach JR. Amyotrophic lateral sclerosis: prolongation of life by noninvasive respiratory Aids [comment]. *Chest.* 2002;122:92–98.
14. Wilson S. Some problems in neurology II. Pathological laughter and crying. *J Neurol Psychopathol.* 1924;4:299–333.
15. Parvizi J, Anderson S, Martin C, et al. Pathological laughter and crying: a link to the cerebellum. *Brain.* 2001;124:1708–1719.
16. Brooks BR, Thisted RA, Appel SH, et al. Treatment of pseudobulbar affect in ALS with dextromethorphan/quinidine: a randomized trial. *Neurology.* 2004;63:1364–1370.
17. Ashworth NL, Satkunam LE, Deforge D. Treatment for spasticity in amyotrophic lateral sclerosis/motor neuron disease. Cochrane Database of Systematic Reviews 2004; 1.
18. Marquardt G, Seifert V. Use of intrathecal baclofen for treatment of spasticity in amyotrophic lateral sclerosis. *J Neurol Neurosurg Psychiatry.* 2002;72:275–276.
19. Stempien L, Tsai T. Intrathecal baclofen pump use for spasticity: a clinical survey. *Am J Phys Med Rehabil.* 2000;79:536–541.
20. Arnulf I, Similowski T, Salachas F, et al. Sleep disorders and diaphragmatic function in patients with amyotrophic lateral sclerosis. *Am J Respir Crit Care Med.* 2000;161:849–856.
21. Ferguson KA, Strong MJ, Ahmad D, George CF. Sleep-disordered breathing in amyotrophic lateral sclerosis. *Chest.* 1996;110:664–669.
22. Gay PC, Westbrook PR, Daube JR, et al. Effects of alterations in pulmonary function and sleep variables on survival in patients with amyotrophic lateral sclerosis. *Mayo Clin Proc.* 1991;66:686–694.
23. Kimura K, Tachibana N, Kimura J, et al. Sleep-disordered breathing at an early stage of amyotrophic lateral sclerosis [comments]. *J Neurol Sci.* 1999;164:37–43.
24. Krupp L. *Fatigue in Multiple Sclerosis: A Guide to Diagnosis and Management.* New York, NY: Demos; 2004.
25. Bourke SC, Tomlinson M, Williams TL, et al. Effects of non-invasive ventilation on survival and quality of life in patients with amyotrophic lateral sclerosis: a randomized controlled trial. *Lancet Neurol.* 2006;5:140–147.

# The Medical
# and Rehabilitative
# Management of Amyotrophic
# Lateral Sclerosis

# 5

# A Comprehensive Approach to Managing Amyotrophic Lateral Sclerosis

**Gabriela Harrington-Moroney
and Jinsy A. Andrews**

Patients with amyotrophic lateral sclerosis (ALS) receive care in a variety of clinical settings. When such care is provided in a comprehensive clinic that specializes in ALS (and possibly other neuromuscular disorders), all of the relevant specialists needed to manage the disease are brought together in one location. When patients are seen in many other types of clinics and practice settings, they will often receive care from these same specialists but in a slightly different rehabilitation setting, often managed within a department of physical medicine and rehabilitation.

The interdisciplinary or multidisciplinary approach provides the most effective management and care for people with ALS. Recent studies have demonstrated that patients who are cared for at ALS centers that provide a multidisciplinary approach live longer and have better quality of life than those who are cared for at a usual doctor's office. The American Academy of Neurology published a guideline in 1999 as to how patients with ALS should be treated based on thorough analyses of medical evidence presented in the medical literature. They are now in the final stage of publishing a new guideline recommending that patients be monitored at a multidisciplinary ALS clinic. An example of a multidisciplinary clinic is the Eleanor and Lou Gehrig MDA/ALS Research Center. At this weekly ALS clinic, patients are seen by a multidisciplinary team consisting of a neurologist, a nurse coordinator, a physical therapist, a speech pathologist, a dietitian, a pulmonologist, and a social worker. Other disciplines, such as gastroenterology, home health care, hospice, orthotics, and a wheelchair specialist, are called on by the neurologist or

69

nurse coordinator on an individual basis. This chapter discusses the responsibility of each of these specialists.

For those who are not receiving care in an ALS clinic, their care may be organized similar to that discussed in the next chapter, which considers the provision of care in a rehabilitation medicine setting.

## The Team Approach

People living with ALS, their family members, and their caregivers all benefit from a comprehensive multidisciplinary approach to care and management because the needs of people with ALS are ever changing. This approach has a positive impact on the ability of people with ALS to function and manage their symptoms (1). Until a curative treatment is found, this holistic and comprehensive approach offers the best physical and emotional support for patients and their families. "A commitment on the part of the patient, family and health care providers to collaborate in a way that can bring meaning and hope to circumstances that make no sense and a sense of wholeness in the face of relentless physical disintegration" (2) is an important aspect of the team approach. "Those who provide health care to patients with ALS need to combine their resources creatively to continue care. . . . The benefits of four independent resources that are used in combination: the ALS clinic, home care, alternate care sites, and hospice care . . . [are essential] . . . for effective management" (3). Ongoing comprehensive evaluation in the clinic setting as well as in the home by the home health care or hospice team provides timely management of the patient's needs.

### Advantages of a Team Approach

The team plays an important role in education and advocacy, makes referrals, and acts as liaisons as needed. The patient and family may wish to add their clergyman and the local ALS support group to the team.

Experience with ALS is vitally important for the successful management and care by the team. At our center, the multidisciplinary approach is provided in a clinic setting that includes evaluations by the neurologist and various other members of the team. This is important for the patients and families because they can see all the clinical experts and receive comprehensive care during their scheduled visit to the center and avoid making separate appointments with each specialist. A block of time is set aside for each patient to be seen privately by each member of the team. A team meeting takes place before the clinic to review each patient's status and needs. The members of the team continue to communicate with each other both during and after the clinic regarding the various needs of the patient. During these sessions, the team members confer about the findings and recommendations. This kind of approach also provides a unique opportunity for health care professionals to become highly experienced professionals who specialize in

**Table 5.1** The Multidisciplinary Team

---

- Neurologist
- Nurse coordinator
- Physical therapist
- Occupational therapist
- Speech pathologist
- Dietitian
- Social worker
- Prosthordontist
- Orthotist
- Pulmonologist
- Respiratory therapist
- Gastroenterologist
- General surgeon
- Psychologist or psychiatrist
- Alternate site coordinator
- Research nurse coordinator
- Research physical therapist

---

ALS. Moreover, such clinics will provide a fertile environment for active clinical research activities.

When a comprehensive team is not available, an alternative is an office visit with a neurologist who has experience in managing ALS and possibly including a nurse coordinator. They will refer the patient to other therapists and disciplines when specific needs are identified and a follow-up appointment with the multidisciplinary team is typically recommended.

## Disadvantages of the Team Approach

One disadvantage to our approach is that the appointment may last 3 to 4 hours and can be tiring for the person with ALS. Also, the cost of a visit may be high if multiple team members are seen. Furthermore, the actual cost of running a multidisciplinary clinic is often not reimbursed by medical insurance, leaving such clinics with a large financial burden. Additionally, the time allocated for each team member may not be sufficient if the patient has multiple issues to discuss and follow-up appointments may be necessary.

## The Team Members

### The Person With ALS

The patient's care and well-being is central to the ALS team. Decision making requires that the patient thoroughly understand the disease process and treatment options. While members of the health care team should work with the patient to set goals for treatment, the final decisions regarding care issues are ultimately decided by the patient. The ALS Association has drafted a Patient Bill of Rights for People Living With ALS (Table 5.2) (4). Its purpose is to inform people living with ALS of their rights as they relate to their health care and health care plan.

### Caregivers

In the early stages of the disease patients may exhibit some symptoms, but they are usually independent with regard to mobility and personal care. As symptoms progress, the patient's ability to function decreases. More assistance with day-to-day care will be needed from friends and more often from family. Family members become the core of emotional and physical support for patients. The person with ALS is usually not considered in need of skilled care as defined by Medicare and the insurance industry. The term *skilled care* implies either that the patient is expected to return to a baseline medical status that existed before the illness or that there will be a positive response to rehabilitation. Private insurance and Medicare do not cover long-term care in the home if no further improvement is expected. Home care visits are terminated after instruction regarding care is provided to patients and caregivers.

The role of caregiver can be both rewarding and overwhelming. Caregivers become important members of the team because they provide the physical and emotional care at home. A caregiver's participation in the ALS clinic creates a necessary link between the health care professionals and the continuity of care. Awareness of the challenges and increasing responsibilities placed on caregivers is very important. They are called on to provide an increasing level of physical and emotional care as the disease progresses. In addition to these demands, responsibilities to children and work outside the home can result in stress and strain that may lead to burnout.

## The Core Team

The following specialists are core members of the ALS team at our center and are always available as resources.

### Neurologist

Neurologists are physicians who specialize in the evaluation and treatment of diseases of the nervous system. They are responsible for making the diagnosis

**Table 5.2** The Amyotrophic Lateral Sclerosis (ALS) Association's Patient Bill of Rights for People Living With ALS

As a person living with ALS, you have a right to the following:

1. Receive comprehensive information about ALS, including treatment options and resources for your health care needs. This includes the right to communicate with your government representatives regarding policies of the FDA, National Institutes of Health (NIH), and other agencies that relate to ALS.

2. Participate in decisions about your health care with the highest level of decision-making possible. This includes the right to discontinue or refuse treatments and therapy.

3. Receive ALS specialty care in a timely manner.

4. Receive health care that is coordinated and individualized for you across the spectrum of home, hospice, hospital, nursing home, outpatient, and work place throughout all the phases of your illness.

5. Access health care benefit coverage and life insurance coverage without discrimination based on your ALS diagnosis or disability.

6. Obtain clear, timely information regarding your health plan, including benefits, exclusions, and appeal procedures.

7. Review your medical records and have the information in your records explained to you.

8. Prepare an advance directive to state your wishes regarding emergency and end-of-life treatment choices.

9. Receive care that is considerate, respects your dignity, and holds information confidential. You have this right no matter what choices you make about treatments and therapy, what your disabilities related to ALS might be, or what your financial circumstances are.

10. Receive maximum support to enhance the quality of your life and have your family involved in all aspects of your health care.

---

of ALS, as well as any underlying disease process. An ALS clinic is directed or led by neurologists who specialize in ALS. They refer those who have an established diagnosis of ALS to be seen in a multidisciplinary ALS clinic. At the Eleanor and Lou Gehrig MDA/ALS Research Center, neurologists usually confirm and discuss the diagnosis of ALS before referring the patient to the ALS clinic. Neurologists prescribe and order symptomatic treatment, often based on the recommendations made by other members of the team. They explain how the disease progresses and discuss the purpose and side effects of any symptomatic or specific treatments for ALS such as riluzole (Rilutek). Currently riluzole is the only treatment approved by the Food and Drug Administration (FDA) for the treatment of ALS.

Neurologists also discuss future treatment alternatives such as percutaneous endoscopic gastrostomy (PEG) tubes for receiving nutrition if the patient develops difficulty taking food by mouth. They explain noninvasive ventilatory support (external ventilator or BiPAP) and the availability of tracheostomy for the person experiencing impending respiratory difficulty or having difficulty managing secretions. The decision to pursue these options is made by the patient following a detailed explanation by the neurologist and the recommendation of various members of the team. In addition, neurologists discuss advance directives such as a Living Will, Durable Power of Attorney for Health Care, and Health Care Proxy. They identify patients who qualify for research protocols and often act as investigators of these studies. Those who are involved in research collect and evaluate data collected from ALS patients and monitor their responses to current methods of treatment and supportive care in their search for new insight into the cause of ALS and potential future treatment.

A potential conflict of interest exists when the treating neurologist is also a research investigator. Clinicians are required to provide the best symptomatic treatment and offer new therapies that may be potentially beneficial. New therapies are studied and proven effective within the context of controlled clinical trials. Clinical trials help develop new effective treatments and help to increase our understanding of ALS. Once a clinical trial is begun, no deviation from the original research plan may occur unless the protocol is formally changed. In some cases this may mean that a patient is given a placebo rather than the drug being tested. In recent years, clinical trials have had complex designs to reduce the chances of getting placebo, reducing time on placebo, and conducting interim analyses while the trial is ongoing to ensure that one group is not doing much better than another. All events related to patient care must be recorded in the patient record, and all major adverse effects must be reported.

## ALS Nurse Specialist or Nurse Coordinator

An experienced and compassionate nurse coordinator is essential for the success of the team approach. The nurse coordinator acts as a liaison between the various members of the ALS team, including the patient, the family or caregiver, and community resources. The nurse coordinator practices under the direction of the neurologist and plays a critical role as a patient advocate.

The patient or family member is referred to the nurse coordinator by the physician once the diagnosis has been made. The nurse coordinator is responsible for providing information through literature and responding to questions about the disease as well as coordinating appointments and consultations with the ALS clinic or with individual members of the team when necessary. Because much of the information may initially be overwhelming, the nurse coordinator is available at future clinic visits or by phone or e-mail to address needs and concerns and to make appropriate referrals so that the person with ALS does not feel abandoned when he or she can no longer come to the clinic. Care is coordinated through communication with a home care or hospice agency when appropriate, and the nurse coordinator continues to be available for psychological support to the patient and family.

The nurse coordinator also discusses issues such as the necessity for a feeding tube (PEG) placement or assistance with breathing (noninvasive vs tracheostomy). At some point, the nurse coordinator ideally should initiate a discussion of advance directives—Durable Power of Attorney for Health Care, Health Care Proxy, and the Living Will. The nurse coordinator monitors the patient's response to treatment along with the neurologist and becomes a resource for other nurses, health care providers, and home care agencies. In addition, he or she coordinates contact with research trials by either referring the patient to a research coordinator for participation in a clinical trial or by overseeing participation in the trial.

## Physical Therapist

Physical therapists evaluate people who have experienced an injury or a disease that has affected their functional status. They assess motion of joints, muscle strength, and endurance. Physical therapists evaluate leg strength and the ability to walk and transfer safely. They can prescribe a program of range-of-motion exercises to prevent contractures of the muscles, which cause pain and loss of function of the joints. Physical therapists may recommend stretching exercises and teach the proper method for either active exercises performed by the patient or passive exercises performed by the caregiver. In the earlier stages of the disease, some mild resistance exercises may be used for the unaffected muscles. Physical therapists also encourage walking, swimming, or performance of usual activities around the house as long as they do not produce fatigue. Patients may be fitted with equipment to ensure safety and/or braces to provide support for weak muscles, such as a cervical (neck) collar or an ankle-foot orthosis for weak ankles. Additionally, the physical therapist assists in the coordination of home safety evaluations, makes referrals for wheelchair evaluations, and, when appropriate, discusses the need for items like Hoyer Lifts and hospital beds.

## Occupational Therapist

Occupational therapists help people to live as fully and as normally as possible within their environment. Occupational therapists in the ALS clinic evaluate arm and hand function and make suggestions to conserve energy. Adaptive skills are taught to help increase or maintain the performance of daily tasks. They also may recommend splints to support weakened muscles and joints. Splints limit or prevent painful and debilitating contractures that would limit the function of weakened arms and hands. Other adaptive devices may also be recommended to make daily activities such as feeding and dressing easier. Occupational therapists teach people with ALS how to conserve energy to prevent fatigue. When wheelchairs become necessary, an occupational therapy evaluation provides the proper dimensions and adaptations.

## Speech Pathologist

Most people with ALS will develop problems with speaking and swallowing at some point, although it is variable as to what stage of the disease this problem occurs. The muscles that control the functions of speaking and swallowing are controlled by nerves that originate in an area of the brain called the medulla, or "bulb" because of its shape. These problems are therefore referred to as *bulbar palsy* and result from weak muscles of the face, throat, and neck. Because the speech and language areas of the brain are not affected, constructing and understanding language and the desire to communicate are not affected by the disease. Speech pathologists evaluate the patient's speech and ability to communicate and recommend communication devices (augmentative alternative communication (AAC) devices) to assist or replace speech weakened or lost as ALS progresses. They also evaluate the ability to chew and swallow, noting the presence of extra saliva, choking and coughing on food and saliva, and the need for extra time to complete a meal. Patients are then taught methods to eat safely and to conserve energy during meals.

## Dietitian

Weight loss may occur as muscles of the mouth and throat weaken because the quantity of food and liquid taken by mouth may not be adequate for proper nutrition and energy requirements. The dietitian assesses the nutritional status of the patient and makes recommendations that prevent aspiration (swallowing down the "wrong tube"), prevent weight loss, and maintain appropriate fluid and calorie requirements. Recommendations may begin with appropriate posture during meals and changes in food consistency, such as a softer diet to make chewing and swallowing easier. Fatigue can cause the patient to stop eating before adequate nutrients have been taken in. Eating smaller amounts more frequently and snacking can prevent fatigue during mealtime. Additionally, nutritional supplements may be recommended. The dietitian will discuss a PEG (feeding) tube as an alternative to taking food by mouth when it is appropriate.

## Social Worker

The social worker is available to assess the emotional status of the person with ALS and the family to determine how they are coping with living with ALS. Living arrangements and home care needs are also discussed. Advance directives will be reviewed at the appropriate time. The social worker can also make a referral if the patient and/or family members need an outside counselor. Coverage for counseling depends on the specifics of each person's insurance coverage.

The social worker is also available to guide the patient and family members with financial resources if assistance is needed. Some patients may utilize the Medicaid program that provides health care insurance for those who lack financial resources. Guidance may be given to apply for Social Security disability (SSD). Patients who qualify for SSD can qualify for Medicare regardless of age.

## The Extended Team

The following specialists are available individually by recommendation of the neurologist as specific needs arise.

### Pulmonologist

A pulmonologist is a physician who specializes in and manages respiratory or breathing problems. ALS does not affect the lungs directly, but it does affect the muscles that control breathing, and shortness of breath or respiratory distress may occur. During each visit at our ALS clinic, we measure the forced vital capacity (FVC)—the amount of air that can be moved in and out of the lungs. The FVC is expressed as a percentage of what is considered normal for each patient based on several variables. The pulmonologist is consulted as early as possible after ALS is diagnosed to establish a baseline respiratory function. If the person with ALS has a history of smoking or respiratory problems such as asthma or chronic obstructive lung disease, the pulmonologist can provide the necessary evaluation. The rate of change of respiratory function can be measured, and interventions or treatments can be prescribed sooner. The pulmonologist will discuss options, including the insufflator-exsufflator (cough assist) machine, noninvasive or external ventilator, tracheostomy, and invasive or permanent ventilator support (breathing machine), and will manage or oversee the care involving these options. At our clinic, pulmonologists also oversee pulmonary therapists who attend our clinic and who also visit the patient's home to provide continuation of pulmonary care to ensure better respiratory management.

### Gastroenterologist or General Surgeon

A consultation with a gastroenterologist, a physician who manages medical problems related to the stomach and intestines, or a general surgeon is recommended when the person with ALS has agreed to have a PEG or feeding tube placed. The decision to have a PEG tube placed is made if chewing and swallowing begin to result in unusual fatigue, if choking frequently occurs, and/or if weight loss is present. Ideally, the PEG tube should be placed while the patient has an adequate forced vital capacity (FVC). The PEG tube is placed with minimal sedation under local anesthetic. PEG placement is usually done on an outpatient basis, but under certain circumstances an overnight stay for observation may be necessary. The dietitian will discuss general nutrition and delivery of nutrition by a PEG tube with the patient and caregivers.

### Prosthodontist

A prosthodontist is a dentist who may be consulted in the presence of dysarthria, or impaired speech. A dental prosthesis may be designed to lift the soft palate, thus increasing the clarity of speech. In some patients, this prosthesis may be particularly useful.

## Research Coordinator

Patients frequently qualify to participate in clinical trials in the search of new treatments in ALS. The neurologist may act as the primary investigator, and a research coordinator oversees the study. The coordinator evaluates patient records to make certain that each participant meets the criteria established by the pharmaceutical company conducting the study and to ensure good clinical practice as determined by the FDA. The coordinator makes certain that all the required information is collected and that patients are followed at the appropriate time intervals. The data must be carefully stored, is kept strictly confidential, and is submitted to the sponsoring agency.

## Psychiatrist and Psychologist

Depression is a natural psychological process when one faces a serious illness such as ALS. It may affect every aspect of a person's life, including his or her personal relationships, work status, and financial status. Marital relationships and other relationships and social issues may be affected. Because physical changes are ongoing, the situation may seem overwhelming at times. Emotional and social adjustments become necessary as the role of each member of the family changes in response to the physical changes of ALS. Members of the ALS team make every effort to provide ongoing support to the patient and family. Antidepressants often provide relief from depression and a psychologist or psychiatrist may be consulted to assist with adjusting to the disease process or to help work out family issues.

## Wheelchair Specialist

A wheelchair specialist is available and is a great asset for patients. After a regular wheelchair evaluation, there is usually a delay of a few months or more before a patient obtains a wheelchair. It involves an evaluation by a wheelchair specialist, a vendor, insurance approval, and construction. Because some durable equipment such as augmentative alternative communication devices and power wheelchairs are very costly, most hospices will not pay for these expensive items because the budget per patient does not allow for it. It is important to have all the required durable medical equipment prior to referral to a hospice service. As previously mentioned, there may be a delay in obtaining the equipment, so it is necessary to begin the evaluation process early and prevent a delay in receiving hospice benefits. A simultaneous evaluation by a wheelchair specialist and vendor would facilitate this process.

## Orthotist

Deformity of the joints can occur as muscle weakness progresses. This leads to a loss of the ability to function effectively. Orthoses, or orthopedic appliances, are typically recommended by the physical therapist or the occupational therapist. The physical and occupational therapist addresses a number of issues concerning the neck, arms, and legs and addresses issues regarding mobility and the ability to function at home or on the job.

Orthopedic appliances are used to support or properly align the joints, the movable parts of the body. Orthoses help to prevent and/or correct deformities or contractures of the joints. Proper support and alignment of the joints relieves the pain that may occur as a result of weakness and deformity.

A referral is made to the orthotist by the physical therapist or occupational therapist, and a prescription for the necessary appliance is provided by the neurologist. The orthotist then designs and builds the orthopedic appliance. One example is a neck brace, or cervical collar, used to support weakened neck muscles. Posture is improved, which makes eating, sitting, standing, and walking easier, and neck pain that results from overworked muscles is relieved. Similarly, an ankle brace or ankle-foot orthosis (AFO) provides support to a weakened ankle, and the ability to walk is improved because the risk of tripping is decreased.

## Home Health Team

Issues about caring for the patient at home usually arise. As care issues become more challenging, the nurse coordinator may arrange for a home health care nurse. Care must be taken to choose a home care team that is knowledgeable about the disease because the needs of a person with ALS are unique. The team makes recommendations that will provide increased safety for the patient and caregivers. During a home visit the home care nurse will evaluate several things: the extent of the patient's disability and his or her ability to function in the home; the need for adaptive equipment such as a hospital bed, equipment for bathing, or a lift; and lifestyle adaptation. The home health care nurse will work with the ALS clinic nurse coordinator. A referral may be made for home visits by a physical therapist, occupational therapist, respiratory therapist, social worker, or home health aide. The nurse, patient, and family members may also address emotional and psychological concerns. The responsibility of caring for the person with ALS often falls to the family members because of variations in coverage or reimbursement by health care plans. Typically, there is a limit to the amount of home care that is covered, making careful planning and use of home care resources necessary. Once the caregiver demonstrates the ability to provide care, insurance no longer covers visits to the home. Should new issues arise, the patient or caregiver may request further services in the home by contacting the nurse coordinator. A referral will again be made to the home care agency by the nurse coordinator. Families with greater financial means may be able to afford privately hired aides for more help in the home.

## Hospice Care

Hospice care was developed to provide support and care for people who are in the last phases of an incurable disease. Patients are referred to hospice by their neurologists or primary care physicians. A recommendation for hospice care may be made by the home care nurse or the nurse coordinator. Patients are either transferred to hospice care from the home health care team or enter hospice care directly. Hospice care requires a team approach and may take place at home or in a nursing facility. A majority of people with ALS remain at home for hospice care. Caregivers must be available, such as family, friends, or the staff of a nursing facility. The emphasis of hospice care is to provide physical and emotional comfort. Comfort is provided to the family as well as the patient, with a focus on quality of life. An important point to note is that patients who have a tracheostomy and are permanently ventilated may not receive hospice care. Should the patient change his or her mind and receive a tracheostomy after entering hospice, he or she is no longer eligible for hospice.

The hospice team is led by a nurse case manager who develops a plan of care for the patient. Other members of the team include the following:

- The medical director who manages the patient care and provides medical services
- The social worker who provides assistance with financial issues, coordinates community services, and provides emotional support
- Pastoral care to meet the spiritual needs of the patient and caregivers
- The home health aide who helps to provide personal services for the patient
- The hospice volunteer

Bereavement support is provided by the hospice team. Care is coordinated with the neurologist and the ALS clinic nurse coordinator. Reports regarding the patient's status are provided by the nurse case manager to the neurologist and the ALS clinic nurse coordinator. Medicare and insurance policies generally provide coverage for hospice care.

## Patient Advocacy Groups

The Muscular Dystrophy Association (MDA) and the ALS Association (ALSA) are the primary advocacy groups for ALS. Certification for MDA centers is provided by the MDA and separately by ALSA at the national level and is based on standards of excellence in the diagnosis of ALS and the delivery of care to the ALS patient. Table 5.3 describes the standards and requirements for certification under the ALSA Center Program.

Varying degrees of financial support are provided to ALS centers at the local level by the local MDA chapter for patient services. Services available to patients include provision of education regarding ALS, support groups, home care con-

**Table 5.3** The ALSA Center Program

---

*Mission of the ALSA Center Program*

To define, establish, and support a national standard of care in the management of amyotrophic lateral sclerosis (ALS), sponsored by the Amyotrophic Lateral Sclerosis Association (ALSA).

Objectives of the ALSA Center Program

To encourage and provide state-of-the-art, multidisciplinary, and interdisciplinary care and clinical management of ALS through

- The involvement of all necessary health care disciplines in the care of the ALS patient and family;
- The offering of multidisciplinary and interdisciplinary care regardless of the ability to pay;
- Collaborative work among centers to enhance ALS patient care techniques.

To select, certify, and support distinguished regional institutions recognized as the best in the field with regard to knowledge of and experience with ALS; and which have neurologic diagnostics and imaging and available on-site licensed and certified ancillary services on clinic days including (but not limited to the following):

- Physical therapy
- Occupational therapy
- Respiratory therapy
- Nursing
- Registered dietitian services
- Doctor of psychology or psychiatry
- Speech and language pathology
- MSW social work services

To establish a cohesive relationship among ALSA centers, ALSA chapters, and ALSA Free Standing Support Groups and the ALSA national organization to fulfill the mission of the ALS Association and its ALSA Center Program.

---

sultants, and medical equipment to borrow for use in the home. The MDA and ALSA are considered as an important part of the team in the multidisciplinary approach to management of ALS.

"The ALS Association (ALSA) is the only not-for-profit voluntary health agency in the United States dedicated solely to Amyotrophic Lateral Sclerosis. The mission of the organization is . . . to raise funds to support cutting edge research, to increase public and governmental awareness, and to assist patients and families in coping with the day-to-day challenges they face living with ALS" (5). MDA and ALSA not only provide funds for research and work to increase public awareness about ALS, but they also provide direct service to patients and their families.

## Database

Critical to the understanding of the disease process is the collection of data or information. Information is stored and shared with health care professionals, providing insight into the disease process as well as response to treatment. Currently, the national database, ALS CARE, stores data from multiple ALS centers, individual neurologists, patients, and caregivers. The data reflect the physical, emotional, and financial effects that living with ALS has on the patient and caregivers. Data given by patients and their caregivers provide insight into the relationship between a patient's financial status and health outcomes. All data are kept confidential. Data are collected for the Cleveland Clinic Foundation ALS Clinic Patient Care Database by the neurologist, nurse coordinator, physical therapist, occupational therapist, speech pathologist, nutritionist, and social worker, which is probably one of the most detailed databases for patient care (6). Similar databases also have been utilized by the University of California, San Francisco.

At the ALS clinic, we have developed a database that promotes *outcome-based management* of the patient (7). The information is collected at specific intervals during patient visits to the ALS clinic. The relationship between medical interventions, or recommendations, and health outcomes, or the patient's response to treatment, is outlined in the database. The interventions are recommended by the neurologist and the other members of the team under the guidance of the neurologist. All members of the team have access to the data collected, which enables them to make further recommendations for patient care based on previous response to care. The collective use of such data allows for higher standards of care by reducing the chance for variability by individual health care professionals as they evaluate the patient and manage his or her care. The data are also used for medical record documentation and outcome-based research.

Information collected in our center's database is specific to the concerns of each member of the team as it applies to the evaluation of the patient and the decision-making process. Information collected by the neurologist and the nurse coordinator would include administrative confidential information, contact information, patient age and gender, onset of symptoms, and the level of diagnostic certainty in the clinical diagnosis of ALS according to the El Escorial World Federation of Neurology criteria. Levels of certainty progress from Suspected ALS to Possible ALS, Probable ALS, and Definite ALS. Differentiation is made between sporadic ALS (SALS) and familial ALS (FALS). A score is given based on the ALS Functional Rating Scale (ALSFRS), which quantifies the severity of the ALS based on motor function in the arms and legs and respiratory function. The FVC is also measured and recorded. Current symptoms, medications, and involvement in clinical trials are listed.

There are strong pros but a few cons to maintaining a database. It is costly and requires constant attention to keep it well maintained. However, the database provides a focused evaluation by health care professionals, which helps reduce variability in the care provided. Medical record documentation is consistent. Research is promoted. On the other hand, collection of data may be tiring for the patient. Additionally, the evaluation process may become time consuming for the health care professionals. The database is a useful tool for all clinicians working with patients to obtain information quickly in providing the best clinical care possible and for research clinicians to obtain critical data required in research. The database also provides current demographic and contact information and is easily accessible to all clinicians.

## Summary

The multidisciplinary approach in caring for someone with ALS requires full and equal participation of the health care providers, family, friends, and the person with ALS. A commitment among the members of the team and effective communication are important elements to providing effective overall care in ALS. This multifaceted approach can help address the constantly changing needs in ALS and help to maintain and promote quality of life.

## References

1. Mitsumoto H, Chad DA, Pioro EP. *Comprehensive Care: Amyotrophic Lateral Sclerosis.* Philadelphia: FA Davis; 1998:305–320.
2. *Patient Bill of Rights for People Living With ALS.* The Amyotrophic Lateral Sclerosis Association, National Office, 21021 Ventura Blvd., Suite 321, Woodland Hills, CA 91364.
3. Mitsumoto H, Borasio GD, Genge AL, et al. The multidisciplinary care clinic: the principles and an international perspective. In: Mitsumoto H, Przedbosrski S, Gordon PH, eds. *Amytrophic Lateral Sclerosis.* New York, NY: Francis and Taylor; 2006:605–632.
4. Chio A, Bottacchi E, Buffa C, et al. Positive effects of tertiary centres for amyotrophic lateral sclerosis on outcome and use of hospital facilities. *J Neurol Neurosurg Psychiatry.* 2006;77:948–950 (Class II).
5. Traynor BJ, Alexander M, Corr Bea. Effects of a multidisciplinary ALS clinic on survival. *J Neurol Neursurg Psychiatry.* 2003a;47:1258–1261 (Class II).
6. Dal Bello-Haas V, Andrews-Hinders D, Richer CB, et al. Development, analysis, refinement, and utility of an interdisciplinary amyotrophic lateral sclerosis database. *Amyotroph Lateral Scler Other Motor Neuron Disord.* 2001;2:39–46.
7. van den Berg JP, Kalmijin S, Lindeman Eea. Multidisciplinary ALS care improves quality of life in patients with ALS. *Neurology.* 2005;65:1264–1267 (Class III).

## Suggested Reading

Miller RG, Rosenberg JA, Gelinas DF, et al., and the ALS Practice Parameters Task Force. Practice parameter: The care of the patient with amyotrophic lateral sclerosis: an evidence-based review. *Neurology.* 1999;52:1311–1323.
Mitsumoto H (section editor). Continuum. *Motor Neuron Disease.* American Academy of Neurology. Baltimore, MD: Williams & Wilkins; 1997.

# 6

---

# Rehabilitation Issues

## Lisa S. Krivickas

Whether you are receiving care in a comprehensive ALS center or in a general community setting, much of the management of the disease will take place under the auspices of rehabilitation medicine. This chapter provides an overview of how care is provided in this setting.

Amyotrophic lateral sclerosis (ALS) is a disease that is now helped by rehabilitation techniques. According to one of the major medical textbooks for the specialty of physical medicine and rehabilitation (also known as physiatry),

> Rehabilitation is defined as the development of a person to the fullest physical, psychological, social, vocational, avocational, and educational potential consistent with his or her physiologic or anatomic impairment and environmental limitations. Realistic goals are determined by the person and those concerned with his or her care. Thus, one is working to obtain optimal function despite residual disability, even if the impairment is caused by a pathological process that cannot be reversed (1).

As researchers develop additional drugs to slow disease progression in ALS, life expectancy will increase and rehabilitation strategies will become even more important.

To fully appreciate the concept of rehabilitation, it is helpful to understand the terminology utilized in the most recent World Health Organization (WHO) model for the International Classification of Functioning, Disability, and Health.

- *Impairment* is a problem in body function or structure.
- *Activity limitation* is a difficulty encountered in executing a task or action because of an impairment.
- *Participation restriction* is a problem experienced by an individual in involvement in life situations because of an impairment or activity limitation.

The term *disability* encompasses impairments, limitations, and restrictions. Having an impairment does not necessarily mean that a person has an activity limitation or participation restriction, and the goal of rehabilitation is to prevent impairments from limiting activity or participation. For example, a person with ALS may have leg weakness or limited range of motion, and these are impairments. The activity limitation may be a loss of independent mobility because of an inability to walk. However, using a power wheelchair removes the activity limitation without altering the impairment. This same person may have the participation restriction of not being able to perform his or her job as a bank manager, but if his or her worksite is made wheelchair-accessible, his or her participation is no longer restricted.

Comprehensive ALS medical care should include rehabilitation to restore the person with ALS to optimal functioning in his or her normal environment and to allow as high a quality of life as possible. For a healthy individual, the highest quality of life attainable is defined as achieving optimal function and the use of all of the assets that he or she has (2). For the person with ALS, this means rehabilitation to the optimal functional performance that is achievable given the stage of the disease.

For people with ALS, rehabilitation is a constantly changing process because of changing physical status. For the rehabilitation professional, rehabilitation of the person with ALS is more challenging than it is for patients with static functional deficits produced by events such as a stroke. One of the most difficult tasks for the rehabilitation team is to predict how quickly the patient's ALS will progress; it is crucial to attempt to do this to stay ahead of the disease. By looking at the course of disease progression, health professionals can help patients avoid purchasing expensive equipment that may be useful for only a very limited period of time. For example, persons who have only moderate leg weakness but whose disease seems to be progressing rapidly should not order a manual wheelchair that takes 10 weeks for customization and delivery; by the time their chair arrives, they may need a power chair.

There are two broad approaches to rehabilitation, one focusing on changing the individual with a disability (restoring function) and the other focusing on altering the environment. These approaches are depicted in Figure 6.1. When individuals acquire physical disabilities as a result of ALS, their environment shrinks. To return them to a more balanced relationship with their environment, we can either remove their impairment or we can expand their environment so that it is no longer too small for them. Unfortunately, at the present time, we cannot cure the ALS (i.e., remove the impairment). Thus, we must use rehabilitation techniques, including adaptive equipment, assistive devices, and environmental controls, to enlarge the environment of persons with ALS so that they can once again function within it.

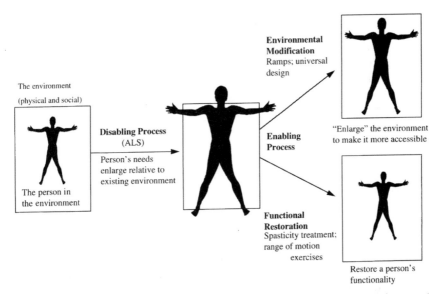

**Figure 6.1** Conceptual overview of enabling–disabling processes. The environment, depicted as a square, represents both physical space and social structures (family, community, society). A person who does not manifest any disability is fully integrated into society and fits within the square. A person with ALS has increased needs (expressed by the size of the individual) and is dislocated from his or her prior integration into the environment, that is, doesn't fit in the square. The rehabilitative process attempts to rectify this displacement either by restoring function in the individual (not yet possible with ALS) or by expanding access to the environment (i.e., providing ramps and assistive devices). Adapted with permission from Brandt EN, Pope AM, eds. *Enabling America.* Institute of Medicine Report. Washington, DC: National Academy Press; 1997.

This chapter is an overview of the concept of rehabilitation as it applies to ALS. Subsequent chapters (Chapters 7–10) provide more specific information regarding various aspects of rehabilitation.

## The Rehabilitation Team

Rehabilitation is a team effort. The team may consist of some or all of the following individuals: physiatrist, neurologist, physical therapist, occupational therapist, speech therapist, respiratory therapist, dietitian, psychologist, social worker, and, most important, the patient and family or caregivers.

Two groups of physicians specialize in rehabilitation: physiatrists, who practice the specialty of physical medicine and rehabilitation, and neurologists with special training in neurorehabilitation. Physical medicine and rehabilitation (PM&R) is a relatively young medical specialty. It developed after World War II because of the need for rehabilitation of veterans with disabling war injuries. As of 2007 there were more than 7,500 board-certified physiatrists in the United States. Physiatrists must complete at least 1 year of general medicine and 3 years of training in PM&R after medical school. They care for a broad range of patients with physical disabilities resulting from many disorders, including neuromuscular diseases, brain injury, spinal cord injury, stroke, orthopedic injuries, burns, arthritis, and amputations, as well as sprains, strains, and other acute musculoskeletal problems. The one characteristic that these diverse groups of patients share is a disability that has compromised their ability to function independently and/or optimally. The physiatrist's goal is to use a combination of medicines, exercise, therapies, and environmental modifications to maximize function.

Neurologists recently have also begun to subspecialize in rehabilitation. Neurologists with expertise in neurorehabilitation receive 1 to 2 additional years of training in rehabilitation after having completed their regular neurology training. They treat patients with disabilities caused by neurologic problems such as neuromuscular diseases, brain injury, spinal cord injury, and stroke. Either the physiatrist or the neurorehabilitation neurologist is best suited to coordinate the overall rehabilitation effort and the work of other team members in the care of the person with ALS.

Physical therapists (PTs) are trained to work with patients with ALS on issues related to mobility and exercise. They assess difficulties with walking and transferring (getting your body from one seat or position to another) and may recommend techniques that improve mobility, assistive devices (such as canes or walkers), foot braces (called ankle-foot orthoses or AFOs), or wheelchairs. They are trained to help patients develop safe and appropriate exercise programs and can teach family members and other caregivers how to physically assist the person with ALS without injuring themselves.

Occupational therapists (OTs) provide some of the same treatments as physical therapists when the physical problem involves the arms rather than the legs. They also often work with physical therapists in prescribing wheelchairs. Occupational therapists evaluate the patient's ability to perform activities of daily living (ADLs), such as dressing, bathing, feeding oneself, and preparing meals, and more complex tasks such as those required for a specific job or hobby. They teach compensatory strategies and recommend assistive devices and equipment that will make it easier for the person with ALS to maintain his or her independence with ADLs. Some occupational therapists will evaluate the skills necessary for driving and make recommendations to improve driving safety or to modify the car to make it easier to operate.

A speech therapist (formally referred to as a speech and language pathologist, or SLP) is important for ALS patients with bulbar symptoms. He or she is trained to work with problems associated with speaking and swallowing. When dealing with speech difficulties, the SLP can teach the person with ALS compensatory strategies both to make him or her more easily understood and to minimize voice fatigue. The SLP can also help the person to evaluate and select alternative means of communication if necessary. Speech therapists evaluate swallowing function both by observing patients while they swallow and by performing radiographic (videofluoroscopy) studies of swallowing. They recommend changes in food consistencies and special swallowing techniques to help prevent aspiration (accidentally getting food into the lungs) and/or choking.

Respiratory therapists teach patients and their caregivers to operate and troubleshoot with equipment used to assist breathing. The therapist may teach patients with weak coughs how to cough more forcefully or to use devices to increase their coughing ability so that they can adequately clear their lungs of secretions. Equipment that the respiratory therapist may assist with includes a manual resuscitation bag, portable ventilators (noninvasive ventilator or so-called BiPAP machines), in-exsufflator ("coughing-assist" machine), and suction machines.

A psychologist may help both patients and their family members adjust to the changes in physical function, family roles, and financial status that often follow the diagnosis of ALS. Many people become depressed after receiving a diagnosis of ALS, and depression may prevent them from using rehabilitation services to maximize their function, independence, and quality of life. The psychologist's assistance may decrease the intensity or length of this period of depression. Acceptance of death and dying is another process with which many patients and families require assistance.

Social workers are a critical member of the rehabilitation team. They help patients navigate through the red tape involved in getting insurance companies to cover rehabilitation services and home assistance. They also provide guidance about applying for Social Security disability benefits, Medicare, Medicaid, and so forth, and they may be able to provide additional information about community services for people with disabilities.

## Rehabilitation Settings

Rehabilitation services can be provided in outpatient clinics, inpatient settings, or in the home. Patients who are fairly mobile usually receive therapies (physical, occupational, speech, etc.) in the outpatient departments of hospitals or in free-standing therapy practices. These settings are preferable to therapy in the home because the therapist is generally able to spend more time with the patient and has more equipment available. Because ALS is relatively rare, many therapists may not have any experience with it. Thus, the ideal therapy setting is the outpatient department of a teaching hospital or a rehabilitation hospital where the therapists at least have experience working with patients with neurologic impairments. Compared with other neurologic disorders, ALS is unique because of its rapid rate of progression. The therapist must remain one step ahead of the disease so that equipment that will not be usable by the time it arrives is not ordered. Therapy in the home setting is often preferable for patients with extremely limited mobility. An advantage of therapy in the home is that the PT and/or OT can assess the home environment and recommend modifications that will improve safety and independence, such as grab bars and ramps. Assessing the patient in the home environment may also demonstrate a need for additional assistive devices, which may not be apparent in the therapy gym. Family members and caretakers can be trained to safely transfer the patient in his or her home setting.

Most people with ALS do not receive rehabilitation in an acute rehabilitation hospital inpatient setting. However, a short "tune-up" stay is appropriate when multiple complex rehabilitation issues need to be addressed simultaneously. To qualify for an inpatient stay (based on the rules of most insurance companies and Medicare), a patient must require intensive therapy for a total of at least 3 hours per day from a combination of at least 2 different therapy disciplines and require medical supervision. An example of a patient suitable for a 1-week tune-up rehabilitation admission might be someone who needs to be fitted for a wheelchair, have family members learn how to transfer him or her safely, learn how to use a ventilator for nighttime ventilatory assistance, and explore augmentative communication systems. All of this could be accomplished during a short intensive inpatient stay, but could easily require 4 to 6 weeks (time that might not be available) on an outpatient basis.

## When Is Rehabilitation Necessary?

Rehabilitation is necessary during all stages of ALS. As the disease progresses, however, rehabilitation strategies and needs change. Most therapies will be intermittent. For example, persons with early ALS may be referred to a PT for help with designing an appropriate aerobic exercise and strengthening program. As increasing spasticity develops, they may return to the PT for a few sessions on stretching and range-of-motion exercises. If a footdrop develops and a brace is prescribed, they may again return for a few sessions of gait training with the new brace. As weakness increases, additional sessions of physical therapy may be necessary to teach the caregiver to effectively transfer the patient.

Insurance carriers will often deny coverage of continuing therapy to patients with ALS because they consider it maintenance therapy since no "improvement" is expected. This is faulty reasoning about which health care providers need to educate insurers. ALS is not a static disease, and additional therapy may be required as function changes. In addition, therapy is sometimes required for the patient to maintain function or to slow the decline in function.

## Exercise and Prevention of Disability

Rehabilitation should begin early in the course of ALS to prevent or delay the onset of disability. This concept is known as *prehabilitation* because it is a preventive form of rehabilitation. One important method of prehabilitation is exercise. Three types of exercise are important for all individuals, whether they have ALS or not: flexibility or stretching exercises, strengthening exercises, and aerobic exercise.

Stretching, or range-of-motion exercise, is very important for people with ALS. Range-of-motion exercises maintain the normal movement of joints and muscles. As muscle weakness develops, joints that are not used will lose their ability to move freely. This may cause pain, which in turn will interfere with function. For example, as shoulder weakness develops, a person can no longer raise his or her arm overhead. If he or she does not make an effort to maintain range of motion in the shoulder joint, the shoulder will become "frozen." Then, if a caregiver tries to assist the person by lifting his or her arm over the head, the person will fail because of pain and tightness of the tissues around the joint. Stretching is also important when spasticity is present. Spastic muscles tend to become permanently shortened—a condition called a *contracture*—when not stretched regularly. This also can limit function and produce pain and discomfort. Patients can be taught specific stretching techniques that actually decrease the severity of—or help to abort—painful muscle spasms.

Few studies have been done on the effect of strengthening exercises in patients with ALS, so their use in ALS is somewhat controversial. One randomized study has addressed the prescription of 30 minutes of aerobic activity versus usual daily activity for patients with early ALS; at 6 months, the group performing the exercise program had experienced a slower deterioration of function, and the investigators concluded that moderate exercise is safe and delays disability over the short term (3). A more recent randomized study looked at the effect of individualized resistance training for 6 months; the patients performing the training had higher functional and quality-of-life scores at the end of the study period, and there were no adverse side effects of the training. This study suggests that resistance training may improve function and quality of life (4). Last, several recent studies in an animal model of ALS have demonstrated a benefit from aerobic exercise.

The stronger a muscle is when a strength-training program is started, the better the muscle responds. I recommend that patients with ALS who are interested begin a strengthening program as soon as possible after diagnosis. Its objective is to maximize the strength of unaffected or mildly affected muscles in an attempt to delay the time when function will be impaired. For example, if some elderly persons must use 90% of the strength of their leg muscles to rise from a chair before they develop ALS, they will be unable to rise from a chair after losing only 10% of their muscular capacity. If other individuals require only 50% of their maximal leg strength to rise from a chair before developing ALS, they will remain independent much longer, even if the disease progresses at the same pace.

Many physicians have expressed concern about the development of overuse weakness as a result of strength training in patients with neuromuscular diseases. There is no good evidence that overuse weakness actually develops in people with ALS who have antigravity strength (the ability to lift a limb against gravity) in their muscles and who exercise at a moderate intensity. I recommend that any weight training or strengthening exercise be performed with a weight that the individual can comfortably lift 15–20 times; this guideline will prevent overworking the muscles with excessively heavy weights. Patients should be instructed to perform sets of 10–15 repetitions. People who weight train often use weights that they can lift only 8 to 10 times before fatigue produces failure; this intensity of weight training is not recommended for people with ALS. Another general guideline is that an exercise regimen is too strenuous if it consistently produces muscle soreness or fatigue lasting longer than a half hour after exercise.

Aerobic exercise is exercise that raises the heart rate and is sustained continuously for a period of at least 15 to 20 minutes. Examples include rapid walking, running, cycling, or using an exercise machine such as a rowing machine, stair-stepper, and the like. Aerobic exercise helps maintain fitness of the heart and lungs, and it is recommended for patients with ALS as long as it can be performed safely without risk of falling or injury. In addition to the physical benefits, this form of exercise often has a beneficial effect on mood, psychological well-being, appetite, and sleep.

## Maximizing Mobility

An important aspect of rehabilitation is helping persons with ALS maintain independent mobility in the community and their environment for as long as possible. Interventions that allow people to maintain mobility include assistive devices such as canes, walkers, braces, wheelchairs, and scooters; medications to decrease spasticity; home equipment such as grab bars, raised toilet seats, shower benches, and lifts; home modifications (ramps, wide doorways); and automobile adaptations such as hand controls.

Both bracing and wheelchairs are best prescribed by multidisciplinary teams. Many rehabilitation centers have brace clinics that are staffed by a team consisting of an orthotist (the person who makes the brace), a physical therapist, and a physiatrist. There is a surprisingly large array of options when it comes to prescribing something as seemingly simple as an AFO, a brace to prevent footdrop. The brace may be constructed of a number of different materials, may have several different types of ankle joints, may have special features built in to help control spasticity, and may even be designed to help control knee motion. An experienced team is best equipped to prescribe the most appropriate brace for a given person.

Many rehabilitation centers use a similar team approach for wheelchair prescription. The wheelchair clinic typically is staffed by a physical therapist, an occupational therapist, and a physiatrist. Numerous options are available in a wheelchair, and, as with the AFO, a multidisciplinary team is best equipped to prescribe the most appropriate (and economic) wheelchair.

## Maximizing Independence With Activities of Daily Living

The term *activities of daily living* (ADLs) describes basic tasks such as bathing, dressing, and feeding oneself. The term *instrumental ADLs* refers to more complex tasks such as shopping, meal preparation, and the performance of household chores. The OT helps people with ALS to remain independent in ADLs for as long as possible. They may be taught energy conservation techniques, provided with dressing aids (buttoners, sock pullers, reachers, Velcro fasteners for clothes), and given adapted kitchen utensils and writing tools (built-up handles, universal cuffs, plate guards, dicem pads). Various hand splints constructed by an OT may improve grip, making ADLs easier to perform.

## Pursuit of Vocation and Avocation

Helping persons with ALS continue to work and pursue their hobbies and interests for as long as possible is another function of the rehabilitation team. The team may be able to assess the worksite and recommend environmental modifications that will allow persons with ALS to continue to perform their job. Voice-activated software may be recommended for people who use computers and have hand weakness. Other modifications might include the installation of ramps and the use of a scooter at work or other interventions discussed previously that allow maintenance of mobility and independence with ADLs.

## Communication and Swallowing

Another area typically addressed by the rehabilitation team is speech and swallowing function. In addition to the speech therapist, a physician and OT are often involved in addressing these issues.

Adequate swallowing function is needed to maintain the nutritional status of persons with ALS unless they have a feeding tube. If nutritional status is not properly maintained, patients tend to burn up muscle for energy and thus lose muscle mass and strength earlier than they otherwise would. Swallowing dysfunction can also precipitate pneumonia and/or respiratory failure when food goes into the lungs instead of into the esophagus and stomach; this is called *aspiration*. A speech therapist or rehabilitation physician often recognizes swallowing difficulties before the person with ALS is aware of them. People with mild swallowing difficulties can be taught compensatory techniques to prevent aspiration and choking. Food consistencies also often require modification.

The ability to effectively communicate is extremely important for psychological and physical well-being. The rehabilitation team can use a variety of tools to ensure that the person with ALS is able to communicate effectively. Interventions include speech therapy to teach techniques to increase intelligibility of speech, palatal lifts, voice amplifiers, and augmentative communication devices, which may be as simple as a letterboard or as complex as a computer with a voice synthesizer.

## Pulmonary Rehabilitation

Preventing and managing respiratory failure associated with ALS is of concern to the rehabilitation team because patients must be able to breath adequately and comfortably to have optimal function and quality of life. As mentioned previously, an important preventive measure is trying to avoid aspiration when swallowing. PTs may instruct patients and family members in methods to assist coughing that allow the lungs to be cleared of mucus and help prevent infection. The rehabilitation team may also recommend physical medicine aids to assist with breathing. These may include machines to assist with coughing, methods of providing range-of-motion exercises to the lungs to prevent them from becoming excessively stiff, and machines to assist with breathing. Although members of the rehabilitation team often work with pulmonary physicians who specialize in ALS, some physiatrists have special expertise in the use of noninvasive ventilation techniques (this term refers to ventilatory support that does not require tracheostomy).

The rehabilitation team may also assist the patient in making decisions concerning whether or not to pursue long-term ventilatory support. Rehabilitation experts have experience working with patients with a variety of diagnoses who require ventilatory support and have a good understanding of the type of family support required, the necessary home equipment, and the level of independence and function the patient will be able to achieve.

## Caregivers' Role in Rehabilitation

The family members and/or caregivers of people with ALS are a critical part of successful rehabilitation interventions. The rehabilitation process must focus on the caregivers as well as on the patient. Caregivers require instruction from PTs in how to properly transfer the patient so that they do not injure themselves. They also require instruction in the maintenance and use of any home equipment provided for the patient. The rehabilitation team should be sensitive to the psychological and physical well-being of caregivers because their ability to assist persons with ALS will have a direct impact on their level of function and independence.

## Assistive Technology

Some rehabilitation hospitals have assistive technology centers that specialize in using technology to help people with disabilities overcome their limitations. Assistive technology centers are staffed by a multidisciplinary team that consists of physicians, PTs, OTs, speech therapists, rehabilitation technologists, and neuropsychologists. These centers provide expertise in augmentative communication, complex seating and wheelchair prescription (i.e., power wheelchairs), environmental control systems (also known as electronic aids to daily living), and worksite modification. Assistive technology allows people to do things like waving a hand to turn on a light, using a puff of air to control a wheelchair, and using their voice to activate an appliance. The assistive technology team determines what assistive equipment will best serve the patient, customizes the device to the patient's needs once it has been purchased, and trains the patient and caregiver to use the equipment. In areas without a consolidated assistive technology program, these services are provided via a variety of different therapists and clinics.

## Case Study

This case study briefly outlines the various rehabilitation interventions used by one patient throughout the course of her illness and illustrates the fact that rehabilitation is an ongoing process. Mrs. A developed right leg weakness at age 50 and her ALS was subsequently diagnosed. She was in good physical condition and had no medical problems before the onset of her leg weakness. Her first rehabilitation intervention was a few sessions of physical therapy to work on gait training with a cane. She soon developed a right footdrop, and an AFO was prescribed. After receipt of her AFO, she returned to physical therapy for a few additional sessions of gait training with the AFO.

She subsequently began to develop weakness in her left leg and both arms, to slur her speech, and to require assistance to rise from chairs, shower, and use the toilet. She was admitted to a local rehabilitation hospital for a 1-week stay and received daily physical, occupational, and speech therapy. Her gait was evaluated while she used a variety of assistive devices, and she was discharged using a rolling walker. Her husband was trained to assist her with transferring in a safe manner so that he would not injure his back. A raised toilet seat and a shower chair were ordered for the home. Her therapists made a home visit and made several recommendations designed to increase her safety and function; these included removing throw rugs, rearranging the kitchen, and obtaining some adaptive kitchen utensils. Mrs. A worked with a speech therapist who evaluated her swallowing and recommended that she avoid thin liquids because she tended to aspirate them. She was taught to slow down and overarticulate her speech so that she could be more easily understood. Mrs. A was also evaluated for a power wheelchair because her disease appeared to be progressing rapidly. Arrangements were made to have a rental power chair available in her home as soon as she thought she needed it. All of these rehabilitation interventions could have been performed on an outpatient basis but probably would have taken at least 4 weeks instead of 1. Because Mrs. A's disease was progressing rapidly, she had multiple rehabilitation needs that were most efficiently addressed with a short inpatient stay.

A few months after Mrs. A's discharge from rehabilitation, she was having such difficulty eating that she had lost 30 pounds. A feeding tube was placed. She also was sleeping poorly and was very fatigued during the day. Her forced vital capacity was only 45% of predicted, and she was advised to begin using noninvasive positive pressure ventilation (BiPAP machine) at night. She and her husband were instructed in the use of the new equipment by a respiratory therapist who made several follow-up visits to their home. She gradually adjusted to using the BiPAP machine all night, and as time went on she began using it for rest periods during the day.

Mrs. A's arm and leg weakness progressed, and she was no longer able to lift her arms over her head. A PT came to the home for 2 visits to teach Mr. A how to assist her with range-of-motion exercises. The therapist also instructed him in some additional transfer techniques because Mrs. A was requiring substantially more assistance with transfers. She was no longer able to walk more than a few steps, and the power wheelchair was rented.

Mrs. A's speech continued to deteriorate so that only 30% to 50% of her words could be understood by those who were not family members. She visited a speech therapist who specialized in augmentative communication, was evaluated using a number of communication devices, and decided to order a dedicated communication device with a voice synthesizer. At the time of this initial visit, she had enough hand strength for direct selection with the communication device.

Within a few months, Mrs. A's arms and hands were too weak to drive her power chair or use the keyboard on her communication device. She also was having difficulty holding her head up and needed better head support for her wheelchair. She made a final visit to the rehabilitation center, where she attended its wheelchair clinic and was prescribed a manual chair that caretakers would have to push. The chair had a high back, a head rest, a ventilator tray, a lap tray for her communication device, and the ability to tilt in space for pressure relief. She also was reevaluated by the speech therapist specializing in augmentative communication; her communication device was modified so that she could use a scanning mode instead of direct selection, and she tried a variety of switches until she found one she could operate.

Shortly after returning home from the rehabilitation center, Mr. A again began to have difficulty transferring his wife because she could no longer assist in any way. Their physician recommended a TransAid lift. A rental lift was obtained, and the PT returned to the A's home to instruct them in using the lift.

This case demonstrates the ongoing rehabilitation needs of patients with ALS. At 5 different times during the course of Mrs. A's ALS, she either attended physical therapy or had a PT work with her in the home. Similarly, she had multiple speech therapy interventions. She also worked with occupational and respiratory therapists and attended a wheelchair clinic. This combination of rehabilitation interventions allowed Mrs. A to remain at home with assistance from her husband and thus significantly improved her quality of life.

## References

1. DeLisa JA. *Rehabilitation Medicine.* Hagerstown, MD: Lippincott-Raven; 1993.
2. Kottke FJ, Lehman JF. *Krusen's Handbook of Physical Medicine and Rehabilitation.* Philadelphia: WB Saunders; 1990.
3. Drory VE, Goltsman E, Reznik JG, et al. The value of muscle exercise in patients with amyotrophic lateral sclerosis. *J Neurol Sci.* 2003;191:133–137.

4. Dal Bello-Haas VD, Florence JM, Kloos AD, et al. A randomized controlled trial of resistance exercise in individuals with ALS. *Neurology.* 2007;68:2003–2007.

## Suggested Reading

Bach JR. *Management of Patients with Neuromuscular Disease.* Philadelphia, PA: Hanley & Belfus; 2004.

Bach JR. *Noninvasive Mechanical Ventilation.* Philadelphia, PA: Hanley & Belfus; 2004.

Carr-Davis EM, Blakely-Adams C, Corinblit B. *Living With ALS: Adjusting to Swallowing and Speaking Difficulties.* Woodland Hills, CA: ALS Association; 2002.

Dal Bello-Haas V, Florence J, Krivickas LS. Therapeutic exercise for people with amyotrophic lateral sclerosis/motor neuron disease. *Cochrane Database Syst Rev.* 2008; 16(2):CD005229.

Kazandjian MS. *Communication and Swallowing Solutions for the ALS/MND Community: A CINI Manual.* San Diego, CA: Singular Publishing Group; 1997.

Krivickas LS, Dal Bello-Haas V, Danforth SE, et al. Rehabilitation. In: Mitsumoto H, Przedborski S, Gordon P, eds. *Amyotrophic Lateral Sclerosis.* New York, NY: Taylor & Francis; 2006:691–720.

Mendoza M, Rafter E. *Living With ALS: Functioning When Your Mobility Is Affected.* Woodland Hills, CA: ALS Association, 2002.

Oppenheimer EA. *Living With ALS: Adapting to Breathing Changes.* Woodland Hills, CA: ALS Association; 2002.

Sanjak M, Paulson D, Sufit R, et al. Physiologic and metabolic response to progressive and prolonged exercise in amyotrophic lateral sclerosis. *Neurology.* 1987;37:1217–1220.

Siegel IM, Casey P. *101 Hints to "Help-with-Ease" for Patients With Neuromuscular-Disease.* Tucson, AZ: Muscular Dystrophy Association; 2005.

# 7

# Physical Therapy

## Vanina Dal Bello-Haas and Jacqueline Montes

As a member of the multidisciplinary rehabilitation team, the physical therapist (PT) plays an important role in assisting the individual with amyotrophic lateral sclerosis (ALS) to maximize functional independence, reduce the effects of disability, and enhance the person's quality of life. This is accomplished through education, rehabilitation programs, psychological support, the provision of appropriate equipment, and referrals to community resources (1). This chapter describes the profession of physical therapy, outlines the role of PTs in managing typical problems encountered by people with ALS, and describes some of the equipment more commonly recommended by PTs for people with ALS.

### Who Are Physical Therapists? What Do They Do?

PTs are health care professionals who are educated at the college or university level and are licensed in the state or states in which they practice. In some states a physician's referral is needed to see a PT, whereas in other states a physician's referral is not needed.

In general, PTs help individuals

1. Prevent and/or address the onset and progression of impairments, activity limitations, participation restrictions, and changes in physical function and health status resulting from injury, disease, or other causes;

2. Restore, maintain, and promote overall fitness, health, and optimal quality of life; and

3. Alleviate pain (2).

As clinicians, PTs engage in examination and evaluation processes that assist in determining the most appropriate intervention for the individual. In an initial examination or reexamination, PTs will take a history to obtain an account of past and present health status and will conduct a systems review to gain additional information about general health. After analyzing all relevant information gathered from the history and systems review, they will administer one or more specific tests and measures to identify existing and potential problems (2). Tests and measures of pain, joint range of motion (ROM), muscle strength, muscle tone, flexibility, posture, edema (swelling), skin integrity, sensation, coordination, balance, transfers, gait, locomotion, endurance, aerobic capacity, and/or safety in the home and community are commonly used by PTs in examining people with ALS.

Based on the data gathered and the findings of the examination, the PT will make a clinical judgment (evaluation), determine a physical therapy diagnosis and prognosis, and design a plan of care. All of the data gathered, the physical therapy diagnosis, prognostic predictions, and patient goals are integrated and incorporated into establishing a plan of care (2). The plan of care for the individual with ALS may include recommendations for therapeutic exercise; interventions for pain, muscle cramps, spasticity, fatigue, and respiratory dysfunction; and prescription of assistive, orthotic, supportive, and/or adaptive devices.

## Therapeutic Exercise

Therapeutic exercise includes a broad group of activities intended to prevent dysfunction and maintain or improve strength, mobility, flexibility, endurance, cardiovascular fitness, breathing, coordination, motor function, posture, skill, and balance (2,3). Therapeutic exercise is an important component of a physical therapy plan of care for a person with ALS, and various types of exercises may be recommended—strengthening, ROM, stretching (flexibility), and endurance.

Range-of-motion and stretching exercises are typically accepted modes of exercise for people with ALS. Range-of-motion exercises involve moving each joint through the normal extent of movement. Active range-of-motion exercises are performed independently, whereas active-assisted range-of-motion exercises involve using an external force (mechanical device or another person) to assist the individual to perform the movement. Passive range-of-motion exercises involve the use of an external force to perform the movement without any voluntary muscle contraction from the individual. Range-of-motion exercises may be recommended to

1. Prevent the development of limited mobility due to muscle shortening and/or tightness in the joint capsule, ligaments, and tendons (contractures); and

2. Maintain joint mobility and muscle strength.

Stretching exercises are designed to lengthen shortened soft tissue, such as muscle, thereby increasing range of motion, but they differ from range-of-motion exercises. With range-of-motion exercises the joint to be exercised is moved, whereas with stretching exercises a position of stretch is maintained for a period of time. Stretching exercises may include manual passive stretching, mechanical passive stretching, and flexibility exercises (self-stretching).

Strengthening exercises may be static (isometric) or dynamic (isotonic or isokinetic). With isometric exercise, the muscle contracts, but joint movement does not occur. Isometric exercises may be prescribed to maintain muscle strength. With isotonic exercises the muscles contract and there is joint movement during the contraction. Isotonic exercises may be concentric (the muscle shortens) or eccentric (the muscle lengthens), may be performed with or without weights or resistance, and are used to increase muscle strength and prevent muscle wasting. Isokinetic exercise involves moving the joint at a constant velocity with varying resistance and requires specialized equipment.

It is not known whether muscles affected by ALS can be improved through strengthening exercises. Thus, strengthening exercises are usually prescribed for unaffected muscles. When designing a strengthening exercise program for someone with ALS, the PT considers 2 factors:

1. Prevention of overuse/overwork fatigue/damage, the permanent or temporary loss of muscle strength due to excessive exercise
2. Disuse atrophy, the lack of use leading to a decrease in muscle mass, strength, and endurance

Research evidence from people with other neuromuscular diseases shows that highly repetitive or heavy resistance exercises can cause overwork damage in weakened, denervated muscle. However, a marked decrease in activity level because of ALS can lead to cardiovascular deconditioning and disuse weakness beyond the amount caused by the disease itself. Therefore, the PT will carefully monitor the intensity of the patient's exercise program to avoid unduly causing fatigue, while simultaneously promoting optimal use of intact muscle groups.

Endurance (aerobic) exercises involve sustained, rhythmic movements of large muscle groups and include walking, swimming, rowing, and stationary bicycling. They may be recommended to increase or maintain aerobic capacity and to prevent deconditioning.

Regardless of the type of exercises prescribed, they should be performed in moderation. You should not exercise to the point of extreme fatigue. For example, fatigue that lasts only a brief time or fatigue that decreases quickly with a brief rest period is acceptable, but fatigue that persists to the next day or that prevents you from performing the usual activities of daily living means that you have overexerted yourself.

The literature describing and examining the efficacy of exercise programs for people with ALS is very limited. Two early case reports demonstrated positive effects of specific strengthening and endurance exercises in individuals with

ALS (4,5). Pinto and colleagues found that people who participated in endurance exercises while on noninvasive ventilation, BiPAP (see Chapter 12), had significantly better function and less forced vital capacity decline over a 12-month period compared with those who did not exercise (6). A recent Cochrane review of exercise for people with ALS identified only 2 studies that examined the effects of strengthening exercises (7). Although the 2 included studies were too small to determine to what extent exercise benefits people with ALS, function as measured by the ALS Functional Rating Scale was statistically significant for the exercise group (7). One study compared a 15-minute, twice-daily moderate-load, endurance-type exercises with the usual activities of daily living in people with early- and middle-stage ALS (8), and the other compared a thrice weekly resistance exercise program (individualized, progressive, moderate load and moderate intensity) with daily stretching exercises in people with early-stage ALS (9). In both studies the investigators did not report adverse effects, such as increased muscle cramping, muscle soreness, or fatigue.

Although functional benefits have yet to be determined, exercise programs may have positive physiologic and psychological effects for patients with ALS, especially when they are implemented before significant muscular atrophy occurs. More research needs to be done in this area.

## Interventions for Pain and Muscle Cramps

People with ALS may experience a variety of symptoms such as pain, muscle cramps, spasticity, and fatigue. Motor neuron degeneration itself does not result in pain, but musculoskeletal changes that occur as a result of weakened muscles can cause pain. Pain may be directly caused by muscle strains, joint sprains, acute injuries (such as from falls); in addition, spasticity, especially if severe, and preexisting conditions such as arthritis can contribute to pain. Indirectly, weakness can produce pain because it may result in shortened muscles (contractures) or hypomobile joints that may cause pain when stretched. Compensatory movement patterns may develop because of muscle weakness; as a result, muscles and surrounding soft tissues and joints may be injured. Strong muscles may be overused, leading to pain, and joints may become unstable or subluxated because of muscle weakness. In addition, poor resting positions may strain muscles or unstable joints. People with ALS most commonly develop pain in the shoulder joint. Because the muscles around the shoulder become weak, a person may have difficulty moving his or her arm. As a result, the soft tissues around the shoulder become tight, causing a "frozen shoulder."

Muscle cramps are common in people with ALS. A muscle cramp is an abrupt, involuntary, and painful muscle shortening that is accompanied by knotting. The exact cause is unknown, but it is thought that cramps are caused by muscle fatigue or loss of flexibility. Muscle cramps are common in the quadriceps (front thigh) muscles, the hamstring (back thigh) muscles, and the gastrocnemius (calf) muscles but can also occur in the abdomen, arms, neck, and jaw (10).

The occurrence of muscle cramps can be lessened by maintaining flexibility, frequent stretching, and massage. Gentle massage and stretching techniques can also help to relieve a cramp while it is happening. Your doctor may suggest quinine or other appropriate medications, if the cramps are not alleviated with these physical measures alone.

Depending on the cause of the pain, the PT may recommend or perform range-of-motion exercises, joint mobilizations, massage, passive stretching, and education about correct positioning and joint protection. In addition, the PT may use physical agents and electrotherapeutic modalities to address the pain. Physical agents include thermal modalities such as superficial heat (hot packs), deep heat (ultrasound), and cryotherapy (cold packs, ice massage). Electrotherapeutic modalities may include transcutaneous electrical nerve stimulation (TENS) and iontophoresis, the introduction of topically applied medication prescribed by a physician into the skin by using electrical stimulation (2). Studies have found that physical agents and modalities are effective in decreasing pain related to acute muscle and bone injuries, pain after surgery, and other types of pain; however, their specific use in people with ALS has not been investigated.

## Interventions for Spasticity

Changes in the brain and spinal cord may cause the muscles to continuously contract. *Spasticity* is a state of sustained muscle tension (resistance) when the muscle is moved passively (10). Typical symptoms, as a result of spastic muscles, are a feeling of stiffness, difficulty moving or performing quick movements, and inability to perform fine motor movements such as fastening buttons and manipulating small objects. People with ALS often complain that these symptoms are worse when they are nervous or cold. Slow, prolonged stretches and passive range-of-motion exercises may help relieve spasticity. A Cochrane review of interventions for spasticity for people with ALS identified one randomized controlled study that found moderate-intensity endurance-type exercises helped decrease spasticity (11). The specific endurance exercises were not described, but clinically it has been found that rhythmical exercises, such as stationary bicycling or swimming, may help to reduce spasticity. Baclofen or tizanidine are oral medications that your doctor may prescribe to help manage spasticity. Often these medications have side effects, such as weakness, fatigue, or sedation. For severe spasticity and intolerable medication side effects, administration of baclofen directly into the spinal cord through a pump may be considered. Botulinum toxin (BTX) injections may also be effective for treating spasticity but, to date, this has not been studied in ALS.

## Interventions for Fatigue

Fatigue is a common symptom of ALS. Some potential causes include overexertion, poor sleep because of breathing difficulties or pain, and depression. Some types of fatigue, in particular, physical fatigue, can be helped by a program of energy conservation. Some suggestions for changing daily routines and lifestyles will minimize fatigue and avoid exhaustion. Principles of energy conservation include the following:

1. *Balancing rest and activity.* Resting is one of the best ways to manage symptoms of fatigue and can be accomplished in various ways: total body rest (nap), resting a specific joint or muscle group, and emotional rest (relaxing). It is important to learn your own tolerance and rest before the point of fatigue, take a time-out if an activity becomes too tiring, and schedule rest breaks into daily routines, such as taking a nap or resting 10 min out of every hour.

2. *Organizing work.* This may include planning ahead, scheduling, setting priorities, and pacing; alternating periods of work, activity, and exercise with rest periods; spreading activities that are difficult or tiring throughout the day; alternating heavy jobs with light ones and change positions often.

3. *Making work easier.* Is the task necessary? Is there an easier way to do it? Sitting while working conserves energy (25% of your energy can be saved). For instance, sitting during food preparation, while talking on the phone, or during grooming activities will reduce the amount of energy needed to perform the activity. It is also important to prioritize and consider if some portion of a task can be done tomorrow or if someone else can do it.

4. *Working in comfort.* This can be accomplished by organizing work areas; placing articles between shoulder and waist level for easy reach; minimizing unnecessary straining, stooping, twisting and bending; and sitting comfortably instead of standing. The use of assistive devices recommended by your PT can help conserve energy. Assistive devices such as walkers and adaptive devices such as ankle-foot orthoses and cervical collars provide support to your body and as a result reduce the amount of energy needed and may improve endurance for walking.

5. *Relaxing.* Stress is fatiguing. It is important to work at a comfortable pace and schedule time to relax. Find pleasant relaxing activities and outlets.

6. *Planning work or play.* Important activities should be done at times of the day when energy is the highest. In addition, plan rest periods when considering daily schedules, and save energy for the activities you most enjoy.

## Assistive Devices—Ambulatory (Walking) Aids

An assistive device for walking is a piece of equipment that is used to provide support or stability while walking. Because of muscle weakness, balance problems, and/or spasticity, the PT may recommend a walking aid to enhance mobility and provide additional support. The PT will help determine which aid will best meet the patient's needs, will determine the correct height for the walking aid, and will provide instruction on its proper use. The type of assistive device recommended is determined by the amount of leg and trunk weakness, mobility and strength of the arms, extent and rate of progression of the disease, acceptance of the aid, and economic constraints. In addition, the PT can also provide information on where to purchase the walking aid. Three main categories of walking aids are canes, crutches, and walkers.

## Canes

Canes provide minimal to moderate support. A cane is carried in the hand opposite to the affected leg and requires good upper extremity (arm) strength. Canes can be used on stairs (Table 7.1).

## Crutches

Few people with ALS use crutches because they often find them too bulky and extremely difficult to manage (Table 7.2).

## Walkers

Walkers provide greater support than canes and crutches, but use up more space. Various types are available and they can be modified to suit your walking environments and needs (Table 7.3).

## Orthotic Devices

An *orthotic device* is used to correct or straighten a deformity or to provide support. Orthoses may be recommended for people with ALS in order to

1. Improve function by offering support to weakened muscles and the joints they surround;
2. Decrease the stress on compensatory muscles;
3. Minimize local or general muscle fatigue;
4. Prevent deformity; and
5. Conserve energy.

Ankle-foot orthoses (AFOs) are probably the most common type of orthotic devices recommended (Figure 7.1). Prefabricated AFOs may be purchased off-the-shelf or they may be custom-made. The orthoses must be lightweight to allow the user to expend the least amount of energy while using the device.

An AFO may be solid or hinged at the ankle joint; each has advantages and disadvantages. A solid AFO is usually prescribed for quadriceps (front thigh) muscle

**Table 7.1** Types of Canes

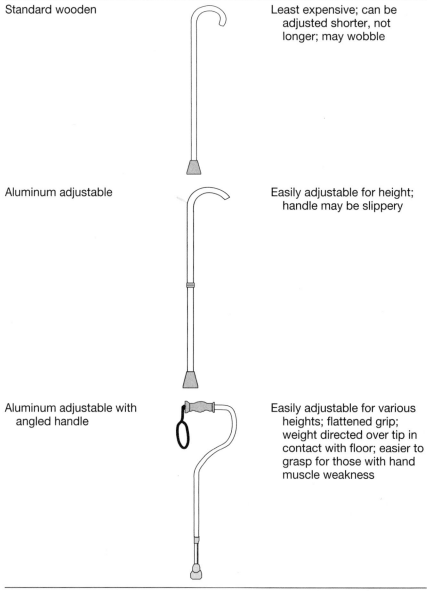

| | | |
|---|---|---|
| Standard wooden | | Least expensive; can be adjusted shorter, not longer; may wobble |
| Aluminum adjustable | | Easily adjustable for height; handle may be slippery |
| Aluminum adjustable with angled handle | | Easily adjustable for various heights; flattened grip; weight directed over tip in contact with floor; easier to grasp for those with hand muscle weakness |

*(Continued)*

weakness in addition to ankle weakness and instability. Because the ankle is held in a fixed position, getting up from sitting, going up and down stairs, and going up inclines may be difficult. A person with mild ankle weakness and adequate knee muscle strength during walking may be prescribed a hinged AFO, which allows a certain degree of ankle motion. The degree of ankle motion can be adjusted de-

**Table 7.1** Types of Canes   (*Continued*)

| | | |
|---|---|---|
| Quad cane | 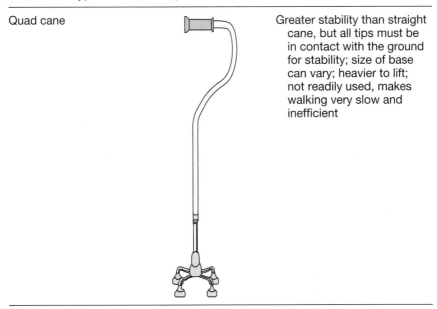 | Greater stability than straight cane, but all tips must be in contact with the ground for stability; size of base can vary; heavier to lift; not readily used, makes walking very slow and inefficient |

pending on your stability and need for support. For people with severe spasticity, antispasticity features can be built in to the AFO.

### Supportive Devices

Supportive devices include therapeutic appliances that are designed to support weak or ineffective joints or muscles. People with ALS may develop cervical extensor muscle weakness (muscles at the back of the neck). Early complaints may include neck stiffness, pain, heaviness, and fatigue in holding up the head. You may also notice difficulties in keeping the head upright with unexpected movements. If weakness is more severe, the head may begin to fall forward (10). The PT may recommend a neck collar to help with this *cervical extensor* muscle weakness. Several different types of collars can support the head, protect weakened muscles, and prevent further deformity.

Cervical collars can be used while in the car to protect against acceleration and deceleration forces or while walking to conserve energy. Regardless of the type, cervical collars should be worn intermittently and not while eating. Wearing the collar should be balanced with periods of rest in a reclined position with head support. The use of cervical support is also practical while working at a computer or while writing, where your trunk is inclined forward.

The type of collar recommended depends on the amount of weakness and the collar's acceptance by the user. A soft, foam collar may be recommended for very

**Table 7.2** Types of Crutches

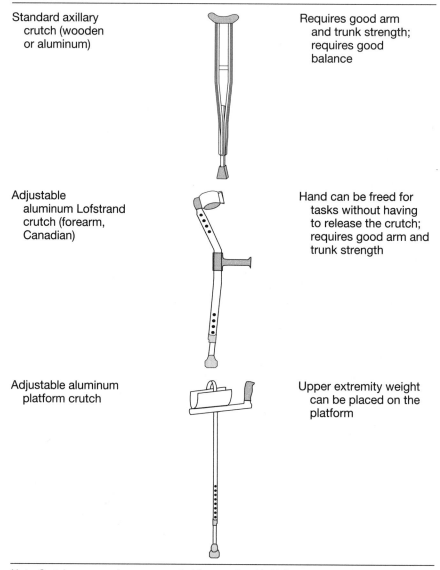

| | | |
|---|---|---|
| Standard axillary crutch (wooden or aluminum) | | Requires good arm and trunk strength; requires good balance |
| Adjustable aluminum Lofstrand crutch (forearm, Canadian) | | Hand can be freed for tasks without having to release the crutch; requires good arm and trunk strength |
| Adjustable aluminum platform crutch | | Upper extremity weight can be placed on the platform |

*Note:* Crutches are rarely recommended for people with ALS.

mild weakness. This type of collar provides gentle support and usually is comfortable and well tolerated. For mild to moderate neck extensor muscle weakness, a low-profile, wire-framed cervical support such as the Headmaster Cervical Collar can be very useful (Figure 7.2).

A semirigid collar, such as the Philadelphia collar or Newport collar may be recommended for moderate to severe weakness. If the user has a tracheostomy, a

**Table 7.3** Types of Walkers

| | | |
|---|---|---|
| Standard aluminum |  | Least expensive; very stable; adjustable; must be picked up and lowered to take steps; may be heavyto lift; not commonly used in ALS |
| Aluminum with wheels |  | Rolls forward easily; does not need to be lifted; may move too quickly |
| Folding aluminum with or without wheels with rear brakes | | Rear brakes secure walker when taking steps; stores easily; portable |
| Specialized wheeled walker (Rollator) |  | Most expensive; covered by insurance; large wheels; good outdoors or on rough ground; often comes with brakes, seat, and a basket |

Miami-J or Philadelphia collar allows for anterior neck access. These collars provide firm support, but they can be very warm and may make the wearer feel confined.

These devices may not be effective when severe or intractable neck droop is present, in which case you may be referred to an orthotist or biomedical engineer for a custom-made neck collar.

## Adaptive Devices

*Adaptive devices* are apparatuses or pieces of equipment that are designed and fabricated to improve the performance of *activities of daily living.*

People with ALS who have leg weakness may find it difficult to get up from a chair. Initially, difficulty rising from a seated position to standing may be helped by placing a firm cushion, 2 to 3 inches thick, under the buttocks in the chair so that the hips are higher than the knees. Or, the chair itself may be raised by placing the legs in prefabricated blocks to make rising easier. Self-powered lifting cushions, such as the UPlift Seat Assist, are relatively inexpensive, portable devices that

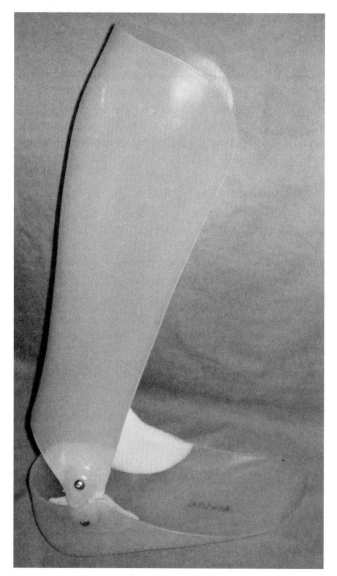

**Figure 7.1** A hinged ankle-foot orthosis. Courtesy of the Department of Physical Medicine and Rehabilitation, City Hospital, Saskatoon, SK, Canada.

provide assistance for rising to standing and gently ease the body's weight into the chair by using hydropneumatics, but the patient's balance needs to be good. These devices can be purchased through several catalog suppliers.

Powered seat lift recliner chairs are also available for rental or purchase. They enable a person to rise to a standing position or recline by activating an electric

**Figure 7.2** Headmaster collar. Courtesy of Symmetric Designs, Salt Spring Island, BC, Canada.

control. This lift function assists with transfers and promotes independence. These devices are partially covered by third-party payers, such as Medicare, and usually well liked.

A transfer board or sliding board is a device made of plastic or wood with a very smooth surface. It can be used if you are unable to stand because of leg weakness, to move from bed to chair, or to transfer in and out of a wheelchair. The transfer board may be used alone if you have adequate arm strength and good sitting balance, or you can be assisted by another person.

People who have difficulty transferring from place to place (bed to chair, chair to a commode, and so forth), even with the assistance of a caregiver, may require a mechanical lift. Lifts most frequently recommended are the Easy Pivot, the Hoyer Lift, and the Trans-Aid Patient Lifter. These lifts are either electrically powered with special batteries or utilize a hydraulic system, and they use a supportive sling system. Mechanical lifts ease the physical demands of transferring, which can often lead to injuries for both patient and caregiver. Ceiling lifts have become available more recently. Ceiling lifts have an electric motor that raises and lowers the patient and is attached to a wheeled trolley that travels along a track that is mounted overhead, normally directly into the ceiling. The main advantage of the ceiling lift is the ease of moving the patient in the horizontal direction, for example, between the bedroom, bathroom, and living areas. Installing a ceiling lift system requires professional advice and installation. Using a lift requires training. The PT can show the caregiver how to transfer someone into a lift device and how to use the devices appropriately.

Chair glides and stairway lifts can be purchased for people who live in multilevel homes but who cannot or should not climb stairs. They are measured and custom-made for individual staircases and are quite expensive. Insurance companies usually do not reimburse for stairway lifts, but some medical supply companies offer rent-to-own options. In addition, local ALS Association chapters and/or Muscular Dystrophy Association chapters may have lifts that have been recycled. Chair glides do not offer much trunk support, which limits their use for people who require support or a recline function for safety. Additionally, you need to be able to get on and off the chair glide, making it more difficult and less practical if you depend on assistance for transfers.

Electric hospital beds can also make moving while in bed and transferring in and out easier. Typically, a semielectric hospital bed has 2 motors: 1 that allows you to move the head of the bed and the other to move the foot. In addition to the bed rails, these features assist in bed mobility. Fully electric hospital beds have a third motor that adjusts the height of the bed. This ability to change the height of the bed surface makes transfers easier and safer.

Other useful devices are transfer belts and swivel cushions/seats. Transfer belts vary in design, but they all allow a caregiver to grasp the belt instead of the individual during transfers. This makes transfers easier on the caregiver and prevents pulling on the arms, which may cause shoulder problems. Swivel cushions/seats are lightweight, cushioned seats that swivel in both directions and make getting in and out of a car easier.

### Interventions for Pulmonary Dysfunction

People with ALS may have difficulty coughing and may develop shortness of breath and/or pulmonary infections. PTs can perform, or show caregivers how to perform, techniques that optimize the cough mechanism and gas exchange and that reduce the accumulation of lung secretions and facilitate their removal.

A person with ALS may find it difficult to generate enough force to cough. This may be due to muscle weakness, the inability to close the glottis, an inability to build up enough pressure in the chest cavity, or the position. Cough effectiveness can be increased by the following:

1. Sitting in a forward-leaning position (sitting is usually best), if at all possible. This pushes up the diaphragm. Some people are able to cough more effectively in a side-lying position.

2. Taking in the biggest breath possible.

3. Placing both hands (one on top of the other) in the center of the abdomen, just below the chest, or encircling the arms around the rib cage (a caregiver can assist at this step), and applying pressure as the breath is let out and a cough is attempted. A variation is to squeeze the arms against the side of the chest.

4. Huffing with the mouth open.

If this is not possible, the PT can show you and your caregiver other techniques to assist with coughing and may recommend the use of an insufflation/exsufflation machine (see Chapter 12).

Postural drainage and manual techniques such as percussion and vibration can decrease the retention of secretions and assist the person with ALS to mobilize secretions. Breathing exercises can be taught that will maximize ventilation (gas exchange within the lungs). In addition, a person with ALS who experiences shortness of breath may benefit from resting in relaxed positions, with the head elevated. Chapter 12 further describes other management options for individuals with pulmonary dysfunction.

## Summary

A PT is an integral member of the rehabilitation team; access to a PT that is knowledgeable about ALS is very important in effectively managing the disease. To address various impairments, activity limitations, and participation restrictions seen throughout the course of the disease, a PT will

- Provide you and your family and caregivers with education and training;
- Order appropriate equipment;
- Refer you to other health care professionals as needed and to appropriate community resources;
- Develop management and intervention plans that address your current and future needs; and
- Provide you and your family with psychological support.

You and your caregiver should feel free to speak to your PT about any questions and concerns.

## References

1. Dal Bello-Haas V. A framework for rehabilitation in degenerative diseases: planning care and maximizing quality of life. *Neurol Rep.* 2002;26(3):115–129.
2. American Physical Therapy Association. Guide to physical therapy practice. *J Phys Ther.* 2001;81(1):9–744.
3. Kisner C, Colby LA. *Therapeutic Exercise: Foundations and Techniques.* 5th ed. Philadelphia: FA Davis; 2007;1–36.

4. Bohannon RW. Results of resistance exercise on a patient with amyotrophic lateral sclerosis. *Phys Ther.* 1983;63(6):965–968.

5. Sanjak M, Paulson D, Sufit R, et al. Physiologic and metabolic response to progressive and prolonged exercise in amyotrophic lateral sclerosis. *Neurology.* 1987;37:1217–1220.

6. Pinto AC, Alves M, Nogueira A, et al. Can amyotrophic lateral sclerosis patients with respiratory insufficiency exercise? *J Neurol Sci.* 1999;169:69–75.

7. Dal Bello-Haas V, Florence JM, Krivickas LS. Therapeutic exercise for people with amyotrophic lateral sclerosis or motor neuron disease. *Cochrane Database Syst Rev.* 2008;2:CD005229.

8. Drory VE, Goltsman E, Reznik JG, et al. The value of muscle exercise in patients with amyotrophic lateral sclerosis. *J Neurol Sci.* 2001;191:133–137.

9. Dal Bello-Haas VP, Florence J, Kloos AD, et al. A randomized controlled trial of resistance exercise in individuals with ALS. *Neurology.* 2007;68:2003–2007.

10. Mitsumoto H, Chad DA, Pioro EP. *Amyotrophic Lateral Sclerosis.* Philadelphia: FA Davis; 1998.

11. Ashworth N, Satkunam L, Deforge D. Treatment for spasticity in amyotrophic lateral sclerosis/motor neuron disease. *Cochrane Database Syst Rev.* 2004;1:CD004156.

12. Dal Bello-Haas V, Kloos AD, Mitsumoto H. Physical therapy for a patient through six stages of amyotrophic lateral sclerosis. *Phys Ther.* 1998;78:1312–1324.

# 8

# Occupational Therapy

## Patricia Casey

The role of the occupational therapist is to improve or maintain the self-care abilities of the person with amyotrophic lateral sclerosis (ALS), and work with the patient and caregiver toward this end. "Occupational therapy helps people live life to the fullest. It does this by helping people of all ages who have suffered illness, injury or some form of debilitation relearn the skills of daily living. By focusing on the physical, psychological and social needs of its patients, occupational therapy helps people function at the highest possible level by concentrating on what's important to them to rebuild their health, independence and self esteem" (American Occupational Therapy Association, 2008).

Occupational therapists are trained to assess functional strengths needed to perform self-care or work activities and choose appropriate assistive devices to help with these tasks. They analyze patterns of performance to find ways to conserve energy and maximize strength and endurance. They set up appropriate exercise programs and train patients and caregivers alike. They use their skills to help patients with ALS and their caregivers to work toward goals that are important in maintaining function as long as is feasible.

Living life always means change, but living with ALS presents unique challenges as progressive physical changes occur. What you and your caregiver see as important shapes the therapy process. Therapists understand and acknowledge that you will change the way you perform a task only if the change makes it easier to accomplish the task. This means that the way you are doing something no longer works. You and your caregiver each have your own strengths and abilities.

Adapting those abilities to meet the changing needs of daily living caused by ALS may not be easy. Occupational therapists can help in this process by focusing on the immediate problems you present to them and guide you to possible solutions. An experienced therapist will suggest fairly simple solutions without offering too much information or too many alternatives at one time.

Adaptations needed for ALS include physical, mechanical, or procedural changes to accomplish activities of daily living (ADLs). Changes may require assistive devices or medical equipment, proper placement of furniture or utensils, or a change in the method of operation, such as pushing or sliding an object instead of lifting or carrying it.

Several factors affect the ability to make changes when the disease progresses. You and your caregivers may have different perceptions of immediate and long-term needs and the degree to which increasing physical limitations will affect your lives. You may be in different stages of the grieving process; denial and depression can make changes difficult. You may have different learning and problem-solving capacities. And your family may have a different lifestyle, social needs, and financial resources than other ALS families.

Progressive physical limitations require the use of a variety of assistive devices. The use of these appliances may mean modifying time, space, and location of activities. Eventually, it may become necessary for your caregiver to perform activities such as feeding, washing, and dressing. Occupational therapy in your home, as well as in the clinic, permits periodic reevaluation to assess your changing priorities, the need for additional information, and your readiness to change your environment to maintain or improve function.

Recommendations for changes are based on your physical limitations rather than on the phase of the disease, because you may present with more or less disability than another person with ALS. Along with physical needs, your therapist must consider the abilities of your caregiver and the availability of insurance or financial resources to purchase assistive equipment and make changes in your living space.

Your caregiver may need instructions on how to assist you safely. Adequate information and instruction will help improve care, reduce anxiety, and decrease the risk of injury to both of you. Written prescriptions from your doctor may be needed for home evaluations and treatments by home health professionals such as occupational or physical therapists. Check with your insurance company or health care system about available services.

The next sections will describe areas of concern requiring solutions. You may or may not experience any or all of them; just in case, they are all included. Table 8.1 lists some Web sites and other resources used for recommendations found in this chapter. Assistive devices and methods that may be helpful for the weakness, atrophy, and deformity that occur include the following:

- Neck supports
- Upper extremity appliances
- Lower extremity appliances

**Table 8.1** Web Sites and Other Resources

| **ALS Organizations** |
|---|
| ALS Association (ALSA): www.alsa.org |
| CAREgiver Chicago: www.CAREgiverMag.com |
| The Les Turner ALS Association: www.lesturnerals.org |
| Muscular Dystrophy Association (MDA): www.als.mdausa.org |

**ALS Medical Equipment**

**Assistive devices:**

Enrichments catalog: www.sammonspreston.com or 1-866-402-8720

**Beasy transfer board:**

www.beasy.com

**Books, electronic:**

Public library lending program

**Clothing adaptations:**

www.silverts.com

www.buckandbuck.com

**Electronic and energy-saving gadgets:**

www.skymall.com

**Hand splints, wrist supports, mobile arm supports:**

Occupational Therapy evaluation

**Hospital beds:**

Invacare

**Mattresses:**

Alternating pressure, thermorest air mattress (L.L. Bean), Roho, gel-foam, temper foam, low air loss

**Patient lifts:**

Invacare, Hoyer, Transaid, Easy Pivot, Sabina

**Ceiling lifts:**

Barrier Free Lift: http://bfl.com

SureHands Lift System: www.surehands.com

**Toilet adaptations:**

Toto Chloe Bidet toilet

**Walkers:**

U-Step Walker: www.ustep.com

(Continued)

**Table 8.1** Web Sites and Other Resources  *(Continued)*

Guardian folding walker with front casters

Guardian Pro202 rolling walker

**Wheelchairs:**

Invacare, Quickie, Permobil; Jay, Roho, Varilite, Ultimate cushions

**Transportation:**

Check your local city/county/state public transportation offices for public use guidelines and fares

**Travel:**

*Frommer's Guide for the Disabled:* information on airline/hotel/transportation for national and international travel

---

- Trunk and hip appliances
- Home modifications
- Techniques for the caregiver
- Collaboration with orthopedics, physical therapy, speech therapy, nutrition, nursing, and social services

## Head and Neck Supports

You may have some weakness in neck muscles that causes occasional headaches, sharp pains in your neck when turning your head, or head drooping. Neck and shoulder weakness often make you want to slide down in the chair to give your back more support and your head a place to rest. Self-care, work, and leisure activities are difficult to perform when neck and shoulder muscles are weak. Neck supports are needed to promote proper positioning, relieve strained muscles, and allow you to continue to perform desired activities.

### Soft Cervical Collar

If you have mild to moderate weakness of the neck and shoulders you may need a *soft cervical collar* or a *firm travel pillow* to provide support, especially when riding in a car (Chapter 7).

### Aspen Collar

The *Aspen collar* is a semirigid plastic frame with foam inserts to provide comfort. It encircles the neck; Velcro straps are used to adjust the fit. It gives most patients support while sitting and riding as a passenger in a car. However, it may restrict jaw movement when eating, swallowing, and speaking. Your therapist and orthotist (brace specialist) can evaluate your needs and measure for the proper size.

## Headmaster Collar

The *Headmaster lightweight tubular frame collar* gives unrestricted neck support with adequate head support while walking.

## Oxford Collar

The *Oxford wire spring support collar* allows some head motion for eating and speaking and gives lightweight support while walking. It also offers unrestricted neck support for suctioning or mechanical ventilation for patients who have a tracheostomy. The chin rest has changeable padding for comfort and cleaning. This collar is custom made by Ballert Orthopedics in Chicago (see "Resources for Patients and Their Families" chapter).

## Sterno-Occipital-Mandibular Immobilizer

A *sterno-occipital-mandibular immobilizer (SOMI)* ensures adequate head and neck control while walking or sitting. It has additional chest and upper back support, and is custom made by an orthotist.

## Upper Extremity Appliances

Upper extremity weakness and atrophy may leave you unable to perform activities that require raising your arms above your waist for dressing, bathing, putting on makeup, shaving, or combing your hair. You may have difficulty placing your hands in a functional position on the table or work area. Weakness in the elbows, forearms, and wrists limits the use of your hands to manipulate tools and utensils for self-care, work, or leisure activities. Intrinsic muscles are the small muscles within the hand that allow pinch, grasp, and coordination. Intrinsic muscle weakness and atrophy affect hand grasp and pinch. Many assistive devices are available for these conditions, but careful selection is required to achieve the desired results, avoid wasting time and money, and reduce frustration for both you and your caregiver.

## Eating Devices

*Lightweight wrist splints* and *utensil holders, foam or cork tubes for utensils, plastic or long-handled utensils, extra-long straws, lightweight large-handled cups, plate guards, suction holders,* and *nonskid pads* are useful items to help you eat independently.

## Dressing, Grooming, and Personal Hygiene Devices

Aids for these activities include *button and zipper hooks, long-handled sponges, lightweight electric shavers,* an *adapted floss holder,* a *rechargeable electric toothbrush with rotary brush,* and *Velcro fasteners.*

## Other Daily Activity Devices

*Key holders, doorknob extenders, light switch extension levers, touch switches, lightweight reachers, self-opening scissors,* and *cardholders* are used to assist with daily needs.

## Mobile Arm Supports

*Mobile arm supports (MASs)* are mechanical devices used to support the entire arm if weakness is moderately severe and feeding yourself or using the computer keyboard is desired. They allow both horizontal and vertical motion. Additional attachments can provide wrist support and allow limited turning upward of the hand. Self-feeding and grooming can be accomplished with the MAS once utensils or other items have been positioned. You can use the computer and portable communication devices more easily with the MAS and attachments because your hands are raised over the keyboards.

*Ergonomic computer forearm supports* used to prevent carpal tunnel syndrome for people who work at computers all day are also available. They resemble the MAS but do not have the same horizontal range for shoulder motions or vertical range for reaching the face and mouth. If wrist muscles are very weak, wrist supports could be added to the forearm trough. These can be used at home or at work on standard workstation surfaces.

## Communication Aids

Aids for writing and reading include the use of a *rubber thumb, pencil grips, writing splints, dry-erase writing boards, book holders, tilt-top over bed table,* and a *lap-style bed table.* Electronic devices include *portable phones with a headset or earphones,* a *speaker phone,* and use *of telecommunication devices for the deaf (TDD) assistance through the phone company.* Devices used to signal your caregiver range from a *small bell* to *an infant monitor system.*

You can use various *augmentative communication electronic speech devices* (ACCs) if your hand function is adequate to operate a keyboard. *Single-switch computer systems* are available if you have difficulty typing. Ask your speech therapist for help with these and other ACCs. If there is a rehabilitation hospital in your area, they may have various devices to try and therapists or an environmental engineer to adapt the devices for hand, head, voice, or other control (Chapter 10).

## Hand Splints

*Resting hand splints* support weak wrist and hand muscles. If you have stiff muscles, you may need a positioning wrist and hand splint (WHO) to prevent the thumb and fingers from curling. Splints can be worn at night to stretch the fingers and thumb and prevent further muscular shortening. If your fingers are very weak, you may need a lightweight WHO to support and protect them. These splints can be custom made or purchased from a catalog. Your occupational therapist will help determine which is better for you.

You may need a small hand splint to facilitate hand grasp and pinch or you may need stabilization of your fingers to perform a specific activity. *Short opponens splints* are useful for these purposes since they strap around the hand to hold the thumb in place for better finger and thumb coordination. Ask your therapist if you need one; it can be custom made for your hand.

## Shoulder Supports

A *simple sling* can be used for support of weak arms and hands to minimize pressure on shoulder and neck muscles as you stand or walk. When you are sitting, your arms can be supported on pillows arranged on an *adjustable-height over bed table*. The table can be set at the proper height to support the weight of your arms and rest your neck and shoulder muscles.

## Trunk and Hip Solutions

### Raised Seat Heights

Initially, if you have difficulty rising from a seated to a standing position you may simply require adding a *firm 2- or 3-inch cushion* to the sitting surface. Sometimes, the simplest solution is to sit on a *firm chair with supportive back and arms*. *Extenders* can be placed under bed legs and chair legs that raise your furniture so that sitting and standing are easier. More often, the purchase or rental of a *power seat lift-recliner chair* will be necessary to provide independent change of position either to a standing, seated, or reclined position.

In the bathroom, you can use a *plastic molded, raised toilet seat*, a simple solution for initial hip weakness. Some raised toilet seats have arms attached to them. Attached arms are useful only if you can push straight down to help yourself to stand. If you have to lean forward to stand they are of no help and may be in your way for toilet hygiene.

A *padded shower commode on casters* with a U-shaped cushion incorporates features you may need for problems of progressive weakness. You can use it by rolling it over the toilet; it adds height to a standard toilet. Others in the household can easily roll it away. It provides a high seat and back support, removable armrests, and a large opening for hygiene purposes. It can be placed at the bedside to avoid the hazards of walking to the bathroom at night for toileting. It can also be rolled into a shower area if you need to remain seated while taking a shower.

### Bathing Devices

Various bathtub seats, benches, lifts, and accessories are available whether you can independently bath or shower or need some help. Two standard aids are a tub grab rail and a raised bathtub seat. The *tub grab rail* can be easily attached to the side of a porcelain or steel tub and gives you a sure grip to hold whether you are stepping in or out of the tub. A *raised bathtub seat* has adjustable-height legs and can be used inside most bathtubs. A *bathtub bench* has two legs inside and two legs outside of the tub so you do not have to stand on one leg to climb into the tub. You seat yourself first on the bench then turn yourself one leg at a time. Benches cannot be used with sliding shower doors; the doors must be removed and replaced with a curtain. Benches also cannot be used if your bathroom vanity sits at a right angle to the bathtub. There is not enough room to turn your legs once you are seated on the bench. A *hand-held shower hose* or *adjustable shower head* that slides up and down for height adjustment are recommended when you are seated.

You can use a *wooden bar stool* in the shower for safety. Most bathtub seats with adjustable legs cannot be raised high enough for use in a shower stall. You may want a *soap or shampoo dispenser* on the wall to avoid dropping slippery containers.

## Lower Extremity Solutions

Lower extremity weakness also affects how you perform self-care and work activities. Occupational therapists coordinate efforts with physical therapists and orthotists who make and fit braces and other supportive devices to keep you safe and mobile. Frequent falls occur when ankle weakness results in dropfoot and weak quadriceps cause the knees to give out.

### Gait Belt

A *gait belt* is essential when your caregiver must assist when you are standing from a seated position, transferring from the bed to a chair, or getting in and out of the car.

### Straight Canes

An *adjustable-height straight cane* with a large rubber tip gives you a steady support when one leg is weak and your walking is unsteady. Four-legged quad canes may be more difficult to use safely because you need to land four points instead of one.

### Ankle-Foot Orthoses

*Lightweight, plastic ankle-foot orthoses (AFOs)* with 5 to10 degrees of plantar flexion (foot and ankle pointed down slightly) can help stabilize walking. People who wear braces and live in apartments or homes with stairs have an additional problem because standard AFOs decrease the ability to climb stairs easily. *Articulating (movable) ankle joints* may be considered when your doctor prescribes braces, but these do not help the knee to lock as well. Careful assessment is required by an orthopedic or rehabilitation physician who will prescribe the correct brace. An orthotist will make the brace and the physical therapist will provide gait training once the brace is fitted properly.

## Rollator Walker With a Seat

If your upper and lower extremities are very weak, *a walker with wheels and a seat* may be helpful. It allows a steadier, smoother gait and provides a seat for rest breaks. The front casters should be able to turn all the way around. Your walk will be less tiring because you will use less energy. You will not need to lift this walker when walking on uneven surfaces, turning corners, or crossing thresholds.

## Wheelchairs

If you become easily fatigued and your walking ability is limited, you will want to consider assistive equipment that will keep you going where you want to go. If you stop leaving your home because your endurance has lessened, your quality of life is limited. You have places to go and people to see; get the appropriate equipment to get there. Your priorities may include continuing work, getting around your home, getting out in the community, and going places with your family or friends for recreation or leisure. Careful selection of manual and power wheelchairs with supportive seating systems should be determined by you, your physician, your therapist, and a rehabilitation technician specialist (RTS). Selection of appropriate features depends on the rate of progression of your disease. Your insurance carrier requires a prescription and justification of medical necessity for all features selected. The wheelchair will be ordered by your physician and determined in consultation with an occupational therapist or physical therapist and an RTS wheelchair and seating specialist. Ask your physician or clinic staff if there is a seating and positioning clinic to which you can be referred.

## Lightweight Manual Wheelchairs

Most patients with lower extremity weakness require a *lightweight manual wheelchair* to provide mobility if their endurance is fair to poor. One that can be placed easily in the back seat or trunk of a car is preferable. Your caregiver's ability to lift and transport a wheelchair must be considered when purchasing such equipment. A suitable *lightweight gel or dense foam cushion* is needed for adequate trunk and pelvic support. A *pressure-relief cushion* is necessary when you are sitting in any wheelchair for more than 4 hours or if you are unable to reposition yourself.

## Recliner Back Wheelchair

A *lightweight high-back wheelchair* may be more supportive than a standard wheelchair for those who have neck and shoulder weakness. It also offers the advantage of easy portability and support for the head, neck, and shoulders. A *standard recliner wheelchair* is bulky and difficult to transport in a car, but it sometimes is useful for people with neck and trunk weakness who remain at home. Transportation may require a *van with a lift*.

### Tilt-in-Space Wheelchair

The *tilt-in-space wheelchair frame* offers more pressure relief for seat, low-back, shoulder, and neck pressure areas than the recliner back. It can be tilted backward periodically to relieve pressure on your low back and tail bone.

### Motorized Scooters (Powered-Operated Vehicles)

People with ALS who are working and socially active may be interested in using *motorized scooters*. The rental or loan of such equipment may be more appropriate if the rate of progression of the disease is slow to moderate. Sitting posture, shoulder and hand function, and hip strength must be assessed to ensure proper seating support. Good trunk control is needed for safety in scooters, as well as good arm and hand strength. An adjustable tiller control or a hydraulic seat may be necessary for reach and safe transfers.

*Be Aware.* Your insurance company may not purchase more than one wheelchair, especially a power wheelchair. You will want them to cover the wheelchair that gives you the most support and service over the course of your disease. Power-operated vehicles (POVs) will not meet long-term needs. You may want to consider purchasing a POV on your own.

### Power Wheelchairs

*Power wheelchairs* with contoured, pressure-relief seating and electronic controllers that can be programmed for changes in hand strength and for adequate neck, trunk, pelvic, and upper and lower extremity support must be measured carefully. This equipment is prescribed by your doctor. Insurance carriers determine which features they will cover. Power wheelchairs are costly but may serve many functions that give you and your caregiver the most independence and highest quality of life.

### Wheelchair Lifts and Racks

*Wheelchair racks* fit on the outside of the car; *wheelchair lifts* fit on the inside of vans. Lifts can operate manually or electrically. Lifts must be fitted for the van once you select the wheelchair you will use long-term. How tall you are, how high you sit in the wheelchair, and how large a van you own are factors that determine which lift to install.

### Ventilator Considerations

Respiratory involvement may cause poor walking endurance (see Chapter 12). You may have already given some thought to the possibility of needing invasive or noninvasive ventilator assistance. Based on these decisions, you need guidance in selecting a power recliner or manual wheelchair with a *ventilator tray*.

## Backup Power in Your Home for Wheelchair/Ventilator Batteries

Check with the wheelchair and respiratory vendors for suitable *backup power generators* that are commercially available for home use.

## Patient Lifts

If you cannot stand, you and your caregiver will need a *manually operated or power-operated patient lift* for lifting you in and out of bed, wheelchair, commode, seat lift recliner chair, or car. This type of lift can place you on the floor, if you desire, or pick you up from the floor if you fall. A *full-size, divided-leg sling* can easily be placed under you and removed without lifting you with some instruction by your therapist. The extra-long model provides head and neck support if you have weak neck muscles.

New *pivot lifts* ease transfers, dressing, and toileting because you lean forward on a chest support with straps around the back, arms, and legs. However, pivot lifts require some trunk stability and may not be suitable if you have severe diaphragm weakness.

## Hospital Beds

You may want to consider an electric hospital bed when you are having difficulty standing from a seated position. A *full-electric hospital bed* (one that rises from the floor electrically) helps you stand and sit safely and saves your energy for other activities. *Half rails* give you adequate support for sitting and standing from the bed; *full rails* may hinder transfers from the bed. If Medicare is your insurance vendor, only the rental of a *semielectric hospital bed* is covered. Semielectric means that only the head and foot of the bed can be adjusted with the hand control; the height of the bed can be set higher but it is not adjustable. Some insurance companies underwrite a queen- or king-size electric bed, but most of these beds do not rise electrically from the floor to assist standing; other insurance plans cover only hospital beds.

You may need a hospital bed if you have difficulty breathing when lying flat on the bed. Being able to raise the head of the bed makes breathing easier, prevents gastric reflux, and decreases the risk of aspirating saliva or food particles.

The hospital bed frame is 80 inches long; an extralong twin bed frame is 80 inches long. If you have enough space in your bedroom both frames can be clamped together to form a king-size bed, allowing you and your spouse to continue sleeping together while providing the power-operated assistance you need for postural support and change of position.

## Skin Protection

When muscle atrophy affects your shoulder and pelvic areas, artificial padding will be needed for sleeping comfort. Also, you need to be comfortable if you spend more time in bed. *Gel and foam mattresses* with *washable sheepskin padding* are commonly used. *Contour neck pillows, foam boots, elbow and heel pads,* and *blanket supports* are also helpful for preventing skin breakdown. You will need an *adequate communication system* at this time, whether activated by *eye blink* or by a *computer system with a head-scanning device.* Low-tech options, such as *flash cards,* are very practical for use by the bedside.

## Home Modifications

Once the decision is made that a wheelchair is needed, easy entrance and exit from the house, car, and office must be considered, as well as the space for turning and the widths of halls and doorways.

### Ramps

*Portable wheelchair ramps* provide the simplest means of negotiating 1 or 2 steps. *Two motorcycle ramps* are usually less expensive than a single wheelchair ramp and readily available at local auto stores. *Wooden or metal ramps* come in all shapes and sizes, depending on the configuration of front doors, walkways, shrubbery, and the location of your house in relation to the sidewalk. Walkways along the side of the house allow space for a long ramp. A *Z-shaped ramp* is necessary when a short front yard or backyard does not provide adequate length for a safe, long incline. A platform that is level with the door frame is needed to rest the wheelchair safely while opening and closing the door. Ramp inclines 1:12 (1-inch incline for every foot of distance) but not more than 1.5:12 are safe and easy to climb for manual or power wheelchairs. Local building ordinances must be taken into account.

### Stair Lifts and Porch Lifts

Trilevel, bilevel, and two-story homes with turning stairways are the most difficult to maneuver, and the solutions depend on family resources. *Hydraulic porch lifts* or *elevators* may be the most economical and the only architectural choice for some homes. *Stair lifts* are a solution for families who are unwilling or unable to move. It is possible to rent stair lifts, which helps in short- and long-term planning. Sometimes, the most feasible solution is to move the bedroom to the most accessible level of the home, making changes for toileting and bathing needs. *Porch lifts* can be installed inside homes to gain access to two levels with easy access to front and back doors, garages, and bathrooms.

### Ceiling Lifts

*Electric ceiling lifts* are commercially available but expensive; send for free videos and get information from the Web sites. Less expensive adaptations have been devised by some families to provide consistent, safe, and easy lifting. One innovative family devised a ceiling lift by using a garage door opener track and motor with an attached swivel bar (from a standard patient lift) and sling. Another family living in a bilevel home installed an I-beam and quarter-ton hoist on the ceiling joists. An attached swivel bar (from a standard patient lift) and sling allowed transport of the patient over the stairwell from top to ground level. The set of lower steps were placed on rollers. When they were rolled out of the way, the wheelchair could be positioned directly below the hoist. This inexpensive renovation (less than $2,000) allowed the family safe and easy access to both levels of their home. It was considerably less expensive than installing an elevator or double stair lift or moving to a one-level home.

## Bathroom Modifications

Selection of assistive bathing equipment depends on the design of your bathroom and your willingness to make minor changes if expensive renovation is not possible. After the front and back doors of your home, the most important doorway is into your bathroom. You must be able to enter your bathroom walking with a walker or sitting in a rolling commode chair (at least 25 inches wide). Manual or power wheelchairs usually do not clear bathroom doors. *Rolling commode chairs* that measure 20 to 21 inches in width clear doors easily. Bathroom doors can be widened with inexpensive *offset hinges*, but some space is needed behind the opened door to accommodate the door and the doorknob.

If you are able to modify your bathroom, *shower stalls* are more accessible than bathtubs for you and your caregiver. A tiled floor with a recessed drain allows access to a remodeled shower area with use of a *walker with wheels* or a *rolling shower commode*. For safety, glass shower doors can be easily replaced with an *expandable shower rod and curtain*. A standard shower stall with a 3 to 4 inch rim can be modified with a *simple wood deck and removable ramp* for access with a shower commode.

## Exercise

Because of the psychological and physical benefits, you should continue to perform the regular exercises you are used to doing. The number of repetitions and weights used should be modified if muscle strain is likely. More benefit is achieved with less weight and more repetitions for shorter periods of time. Consider your daily schedule, the amount of time and energy you need to accomplish necessary activities, and balance activity and rest periods each day. Table 8.2 summarizes an appropriate exercise program that is designed for basic mobility and function and can be performed with or without the assistance of your caregiver. Table 8.3 describes how to conserve energy. Consult with a dietician to ensure that you do not lose weight because of poor energy intake and expenditure. Your food intake should balance your activity and exercise needs.

**Table 8.2** Exercises for Patients With ALS

**Breathing**

- Breathe in a big breath through your nose, with your mouth closed.
- Pucker your lips as if you are going to whistle.
- Slowly blow out as long as you can, pulling your abdomen in as best as you can.
- Repeat only 3 times at any given time.
- You may do this exercise once every hour during the day (10–15 times per day).

**Arm Exercise**

This is a gentle exercise to maintain your range of motion and prevent stiffening of the shoulder joints. The motions gently stretch the ligaments and tendons around the shoulder joints. You will feel stretching or pulling in your muscles, but you should not feel sharp pains. If you do experience pain, stop and gently lower your arms. Call your physician.

- Lie on your back on your bed; scoot down on the bed so you have enough room to raise your arms over your head.
- Raise both arms over your head with your elbows bent. Use one hand to help lift the other if needed. If your shoulders are stiff, raise your arms as far as they will go.
- Rest your hands on your chin; press your elbows and shoulder blades into the pillow; count to 3, relax. Move your hands to your forehead; press your elbows and shoulder blades into the pillow; count to 3, relax. Move your hands to the top of your head; press your elbows and shoulder blades into the pillow; count to 3, relax.
- Gently make small forward and backward circles (5–10 in each direction) at the shoulder when your hands are on the top of your head; move down to your forehead, repeat circles; then move down to your chin, repeat circles. Relax both arms.
- Raise your arms in this manner once in the morning before you get out of bed and once in the evening before you go to sleep.

**Leg Exercises**

These exercises can be done once an hour while you are sitting in a firm chair. They will help maintain the strength in your hip, knee, and ankle muscles that is needed for standing and transferring.

- Raise each leg with knee straight and your toes pulled toward you as far as they will go. Rotate your foot 3 times each way. Lower that leg.
- Raise the other leg. Do the same motions with the foot on that leg.
- Repeat these exercises at least once per hour, alternating legs 3 times.
- If you cannot raise your straightened leg off the floor, rest your heel on the floor and practice pulling your toes toward you and completely locking your knee.

*(Continued)*

**Table 8.2** Exercises for Patients with ALS   (*Continued*)

**Hand Exercises**

- Turn both palms up. Arms should be held with elbows against your ribs. Pretend you are pulling your fingers into a ball of clay and you want to make fingerprints in the clay. Count to 5 as you pull your fingers and thumb around the ball of clay. Aim your thumb toward your little finger. Don't forget to look at each finger while you are pulling.
- Turn your hands over both palms down. Pretend you are pushing your fingers into the clay until they are fully outstretched. Count to 5 as you stretch. Then, with fingers extended, pull your wrist back. Feel the stretch.
- This exercise can be repeated once an hour.

**Walking**

- Walk every hour. Make an imaginary exercise path inside your home or office. Stand up and walk every hour. Go as far as you are comfortable, 1 minute, 5 minutes, or 10 minutes.
- Stand by your walker, desk, or kitchen counter for balance and shift weight from one foot to the other for 5 minutes every hour if you cannot walk.

**Table 8.3** Guidelines for Conserving Your Energy

You can help yourself by taking charge of how you perform the things you need to do everyday. How you perform the tasks of daily living can affect how you feel the rest of the day.

- Consider what routines are necessary. Decide what you can do, what someone else can do, and what can be eliminated from the routine. Examples: dressing routine, grooming needs, and time for shower or bath.
- Consider timing or scheduling of activities. Your time and schedule, as well as your caregiver's time and schedule, are equally important. Plan activity and rest periods; pace yourself.
- Consider the best use of your energy. When you climb a mountain, you also have to have enough energy to return to base camp. Use assistive devices to help reduce fatigue and frustration. Examples include walkers with wheels, wheelchairs for distance (shopping), handicapped parking cards or special license plates.
- Eat high-energy foods in small amounts every 2 to 3 hours since muscles become more readily fatigued. Talk to your dietician for appropriate choices.
- Place frequently used items in the most convenient place. Place heavier items on the lowest level that you can reach. This is especially important in the bathroom, kitchen, and office.

(*Continued*)

**Table 8.3** Guidelines for Conserving Your Energy   (*Continued*)

---

- Purchase gadgets or other energy-saving devices after recommendation from someone who is knowledgeable about their actual success rates. Otherwise, you have wasted time and money. Good information can be found at support groups. But please keep in mind—not all suggestions at support groups will fit your specific problem or situation. Check with your ALS clinic staff. They usually have heard all the comments or complaints about certain items or resources. Your occupational therapist can help sort out the good advice and apply specific recommendations or techniques to you to meet your needs.

---

## Summary

ALS initially forces you to adapt to your environment. As weakness increases, however, the environment must be adapted to fit the needs of you and your caregiver, to help you function as independently as possible, and to make living easier for both of you. Each patient and family has its own priorities. Each has its own style, unique sense of timing, and available resources. The occupational therapist works with you and your caregiver in this dynamic process to help you live life to the fullest. Be sure to consult with the occupational therapist at clinic visits to review your current needs and receive helpful up-to-date information about living with ALS.

## Resources

*Everyday Life With ALS: A Practical Guide.* Tucson, AZ: Muscular Dystrophy Association; 2005.

*Living With ALS. A Series of Manuals.* Woodland Hills, CA: ALS Association; 2003.

Richman J, Casey P. Multidisciplinary approach to management and support of patients. In: Kuncl R, ed. *Motor Neuron Disease.* New York: W.B. Saunders; 2002.

# 9

# Wheelchair Selection

## Ronit Sukenick and John T. Calcavecchia

The prospect of obtaining a wheelchair can be daunting. Gone are the days when you go to your neighborhood drugstore and pick out your wheelchair from a shelf filled with one-size-fits-all models. With the recent advances in technology and the savvy of today's health care consumers, wheelchairs can now be custom-prescribed and custom-built for the individual user. This means choices for you as a consumer—and plenty of them! Be aware, because many models are not appropriate for an patient with amyotrophic lateral sclerosis (ALS). This chapter takes you through the process of selecting a wheelchair system and answers some questions most commonly asked by consumers.

### Goals of Seating and Mobility

Wheelchairs can be invaluable in improving quality of life and preventing secondary complications caused by immobility. Whether they are used intermittently or daily, wheelchairs can achieve many different goals depending on the needs of the individual. An appropriate seating system will

- Provide alternate means of mobility when ambulation is no longer safe or possible because of balance, strength, and/or endurance deficits;
- Provide support to weakened neck, trunk, and/or pelvic muscles;
- Provide pressure relief, reducing the risk for skin breakdown and pain;

131

- Improve sitting tolerance; and
- Improve respiratory efficiency by maintaining an upright seated posture and reducing the need for overexertion.

## When Is it Time to Get a Wheelchair?

When is the right time to get a wheelchair? Good question—and a difficult one at that. Should you wait until your doctor tells you it is time? Should you wait until you are at risk for falling when you walk? Probably not. Reflect back on your lifestyle over recent weeks, or months, or over the past year. Have you given up activities that are enjoyable or meaningful to you because you have difficulty walking? Is most of your strength and energy being used up for locomotion? If your answer to either of these questions is yes, consider this—if using a wheelchair allowed you to conserve precious energy or to resume activities that you value, would it be worth it? This is a very individual decision and one that only you can make based on your personal values and beliefs. Consult your loved ones—they often have useful insight.

For some people, the need to use a wheelchair seems to be a marker of how far the disease has progressed and from that moment on "things can only get worse." Your decision to use a wheelchair need not be a self-imposed, lifelong sentence of sitting. Early on in the disease process, a wheelchair may be used intermittently for traveling long distances such as the local mall or park—a wise way to conserve energy. Some worry that using a wheelchair will lead to the loss of the ability to walk. Instead, walking despite balance or endurance deficits many lead to exhaustion or a fall and, in turn, to the loss of the ability to walk even in the best circumstances. The risk and benefits of continued ambulation should be weighed to determine the appropriate use of a wheelchair.

If you currently do not need a wheelchair for regular use, it may be premature for you to purchase a permanent wheelchair system. In this instance, obtaining a wheelchair on a temporary basis (short-term rental or loan from your local ALS Association [ALSA] or Muscular Dystrophy Association [MDA] chapter, church, friends, or family) makes sense. In this way your resources (personal or medical insurances) remain intact for your future needs. If you are undecided about whether you need a wheelchair, the temporary use of one is a great way to test the waters and see whether it makes a difference in the quality of your life. When you find yourself using the wheelchair regularly to perform activities throughout the day or week, it might then be the right time to consider purchasing a permanent wheelchair that is customized to your individual needs.

## Can't I Just Go to the Store and Pick Out a Wheelchair?

Yes, you can. The risk that you take in selecting and purchasing a wheelchair directly from a salesperson is that you purchase a piece of equipment that is not the most appropriate choice for you, particularly as your symptoms change. Model

"XYZ" may be impressive from a showroom floor, but it may not meet your future needs. If you use your insurance benefits to purchase a wheelchair system that is not an appropriate choice, your insurance source may deny covering a second wheelchair (because they expect that the first one they paid for should be meeting your needs). The expectation is that you will get it right the first time—this can be an expensive lesson to learn.

It may require a bit more time and effort on your part, but by seeking the input of a skilled professional you can be better assured you will receive a wheelchair system that is tailor made to meet your individual needs both now and in the future. Look for a wheelchair/seating clinic in your area; you may find one at many inpatient and outpatient rehabilitation centers. If no such clinic exists in your area, inquire at local hospitals that have an outpatient physical and occupational therapy department. The Rehabilitation Engineering Society of North America (RESNA) is an interdisciplinary association that is devoted to the advancement of assistive technology. RESNA publishes a list of their membership that can help you locate a certified assistive technology supplier (ATS) who specializes in wheelchair evaluations in your area.

Clinic-based wheelchair evaluations are most commonly done by an occupational therapist (OT) and/or a physical therapist (PT). He or she may work alone or in conjunction with a treatment team, which can consist of a physician, a rehabilitation engineer (who specializes in the design of the equipment), and/or a rehabilitation technology supplier (who will sell you the equipment and process your wheelchair through your insurance company). Even if there is no seating specialist in your geographic area, seeking the professional input of an OT or a PT is invaluable to the selection process. Your therapist may not know everything there is to know about wheelchair pieces and parts, but he or she is trained to evaluate your physical and functional status; a wheelchair vendor can fill in the blanks about what equipment will best fulfill these needs.

It is essential that you obtain a physician's prescription for the therapy evaluation *before scheduling;* you will be required to produce this documentation for your evaluator. Also, most medical insurance companies require a physician's prescription and face-to-face examination to consider funding the cost of the therapy visits required to complete the full evaluation of your wheelchair system needs.

## What Does a Wheelchair Evaluation Involve?

Depending on the complexity of your needs and the complexity of the device, a thorough wheelchair evaluation can take one or more clinic visits. Your initial contact with the evaluator will involve information gathering and should include the following:

- A thorough review of your medical history, including your ALS symptoms (your pattern of muscle weakness, spasticity, breathing and swallowing problems, weight loss, pain, and so forth), your vision, and any orthopedic issues.

- An evaluation of your ability to complete activities of daily living that are part of your everyday routine, such as eating, dressing, bathing, toileting, transferring between seat surfaces, home management, work-based tasks, and leisure activities.
- A discussion of the physical environments (indoor and outdoor) in which you will be using the device—home, workplace, church, local neighborhood, special events, and so forth. General physical layouts, specific door frame measurements, table and desk heights, vehicle information (for transport), and descriptions of any transitions (ramps, thresholds) are all valuable.
- A review of any mobility devices that you are currently using. How and where do you use them? How long have you had them? How were they purchased and from whom? Do the devices still meet your needs?
- Trials of many variations of equipment to determine your level of function and what seating and positioning system will meet your needs today and in the future.
- Your goals—what do you want to be able to do?

The more information you can provide the better. Don't forget to take your medical insurance information to the evaluation; in fact, it is a good idea to contact your insurance carrier *before* the evaluation to verify your coverage for durable medical equipment. In addition, your supplier can complete a preverification of insurance coverage prior to the evaluation. A good understanding of any potential out-of-pocket expense before the evaluation can certainly influence your decision making.

The evaluator will then complete a hands-on physical evaluation, during which he or she will assess your

- Sitting balance;
- Sitting posture and spinal alignment;
- Range of motion at all major joints (including ankles, knees, hips, back, shoulders, elbows, wrists, hands, and neck);
- Arm and leg strength and muscle tone;
- Neck strength and head positioning;
- Hand function; and
- Body measurements (to ensure a good fit of the wheelchair).

The information gleaned from the interview and physical evaluation is critical and heavily influences the recommendations your evaluator will make with regard to options in wheelchair styles and postural supports appropriate for you. The evaluation process is also meant to be collaborative. There should be open and honest dialogue between you and your therapist so that the best decisions possible will be made.

## What Kind of Wheelchair System Is Right for Me?

A wheelchair system consists of the wheelchair itself—the base—and the postural supports—the seating—on or into which you sit.

## Wheelchair Base Types

### Manual Wheelchairs

Manual wheelchair frames consist of two small front wheels, called casters, that swivel and are used to steer the wheelchair, and two larger rear wheels. The back and seat surfaces are fabric (nylon or vinyl) unless otherwise specified. Arm and foot supports come with the wheelchair for your comfort and convenience. There commonly are rear push handles that allow someone else to push you in the wheelchair. Although manual wheelchairs can be self-propelled by using the arms and hands, the legs and feet, or both, it is generally not recommended for people with ALS to self-propel a wheelchair because of the high energy cost.

Manual wheelchairs are categorized as follows:

1. *Standard weight.* Standard wheelchairs are heavy-duty wheelchairs that typically weigh between 40 and 50 pounds—the ones that you most often find offered as courtesy wheelchairs at the local shopping mall, hotel, or hospital. These frames tend to be very durable (almost indestructible) and are made from low-grade steel. The weight of the frame, however, can make these wheelchairs difficult to push, to lift, and to load into your vehicle for transporting. They are the least expensive option in manual wheelchair frames and provide no positioning benefits for people affected with ALS.

2. *Lightweight.* Lightweight wheelchairs typically weigh between 30 and 40 pounds. The frames are made from strong lighter metals such as aluminum. The lighter weight makes them attractive for ease of propulsion (energy conservation) and transporting. There typically are more options available on lightweight frames (compared with standard frames) to allow customization of the wheelchair for your needs.

3. *Manual positioning chairs.* These positioning chairs are called Tilt-N-Space chairs. These chairs provide the best positioning for people with muscle weakness and for individuals who have a pressure sore or are at risk for a pressure sore. A Tilt-N-Space chair will distribute weight from your seat to your back, allowing blood to flow in weight-bearing parts of your body.

4. *Ultralightweight.* Ultralightweight wheelchairs are most often prescribed for very active users (including wheelchair athletes) or for those whose limited energy reserves severely restrict their activity. The frames are constructed from extremely light, more expensive materials

such as titanium or carbon fiber, which keeps the weight well under 30 pounds.

5. *Transport.* Lightweight transport wheelchairs have four small wheels and are foldable, making them perfect for transporting in the trunk of a car. Caregivers will find them easy to push, but they cannot be self-propelled. They are useful for short outings such as doctor appointments or trips to the mall for those who do not require postural support.

## Power Wheelchairs

A power wheelchair base consists of two direct drive motors (one to power each drive wheel of the wheelchair), two deep-cycle rechargeable batteries, and the electronics or the "brains" of the wheelchair. A power wheelchair is operated by using a drive control, most commonly a joystick (similar to video game joysticks).

Power wheelchairs are categorized according to the placement of the drive wheels that power the wheelchair:

1. *Rear-wheel drive (RWD).* On an RWD power wheelchair, the drive wheels are positioned to the rear of the base, behind you. RWD power wheelchairs tend to be quite stable because your weight and the weight of the wheelchair usually are well distributed across the total length of the wheelchair. As such, they are able to smoothly handle changes in gradient, such as ramps and curb cuts. RWD power wheelchairs, however, require more space to maneuver in terms of turning radius (compared with a mid- or front-wheel drive power wheelchair) and therefore may not offer the accessibility needed to navigate within small or cluttered environments or to make tight turns from narrow hallways. RWD power wheelchairs are not usually a good choice for people with ALS because they are more difficult to drive.

2. *Mid-wheel drive (MWD).* The drive wheels on MWD wheelchairs are positioned directly under you. This effectively allows the wheelchair to spin on its base much like a lazy Susan. MWD power wheelchairs offer the smallest full (360°) turning radius and therefore provide optimal access in tight spaces such as galley-style kitchens or bathrooms. The MWD wheelchairs have two small caster wheels on the back and two small caster wheels in the front. These wheels are usually about 6 inches in height and offer stability when driving up and down hills. The MWD chair is a popular choice for people with ALS mainly because it is easier to drive in smaller halls and apartments.

3. *Front-wheel drive (FWD).* The drive wheels on a FWD power wheelchair are located in the most forward position of any other power wheelchair base. This style of wheelchair base offers optimal stability similar to a MWD chair, so no antitip devices are needed. FWD power wheelchairs navigate environmental obstacles such as curbs better than MWD

or RWD wheelchairs do, and they offer maneuverability and accessibility comparable to that of a MWD wheelchair.

All power wheelchair bases can include up to 4 power seating functions: tilt, recline, power legs, and seat elevation. In addition, an attendant control can be mounted behind the chair for the caregiver. Each has the ability to accept alternative drives (driving without using a standard joystick) at any point after original delivery. It is very important that your evaluator and supplier build the chair to address your current needs, but they must never lose sight of what you will need as the disease progresses. To start, only a few power features may be used more often than others, but as the disease progresses, all the power features will be ready when you need them.

Tremendous technological and design advances have been made in the power wheelchair industry over recent years. The technology exists to allow you to operate a power wheelchair with almost any part of your body, including your head, chin, arm, finger, foot, tongue, or even your breath. Although hand-operated joysticks are standard, careful consideration must be given to what type of drive control will work best for you, based on your abilities and disease symptoms.

The electronics that run the drive control are mini, onboard computers. The wheelchair is programmed to operate in accordance with your abilities, needs, preferences, and environmental demands. There are varying levels of sophistication in the electronics packages that are used on power wheelchair bases. With more basic electronics packages, you may be able to adjust only the maximum speed. On the other hand, high-end electronics can offer you complete freedom in programming all parameters of how your wheelchair system will perform, including maximum speed, acceleration and deceleration, turning speeds, torque, and so forth. Additionally, power control of tilt, recline, seat elevation, and leg elevation are available. This allows the operation of the wheelchair to be fully customized to match your changing physical abilities. Some of the high-end electronics packages will also interface with other assistive technologies. Interfaces can permit your wheelchair control device to also run your computer, television, and lights.

## Which Is Better for Me—A Manual Wheelchair or a Power Wheelchair?

There are many factors to consider when deciding between a manual wheelchair and a power wheelchair. If you choose to purchase a manual wheelchair, you will likely have to rely on someone else's assistance to move from one place to another and to adjust your chair's features, such as tilt, recline, and leg elevation. Power wheelchairs allow for independent mobility and adjustment of your chair's power features. This is a *very important and personal* decision—one that only you and your family can make. Power wheelchairs certainly cost more than manual wheelchairs, and the more sophisticated your power wheelchair system, the greater will be the cost. If you are required to make an out-of-pocket contribution toward the purchase price, the cost of a power wheelchair system may be prohibitive. As discussed earlier, it is important to complete a preverification of your insurance prior to the evaluation because many insurance companies will pay for a power wheelchair with little or no cost to you. For example, Medicare will pay 80% and, if you have a secondary insurance, they will pay the 20% balance. Get the facts before your evaluation and discuss your insurance coverage with your therapist and supplier.

Consideration must be given to how you will transport the device. How will you lift and load the device into your vehicle? Which vehicle do you travel in most? How large is the trunk or cargo area? Certainly, in the area of transportation, manual wheelchairs are more portable than power devices. A number of power bases are marketed as "portable," but they generally require some assembly and disassembly; taking apart and putting together a power wheelchair system may be a major inconvenience and not practical to do on a regular basis. In addition, despite the portability of a power base, someone still needs to be capable of lifting the motors and wheelchair frame (which together may range in weight from 30 to more than 60 pounds) in and out of your vehicle. One alternative would be to purchase a power hoist for your vehicle. Another choice would be to purchase a lift-equipped van that is designed for wheelchair transportation. Either of these options can involve a significant out-of-pocket expense because many insurance sources do not consider vehicle modification a medical necessity. Another option would be to purchase (or borrow) a second wheelchair (a manual one) for community outings. It is important to note that power chairs that can be taken apart are not recommended for people affected with ALS because they offer no positioning benefit and are often unsafe. Consult with your therapist before making a purchase.

### Power-Operated Vehicles

The term *power-operated vehicle* refers to a category of devices more commonly known as "scooters." Power scooters typically have 3 wheels (although 4-wheeled models are available), a platform base, a tiller-style drive control that typically has handle bars (similar to those of a bicycle), one or more motors, and one or two deep-cycle rechargeable batteries. The throttle is usually either a thumb throttle or a squeeze throttle—either, however, requires relatively good hand control and muscle endurance to safely operate the device. Some scooters have joystick or switch controls that look very similar to light-duty power wheelchairs. However, unlike a power wheelchair, the seating and drive devices cannot be customized or redesigned as symptoms change. It becomes infinitely more difficult to steer and maneuver this type of device when arm, hand, and/ or back weakness worsen. Additionally, the seat of a scooter requires that you maintain an erect sitting posture and cannot be adapted to accommodate trunk or neck weakness that may eventually make sitting without support impossible. Although this type of device may be well suited to you in the early stages of ALS, perhaps when long-distance walking is difficult, the use of a scooter may be limited in later months or years as your muscle weakness progresses. This may cause problems with the funding of a new device if your medical insurance was involved in the previous purchase of a scooter; most insurance companies consider a scooter a power mobility device and, therefore, may not fund a second power wheelchair device.

## Customizing the Wheelchair Features for You

Prescription wheelchairs are built at the factory to meet your individual specifications. Once you have decided on a type of wheelchair base, manual or power, you and your evaluator and your certified supplier will begin customizing the features and options to meet your personal needs.

### Wheelchair Dimensions

The size of the wheelchair is heavily influenced by your height, weight, and body dimensions. However, accessibility is also a consideration. For example, your hip width may measure 18 inches, but a wheelchair with an 18-inch-wide seat may be too wide overall to fit through your doorways. A 16-inch-wide seat may be a bit skimpy, but it may keep the wheelchair narrow enough to allow free movement around your home.

### Wheels

1. *Mag (molded)*. The term *mag* refers to magnesium, which was originally used to create a wheel in the molded style. Mag wheels are now made of a solid or composite material, usually nylon, plastic, or aluminum. Mag wheels are standard on all power wheelchairs but are an option on manual wheelchairs. They are virtually maintenance-free and require only periodic cleaning. There is no risk of corrosion in damp conditions because they are made of synthetic materials. However, they are slightly heavier and have more limited shock-absorption qualities than a spoked wheel.
2. *Spoked*. Spoked wheels resemble bicycle tires and are available only on manual wheelchairs. They are lighter than mag wheels but require more maintenance, including periodic adjustment of the spokes (to maintain proper tension) and replacement of broken or bent spokes. Additionally, spoked wheels are more difficult to maintain in damp climates because of the risk of corrosion.

Removable or quick-release rear wheels and/or casters are an option on some manual wheelchair frames. This feature can be useful in making the frame lighter for lifting, or smaller for transporting in vehicles with smaller cargo areas.

*Tires*

1. *Polyurethane.* Polyurethane or solid-rubber tires do not require air and therefore are considered maintenance free. They roll easily on smooth surfaces, but they offer little shock absorption on rough or uneven terrain and less traction on wet surfaces. They also are heavier than an air-filled tire. Manual wheelchairs may be ordered with polyurethane tires front and back, but they are offered only as a caster option for power wheelchairs.

2. *Pneumatic.* Pneumatic tires are air-filled inner tubes with a tread. They offer the best shock absorption and optimal maneuverability and traction on rough or uneven terrains. However, just like the tires on your car or bicycle, they require regular maintenance to maintain air pressure, and there is a risk of getting a flat.

3. *Flat free.* In a flat-free tire, a solid insert replaces the inner air tube. With this, you have a no-maintenance tire with the benefit of a tread for traction. Flat-free tires are somewhat heavier than air-filled tires and offer slightly reduced shock absorption, but for many users the benefits (no flat tires and no maintenance of tire pressure) outweigh these drawbacks.

## Wheel Size

Standard rear wheels used on adult manual wheelchairs are 24 inches in diameter, although 22-inch and 26-inch tires are also available. The choice of wheel size, in part, is determined by your body size (how well you are able to reach the wheel), but ease of propulsion and overall seat height (the larger the wheel, the higher the seat height) are also considerations. Large rear wheels (at least 20 inches in diameter) are paramount if your family or friends will be "bumping" you in the manual wheelchair up and down stairs (consider places where you travel where there are no ramps)—smaller wheels are unable to climb the gradient between most steps.

Standard rear wheels on direct-drive power wheelchairs are usually 12 or 14 inches in diameter. Either size is capable of handling outdoor terrains without difficulty.

## Wheel Locks

Wheel locks are used to prevent rolling of the wheelchair at rest. *Wheel Locks Are Not Brakes!* They are not designed to slow down or stop a moving wheelchair—in fact, you may incur injury if wheel locks are used in this manner. The wheel locks on a manual wheelchair are most commonly located in front of the rear wheels, just below the level of the seat. They may be push-to-lock or pull-to-lock operated. Pull-to-lock wheel locks generally move the wheel lock lever out of the way for side-to-side transfers in and out of the wheelchair. Extension handles for wheel locks are helpful if your hands are weak because they reduce the amount of power needed to engage the wheel locks.

Power mobility devices (wheelchair and scooters) are equipped with an automatic braking system that allows them to stop and remain stationary on flat surfaces, as well as inclined and declined surfaces.

## Caster Size

Casters also come in different sizes, and size must be specified on the prescription.

1. *Larger casters* (8 inches). Eight-inch casters are better able to overcome environmental obstacles, such as cracks in the sidewalk or the gap in the elevator, but they require more space to maneuver. They are well suited to outdoor use.
2. *Smaller casters* (6, 5, 3 inches, etc.). Smaller casters increase the turning maneuverability of the wheelchair, but greater personal strength is needed to get across door thresholds or to overcome other environmental obstacles.

## Back Height

The height of the back support provided by the wheelchair is dictated by the length of your upper body and the strength of your trunk. On some wheelchair styles, the rear back posts are height-adjustable, which offers you the option to later raise the height of the back support (a few inches maximum) if necessary. Typically, back support that is lower requires good trunk strength and balance.

## Seat Height

Seat height is measured from the floor to the level of the seat surface and is determined in part by your lower leg length as well as by whether you want your feet to contact the ground (for foot propulsion of a manual wheelchair frame or for transfers). Seat height is an important consideration for environmental access, including knee clearance under tables and vehicle access. Don't forget to factor in the thickness of your seat cushion when calculating the overall seat height of your wheelchair system.

## Armrests

When well fitted, armrest supports should support the forearm without raising or lowering the shoulders and should increase your stability and balance when sitting. They also provide a surface to push against to relieve sitting pressures (push-ups) and to transfer out of the wheelchair. When deciding on an armrest style, consider whether you will want the armrest support to swing out of the way/flip back and/or remove from the wheelchair frame altogether (relative to your transfer method, need for tabletop access, etc.).

1. *Swing-away.* Swing-away armrest supports typically are tubular with a layer of thin foam padding. They are the lightest style of armrest support, but they also tend to be the least durable over time.

2. *Full-length.* As the name implies, full-length armrests run the full length of the seat. Full-length armrest supports provide a greater surface area on which to rest your arms, which may affect your comfort. The longer pads may assist you in using your arm strength to rise to standing or to control a descent into the wheelchair. Additionally, this style of armrest is more conducive to using a lap tray support. However, the length of the pad may prevent you from gaining close access to tabletop surfaces for eating meals, using a computer, and so forth, unless the armrests are moved out of the way.

3. *Desk-length.* Desk-length armrests are shorter and allow you tabletop access with the armrests in place. The shorter length of the armrest may make independent or assisted transfers in and out of the wheelchair more difficult because you must reach farther behind your body to access the support surfaces. They also allow you to get closer to tables or desks.

Both full-length and desk-length armrests may be ordered with either fixed height or a height-adjustable feature. Because fixed-height armrests are non–height adjustable, they are slightly lighter in weight than height-adjustable armrests. The height of the fixed armrest should allow you to use the support without reaching. Adjustable-height armrests are needed if fixed-height armrests are too low for you.

### Foot Supports

Foot supports or footrests are used to support the legs and protect the feet from dragging on the ground or getting caught in the front casters. When the footrests are adjusted appropriately, your hips and knees are level; the weight of your thighs should then be evenly distributed on the seat surface, which will add to your comfort. If the footrests are adjusted to be too short, you may experience excessive pressure on your buttocks, your feet may slip off the footplates when traversing bumpy surfaces or during quick changes in direction, or your legs may roll outward (frog's legs) or inward (knock-knees). Conversely, if they are adjusted to be too long, you will experience excessive pressure behind the knees and possibly lower-back pain. It is ideal for the footplate to have at least 2 inches of clearance from the ground to clear uneven surfaces.

Most footrests can swing out of the way and/or be removed altogether, which provides for less interference during transfers in and out of the wheelchair. The angle at which the footrests protrude forward may be specified for 70°, 80°, or 90° on some models, depending on the flexibility of your knees, which position is most comfortable, and your accessibility needs—the farther they stick out, the more overall space is needed to turn and maneuver the wheelchair. Tapered footrests are available on some models; these position your feet closer together and may improve your accessibility (by requiring less space for turning). The footplates on tapered footrests tend to be smaller than those on nontapered front rigging and may not provide a large enough surface to adequately support your feet.

Footrests with an elevating feature are called *legrests*. They allow the lower leg to be elevated slightly if swelling, knee pain, or knee range of motion is a problem. Legrests do add weight and greater length to your wheelchair system, which may affect accessibility.

### Seat Cushions

Wheelchair seat cushions are designed and selected to provide dynamic stability—meaning they provide a stable base at the pelvis from which activity can be performed by using your arms or head. Additionally, they are used to keep you comfortable when sitting for long periods in the wheelchair by better distributing pressure incurred on your buttocks and thighs. People who spend a greater time sitting in a wheelchair usually require greater pressure relief than those who use a wheelchair only occasionally. Wheelchair seat cushions are made from a variety of materials. The most common seat cushions are made from foam (polyurethane, latex, or viscoelastic). The foam compresses to conform to the contours of your body when you sit. Foam cushions tend to be lightweight, low-maintenance, and the least expensive. Foam does break down over time, losing its ability to spring back and provide support. Foam cushions that are used daily need to be replaced yearly. Other seat cushion mediums include gel, viscous fluid, water, and air. These cushions are designed to "float" bony areas, such as your tailbone or sitting bones, and to prevent them from butting up against a firm surface, which can obstruct the circulation of blood to the skin. These cushions offer greater pressure relief, which, in general, means less pelvic and trunk stability; a balance between pressure relief and stability determines the most appropriate cushion. Although these cushions are designed to allow you to sit more comfortably for longer periods, they certainly do not replace the need for you to move between seat surfaces periodically throughout the day to avoid the development of pressure ulcers. These types of cushions are more expensive than foam cushions, and some makes and models require routine maintenance. However, with appropriate care they may not need replacing for years.

When selecting wheelchair seat cushions (and covers), we must determine what level of sitting tolerance you have currently. The clinician will always keep in mind what is the best cushion to meet your current needs while planning for what you will need as the disease progresses. Important note: A gel or air cushion is often recommended.

- Do you have any soreness in your buttocks or thighs?
- How much time will you be sitting?
- Can your weight shift independently?

Below are some cushion features that should be considered:

- The weight of the cushion (in particular, if you are self-propelling in a manual wheelchair).
- The ability of the cushion to repel fluids, bodily (perspiration, urine, etc.) or otherwise.

- The air exchange properties of the cushion (remember what it is like to sit on vinyl car seats on a hot day!).
- How the cushion is cleaned—many may be wiped clean with a cloth by using a gentle cleanser such as dishwashing liquid, and others can be thrown right into your washing machine!

The surface of a wheelchair seat cushion may be flat (planar) or may have some shape (contoured). Your evaluator will offer valuable input as to which style of seat cushion he or she would recommend for you based on the results of the physical evaluation (i.e., depending on how much support and positioning you require to maintain good sitting posture). You also will want to consider ease of movement in sitting—seat cushions with contours can restrict your lower body movement.

## Back Supports

The purpose of a wheelchair back support is to maintain the natural curves of your spine. Wheelchair systems, particularly manual ones, often have an upholstered or fabric back support. This may be adequate for the occasional or light user. An upholstered back support is light and allows a collapsible frame to be easily folded. However, the fabric does stretch or hammock with use and requires replacing at routine intervals, depending on how much the wheelchair is used.

An upholstered back support may not provide enough support for many people who experience weakness and/or fatigue of the back muscles. A wide variety of backrest inserts can be used in addition to the upholstery or can replace it altogether. An insert that is used in conjunction with the upholstery has the added benefit of being transferable to any wheelchair or chair (at home, in your car, etc.). An insert that replaces the upholstery consists of a firm padded shell; it must be removed before a collapsible wheelchair frame can fold. This may sound inconvenient, but, in fact, assembly and disassembly are relatively quick and easy. For those who use more than one wheelchair system, this also allows the back support to be transferable between wheelchairs (using extra hardware packages). These inserts generally offer the greatest amount of support. Like seat cushions, back supports may be flat or contoured, depending on your needs, and may be padded with different mediums such as foam, fluid, or air. Again, your evaluator will likely offer his or her recommendation based on the results of the physical evaluation (i.e., depending on how much support and positioning you require to maintain good sitting posture).

## Head Supports

Head supports or headrests can be added to most wheelchair systems and are used to prevent the head from falling backward into hyperextension (unlike a cervical collar, which prevents the head from falling forward onto your chest). Detachable or flip-down hardware is most convenient because it allows the head support to be moved out of the way, particularly for assisted transfers in and out of the wheelchair. Headrests also may be flat or contoured. Many of the contoured supports are adjustable if the prefabricated shape does not match what you need. The headrest should support your head well both at the base of the skull and at the back of your head. Headrests can be modified and used as an alternative drive in place of a joystick if you have significant weakness in your hand that makes driving difficult or unsafe. A headrest can be used as a replacement of your joystick, called a "Head-Array."

### Pelvic Positioning Strap

A pelvic positioning strap, or lap belt, is used to help keep your hips positioned to the rear of the seat if sliding forward is a problem. It is not intended to be used as a restraint device like the seatbelts in your car.

### Trays

A lap tray or tray table is a portable tabletop surface that attaches to your armrest supports via Velcro strapping or quick release clamping hardware. A lap tray is useful for arm and hand positioning if standard armrest supports are inadequate. It also allows for easy transport of a communication device, a laptop computer, and so forth.

If you plan to use a machine to assist with your breathing (e.g., BiPAP, ventilator), make certain that your wheelchair system can be equipped with a means for carrying the device.

### Antitippers

Antitip devices are standard on power wheelchairs (except FWD) but are an option on most manual wheelchairs. These devices are a safety feature designed to decrease your risk of tipping directly backward or forward. They may be mounted on the front (MWD) or the rear of the wheelchair frame (manual, RWD). For MWD power wheelchairs, these front-mounted antitip devices can pose problems in some situations—they can get in your way during transfers in and out of the wheelchair, they can limit the angle of incline that can be traversed (such as ramps), and they can prohibit you from traversing obstacles (usually more than 3 to 5 inches high) (refer to "Power Wheelchairs—Mid-wheel drive (MWD)" for more details). Front-mounted antitip devices can be adjusted upward and can be equipped with suspension systems, but this will increase the forward rocking of your MWD power wheelchair.

### Tilt and Recline Features

Postural adjustments in a wheelchair system may be made by changing your body position relative to gravitational pull. When you sit fully upright, the force of gravity pulls directly downward through your head, neck, and trunk. If your muscles are weak or easily fatigued, this can result in poor sitting posture—slouching forward or listing to the side. By adjusting your body position relative to the force of gravity, you may actually succeed in maintaining a better, more erect sitting posture. There are generally two ways to achieve this:

1. *Recline.* When you recline, you open up the angle between the seat and back surfaces. Essentially your buttocks and thighs stay where they are, while your head, neck, and trunk lean back.

2. *Tilt-in-space.* When you are tilted, your seated position remains constant, and the entire system is tipped or angled backward. Your seated posture is the same when vertical as when tilted.

Tilt-in-space and recline features may be used alone or in combination with one another. They may be fixed (i.e., nonadjustable) or adjustable. Some of the benefits of using postural adjustments (tilt or recline) include the following:

1. *Pressure relief.* When you recline back, you increase the surface area of your body used for weight bearing. With tilt, you displace the pressure from your buttocks and thighs to your back.

2. *Gravity-assisted positioning.* With either tilt or recline, gravitational pull can be manipulated to pull you into the seat and the back and head supports (versus pulling you forward and out when you are sitting fully upright). This is a particularly good tool for positioning the head and neck. Tilt and/or recline may assist to reduce or eliminate the need for a chest harness (which can interfere with ease of breathing) to prevent forward instability of your trunk if your muscles are very weak.

3. *Sitting tolerance.* Tilt or recline can increase the overall length of time you are able to remain sitting. Because your position can be adjusted for comfort and in accordance with your level of fatigue, you can conceivably increase your sitting tolerance and reduce time spent lying down.

Your evaluator will consider a number of other medical issues when recommending tilt, recline, or both, including your transfer method, hip range-of-motion limitations, muscle spasticity, and so forth.

Tilt and recline features can be manually operated (i.e., you need someone's assistance) or power-operated (i.e., you can adjust your posture independently) and should always be used in conjunction with the appropriate head support.

### Seat Elevators

Power-operated seat elevators or seat lifts are available on some power bases. A power-operated seat lift allows you to raise the height of the seat surface approximately 6 to 8 inches from its lowest position. This feature may be used to assist you to safely transfer in and out of the wheelchair if leg weakness is a problem. It also allows you access to tabletops, countertops, and cupboards from a seated position if it is no longer safe for you to stand.

Seat elevators are not covered by Medicare although private insurances have covered them with strong documentation to support the need. Ask your therapist and supplier to review your insurance coverage.

### Power and Manual Elevating Leg Extensions

This feature is available on most power-steering systems as this will allow you to elevate your legs to different positional degrees. This is often recommended when you have swelling in the lower legs and ankles. When used in conjunction with tilt and recline, and when raised a few degrees above your heart, it assists in decreasing swelling in the lower extremities.

### Batteries and Battery Chargers

Batteries are used to power the drive motors of power wheelchair bases and to operate power options on your wheelchair system such as tilt, recline, or a seat lift feature. The batteries used on wheelchair systems are deep-cycle, rechargeable batteries and are designed to be regularly discharged slowly over time and then re-charged. They differ from the batteries that you use in your car, which are designed for quick bursts of power (to start the car) followed by recharging with an alternator. Marine batteries often are not deep-cycle batteries. How long does it take to recharge? You should always refer to the manufacturer's listed time in the owner's manual. I recommend that you set up a docking station in your home where the power charger will be at all times. This is where your power wheelchair will stay while you are not using it. You should charge the battery every night. The charging time usually lasts for about 4 to 6 hours on a low-power battery. Again it is important to follow the owner's manual because charging times may be different.

Deep-cycle batteries can be wet lead acid or sealed lead acid, typically called *gel cell*. Wet lead acid batteries are generally less expensive than sealed lead acid or gel cell batteries, and they also offer longer running time. However, wet batteries require higher maintenance than sealed lead acid and gel cell batteries and are a potential safety hazard because of the risk of contact with battery acid. Only gel cell batteries are approved for airline travel at this time. Batteries will usually last for approximately one year before they need replacing, although this may vary depending on how much you use your wheelchair and on the inherent features of the batteries themselves—some simply last longer than others! You typically can get a full day's use from a single charge; if not, it may be time to replace the batteries.

Battery chargers can be onboard or off board. Onboard chargers are convenient in that you can plug in your wheelchair for charging almost anywhere there is an available electric socket. Onboard chargers may be preferable if you travel a lot.

*All new wheelchair systems come with an owner's maintenance manual that provides invaluable information regarding the features you have selected for your wheelchair system and their care and maintenance. Review this manual with care.*

## Which Manufacturer Should I Choose?

When deciding on a particular manufacturer for your wheelchair, it is important to consider not only cost but also the warranty, local servicing, and availability of parts. You will want repairs done expeditiously, and waiting for parts from halfway around the world can put a crimp in your plans! Your therapist and the supplier will have more information regarding what manufacturer you should choose. The repairs are usually completed by the supplier and they would process them through your insurance company. It would be wise to ask your supplier about their repair policy. There are some suppliers who only sell equipment and don't repair it.

## Will My Insurance Pay for My Wheelchair System?

Most medical insurance sources will consider funding wheelchair equipment, provided the equipment is considered *medically necessary*—in other words, the expense is justified by your medical condition. This is where the knowledge and skill of your evaluator and supplier become integral. He or she often will assume the responsibility for preparing the justification strategy or documentation that systematically outlines the medical need for all the pieces and parts of your system. The more thorough the medical documentation, the less likely your need(s) will be questioned, and the more likely your insurance coverage for the purchase will be optimized. Most (if not all) insurance sources require a medical prescription for the wheelchair system, so talk to your physician in advance.

Carefully consider your options. If you are at all interested in power mobility, reserve your medical insurance coverage for the purchase of a power wheelchair. Choose a system that is modular, where changes can readily be made relative to your changing abilities—it is far easier to justify the medical need for modifications to an existing wheelchair system than it is to justify the need to replace the system altogether.

Obtaining a customized wheelchair, whether it is power or manual, can be lengthy. The industry average is longer than 3 months; therefore, it is a good idea to begin the process as early as possible. Physicians will often prescribe a wheelchair before significant weakness is apparent.

### Medicare

As your primary insurer, Medicare generally will pay for 80% of a preestablished fee for your wheelchair. You or your coinsurance(s) (if you have any) will be responsible for the remaining 20% of the cost. You should review your plan because some coinsurances have a maximum benefit and you would be responsible for the balance after your coinsurance has been met.

With manual wheelchair frames, Medicare operates under a *capped rental program*. This means Medicare pays your dealer (the company from whom you purchase your wheelchair) a monthly fee, which is intended over time to cover the purchase cost of the frame as well as the cost of routine maintenance and repairs. These payments continue for 15 months. However, before the full 15 months have expired, you should receive written notification from your equipment dealer asking whether you wish to continue renting the wheelchair or if you wish to purchase it. In the event that you opt to purchase the wheelchair, the payments that Medicare has made thus far are converted toward the purchase, and the wheelchair becomes part of your estate. Medicare generally will continue to cover the cost of maintenance and repairs that are considered "reasonable." If you choose to continue renting the wheelchair, Medicare will continue to pay for routine servicing of the wheelchair, but it will have to be returned to your dealer when you no longer need it. Most therapists and suppliers do not recommend renting power or manual equipment because these are not appropriate for people needing customized equipment. Often families will rent a manual chair as an interim as they wait for their customized equipment to be delivered and then return the rental when the new wheelchair arrives. Medicare will not pay for both a rental and a new wheelchair.

Medicare usually purchases power mobility bases (wheelchairs or scooters) outright and usually will cover the cost of routine servicing and repairs. Seating items such as seat cushions and customized back supports, whether used on a manual or a power mobility base, are considered items covered by Medicare because of the intimacy of contact associated with their use.

As of April 2007 Medicare requires that everyone in need of a power wheelchair must have a face-to-face examination with his or her doctor, who must chart the discussion in his or her notes. In addition, the supplier must complete an in-person home evaluation for power and over-the-phone evaluation for manual wheelchairs. This information will be requested by your supplier as part of the authorization process. The supplier cannot provide equipment until this requirement is met, extending the waiting time.

If families decide that hospice is the best option, it is important to note that Medicare will not pay for equipment if you enroll in hospice. Before enrolling call your therapist and supplier because they will give you guidance. Most therapists understand how hospice works. Discussing your hospice intentions at the initial evaluation will be extremely beneficial to you and your family.

## Medicaid

As your primary insurer, Medicaid usually will pay for most or all of the cost of a wheelchair system that is considered medically necessary, although every state has its own policies and procedures. Detailed medical justification and pre-authorization are common in most states, so the process of obtaining coverage for purchase of a wheelchair can be quite lengthy (months). If you choose a reputable supplier who understands your state Medicaid program, the process can be much quicker.

## Private Medical Insurance Policies

Private insurance coverage for durable medical equipment such as wheelchairs varies greatly—from no coverage at all to 100% coverage. Verify the specifics of your policy either by reviewing your contract at home or by contacting your insurance provider directly.

## Coinsurance

If you are fortunate enough to have more than one medical insurance source, the secondary and tertiary coverage sources often will consider paying for the portion of the cost of your wheelchair system that is not covered by your primary provider. Coinsurance sources typically will not pay for a wheelchair system if the claim has been denied by your primary insurance provider.

### How Long Will It Take for Me to Get My Wheelchair?

The medical review process begins once the necessary documentation is provided to your insurance source. During the review, your primary insurance source reviews the claim and determines your eligibility to receive this insurance benefit. This internal review process by your insurance carrier can take from a few weeks to several months to be completed. The ordering, shipping, and fitting of your system can add another few weeks to the process, so be proactive relative to obtaining your wheelchair. Anticipate your future needs as best as you can, and do not wait until you are in crisis before you initiate getting a wheelchair.

### What If My Insurance Denies My Claim?

In many cases when insurance sources deny requests for funding of wheelchair systems, it is because they need additional information (i.e., the medical necessity on the original claim was not clear enough). You may request that your claim be re-reviewed by your primary insurer, at which time additional relevant information should be submitted relative to your medical need for the equipment. Self-purchase remains an option in the event that insurance funding is denied. Alternative funding sources include the Department of Veterans Affairs (for some veterans), charitable funding from the MDA and local social service agencies, and donations from family, coworkers, and/or friends.

### Where Should I Buy My Wheelchair?

Some insurance sources allow you to use the dealer of your choice, whereas others, particularly health maintenance organizations (HMOs), have preferred providers for durable medical equipment. For you as the consumer, this means your coverage (percentage of the total cost of the wheelchair system paid by your insurance) is better if you use one of the equipment dealers specified in the list of preferred providers. If you choose to use a dealer outside this provider network, you likely will incur a penalty (which often amounts to greater out-of-pocket expense). Your medical insurance source can provide you with a list of preferred providers in your area.

Certain industry standards can be used in researching a reputable wheelchair dealer in your area. Find out if the company you are considering is approved by the Joint Commission for Accreditation of Healthcare Organizations (JCAHO). JCAHO is an independent, not-for-profit organization whose mandate is to establish minimum professional standards for the industry and to regularly evaluate the compliance of the company against these standards. JCAHO accreditation is recognized throughout the health care industry as representative of quality service. You also may wish to inquire whether the dealer has employees who are members of the National Registry of Rehabilitation Technology Suppliers (NRRTS).

NRRTS was established to credential individuals who provide rehabilitation technology equipment such as wheelchairs. It has standards of practice and ethics to which each member must adhere in order to maintain membership. In addition, seek the frank opinions of other consumers who use wheelchairs. If you do not know anyone personally, check with your local ALS Association. Use the Internet. Ask your evaluator who he or she recommends in your area. Inquire about each company's reputation regarding customer service, reliability, and both routine and emergency maintenance issues. Will they offer you a test drive of the wheelchair equipment you are considering? Although the trial equipment may not have the exact features and proportions for you, a test drive will provide invaluable information about the equipment that you cannot possibly learn from a brochure—how the equipment drives, its maneuverability, how well it fits into your home or car, and so forth.

## Summary

Consumers need to be proactive with regard to their personal well-being. Selecting a wheelchair system can be challenging, but, like anything else, the more information you have, the more educated your decisions will be. A carefully selected wheelchair system will allow you to continue at your maximal level of independence and comfort—certainly for much longer than an inappropriate wheelchair system.

## Suggested Reading

Brubaker, CE. Ergonomic considerations. *J Rehab R&D.* 1990;(suppl 2):37–48.

Dicianno BE, Tovey E. Power mobility device provision: understanding Medicare guidelines and advocating for clients. *Arch Phys Med Rehabil.* 2007;88(6):807–816.

Health Care Financing Administration. *Region B DMERC Supplier Bulletin.* Indianapolis, IN: AdminaStar Federal; 2007.

Joint Commission on Accreditation of Healthcare Organizations. Facts about the Joint Commission on Accreditation of Healthcare Organizations. www.jcaho.org. Accessed July 13, 2008.

Kreutz D. Airline Travel With a Power Wheelchair. *Directions.* 2008;3:42–44. http://www.nrrts.org. Accessed July 13, 2008.

National Registry of Rehabilitation Technology Suppliers. NRRTS. http://www.nrrts.org/. Accessed 2008.

Perr A. Elements of seating and wheeled mobility intervention. *OT Pract.* 1998;3(9):16–24.

Rehabilitation Engineering and Assistive Technology Society of North America. RESNA. 1999. www.resna.org.

Roesler, T. Sitting around: Wheelchair cushion evaluation and education in pressure sore prevention. *TeamRehab.* October 1997;31. http://www.wheelchairnet.org/WCN_Prodserv/Docs/TeamRehab/TRRArchive.html. Accessed July 13, 2008.

Trail M, Nelson N, Van JN, Appel SH, Lai EC. Wheelchair use by patients with amyotrophic lateral sclerosis: a survey of user characteristics and selection preferences. *Arch Phys Med Rehabil.* 2001;82:98–102.

United States Department of Transportation. New horizons: information for the air traveler with a disability [on-line]. 2004. http://airconsumer.ost.dot.gov/publications/horizons.htm. Accessed July 13, 2008.

Warmoth M, King S. Coming together: a multidisciplinary mobility clinic can eliminate delays and hassles. *ADVANCE for Directors in Rehabilitation.* 2008;17(6):23. http://rehabilitation-director.advanceweb.com/.

# 10

# Managing Communication and Swallowing Difficulties

### Lisa Adams, Marta Kazandjian, and Winston T. Cheng

The speech-language pathologist (SLP) is an integral part of the interdisciplinary amyotrophic lateral sclerosis (ALS) team that will help the patient to manage the disease through its course. The SLP will work with the patient and caregivers in addressing two functions that have significant impact on quality of life and well-being—communication and swallowing. The role of the SLP in ALS extends beyond traditional speech therapy, in which the goal is to provide stimulation, exercises, and activities to regain lost functions or return to baseline levels. In ALS, the philosophy of maintenance and compensation frequently underlies the treatment strategies used to address the main goals of ensuring effective communication across settings and safe and efficient swallowing.

Frequently, speech may be disrupted because of the weakness of muscles involved in speaking and/or tracheostomy and ventilator dependence. Strategies are available to allow the person with ALS to continue to use speech as an effective means of communication for as long as possible. Techniques to supplement or augment speech/verbal communication can also be used to assist the person with ALS to communicate messages when speech becomes increasingly difficult to understand. If the person with ALS is experiencing respiratory difficulty, communication management may involve working closely with the respiratory therapist and physician to allow airflow through the upper airway or voice box to both speak and safely swallow. This is often needed for patients who require a tracheostomy tube. The SLP may use techniques such as tracheostomy tube cuff deflation and one-way speaking valves to achieve these goals, but not all patients will benefit from these modifications.

A change in swallowing function may also be an early symptom of ALS that co-occurs with changes in speech. This problem arises as the muscles involved in speech and swallowing become weak. The speech pathologist will help the patient understand the degree and nature of the swallowing impairment by performing simple objective tests. As the disease progresses, dietary changes and swallowing maneuvers can be used to avoid choking and *aspiration* (the entrance of food or liquid into the lungs). Strategies to address issues related to increased secretions in the mouth or drooling are also available.

Some people with ALS may also present with cognitive changes related to fron-totemporal dementia. The deterioration occurs mainly in functions such as main-taining attention to a task, recalling words, following complicated directions, and controlling impulses and mood. The SLP will take these cognitive changes into consideration because they can have a significant impact on the communication and swallowing management of the patient with ALS.

It is the role of the SLP who specializes in diseases such as ALS to con-tinually reevaluate communication and swallowing needs as they change. This proactive approach will enable you to work with the SLP to anticipate problems before they occur. In a proactive approach there is always a plan to maintain or compensate for the loss of function. This chapter discusses the various manage-ment techniques used to facilitate communication and swallowing throughout the disease process, as well as discussing the other team members who assist in meeting these goals.

## Early Communication Management

*Dysarthria* may be diagnosed in a person who presents with changes in speech clarity or voice. The characteristics of a person's dysarthria will vary depending on which group of speech muscles are affected. Weakness of breathing muscles may result in a softer voice and difficulty in projecting the voice or yelling. Some people notice changes in their voice function during activities such as singing. If the muscles of the voice box are too tight (spastic) or too loose (flaccid), the voice may sound tight and strained or breathy and hoarse. If there is reduced movement of the soft palate to prevent voice energy from escaping through the nose when talking, a hypernasal speech quality can be observed. Last, if there is weakness and slow movement of the muscles of the tongue and lips, slurred (drunk-like) speech quality and/or slowing down of speech rate may result. In the early stage, a person may only exhibit speech or voice difficulties toward the end of the day or when he or she is tired. The speech/voice disturbance may only be present or predominant in one area, and strategies are available to address each specific problem.

Reduced loudness of voice and needing to use more energy to talk can occur as a result of weakness of the breathing muscles. A person with ALS may also experience running out of air midsentence and needing to take frequent breaths when talking. These problems can easily be alleviated by using a portable voice amplifier that comes in various sizes. Although a collar or lapel microphone is more discreet, using a headset microphone with the amplifier is recommended. The close distance between the microphone head and the person's mouth eliminates the need to use more effort when talking, allowing the person to talk for a longer time without getting fatigued. Another benefit of a head-mounted microphone is that the voice is constantly amplified even if the person moves or turns his or her head. The voice amplifier can also be useful for those with a hoarse or strained voice who experience difficulty being heard, especially in noisy environments.

Many people have difficulty abandoning the practice of speaking to each other from distant rooms. This communication pattern creates frustration for both parties. A powerful amplifier or intercom in the home may be helpful in this case. A strategy of *breath grouping* is also highly effective for people who run out of air during speech, which usually occurs because a lengthy sentence is produced on one short breath. As a result, the beginning of the sentence is understandable, but the end is not. The breath-grouping strategy limits the number of words produced per breath to only about 3 or 4. A new breath must be taken for each group of words. With this technique, overall speech rate is reduced and intelligibility and volume are improved by the added airflow and breath support.

Some people with ALS have fairly good articulation or pronunciation, but they sound as if they are talking through the nose or are hypernasal because of excessive air loss through the nose. Reduced clarity and projection of speech can result. If this is the case, a device designed to lift up the soft palate or *velum* may be appropriate. This device is called a *palatal lift* and is custom-produced by a prosthodontist. It is the same as a retainer or an upper denture, except that the wax part of the denture extends further back in the mouth to lift the soft palate, as illustrated in Figure 10.1. Palatal lifts are expensive and often require multiple fittings before they are completed to ensure that airflow is stopped and comfort is maintained. Some people report restoration of louder and more understandable speech when using this device. The palatal lift may decrease the feeling of breathlessness caused by the loss of air from the nose and reduce fatigue caused by talking. Unfortunately, speech muscle deterioration can occur quickly in some people, and a palatal lift may be a short-lived therapeutic option. This may also be contraindicated for those with a hypersensitive gag reflex.

Speech clarity may be further complicated by difficulty articulating words. The SLP can introduce compensatory strategies that will improve the intelligibility of speech so that there can be a more successful exchange of messages between the person with ALS and a variety of communication partners. These strategies can also reduce the amount of effort you use in talking. They can be classified into *speaker strategies* and *environment/conversational partner strategies*. Examples of these are as follows:

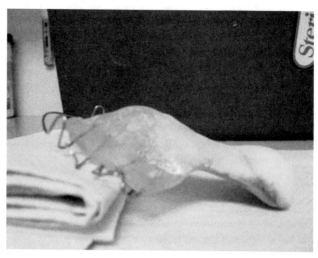

**Figure 10.1** An example of a palatal lift. Photo courtesy of Winston Cheng.

### Speaker Strategies

1. Speak at a slower rate and exaggerate the pronunciation of each word to allow proper movements of the speech muscles.
2. Take a breath after every 3 to 4 words. Avoid the habit of talking until you are completely out of air.
3. Schedule periods of voice rest (i.e., 15 to 20 minutes of no talking) when you start to notice that your speech is getting worse during conversation to allow the speech muscles to rest and recuperate. Do not overuse the muscles.
4. Schedule important conversations and phone calls during the time when your speech is at its best, usually midmorning.

### Environment/Conversational Partner Strategies

1. Make the speaking environment optimal. Avoid talking in noisy and dimly lit areas.
2. Avoid talking when your conversational partner is far from you or not facing you.
3. Encourage conversational partners with hearing loss to use hearing aids or an amplification device so that you won't need to use a loud voice and exert more effort when talking to them.
4. Ask your conversational partner to provide feedback of what they understood from your message (e.g., "You are saying something about Vermont. . . .") so that you only repeat the parts of the message not understood instead of the whole message.

Using the above strategies can be beneficial in the early stage to reduce the amount of frustration that can be caused by a breakdown in communication. Another compensatory technique is referred to as *speech supplementation,* in which an alphabet board is used as an adjunct to speech. The person points to the first letter of each word as the word is produced. If the word is not understood after 2 or 3 attempts, it is spelled out on the board. Many people who have adequate use of their hands will write to supplement messages that are not easily understood. Magic Slates or easily erasable boards are helpful. An occupational therapist might assist in recommending methods of maintaining writing through assistive devices or splinting if hand or finger weakness exists.

There has been limited research regarding the effectiveness of exercise in strengthening or maintaining muscle strength in ALS. Little to no research has addressed the specific use and benefit of oral-motor-strengthening exercises in this population. The primary concern for the use of oral-motor exercises is that they will result in fatigue of the already deteriorating muscles, which potentially might further reduce speech clarity. Encouraging ongoing use of the speech musculature through speech itself is considered the best method for maintaining muscle movement. SLPs will provide the patient with strategies as the person's speech and voice change to improve message transfer and make it possible for the person to continue to use speech as the primary mode of communication. Little research specifically discusses the benefits of oral-motor exercises to maintain muscle function for speech purposes. Muscle fatigue is a primary problem in ALS. Quite often, deterioration of speech after prolonged talking or when tired is an early symptom of ALS. Engaging in an exercise program may result in even more fatigue and prevent a person from using speech for real-life communication. To put it another way, if a patient uses up the "energy reserve" of his or her speech muscles doing speech exercises, he or she may not have enough reserve left for actual conversations/communication. Ongoing use of the speech musculature during speech itself is often the best strategy for maintaining function as long as possible.

During the early stage of dysarthria, an SLP may also discuss voice recording or voice banking. This is the process in which a person with ALS records his or her speech for later use. If the person requires the use of a communication device, these recordings can then be transferred onto the device so that it will speak the person's own voice instead of a computerized voice. Communication devices will be discussed in more detail in the next section. Because it is impossible to predict all of the sentences a person will be saying later on and because of storage limitations on the speech devices, we recommend limiting recordings to frequently used phrases/sentences and signature expressions. Voice banking can easily be done by recording each of the phrases/sentences as a separate *.wav file* by using a portable digital audio recorder/dictation device, widely available in electronic stores. Voice recording can also be done on the computer by using a microphone and preinstalled program such as Windows Media Player.

Researchers at the Nemours Speech Research Laboratory in Delaware have developed and are currently testing the Model Talker (www.modeltalker.com).

The center currently provides a free service in which a person with ALS reads a predetermined list of words/sentences and a customized synthesized voice with the features and characteristics of the person's speech/voice patterns is created. This customized voice can then be used with most communication devices on the market.

## Middle-Stage Communication Management

As speech musculature weakens and verbal communication becomes more difficult to understand, reliance on supplemental or *augmentative methods of communication* increases. Augmentative communication refers to the use of nonverbal and/or nonvocal communication strategies in addition to or as an alternative to speech. These strategies may include spelling messages on an alphabet board, pointing to items on a communication board with a list or picture symbols of frequently used messages, or using a computer that speaks, known as a speech-generating device (SGD). In middle-stage communication management, these techniques are often coupled with the use of speech for messages easily understood by familiar communication partners such as family members. The SLP who specializes in augmentative communication technology will work closely with the patient to meet his or her communication needs as physical motor function changes. An *augmentative-alternative communication (AAC) evaluation* is often recommended during this stage of the disease.

The AAC evaluation includes an assessment of the patient's current and anticipated level of speech capability, visual and hearing acuity, and physical-motor functioning. Additionally, the patient's cognitive-linguistic function is evaluated at this time to determine the ability to use specific communication strategies and techniques to augment verbal communication. During the evaluation, the SLP provides the person with ALS opportunity to try out various AAC devices and options to determine the most appropriate option(s) for the patient.

Depending on a person's experience with typing and computer technology, it may take some time before a person can adjust and be an effective AAC user. Further, some of the devices and accessories can be expensive. Health insurance may cover some or all costs related to renting or purchasing an AAC device, but the approval process may take time. At times, it may take a few months before a person receives the device after the order is placed. This can be especially problematic if speech functions are deteriorating rapidly. Therefore, having an AAC evaluation early is highly recommended.

There are some general guidelines regarding timing of AAC evaluation in persons with ALS. These guidelines were based on recent research showing that the slowing down of a person's speech rate is a key and reliable indicator of speech intelligibility or clarity in people with ALS. Speech rate refers to the number of words one can speak per unit of time. The normal rate is up to 200 words per minute (wpm). Research has found that rapid deterioration of speech intelligibility occurs once a person's speech rate slows down to 125 wpm (1). The recommendations are as follows:

1. Regular monitoring of speech rate and intelligibility is recommended once speaking rate slows down to 150 wpm. If regular visit to an SLP is not possible, monitoring via the telephone is suggested.
2. An AAC evaluation is strongly recommended if the speaking rate slows down to 125 wpm, even though a person's speech is understood more than 90% of the time (90% intelligible).
3. If, at any time, speech intelligibility falls below 90%, an AAC evaluation should be performed.

The AAC evaluation can be conducted in a clinic, a hospital, or the home. If persons with ALS have difficulty ambulating or are nonambulatory, they should be optimally seated and positioned in the place they spend most of their time (i.e., easy chair, wheelchair, bed) so that the most common real-life communication situation can be replicated. The SLP, often with the assistance of an occupational therapist or a physical therapist, will assess any available motor movements to determine the one that is most *functional*. A functional motor movement may be any small movement of a muscle or body part that can be readily controlled consistently and reliably. The physical motor movement can then be used to control the AAC system. This movement is referred to as an *access method*. This access method may change as the disease progresses and motor movement becomes less reliable.

*Direct selection* is often the access method of choice during this stage of communication function. It is considered the quickest method of access because a body part, such as a finger for pointing or typing, selects the desired letter or key. It is sometimes necessary to provide adaptive equipment to make the arm or hand functional. For example, if the shoulder or wrist is weak, assistive devices to support the arm may make the hand and fingers more reliable for typing and using as a direct selection method. Assistive devices are prescribed and implemented by the occupational therapist or physical therapist. Occupational and physical therapists will work closely with the SLP as physical motor function changes in an effort to maintain and compensate for decreased muscle strength and allow continued access to the speech device.

## Low-Technology Options

Communication options have a range of sophistication and complexity. The specific communication needs and physical abilities often will determine which AAC device/options are chosen. Other factors to consider include communication partners, the various environments in which communication will take place, vocational needs, literacy, physical ability, and so forth. Low-technology options involve handmade or prefabricated alphabet-phrase boards or picture boards. These boards may be small enough to fit in a pocket and can be used in combination with speech or as an alternative to speech with unfamiliar listeners. The Eye Link

(Figure 10.2) is another example of a low-technology option that uses eye gaze as a direct selection method. Eye gaze is an extremely useful method of selection for patients who want to communicate rapidly but cannot point with a finger. This device, which is commercially available or can be created at home, has letters of the alphabet organized on a piece of clear plastic. The listener holds the clear plastic with the letters facing the person with ALS. He or she looks directly at each letter of his message. The listener or communication partner follows the patient's eyes and "links" eye gaze as each letter is deciphered and words are spelled out. The process continues for each letter until the message is completed.

## High-Technology Options

During middle-stage communication management, the person with ALS may begin to have significant difficulty with speech, especially with unfamiliar listeners or in noisy environments. However, he or she may still be physically active, either walking or moving about in a wheelchair. The following section reviews options that allow for maintaining communication through computerized speech, over the phone, and through writing.

Many people with ALS seek assistance in maintaining phone use even when speech becomes too difficult to understand when not speaking face to face. If he or she has finger use for typing, a Telecommunications Device for the Deaf (TDD/TTY) may be considered. Although this device is designed for people who are deaf, it may help to maintain phone use for those who are speech impaired. The user types in the message instead of speaking over the telephone. The message is sent to another TDD and can be read on a display. If the communication partner does not have a TDD available, a third party or a relay operator reads the message aloud. The communication partner replies verbally to the patient. The telephone company offers this service through their "Services for People With Disability." For patients who have sufficient physical motor control, sending text messages on cellular phones or using a BlackBerry can also serve as an alternative means of communication.

Many patients use desktop personal computers or a laptop for work or pleasure, primarily to produce written text, to send electronic mail, or to use online services. People with a moderate degree of physical motor deterioration and who still have hand function can use a personal computer with ongoing modifications. People who have difficulty controlling the movement of a mouse or manipulating the click button on the mouse can explore alternatives to the standard mouse. One alternative is a trackball, which can be rolled in a variety of directions by using very small finger movements. Many programs are now equipped with a dwell feature in which an icon is automatically clicked on when the mouse cursor is left in one area for a specified amount of time. Many alternative mouse products can be purchased in standard computer stores.

When alternatives to the standard mouse are used, they are commonly coupled with *onscreen keyboards* to allow ongoing direct selection. Communication software programs are available that bypass the standard keyboard and allow a person

Communication
partner

Patient

1. Hold sheet in front of the patient
2. Have patient focus on the first letter of the word desired
3. Move sheet until your eyes "link" with the patient's
   through the desired letter
4. Check with the patient to see if you are correct
5. Continue the process until you get the message

**Figure 10.2** Instructions for using an Eye-Link. From Dikeman KJ, Kazandjian MS. *Communication and Swallowing Management of Tracheostomized and Ventilator Dependent Adults.* 2nd ed. Belmont, CA: Delmar Learning; 2003:211. Reproduced with permission. www.cengage.com/permissions.

with limited physical motor control of the hands and/or fingers to type by selecting each desired letter shown on the computer screen. Those who do not have good hand function but who maintain good head and neck movement may be able to operate a computer through the use of a head-pointing device. With this technology, the user wears a small reflective sticker, usually on the tip of the nose, forehead, or chin. A sensor attached to the computer senses this sticker and interprets its movement on the computer screen as mouse movement. Therefore, the mouse is controlled by small movements of the head. The mouse click can be accomplished via the dwell feature. Specialized software is also available that provides *keystroke-saving options.* These options enhance the speed with which a person can type by providing *word prediction* and *abbreviation expansion.* Word prediction is a typing or rate enhancement tool in which the software attempts to guess what the user is trying to say. As he or she types, a prediction box appears on the screen. The user checks to see if the correct word or phrase is being predicted from the few letters that have been typed. If the word is available in the box, the user needs only to choose a single number. This saves time and energy for the typist. Abbreviation expansion is a method of abbreviating frequently used word, phrases, and sentences. Lengthy items can be retrieved by simply typing in 2 or 3 letters. For example, TM = "Hi, this is Tom Murray. I am using a computer to help me communicate with you." This type of software is designed to work well with other standard computer software programs. An additional benefit to using specialized communication software is that *environmental control* options are often built into the software. Environmental control is a function that allows the computer user to manipulate appliances in the environment through the computer. This may include lights, television, or an electric bed. Each appliance is fitted with a small module that permits it to be controlled by a computer. This may be highly beneficial for individuals who continue to work and require increased independence in manipulating the environment.

For people with limited hand functions but with fairly intact speech and voice functions, they can type a document or e-mail on the computer by using *voice recognition software,* which converts the user's speech into text form on the computer. This may be used as a temporary option before speech intelligibility deteriorates.

Although the personal computer is an excellent tool for in-home use, it does not address the communication needs of the person with ALS who needs to communicate in other settings. When speech becomes too difficult to use with less familiar people or in groups, a portable communication device is recommended, typically a speech-generating device (SGD). SGD, as the name implies, refers to devices that produce speech. This may be a *notebook or laptop computer or a tablet.* An SGD can be a *dedicated communication system.* "Dedicated" means the system was developed solely for use by people who are communicatively impaired. The degree of portability needed will vary from person to person. For some individuals who are still walking, *portable* means a device that is small and lightweight enough to be carried around freely by hand or small enough to be carried in a handbag. Other devices, such as a laptop computer, may be too heavy for the ambulatory person with ALS to carry, but they can be *mounted* or fixed on a wheelchair.

A dedicated communication system will run for 8 to 10 hours on a single battery charge, making it easy to use in all communication settings. Most SGDs include high-quality synthetic speech output that substitutes for the user's actual voice. Many highly portable devices also offer *digitized speech* as an alternative to synthetic speech. Digitized speech is a recording of a person's voice and therefore has a more authentic voice quality than synthetic speech (see "Early Communication Management" section for more information). However, devices using digitized speech are usually limited to a finite number of minutes of speech output and will speak only a preset group of messages. This differs from synthetic speech, which offers a *text-to-speech* option in which any message the person types is spoken aloud. There is no limit to the number of messages that can be spoken. Users can explore devices that offer both digitized speech and synthetic speech as options. The SGD may also offer printed output, which is known as *hard copy*. Most devices do not print on their own and must be coupled with a full-sized printer to produce written output. In some cases, a device may print remotely when interfaced with a router. Some SGDs offer an enhanced two-way screen so that a message can be read when facing the person, as shown in Figure 10.3. This unique feature allows normal face-to-face communication to take place instead of side-by-side message transfer.

Although dedicated SGDs meet the communication needs of many people with ALS, the specific features that are desired by the person with ALS must be carefully considered. Some SGDs are keyboard-based. Figure 10.3 is an example of this type of SGD. These devices are better designed for individuals who have hand and finger

**Figure 10.3** An example of a portable communication device with a two-way message display. Photo courtesy of Zygo Industries, Inc. Manufactured by Toby Churchill Ltd., U.K. Distributed in North America by Zygo Industries, Inc.

function. The device may or may not continue to be usable when these movements deteriorate. Other SGDs feature a touch screen on which a user can either communicate by typing his or her message on the on-screen keyboard or by pressing buttons that speak preprogrammed messages (Figure 10.4). The latter makes communication more efficient because the number of keystrokes is reduced. For example, when a user presses a button on his or her SGD, it will automatically speak "Good morning! I'm glad to see you today," instead of the user needing to type the full greeting. Because some devices are designed to be small and highly portable, they are not equipped with all the features of a less portable system, such as a large screen or a louder and clearer voice output. Some devices are too small and may not be useful for a long time. Controlling a very small device may become impossible once hand and finger functions start to deteriorate. A dedicated SGD will not have the option to run a variety of software programs, although some SGDs can provide e-mail and Internet access. E-mail and Internet access allow even the most physically disabled person to communicate with an unlimited number of people around the world without ever leaving home. The Internet, or information superhighway, provides vast resources for people to obtain information on an unlimited number of subjects.

To obtain all of the advantages of a personal computer, you may need to select a speech device that is not solely dedicated to communication but combines the

**Figure 10.4** An example of a speech-generating device with touch-screen keyboard and preprogrammed message buttons. Photo courtesy of Dynavox Technologies, Pittsburgh, PA. 1-866-DYNAVOX.

features and flexibility of a laptop computer with the advantages of communication software. This type of system may be more appropriate for users who use multiple software programs (e.g., spreadsheets).

When selecting an augmentative communication system or an SGD, it is advisable to select a versatile SGD that can be modified or adapted as a person's needs change so that a person with ALS can continue to use the SGD for effective communication throughout the disease process.

## Late-Stage Communication Management

In the late stages of ALS, speech as a reliable mode of communication is often lost. Significant physical motor weakness throughout the body may prevent persons with ALS from using their hands or fingers as a method of directly accessing a communication device. However, residual or minute motor movements throughout the body may be used to control an SGD, such as a slight bend of a finger, a head turn, a jaw clench, an eyebrow raise, or any movement of the eyes. At this point, many patients are fitted with a *switch*. Each time they act on the switch, an activation signal is sent to the device. The switch can be fit anywhere on the body where there is a consistent, reliable motor movement, including areas of the face and eyes. Switches work in various ways. Some must be activated by pressure, whereas others react to minute movements and will sense a head turn, finger bend, or deep muscle movement. An *infrared switch* is an example of a switch that can be triggered by small movements. This type of switch casts out a beam of light. The user must execute a small motor movement, such as an eye blink or a downward movement of the eye, to break the beam of light. Figure 10.5 shows an infrared switch mounted on a headband. Once fitted with a switch, the person can control an electronic communication system by using only a single, small motor movement. Fitting the person with a switch requires experience and is best done by a speech-language pathologist, occupational therapist, or rehabilitation engineer who has a good working knowledge of switches and switch interfaces. Accurate positioning of the switch is crucial and may require input from several members of the treatment team.

In cases in which the patient cannot reliably control a switch with a body part, an eye gaze system may be considered. Electronic eye gaze systems enable a person to select letters by looking at them. Eye movements are electronically tracked, and a selection is made when the patient sustains eye gaze at an item for a predetermined amount of time. This high-level technology allows very disabled users to use a rapid direct selection technique for communication. Figure 10.6 shows a current electronic eye-gaze system for use by patients with ALS.

## Coded Systems

Switch access is provided when direct-selection techniques are no longer functional and alternate access methods are required. A switch is a piece of equipment

**Figure 10.5** A fiberoptic infrared switch mounted for use with an eye blink. Photo courtesy of AMDI, Inc.

that allows a person to bypass the keyboard. One technique that may be beneficial to a person who can activate 1 or 2 switches is *coding*. In a coded system, the person uses a code that is deciphered by the listener. The code is a combination of smaller units that stand for larger units, such as letters of the alphabet or phrases on a board. Use of a brief code to represent longer messages saves time. Coding is very useful for people who want to access a large amount of language rapidly but do not have the physical ability to accomplish it. The most commonly used code is *Morse code.* The individual using Morse code may be able to activate a buzzer system. When the buzzes are combined, they stand for letters of the alphabet. Coding

**Figure 10.6** An electronic eye-gaze system. Photo courtesy of Eye Response Technologies, www.eyeresponse.com.

can be used in a low-technology, nonelectronic system, such as an *E-Tran* (shown in Figure 10.7). It also can be used as a way of accessing an electronic or computerized communication system. When using Morse code, the series of buzzes are automatically converted by the computer into letters of the alphabet.

## Scanning

*Scanning* is another access method used by people who have functional residual motor movement but cannot rely on direct selection options because of severe physical motor weakness. Scanning with an alphabet board is a widely used

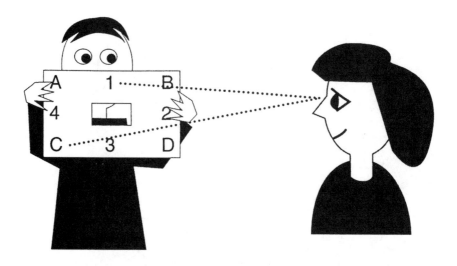

| A. Medical | B. People |
|---|---|
| 1. Call the doctor | 1. Call my husband |
| 2. Am I doing OK? | 2. I miss my kids |
| 3. Please suction me | 3. Have you seen Kris? |
| 4. I need more medicine | 4. Who are you? |
| C. Daily Needs | D. Feelings |
| 1. Please reposition me | 1. I'm sorry |
| 2. I'm hot | 2. I love you |
| 3. I need another tissue | 3. I'm happy to see you |
| 4. I'm hungry/thirsty | 4. Bug off! |

**Figure 10.7** An example of encoding through the user of an E-Tran. From Dikeman KJ, Kazandjian MS. *Communication and Swallowing Management of Tracheostomized and Ventilator Dependent Adults.* 2nd ed. Belmont, CA: Delmar Learning; 2003:215. Reproduced with permission. www.cengage.com/permissions.

method of communication for nonspeaking patients. During scanning the alphabet is accessed in groups. When row-column scanning is used, as illustrated in Figure 10.8, each row of letters is scanned until the desired row is presented. The user then executes a predetermined motor movement, such as upward eye gaze, to select that row. Each letter within the row is scanned until the desired letter is presented. The patient then executes the motor movement to select the letter. The process is repeated until each letter of the word is selected. Lengthy messages can also be spelled.

Scanning can also be accomplished electronically with a computer-based communication system. Many SGDs offer scanning as a method of input, but this should be investigated before purchase. Specialized computer software for desktop or laptop computers generally offers scanning as a method of input. To use an SGD via scanning, the user's functional motor movement must be paired with a switch. The switch controls a moving cursor on the screen. Each time the switch is activated, the cursor movement is stopped and the selection of a letter, word, or number can be made.

Many people with ALS use multiple communication systems, including low- and high-technology devices, to meet specific communication needs in specific communication environments. For example, a low-technology row-column scanning alphabet board may be used for easy message transmission from bed, a portable speech-generating device when out at a social gathering, and a desktop computer with modifications to complete work-related tasks. The SLP who specializes in

**Figure 10.8** An example of row-column scanning . Adapted from Fishman I. *Electronic Communication Aids, Selection and Use.* San Diego, CA: College-Hill Press; 1987:71. Copyright by I. Fishman.

augmentative and alternative communication should assist the patient in the selection of a variety of appropriate methods of communication at each stage of the disease so that the patient's individual communication needs are always being met.

### Brain-Computer Interface Devices

If physical motor deterioration has resulted in the loss of all controlled voluntary movement in any part of the body and, therefore, single switch use is not an option, the patient is considered *locked in,* Research in communication technology for this locked-in population has moved toward the use of brain-computer interface (BCI) devices (2). BCI is a system that uses electrodes to transmit brain wave activity presented by an electroencephalogram (EEG) to a computer. The computer monitor presents a matrix with a number of communication choices such as the alphabet. The user has to concentrate on a single item of the matrix for a selection to be recognized. BCI has been studied as a potential mode of communication in the ALS population. As the technology becomes more accessible and more research is conducted the system may eventually become an alternative communication option.

### Strategies to Facilitate the Use of Augmentative Communication in the Presence of Cognitive-Linguistic Impairment

In addition to changes in physical motor function, changes may occur in the cognitive-linguistic abilities of some patients with ALS. *Cognition* refers to thought processes and the ability to follow directions, use memory, pay attention, and recall words. *Linguistic* is the process of using language to put thoughts into words. Recent literature has shown that as many as 50% of patients with ALS may show signs and symptoms of deteriorating cognitive ability in varying degrees (3). The deterioration occurs mainly in functions such as maintaining attention to a task, recalling words, following complicated directions, and controlling impulses and mood. The specific behavioral abnormalities, often referred to as frontotemporal dementia, can coincide with ALS. These cognitive changes can have a significant impact on the communication management of the patient with ALS.

The patient with ALS who has cognitive-linguistic impairment may present with more challenges to the SLP during the teaching phase of the augmentative communication training. This patient may be more resistant to alternative communication options and more focused on the presenting bodily discomfort of the disease. Providing this patient with small tangible successes in communication may improve the willingness to move to the next level of technology. For example, using a content-specific phrase board to successfully communicate ideas and wishes during a family event may provide the positive feedback necessary to advance to other more complex modes of communication. Memory deficits have their own challenges during training and implementation of an augmentative system. Switch access training requires memory and sequencing. Scanning options provide the greatest challenge. The patient might benefit from a combination of auditory and visual feedback such as symbol/word combinations and synthetic speech output during the scanning process. The SLP should expect to spend more time training the patient with cognitive-linguistic impairments as the need for modifications arises. An SLP should also be aware of issues relating to acceptance and compliance in the use of an SGD that may be more pronounced in a patient with cognitive-linguistic impairment.

Appendix A provides a visual overview of the strategies to enhance communication as the patient with ALS moves through the disease process.

## Funding Communication Systems

Once the SLP and the patient have determined the specific type or types of augmentative-alternative communication systems needed to best meet the patient's needs, the SLP who specializes in alternative and augmentative communication techniques will formulate a prescription for the communication device and accessories. This prescription is often in the form of an evaluation, detailing the patient's physical motor status and current method of communication, and naming the desired device, software package, and accessories such as a switch or a wheelchair mounting system if needed. The managing physician then approves this prescription. Once this is accomplished, the SLP can seek an appropriate funding source to assist in payment for the communication equipment. The funding process varies widely from state to state. Some people with ALS are entitled to communication equipment through their state Medicaid or Medicare program. If the patient is privately insured, his or her insurance company should be approached to determine whether communication equipment can be funded. Policies on granting communication equipment vary widely from one insurance company to another.

Other funding sources may also be explored, including local churches or temples and organizations that perform charitable works such as fund-raising. Patients and caregivers may receive important information and funding assistance through their local ALS Association chapter and the Muscular Dystrophy Association (MDA). Some chapters may provide equipment loan banks for communication devices and other daily care items. Some people with ALS purchase second-hand equipment from an individual who no longer can use it. The SLP who frequently works in the area of ALS acts as the patient's primary advocate in the area of funding. The patient may also use the services of a public interest attorney in appealing to state and private organizations.

## Tracheostomy

At times, speech articulation remains intact but the presence of a *tracheostomy tube* creates an interruption in speech production. A *tracheostomy,* or the surgical creation of a hole in the trachea (upper airway) through the neck, is performed to provide assistance in breathing and to remove secretions. A tracheostomy tube is placed through the hole, below the level of the *vocal cords,* as shown in Figure 10.9. Air must go through the vocal cords for voice or sound to be produced.

Some tracheostomy tubes contain a *cuff.* This is a balloon on the end of the tube that, when inflated, prevents air that is coming out of the lungs from escaping up through the vocal cords, mouth, and nose. This results in a condition known as *aphonia,* or the absence of voice. Figure 10.10 illustrates airflow that is passing around the tracheostomy tube cuff during *de*flation and air that is stopped from reaching the vocal cords during cuff *in*flation. When the tracheostomy tube cuff is deflated fully or even partially, air can potentially be directed upward around the sides of the tracheostomy tube, through the vocal folds, mouth, and nose. Speech can be produced when the tracheostomy tube is occluded by a finger or other device that stops the air from moving out the tracheostomy tube. Tracheostomy tube cuffs are designed for two purposes: to stop large amounts of oral secretions from being *aspirated* or entering the lungs and to allow a patient to receive the correct amount of air that a mechanical ventilator or respirator is set to provide. Cuffs are not designed to stop large amounts of food or liquid from entering the lungs.

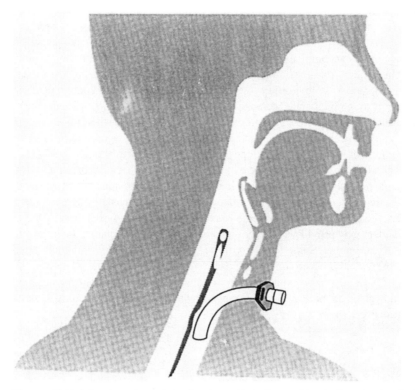

**Figure 10.9** A tracheostomy tube in place. Note its position below the level of the vocal cords. From Dikeman KJ, Kazandjian MS. *Communication and Swallowing Management of Tracheostomized and Ventilator Dependent Adults.* 2nd ed. Belmont, CA: Delmar Learning; 2003:54. Reproduced with permission. www. cengage.com/permissions.

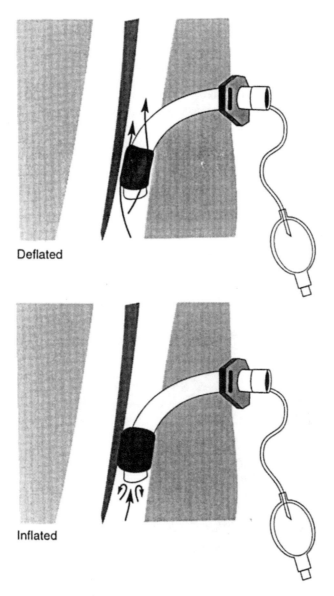

Deflated

Inflated

**Figure 10.10** A cuffed tracheostomy tube in place. Arrows indicate upward airflow. From Dikeman KJ, Kazandjian MS. *Communication and Swallowing Management of Tracheostomized and Ventilator Dependent Adults.* 2nd ed. Belmont, CA: Delmar Learning; 2003:72. Reproduced with permission. www. cengage.com/permissions.

Speech and safe swallowing can be facilitated by deflation of tracheostomy tube cuffs. When even a small amount of air is removed from the cuff, the tracheostomy tube cuff can move more easily within the neck. This allows the person to return to a more normal pattern of swallowing and to potentially produce voice. The SLP works closely with the respiratory therapist and physician to allow air to travel up through the vocal cords or voice box while ensuring that the patient on a ventilator maintains breathing.

When a patient is able to tolerate full cuff deflation, a one-way speaking valve can be considered to assist in verbal communication production. One-way valves stop air from escaping out the tracheostomy tube by redirecting the air that is breathed in, or *inspired,* and allowing it to travel up to the vocal cords. Figure 10.11 illustrates the airflow that is used for speech production when a one-way valve is placed on the tracheostomy tube. One-way valves can be used for patients who are on or off ventilators. A patient is considered a candidate only if full cuff deflation is accomplished and there is sufficient oral motor strength to mouth understandable words.

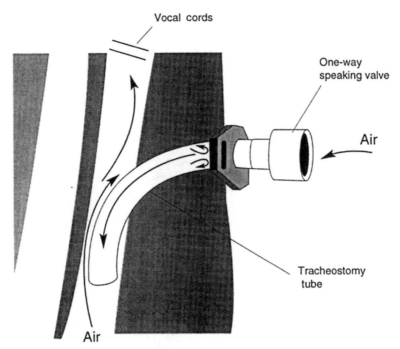

**Figure 10.11** The redirection of airflow when a one-way valve is in place on the tracheostomy tube. From Dikeman KJ, Kazandjian MS. *Communication and Swallowing Management of Tracheostomized and Ventilator Dependent Adults.* 2nd ed. Belmont, CA: Delmar Learning; 2003:165. Reproduced with permission. www.cengage.com/permissions.

## Swallowing Disorders

The loss of motor movement that results in the progressive deterioration of speech also typically results in the progressive deterioration of swallowing. The normal swallowing process is interrupted by changes in the strength and range of movement of the lips, tongue, jaw, soft palate, and vocal cords, as illustrated in Figure 10.12. Impairment in swallowing function is known as *dysphagia.* The swallowing ability of a person with ALS changes gradually. The progressive weakening of each of the oral motor structures yields its own set of problems. The loss of lip strength may make it difficult to hold food, especially liquids, in the mouth. The loss of tongue strength alters the normal movements of the tongue that are required to safely swallow foods. This includes the side-to-side movement the tongue makes that enables food to be swept onto the molars for chewing. If this movement is not accomplished, food will remain unchewed. It also includes the upward movement of the tongue that enables food to be pushed toward the back of the mouth. People with ALS often have to manage this backward food propulsion by using many swallows. When viewed by the SLP, the patient appears to be "pumping" the tongue to get it to do its work. If the tongue is weak, food may not be gathered into a *cohesive bolus,* or mass. This may result in small food particles being deposited into the crevices around the lips or

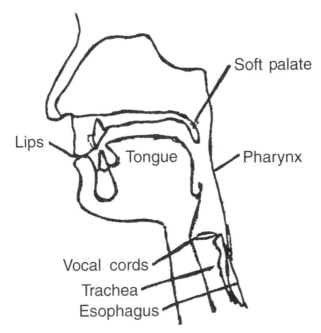

**Figure 10.12** A schematic of selected structures involved in the swallowing process.

adhering to the hard palate or having particles of food left on the tongue after swallowing.

As food leaves the mouth, the soft palate closes to keep food from entering the nasal cavity and being pushed out the nose. The food or liquid enters the throat or *pharynx,* and the next stage of swallowing begins. It is at this point that the actual swallow occurs. The back of the tongue has moved backward, and the muscles of the pharynx begin to contract to push the food downward. At the same time, the entrance to the windpipe or larynx closes tightly as the *larynx* moves upward. The *vocal cords* are contained within the larynx and must close to ensure that the food or liquid, which passes directly over the larynx, does not spill into the lungs. If these precisely timed events do not occur in the appropriate order, the patient will no longer produce a safe swallow. ALS results in many changes in the strength and speed of the structures, which contributes to an unsafe swallowing pattern during this stage of the swallowing process. As the muscles of the pharynx weaken, food may not be effectively pushed downward into the *esophagus* and finally into the stomach. The result may be a feeling of food sticking in the throat. Liquids may need to be taken to assist in moving the food through the throat and esophagus. However, if the finely timed event of vocal cord closure does not occur, choking or coughing may result as food or liquid enters the larynx instead of moving normally through the pharynx and into the esophagus and stomach. The entry of food or liquid into the larynx and lungs is referred to as *aspiration.* The entrance of any substance other than air has the potential of causing an infection. Some patients may develop *aspiration pneumonia* if this occurs only once; others may be at high risk after several episodes of large-scale aspiration. It is difficult to judge how much is too much aspiration before a particular patient experiences a pneumonia. Repeated episodes of coughing when eating or drinking may indicate a risk of food or liquid entering the lungs and requires a comprehensive swallowing evaluation by an SLP.

## Evaluation of Swallowing Disorders

The philosophy of managing swallowing problems in ALS is to teach the patient about the potential problems before they occur and to circumvent them by using compensatory strategies for as long as possible. The goal is for the patient to continue to eat and drink by mouth safely and efficiently for as long as possible. In the early stages of swallowing impairment, the problems may be highly visible and easy to diagnose and manage. As the disease progresses, it may become more difficult to diagnose the exact nature of a problem because the structures for swallowing are not readily visible. To fully understand what aspect of the swallowing process is being disrupted, the SLP has to view the structures for swallowing. This is most easily accomplished by performing an examination known as *videofluoroscopy* or *modified barium swallow.* During this examination, the patient is asked to chew and swallow a variety of food textures ranging from liquid to smooth to coarse. The foods are impregnated with *barium,* a substance that can be tracked on an x-ray. A video x-ray examination is then taken of the patient chewing and swallowing foods. This examination shows the movement of food from the mouth to the esophagus and allows the SLP and the radiologist to determine those aspects of the swallow that are most difficult for the patient and whether aspiration of foods is occurring. The videofluoroscopy is a very beneficial tool to use when the goal is safe preservation of the swallow for as long as possible. It allows the SLP to determine whether some type of a compensatory swallowing strategy can circumvent a problem and to actually experiment with that strategy during the examination to assess its benefit.

The SLP must often justify the need for this examination to the managing physician, who views the loss of swallowing and the placement of a feeding tube as an inevitable part of ALS. Although the progressive loss of swallowing is accepted by the SLP as a possibility, the larger goal is to maintain swallowing as a means of improving the overall quality of life with ALS. The videofluoroscopy may allow the patient to continue eating safely even if full nutrition and hydration cannot be maintained by mouth. The patient may choose favorite items and eat small quantities for pleasure, while also using the strategies that have been determined as effective during the evaluation. In many clinical settings, videofluoroscopy may not be available or recommended when the clinical signs of aspiration are already evident. Examples would include episodes of pneumonia or upper respiratory tract infections, frequent coughing during eating or drinking, and significant weight loss. When these signs are present, the SLP may be able to determine the appropriate management techniques for safer swallowing. If the SLP is unable to use the videofluoroscopy as an assessment tool, another possible tool is a *fiberoptic endoscopic swallow study*. During this examination, a flexible fiberoptic scope is passed through the nose and suspended above the larynx, as shown in Figure 10.13. Vegetable dye is added to food and liquid. This tool allows the SLP to view the dyed food and liquid moving through the pharynx while observing the effectiveness of vocal cord closure and protection of the trachea (windpipe) and lungs.

The SLP may also view the structures after the patient has swallowed foods impregnated with dye. Residue of the dye will be visible in high-risk areas around the vocal cords if the patient is not swallowing safely. If the patient has a tracheostomy tube in place, secretions suctioned from the tube may be tinged with dye if the food has been aspirated into the trachea during the fiberoptic endoscopic swallow study.

Videofluoroscopy and fiberoptic endoscopic swallowing study allow the SLP to obtain further information about the nature and extent of the swallowing impairment and to determine which treatment strategy will allow safe swallowing to continue. Both of these procedures can also be powerful tools in illustrating the risks of certain food consistencies to the patient and their caregivers and assisting them in choosing the safest way to maintain nutrition and hydration. If the swallowing disorder is severe enough to pose a health risk to the patient, these procedures may help them make an educated decision regarding nonoral methods of nutrition or hydration such as feeding tube placement.

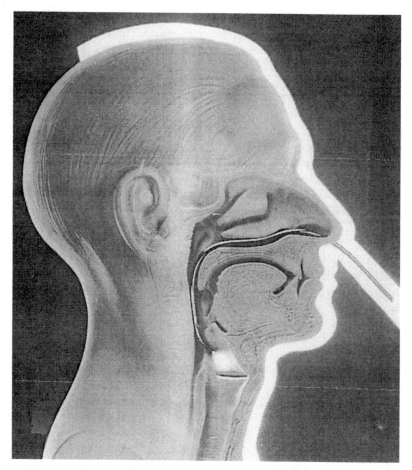

**Figure 10.13** The flexible fiberoptic scope in place for viewing the pharynx. Photo courtesy of Kay-Pentax.

## Management of Swallowing Disorders

The gradual loss of swallowing, like the gradual loss of speech, presents a challenge to the SLP in attempting to stay one step ahead of the disease. Swallowing problems should be anticipated, and an update about the swallowing ability of the person with ALS should be consistently provided so that changes can be recognized. Dietary management can be one way to prevent problems and prolong safe swallowing. The SLP should consult a *registered dietitian* to assist with the diet so that the patient has adequate caloric intake and his or her nutritional needs are met. People with ALS often eliminate difficult food consistencies from their diet as swallowing deteriorates. If solid food becomes difficult to chew, prechopped or mashed foods can eliminate the need for extensive chewing. Foods that do not contain small pieces and are well moistened will move toward the back of the mouth easier. When foods are held together by a cohesive food substance, such as mashed potatoes, it is less likely that the patient will breathe the food into the lungs. Thin, liquid consistencies present a particular challenge. Thin liquids are difficult to keep in the mouth, and they are difficult to control when swallowing, thereby resulting in coughing or choking. People with ALS often benefit from thickening liquids to a nectar- or honey-like consistency. Several thickening substances are available that do not greatly alter the taste of liquid and allow the patient to achieve the safest consistency. As the muscles of swallowing get weaker, the person with ALS may take an increasing amount of time to finish a meal, which can result in fatigue and loss of appetite. Eating several small meals throughout the day instead of 3 large meals can reduce the fatigue that accompanies eating. Many people with ALS tend to experience more dysphagia symptoms later in the day when the muscles of the mouth and throat are more fatigued. Taking a few minutes to rest or nap before meals can recharge the muscles and make swallowing safer and more efficient. Swallowing pills/medications can also pose a problem. It is advisable to take a pill with some pureed food (pudding, applesauce) or to crush the pills and mix them with puree for the patient to swallow medications more safely.

The person with ALS may also attempt to manage swallowing problems by using *compensatory swallowing techniques.* These techniques have been evaluated for their effectiveness via objective assessment, including videofluoroscopy and the endoscopic swallow examination. One technique involves placing food toward the rear of the mouth by using a syringe or special spoon to reduce the use of tongue pumping. Another technique involves teaching the patient to hold his or her breath and bear down during the swallowing process, which may forcibly close the vocal folds for better protection. Utilizing chin tuck posture when swallowing may be recommended for a patient who does not swallow readily (i.e., delayed swallowing), which results in food or liquid falling into the throat prematurely. Delayed swallowing can cause liquid or food particles to be aspirated, and chin tuck is designed to reduce or eliminate this risk. This technique may be beneficial during earlier stages of swallowing impairment; however, as the muscles of the lips and tongue become weaker, chin tuck may result in dribbling or loss of food/liquid or increased fatigue during meals because the patient needs to work against gravity in pushing food or liquid to the back of the mouth for swallowing. Another technique teaches the patient to swallow many times to clear residue from the throat. Yet another technique teaches the patient to cough after the swallow to clear any residue that may have fallen around the vocal folds. These techniques may be fatiguing, however, and should be used with caution. Through the use of careful testing, dietary management, and compensatory swallowing techniques, the patient may continue to swallow safely until a significant amount of motor deterioration has occurred. At that time, an alternative method of feeding such as a gastrostomy tube may be recommended. The placement of a gastrostomy tube may be recommended when the patient cannot manage to safely take a sufficient amount of food by mouth to maintain adequate nutrition and hydration. However, small amounts of oral intake can be continued in the presence of a gastrostomy tube. This will provide another source of pleasure and improve the quality of life for the individual with ALS.

For people with ALS with accompanying frontotemporal dementia, learning and consistent use of the techniques and strategies mentioned above can be challenging. Because of reduced attention and impulse control, the person with ALS may require little to full supervision during meals to ensure compliance with the strategies. Frequent reminders to take small bites and sips and to use the appropriate safe swallow techniques may be required. As with learning to use an alternative communication system, pictures and/or written reminders in concise, plain language can be used to reinforce verbal cues to ensure safety during meals. If the frontotemporal dementia is severe, inspecting a person's mouth after eating to check for residual or nonchewed food may be beneficial to prevent risk for aspiration or choking.

## Management of Problems With Saliva

Many people with ALS complain about two things relating to their saliva. Some people report that they have significantly increased amount of saliva in the mouth, requiring them to wipe their mouth constantly or making it difficult for them to talk. *Sialorrhea* is the medical term for drooling. There is no research evidence showing that patients with ALS produce more saliva than normal. The problem is probably related to the person having difficulty in swallowing as frequently, causing saliva to accumulate in the mouth. Medications such as *amytriptyline, glycopyrrolate,* or a transdermal patch used for motion sickness can be recommended to address this problem. In extreme cases, injection of botulinum toxin type B or radiation of the salivary glands may be performed. These treatments may have side effects and their effectiveness varies from person to person. The physician will be able to determine what is most appropriate given a person's presentation and medical history (see Chapter 4).

Other people with ALS complain of copious and thick secretions/phlegm in their throat, which interferes with talking and/or swallowing. A wet/gurgly sound (i.e., sounding like one is underwater) coming from the throat may also be heard during breathing. Throat clearing, coughing, and hacking may not get rid of the secretions, especially when there is weakness of the breathing and throat muscles. A number of strategies may be helpful in making the secretions thinner, and thereby making it easier to swallow or to spit out the secretions. Ensuring adequate hydration (6 to 8 glasses of water per day) if possible, inhalation of steam, use of a humidifier at home, over-the-counter cough medicine with guaifenesin (e.g., Robitussin), taking *papain* or *bromelain* enzyme (by drinking papaya or pineapple juice, taking enzyme tablets, or putting a swab of meat tenderizer on the tongue) are some of the strategies that may be helpful. Sometimes, a suction machine (similar to the one used in a dental office) and/or a cough-assist machine may be recommended to address problems related to secretions (see Chapter 12).

*Xerostomia* or dryness of the mouth is also not uncommon in people with ALS. They may drink fewer liquids because of swallowing problems or the need to prevent going to the bathroom frequently. Mouth dryness is a side effect of some of the medications taken by people with ALS. Drinking an increased amount of caffeinated or alcoholic drinks can also result in xerostomia. Exposure to dry air, such as when using a BiPAP machine or oxygen, may also exacerbate this problem. Xerostomia can make a person feel uncomfortable and it can also interfere with talking and swallowing. Ensuring adequate hydration and using steam inhalation and over-the-counter mouth moisturizers are helpful to address this problem.

## Conclusion

ALS challenges the therapist's training in the area of rehabilitation. A philosophy of maintenance and compensation must be used if the person with ALS is going to be treated by the SLP. Technology is constantly opening new doors to provide improved quality of life through communication for the person with ALS and has made communication a reality for everyone with ALS throughout the disease process. The provision of high-quality synthetic and digitized speech devices, written output, and access to on-line services can restore a high degree of independence. The philosophy of maintenance and compensation can also be applied to the changes in swallowing that occur in ALS so that another aspect of the patient's functioning can be preserved for as long as possible. By working with a team of highly trained professionals, the person with ALS can manage the disease from a position of knowledge and strength. Through ongoing education and research, the highest quality of life can be maintained for individuals with ALS.

**Appendix A**

# Strategies to Enhance Communication

Slowing rate of Speed

Overarticulation

Breath Grouping

Palatal lift

Amplification

Splint to Assist Writing

TTY for Telephone Use

ABC Board

List of Frequently Used Messages

Content-Specific Phrase Boards

Non-Electronic Eye Link

Switch Access

On-Screen Keyboard

Coded Systems

Electronic Communication System

Infra-red Switches

Environmental Control

Scanning

Electronic Eye Gaze System

Brain Computer Interface

Disease Stage Process

Early

Middle

Late

# References

1. Ball LJ, Beukelman DR, Pattee GL. Communication support for persons with ALS: a fact sheet. *Augmentative Commun News.* 2005;17(2):8.
2. Arbel Y. Brain-computer interface: transforming electrical brain activity into communication. *The ASHA Leader.* 2007;12(12):14–15.
3. Ringholz GM. Prevalence and patterns of cognitive impairment in sporadic ALS. *Neurology.* 2005;65(4):586–590.

# Suggested Reading

Beukelman DR, Yorkston KM, Dowden PA. *Communication augmentation: a casebook of clinical management.* San Diego, CA: College-Hill Press; 1985.

Dikeman K, Kazandjian M. *Communication and Swallowing Management of Tracheostomized and Ventilator Dependent Adults.* 2nd ed. Belmont, CA: Delmar Learning; 2003.

Esposito SJ, Mitsumoto H, Shanks M. Use of palatal lift and palatal augmentation prostheses to improve dysarthria in patients with amyotrophic lateral sclerosis: a cases series. *J Prosthet Dent.* 2000;83:90–98.

Fishman I. *Electronic communication aids and techniques.* Boston, MA: College-Hill Press; 1987.

Kazandjian M, ed. *Communication and swallowing solutions for the ALS/MND community.* New York, NY: Communication Independence for the Neurologically Impaired; 1997.

Kennedy PR, Adams KD. A Decision tree for brain-computer interface devices. *IEEE Trans Neural Syst Rehabil Eng.* 2003;11(2):148–150.

Yorkston KM, ed. *Augmentative communication in the medical setting.* Tucson, AZ: Communication Skill Builders; 1992.

# 11

## Nutrition Intervention

### Kate E. Dalton

Many aspects of nutrition management need to be addressed to maintain a high quality of life. Many patients with amyotrophic lateral sclerosis (ALS) are at risk for compromised nutrition due to (a) weight loss, (b) difficulty chewing and swallowing (1), (c) dehydration, (d) difficulty feeding oneself, or (e) improper feeding tube management. Because malnutrition can accelerate the progression of the disease (2) it is important for registered dietitians to assess patient nutritional status frequently and work with patients and caregivers to intervene as necessary.

Registered dietitians are nutrition experts and play an important role in the multidisciplinary clinic. In the United States, dietitians are registered with the Commission on Dietetic Registration and are only able to use the label *Registered Dietitian* when they have met strict, specific educational and professional prerequisites and passed a national registration examination.

### Role of the Dietitian in ALS Care

Registered dietitians provide nutritional counseling through diet management to promote adequate nutrition while preventing malnutrition. They

- Assess nutritional needs based on disease progression;
- Identify malnutrition;
- Recommend changes in diet to assist in the treatment of the disease.

185

- Adapt the consistency of foods and liquids when swallowing becomes difficult.
- Provide suggestions to maximize calorie and nutrient consumption.
- Recommend alternate forms of nutrition, such as tube feeding, if the patient is unable to obtain adequate nutrition by mouth.
- Provide education on care and administration of tube feedings.

As a multidisciplinary team member, the registered dietician works with all team members to improve and maintain patient quality of life and general wellness.

Working with speech pathologists, registered dietitians can identify swallowing weakness that interferes with safe food or fluid intake. Speech pathologists perform examinations to identify the source of chewing and swallowing problems and help the dietitian to recommend modifications in the daily diet, depending on individual needs.

## Assessing Medical History

Other medical illness can be an obstacle to providing adequate nutrition and change in diet. Any history of heart disease, diabetes, cancer, renal disease, stroke, or other conditions should be discussed with the dietitian. The dietitian can help assess whether past dietary restrictions should be continued, liberalized, or discontinued based on current nutritional needs. It may be appropriate to make adjustments to existing diet restrictions if the patient experiences poor food or liquid consumption, chewing or swallowing problems, or weight loss. Changes should be made only after consultation with a registered dietitian and the patient's primary care physician.

## Follow-Up and Reassessment

Regular follow-up with the dietitian can help ensure success of the current regimen and address new issues that occur between assessments. Weight is checked at each visit and chewing and swallowing are reevaluated as necessary. Reassessment may result in changes to the patient's diet prescription and oral supplementation or in recommendation for tube feedings and high-calorie recipes. Follow-up can also result in a continuation of the current diet regimen. Each follow-up visit, usually in 3-month intervals, addresses issues needed to maintain an optimal nutritional status.

## Weight Loss

It is important for an individual with ALS to maintain a stable weight. Weight is maintained when caloric intake is equivalent to the calorie output or expenditure. Many patients with ALS lose weight because they are in a negative caloric balance that theoretically can cause the body to utilize glycogen and protein stores for energy and therefore accelerates the breakdown of muscle. Because ALS leads to muscle weakness and atrophy, it is important to ensure that patients with ALS meet their energy requirement and do not lose weight. It is difficult to manipulate the energy expenditure of a patient with ALS, but adjustments can be made to increase energy intake.

## Assessment

Dietitians use body weight, percentage weight loss, and body mass index to assess nutritional status (3). A patient's normal body weight, as opposed to ideal body weight, is most useful in evaluating the health and nutritional status of a patient with ALS. Daily energy and protein requirements can be estimated by the Harris-Benedict formula (4) and by the healthy adult protein requirements multiplied by a reference factor associated with disease (5). In patients with ALS, however, this method may be inaccurate and under- or overestimate the dietary need. Therefore, the best way to determine whether patients are meeting their energy needs is to regularly track weight, ideally once a week. If possible, dietary intake should be assessed by using the 24-hour recall method (3), which consists of obtaining information on food and fluid intake for the previous day and is based on the assumption that the intake described is typical of daily intake.

## Recommendations

Consuming enough calories to maintain weight is the primary concern of dietitians working with ALS. It is currently unknown whether a specific balance of calories (carbohydrate, protein, and fat) could slow disease progression; as a result, it is suggested to follow the Acceptable Macronutrient Distribution Ranges (AMDR) of 45–65% calories from carbohydrates, 10–35% protein, and 20–35% fat established by the United States Department of Agriculture (USDA) (5). Increasing calories in the diet can be accomplished by eating frequent meals and larger portions or consuming more calorie-dense foods. Both carbohydrates and fats can be added to boost caloric intake and maintain a well-balanced diet. Unsaturated fats, such as olive and canola oils, nuts, seeds, peanut butter, and avocados, are preferable provided swallowing problems do not restrict food intake. These foods do not promote cardiovascular disease. Whole milk, butter, cream, and cheese can also be added to prevent weight loss. If the patient with ALS has a history of cardiovascular disease or diabetes, it is important to let his or her primary care doctor know that a change in diet is planned. In general, it is more important to liberalize intake and maintain weight in ALS than to restrict the diet because of another disease risk. In addition to adding fats to the diet, carbohydrates such as dried fruits, starch vegetables, dense whole grain breads and cereal, and hearty bean soups can boost caloric content. Drinking beverages is an important method to add calories and can help with hydration. High-calorie drinks include milk shakes, milk, and 100% fruit juice. When using commercial supplements, patients should read the labels to find the most calorie-dense formula, usually the "plus" version. The "high protein" versions of these supplements often have fewer calories and, because it is the neuron that is not functioning properly in ALS, the increase in protein will not necessarily promote muscle protection. If the patient has a poor appetite, an appetite-stimulant medication such as magestrol acetate or Marinol can be prescribed.

Frequent weight checks are essential in the assessment of the effectiveness of a change in diet. The patient should be weighed at home weekly and every 3 months at the ALS clinic visit. For example, if a patient is maintaining weight, then the patient is in caloric balance and does not need a dietary change. On the other hand, if a patient loses 4 pounds over a month, then an increase of 500 calories per day would help stop the weight loss. For a list of ways to increase calories, see Table 11.1.

### Chewing and Swallowing Difficulty

Chewing and swallowing may become more difficult because ALS may weaken jaw, throat, tongue, and lip muscles. It also may take more time and energy to fin-

**Table 11.1** Boosting Calories

| *Instead of . . .* | *Try . . .* |
|---|---|
| Hot cereal | Hot cereal with butter or margarine, cream and honey, or sugar |
| Plain eggs | Scrambled eggs with butter or margarine, melted cheese, and cream |
| Plain pancakes | Pancakes topped with plenty of syrup, whipped cream, butter, or margarine |
| Baked potato | Potatoes mashed with cream and butter or margarine; or topped with sour cream, Parmesan, Romano; or other cheeses and butter or margarine |
| Fresh apple | A peeled, cored apple baked with brown sugar and butter, topped with cream |
| Regular pudding | Pudding made with cream and topped with whipped cream |
| Plain ice cream | Premium ice cream topped with your favorite flavored syrup and marshmallow cream |
| Milk (if thin liquids are tolerated) | Make thick milkshakes by adding ice cream, your favorite syrup, and an instant breakfast mix |

ish a meal. If chewing becomes difficult, it is important to change the texture of foods to make them easier to chew. If swallowed liquids or food accidentally enter the windpipe leading to coughing, then the consistency of the food needs to be changed to prevent further aspiration that might cause pneumonia.

## Assessment

Chewing and swallowing problems are assessed with questions such as How long does it take you to eat a meal? Are you having difficulty chewing, swallowing, or moving food around in your mouth? and Do you cough on thin liquids such as water or on dry, crumbly foods such as crackers or popcorn? Difficulty with chewing and swallowing also increases the time it takes to complete meals. People who take longer than 20 to 30 minutes to complete a meal may have difficulty with chewing and/or swallowing. A speech pathologist can examine and evaluate swallowing to identify problems and recommend consistency changes (see Chapter 10).

## Recommendations

Depending on the severity of the muscle weakness, the texture of the diet will usually change to *mechanically softened,* consisting of chopped meats, casseroles, well-cooked vegetables, and soft fruits. For more severe weakness a *pureed diet* may be recommended, which provides a blended consistency for all food items. Foods can be moistened with gravy, butter, or sauces to make them easier to swallow. Dry and crumbly foods such as crackers, potato chips, pretzels, and muffins may cause problems and should be avoided (Tables 11.2 and 11.3).

**Table 11.2** Selecting Easy-to-Swallow Foods

| FLUIDS: 6 TO 8 8-OUNCE CUPS PER DAY | |
| --- | --- |
| **Select** | **Select only if thin liquids are tolerated** |
| Sherbet and sherbet shakes | Water |
| Ice cream | Coffee |
| Milk shakes | Tea |
| Gelatin | Soft drinks |
| Pudding | Thin juices |
| Fruit ice | Hot chocolate |
| Orange juice with gelatin added | Thin soup |
| Pureed fruits | Chunky-style soup |

*(Continued)*

**Table 11.2** Selecting Easy-to-Swallow Foods  (*Continued*)

### PROTEINS: 2 TO 3 SERVINGS PER DAY

| Select | Avoid |
| --- | --- |
| Moist, ground, or pureed meat and poultry | Tough, dry meats |
| Tender fish without bones | Dry poultry or dry fish |
| Eggs | Peanut butter |

### DAIRY: 2 TO 3 SERVINGS PER DAY

| Select | Avoid |
| --- | --- |
| Creamy cottage cheese | Dry cottage cheese |
| Yogurt | Ice cream with nuts, raisins, or candy |
| Ice cream without nuts, raisins, or candy | |
| Milk, buttermilk (if thin liquids are tolerated), and milkshakes | |

### STARCHES: 6 TO 11 SERVINGS PER DAY

| Select | Avoid |
| --- | --- |
| Bread or toast buttered or dunked in liquid | Crumbly bread |
| Cold cereal soaked in milk or cream | Hard rolls |
| Cooked cereal | Bread with nuts, seeds, coconut, or fruit |
| Pancakes | Bread with cracked-wheat particles |
| Pasta | Sweet rolls |
| Casseroles | Waffles |
| Rice with gravy or sauce | Doughnuts |
| Moist cookies or quick breads without coconut, raisins, or nuts | Coffee cake |
| | English muffins |
| Baked, mashed, or boiled potatoes with gravy, cream, or margarine | Dry cereal flakes |
| | Dry toast, crackers, Melba toast, dry rice, or dry cookies |

(*Continued*)

**Table 11.2** Selecting Easy-to-Swallow Foods *(Continued)*

### FRUITS: 2 TO 4 SERVINGS PER DAY

| Select | Avoid |
|---|---|
| Soft, fresh, or canned fruits with seeds, pits, and skin removed | Raw fruits with skins |
| Chilled applesauce or pureed fruit | Stringy pineapple |
| Poached fruit in gelatin | Dried fruit |
| Ripe bananas | |

### VEGETABLES: 3 TO 5 SERVINGS PER DAY

| Select | Avoid |
|---|---|
| Soft, canned, or well-cooked vegetables | Raw vegetables |
| fresh or frozen vegetables | Firm or stringy cooked vegetables |
| Scalloped tomatoes | vegetables with hulls (such as corn, spinach, or firm peas) |

### SOUPS

| Select | Select only if thin liquids are tolerated |
|---|---|
| Thick soups such as cream soups or thickened broth-based soups (any vegetables should be well-cooked) | Broth and thin soups |

### DESSERTS

| Select | Avoid |
|---|---|
| Fruit whip | Dry, crumbly cakes and cookies |
| Gelatin | Desserts with raisins, nuts, seeds, or coconut |
| Cobblers | |
| Apple or peach crisps | |
| Moist cookies without nuts or raisins | |
| Custards | |
| Puddings | |
| Hard frozen sherbet or ice cream | |

*(Continued)*

**Table 11.2** Selecting Easy-to-Swallow Foods   (*Continued*)

### FATS, SNACKS, AND OTHER FOODS

| Select | Avoid |
|---|---|
| Butter or margarine | Popcorn |
| Gravy | Potato chips |
| Sour cream | Corn chips |
| Melted cheese | Pickles |
| Honey | Seeds |
| Jelly | Whole spices |
| Plain chocolate without nuts | Nuts |
| Chocolate mint patties | |

**Table 11.3** Creating the Best Texture

**To thicken foods and liquids, try . . .**

- Adding mashed potatoes, potato flakes, sauces, or gravies to pureed vegetables, casseroles, or soups
- Adding plain gelatin, cooked cereal, or flaked rice cereal to pureed fruits
- Cooking canned fruit with tapioca or corn starch to create a thick pie-filling texture

**To thin foods or to make dry foods moist, try . . .**

- Adding broth, gravies, sauces, milk, cream, butter, or margarine to hot foods
- Adding fruit juices, pureed fruit, cold milk, cream, yogurt, or liquid plain gelatin to cold foods

**To make your foods softer, try . . .**

- Using your favorite foods in casserole recipes when suitable
- Grinding meats with vegetables in a blender or food processor
- Mashing fruit or vegetables
- Cooking meat in broth or soup to keep it moist
- Poaching fish in milk to keep it soft

Thin liquids cause coughing because they move too quickly through the mouth, not allowing enough time for the throat valve muscles to seal off the airway. Thick liquids are easier to swallow because they have a slower transit time and allow throat muscles to contract appropriately. Commercial thickeners can be added to thin liquids in the absence of naturally thick alternatives. Commercial thickeners can be purchased without a doctor's prescription and are generally tasteless and simple to add to drinks. These products can come in gel or powder forms and should be added gradually to liquids until the desired consistency is achieved. Some individuals complain of a bad taste when adding thickener to water; adding flavors such as lemon or lime juice to the thickened water may improve the taste. There are also commercially available prethickened products such as coffee and water, which can be purchased through medical nutrition suppliers. Naturally thick alternatives include milkshakes, ice cream, cream soups, puddings, tomato juice, nectars, and gelatin (Table 11.2).

Progressive difficulty with chewing or swallowing, increased time to consume meals, and weight loss may indicate that meeting nutritional needs by mouth may no longer be possible. When these signs begin to appear, it is important to discuss with a physician the option of having a feeding tube placed. Tube feedings may be safer and easier than trying to meet nutrient needs through eating and drinking by mouth. We will explore the feeding tube in further detail later in the chapter.

## Hydration

Adequate fluid is needed to replace normal body losses, prevent dehydration, and ensure good digestion and intestinal function. Patients with difficulty swallowing are at high risk for dehydration, because fluids are always more difficult to swallow than solid food. Many patients who have difficulty walking restrict their fluid intake because it is a challenge for them to get to and from the bathroom, placing them at risk for dehydration. As discussed earlier, if a person is having difficulty swallowing, thickened liquids can prevent choking and provide adequate hydration. The importance of water/fluids cannot be overemphasized for protecting the airway lining and, in general, normal metabolism of the entire body.

## Assessment

Hydration requirements can be calculated by using maintenance and age-related values (6). Using the 24-hour dietary recall the dietitian can determine how much fluid a person is consuming and if it is adequate to meet his or her nutrition needs (3). However, the best way to assess inadequate intake is to monitor for signs of poor hydration such as constipation, increased thickness of saliva, dry mouth, and decreased urination. Bowel function is discussed below.

## Recommendations

Good hydration is maintained by drinking at least 6 to 8 cups of noncaffeinated fluid per day. If swallowing thin liquids makes this goal difficult to achieve, thicker foods such as eggnog, yogurt, pureed fruit, ice cream, sherbet, pudding, frozen shakes, frozen juices, or frozen sodas can help increase hydration.

## Bowel Function

Constipation may occur in patients with ALS because of reduced physical activity, dehydration, medication use, and weakness of the muscles that assist the bowel to move. Also, the fiber content of the diet may drop if softer foods are eaten, making it difficult to maintain the bulk of the stool for regular bowel movements. This change in normal bowel function can lead to enormous discomfort. It is important for patients to discuss signs of constipation with the dietitian during the nutritional assessment. The dietitian, ALS nurse, and physician will collectively plan appropriate symptom management (see Chapter 4).

Diarrhea can occur as a result of a particular food, a viral illness, or a tube-feeding formula. It is necessary to replace the hydration that is lost by increasing fluid intake. Problems in these areas should be discussed with a dietitian so that diet or tube-feeding modifications can be considered.

### Assessment

Some people find it hard to talk about being constipated. Patients may feel embarrassed or upset by the problem or worry about what is causing it. It is important, however, for them to communicate with their dietitians, who may be able to suggest ways to relieve symptoms. Dietitians will often ask questions, such as When did you last open your bowels? What do your stools look like? Are they hard? What are your normal bowel habits like? and How frequent are your bowel movements?

### Recommendations

The key to maintaining bowel function is to create a regimen of hydration, fiber intake, and medication. As discussed above, adequate fluid intake helps to relieve constipation and maintain hydration. Soft, fiber-containing foods and bulking agents can also be tried. When constipation first occurs, drinking an 8-ounce glass of warm prune juice might provide the solution. If prunes do not help or if the patient does not like prune juice, then an over-the-counter stool softener can be taken daily to help soften the stool. For more resistant constipation an additional over-the-counter laxative can be added at night. Laxatives, which increase the peristalsis of the intestine, are taken in the form of a fiber supplement such as Metamucil, or as a medication such as Ex-Lax. If the constipation persists, then a prescription medication or enema can be tried. It is important to add interventions gradually, every 2 to 3 days, to avoid overstimulating the gut and creating diarrhea. If these methods do not work, the dietitian, nurse, and physician will work together to find an alternative treatment.

If diarrhea occurs as the result of consumption of a particular food, such as milk, that food should be omitted from the diet. Medical treatment may be needed if the diarrhea is caused by disease rather than diet. Increasing fluid intake is also appropriate to help replace fluid losses from diarrhea.

## Difficulty Feeding

Patients with arm weakness have difficulty feeding themselves. They can feel frustrated with this loss of independence and may avoid eating, which leads to weight loss. Many complain that eating a meal is less satisfying, which in turn leads to a decrease in caloric and fluid intake and weight loss.

### Assessment

Dietitians will often ask the following questions: How long does it take to complete a meal? Have you been assessed by an occupational therapist? What part of the process is the most difficult—the lifting or the manipulating of utensils, such as in cutting?

### Recommendations

Occupational therapists are able to identify and make recommendations that simplify feeding. There are many different adaptive devices that can assist and prolong independent feeding (see Chapter 8). Devices can be purchased from a medical supply company or can be made by modifying standard utensils. Thicker handles can ease the ability to grasp and manipulate utensils. Lightweight utensils, such as shrimp forks substituted for standard forks, can ease the ability to lift food to the mouth. For help with cutting, a pizza wheel can be used for most food items. Reducing the distance from one's food to one's mouth also eases the burden of feeding. Propping two telephone books under each elbow and placing a tray of food a few inches away from the mouth relieves the arms from having to work as hard to lift a utensil. Alternatively, there is an assistive device called an arm swivel that assists arm movement more easily but is often not covered by insurance. If consuming a meal takes longer than 45 minutes, caregiver assistance should be considered. Patients will often become fatigued through a meal. At the first sign of fatigue, caregivers should assist, which will also allow the patient to reduce caloric expenditure.

## Tube Feeding

Tube feedings are an alternative way to meet nutritional needs if eating by mouth has become difficult, dangerous, or insufficient. The option of having a feeding tube placed should be discussed when it becomes apparent that eating is affected

by weakness. Symptoms such as taking longer to finish meals, coughing or choking on foods or beverages, difficulty moving food around in the mouth, or difficulty
chewing are evidence that eating is becoming more difficult and that maintaining
intake by mouth alone may no longer be feasible. It is very important to realize
that receiving a feeding tube early in the disease might provide a better outcome
(7–9). Weight loss, a more objective sign that adequate caloric intake is not being
achieved, also indicates that tube feeding may be necessary. It has been suggested
that a weight loss of 10% of usual body weight, along with signs of chewing and
swallowing difficulty, should be the starting point for discussions regarding the
need for a feeding tube (3). Weight loss of more than 10% of one's usual weight
over a short span of time (2 to 3 months or less) or of more than 20% overall is
considered severe.

At this time there is little evidence-based research on the timing and safety
of feeding-tube placements. However, according to the American Academy of
Neurology Practice Parameters, patients should get a percutaneous endoscopic
gastrostomy (PEG) tube (which will be described later in the chapter) if there is
significant dysphasia or weight loss and before their forced vital capacity (FVC) is
less than 50% of predicted (9). This recommendation is based on previous studies
showing that patients with ALS who had low vital capacity at the time of the PEG
procedure did poorly afterward (7). It does not mean that the procedure cannot
be done in those who have low breathing capacity, but the risk is not negligible.
It is best to have the procedure done by a gastroenterologist or a general surgeon
experienced in ALS. It is essential to have close follow-up by the doctor who performed the procedure and by a dietitian. If a feeding tube is elected, however, the
sooner the procedure takes place, the better, in part because of the recovery time
after the feeding tube is placed. Furthermore, a good breathing capacity will ensure
a smooth procedure. Once a feeding tube is inserted, the patient can continue to
eat orally but can use the tube for medicine, hydration, and supplemental nutrition
(see Figure 11.1).

## Why Should Patients Consider PEG Tube Feeding?

PEG is an efficient way to provide necessary nutrition and water for anyone who
has difficulty eating by mouth. Patients consider a PEG tube feeding because it sta-
bilizes the weight and might lengthen life; alternative nutrition support can correct
the energy depletion associated with pre-PEG placement (10). The procedure of
inserting a PEG tube is simple and minimally invasive, and good nutrition can
greatly improve strength (8,10).

All necessary daily calorie requirements and water can be given through a feeding tube, but this does not mean that patients cannot also eat by mouth. In fact,
patients frequently are allowed to eat as long as they feel comfortable. They need
not struggle to eat to maintain their calorie and water requirements but can enjoy
foods for pleasure. Many patients are reluctant to consider such a procedure; some
patients do not wish to even discuss it or want to delay the decision because an

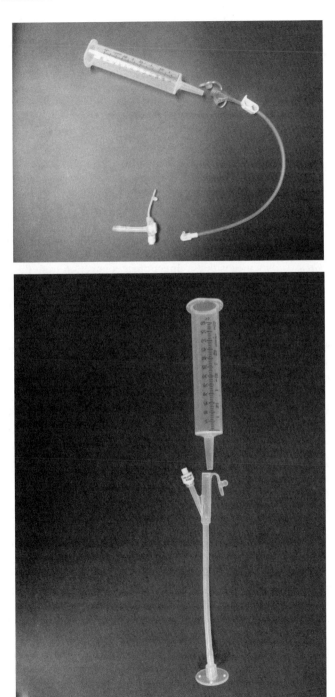

**Figure 11.1** Percutaneous endoscopic gastrostomy (PEG) tubes.

artificial route to take nutrition is not appealing. It is common for patients to defer the decision until a physical necessity arises. When this occurs, however, the procedure may become risky because breathing capacity may be reduced and malnourishment may have weakened the body's overall defenses.

## Types of Feeding Tube Procedure

Gastrostomy tubes are commonly used for people with ALS. They are placed directly into the stomach through an incision in the outside of the abdominal wall. They can easily be kept out of sight when not in use and generally do not cause physical discomfort or irritation after the original incision has healed.

The most common gastrostomy tube, referenced above, is called a *percutaneous endoscopic gastrostomy* (PEG) tube. *Percutaneous* indicates a tube that is positioned through the skin surface of the abdomen. *Endoscopic* means that the procedure is performed under a scope through a thin and long flexible tube from the mouth. *Gastrostomy* means that a direct open connection from the outside of the body is placed to the stomach. This tube is inserted by a gastroenterologist or surgeon who often uses only a local anesthetic and minor sedation. The procedure can take place in conjunction with an overnight hospital admission or it can be performed in an outpatient endoscopic suite. For patients who have respiratory difficulty or other medical issues an overnight observational stay is recommended. A small amount of formula is initiated through the tube the day after the procedure and then gradually increased.

Feedings usually are administered in a 4- to 5-feedings-per-day schedule (depending on food intake) and each feeding takes about 5 minutes to infuse using the force of gravity via a large syringe or 20 to 30 minutes dripping from a tube-feeding bag. After about 2 weeks, the temporary feeding tube can be replaced by a permanent traditional feeding tube or a mic-key button tube. The mic-key button is preferable for patients who are active because the device is flush with the skin; an attachment tube is used to administer the feeding.

An alternative to the PEG procedure is the radiologically inserted gastrostomy (RIG) method (11). The pre- and postprocedures are similar, but the insertion process differs in that the RIG is carried out under x-ray by a specialized doctor called an *intervention radiologist.* During the RIG placement, air is pushed into the stomach through a tube that extends from the nose; inflating the stomach slightly helps to place the tube accurately. The radiologist inserts a thin, hollow needle through the skin and into the stomach. The feeding tube is passed through the opening. Once the tube is in place a small amount of dye is flushed into the tube so that the radiologist can view the RIG placement under an x-ray machine to ensure the tube is securely in place. The entire technique is done solely under local anesthesia. Previously, RIG was thought to be the safer method for patients with ALS who have low respiratory capacity (12); however, recent literature comparing PEG with RIG states that the difference between the outcomes of the procedures is not significant (13,14). The decision to have either a PEG or RIG placed should be based on the ALS physician's familiarity with the procedure and the ability to communicate with the doctor performing the gastrostomy.

Jejunostomy tubes, which are inserted directly into the small intestine instead of the stomach, are also available but are less common. Jejunostomy is preferable when gastroesophageal reflex or regurgitation is an impending problem. These tubes require slower infusion rates and a different formula than gastrostomy tubes. The physician who inserts feeding tubes also discusses different options for the type of tube, because every patient's situation is different. It is important to have a gastroenterology consult before the real procedure is done.

Nasogastric tubes extend from the nose into the stomach and are often used for short-term feedings, that is, a few weeks or less. They may cause irritation to the throat and nasal passages over longer periods and are somewhat obtrusive to the user; they are not the typical tube used for long-term feeding as is necessary with ALS (15). Tube types and their advantages and disadvantages are summarized in Table 11.4.

**Table 11.4** Advantages and Disadvantages of Feeding Tubes

| Tube type | Usual feeding schedule | Benefits | Limitations |
|---|---|---|---|
| Nasogastric (NG) | Feedings can be given in bolus form (large doses in a relatively short time) several times each day. | Least traumatic to the body for placement. | Irritating to the nasal cavity over time (so usually only used for a few weeks duration). May be considered obtrusive because it dangles from the nose. |
| Percutaneous endoscopic gastrostomy (PEG) and radiologically inserted gastrostomy (RIG) | Usually bolus feedings, several times each day. Uses local anesthesia and muscle relaxants. | Minimal trauma, may require hospitalization. Otherwise, generally well tolerated. | Requires some sedation; therefore, pulmonary function is a concern. |
| Jejunostomy (J tubes) | Feedings must be run slowly over several hours, usually at least 12 h/d, continuously. | Placement of the tube lower in the gastrointestinal tract may or may not reduce risk of aspirating feedings. | If surgically placed, will require general anesthesia. If placed endoscopically, the anesthesia is minimized. Feeding scheduling options most limited. |

## Feeding Tube Placement

### Before the Procedure

Before the procedure, the physician will review the patient's medical history, give instructions regarding medications, and answer any questions. The physician then schedules the procedure and gives preprocedure instructions.

### What Patients Can Expect When Getting a Feeding Tube

On the morning of the procedure, patients report to the designated procedure area at the hospital. They should not eat or drink for 8 hours before the procedure. They are asked to change into a hospital gown and to remove eyeglasses and dentures. A nurse or a doctor reviews current medications with them and takes a brief medical history and monitors their vital signs. An intravenous catheter is placed in one of the patient's arms.

When the physician is ready, the patient is taken into a procedure room that has the equipment necessary for feeding tube placement. A blood pressure cuff is placed on the arm and a pulse oximeter, which measures the amount of oxygen in the blood, is placed on the fingertip. The blood pressure, heart rate, and blood oxygenation are measured every 5 to 10 minutes during the procedure.

The physician sprays a numbing medication into the back of the patient's throat and administers medication intravenously to cause a sleepy, comfortable feeling during the PEG placement. A plastic mouthpiece is inserted into the mouth to provide an opening through which the doctor passes the endoscope down to the stomach. The endoscope does not interfere with breathing.

After the endoscope reaches the stomach, the physician finds the correct position for the insertion of the tube, injects medication to numb the area, and makes a small incision through which to pass the tube. The flexible tube is then passed through the endoscope, into the stomach, and out of the incision, so that the end of the tube is on the outside of the stomach. Bumpers are placed on both the outside and the inside of the stomach to help ensure that the tube does not become dislodged. The tube can then be capped or connected to feedings. The procedure takes approximately 15 minutes.

If the patient has respiratory muscle weakness, the procedure may be carried out by using a noninvasive positive pressure ventilator, a respiratory device that assists with breathing. The device includes a mask that is placed over the patient's nose to assist in moving air into the lungs, which can help make the procedure more comfortable and lessen the risk of respiratory complications during and after the procedure.

The insertion site is covered with an antibiotic ointment and gauze is placed over the incision. The patient is then transferred to a recovery area, where vital signs are monitored for several hours to ensure that the procedure was successful and to allow the sedating medication sufficient time to wear off. Medications are available to relieve pain, should it occur. The patient may or may not be transferred to a unit in the hospital for an overnight stay. After discharge from the hospital, a home visit with a nurse is scheduled to ensure that the feeding procedure is understood and that the PEG site is healing well.

The day after the PEG placement, sterile water is placed through the new tube to ensure that it is functioning properly. If the patient's stomach tolerates the water without problems, then a tube feeding containing a nutritional supplement is given by the visiting nurse. A nurse teaches the patient and the caregiver how to administer the feeding and what type and amount of nutritional supplement to use. The nutritionist will offer advice on the daily calories and amount of water necessary to meet nutritional requirements. A nurse then shows the patient how to care for the tube and the insertion site, usually by washing it with soap and water.

## Use of Feeding Tube

Once a feeding tube has been placed, the doctor or dietitian prescribes a formula based on a calculated nutritional need. He or she schedules visiting nurse services and formula delivery. The visiting nurse goes to the patient's house within 24 hours after the procedure to provide instructions on the proper use and care of the feeding tube. The nurse also informs the patient and caregivers about how to solve potential problems such as a clogged tube, diarrhea, constipation, abdominal discomfort, or nausea. When the patient is admitted to the hospital, this is done during the hospital stay. The tube feeding vendor typically delivers a one-month supply of formula and syringes, followed by similar deliveries each month.

Patients care for a PEG tube by flushing it with water daily and each time the tube is used (whether for feeding or for medication administration). Patients should call their physician if they experience vomiting, irritation, or redness at the PEG site or accidental removal of the PEG tube. The doctor who performed the procedure usually provides full instructions as to what to do for any unusual occurrence. Tube feedings are easy to manage when the steps of the feeding process and potential problems have been discussed before going home from the hospital. Tube feeding schedules and formula types can be adjusted as needed with the help of a dietitian or doctor once the tube is being used at home. If changes in bowel habits occur, patients should speak with their dietitian to ensure that hydration and nutritional requirements are being met.

Diarrhea may be caused by a concentrated formula (more than 1 calorie per milliliter), the rate at which the tube feeding is being administered, or too high a volume. A dietitian can make recommendations to change the formula, rate, or volume to alleviate the diarrhea and continue to meet fluid, calorie, and protein needs.

## Conclusion

As discussed, the main concerns of nutrition in ALS are weight loss, difficulty with chewing and swallowing, dehydration, change in bowel function, difficulty feeding, and feeding tube intervention. With each of these concerns comes assessment by a registered dietitian and intervention to attain a better quality of life.

# References

1. Kasarskis EJ, Berryman S, Vanderleest JG, et al. The nutritional status of patients with amyotrophic lateral sclerosis: relation to the proximity of death. *Am J Clin Nut.* 1996;63:130–137.
2. Desport JC, Preux PM, Truong TC, et al. Nutritional status is a prognostic factor for survival in ALS patients. *Neurology.* 1999;53:1059–1063.
3. Rio A, Cawadias E. Nutritional advice and treatment by dietitians to patients with amyotrophic lateral scelrosis/motor neurone disease: a survey of current practice in England, Wales, Northern Ireland and Canada. *J Hum Nutr Diet* 2007;20:3–13.
4. Harris JA, Benedict FG. *A Biometric Study of the Basal Metabolism in Man* (Publication 279). Washington, DC: Carnegie Institution of Washington; 1919.
5. Dietary Reference Intakes (DRI) for energy, carbohydrate, fiber, fat, fatty acids, cholesterol, protein and amino acids (macronutrients). *A Report of the Panel of Macronutrients, Subcommittees on Upper Reference Levels of Nutrients and Interpretation and Uses of Dietary Reference Intakes.* Washington: National Academy Press; 2005.
6. Thomas B. *Manual of Dietetic Practice* (3rd ed.). Oxford: Blackwell Science; 2001.
7. Kasarskis EJ, Scarlata D, Hill R, et al. A retrospective study of percutaneous endoscopic gastrostomy in ALS patients during the BDNF and CNTF trials. *J Neurol Sci.* 1999;169:118–125.
8. Chio A, Finocchiaro E, Meineri P, et al. Safety and factors related to survival after percutaneous endoscopic gastrostomy in ALS. ALS Percutaneous Endoscopic Gastrostomy Study Group. *Neurology.* 1999;5:1123–1125.
9. Miller RG, Rosenberg JA, Gelinas DF, et al. Practice parameter: the care of the patient with amyotrophic lateral sclerosis (an evidence-based review): report of the Quality Standards Subcommittee of the American Academy of Neurology: ALS Practice Parameters Task Force. *Neurology* 1999;52:1311–1323.
10. Mazzini L, Corrà T, Zaccala M, et al. Percutaneous endoscopic gastrostomy and enteral nutrition in amyotrophic lateral sclerosis. *J Neurol.* 1995;242:695–698.
11. Chio A, Galletti R, Finocchiaro C, et al. Percutaneous radiological gastrostomy: a safe and effective method of nutritional tube placement in advanced ALS. *J Neurol Neurosurg Psych.* 2004;75:645–647.
12. Thornton FJ, Fotheringham T, Alexander M, et al. Amyotrohpic lateral sclerosis: enteral nutrition provision-endoscopic or radiologic gastrostomy? *Radiology.* 2002;2:713–717.
13. Desport JC, Mabrouk T, Boullet P, et al. Complication and survival following radiologically and endoscopically-guided gastrostomy in patient with amyotrophic lateral sclerosis. *Amyotroph Lateral Scler Other Motor Neuron Disord.* 2005;6:88–93.
14. Laasch HU, Wilbraham L, Bullen K, et al. Gastrostomy insertion: comparing the options-PEG, RIG or PIG? *Clin Rad.* 2003;58:398–405.
15. Scott AG, Austin HE. Nasogastric feeding in the management of severe dysphagia in motor neuron disease. *Palliat Med.* 1994;8:45–49.

# 12

# Respiratory Management

## Robert C. Basner

Amyotrophic lateral sclerosis (ALS) is associated with a progressive loss of strength of the respiratory (breathing) muscles, in particular, the diaphragm, the major muscle of breathing. This loss of strength of the respiratory muscles also involves the muscles that allow for adequate coughing and clearing of the airways of normal mouth, nose, and airway secretions and mucus, and the muscles that allow safe swallowing of foods and liquids. Such progressive weakness leads to failure to achieve adequate breathing and is responsible for most deaths in patients with ALS. Patients with ALS have important respiratory management needs throughout the course of their illness. Accurate and proactive respiratory management, including preventive as well as treatment measures, is considered as able to prolong life as well as improve the quality of life in patients with ALS. Patients with ALS and their family and caregivers should feel empowered that there are many things to be done to help preserve breathing function, and to prevent and treat respiratory difficulties associated with this disorder.

This chapter will present a brief background regarding the major respiratory functions including ventilation and oxygenation, a discussion of what goes wrong with these functions when a patient develops ALS, and a discussion of the major respiratory goals for the patient with ALS. The content of this chapter does *not* take the place of being individually evaluated by experts in ALS, preferably in a multidisciplinary center with experts in pulmonary care as well as the other major aspects of motor neuron disorder.

## What Is Ventilation? What Is Oxygenation?

A necessary job in life is to conduct fresh air containing oxygen ($O_2$) from the environment into the lungs, where it can, in turn, diffuse into the bloodstream and circulate to the vital organs of the body. In doing so, the lungs also take up carbon dioxide ($CO_2$), produced during normal functioning of the cells of the body, and conduct it out of the lungs and into the environment. The conduction of fresh air into the lungs and carbon dioxide out of the lungs is the process of *ventilation*. The goal throughout life is to use as little work as possible to ventilate, and, in fact, most persons are unaware that this process of ventilation is occurring in them 10 to 20 times per minute.

Normal ventilation requires good respiratory muscle function, which includes both an inspiratory (inhalation) and expiratory (exhalation) phase. Normal inspiration is active, and requires use of the muscles that expand the chest and allow ventilation, particularly the diaphragm. The expiratory phase of breathing is, to a great extent, although not completely, passive. A certain amount of muscle strength is necessary, however, to ensure complete emptying of the lungs; this strength is derived from muscles of the abdomen and chest wall. With normal ventilation, the oxygen needs (*oxygenation*) of the body are met, provided the movement of the oxygen into the blood is not blocked once it is in the lungs, as may occur with diseases of the lungs or heart. *Oxygen saturation* refers to how well the oxygen content of the blood matches with oxygen capacity; this should normally be above 90%.

## Problems With Ventilation and Oxygenation in ALS

Weakness of the breathing muscles will lead to worsening ventilation, as well as to further weakening of the muscles because of the need to use extra energy to push the breathing muscles to achieve sufficient ventilation. As the major muscle of breathing, the diaphragm, becomes weakened, one may become aware of difficulty in inspiration. Signs and symptoms of respiratory difficulties related to weakness of the breathing muscles in ALS may include any or all of the following: generalized fatigue; fast breathing rate (generally above 20 breaths per minute); fast heart rate (generally above 90 beats per minute); shortness of breath (also called breathlessness, air hunger, or dyspnea), in particular, when exerting oneself or when laying down; a sensation of having to work hard to breathe; use of accessory muscles of breathing, such as the shoulder and neck muscles; inward movement of the abdomen on inspiration (normally the diaphragm pulls down and the abdomen comes out with inspiration). Poor sleep may also occur. When the disorder reaches the point where the patient can no longer achieve adequate ventilation to meet his or her body demands, symptoms and signs of low ventilation (*hypoventilation*) may occur. As ventilation decreases, $CO_2$ will increase and $O_2$ will fall. Problems associated with hypoventilation therefore include lower-than-normal oxygenation of the body (*hypoxia*) and buildup of $CO_2$, which may cause headache, confusion, acidic blood with impaired blood vessel function, shortness of breath, drowsiness, or even coma at extremely high levels. Such severe hypoventilation is considered *respiratory failure*. It is good to remember, though, that even as the characteristic progression of the disorder causes the $CO_2$ in the blood to rise mildly because of impaired ventilation, while the $O_2$ decreases proportionately, these levels are generally quite adequate to meet the usual demands of the body at rest, including those of the brain and heart; with exercise or other exertion such demands may not be met. Most patients with ALS, even with severely decreased respiratory muscle strength, will not suffer from a greatly elevated $CO_2$ or greatly decreased $O_2$ at rest until very late in the course of the disorder, unless pneumonia or other cause of a breathing problem occurs. When a decreased $O_2$ level is identified in ALS, it is usually due to a ventilation problem, and assisted ventilation should decrease the $CO_2$ levels and raise the $O_2$ levels sufficiently in most cases, as noted above. Pneumonia or another lung or heart problem may cause such problems to rapidly worsen at any point in the course of the disorder. Examples of nonventilatory causes of low $O_2$ include pneumonia, partial collapse of part of the lungs (atelectasis), heart failure, and chronic obstructive pulmonary disease (COPD). A pulmonary specialist should be consulted to help determine the cause of any of these symptoms. Certain blood tests, a chest x-ray, and pulmonary function testing are some of the methods that the physician may use to investigate this.

With this background in mind, the following pages will discuss the major goals of respiratory management in the patient with ALS:

- Protect the airway; keep the airway clear of mucus and other secretions (includes prevention of choking and aspiration)
- Cough assist
- Improve lung expansion and prevent partial lung collapse
- Prevent lung infection (pneumonia and bronchitis)
- Preserve and assist ventilation
- Prevent shortness of breath and related anxiety

Note that these goals are very much related to one another in patients with ALS, and the patient should be working to achieve all of these goals throughout the course of the disorder.

## Protect and Keep the Airway Clear of Mucus and Other Secretions

Protecting the airway must be considered a priority in patients with ALS, whether or not primarily mouth and throat muscle (bulbar) weakness exists. One of the most feared complications of ALS, in particular when there is weakness of the muscles of swallowing and speech, is choking due either to swallowing food or liquids into the trachea (windpipe) or to the inability to get mucus and normal mouth and airway secretions out of the airway. This usually occurs in the later stages of the disorder but can occur at any time, sometimes in a sudden fashion. This is called *aspiration,* and it may be a sudden catastrophe or a chronic condition, with pneumonia being a common result.

Increased saliva production, with difficulty swallowing it and resultant drooling (*sialorrhea*), can predispose to aspiration and be a troubling symptom itself, causing dependence on suctioning devices and sometimes sleep interruption. Suctioning devices may be used to suction out the mouth and back of throat, taking care not to cause choking, gagging, or damage to the soft tissues at the back of the throat. Deeper suctioning is generally not advisable; if such suctioning seems necessary, the patient should be assessed in a medical facility. Treatments to improve sialorrhea often include *anticholinergic* medications, either oral or with a skin patch. Commonly used medications of this kind include scopolamine, hyoscine (Levsin), and glycopyrrolate (Robinul). Botulinum toxin injections can temporarily decrease salivary gland functions, but this is still considered an investigational procedure. If these fail, radiation of the parotid gland can be considered.

One needs to be careful about overdrying the secretions to the point where they may become thick and tenacious, and therefore more difficult to move and clear from the airway. Thick secretions may also occur from an infection or failure to clear natural airway secretions over time so that they pool in the airway. Such secretions may cause outright blockage of the upper airway. To treat this, adequate hydration is of primary importance. Along with this, expectorants, or agents that improve movement of secretions up the bronchial passages, such as Guaifenesin (e.g. Robitussin or Mucinex) may be helpful.

Nebulized solutions including saline, or dilators of the bronchial tree as used in patients with asthma, may be used to loosen and mobilize secretions and may be particularly effective if used preceding use of the cough assist device. These medications may have different effects on airway clearance and must be selected with care; for example, bronchodilators, such as albuterol, may be more likely to improve movement of the secretions up and out of the airway, whereas the anticholinergics, such as ipratropium, may decrease such clearance but achieve decreased or dryer secretions. These inhaled bronchodilator solutions have potential side effects, including increased heart rate and blood pressure, and generally should not be used if there is glaucoma.

Acetylcysteine (*mucomyst*) may also be used as a nebulized solution if other agents and attempts at airway clearance are not effective. Acetylcysteine should generally be used after a bronchodilator because it may cause the airways to spasm and close.

If postnasal drip is part of the cause of problematic secretions into the airway, local nasal sprays or systemic medications to constrict the nasal muscosa (such as phenylephrine) should be considered. Occasionally a choking sensation may occur when secretions drip into the back of the throat and cause reflex spasm of the vocal cords; lorazepam may be useful in that situation.

Avoidance of aspiration of food, liquids, and nose and mouth secretions into the airway protects both against sudden choking episodes and aspiration pneumonia. When these methods are not satisfactory in creating a clear airway, the decision to undergo tracheostomy may need to be considered. Such a procedure allows for improved ability to provide deep suctioning and clearance of secretions from the airway (see "Tracheostomy-Assisted Ventilation," below).

## Assisted Cough

A normal cough is critical for airway clearance; the gag reflex offers further protection. Each of these is compromised progressively during the course of ALS. Many patients are not aware that they need assistance with clearing secretions when their reserve is low; others may be aware of frequent difficulty with this. All, however, may benefit from cough assist to prevent lung and airway infection and clogging when lung function has decreased to low levels, with early initiation of assisted cough generally considered the best strategy whether or not the patient is symptomatic. Methods of breathing to assist cough can be learned, which may allow for "air stacking," thus starting the cough at higher lung volumes, which produces a greater ability to cough effectively. In many cases this can be accomplished with a simple bag-and-valve device. In many cases, however, inability to cough and clear the secretions in the airway necessitates a cough assist device to optimally allow for airway clearance. Also referred to as an *insufflator-exsufflator,* this is a machine that combines positive pressure to enhance lung volume and negative pressure to facilitate clearing of the airway. The patient wears a mask over the face that is attached to the machine. A cough assist device serves a dual purpose: airway clearance (thus decreasing risk of pneumonia and choking) and increasing lung expansion to prevent partial lung collapse. Therefore, cough assist treatments may benefit the patient with ALS even if clearing secretions and mucus is not a major problem at that point. This treatment is *not* intended to make the patient cough (and should not). Rather, it provides the function that coughing can no longer do in patients with ALS who can no longer do the 2 things necessary to generate a cough: close the vocal cords to build up pressure in the chest and generate a sufficient pressure in the chest to expel secretions. The increasing inspiratory lung volume in the time it is used takes the place of the sigh that all people do throughout the day and night, which reflexively expands the lung and prevents the lower lung units from collapsing.

Often the cough assist will be most beneficial when preceded by a nebulizer treatment with saline or a medication that helps loosen and moisten secretions as discussed above. Care must always be taken with such a device to avoid bringing up a large plug of mucus into the airway that cannot be dislodged and therefore causes choking, and it is also possible that secretions are brought up by the suction part, then deeper into the lungs by the positive pressure. Thorough training by a respiratory therapist when the device is set up in the home is necessary, as is review of the technique once it is begun.

## Improve Lung Expansion and Prevent Partial Lung Collapse

It has already been discussed how the use of methods to promote cough and airway clearance will help to keep the lungs expanded and partial lung collapse from occurring as the breathing muscles weaken during the progression of ALS. This in turn will directly help to improve and preserve ventilation and oxygenation, as well as help to prevent the development of lung infection. Assisted ventilation will also directly improve lung expansion. Prevention of pneumonia and assisted ventilation are discussed next.

## Prevent and Treat Pneumonia and Bronchitis

Pneumonia, or infection of the lungs, can be a life-threatening complication in a patient with ALS who has little respiratory reserve. Pneumonia is generally a more severe infection than bronchitis, in that it involves the deep airspaces of the lungs, and can severely interfere with the ability to move oxygen into the blood. Bronchitis, an infection of the bronchial tree, can also cause similar symptoms and severe problems with breathing. These infections usually are viral or bacterial, although other organisms including tuberculosis can also cause infection. Pneumonia may occur in the patient with ALS as bacteria or virus breathed in from someone who has the infection or is harboring the germ. Aspiration has already been discussed as a possible precipitant of life-threatening lung infection or choking.

Signs and symptoms of pneumonia may include chills, fevers, night sweats or shaking chills, cough, chest pain particularly with deep inspiration, worsening shortness of breath and sensation of an increased work of breathing, low $O_2$ levels, increased breathing rate, increased heart rate, low blood pressure, and decreased appetite. Some patients may develop a low body temperature. Clinical evaluation will likely include a chest x-ray and blood count; sputum or blood cultures may also be needed. At times, treatment with an oral antibiotic may be sufficient, but proper follow-up is necessary; otherwise, intravenous antibiotics may be necessary.

Pneumovax injection, generally given every 10 years, and yearly influenza immunizations are generally recommended to help prevent pneumonia in the patient with ALS, unless an allergy to one of the products is known.

## Preserve and Assist Ventilation

Weakening of the diaphragm and other respiratory muscles is progressive and irreversible in ALS; no treatments are currently available that can be reasonably expected to restore lost muscle strength and function. Therefore, the main goal of ALS treatment is to preserve respiratory muscle function for as long as possible and assist ventilation when such function declines to the point where it is causing symptoms or signs of respiratory insufficiency. Ventilatory assistance is used for both purposes; in fact, it is felt that by assisting ventilation one can not only prevent signs and symptoms of respiratory insufficiency but also perhaps prolong the strength of the respiratory muscles over the course of the illness.

Preserving respiratory function includes the following: avoid tiring the muscles, either by exerting to the point of exhaustion or feeling greatly short of breath; avoid sleeping without necessary assisted ventilation; and allow for the lungs to expand maximally throughout the course of the day, thus preventing collapse of the lungs as they function at a consistently low capacity. Both assisted ventilation and use of cough assist methods can aid with such expansion. It is important for the patient with ALS to remain active to allow for best overall function of the respiratory system. Assisted ventilation during sleep is particularly important and is discussed separately below. Adequate nutrition is also considered important to preserve respiratory muscle function and is discussed below.

Once the patient has reached the point of needing to work particularly hard to maintain adequate ventilation, inability to maintain ventilation will worsen the respiratory symptoms that have been discussed, and may as result in inadequate oxygenation and ability to clear carbon dioxide from the body. Further, more oxygenated blood will be used for the muscles of breathing and less will be available for the other needs of the body. Assisted ventilation is indicated at this point to preserve adequate ventilation. There are basically two types of assisted ventilation: noninvasive and tracheostomy-assisted ventilation.

## Noninvasive Ventilation

Nocturnal noninvasive positive pressure ventilation (NIV), which is positive airway pressure delivered via a compact pressure-cycled system, may improve overall survival when begun in patients with ALS who have a lung volume capacity (vital capacity) of less than 50% of predicted and may preserve respiratory muscle function and quality of life. When patients keep up with nutrition, hydration, and airway clearance, NIV can often provide adequate assisted ventilation for patients with ALS until well into the last stages of the disorder.

Shortness of breath alone is often reason enough to begin a trial of NIV. There are also specific criteria used by specialists and generally mandated by insurance providers, including measurement of low inspiratory muscle pressures, a vital capacity less than 50% of predicted, or specific levels of awake increased $CO_2$ or low levels of $O_2$ during sleep.

Depending on the physician seen and the respiratory services involved, patients may be exposed to a bewildering array of such devices, such as volume-cycled, pressure-cycled, and bilevel units, sometimes being advised to use one for awake NIV and another for sleeping. This should not be so complicated or confusing. Basically, the idea is to have a small machine that can be placed by the patient's bedside or chair. It delivers air from the room under pressure into the patient's airway and lungs, using a soft tubing attached to a mask fitting over the nose, or a soft interface inserted directly into the nose (*nasal pillows*) or held in the mouth. Usually the push of air into the nose or mouth and down into the lungs is triggered by the patient's own respiratory efforts, allowing for less work on the part of the patient to breathe. Speech is usually possible during the exhalation phase of breathing. It is not clear that any specific type of positive pressure ventilator is most effective awake or asleep, and the decision regarding what pressure or volume should be used is often made based on the experience of the clinician and the patient's comfort. Although patients may need a fair amount of time to get used to such ventilation, they should immediately feel that NIV is improving their work of breathing.

All such ventilators can be attached to a wheelchair to allow the patient to leave the home while maintaining assisted ventilation. Special mouthpieces can be used for providing such ventilation (sometimes referred to as *sip and puff*), which allows the patient freedom from having to use a nasal mask or nasal pillows during the day when awake. To use such ventilation, a patient needs a special portable ventilator rather than the usual bilevel positive air pressure (BiPAP) machine. Many patients with ALS will not be able to keep their mouth closed during sleep with NIV, resulting in air leaking from the mouth. A larger mask (full-face mask) that covers the nose and mouth, or a chin strap used with a nasal mask, may be helpful in that situation. Often a patient uses a full-face mask at night, and nasal pillows or a mouthpiece when awake. Many different types of interfaces are available for patients to effectively use this assistive device. Oxygen may be added to the breathing circuit as necessary and as determined by the physician (see below); humidification is usually attached to moisturize and warm the air being delivered to the patient's airway.

A respiratory therapist will usually set up the NIV based on the physician's orders, but ongoing evaluation is necessary as breathing strength declines. A pulmonologist (a physician expert in respiratory disorders) experienced with using NIV in patients with ALS should be involved in setting up and monitoring the NIV. Decisions regarding the use of NIV include what type of machine to use and at what pressure levels; levels that are too high may cause discomfort, air leak, and inability to sleep, while levels that are too low may simply result in inadequate ventilation. Although comfort is a primary concern regarding the use of NIV, patients should be aware that using NIV based only on how they feel that they are benefiting may result in a significant degree of failure of adequate ventilation during sleep.

NIV is usually first used during sleep because sleep is the time when breathing is most challenged as noted below under "Sleep, Breathing, and ALS." A sleep study overnight in the sleep center or at home, which measures breathing function, $O_2$ and $CO_2$ levels, and sleep quality, may be requested to determine how effective the NIV actually is, and to directly adjust it to the ventilation needs of the patient during sleep.

Many patients wonder whether they should use the NIV when they are awake, and if so, for how long a session. In general, one should use it when feeling short of breath. It is not known whether early use of such NIV (that is, before there is a severe decrease in muscle function or the patient is symptomatic) will preserve respiratory muscle function. It is also possible that using NIV when it is not clearly needed may stretch and weaken rather than strengthen respiratory muscles in patients with ALS. Even patients with difficulty swallowing and handling airway secretions may be able to benefit from NIV, although particular care must be taken in this situation to avoid aspiration, and many such patients will not find NIV helpful or even tolerable.

Patients should not feel that using assisted ventilation makes one dependent on the ventilator, and that once it is begun patients will not be able to come off it. Rather, one may become dependent on the NIV because of the progression of respiratory muscle weakness. NIV may in fact become a 24-hour-a-day treatment; that is, the patient can use the ventilation when awake and sitting up, even while working, and throughout the night while sleeping. We see a number of patients who live fully by using 24-hour-a-day NIV. However, it is necessary to remember that the use of NIV when a patient cannot maintain adequate awake ventilation on his or her own does not guarantee that failure of the treatment and sudden death awake or in sleep will not occur. In such a case it must be clearly understood by the patient, caregivers, family, and clinician that this possibility exists. All must be knowledgeable partners regarding what the specific limitations and parameters of the equipment are (e.g., battery lifetime if the patient is using such treatment out of the home) and agree that this risk is in fact consonant with the overall plan for the patient. The alternative to NIV in this setting is tracheostomy-assisted ventilation, discussed below.

## Tracheostomy-Assisted Ventilation

Tracheostomy-assisted ventilation involves the surgical placement of a soft tube directly into the trachea (windpipe) just below the vocal cords. Ventilation is then given by directing the pressurized air from the ventilator directly into the tracheostomy (trache) tube. The trache tube usually has a cuff at the end that is inflated by air to allow it to sit snugly in the patient's trachea. The actual ventilator unit is typically compact and portable, similar to a unit used for NIV.

Tracheostomy-assisted ventilation is generally considered for two reasons: when it is no longer possible to adequately ensure that the upper airway can be cleared of secretions and mucus that may block the entry of oxygen and thus cause sudden death; or when it is no longer possible to provide adequate ventilation with NIV because of the progression of respiratory muscle weakness or weakness of the muscles that keep the airway from collapsing. When used primarily for airway protection and clearance, it may be possible to close (cap) the trache tube during awake periods without using ventilation, while opening it only at night during sleep periods. As with NIV, tracheostomy-assisted ventilation is generally not indicated early in the course of the disorder; there is no evidence that this will prolong life.

Tracheostomy-assisted ventilation can also be considered in a patient who might be able to benefit from ventilatory support but cannot tolerate the use of NIV. Overall in the United States, only a small minority of patients with ALS receive trache-assisted ventilation. Such assisted ventilation may help prolong life well beyond the time that would be possible without the use of a trache in many patients. However, the use of a trache is not a guarantee of a lengthy lifespan; even with skilled care, plugging of the trache tube with mucus secretions may cause sudden failure of breathing, and aspiration and pneumonia may occur even with the trache in place. Pain and infection at the site may also occur. Nonrespiratory problems that are not prevented by the trache-assisted ventilation, including heart and blood pressure failure, may also occur. Patients who consider such ventilation must also consider that assisted ventilation via a tracheostomy is likely to result in ability to maintain adequate oxygenation and life well after all major muscles of the body have severely weakened or failed and the ability to communicate has become severely compromised or is even absent. Costs for such ventilation are high, primarily because of the need for skilled caregivers (see Chapter 13).

## Other Types of Assisted Ventilation

Numerous centers are currently investigating the possibility of placing electrodes into the diaphragm to stimulate (pace) the nerves to move the diaphragm and thus allow assisted breathing without the use of a ventilator. It has been suggested that such treatment can strengthen the diaphragm in ALS. Such pacing remains an experimental procedure at the time of this writing.

## Prevent Shortness of Breath and Related Anxiety

The feeling of shortness of breath (or breathlessness, air hunger, dyspnea) can be associated with much anxiety and even fear. The dyspnea that patients with ALS may feel generally comes from several sources, including the respiratory system sensing the need to breathe deeper to generate more ventilation, as well as the sensation of high $CO_2$ levels, sometimes combined with the sensation of low $O_2$ levels. Lung and heart problems may add to such feelings of air hunger. Therefore, treatment of shortness of breath and the related anxiety must be individualized and should generally include a trial of assisted ventilation. Occasionally, supplementation of oxygen may be helpful. Medications that may be helpful in this setting, in particular if the patient is already using maximal ventilation or cannot tolerate ventilation, include oral benzodiazepines (such as valium, lorazepam, and midazolam), sublingual (under the tongue) benzodiazepines, and inhaled opioids. For severe breathlessness and the anxiety related to it, opioids (including morphine) can be given intravenously, by skin patch, by injection, by mouth, or by feeding tube. All of these, however, may depress breathing drive.

## Respiratory Management in ALS: Other Frequently Asked (and Not Asked) Questions

### Percutaneous Endoscopic Gastrostomy

Percutaneous endoscopic gastrostomy (PEG) has become an important part of preserving ventilation and airway clearance and avoiding pneumonia in ALS. It is considered that preserved respiratory muscle strength and function will be optimal if caloric needs are met; at the same time, there is decreased risk of aspiration if one can get sufficient calories without having to force oral feedings. Thus, PEG placement is generally recommended when necessary to prevent pneumonia and preserve caloric intake. Early intervention with PEG has been shown to prolong survival to some extent. PEG placement is usually considered if there are consistent or progressive difficulties with swallowing, or if the forced vital capacity (FVC) decreases to 50% of the predicted range. However, PEG placement and use is not without potential complications, including infection and bowel dysfunction. During placement, which is usually done with local anesthesia, patients need to be flat and receive mild sedation, each of which may contribute to poorer ventilatory function and the risk of respiratory compromise and even respiratory failure. Therefore, it is usually recommended that PEG placement be done relatively early in the course of the disorder, even before the PEG is actually necessary for feeding. It is, however, also possible to put in a feeding tube at a more advanced stage either by special radiology methods or surgery.

## Pulmonary Function Testing

Pulmonary function testing, or PFT, is often performed at successive visits with patients with ALS, both to assess the rate of decline in the individual patient and to help plan the initiation of treatments such as cough assist, NIV, and PEG. The decline of lung function in ALS has been measured as 2% to 5% per month.

In general, this testing involves portable hand-held machines in the office, and includes FVC and maximal breathing muscle pressures (MIP and MEP) while seated and also often while lying down. These tests are sometimes performed through the nose during a maximal sniff maneuver. Such testing is sometimes performed in a hospital pulmonary function laboratory. Particularly if a lung disorder other than the muscle weakness of ALS itself is suspected. These tests are chosen because they give a fair estimation of respiratory reserve and function and measure to what extent the respiratory muscle weakness is affecting the ability to maintain adequate ventilation. However, no single such test or set of tests gives definitive information regarding the prognosis of a patient with ALS, and it is emphasized that patients and their families should *not* feel that a low FVC or maximal muscle strength testing score means that respiratory failure or death will occur very soon. Although a decline in such function usually does indicate progressive weakness of breathing, there is enough reserve in the ventilatory system so that many patients can ventilate adequately, at least for the amount of effort they generally expend, even when the FVC is extremely low and, in fact, no longer measurable because of the inability to perform the maneuver. Further, patients may have severely compromised muscle strength with a relatively high FVC.

## Sleep, Breathing, and ALS

There are numerous respiratory considerations for the patient with ALS concerning sleep. Sleep is a time wherein the muscles of breathing as well as the "drive" from the brain to breathe decrease; therefore, the patient with ALS is at risk of worsening hypoventilation when asleep. Further, there is more need to work the muscles of breathing to compensate for this, generally risking ongoing taxing and eventual greater weakening of the respiratory muscles. Therefore, sleep is a time when ventilation and oxygenation may be most impaired, even more so than if the patient were exercising. Patients with ALS and those involved in their care should therefore be aware that sleep is a situation that specifically challenges the ability to breathe, in terms of the cough reflex, handling of airway secretions (drooling, decreased ability to swallow), positioning that puts the respiratory muscles at a mechanical disadvantage, as well as the ability to maintain regular breathing rhythm. Patients with ALS may also have sleep apnea, a condition of repeated episodes of breathing stopping, or being obstructed in the throat, during sleep. Failure to maintain normal blood oxygenation and carbon dioxide levels during sleep could also place stress on the breathing muscles and the heart as well as disrupt sleep, thus causing insomnia, fatigue, decreased alertness, decreased sense of well-being, and morning headache. For all of these reasons, noninvasive ventilation, when begun, is typically used during sleep, as noted in the section "Noninvasive Ventilation". Sleep studies in the hospital laboratory are sometimes ordered as necessary, in particular when a disorder other than ALS itself is suspected, such as sleep apnea.

## Oxygen

Oxygen does not specifically improve ventilation, or the work of breathing, and in many cases may decrease the drive to breathe. Therefore it must be used cautiously, in general, when there is persistent decrease in the oxygenation of the blood as measured by the saturation or by a blood gas, which cannot be reversed with assisted ventilation. Oxygen should be given only at the lowest level that keeps oxygen saturation above 90%. Most often, $O_2$ is added to NIV or given in the setting of palliative care. Most patients do not have failure of awake oxygenation until very late in the course of ALS, unless there is evidence of severe respiratory problems such as pneumonia.

## Other General Care Issues

It is not clear that pulmonary rehabilitation programs that may be helpful in certain lung diseases, such as COPD, are helpful in ALS. However, patients with ALS should not avoid exercise; rather, they should keep active, thus exercising the lungs, as long as they do not exercise to the point of severe shortness of breath or fatigue, as noted earlier. Once a patient with ALS is immobilized, risk of developing a clot in the veins of the lower extremities needs to be considered; painful swelling of the legs, particularly one greater than the other, should be immediately reported to the physician, because such clots can travel to the lungs (pulmonary embolism) and cause severe illness or even death. Compression stockings may decrease this risk to some extent; in cases of proven deep venous clot, blood thinners are generally prescribed.

Maintenance of adequate nutrition and normal blood electrolytes, and avoidance of medications that may interfere with breathing drive, particularly during sleep (such as certain sleeping aids, including all benzodiazepines), are all part of the necessary respiratory considerations in patients with ALS. When ALS is diagnosed, it is also important to remember that patients may have additional lung or heart disease that affects respiratory management. For all of these reasons, a multidisciplinary center, which includes pulmonologists and neurologists as well as nutrition and speech and swallowing experts, is the preferred way to approach the respiratory treatment of the patient with ALS.

# 13

# Life Support: Realities and Dilemmas

## Mark B. Bromberg and Estelle S. Harris

Amyotrophic lateral sclerosis (ALS) is a disease of motor nerves. Weakness begins in one area of the body and progresses to other areas. At some point, the muscles of respiration become weak, breathing becomes impaired, and death eventually comes from respiratory failure.

The rate of progression of weakness is gradual. This provides time for patients to reflect on their lives, including their mortality. This, in turn, gives them the opportunity to make decisions regarding their death. Although death is a necessary consequence of living, it is the one universal experience for which no sage advisor is available for consultation. Because of the very personal issue of mortality, questions about respiratory failure and respiratory support are uncomfortable topics for people with ALS, their families, and health care providers. This makes counsel and management of respiratory failure one of the greatest challenges for all involved.

This chapter focuses on realities and dilemmas. The most important reality in ALS is the predictable progression to respiratory failure. The essential dilemma is the choice of whether to support respiration artificially with a breathing machine or to pass away as part of the course of the disease. Intertwined with the reality of failure and the dilemma of support are a number of other related issues that affect patients and caregivers. A primary role of health care providers is to give you and your family full information about respiratory failure and artificial respiratory support.

ALS affects every patient, caregiver, and family member in a different way. It is during discussions about respiratory failure that the range of issues in ALS becomes apparent. Health care providers can guide you and your family through the decision process. During this process, the patient's wishes should be held high, but at the same time consideration should also be given to caregivers and family.

This chapter is divided into 3 sections. The first section discusses the *realities* of respiratory failure. It is important for both patient and health care provider to recognize early symptoms of respiratory failure. Patients learn from a variety of sources that death in ALS occurs from respiratory failure. However, it is our experience that patients rarely understand the mechanism, time course, and physical events that occur with respiratory failure and death in ALS. Having specific information about these difficult issues can help to resolve fears.

The second section discusses the *equipment* that is used to assist or support respiration. An understanding of the choices and equipment is important for the patient and family in making decisions.

The third section discusses the *dilemmas* of making choices. Assisted or supported ventilation can relieve symptoms of respiratory distress and can prolong life for the patient but is physically limiting because of the equipment. It also poses dilemmas for the caregivers in the form of increased responsibilities and decreased freedom. The cost of supported ventilation in the home can be formidable and can present a financial dilemma. Finally, when a patient is dependent on mechanical ventilation, ALS continues to progress with greater weakness, and the decision to discontinue respiratory support at some point may be the ultimate dilemma for the patient, family, and clinician.

## The Realities of Respiratory Failure

This section discusses the symptoms of respiratory failure, how they occur, and how people die of ALS.

### Muscles of Respiration

The muscles of respiration are part of the skeletal muscle system. The diaphragm is the major muscle of inspiration. The external intercostal muscles (muscles between the ribs) and the strap muscles in the neck are the secondary or accessory muscles of respiration. Muscles of respiration, like limb and bulbar muscles, are activated or innervated by lower motor neurons. In ALS these neurons degenerate and die. The loss of motor neurons causes muscles to become weak. The lower motor neurons for the diaphragm start in the upper portion of the cervical spinal cord, segments C3–C5, and travel to the diaphragm in the phrenic nerves.

It is not possible to determine when weakness of the diaphragm first begins, because a muscle does not become perceptively weak until 40% to 50% of the motor neurons going to it have died. The delay in weakness is due to what is termed *collateral reinnervation,* the body's attempt to compensate for motor nerve loss. It is a process whereby a surviving neuron grows new branches to reinnervate muscle fibers that have lost their connection after a motor neuron dies. When only a few motor neurons have died, collateral reinnervation can compensate well, and the muscle remains strong. As more motor neurons die, collateral reinnervation cannot keep up, and the muscle becomes weak. Weakness will begin earlier in rapidly progressive ALS because muscle fibers are denervated at a faster rate than they can be reinnervated.

Although collateral reinnervation is an important compensation process, once it begins to fail, the symptoms of respiratory failure become apparent and progress.

## Respiratory Muscle Fatigue

Respiratory failure occurs when the diaphragm can no longer maintain adequate ventilation. An additional factor is muscle fatigue. Normally, the diaphragm never becomes fatigued, even after heavy breathing during exercise. However, in ALS, the diaphragm will fatigue when it becomes weak, particularly if extra physical effort is exerted.

In most people with ALS, the diaphragm tends to weaken only relatively late in the course of the disease, after other muscles have become very weak. For example, patients who have almost no movement of legs or arms may be able to breathe comfortably when sitting. In these situations, although the diaphragm is weak, it is strong enough to keep up with their reduced level of physical activity and respiratory needs. If patients exert extra physical effort, however, they may experience fatigue of the diaphragm. One common situation is shortness of breath resulting from the effort of bathing or dressing. Shortness of breath may also be experienced when lying down. In the upright position, the diaphragm moves downward in the chest and does not push the abdominal organs out of the way. In the lying position, however, the diaphragm must work harder because of the resistance in pushing against the organs. Thus, a weak diaphragm becomes fatigued when a patient is lying down, causing a feeling of shortness of breath and the need to sit up.

## Dyspnea

Over time, as muscle strength decreases, it is common for patients to experience shallow respirations and greater work of breathing. Shortness of breath, known also by its medical term *dyspnea,* is described by patients "as a complex of symptoms which can be variable and include an uncomfortable awareness of breathing, a panicky feeling of being smothered, a feeling of increased effort or tiredness in moving the muscles of the chest, or a sense of tightness or cramping in the chest wall." Dyspnea results from a combination of impulses relayed to the brain from nerve endings in the chest muscles, rib cage, lungs, and diaphragm, combined with the patient's perception and interpretation of these sensations.

Dyspnea can occur in many situations but most commonly falls into one of three categories. Patients may have an underlying lung disease like emphysema or asthma, an abnormality of the muscles of breathing as in ALS, or a systemic disease like heart failure or severe anemia. Dyspnea can be improved by treating the underlying causes: inhalers and oxygen in the case of emphysema, assisted venti-lation (see below) for muscle weakness, or treatment of the sensation of dyspnea with medications (i.e., morphine). However, dyspnea, like pain, is a subjective symptom, meaning it cannot be measured like oxygen or carbon dioxide levels in the blood (see below) by a laboratory test.

## Oxygen and Carbon Dioxide

The job of the diaphragm and respiratory muscles is to move air in to and out of the lungs. During inspiration the lungs bring in fresh air containing oxygen, and during exhalation the lungs eliminate carbon dioxide. In the lungs, oxygen is taken up into the blood and is used by the body's cells for energy production. In contrast, carbon dioxide, a waste product of cellular energy production, moves from the circulating blood into the lungs and is removed from the body by exhalation.

When diaphragm muscle strength decreases it is common for patients to ex-perience shallow respirations. The body compensates for smaller air exchange by increasing the number of breaths per minute. Initially the body compensates well, but as weakness progresses and carbon dioxide production is greater than the lungs can eliminate, an excess of carbon dioxide accumulates in the blood. Symp-toms associated with increased carbon dioxide and respiratory failure (termed *hy-percapnic respiratory failure*) include dyspnea, morning headaches, and daytime sleepiness. Patients with ALS who have hypercapnic respiratory failure often have lower oxygen levels because of the overall decrease in lung gas exchange. This can be treated with assisted or artificial ventilation (see below). Oxygen replacement alone will not treat the retained carbon dioxide and it has been shown to worsen some sleeping disturbances (see below). It is important to realize that patients with ALS may also have some degree of underlying lung disease (i.e., asthma, obstruc-tive sleep apnea, or emphysema), which, in conjunction with muscle weakness, results in more severe symptoms and/or earlier onset of respiratory failure.

To relieve the physical abnormalities and symptoms associated with respiratory failure, it is often necessary to help the diaphragm with assisted ventilation or to completely take over for the diaphragm with artificial ventilation. A weak dia-phragm can also be helped by reducing the amount of energy used during activi-ties, such as by resting while bathing or dressing or sleeping in a reclining position rather than flat in bed. When these changes do not relieve shortness of breath, it is often necessary to use assisted or artificial ventilation.

### Sleep Disturbances

Sleep is a time of particular concern in ALS because a number of changes occur that may affect breathing. One is a change in body position. A person may not be aware that he or she has turned over onto his or her stomach during the night, a change that can lead to diaphragm fatigue. A second change during sleep is that breathing naturally becomes a little irregular; if the diaphragm is weak, it may not be able to keep up. The third and most important change occurs during the period of sleep characterized by rapid eye movements (REM sleep). The body is in its most relaxed state during REM sleep. All muscles are quiet except for those that move the eyes and the diaphragm. This includes the muscles that help keep the throat open to allow free movement of air. Thus, the work of breathing increases during REM sleep, and the diaphragm may fatigue in people with ALS. When the diaphragm fatigues, not enough fresh air comes in and not enough carbon dioxide goes out. A patient will not go through all the normal stages of sleep but will be aroused to a lighter stage of sleep. At the lighter stages of sleep, the muscles that keep the throat open become active and the patient moves more air in to and out of the lungs more freely. The patient then drifts back into deeper sleep and greater muscle relaxation. This cycle can repeat up to hundreds of times during the night. Patients may not be aware of these arousals but will receive insufficient deep sleep and will experience sleepiness during the daytime as a result of chronic sleep deprivation.

Although this situation does not happen to everyone with ALS, it is important to look for signs of disturbed sleep. The first sign may be headache on waking in the morning. This headache is presumably due to excess carbon dioxide from poor movement of air in to and out of the lungs during the night. Another symptom is excessive daytime sleepiness, falling asleep during the day when one does not want to. Examples include falling asleep while dressing and eating or while talking to family and friends.

There are several ways to investigate the cause of disturbed sleep in patients with ALS when it may be due to respiratory compromise. The physician can order a simple test called *overnight oximetry,* which can be performed in the home. Nocturnal oximetry measures the percentage of oxygen in the blood during sleep. A clip with a sensor is placed on the patient's finger, and a wire goes to a small machine that records heart rate and oxygen saturation in the blood. The results can be printed on a strip of paper for the physician to review. If there are periods of low oxygen during sleep, called desaturations, the neurologist may recommend additional testing or suggest that the patient try assisted breathing. The additional test is called a *sleep study* or *polysomnogram.* This test usually requires the patient to sleep for 1 or 2 nights in a special room in the hospital or clinic.

It is important to emphasize again that unless a patient with ALS has lung disease, such as emphysema from smoking, desaturations and respiratory events during sleep will not be easily treated with extra oxygen alone. Some studies even suggest that oxygen alone can increase the duration and severity of the respiratory events during sleep. The optimal way to treat nocturnal respiratory events is with assisted or artificial ventilation. The neurologist may manage this or have the patient see a pulmonologist (lung doctor).

## Measurement of Respiratory Weakness

It is more difficult to measure diaphragm weakness than to measure arm or leg weakness. The most useful test is to measure how much air can be forcefully exhaled. This measurement is called *forced vital capacity,* or FVC. A patient will be asked to take in as deep a breath as possible and then blow out as hard and as long as possible—similar to blowing out all of the candles on a birthday cake with lots of candles. To measure the amount of air exhaled, the patient blows into a tube that is attached to a machine called a spirometer. It is important that all of the air go into the spirometer mouthpiece, and a clip may be placed on the nose to prevent a loss of air.

The amount of air exhaled is measured in liters (a liter is a little less than a quart) and is compared with the FVC for people of the same gender, age, and height. This is called the percent of predicted FVC (% FVC). Normally, a person starts out with a predicted FVC of 90% to 100%. As the diaphragm weakens, the % FVC will fall. It is important to understand that the measurement of FVC can be difficult to perform accurately. It takes coordination to place the mouthpiece in the mouth at the right time. It also requires a big effort to blow out all of the air. As a result, % FVC predicted values are not absolutely accurate, and a patient should not be overly concerned about small changes. What is important is a trend of falling values.

## Progression of Weakness

ALS is a progressive disorder, and progression of diaphragm weakness is the most important issue. As discussed earlier, diaphragm weakness frequently occurs relatively late in the course of ALS. It is customary to measure % FVC at every clinic visit. For both limb muscles and the diaphragm, the rate of loss of strength tends to be constant for an individual patient. However, it is not possible to accurately predict when respiration will become a problem. Generally speaking, respiratory issues should be discussed at the time the FVC reaches 50% of predicted. However, the % FVC is not the only thing to follow, and it is also important to consider the symptoms of shortness of breath and respiratory failure that were discussed earlier. As the % FVC falls or the patient has symptoms of shortness of breath, both the realities of respiratory failure and how to manage these realities should be discussed.

### Respiratory Failure

Many people with ALS are concerned about how they will die. They frequently worry that they will suddenly choke to death or will suddenly be without air and gasping. It is our experience that most patients with ALS pass away peacefully, frequently in their sleep. Choking very rarely causes death in ALS. Aspiration of food leading to pneumonia is also rare. A small number of patients may be anxious or restless or have "air hunger" late in the course of their disease. These symptoms can usually be managed medically. If a patient wishes to have respiration supported, machines are available to relieve the symptoms. If a patient does not choose to have respiration supported, medications can be given to make the patient comfortable as death occurs.

Sometimes a patient will be very short of breath and want to have his or her respiration supported for a limited period (several days) to allow time to put or her affairs in order and to say goodbye. Under these circumstances, a patient can go on a breathing machine temporarily. When the patient is ready, he or she can be allowed to pass away in complete comfort. Medications will be given to make the patient physically comfortable and unaware of his or her surroundings. Only at that point will ventilator support be withdrawn.

As this time approaches, it is important that the neurologist discusses the issues of respiratory failure very frankly with the family, including options, the patient's wishes, and hospice services. It is useful to have hospice services to help with patient care at the late stages of ALS, or any disease. If air hunger occurs with ALS, hospice personnel have experience with relieving the symptoms with medication. In addition, a hospice nurse is always available and can assist the patient and family at any hour.

## Assisted and Artificial Ventilation

Although the natural course of ALS ends in death from respiratory failure, it is important for the patient with ALS and the family to understand that the reality of death can be postponed or prevented by artificial ventilation. This section discusses the various forms of ventilation.

When the diaphragm becomes weak and begins to fail, the only effective way to manage respiratory failure is by mechanically assisting or supporting ventilation. There are two general types of mechanical ventilation, invasive and noninvasive. These two types are discussed separately.

### Invasive Ventilation

The term *invasive ventilation* is used because a cannula, or breathing tube, must be placed in the patient's trachea (windpipe). This is also called a *trache* tube. A tracheal cannula is used because it is the only practical and comfortable way to provide air to the lungs 24 hours a day for a long period. If artificial ventilation is urgently needed, a temporary tube may be placed in the trachea through the mouth. This is called an endotracheal tube. An endotracheal tube can only be used for about 2 to 4 weeks; if needed beyond this time, a tracheostomy (placement of the trache tube) is performed by a surgeon during a simple operation. With invasive ventilation, a breathing machine automatically provides all the *air exchange* needed and can completely take the place of the diaphragm. Other terms that are used for invasive ventilation are *artificial* or *supported* ventilation. A patient can live for many years with invasive ventilation and good care.

The breathing machines used for invasive ventilation are called ventilators (vents) or respirators. They are small devices that are about the size of a bread box. There is a flexible plastic tube that goes from the machine to the tracheal cannula. The controls on the machine are simple, and the machines are reliable. The patient and family learn about mechanical ventilation and become comfortable with the ventilator and caring for the patient during an initial hospital stay. Thereafter, they work with a pulmonologist and a respiratory therapist from a home care agency or with a respiratory therapist from the hospital for ongoing care issues. Ventilators are powered by household current or a battery and thus are portable. Emergency issues must also be considered in the event of a power failure, including extra backup batteries and a portable generator. Patients should inform the local power company and fire department that someone in the household is dependent on a ventilator. Further, it is wise to have a backup ventilator in case of mechanical failure.

A frequently asked question is "What is it like being on artificial ventilation?" Descriptions from patients who have been on artificial ventilation for a limited period, although they are not patients with ALS, are informative. Initially, there may be some anxiety associated with intubation and mechanical inflation of the lungs. Because some respiratory muscle function is present when ventilation is started, there usually is a period of adjustment during which the natural rhythm of respiration fights with the artificial pattern of mechanical ventilation. In ALS, however, the feeling of air hunger that prompted the artificial breathing machine will disappear immediately, and the patient will feel relief.

Some physical discomfort may occur while on invasive ventilation. Supported ventilation remains permanently artificial, and the ventilator cannot provide for sighs, gasps, or sneezes, which have been described as part of the "respiratory vocabulary." Because the patient will not be able to adequately cough up secretions from the lungs, someone must help to suction out secretions. This requires placement of a small rubber tube inside the tracheal cannula. The rubber tube is connected to a suction device, and the secretions are aspirated by a vacuum. Suctioning brings relief from the discomfort of secretions but may be an uncomfortable procedure. Although suctioning usually is done infrequently, it may be needed often under certain circumstances, such as when a patient has a cold. A second device called a *cough assist machine* is an alternative way of eliminating airway secretions. The cough assist machine is a small pump that pushes a fairly large volume of air into the lungs and then rapidly reverses to a negative pressure vacuum that rapidly sucks the air and secretions out of the lung. The cough assist machine can be attached to the tracheal cannula directly or attached to a mask for patients not using invasive ventilation. The cough assist machine appears to decrease the need for direct suctioning and helps to prevent recurrent airway collapse secondary to secretions.

After the initial fears and tribulations of artificial ventilation are dealt with, there is an adjustment period of a different type in which a patient begins to reestablish self-worth, regains control, and begins to think about and make decisions concerning the future. At this time, the reality of all that is involved with artificial ventilation becomes apparent. This transition has been described as "getting on with life." This getting on applies to the whole family. Factors include adjustments in lifestyle and physical living arrangements in the home, reestablishing work and recreational interests, and integrating these with the interests and activities of the rest of the family. The transition phase must be an active and continuous process because more adjustments become necessary as the patient's strength and function continue to decline with the passage of time.

Another question is whether a patient with ALS will be able to speak while on artificial ventilation. If a patient was able to speak just before starting artificial ventilation, he or she will not be able to speak right after placement of the tracheal tube. Several weeks later, the first tube can be replaced by a special tracheal tube that allows leakage of air, and a patient can learn to speak with some practice. More commonly, people who need invasive ventilation already have difficulties with speech. The strength to make speech sounds eventually will be lost, and a patient will have to use other means to communicate. These include responding to yes-no questions and alphabet boards or use of computer-assisted communication systems (see "Managing Communication and Swallowing Difficulties" chapter).

## Noninvasive Ventilation

Assisted or noninvasive ventilation (NIV) does not require a tracheal tube. Instead, the machine connects to an interface, which can be a small mask fitted over the nose or a larger one fitted over the nose and mouth, or a cannula secured under the nose (nasal pillows). The machine does not usually provide the entire volume of air needed but just assists the patient. NIV is used mainly to decrease the work of breathing and to relieve the symptoms of dyspnea associated with diaphragm fatigue. Given difficulties with ventilation and sleep disorders during sleep, noninvasive ventilation is most commonly used at night. Other frequently used terms for NIV are noninvasive positive pressure ventilation (NPPV), bilevel ventilation, or BiPAP ventilation. These terms are used because, in NIV, air is given to the patient at two levels: a lower level during expiration and a higher level during inspiration. In this way, the patient gets more air during inspiration. Strictly speaking, BiPAP is a brand name for a particular company's model of bilevel noninvasive ventilation machine.

The bilevel ventilator is small (the size of a bread box) and is powered by household current. Plastic tubing goes between the machine and the interface masks. It is important that all of the air from the machine goes into the patient's lungs, and the fit of the mask or nasal pillows is very important. Just as there are many different shapes of people's faces, there are many different shapes of masks and nasal pillows. Sometimes the mouth is held closed by a strap to prevent leakage of air through the mouth. It is important for patients to work with a respiratory therapist to find a comfortable system. This may require several different trials, and a patient may need to alternate between different interfaces.

A similar question—"What is it like to be on bilevel ventilation?"—is asked about NIV. Patients describe several different sensations. Some patients are distressed at having a mask placed over the mouth and nose and may also be distressed at having a stream of air forced on them. However, for the majority of patients, bilevel ventilation decreases the sensation of dypspnea, improves sleep quality, and increases daytime energy levels. NIV gives a patient time to adjust to the events of ALS.

Some people have difficulty getting used to bilevel ventilation. Several factors may predict successful use. The most important one is weakness of bulbar muscles. Patients who have weak speech and swallowing tend to have a harder time with bilevel ventilation than those who have good bulbar function. The most important recommendation is that patients relax when they first try bilevel ventilation. Because there are two settings (the pressure for the stream of air during exhalation and the pressure for the stream of air during inhalation), it is wise to set these two pressures low when a patient first tries bilevel ventilation and to turn the pressures up slowly. Some physicians and respiratory therapists let patients adjust the settings themselves in order to give them control. Some patients feel closed in with the mask, especially at night. It may be helpful to start noninvasive ventilation in the daytime, beginning with 30 minutes, and slowly advancing as comfort dictates. The minimum goal is to use noninvasive ventilation at least 4 or more hours per night. Because it can take some time to get used to bilevel ventilation, many neurologists recommend starting NIV early, before a patient actually needs it during sleep.

Can bilevel NIV be used to support ventilation full-time; that is, can bilevel ventilation be used in place of invasive ventilation? Yes, it can. As patients require more and more time on bilevel ventilation, they can approach full-time use. A recent survey of patients on full-time NIV shows that they are satisfied with this arrangement. However, as the respiratory needs increase with progression of diaphragm weakness, the higher air pressures needed may cause air leakage around the mask, and this is the ultimate limitation of NIV. Thus, many people who use full-time NIV eventually convert to a trachea cannula and invasive ventilation.

There is a new method of assisting the diaphragm that is currently experimental but may be approved within the next few years and be more widely available. It is based on implanting stimulating electrodes directly into the underside of the diaphragm (abdominal side) during a laparoscopic surgical procedure. The electrode leads are tunneled through the skin to the outside and are connected to a stimulator box. The stimulation current is adjusted to electrically pace the diaphragm. This can be used at night to take the place of noninvasive ventilation. It must be emphasized that the electrodes activate the phrenic nerves entering the diaphragm, and as phrenic nerve fibers degenerate with ALS progression, the pacing becomes less effective; it is not a substitute for artificial ventilation at late stages of respiratory failure.

## The Dilemmas of Respiratory Failure

The dilemmas of respiratory failure relate to making decisions about ventilation. No two people with ALS have the same issues or concerns, and no two people will have the same set of dilemmas. However, certain issues are common to all patients with ALS, caregivers, and families. This section follows the changes in respiration and discusses the dilemmas and decisions that need to be addressed (see also "Respiratory Management" chapter).

## The Choice of Noninvasive Ventilation

Insurance coverage for bilevel ventilation is not a problem for most people with ALS. It is hoped that NIV will make a patient more comfortable, give him or her a better night's sleep, and perhaps give him more energy or endurance during the day. Early use of bilevel ventilation may extend the life of a patient with ALS. Despite these benefits, some patients choose not to use bilevel ventilation. Others try bilevel ventilation but are not comfortable with the mask and stop using it. This is a reasonable decision.

Patients may ask what happens next if they do not choose or cannot use NIV. Not much happens immediately. Most patients are able to continue for some time without any changes. They will continue to be sleepy during the day. They may try different sleeping positions at night, such as sleeping in a reclining chair. They may take more frequent naps. They also will have both good days and bad days. Eventually, they will become short of breath more easily and will have to make decisions about invasive ventilation.

## The Choice of Invasive Ventilation

The most important dilemma for a person with ALS is whether to choose invasive or artificial ventilation when shortness of breath becomes uncomfortable. The number of patients who are supported by invasive ventilation is not known, but estimates from a regional survey in the midwestern United States and a national survey suggest that 5% to 8% of patients with ALS are placed on full-time invasive ventilation. It is important to understand that some of these patients intentionally chose artificial ventilation, while others were placed on artificial ventilation during a medical emergency. Choosing to be placed on artificial ventilation or choosing not to be placed on it in an emergency is an important issue for patients with ALS and their families to consider.

When patients on artificial ventilation are questioned, the majority report being informed about this issue, but only a few patients chose artificial ventilation in advance. Most patients on artificial ventilation were forced into making a choice, or their families had to make the choice for them, under emergency medical conditions.

In most ALS clinics, arrangements can be made to honor a patient's choice against invasive artificial ventilation if an emergency arises. Without such arrangements, if a patient wishes not to be artificially ventilated, the emergency medical team should not be called. In some communities, documents can be filled out that allow for an emergency medical team to honor a patient's wishes to decline invasive ventilation, and they would then focus on helping make the patient comfortable.

## Dissemination of Information About Respiratory Failure and Support

It is hoped that every patient with ALS will be able to think about respiratory failure and make a decision about supporting ventilation. It is also hoped that the patient will receive full information from his or her neurologist or pulmonologist during the decision-making process. It is important that the patient's family be a part of the discussion and process. We know from experience that this process is very difficult for a number of reasons.

First, there is only so much information that a patient and family can process during a single clinic visit. Most patients with ALS state that they desire as much information as possible from their physicians. However, respiratory failure is a frightening idea early in the course of the disease, and patients may not think that respiratory failure is a real possibility for them. As weakness progresses, however, it is important for patients to request information. Although discussions about artificial ventilation may cause sadness and anxiety, it is important to have detailed information. This includes descriptions of the symptoms and signs of respiratory failure, a description of what it is like to be on artificial ventilation, and an understanding of the manner of death from respiratory failure. Strange as it may seem, this process is often satisfying and may be reassuring to patients as they consider their choices.

Second, it is important to keep in mind that the request by patients for full information also presents a dilemma for the neurologist or pulmonologist. Doctors have personal thoughts and feelings about artificial ventilation, as well as sadness as a patient becomes weaker. These feelings may show through as the physician describes life on a ventilator. A doctor's feelings can influence a patient's decisions. One survey of patients with ALS and their ALS clinic neurologists showed that patients were more likely to choose artificial ventilation if their neurologists had strongly positive feelings about it.

Third, patients have difficulty discussing their feelings about artificial ventilation. Only half are able to do so. Patients most commonly talk with their spouse. Although these feelings are expressed less often with their physician, patients generally feel comfortable and in control during these discussions. Despite the fact that a majority of patients seen in an ALS clinic receive information about respiratory failure and support, and half of them discuss these issues, 30% prefer to leave care and treatment decisions to their physicians. It is not clear whether neurologists are aware of this preference.

## Patient Decision Making

It is important that ALS patients be encouraged to make a decision about artificial ventilation in a timely fashion. An approach used in our Motor Neuron Disease Clinic is to discuss decisions about artificial ventilation in terms of a neutral document, the Durable Power of Attorney for Medical Affairs. We make the argument that all people of legal adult age (older than 18 years) should designate someone to manage their medical treatment if they should be unable to answer for themselves. This approach shifts the focus from the patient with ALS and encourages everyone to fill out a Durable Power of Attorney for Medical Affairs. This document does not require an attorney or lawyer and does not cost anything. Every hospital should have the forms available.

Reaching a decision about artificial ventilation is difficult, and patients should be given permission to change their minds as their experience with ALS grows and circumstances change. The emphasis in our clinic is to keep the patient in control of the decisions. We also stress that there are no right or wrong decisions with regard to artificial ventilation.

## Patient Indecision

When a patient does not make a decision about supporting ventilation, the family and clinician are faced with the dilemma. One clinician's approach is to classify symptomatic treatment in ALS as either "ordinary" or "extraordinary." In this scheme, invasive ventilation is considered an example of extraordinary treatment, and a patient's indecision or "no decision" can be interpreted as a decision against the extraordinary therapy of artificial ventilation. However, many physicians believe that a patient's "no decision" means that the physician must do everything technically possible for the patient. This can result in starting invasive ventilation under emergency conditions.

## Stopping Ventilator Support by the Patient

Stopping ventilatory support becomes an important issue for any patient using noninvasive or invasive ventilation. As the diaphragm weakens, a patient will require more ventilator support. For example, if NIV is used just at night, eventually it will be needed during the day. With more experience with NIV, it has become clear that it can be used full-time by some patients. At this point, patients may request invasive ventilation because it is more comfortable.

Weakness in all muscles will progress on artificial ventilation. In the extreme, patients will lose all movement, including the ability to communicate, even by eye movements or blinking or controlling a computer. This is called a *locked in* state. Many physicians believe that this can be a very distressing situation for the patient. It clearly is desirable to know a patient's wishes before he or she loses the ability to communicate.

Some patients consider stopping artificial ventilation when weakness progresses to a certain level. This level varies from patient to patient. For some, it is when communication is no longer possible, whereas for others it is when a certain goal or event in life has been met. This sounds like a frightening situation, but it is important to emphasize that removing a patient from a ventilator can be done so that the patient is completely comfortable and experiences no air hunger or distress.

## Stopping Artificial Ventilation by the Family

The dilemma of stopping artificial ventilation can fall to the family when a patient's wishes are not known and he or she loses the ability to communicate. This is an avoidable burden if the patient makes his or her wishes known in advance.

## Dilemmas of the Caregiver

Respiratory failure in the patient with ALS also causes dilemmas for caregivers. Most patients on artificial ventilation, either noninvasive or invasive, are cared for at home, which offers substantial psychological benefits compared with life in an institution. As the patient requires more and more time on the ventilator, however, management becomes a full-time, 24-hour job. Most caregivers are spouses, and the overall burden of management falls on them. The task of home ventilatory care usually is divided among several people. On average, it takes 3 to 4 people per day to care for an invasive ventilator–dependent patient. The average daily time spent by family members in patient care is 9 hours, and the balance of care comes from outside personnel if finances permit. Although hiring outside personnel brings relief, it is not without stress. Stresses include finding and interviewing candidates, assessing their level of competence, and determining the reliability of their attendance. Qualifications alone are not sufficient because experienced personnel may be burned out from previous work with patients on ventilators.

The impact on the spouse and family is largely hidden from discussion. With the trend for families to assume more of the burden of long-term patient care, questions about the psychological, ethical, and moral limits of their obligation should be considered. Half of the home caregivers in one survey consider the time commitment to be a major burden. The initial enthusiasm frequently wanes, and anger and resentment are common. Anger may be directed toward the patient. Previously established patterns of coping are often used, and family conflicts may become channeled through the patient. Anger also may be directed back to the caregiver. The anger, in turn, often generates guilt, and home caregivers frequently suffer in silence. As a consequence, many caregivers experience ill health.

It is important to note that after living with these difficulties, most caregivers surveyed were happy that their patient with ALS chose artificial ventilation. This finding may reflect, in part, the complex and ambivalent nature of feelings toward the patient. Caregivers' experience with artificial ventilation did impact their attitude toward artificial ventilation, however; and one study showed that only half would choose artificial ventilation if they developed ALS themselves.

## Financial Dilemmas

Financing artificial ventilation can be formidable. First, it is less costly to care for ventilator-dependent patients in the home than in a hospital. Monthly home costs vary widely, from a low of $500 to a high of $35,000. The major factor affecting cost is the need to hire outside personnel. The major financial concern for the family is the amount of insurance coverage. Data from a survey showed that 83% of the monthly costs listed previously were covered by insurance, with more than half of the families receiving full coverage. When incomplete, insurance coverage was usually denied for outside personnel, and the uncovered monthly expenses ranged from $100 to $7,000. The less insurance companies pay for, the more the burden of home care shifts to the spouse and family (see "Financial Realities" chapter). The amount covered by insurance companies varies but is based on the coverage for durable medical equipment. Durable medical equipment refers to all items, such as wheelchairs and, in this case, ventilators. Many patients with ALS are insured under Medicare. Medicare will cover 80% of charges until out-of-pocket expenses are maximized, and then it will cover 100%. If there is a secondary insurance company, it will often cover copay charges. It is wise to review individual insurance policies for accurate information.

It is important to note that hospice services cannot cover ventilator patients, and if a patient is on hospice and goes on to use artificial ventilation he or she must be discharged from hospice.

## Summary

The full spectrum of dilemmas associated with respiratory failure is formidable in both number and complexity. Nonetheless, they can all be managed. Patients with ALS and families who choose artificial ventilation generally are satisfied with their choice—such is the will and power of the human spirit to deal with and overcome obstacles.

Understanding the full spectrum of dilemmas encourages discussion between patient, family, and health care professionals. A full presentation and open discussion are very important for the well-being of those who choose and those who refuse artificial ventilation.

The reality of respiratory failure in ALS profoundly affects everyone involved with the disease. The dilemmas are shared by all. The opportunity to make decisions regarding the manner of one's death is a unique feature of this disorder. Although these decisions may be frightening, they reflect a control over life, which becomes an important issue in light of the technologic advances in medicine. These decisions should be considered the right of every person. In ALS, full information should be made available by health care providers in a neutral manner. Educational materials about respiratory failure and artificial ventilation are available to assist in dissemination of information. Decisions by the patient should be encouraged and supported, and they should be made known informally to the family and formally in a document such as a Durable Power of Attorney for Health Care. Health care providers are obligated to honor these decisions.

# 14

# Alternative Therapies for Amyotrophic Lateral Sclerosis

## Richard S. Bedlack, Nada El Husseini, Nazem Atassi, Justin Mhoon, Laurie Gutmann, Terri Heiman-Patterson, Stacy Rudnicki, and Jeremy Shefner

In this chapter, *alternative therapies* are defined as treatments, for which there is no good evidence, that patients with ALS use instead of or in addition to treatments that are proven and recommended by ALS experts. There are 3 key considerations in understanding this definition. First are the concepts of *ALS experts* and *good evidence*. Second is the fact that there *are* proven treatments for ALS. Third is the observation that many patients with ALS opt to expose themselves to treatments that are either unproven, or even disproven, often against the advice of ALS experts. Each of these important points deserves further discussion.

### ALS Experts and Good Evidence

ALS experts are neurologists that devote most or all of our careers to caring for patients with ALS and to researching the disease. Our formal education typically includes 4 years of college, 4 years of medical school, a 1-year medicine internship, 3 years of neurology residency, and 1 or 2 years of neuromuscular fellowship. In addition many of us have completed masters or doctor of philosophy programs to get special training in research methods, and most of us have diagnosed and treated hundreds of patients with ALS and participated in many types of ALS research studies. Our years of formal training and our years of hands-on experience have taught us how to critically evaluate potential ALS treatments, and when to recommend them to our patients. Without this training, it is very difficult to know what treatments are reasonable to try for ALS. Beyond this professional commitment,

ALS experts also have a strong personal commitment to our patients and their families. Our number one goal is to partner with our patients to ensure the best possible outcome. Unfortunately, there are non–ALS experts out there with different motivations, such as profit, behind their recommendations. It is not always easy to determine someone's motivation when they are recommending something to you.

How do ALS experts decide what treatments to recommend to our patients? We look at the strength of the evidence behind them. The strongest evidence, and indeed the only way to know for certain whether a particular treatment helps or harms, is to study it in a large, randomized, double-blind, placebo-controlled clinical trial. A *large* number of patients are needed because the progression of ALS is naturally very different between different patients. Some patients with ALS progress over just a few months, whereas others survive for decades. The more patients there are in a study, the less likely it is that the naturally occurring differences between individual patients will influence the results. *Randomization* refers to a process for assigning the different treatments being compared in the trial; this process maximizes the chances that the groups of patients assigned to the different treatments will be similar at the start of the study. For example, one group should not be much older, or much sicker, at the start than the other, or otherwise this might be the reason for any difference between groups at the end. *Double-blind* means that neither patients nor the team performing measurements in the study know who is getting which treatment. This minimizes the chances that enthusiasm or excitement about one treatment over the other could influence the result of the study. Finally, a *placebo control* is important in ensuring that any differences observed at the end of the study are truly due to the specific treatment being given, rather than to patient expectations or to some other aspect of care being delivered. More information on clinical trials is available for interested readers in other parts of this book and online (1).

Not every treatment being touted for use in ALS has been evaluated in a large, randomized, double-blind, placebo-controlled trial. The next best evidence would come from a smaller but similarly rigorously designed trial. Below that would be evidence from a large carefully followed series of patients whose outcome was compared with a series of similar patients cared for in a similar way, except for the treatment under study. Lower still would be a treatment shown to work in well-designed studies using an animal model of ALS; unfortunately some medications that seemed to work well in ALS animal models have not worked in patients with ALS. The worst evidence is that from one or a few case reports. This type of evidence should never be used to justify a treatment for ALS. The danger with concluding anything from individual case reports is that, as mentioned above, the progression of ALS is naturally tremendously different between different patients. Thus, a patient who survived a long time on a particular treatment may have done just as well (or indeed even better!) without it. Finally, at the lowest level, there are treatments that are proposed to help based on how they work, and on what we know about the mechanism of ALS, with no data from animals or patients with ALS. Again, this type of evidence should never be used to justify a treatment for ALS but rather to plan studies in animals or large trials in humans.

## Proven Treatments for Patients With ALS

In the 130 years since ALS was first described, much has been learned about the disease, including ways to slow it down. One of these is a medication, riluzole (also called Rilutek), which affects sodium channels and a chemical called glutamate. Two large, randomized, placebo-controlled trials have proven beyond a doubt that this medication prolongs survival in patients with ALS (2). Other treatments typically recommended by ALS experts are devices such as feeding tubes and BiPAP; the evidence that these prolong survival comes from series of patients with the devices that were compared with those without (3,4). Finally, there are the multidisciplinary ALS clinics themselves. It turns out that series of patients attending these types of clinics live longer and have preserved quality of life to a greater degree than series of patients who do not attend these types of clinics (5).

## Patients With ALS Choose Alternative Therapies, and Why

It is clear that patients with ALS often choose to try an alternative therapy, frequently against the advice of their ALS expert. Surveys of patients with ALS and of ALS experts agree that more than half of the patients with ALS will try one or more alternative therapies at some point. Wasner and colleagues showed that, of those that try alternative therapies, approximately 10% believe they will find a cure, more than 20% believe they will find something to make them better, and approximately 50% believe they will find something to slow the progression of their disease (6). Patients who try alternative therapies express significant frustration over the fact that there is no treatment proven to stop or reverse ALS. They also report peer pressure from family members or friends and sometimes express the idea "I have ALS, what further harm could come to me?" As will be pointed out in the next sections, it is certainly possible for further and substantial harm to come from pursuing an alternative therapy.

## Specific Alternative Therapies Often Used
## by Patients With ALS

In this section, we report on the most popular alternative therapies for ALS currently being used by patients in North American ALS clinics. These alternative therapies are presented in alphabetical order.

### Acupuncture

It is not clear that acupuncture could influence any of the events thought to be important in how ALS starts or progresses. Nonetheless, in one survey of patients with ALS, almost half of the patients had tried acupuncture (6). There are no trials of acupuncture in ALS, no large case series, and no animal studies. There have been individual cases of patients reporting benefits, including improved cramps and even improved pulmonary function. Some of us have attempted to quantify these reported improvements, without success. There are definite risks to acupuncture; bleeding, infection, punctured lungs, punctured bladder, and punctured kidney have all been reported. A typical treatment costs approximately $100 and may or may not be covered by insurance.

## Amalgam Removal

Exposure to mercury has been a health concern for many years. At high concentration all forms of mercury have been shown to affect the human body. The main forms that we are exposed to are organic mercury, inorganic mercury, and mercury vapor. Organic mercury exposure mainly comes from our diet, in particular, from consuming large quantities of shark, tuna, or swordfish. Batteries and occupational exposures are the main source of inorganic mercury toxicity. Mercury vapor exposure mainly comes from dental amalgams (7).

The clinical presentation of mercury toxicity varies depending on the type of mercury and the intensity of the exposure. Exposure to enough mercury vapor can cause tremors, gingivitis (gum inflammation), peripheral neuropathy, lung and kidney problems, and behavioral changes (such as shyness, insomnia, memory loss, and uncontrolled blushing and perspiration). Organic mercury toxicity results in neurologic complaints such as memory problems, visual disturbances, ataxia, hearing loss, movement disorders, and mental deterioration. Acute inorganic mercury toxicity is manifest mainly by gastrointestinal complaints like nausea, vomiting, blood in the stool, and abdominal pain. Chronic exposure to inorganic mercury can cause renal failure, dementia, erythema of the palms and soles, irritability, decreased muscle tone, high blood pressure, and weight loss (7). Note that none of these presentations sounds much like ALS!

Dental amalgams are a combination of 50% mercury and 50% metal powder (usually copper, zinc, tin, and silver) are used for filling cavities and certain dental reconstructions. More than 100 million Americans have had amalgam fillings placed. The amalgam alloy is very stable and poses little risk. However, studies show that mercury vapor released during the initial implantation or extraction or by chronic chewing of fillings can increase the concentration of mercury in blood and urine. The level of mercury is directly proportional to the number of amalgam fillings; for every 10 surface increase in amalgams, the urinary mercury concentration increases by 1 µg/L. Normal urine mercury levels are less than 2 µg/L (8). There is controversy over the smallest possible amount of mercury exposure that can cause symptoms, but most experts think one needs at least 50 µg/L and perhaps as much as 300 µg/L to produce problems. Amalgams would thus not appear to cause a large enough increase in body mercury to reach harmful levels (7). Numerous studies have compared patients with and without amalgam fillings and found no difference in problems that could be attributed to mercury (8).

Recent concerns have been raised about the dangers of chronic exposure to low levels of mercury. Some claim that these low levels can exacerbate or even cause neurologic diseases such as Alzheimer's disease, multiple sclerosis, and ALS. Others claim that removing dental amalgams can actually stabilize or reverse the effects of these diseases. These claims are not based on scientific evidence but on rare case reports and personal testimonies. In fact, several large epidemiologic studies have failed to show an association between mercury exposure, including dental amalgams, and the development of neurodegenerative disorders like ALS (7,8); some studies do show that removal of amalgam fillings decreases the baseline level of mercury in the body, but this does not result in a significant change in symptoms.

The replacement of mercury amalgams is expensive and painful; it often requires root canals for larger fillings. Typical cost for having 10 amalgam surfaces replaced with nonmercury fillings can range from $2,500 to $5,000. This includes the price of an office visit, dental x-rays, replacement fillings, and root canals. In addition to the cost, the grinding process that is required actually increases the amount of mercury vapor in the mouth and causes a temporary spike in blood mercury concentrations (7).

## Atypical Lyme Disease Treatment

One of the diseases that people with ALS are often concerned that they might have is chronic Lyme disease. Although Lyme disease can affect the nervous system and may cause some weakness in some patients, the weakness is really the only similarity between Lyme disease and ALS. Lyme disease is typically accompanied by a rash and joint pains, which are not part of ALS. When it affects the nervous system, it causes prominent sensory symptoms (pain and numbness); again, these are not usually part of ALS. As Lyme disease and ALS progress, they become less and less similar. Despite these dissimilarities, approximately 20% of our patients ask us about getting tested for, and sometimes treated for, atypical Lyme disease.

Patients should be cautious about going to centers that specialize in Lyme disease diagnosis. Some of these specialists use a lab that they may own or at least have financial interests in to test all their specimens. The testing in these labs may have a very high positive rate, with many patients then requiring treatments that they may only be able to receive at that particular center. This may include a combination of antibiotics, steroids, and/or anticoagulants. These treatments do have side effects. The treatment for chronic Lyme disease can cause side effects including diarrhea, loss of appetite, weight loss, infections that are resistant to the antibiotics being used, and yeast infections. Precautions can be taken to avoid some of these side effects, but for a patient who has ALS, not Lyme disease, these side effects can hasten the progression of the disease, especially if weight loss or infection occurs. These treatments can also be very expensive, sometimes thousands of dollars, and insurance is unlikely to cover them.

The ongoing ALS trial using ceftriaxone, a potent antibiotic that crosses the blood–brain barrier and has been used in treating nervous system Lyme disease, has again raised the question of an infectious cause for ALS. Antibiotics in this family also have a protective effect on cells, especially astrocytes (which live next to motor neurons in the brain and spinal cord and act as their bodyguards), separate from their antibiotic effect. There are some statements on the Web and in some handouts, though, that imply that the neurologic community is not being honest with the public and that this trial proves that ALS is a form of Lyme disease. This is *not* why ceftriaxone is being used in an ALS trial.

## Chelation

Mutations of the SOD1 gene encoding CuZn superoxide dismutase enzyme (SOD) are found in 20% of patients with familial ALS who, in turn, represent at most 5% of all ALS cases. These mutations are also present in up to 5% of people with sporadic ALS. CuZn SOD is an enzyme that functions as a protective antioxidant that, if mutated, becomes pro-oxidant and destructive to motor neurons. Copper functions as the catalytic center of the enzyme and may be crucial for its function. Hypothetically, chelation therapy, by depleting copper, may inhibit oxidative mechanisms and thus alters the disease course. To test this hypothesis experiments were done on transgenic mice with altered SOD gene by giving them penicillamine, an orally available copper chelator. The result was that chelation therapy delayed disease onset but did not extend survival (9).

Animal experiments further suggest that various metals such as cadmium and inorganic mercury are toxic to motor neurons, including those in the spine and brain stem. Lead poisoning can produce a lower motor neuron disease in humans (accompanied by many other problems that are not typical of ALS, including low blood counts and blue gums). Population-based studies have failed to show any association between reported metal exposure and ALS (10). Attempts to measure blood levels of essential and toxic metals in patients with ALS have lead so far to contradictory results (11–16). A very recent study actually showed that elevated bone lead levels were associated with *longer* survival in patients with ALS (17)! Although of low diagnostic yield, analysis of blood or urine metals is still sometimes performed in the clinical assessment of people suspected to have ALS. Inadequate specimen handling can lead to misleading results in laboratories that perform metal analysis infrequently. It is also postulated that blood and urine levels of these metals may not be truly representative of the concentration of these metals in the motor neurons. The metal may be bound to other organs so a low metal level in blood may not give an indication of previous or chronic low-level exposure to the metal. The finding of an increased metal concentration may lead to inappropriate attempts at chelation therapy, which can be deleterious in ALS and may result in more of the metal being deposited in the nervous system after the metal has been mobilized from other organs (18). Investigations in animals confirmed that hypothesis, because the level of mercury in motor neurons increased after treatment with a chelator (19). In a case report of a woman with a diagnosis of ALS, in whom increased blood and urinary levels of mercury were found secondary to a known source of chronic mercury exposure, chelation therapy for 4 weeks did not alter the disease course. In that patient the urinary level of mercury decreased with chelation therapy, but the blood and spinal fluid levels were not affected (13).

Chelation therapy has real risks: abnormal heart rhythm, kidney failure, respiratory failure, seizures, allergic reactions, and even death have been reported during chelation. It typically costs a few thousand dollars for the first month, and a hundred or so for maintenance therapy every month thereafter. It is unlikely to be covered by insurance.

## Chinese Herbs

Chinese herbs are treatments used in traditional Chinese medicine. These preparations consist of complex combinations of herbs, minerals, and plant extracts. Some practitioners believe that herbs have the power to prevent and treat ALS, though no clear rationale for these beliefs has emerged. No reliable studies in the medical literature have shown that Chinese herbs have any positive effect on ALS. Most of these claims are based on individual cases that lack the standards of making the correct diagnosis or measuring response to treatment. Herbal treatments cost $30 to $1,000 per month and are not covered by insurance. Because of the variety of herbs used in Chinese herbal medicine, a potential exists for negative interactions with other prescribed drugs. Actual amounts per dose may vary between brands or even between different batches of the same brand. In addition, some herbal preparations contain other ingredients that are not always identified. Fatal organ failures and allergic reactions are potential side effects of some of these preparations. Tests of Chinese herbal remedies by the California Department of Health found that nearly one third contained prescription drugs or were contaminated with other toxins (20).

## Eric Is Winning

This complicated and expensive alternative treatment regimen is outlined in a book titled *Eric Is Winning* by Eric Edney (21). Edney is convinced that neurodegenerative diseases, including ALS, are caused by the same thing: pesticides and heavy metals. He himself professes to have been cured of ALS through a 2-phase treatment strategy incorporating a series of alternative treatments, some of which have been already discussed. The objective of phase 1 is to stop the progression of illness and that of phase 2 is to restore the body.

In phase 1 the person living with ALS is encouraged to begin therapy by purifying the colon, liver, and kidneys with colloidal silver, clay, and psyllium along with water, colon hydrotherapy, and enemas, if necessary. Subsequently the body is detoxified by using chelation, bentonite clay foot baths, ionic cleansing foot baths, and colon hydrotherapy. It is further recommended that the patients with ALS (PALS) divorce their present medical doctor and find a doctor who does alternative medicine. Although the cost of these treatments cannot be calculated exactly, following the recommendations of the author will cost at least $1,800 in equipment (alkalinizer, colloidal gold generator, ionizing foot bath) and $150 per month in supplies. In addition, hair analysis is recommended ($100). If someone decides to undergo chelation in the physician's office, the cost is estimated at a minimum of 30 treatments at approximately $100 per treatment or $3,000 total. Some alternative specialists recommend up to 40 treatments and repeat courses of chelation if the patient progresses.

In a literature search using a standard search engine for the medical literature, Medline, there were no studies that examined the efficacy on ALS disease progression of any of these regimens. As mentioned above, chelation in ALS shows no definite beneficial effect heavy metal load. Furthermore, "colon cleansing" with sodium phosphate solutions can cause acute kidney failure, bentonite clay is used in animals to create models of skin inflammation and is damaging to lung cells, and colloidal silver has caused a blue tinge to skin and has been linked to seizures. A summary for many of the treatments outlined in *Eric Is Winning* can be found on the Web site Quackwatch.com (22).

After the detoxification, the patients are encouraged to eliminate all toxins in the environment, including having their amalgam fillings removed (see above), and to eat only organic foods. In addition, prescription drugs are considered toxic and it is recommended that people adhering to Eric's regimen avoid them. This includes riluzole, the only Food and Drug Administration (FDA)-approved drug that has shown efficacy in a placebo-controlled trial. Patients with ALS are to use clay, papaya enzymes, and pomegranate juice to alkalinize the pH of their body and take supplements and antioxidants. Again, despite interest in antioxidants as a treatment for ALS, there has been no definitive trial demonstrating an improved survival; high doses of vitamin E may in fact be harmful (see below). The cost of antioxidants can be as much as $130 per month with a modest regimen, and alkalinization supplies and supplements are another $60 monthly. Glutathione is also recommended as part of these treatments, but it is generally given as part of the infusions in a physician's office and costs will vary.

In the second phase of the treatment, the goal is to restore the body to a more normal condition. This includes "live-cell therapy," vitamin $B_1$, human growth hormone shots, Starbucks Chai Soy Milk Latte, and laser beam therapy. Live-cell therapy is not stem cell therapy but rather animal embryo live-cell extracts that cost $925 for a 2-month supply. The vitamin $B_1$ taken the way Eric Edney recommends would cost about $200 per month. The growth hormone is $300 per month, and the Latte is $60 monthly. The cost of laser treatments is not clear.

Clearly, there are many dangers in this particular alternative treatment regimen, with no good evidence of any effectiveness for any component of it and an estimated cost over the course of the illness of $39,800. This cost analysis does not include glutathione treatments or the laser treatments.

## Glyconutrients

Glyconutrient is a marketing term used to describe a group of sugars that are used by cells to make glycoproteins (proteins with a sugar part attached) and glycolipids (lipids with a sugar part attached). These compounds are important in the communication that occurs between cells. In recent years, various combinations of these sugars have been sold as dietary supplements with a supposed wide range of health benefits, including treating ALS.

There are no controlled studies in the medical literature to show that taking glyconutrient supplements has any effect on ALS or other disorders. The few individual case reports often mentioned by promoters of such products have appeared mainly in obscure medical journals or cannot be found in published medical literature. The companies that make these supplements are not required to prove to the FDA that their supplements are safe or effective, as long as they do not claim the supplements can prevent, treat, or cure any specific disease. Some of these products may not contain the amount of the substance that is written on the label, and some may include other substances (contaminants). They cost $100 to $150 per month, and are not covered by insurance.

## High-Dose Vitamins

Multivitamins are routinely used by many healthy individuals, as well as by those with a variety of diseases. Many patients with ALS wonder whether high doses of a variety of vitamins are potentially useful. Because the most common genetic mutation causing ALS is in the SOD1 gene, and SOD1 is a protein that acts as an antioxidant, vitamins that also have antioxidant properties seem especially attractive. Vitamin E is one such vitamin, and an animal study showed that high doses of vitamin E mildly altered disease onset in a mouse model of ALS. A study of a large series of cases showed some possible potential benefits in reducing death from ALS. However, a systematic review of vitamin E use, as well as acetylcysteine, L-methionine, and selenium, showed no effect on disease course in patients with ALS (23). Other vitamins, such as vitamin C, $B_1$, and $B_6$, also do not alter the course of ALS. A recent multicenter study testing coenzyme Q10 (CoQ10) to determine the need for a large study turns out to be futile for the further study, implying that a large dose of CoQ10 is unlikely beneficial.

Importantly, like other substances, excess administration of vitamins can clearly be harmful. In a large study of vitamin E use in healthy individuals, it was found that there was a greater incidence of death in those subjects with a history of vitamin E use. Vitamin $B_6$ can cause a painful neuropathy when taken at high doses. Thus, the most prudent approach is to maintain good nutrition, take multivitamins if it has been your preference prior to contracting ALS, but not to add large doses of substances that have not shown benefit but could cause additional health risks.

## Stem Cells

Stem cell therapy has received quite a lot of attention in the lay press in recent years. On the surface, it sounds like a wonderful idea: replace the dying motor neurons with stem cells that could transform into motor neurons and take over their function. There are, however, a number of obstacles to be overcome. Not only do the stems cells have to gain access to the appropriate areas of the brain and spinal cord, they would need to be transformed into the motor neurons. An even bigger challenge is that replacing motor neurons would not, in and of itself, fix the underlying problem, because motor neurons have lengthy connections through the brain and spinal cord on the way to giving rise to nerves that supply the muscles and allow them to function. Therefore, currently the hope of stem cell therapies in ALS is to improve the environment surrounding the motor neurons and to help at-risk motor neurons survive longer.

There was abundant publicity, particularly through the Internet, regarding a program in China for stem cell therapy, not only for ALS, but also other neurologic disorders. To date, there have been no peer-reviewed reports of this work appearing in the English literature from the study investigators. However, at the 2007 meeting of the International Symposium on ALS/MND, a group from Holland reported the outcome regarding 12 Dutch patients who traveled to China to have embryonic stem cells injected into the brain and who were examined before and after their trip. The Chinese program was run by Dr. Huang at the Institute of Beijing. Cells were obtained from miscarriages at 4 to 5 months. Patients paid out of pocket for the procedure, which cost, on average, between $30,000 and $40,000. There was no ethics committee involved in the study, and no proof that the cells survived. Of the 12 patients, 7 had a brief, transient improvement in strength that occurred immediately after the procedure, followed by progression of their disease. The 5 who had no immediate benefit also continued to progress. Of the 12, 1 experienced a blood clot and another 1 developed a pneumonia. At least 1 other patient is reported to have suffered a serious side effect, permanent ringing in the ears, after this procedure. The Chinese government has since closed the clinic (24).

Clearly, using stem cells to treat ALS is in its infancy, and much more scientific work will need to be done before we know whether it will prove to be helpful or harmful.

## How to Assess Other Alternative Therapies for ALS

New alternative treatment options appear all the time. How should patients and their families decide if any are worth pursuing? The easiest and safest method is to discuss them with an ALS expert who has the years of education and experience to help you. If this is not possible, consider the strength of the evidence being presented for the alternative treatment option. Only a randomized, double-blind, placebo-controlled trial gives definitive proof of effectiveness.

There are some definite red flags for patients and families to consider. If any of these are present, we strongly advise against using the alternative treatment being considered. First, avoid it if the only evidence for it is individual case reports of clinical benefits. Remember, ALS is naturally highly variable, so case reports are virtually useless as evidence of effectiveness. Second, beware of new therapies that will cost you large sums of money. When ALS experts do a research study of a potential new treatment, it is usually free. Sometimes we will even pay your travel expenses! Third, beware of someone presenting a new therapy for ALS who wants to collect your money, treat you, and then never see you back for a follow-up testing. Anytime an ALS expert embarks on a study of a new treatment, we will want to see you back for careful follow-up testing afterward. Finally, beware of alternative therapies that are touted as cure-alls for multiple diseases that seem to share little in common. Chelation, for example, is touted as an effective treatment for diseases as diverse as autism, ALS, atherosclerosis, multiple sclerosis, Alzheimer's, and Parkinson disease.

## Conclusion: A Cautionary Tale

A few years ago, the ALS community was very excited about the drug minocycline. This old antibiotic had a lot of mechanisms of action that seemed to be relevant in ALS. In ALS animal models, minocycline prolonged survival. It seemed to be well-tolerated in patients with ALS. Thus, a large, double-blind, placebo-controlled study was initiated to determine definitively whether the drug could slow ALS progression. It was surprisingly difficult to enroll patients in the study. The reason was that many patients decided to use minocycline as an alternative therapy for their ALS and were getting non–ALS expert physicians to prescribe it for them. When we finally finished the study in late 2007, we discovered that patients with ALS who took minocycline progressed 25% faster than patients who took placebo! This is just another example of the many harms that can come from using alternative therapy for ALS against the advice of your ALS expert. We are always willing to discuss alternative therapies during or between your clinic visits with us.

## References

1. *Understanding Clinical Trials*. http://clinicaltrials.gov/ct2/info/understand. Accessed August 2, 2008.
2. Miller R, Mitchell J, Lyon M, Moore D. Riluzole for amyotrophic lateral sclerosis (ALS)/motor neuron disease. *Amyotroph Lateral Scler*. 2003;4(3):191–206.
3. Massine L, Corra T, Zaccala M, et al. Percutaneous endoscopic gastrostomy and enteral nutrition in amyotrophic lateral sclerosis. *Neurology*. 1995;242:695–698.
4. Aboussouan LS, Khan S, Meeker DP, et al. Effect of noninvasive positive-pressure ventilation on survival in amyotrophic lateral sclerosis. *Ann Intern Med*. 1997;127:450–453.
5. Traynor BJ, Alexander M, Corr B, et al. Effect of a multidisciplinary amyotrophic lateral sclerosis clinic on ALS survival: a population based registry 1996–2000. *J Neurol Neurosurg Psychiatry*. 2003;74(9):1258–1261.
6. Wasner M, Klier H, Borasio G. The use of alternative medicine by patients with amyotrophic lateral sclerosis. *J Neurol Sci*. 2001;191:151–154.
7. Clarkson TW, Magos L, Myers GJ. The toxicology of mercury—current exposures and clinical manifestations. *N Engl J Med*. 2003;349:1731.
8. American Dental Association. http://www.ada.org/public/media/presskits/fillings/testimony_marshall.pdf. Accessed July 21, 2008.
9. Hottinger AF, Fine EG, Gurney ME, et al. The copper chelator d-penicillamine delays onset of disease and extends survival in a transgenic mouse model of familial amyotrophic lateral sclerosis. *Eur J Neurosci*. 2006;9(7):1548–1551.

10. McGuire V, Longstreth WT Jr, Nelson LM, et al. Occupational exposures and amyotrophic lateral sclerosis: a population-based case-control study. *Am J Epidemiol.* 1997; 145(12):1076–1088.

11. Kapaki E, Zournas C, Kanias G, et al. Essential trace element alterations in amyotrophic lateral sclerosis. *J Neurol Sci.* 1997;147(2):171–175.

12. Pamphlett R, McQuilty R, Zarkos K. Blood levels of toxic and essential metals in motor neuron disease. *Neurotoxicology.* 2001;22:401–410.

13. Praline J, Guennoc AM, Limousin N, et al. ALS and mercury intoxication: a relationship? *Clin Neurol Neurosurg.* 2007;109(10):880–883.

14. Kamel F, Umbach D, Munsat T, et al. Lead exposure and amyotrophic lateral sclerosis. *Epidemiology.* 2002;13(3):311–319.

15. Mitchell JD. Heavy metals and trace elements in amyotrophic lateral sclerosis. *Neuorol Clin.* 1987;5(1):43–60.

16. Louwerse E, Buchet J, Van Dijk M, et al. Urinary excretion of lead and mercury after oral administration of meso-2,3-dimercaptosuccinic acid in patients with motor neurone disease. *Int Arch Occup Environ Health.* 1995;67(2):135–138.

17. Kamel F, Umbach D, Stallone L, et. al. Association of lead exposure with survival in amyotrophic lateral sclerosis. *Environ Health Perspect.* 2008;116(7):943–947.

18. Costa A, Branca V, Pigatto PD, et al. ALS, mercury exposure, and chelation therapy. *Clin Neurol Neurosurg.* 2008;110(3):319–320.

19. Ewan K, Pamphlett R. Increased inorganic mercury in spinal motor neurons following chelating agents. *Neurotoxicology.* 1996;17:343–349.

20. Aubrey Organics. http://www.organicanews.com/news/article.cfm?story_id=153. Accessed October 24, 2008.

21. *Eric Is Winning.* http://www.ericiswinning.com. Accessed July 20, 2008.

22. *Quackwatch.* http://www.quackwatch.org. Accessed July 30, 2008.

23. Orrell RW, Lane JM, Ross MA. Antioxidant treatment for amyotrophic lateral sclerosis / motor neuron disease. *Cochrane Database Syst Rev.* 2004(4):CD002829.

24. Van den Berg L. Unproven cell-based treatments for ALS/MND: lessons from Beijing. *Amyotroph Lateral Scler.* 2007;8(S1):32.

# 15

# Clinical Therapeutic Trials

## Theodore L. Munsat

The development of effective treatments for neurologic disease, or *neurologic therapeutics,* has generally lagged behind drug and clinical trial development in other fields of medicine because of a tradition of therapeutic nihilism that until recently has delayed the development of effective amyotrophic lateral sclerosis (ALS) drugs. This lack of interest in developing effective treatments resulted from an emphasis on diagnosis and lesion localization rather than treatment. This perspective characterized the practice of most of the founders of modern neurology. For example, the first placebo-controlled trial (a study in which some people are treated while others are given sham [placebo] treatment) in all of neurology was not carried out until 1967, more than 10 years after the importance of placebo control was demonstrated in other branches of medicine. There is a general consensus that neurologic therapeutics is approximately 10 to 15 years behind such disciplines as cancer chemotherapy or AIDS, diseases that share many features with ALS. However, after a slow start, neurology has developed an increasingly productive interest in new therapies, as well as in the design of effective trials, and this has certainly been of benefit for those with ALS.

Of particular importance in this regard is the work done by the World Federation of Neurology (WFN) to develop an international consensus on how to diagnose ALS and how to design clinical trials. This consensus has already resulted in trials that are increasingly scientifically sound, more cost-effective, and, above all, more able to separate treatments that truly work from those that do not. This information can be accessed on the Web site of the WFN Research Group on ALS at www.wfnals.org. This site contains other useful information for those interested in ALS clinical trials.

This chapter deals with certain general issues that are of particular interest and concern if you are considering entering a clinical trial of an experimental drug. Details relating to specific current and future trials are discussed in the next chapter.

## Why Are Clinical Trials Necessary?

A clinical trial is not needed when a drug or treatment is so effective that its benefit is immediately apparent to both patient and treating physician. The effectiveness of penicillin for certain infections is often cited as an example where the benefit was so clear and so dramatic when it was first used that a trial was not needed to show that it worked. Unfortunately, most drugs are not that effective. If we were lucky enough to discover a drug that stopped the progression of ALS, let alone reversed the damage, it would be immediately apparent to all within a few months, and an expensive, long, and statistically complicated clinical trial would not be needed. But it is unlikely that such a drug will be discovered in the near future. Rather, we most likely will be identifying drugs that have a modest slowing effect on the course of motor nerve damage such that the benefit may not be apparent to either the patient or the treating physician. This has been the case with riluzole, the first and, to date, the only drug that has been shown to slow the neurologic damage in ALS and the only drug to be approved by the Food and Drug Administration (FDA) for the treatment of ALS. To obtain government approval for riluzole, a long, difficult, and expensive trial process was necessary to demonstrate its modest benefit.

One might understandably ask why it is necessary to work so hard to demonstrate what only a modest benefit from a drug is when what we really need is something that has substantially greater benefit. It is reasonable to suggest, as many have, that a true cure for ALS must await a more complete understanding of the cause of the disease. However, recent research has revealed that the cause of ALS is much more complex than previously thought and involves several related pathologic processes, not a single one of which could be ameliorated with a single drug. In addition, it is quite likely that different factors are operative for different patients or groups of patients—that is, ALS may be a family of related diseases rather than a single disease. Consequently, it is most likely that, as in cancer, the initial effective treatments for ALS will only result in small gains, similar to what we have seen with riluzole. However, it also is likely that if enough small gains are linked together by using combinations of drugs or drug cocktails, each component of which produces only small benefit, we might achieve significant slowing, if not arrest, of the ALS process. This is exactly the history of the significant gains that have been achieved in treating both cancer and AIDS. If this reasoning is correct, it then becomes very important to be able to identify drugs that may indeed show only minimal benefit. It is equally important to begin simultaneously testing various combinations of drugs, something that has been disappointingly slow to develop.

## The Different Types of Clinical Trials

Clinical trials of new drugs are always preceded by extensive studies in animals to determine whether the drug produces any damage to normal tissue and to determine what doses of the drug might be used in humans. If an *animal model* of the disease is available (that is, a disease that appears to have features similar to the human disease), information about possible effectiveness of the drug in humans might also be obtained. For example, the recent availability of *transgenic* mouse models of inherited ALS may become useful in defining new treatments. Human trials are typically carried out in various stages or phases.

- Phase 1 trials are often carried out in healthy volunteers and are designed mainly to determine whether the drug is safe in humans and what side effects occur with different doses. These trials are done in relatively small groups of subjects. Phase 1 trials rarely give useful information about whether the drug will be effective in ALS. This information is collected from phase 2 and phase 3 trials.
- Phase 2 trials are typically done in a few centers that specialize in ALS and may be placebo controlled. These are preliminary trials in patients with ALS and aim to determine not only whether the drug is safe but also whether it appears to have a beneficial effect on the disease. If the results of these studies are encouraging, phase 3 trials are performed next.
- Phase 3 trials are carried out in many ALS centers and often involve 1,000 or more patients. The goals of these large, placebo-controlled trials are (a) to further determine the safety of the drug in large numbers of different patients with ALS, (b) to determine whether the drug is better than placebo or existing best medical treatment, and (c) to prepare a case for FDA approval of the drug so that it can be marketed by the pharmaceutical company that holds the patent.

As you can see, these various steps define a gradual, graded process of bringing a new drug to the patient—a drug that is both safe and effective. Some have argued, with possible justification, that the process leading to drug approval is too slow and too bureaucratic, especially for a disease as serious as ALS. This perspective states, "I'm going to die soon anyway so what difference does it make if the drug isn't fully evaluated?" The most persuasive counterargument points out that unregulated or poorly studied drugs have caused harm in the past and that the mandate and ethical responsibility of the FDA is to make certain that a harmful drug is not approved and to make certain that the drug is indeed beneficial.

After a drug is approved for marketing, the drug company has a continuing responsibility to make certain that longer-term use is still safe. This process is often formalized in a phase 4 study, which collects information about the drug's safety and benefit over many years.

## The Role and Necessity of Placebo Controls

During World War II evaluation of seriously injured battlefront soldiers showed that many experienced little or no pain during the heat of battle. It became apparent that the quality and severity of pain varied greatly depending on emotional state. These observations led to a growing understanding that many physical symptoms could be significantly influenced by a person's state of mind or psychologic condition. In the middle and late 1950s a series of studies in Great Britain and the United States demonstrated that many patients showed a beneficial response to sugar pills if they believed that the pills were of potential benefit. This placebo response has been studied in great detail. It is clear that a patient's will to get better—the desire to have a treatment work—may by itself have a powerful effect on his or her physical, psychological, and even biochemical condition. Some physicians regularly give patients placebo tablets as a form of symptomatic treatment. For example, it has been well documented that people in a clinical trial who are taking placebo do better than those who receive no treatment. As soon as someone begins a clinical trial, important changes in their physical and emotional condition occur, changes that could be attributed to the new drug being tested.

This finding immediately posed the problem of how to determine whether the apparent benefit of a new drug was in fact due to the drug itself or to the placebo effect. The answer was to give one group of patients the active medication and another the placebo—without anyone knowing who was receiving which. It is now generally accepted that the "gold standard" for clinical trials is the placebo-controlled, double-blind, randomized trial. *Double-blind* refers to the fact that neither the patient nor the physician running the trial is aware of who is receiving active medication and who is receiving placebo. If the physician knew which patients were in the treatment group and which were in the placebo group, he or she might manage them differently. If a problem develops that might be related to the medication being tested, the "code" can be broken, a determination made as to whether the patient was taking drug or placebo, and appropriate action taken.

The term *randomization* refers to the process by which patients are assigned to either the treatment group or the placebo group. Patients are assigned by a chance procedure, usually computer-determined, in an attempt to make each of the 2 groups as similar as possible in regard to gender, age, severity of disease, and so on. When entering a trial, the patient must agree to be enrolled in either of the 2 groups depending on his or her assignment, a process that cannot be compromised in order to ensure the scientific effectiveness of the trial. However, it is common practice to allow patients to begin active treatment at the end of a trial if they had been in the placebo group and for patients who had been receiving active drug to continue taking it if they so desire.

The use of placebo controls in trials of new ALS drugs has been somewhat controversial. Most investigators and federal regulatory agencies have insisted on the use of placebo controls in all trials. This position holds that there is no other way to make certain that a drug is truly effective, especially when its benefit is modest. On the other hand, most patients and some investigators maintain that in certain circumstances there may be other kinds of controls that are satisfactory. For example, historical controls might have a role in screening drugs when a fast and inexpensive, but possibly flawed, answer is acceptable. In this situation, the group of patients being treated with the new drug is compared with a similar group of patients who have been seen in the clinic in the past but have not been treated with any specific medication. Thus, we use the history of untreated patients as a control group. Although this approach has obvious advantages, it also presents major problems because an exact match of treated patients and controls is not possible.

With the advent of riluzole, the situation has changed dramatically and at the same time has become more complicated. It is universally accepted that a physician has the responsibility to make certain that none of his or her patients are denied effective treatment for their illness. This causes a significant dilemma if placebo is used in a clinical trial when an FDA-approved drug is available. For example, is it appropriate to place patients on placebo and thus deny them riluzole while taking part in the study of a new drug?

Current views on the physician's responsibility to the patient can be traced to the Nuremberg trials, which, among other things, judged the responsibility of Nazi physicians who had performed various medical experiments on concentration camp victims. The judges of this trial established 10 principles of medical research that they believed should determine physician–patient relationships during a research program. This became known as the Nuremberg Code and eventually resulted in important changes in how trials are conducted. In the past, patients typically were expected to be passive, silent, and subservient to the wishes of the physician or researcher. The doctors knew best, what they advised was in the patient's best interest, and they should not be questioned. As a corollary, the general perception was that the important goal was finding effective treatment for diseases in humans for the good of society in general and that almost any reasonable sacrifice was acceptable with this altruistic goal in mind. The welfare of the individual patient was considered secondary to the welfare of the much larger group of patients in society who had that particular disease.

The Nuremberg Code clearly and dramatically changed this dynamic, such that the individual patient now became the focus. It was suggested and recommended that the physician's primary responsibility was to a specific individual patient and not to a less well-defined societal need. The two most important concepts expressed in this code and now included in every human drug study are (a) the patient must be fully informed about all aspects of the trial, and (b) the patient has the right to withdraw at any time he or she wishes without penalty.

The principles espoused in the Nuremberg Code were further developed in the Declaration of Helsinki, which was adopted by the World Health Organization of the United Nations in 1964. This document further defined and elucidated the rights of patients enrolled in a clinical trial, again emphasizing that the patient's welfare must always supersede a perceived benefit to society as a whole. It states that "in any medical study every patient, including those of a control group, if any, should be assured of the best proven diagnostic and therapeutic method."

Unfortunately, the rights of the individual patient and the desire to have a scientifically sound research clinical trial at times can be at odds and result in dilemmas that are difficult to resolve. Nowhere has this been more apparent than with the use of placebo. Many physicians carrying out clinical trials in ALS maintain that because riluzole has been accepted by the regulatory agencies and scientific community as a drug that is both beneficial and safe, it is unethical to deny it to any patient who wishes to receive it. This would include patients receiving placebo as a control in a drug trial. This view holds that it is unethical for a doctor to advise a patient that placebo is appropriate because the drug being tested may benefit society as a whole and that the patient has an obligation to act in behalf of this greater good. On the other hand, other investigators have taken the position that the only way to determine whether a new drug works is with a placebo control. They point out that because the benefit from any new drug is likely to be small, testing it against another drug with modest benefit (i.e., riluzole) may hide a beneficial effect.

Some recent trials have been interested in determining not whether the new drug is better than nothing at all but whether the new drug is better than existing treatment. In these trials, the investigational drug is tested against riluzole, which is used as a control. However, random assignment to either of the two drugs is still necessary.

## Institutional Protection of the Patient

All clinical trials must undergo careful scrutiny by a special committee before approval for the trial is given. In our hospital it is called the Human Investigation Review Committee and is composed of physicians, scientists, lawyers, ethicists, and patient advocates. This committee has the responsibility of ensuring that every clinical trial it approves meets strict scientific and ethical criteria. It ensures that the research is being carried out by competent investigators and that the information obtained will remain confidential. It especially protects the rights of minors and those who are mentally unable to understand the nature of the trial. The committee makes certain that any risks involved are defined and that they are outweighed by potential benefit to the patient. Women of childbearing age are given special attention. It carefully monitors the conduct of the trial once it begins and may order the trial to stop if untoward or unexpected results occur.

## Informed Consent

The Nuremberg Code principle, which states that any patient involved in a drug trial must be fully informed about all details of the study, is now incorporated into every clinical trial. This is usually done with an informed-consent document that is signed by the patient after a detailed explanation of the trial and after ascertaining that the patient does indeed understand his or her rights and the nature of the trial. People who are ill, especially with a life-threatening disease such as ALS, are particularly vulnerable and often desperate for any possible benefit. As a result, they may unknowingly act against their own best welfare. Sometimes the physician's explanation of a trial to the patient is made in the presence of another person, who acts as the patient's advocate to ensure that he or she fully understands what he or she is about to sign. The consent form describes the goals of the study, potential hazards, and what procedures will be required of the patient. It clearly states that the trial participant may drop out of the study at any time with or without explanation. It explains who is responsible for paying for the care needed if medical harm occurs to the patient as a result of his or her participation in the study. It should contain information about who should be contacted if a problem develops. Consent forms recently have included information about possible physician conflicts of interest that relate to the study, such as receiving payment for enrolling patients. Patients may or may not receive payment for taking part in the study, and this also is described in the informed-consent document.

## The Patient's Obligations

Although the main obligations of the informed-consent process are properly placed on the physician or researcher, it is important to understand that patients also accept certain responsibilities when they agree to enter an experimental clinical trial. Although patients properly have the right to withdraw from a trial at any time, they should be aware that their full participation and cooperation are essential for the completion of a successful trial. When a consent form is signed, patients have implicitly agreed to meet all their responsibilities such as obligations to get tests done, have blood samples drawn, make the necessary clinic visits, and so forth. They should not discuss anything about the study with other patients, especially any side effects of the medication received. Above all, they should make every attempt possible to complete the study despite any inconvenience, because incomplete information can result in a serious problem interpreting the study results. Many patients make attempts to find out whether they are receiving active drug or placebo, a course of action that may be harmful to the success of the study.

## Clinical Trials and the Internet

As with all new technologic advances, the advent of Internet-based communications has provided both opportunities and dilemmas. The wealth of information related to ALS already on the Internet can be overwhelming and difficult to fully understand. This undoubtedly will increase with the passage of time. It has provided an unprecedented way for both rapid and current data to be provided to patients and their families. Above all, it has allowed patients to communicate with each other and provide not only psychological support but also meaningful and helpful ways to deal with the multiple problems caused by the disease. It has helped them understand that they are not alone with the burden they must bear, and this by itself has a strengthening effect. The Internet has allowed physicians, other health care providers, and voluntary health agencies such as the Amyotrophic Lateral Sclerosis Association (ALSA) and Muscular Dystrophy Association (MDA) to communicate with patients with ALS in a rapid and inexpensive manner. It has provided an unprecedented avenue for clinical and basic researchers to communicate research results with each other. There is growing interest in using the Internet to record data from clinical trials; this would markedly reduce the paperwork required and speed the completion of these trials.

Simultaneously, however, it has raised a number of issues that have proven troublesome. Communication on the Internet is essentially unregulated. Anyone can say almost anything they wish, well-meaning or otherwise. This obviously creates the opportunity for a lot of mischief as well as well-intended misinformation. For example, patients occasionally have suggested that they have benefited from treatments that clearly have no therapeutic potential. Undoubtedly, they have experienced a placebo effect. Similarly, claims of benefit have been made by companies selling products that have not been properly studied. Of more concern are claims of benefit from treatments that are potentially dangerous or could intensify weakness already present.

The key to evaluating the validity and usefulness of information provided on the Internet rests with an understanding of the source of that information coupled with an understanding of the disease itself. Every person with ALS and his or her family members should become as knowledgeable as possible about what is known and not known about the cause and treatment of ALS. When reading anything on the Internet, it is essential to find out who wrote it and where it comes from. Information from established voluntary health organizations such as ALSA and MDA is carefully reviewed for accuracy before it is put on the Internet. Similarly, information from established academic health and research centers has been carefully considered before putting it out for the world to see. Patient-generated information has been extremely useful most of the time, but it should be understood that a person with ALS is understandably not an unbiased observer. Be very careful about therapeutic claims made by any company that stands to benefit financially by the sale of its product. Above all, check with your ALS physician about any questionable information you receive before you act. Similarly, be very careful about what information you yourself put onto the Internet. Make certain it will be of true value to other patients or health care providers.

## The Future

Therapeutic trials in ALS have suffered greatly from the lack of a biologic marker that would indicate whether the disease process is slowed after administration of a drug. Although we have clinical indicators of disease progression, such as change in muscle strength, this is an indirect measure and is relatively insensitive. In diabetes, the blood sugar level indicates the benefit or lack of benefit of a specific drug that is being tested. In AIDS, certain tests can be done on white blood cells to indicate the same thing. Unfortunately, no such test is available for ALS. This has been a major hurdle in understanding whether a new treatment is effective. The entire process of clinical therapeutic trials will be significantly speeded up should such a test become available, and many laboratories are working on the problem.

It is clear that a more perfect understanding of the multiple causes of ALS will eventually lead to more effective treatment. However, as we wait for the further elucidation of this difficult disease, we should not relax our efforts in finding better treatments. The advent of riluzole, the first effective drug for ALS that has a scientific basis, has undoubtedly heralded the beginning of a new age of treatment. The single most pressing need is to begin the process of carrying out trials that simultaneously administer multiple drugs, each of which has demonstrated benefit alone or has a strong potential for doing so. These trials are long overdue.

Although it is not possible to predict exactly when more effective treatment for ALS will become available, it is clear we have recently entered a new era of drug treatment that offers great hope for all those who are fighting the good fight.

## Suggested Reading

Bernat JL, Goldstein ML, Ringel SP. Conflicts of interest in neurology. *Neurology.* 1998; 50:327.

Eisen A, Krieger C, eds. *Amyotrophic Lateral Sclerosis: A Synthesis of Research and Clinical Practice.* New York: Cambridge University Press; 1998.

Giffels JJ. *Clinical Trials: What You Should Know Before Volunteering to Be a Research Subject.* New York: Demos Vermande; 1996.

Hampton JR, Julian DG. Role of the pharmaceutical industry in major clinical trials. *Lancet II.* November 28, 1987;1258.

Munsat TL, Hollander D, Finison L. Clinical trial methodology. In: Leigh PN, Swash M, eds. *Motor Neurone Disease.* London: Springer-Verlag; 1995.

Rothman KJ, Michels KB. The continuing unethical use of placebo controls. *N Engl J Med.* 1994;331:394.

Shuster, E. Fifty years later: the significance of the Nuremberg Code. *N Engl J Med.* 1997; 337:1436.

# 16

# Clinical Trials in Amyotrophic Lateral Sclerosis

**Petra Kaufmann**

Finding a cure for amyotrophic lateral sclerosis (ALS) is the ultimate goal of all ALS research. Therefore, laboratory research and patient-oriented research go hand in hand. Bringing discoveries from the laboratory to People with ALS (PALS) is sometimes referred to as *translational* research. Clinical trials are one of the last steps in translating a discovery into an actual treatment for patients.

Recent decades have seen remarkable progress in laboratory research. Several pathways have been discovered that are thought to be part of the disease process. Understanding the steps that lead to the loss of motor nerve cells in ALS brings us closer to finding a treatment. From understanding the disease process, researchers can sometimes tell which treatments may be worth trying. For example, if free radicals are thought to play a role, then researchers can try antioxidants. The steps in the disease process can be targets for new treatments.

Even if a laboratory discovery does not suggest a particular treatment, researchers can now search for medications differently. They can start with a large number of new drugs, a so-called library. They can then set up an experiment that is repeated over and over with each of the drugs. This has become possible because robotic technology is available in laboratories. In the past, it would have taken a long time and it would have been very expensive to have someone repeat an experiment over and over, often several hundreds of times. With robotic technology, this process can be done at high speed. Therefore, testing a library of new drugs is now possible and is often referred to as *high-throughput* screening.

The next step is to follow up on the discovery of a potential treatment with more experiments. These experiments confirm the results in different ways. Also, these experiments help researchers to better understand how exactly the new drug works.

After confirmatory experiments, new drugs are often tested in animals to see whether they work. However, in ALS this has been somewhat disappointing recently. Researchers have used a genetically engineered mouse model. This mouse model carries a mutation in a gene encoding superoxide dismutase (SOD). This gene is linked to the disease in some PALS who have a familial form of ALS. However, it has not been very predictive of success. In other words, many drugs have helped the mice but then failed in clinical trials. Because there are no other animal models available, there is now a debate in the ALS community about how mouse studies could be improved so that they better predict success in PALS. The potential improvements include that the mice are not treated before they develop symptoms, because that would not be a realistic model for people with ALS. Also, researchers have suggested that prior to trials in people, more animals should be tested at different doses and under very standardized conditions.

Once a drug looks promising based on laboratory research and perhaps based on animal research, it is often considered for testing in PALS. In addition to these scientific experiments, PALS and physicians often hear reports of a new treatment having been beneficial to a small number of PALS. Although we all hope that these reports will translate into an effective treatment soon, it is difficult to come up with sound treatment recommendations based on these laboratory experiments or uncontrolled clinical reports. We may be facing a dilemma, because many new drugs need testing, but resources and the number of potential trial participants are limited. The essential question then becomes how we can conduct very efficient clinical trials (1). The following text tries to answer some of the frequently asked questions regarding ALS clinical trials.

## Frequently Asked Questions About Clinical Trials

• Why do we need clinical trials?

Clinical trials are needed to evaluate new promising treatments. Good clinical trials can help us decide whether a new treatment actually helps PALS. Without data from clinical trials, PALS and those caring for them can find themselves in a difficult situation. Several new treatments are often discussed at any given time as having some promise, but it is impossible to know which ones are safe and beneficial in ALS without adequate data. We all hope to find a good treatment for ALS. There is, however, the possibility that a new drug makes patients worse. There are several ALS trials in which those taking the new drug on average did slightly worse than those taking placebo (a sugar pill), for example, topiramate, ciliary neurotrophic factor (CNTF), minocycline, pentoxyfilline, indinavir, and TCH346. Although these negative results were disappointing, the clinical trials were important because they gave PALS the much needed information that these drugs are not worth taking for PALS. In addition to providing essential information to PALS and those caring for them, clinical trials also fulfill a regulatory requirement.

The Food and Drug Administration (FDA) requires evidence from clinical trials in order to approve drugs. FDA approval allows doctors to prescribe a medication and is also a prerequisite for most insurance coverage. We are in a good period for ALS drug development because the increasing understanding of the mechanisms underlying the nerve cell loss in ALS has led to several candidate drugs. However, the progress has also led into a period of increased need for clinical trials.

- What are some of the key factors that make clinical trials work?

Randomization is a key concept in clinical trials. If we want to decide whether a new drug "A" is better than placebo "P," we need to make sure that patients taking "A" are as similar as possible to patients taking "P." Only if the two groups are very similar can we assume that any emerging difference is an effect of our treatment. If doctors and patients had to decide which treatment arm ("A" or "P") a trial participant should be assigned to, chances are that the two groups would look quite different. Because of this human factor, the sicker patients for example would be more likely assigned to treatment "A" than to placebo. The resulting differences between groups could lead to false conclusions about the effect of the new treatment to be tested. Randomization is a way to address this problem: Patients are not selected for group "A" or "P" by a person, but rather randomly, by chance. This can be accomplished by drawing the group assignment for each participant out of a "hat" containing all possible assignments. Nowadays, randomization is usually accomplished by telephone or computer systems. Randomization, when successful, results in two groups ("A" or "P") that are very similar. Comparing the treatment effect in two very similar groups is one of the key features of a good clinical trial.

Control groups are a key concept in clinical trials. A control group is a group of patients who do not receive the new treatment to be tested. Instead, they receive standard care or sometimes another treatment. The effect of the new treatment can thus be compared with the effect of standard treatment in the control group. If there were no control group, then we could not really decide whether a new treatment is better or worse. This is because we cannot know how patients would have fared without being treated. We can either observe how someone does with a new treatment or without a new treatment, but we cannot observe things both ways. Thus, having a control group in clinical trial is essential.

- Why do we need a control group on "placebo" treatment?

Many PALS when they first hear about clinical trials very understandably think that they do not want to take a chance of being on placebo while they have a progressive disease such as ALS. Placebo treatment and blinding are important concepts for successful trials. Placebo is a sugar pill that looks and tastes just like the new active drug. However, a placebo does not contain any active ingredient. Blinding refers to a clinical trial method that does not allow the patient or study doctor knowledge of the treatment. In other words, the patient and doctor do not know whether the patient was assigned to active drug or placebo. Because both of them do not know, this is called double blind. If only one of them does not know, this is called single blind. A single-blind design is not often used because it is difficult for the doctor and patient to keep this knowledge from each other. They may find it hard not to talk about the treatment or they may unknowingly communicate the assignment in their attitudes.

Placebo and blinding are used in randomized trials because we all desperately want to find an effective treatment for ALS. It is therefore part of our human nature that we want to believe that a new drug helps. However, it is important to face the reality that most new drugs do not help, and that some even make patients worse. To avoid exposing everyone to a new drug of unknown effect, we need ways to test the new drug. For believable results, we need to control the human factor that leads us to believe that every new drug is better, even if it is not. Therefore, blinding and placebo are needed. The participating PALS and doctors will likely all feel some positive effect of any trial medication. Through blinding we can then decide whether there is any additional, true effect that can be attributed to the new treatment. This is the reason the randomized, placebo-controlled study is considered as the gold standard for clinical trials.

- Have researchers tried to avoid placebo controls in trials?

Yes, researchers have tried to avoid placebo. The discussion regarding placebo continues as PALS, their families, and everyone who cares for PALS understands how difficult it is to enroll into a placebo-controlled trial. However, based on the reasons outlined in the previous paragraph, uncontrolled trials cannot give us the much needed answers as to whether a new treatment actually helps or does harm.

Trying to maintain a trial that would give us meaningful results while avoiding a placebo-control group, researchers have tried to observe patients for a certain time without treatment and then to observe the same patients while being treated. However, that was difficult because a patient's health does not always change at the same rate. The disease course is not always predictable. Therefore, we cannot be sure that any two time periods are comparable enough to allow for conclusions from such a clinical trial. Also, when a treatment is given during the initial period, then a carry-over effect can occur into the period without treatment and make it difficult to judge the actual treatment effect. Therefore, this so-called cross-over design is not much used in ALS.

Another approach to avoiding a control group is to compare a group of patients who are receiving new treatment with a previous group of untreated patients. The problem with this approach is that the previously untreated group may not be comparable enough to the treated group. This has happened several times in clinical trials and it makes it impossible to interpret the results. With the constant advances in medical care, patients do a little better over time, even if there is no major breakthrough. This makes it likely that any currently observed patient group will do better than a previous group, regardless of any new drug treatment. The risk is that we may falsely call any new treatment effective. Therefore, trials without current control groups are typically not acceptable to the FDA.

- Why do clinical trials need protocols that patients and doctors have to follow?

Study protocols are important for clinical trials. They are laying down the rules for the study. Protocols have to be decided before the clinical trial begins. After the start, protocols can typically not be changed. We might be tempted during a trial to change the rules because we think we learned how we may have a better chance to see a treatment effect. However, this is a slippery slope because we may end up manipulating the results, willingly or unwillingly. Therefore, protocol changes are taken very seriously in ongoing clinical trials. They typically require approval of an independent oversight committee. For a successful clinical trial, it is important that participants and study doctors adhere as much as possible to a protocol that has been set in advance.

- What are the different phases of drug development?

The path from a laboratory discovery to having a new treatment on the pharmacy shelf is divided into four phases. The previous definitions of important trial concepts mainly referred to phase 3 trials. In the following, the characteristics of each of the trial phases are briefly described.

*Phase 1* trials are often done in healthy volunteers but can also include patients. Phase 1 trials are often first-in-man trials. This means that a new drug has been given to animals, but not to humans. The purpose of a phase 1 trial is to make sure that the new drug is safe and well tolerated before it is given to a larger group of patients. A related question is which dose is well tolerated. To answer these questions, typically a small number of participants, for example, 3 people, are given a single low dose of a new drug. If this turns out to be safe, then another small group of people is given a somewhat higher dose of the drug. In this way, the dose given is gradually escalated until problems occur. This highest dose is called the *maximum tolerated dose*. Once we know the maximum tolerated dose, then multiple doses are given, again to a small number of people only. Another important question that is often addressed in phase 1 is what drug levels can be achieved with a given dose. Therefore, phase 1 studies often involve repeated blood drawing after a participant takes medication.

Most phase 1 studies are done for new drugs that have not previously been given to humans. However, sometimes studies are called phase 1 studies when they gather information on the highest tolerated dose in PALS specifically.

*Phase 2* studies are typically needed to learn about the safety of the new drug when taken over a longer period of time. In phase 2, researchers also learn more about the effect of drugs on PALS specifically, even when the drug has already been used for other indications. Sometimes, we also study in phase 2 how a drug will interact with other medications, such as riluzole.

More importantly, phase 2 studies give us an early signal of possible drug benefit. Sometimes, phase 2 studies have several dose arms to give us some preliminary information as to which dose might work best. Phase 2 studies typically involve 50 to 200 participants. When there are several promising new treatments emerging from laboratory research, we cannot leave large, definitive phase 3 trials for all of them. This is because phase 3 trials take a long time and require large resources. Therefore, it is strategically important to select those new drugs that should be taken to phase 3 with priority. In phase 2 studies, we frequently aim to find out if it is futile to move a new drug into phase 3. It may seem counterintuitive to conduct a trial looking for futility, when we really want to find something that works. However, finding which drugs are unlikely to ultimately succeed can be an important step in drug development.

*Phase 3* trials are large clinical trials designed to study whether a drug is effective against ALS. They are typically randomized, placebo controlled, and double blinded. They often involve several hundred participants. Therefore, they usually require many ALS centers in North America or internationally to participate. Successfully implementing a phase 3 trial for ALS requires large resources and the collaboration of many ALS researchers and patient groups. An independent committee is appointed to oversee safety and data quality. This committee is called the Data and Safety Monitoring Board, or DSMB. Monitors visit the participating ALS centers to make sure that the data are accurate. This level of oversight and quality control is necessary so that the results will convince patients and doctors about the new medication. Also, the FDA requires positive evidence from two independent randomized control studies for drug approval.

- Why does drug development take a long time?

People living with ALS understandably question why it often takes years to move from a laboratory discovery to a clinical trial result. Everyone involved with ALS shares a sense of urgency. However, several factors contribute to the time currently needed to test a drug all the way from the laboratory to phase 3. First and most importantly, we need to safeguard participants. Although ALS is a serious condition, the potential risks of a new drug to the health of trial participants need to be justified. In other words, the relationship between risk and potential benefit has to be ethically acceptable. This means that we usually have to go step by step because short cuts would potentially place a larger-than-needed group at risk. Other factors that contribute to the overall drug development time are regulatory requirements. Every step has to be approved by the FDA and by the Institutional Review Boards, or IRBs, of the participating ALS centers. This again serves to protect trial participants. Obtaining funding for ALS trials can be challenging, and lack of funding contributes to delays in drug development. For diseases more common than ALS, the pharmaceutical industry often funds phase 3 trials. For ALS, this may not be the case because the industry may perceive the market incentives as insufficient. However, many companies recognize that a drug approved for ALS may also have potential for other, more common neurodegenerative diseases. Government funding and funding by patient groups is very important to move ALS clinic trials forward.

ALS is designated as an *orphan disease*. Orphan disease status can be granted to a disease that affects less than 200,000 people in the United States. This orphan status provides incentives to drug developers. ALS can also be on a fast track with the FDA. This means that the FDA can give ALS an accelerated drug evaluation under special circumstances. This is good news for ALS drug development.

Recruiting participants for ALS trials may take a long time. This may be due to insufficient trial access or lack of interest in the trial among PALS.

Retention can be insufficient and thus jeopardize the success of an entire trial. This can contribute to delays in overall drug development. Retention means that patients who enroll in a trial complete the study as per protocol.

- What can PALS, families, advocacy groups, and researchers do to speed up clinical trials?

All stakeholders can work together to increase funding for ALS clinical trials. They can ask regulatory agencies such as the FDA to expedite the approval process for ALS drugs. If a large proportion of PALS participate in trials, the recruitment time is shortened. To increase recruitment, researchers and PALS need to make sure that trials are as accessible and user-friendly as possible. For example, participating ALS centers need to be sufficiently numerous and geographically well distributed. The visit schedule needs to be feasible for most PALS and their families. PALS and their families can help if they try to stay with a study that they had committed to.

- What is the ethical framework underlying a clinical trial?

For a clinical trial to be ethically acceptable, there has to be *equipoise* regarding the medication. Equipoise essentially means that we truly do not know whether the new treatment is any good. If doctors knew for sure that a new treatment was helpful, then it would not be ethical for them to withhold it from their patients. When physicians, PALS, and the FDA want to make sure that a new treatment really works, they need evidence from clinical trials. On the other hand, it would likely be considered unethical as well if doctors conducted a clinical trial if they did not have a good reason to try a new drug. These reasons are often based in the understanding of the drug's mechanism, in laboratory results, animal data, and experience with the new drug in other diseases.

Another key concept that makes a trial ethically acceptable is that it has to be designed so that the important questions can be answered at the end of the experiment. If a trial is poorly designed or implemented, then the PALS and doctors who give their time and effort do not actually contribute to advancing knowledge on the new drug in ALS. Participating in a trial and complying with a study protocol is a big effort, so that those who generously make this effort should be able to expect that their contributions will advance knowledge in a meaningful way. Uncontrolled trials can answer some important preliminary research questions, but they can rarely tell us if a new drug is actually effective. Before enrolling into an uncontrolled efficacy trial, PALS and their families should carefully consider the study design and consult their doctors and patient advocacy groups for guidance. Institutional review boards are also important in this process because they provide oversight and give approval to studies based on their safety, scientific merit, and ethical framework.

• Does so-called alternative medicine have an impact on clinical trials?

Given that traditional medicine and academic research have failed to date to find a cure for ALS, it is understandable that many PALS look toward unconventional approaches and alternative medicine. However, it is important to keep in mind that very little is often known about these treatments and that many of the claims made are difficult to confirm. PALS should be particularly cautious before committing to any treatment that requires a large financial investment. This may mean that someone significantly benefits financially who may not put patients first. If a really good treatment were available, physicians would want to use it and it would probably be tested in a trial. Also, PALS should be careful with risky and invasive treatments. With good care, we can do a lot nowadays to maintain function, extend life expectancy, and improve the quality of life for PALS. Individual PALS who undergo an unconventional and perhaps risky treatment understandably put much hope into it and may therefore be inclined to see benefit, when in fact it might turn out that it did not have any real or lasting effect. Therefore, before agreeing to expensive or risky unconventional treatments, PALS should gather information and get advice from patient advocacy groups and their treating physicians to protect themselves. It is said that millions are spent each year by PALS on unconventional treatments and that these millions could make a big difference in accelerating research toward a cure. And, alternative medicine approaches can also slow down recruitment into clinical trials.

• Why should a patient consider participating in a clinical trial?

PALS should consider trials because we are in a difficult situation: We have only one approved drug for ALS, riluzole, with modest benefit. We desperately need a second effective medication. Clinical trials are the fastest way to find a more effective medication for ALS. Participating in a clinical trial is an important decision for PALS. First, there is, of course, the hope of personal benefit. Trial participation can give patients access to new treatments with potential benefit. However, there is no guarantee for benefit. Also, in most trials, many participants will not receive the active drug, but will instead receive a placebo. The personal advantage of this arrangement is the built-in safety factor. Most trials have an independent board that monitors safety. Rarely, trials can be stopped early if the drug is found to be unsafe or if it is very unlikely that the drug is effective. Theoretically, if there is overwhelming evidence early on that the drug is effective, the protocol may be stopped early or may be modified to allow more PALS access to active study drug.

A secondary motive for trial participation can be the wish to accelerate ALS research and to help others affected by ALS. This is certainly the case in phase 1 studies, where the short treatment period makes personal benefit unlikely. Altruism is a powerful force that has led to many advances. In medicine, HIV trials are a good example. The willingness of a large proportion of patients to commit to clinical trials has resulted in greatly improved treatments for those infected with HIV. Although individual patients were initially opposed to placebo-controlled trials, they soon came to recognize that, as a group, they would improve their outlook by giving their time and effort to clinical trials. HIV disease has gone in one decade from having a very poor prognosis to being a rather treatable disease.

Finally, independent of motives and treatment assignment, many patients find it rewarding to participate in a clinical trial. Trial participants often develop a close relationship with the health care team they work with throughout the trial. Also, trials convey hope for ALS. The choice to participate in a clinical trial often gives patients and their families a sense of choice and control.

- Once participating in a trial, what can PALS and families do to make it successful?

PALS and researchers are partnering in clinical trials to achieve a common goal, finding an effective treatment for ALS. PALS and their families should make sure that they understand what the trial is testing and what the risks and benefits are. This information is available in the consent form. Also, PALS and their families should make sure that their questions are answered by the study team. PALS should enroll in a clinical trial only if they are ready to make this commitment, which should not be made too easily. Also, they should make sure that they have a family member, friend, or caregiver who can support them in their participation. It is very important for the validity of trial results that participants continue to follow up with the study team, even if they end up stopping the study medication. They should still complete all the tests that are part of the trial. For example, if only those people came back for study visits who are doing well, but not those who are doing poorly, then the study might falsely conclude that the new drug is beneficial when in reality it is not. Therefore it is very important that participants return for all study visits. PALS who know at the onset that they will likely not be able to complete the study visits should consider forgoing participation so that others can have the opportunity to participate who are more likely to complete all visits. While participating in a trial, PALS can also help by letting the study team know about any health-related events.

## Riluzole, a Medication With Proven Benefit in Clinical Trials

Riluzole is the only drug approved by the FDA for the treatment of ALS. It is thought to lessen the nerve cell damage associated with glutamate. This kind of nerve cell damage is believed to play a role in ALS, so clinical trials were initiated in PALS. This happened before riluzole was tested in mouse models. However, after riluzole was shown to have an effect in people with ALS, it also turned out to be beneficial in mice (2–4).

*The first, randomized, double-blind, placebo-controlled trial* included 155 patients. At the end of the 12-month treatment period, 74% of those treated with 100 mg of riluzole daily were still alive, compared with 58% in the placebo group. This represented a statistically significant survival benefit. The survival difference between treatment groups was larger for bulbar onset patients than for limb onset patients. At the end of the placebo-controlled observation period, the survival benefit was smaller but continued to be significant for the entire study population and for the bulbar onset patients, but not for the limb onset patients. The rate of muscle strength deterioration was significantly slower in the riluzole group. Other functional outcomes, including quality-of-life measures, were not different between treatment groups (2).

*A second phase 3 trial* in 959 patients with ALS tested 3 dose arms: 50 mg, 100 mg, and 200 mg daily. After a mean follow-up time of 18 months, 50% on placebo versus 57% receiving 100 mg of riluzole daily were alive. The 100-mg dose had the most favorable efficacy and safety profile. There was no difference in the rate of decline for the secondary outcome measures including muscle strength (5).

*A third, randomized, controlled riluzole clinical trial* included 168 patients who did not meet the inclusion criteria for the large, confirmatory riluzole trial (5). Patients who were elderly or who had advanced-stage disease were randomly assigned to 100 mg of riluzole daily or placebo and treated for 18 months. The safety profile in this sample was similar to that observed in the previous trials (2). The study could not include enough patients to reach sufficient power, and no survival difference between treatment groups was observed (6).

*A fourth randomized, controlled riluzole trial* in Japan involving 195 patients had negative results. The primary outcome was a composite measure of disease progression.

*The evidence-based and systematic Cochrane review* reports a meta-analysis of randomized riluzole trials with tracheostomy-free survival as the primary endpoint (876 riluzole-treated and 406 placebo-treated patients) (7). A meta-analysis means that the authors combine information from trials and analyze the results. For the homogeneous group included in the two initial randomized trials (2,5), 100 mg of riluzole daily provided a significant survival benefit. This benefit fell short of significance when the more advanced or elderly patients from the third trial (6) were included in the analysis. Based on their meta-analysis, the authors concluded that riluzole at 100 mg daily is reasonably safe and prolongs survival by about 2 months (7).

Riluzole overall is well tolerated. The most common adverse events observed in the controlled trials were nausea (15%) and asthenia (18%). Less common adverse events included dizziness and gastrointestinal events. Open-label studies have found the same adverse events at lower frequencies and have not uncovered any additional, unexpected adverse events.

Caution is warranted in patients with liver disease. In 10% to 15% of riluzole-treated patients, serum liver levels increased (8).

## Recent ALS Clinical Trials

In recent years, there have been a number of randomized, controlled phase 2 and 3 trials for ALS. The following is a list of some of the recent, larger clinical trials organized by the mechanism they target. The list is incomplete, omitting many smaller trials and past trials. More extensive listings of ALS clinical trials are available elsewhere (9–11).

## Targeting Oxidative Stress

Several research findings suggest that oxidative stress contributes to motor neuron degeneration in ALS. Drugs with antioxidant properties that have been studied in the treatment of ALS include vitamin E (α-tocopherol), coenzyme Q10, *N*-acetylcysteine, and selegiline. Many patients with ALS are taking antioxidants with the hope of slowing disease progression. The rationale for their use is compelling, but there is no significant evidence to date to support the benefit of these antioxidants (12). Several trials based on antioxidant strategies are ongoing or in planning.

## Antiglutamate Strategies

An accumulating body of evidence suggests that glutamate, an excitatory neurotransmitter, may contribute to motor neuron death in ALS. *Branched-chain amino acids* can activate glutamate dehydrogenase, but the results of several clinical trials have been negative. Although an earlier trial of gabapentin, another antiglutamate drug, was promising, a second study of 3,600 mg of gabapentin daily in 204 patients with ALS was unable to document a significant difference between the gabapentin and placebo groups (13). Two randomized clinical trials of *lamotrigine* in 30 and 67 patients with ALS, respectively, did not find evidence of a functional benefit in ALS (14,15). *Topiramate* was not beneficial in an ALS clinic trial (16). Overall, antiglutamate strategies remain an important focus of ALS research, especially following the positive riluzole trial results (see above).

## Targeting Mitochondrial Function and Energy Metabolism

Mitochondrial impairment is thought to play an important role in the pathogenesis of ALS. *Creatine,* a natural compound central to energy metabolism, showed promise in the mouse model of ALS (17). However, the results of two randomized, controlled clinical trials were negative. A well-designed study of 10 mg of creatine in 175 patients with ALS showed no survival benefit in a 16-month study (18). A phase 2 trial of high-dose coenzyme Q10 in ALS showed insufficient evidence of benefit to warrant phase 3 testing in ALS.

## Nerve Cell Rescue by Growth Factors

Based on their survival-promoting effects on motor nerve cells in culture and in animal models, nerve cell growth factors have emerged as possible treatments for ALS. These include insulin-like growth factor-1 (IGF-I), brain-derived neurotrophic factor (BDNF), ciliary neurotrophic factor (CNTF), glial cell-line-derived neurotrophic factor (GDNF), and vascular endothelial growth factor (VEGF). The preclinical studies were rapidly followed by a number of randomized, controlled clinical trials. A large, randomized, controlled phase 3 trial of 1,135 patients with ALS evaluated FVC change and survival in *BNDF*-treated patients compared with the placebo group (19). The primary analysis was negative, but secondary analyses suggested benefit. *IGF-1* was studied in a randomized trial of 266 patients over 9 months with a functional primary outcome (Appel scores). A second study in 183 patients with ALS with a similar design did not confirm this result (20), but a meta-analysis of both trials suggests a modest effect (21). A third *IGF-1* study in the United States turned out to be negative. *CNTF* was studied in two large, randomized, placebo-controlled clinical trials including 730 (22) and 570 (23) patients, respectively. Adverse events were more frequent than anticipated in both trials, and no treatment benefit was shown.

*Sanofi SR57746A (Xaliproden)* is a small peptide with both neurotrophic and neuroprotective properties as well as good brain penetration. Two randomized, controlled clinical trials have been completed, one evaluating xaliproden alone, the second evaluating xaliproden in combination with riluzole. The results of the trial were negative overall but suggested a trend toward a beneficial effect of the 1-mg dose on pulmonary function (24).

## Mitigating Motor Neuron Apoptosis and Autophagy

Evidence suggests that cell death or *apoptotic* pathways are activated in ALS contributing to motor neuron degeneration (see Chapters 11 and 15). *Minocycline,* a drug with a presumed effect on cell death, was not beneficial in a phase 3 trial (25).

*TCH346* (Novartis) also is thought to prevent nerve cell death, but a phase 3 clinical trial failed to show a significant treatment benefit (26).

Lithium is thought to have an effect on *autophagy*, a mechanism of cell removal, as well as on mitochondrial function in motor neurons. It was recently reported to show benefit in a transgenic mouse model of ALS but also in a small series of patients with ALS. The study in patients with ALS was so small that it is difficult to judge if the benefit possibly occurred by chance (27). Therefore, larger controlled trials are needed to evaluate the effect of lithium in the treatment of ALS.

## Antiviral Strategies

Infectious causes including viral etiologies have been implicated in the pathogenesis of ALS. In a pilot study of indinavir prescribed to patients with sporadic ALS no clear benefits were found, although the number of patients was too small to make definitive conclusions. Patients who were on indinavir had more side effects such as kidney stones and significant gastrointestinal symptoms (28). Treatment with the HIV protease inhibitor ritonavir in combination with hydroxyurea (a medication used in hematology/oncology as well as HIV multidrug treatment) is currently under investigation.

## Targeting Inflammation and Microglial Activation

Inflammation and activation of the cells surrounding nerve cells in the brain (microglia) may be involved in ALS. A randomized clinical trial in 300 patients with ALS evaluated the efficacy of *celcoxib,* and found no difference for the primary outcome measure, the decline in muscle arm strength (29). *ONO-2506* is supposed to have a similar mechanism and is currently being evaluated in Europe.

Neurovaccination strategies targeting the inflammatory processes that may contribute to motor neuron degeneration have been suggested in the treatment of ALS. *Glatiramer acetate,* a polypeptide mixture that has been approved by the FDA for the treatment of multiple sclerosis, has demonstrated moderate benefit in the transgenic mouse model of ALS and was well tolerated in early trials in humans (30). A large controlled study is underway in Europe.

## Other Neuroprotective Strategies

The xanthine derivative *pentoxyfilline (EHT 0201)* is thought to have neuroprotective properties based on preclinical studies and has recently been evaluated in a phase 2 trial as a potential treatment for ALS. Four hundred subjects were enrolled within 4 months and treated with EHT 0201 as an add-on therapy to riluzole. The study period was 18 months with patient survival regardless of tracheostomy/ventilation status as the primary efficacy endpoint. No difference was found between treatment groups (31).

*Tamoxifen,* an anti–breast cancer agent, was overall well tolerated in ALS but was associated with frequent hot flashes in a pilot study. There was a suggestion of benefit, but it was a small study so that further evaluation is under consideration (32).

*Ceftriaxone* is an antibiotic that has been identified as a candidate treatment for ALS. A National Institutes of Health (NIH)-funded, double-blind, placebo-controlled clinical trial of ceftriaxone in 600 patients with ALS is underway.

*Sodium phenylbutyrate* is a medication approved for people with rare inborn errors of metabolism called *urea cycle disorders.* It is thought to affect the way genes are translated into proteins in our cells. In mice, it was reported to increase survival (33). Although it was well tolerated in early trials in humans, there has not been a larger study to test its effect in ALS.

*Arimoclomol* is believed to function by a mechanism that stimulates a normal cellular protein repair pathway. It is slated for efficacy testing in ALS soon.

*KNS-760704* (Knopp) is a small molecule similar to pramipexole, a medication for Parkinson disease. In a phase 1 study, it was safe and well tolerated. A phase 2 study is anticipated to begin in 2008.

Antisense oligonucleotides are molecules that can downregulate genes in the brain. They can be designed to target many different genes, including the one found in familial ALS, superoxide dismutase 1 (SOD1). When these special antisense oligonucleotides are infused into the nervous system of mice with ALS, they decrease SOD1 protein and slow disease progression. This approach has potential but requires a large number of research steps before it can be tried in PALS.

*Stem cell therapy* has not been evaluated in controlled clinical trials. Preliminary, small open-label trials in patients with ALS have been reported at motor neuron disease conferences, using allogenic hematopoietic stem cells (16) or autologous cultured bone marrow mesenchymal stem cells that were directly injected into the lumbar spinal cord (20, 34). These efforts are in very early stages and require extensive basic research, animal studies, and feasibility studies before their efficacy can be evaluated.

## Conclusion

The impressive series of large, randomized multicenter trials for ALS has resulted in the approval of riluzole, the first medication effective in the treatment of ALS. Although riluzole conveys only modest benefit, having a medication available to treat the disease has changed the practice of ALS care and has given us hope that better treatment can be identified through clinical trials.

Although it is disappointing that the results of many recent ALS trials have been negative, these trials have resulted in progress toward a cure. The clinical trials methodology and infrastructure have seen many improvements during the past decade. Patient advocacy groups and researchers are increasingly working together to raise funds for trials and to increase the awareness among patients of clinical trial opportunities.

Drug discovery is a difficult and costly process. If out of a very large chemical library only 100 drugs reached phase 1, then of those 100 drugs only one would ultimately be successful and approved by the FDA. In ALS drug discovery, we have tested more than 30 drugs in the last 18 years and, in fact, one drug has been approved. However, we obviously need far better treatments for ALS. Drug discovery in ALS is urgent and is the ultimate goal of most ALS research.

Controlled clinical trials are still considered the fastest and safest way to evaluate new treatments for ALS. We believe that through good clinical trials and a joint effort of all stakeholders, clinical trials will soon help translate research progress into better treatment for patients living with ALS.

## References

1. Mitsumoto H, Gordon P, Kaufmann P, et al. Randomized control trials in ALS: lessons learned. *Amyotroph Lateral Scler Other Motor Neuron Disord.* 2004;5(Suppl 1):8–13.
2. Bensimon G, Lacomblez L, Meininger V. A controlled trial of riluzole in amyotrophic lateral sclerosis. ALS/Riluzole Study Group. *N Engl J Med.* 1994;330:585–591.
3. Gurney ME, Cutting FB, Zhai P, et al. Benefit of vitamin E, riluzole, and gabapentin in a transgenic model of familial amyotrophic lateral sclerosis. *Ann Neurol.* 1996;39: 147–157.
4. Ishiyama T, Okada R, Nishibe H, et al.. Riluzole slows the progression of neuromuscular dysfunction in the wobbler mouse motor neuron disease. *Brain Res.* 2004;1019: 226–236.

5. Lacomblez L, Bensimon G, Leigh PN, et al. Dose-ranging study of riluzole in amyotrophic lateral sclerosis. Amyotrophic Lateral Sclerosis/Riluzole Study Group II. *Lancet.* 1996;347:1425–1431.
6. Bensimon G, Lacomblez L, Delumeau JC, et al. A study of riluzole in the treatment of advanced stage or elderly patients with amyotrophic lateral sclerosis. *J Neurol.* 2002;249:609–615.
7. Miller RG. Role of fatigue in limiting physical activities in humans with neuromuscular diseases. *Am J Phys Med Rehabil.* 2002;81:S99–S107.
8. Bensimon G, Doble A. The tolerability of riluzole in the treatment of patients with amyotrophic lateral sclerosis. *Expert Opin Drug Saf.* 2004;3:525–534.
9. Murray B, Mitsumoto H. Drug therapy in amyotrophic lateral sclerosis. *Adv Neurol.* 2002;88:63–82.
10. Bhatt JM, Gordon PH. Current clinical trials in amyotrophic lateral sclerosis. *Expert Opin Investig Drugs.* 2007;16(8):1197–1207.
11. Mitsumoto H, Gordon P, Kaufmann P, et al. Randomized control trials in ALS: lessons learned. *Amyotroph Lateral Scler Other Motor Neuron Disord.* 2004;5(suppl 1): 8–13.
12. Orrell R, Lane J, Ross M. Antioxidant treatment for amyotrophic lateral sclerosis/motor neuron disease. *Cochrane Database Syst Rev.* 2004:CD002829.
13. Miller RG, Moore DH 2nd, Gelinas DF, et al. Phase III randomized trial of gabapentin in patients with amyotrophic lateral sclerosis. *Neurology.* 2001;56:843–848.
14. Ryberg H, Askmark H, Persson LI. A double-blind randomized clinical trial in amyotrophic lateral sclerosis using lamotrigine: effects on CSF glutamate, aspartate, branched-chain amino acid levels and clinical parameters. *Acta Neurol Scand.* 2003;108:1–8.
15. Eisen A, Stewart H, Schulzer M, et al. Anti-glutamate therapy in amyotrophic lateral sclerosis: a trial using lamotrigine. *Can J Neurol Sci.* 1993;20:297–301.
16. Cudkowicz ME, Shefner JM, Schoenfeld DA, et al. A randomized, placebo-controlled trial of topiramate in amyotrophic lateral sclerosis. *Neurology.* 2003;61:456–464.
17. Klivenyi P, Ferrante RJ, Matthews RT, et al. Neuroprotective effects of creatine in a transgenic animal model of amyotrophic lateral sclerosis. *Nat Med.* 1999;5:347–350.
18. Groeneveld GJ, Veldink JH, van der Tweel I, et al. A randomized sequential trial of creatine in amyotrophic lateral sclerosis. *Ann Neurol.* 2003;53:437–445.
19. A controlled trial of recombinant methionyl human BDNF in ALS: the BDNF Study Group (Phase III). *Neurology.* 1999;52:1427–1433.
20. Borasio GD, Robberecht W, Leigh PN, et al. A placebo-controlled trial of insulin-like growth factor-I in amyotrophic lateral sclerosis. European ALS/IGF-I Study Group. *Neurology.* 1998;51:583–586.
21. Mitchell JD, Wokke JH, Borasio GD. Recombinant human insulin-like growth factor I (rhIGF-I) for amyotrophic lateral sclerosis/motor neuron disease. *Cochrane Database Syst Rev.* 2002:CD002064.
22. ALS CNTF Treatment Study Group. A double-blind placebo-controlled clinical trial of subcutaneous recombinant human ciliary neurotrophic factor (rHCNTF) in amyotrophic lateral sclerosis. ALS CNTF Treatment Study Group. *Neurology.* 1996;46:1244–1249.
23. Miller RG, Moore D, Young LA, et al. Placebo-controlled trial of gabapentin in patients with amyotrophic lateral sclerosis. WALS Study Group. Western Amyotrophic Lateral Sclerosis Study Group. *Neurology.* 1996;47:1383–1388.
24. Meininger V, Bensimon G, Bradley WR, et al. Efficacy and safety of xaliproden in amyotrophic lateral sclerosis: results of two phase III trials. *Amyotroph Lateral Scler Other Motor Neuron Disord.* 2004;5:107–117.
25. Gordon PH, Moore DH, Miller RG, et al. Efficacy of minocycline in patients with amyotrophic lateral sclerosis: a phase III randomised trial. *Lancet Neurol.* 2007;6:1045–1053.

26. Miller R, Bradley W, Cudkowicz M, et al. TCH346 Study Group. Phase II/III random-ized trial of TCH346 in patients with ALS. *Neurology* 2007;69(8):776–784.

27. Fornai F, Longone P, Cafaro L, et al. Lithium delays progression of amyotrophic lateral sclerosis. *Proc Natl Acad Sci USA*. 2008;105:2052–2057.

28. Scelsa SN, MacGowan DJ, Mitsumoto H, Imperato T, LeValley AJ, Liu MH, DelBene M, Kim MY. A pilot, double-blind, placebo-controlled trial of indinavir in patients with ALS. *Neurology*. 2005 Apr 12;64(7):1298–1300.

29. Shefner JM, Cudkowicz ME, Schoenfeld D, et al. A clinical trial of creatine in ALS. *Neurology*. 2004;63:1656–1661.

30. Angelov DN, Waibel S, Guntinas-Lichius O, et al. Therapeutic vaccine for acute and chronic motor neuron diseases: implications for amyotrophic lateral sclerosis. *Proc Natl Acad Sci USA*. 2003;100:4790–4795.

31. Meininger V, Asselain B, Guillet P, et al. Pentoxifylline in ALS: a double-blind, ran-domized, multicenter, placebo-controlled trial. *Neurology* 2006;66(1):88–92.

32. Brooks B, Sanjak M, Roelke K, et al. Phase 2B randomized dose-ranging clinical trial of tamoxifen, a selective estrogen receptor modulator (SERM), in the treatment of amyo-trophic lateral scleroris (ALS): sensitivity analyses of discordance between survival and functional outcomes with long-term follow-up. 16th International Symposium on ALS/MND. *Amyotrophic Lateral Sclerosis* 2005;6(suppl 1):118.

33. Ryu H, Smith K, Camelo SI, et al. Sodium phenylbutyrate prolongs survival and reg-ulates expression of anti-apoptotic genes in transgenic amyotrophic lateral sclerosis mice. *J Neurochem*. 2005;93:1087–1098.

34. Chio A, Mora G, Leone M, et al. Early symptom progression rate is related to ALS outcome: a prospective population-based study. *Neurology*. 2002;59:99–103.

# 17

# The Amyotrophic Lateral Sclerosis Patient Care Database

**Robert G. Miller, Stacey M. Champion,
Dallas A. Forshew, and
Frederick A. Anderson, Jr.**

Care for patients with amyotrophic lateral sclerosis (ALS) has traditionally been based on the experience of clinicians, the advice of leaders in the field, and reports about individual patients. Although these can be valuable, they are insufficient for establishing the standard of care for patients with ALS. In 1999, in an attempt to offer recommendations for care that were based on research studies, the American Academy of Neurology (AAN) published practice parameters for ALS that provided strategies based on scientific and medical evidence. In addition, the Cochrane Collaboration has analyzed more recent studies to provide additional guidelines for treating patients with ALS. These reviews offer further insight but do not allow for monitoring the results of various treatment protocols. To this end, a large, multicenter, long-term database was established to examine the impact of proper treatment of ALS symptoms and patient responses. The goal of the ALS CARE database was to create a more uniform and excellent treatment standard. By tracking outcomes, the database provided a clearer picture of the effectiveness of different therapies and thereby helped to increase the overall standard of care. Secondarily, the ALS CARE database has provided data that can be used to guide future clinical research. Much has been learned from the ALS CARE database and, with time, its usefulness has increased.

The ALS CARE team was made up of an advisory board of leaders in the ALS community including neurologists, nurses, statisticians, and a representative from the ALS Association. Bylaws that address the goals and guidelines of the ALS CARE database and a protocol for the collection of data were established.

**Table 17.1** Variables Reported in Amyotrophic Lateral
Sclerosis (ALS) Patient Care Database Quarterly Reports

Patient characteristics (e.g., duration of symptoms, age)

Clinical measures (e.g., ALSFRS [ALS Functional Rating Scale] score, forced
    vital capacity)

Type of insurance

Diagnostic criteria

Medications

Feeding modalities

Respiratory interventions

Quality of life

Satisfaction with medical care

Caregiver burden scores

All practicing neurologists in North America were invited to join the database
and contribute data pertaining to the diagnosis, prognosis, and treatment of patients with ALS. Patients and caregivers also completed forms (Table 17.1) that
included demographics, quality of life, and other disease-specific items. Data
were collected at the time the patient signed up to be included in the database and
at follow-up intervals of 6 months. A Study Coordinating Center at the University
of Massachusetts Medical School (Worcester) is responsible for data analysis,
management, and maintenance of confidentiality. Physicians receive confidential
feedback about their patients and national practice patterns across the database.

## Methodology

### Health Professional Form

Neurologists completed a 2-page form that included information about symptom
duration, severity, and current management. Details of the forms have been published (see Miller et al., 2003, in the Suggested Readings). The forms may be
viewed at http://www.outcomes-umassmed.org/ALS/data_forms.cfm.

### Patient Form

Patients completed a form that took about 15 minutes, including questions about
medications, therapies, disease severity, quality of life, satisfaction with care, and
the financial impact of ALS.

## Caregiver Form

For the caregiver, questions included the caregiver's relationship to the patient, employment status, and the effects of caregiving on the caregiver's physical and emotional health.

## Completion Form

The Completion Form served to correct the diagnosis if the patient is found to not have ALS and also provided information about the dying process.

## Data Analysis and Reporting

Once forms were completed, they were sent to a central data coordinating center where the information was entered into a computer database. Confidential quarterly reports were sent to participating neurologists. The reports included data on adherence to the practice parameters of the AAN, the use of therapeutic interventions, correlation between measures of quality of life and scores related to the patient's ability to perform certain physical tasks such as walking, and patient satisfaction with care.

The ALS Patient Care Database data coordinating center is also responsible for protecting the confidentiality of the data submitted. Neurologists participating in the database were assigned a confidential identification number. They, in turn, assigned confidential numbers to the patients in the database. Caregivers gave only their initials when completing forms. Thus, participants cannot be identified.

# Results

Since inception in September 1996, the ALS CARE database has enrolled over 5,600 patients from 387 neurologists at 107 clinical sites across North America. Patients are 93% white and 61% are male. The average age is 58 years. Only 6% of patients have the familial form of ALS. Obtaining follow-up information from patients throughout the course of their disease has been challenging. The number of patients at 6-, 12-, 18-, and 24-month follow-ups decreased from 1,838 to 1,334, 736, and 682, respectively.

Several trends in ALS care have emerged. The diagnosis of ALS for these patients was based on a variety of tests. The most commonly employed diagnostic tests were electromyography (EMG) and nerve conduction studies (87%), followed by imaging of the spine (MRI) (56.8%), thyroid function (50.8%), serum immunoelectrophoresis/serum electrophoresis (searching for abnormal proteins in the blood) (47.2%), brain imaging (MRI) (50.4%), ganglioside (GM-1) blood antibody (38.1%), heavy metal screening (31.2%), and lumbar puncture (spinal tap) (19.7%). After their initial diagnosis, 86% of patients sought a second opinion.

The average patient was in the intermediate stages of the disease at the time of enrollment in the database. Those patients who were enrolled within 6 months after symptom onset had an average forced vital capacity of 75% of predicted, and an average ALS Functional Rating Scale (ALSFRS) score of 28. Forty percent of patients self-reported full independence in activities of daily living.

Concerning drug therapies, riluzole (Rilutek) was used in 52% of patients in the ALS CARE database at the time of enrollment. Other medications included gabapentin (14%), creatine (39%), high-dose vitamins or antioxidants (48%), non-traditional medications (15%), and other unspecified medications (42%). During the most active enrollment period, gabapentin and creatine were both being studied in drug trials to see whether they would slow down the rate of new weakness in ALS. The drug studies for both gabapentin and creatine showed that they did not help ALS. At the time of enrollment, 89% of patients were satisfied with their medical care. Patients who used various therapies and reported satisfaction with those services are listed in Table 17.2.

## Trends Over Time

The ALS CARE database allows us to detect changes in patient care over time. The 1999 publication of the AAN practice guidelines for managing ALS had a significant impact on patient care, as shown by the analysis of changes in patient management over an 8-year period since inception of the ALS CARE database (Table 17.3). Thus, the database is a valuable tool to determine whether progress has been made in the integration of evidence-based recommendations into patient care and to target areas for further progress. For example, the use of riluzole increased from 45% in 1998 to 61% in 2002 ($P < .0001$). Similarly, only a fraction of patients were being treated for ALS symptoms such as constipation, cramps, depression, disturbed sleep, spasticity, and increased saliva. However, based on patient reports, most therapies offered benefit and it is likely that a greater proportion of patients could benefit from symptomatic treatment.

Initial results from the ALS CARE database suggest that treatment utilization in general has increased in recent years (Table 17.3). For example, symptomatic

**Table 17.2** Services Used by Patients

| Service | Patients using service, % | Find service helpful, % |
|---|---|---|
| Physical therapy | 46 | 84 |
| Occupational therapy | 31 | 79 |
| Speech therapy | 22 | 66 |
| Home nurse | 20 | 85 |
| Dietary (nutrition) | 19 | 83 |
| Social work | 17 | 76 |
| Psychology/psychiatry | 11 | 69 |

**Table 17.3** Changes in Management of Patients With ALS Since Inception of ALS CARE

| Parameter | 1997 | 2004 |
|---|---|---|
| **PARAMETERS THAT INCREASED** | | |
| Patients enrolled in ALS CARE within 6 mo of diagnosis, % | 31 | 61 |
| Patients taking riluzole, % | 45 | 56 |
| Patients taking medication for drooling, % | 12 | 17 |
| Patients receiving treatment for emotionality, % | 28 | 42 |
| Patients receiving treatment for depression, % | 23 | 42 |
| Patients receiving treatment for sleep disturbance, % | 17 | 29 |
| Patients receiving PEG when FVC was <50% of predicted, % | 3 | 16 |
| Patients receiving NIV when FVC was <40% of predicted, % | 5 | 9 |
| Use of nutritional supplements, % of patients | 9 | 19 |
| Use of physical therapy, % of patients | 31 | 43 |
| Use of occupational therapy, % of patients | 19 | 31 |
| Patients with depression, % | 39 | 45 |
| Mean delay between first symptom and diagnosis, mo | 13 | 14 |
| **PARAMETERS THAT DECREASED** | | |
| Patients enrolled in a clinical trial at the time of enrollment in the ALS CARE database, % | 34 | 8 |
| Patients who died at home, % | 49 | 42 |
| Patients taking gabapentin, % | 13 | 4 |

ALS, amyotrophic lateral sclerosis; FVC, forced vital capacity; NIPPV, noninvasive positive pressure ventilation; PEG, percutaneous endoscopic gastrostomy.

medications for ALS symptoms such as constipation, cramps, depression, disturbed sleep, spasticity, and excess saliva were underutilized prior to the adoption of the AAN guidelines. This realization led to the revision of the ALS CARE survey forms to obtain more information regarding these issues.

One of the most common symptoms reported by patients in the ALS CARE database is depression. Since the start of the database in 1996, the percentage of patients with symptoms of depression has ranged from 39% to 45%, suggesting that it is a consistently burdensome issue. Not surprisingly, patients with ALS who have depression tend to score lower on quality-of-life scales than patients with ALS who do not, despite similar degrees of physical decline. As recognition of depression among patients with ALS has increased, so has its treatment (Table 17.3).

Similarly, awareness and treatment of pseudobulbar affect, an excess of crying or laughing beyond what the person is really feeling, has been enhanced by the guidelines (Table 17.3). The proportion of patients treated for this symptom has risen significantly from 29% to 44% (Table 17.3). Similarly, prior to the AAN guidelines, 54% of patients were offered medication to treat drooling, and treatment rose to 75% of patients after the publication of the AAN guidelines.

Thus, symptomatic treatment has increased since inception of the ALS CARE database, and it is quite possible that a greater proportion of patients could benefit from such treatments.

A feeding tube or percutaneous endoscopic gastrostomy (PEG) was recommended in the AAN guidelines for patients with swallowing difficulty. To reduce the risk of the procedure, it was recommended that the PEG be placed before the vital capacity (breathing test) decreased to less than 50% of predicted. After the publication of the AAN report, the proportion of patients for whom PEG was recommended by their physician increased from 12% to 22%. However, only 43% of these patients went through with the procedure, the rest citing reasons such as belief that their swallowing was still adequate (54%), disdain for PEG (11%), and having insufficient information to make a decision favoring PEG (4%). Patients who used a PEG used more assistive devices, more often received multi-disciplinary care in a specialized ALS clinic, had greater utilization of home care nurses and aides, and had more physician and hospital visits. The use of PEG was variable among ALS clinics, ranging from 0% to 52%, suggesting that the belief of the clinic team may play a role in the patient decision. Follow-up study revealed that PEG had an average positive impact for 79% of patients overall, but in only 37% of patients who received PEG late in the disease course. This suggests that patients who got the PEG earlier believed that they received greater benefit from it than patients who waited.

The AAN guidelines recommended assistive breathing devices, or noninvasive ventilation (NIV or BiPAP), for patients with breathing symptoms and a forced vital capacity below 50% of predicted. After the publication of the guidelines, use of NIV increased from 9% to 21%. The primary reasons for the continued under use of NIV are unclear; however, some patients, especially those with speech and swallowing impairment, find that NIV is more difficult to use at first. NIV use in the ALS CARE database was higher among males and among individuals with a higher income. Patients who used NIV were also more likely to have PEG tubes and to take riluzole, suggesting openness to all treatment, compared with nonusers. Those who used NIV had a higher 5-year survival rate (53%) than those who did not use NIV (38%) and reported a better quality of life.

Thus, although use of symptomatic treatments, PEG, and NIV have increased in recent years, persistent underutilization of these effective therapies is a targeted area for improvement in treating patients with ALS.

## Limitations of the Database

There are certain limitations as to what the ALS Patient Care Database can show. It is an observational study that tracks the use of a variety of interventions in routine clinical practice. Because patients enrolled in this database are not randomly assigned to a particular treatment, they are likely to be dissimilar across treatment groups with regard to important characteristics including age, sex, other medical conditions, and so forth. There is also some question as to whether the population within the database is representative of the patient population at large. For example, some clinics may not enroll all of their patients with ALS into the database, which may not reflect the clinic's overall ALS patient population. Although the demographic data in this database appear to be similar to other large natural history studies and to the populations in large clinical trials with respect to gender, age, duration of symptoms, and incidence of familial disease, these data represent the results of participating clinics that may not be representative of all North American patients with ALS.

## New Directions: ALSconnection

In order to get a more accurate view of the ALS experience across North America, a patient registry should reach into rural areas and be accessible to those patients who receive care outside of large ALS clinics. An online patient registry called ALSconnection (www.alsconnection.org) was created with this important effort in mind. ALSconnection has the potential to give every ALS patient with Internet access a voice about the quality of patient care in North America.

ALSconnection is a Web site that allows a 2-way flow of information about ALS. Patients can enter their own information into the online database, and they can also find valuable guidance on how to manage different aspects of their disease. This resource is especially important to patients who do not have access to ALS specialty clinics. ALSconnection offers helpful articles written by ALS experts that work with patients on a daily basis. The articles address such issues as proper nutrition, good nighttime breathing, heartburn, depression, and how to make a bathroom more ALS friendly. There are also updates and links about new research, including clinical trials, and summaries of international research meetings.

This Web-based survey consists of over 200 questions that have been adapted from the ALS CARE paper-based questionnaire. The goal of this survey is to learn about many different aspects of the ALS experience straight from the source, the patient. The survey includes questions about symptoms, medications, disease severity, quality of life, satisfaction with care, and the financial impact of ALS. It is important to know how things change for patients over time;

therefore, participants are sent an e-mail reminder to update their profile every 6 months.

Because ALSconnection is a secure database of private patient information, it requires the oversight and approval of an institutional review board (IRB). IRBs are committees made up of scientists, health care workers, and other community members who do not have a stake in the research being conducted and can ideally serve as unbiased guardians of patient rights and privacy. The IRB overseeing this study requires that each patient sign a 3-part electronic consent form prior to entering data. The consent forms are there to make sure that patients understand their rights, that they understand the research project and why it is being conducted, and that they are voluntarily sharing their health information. Every patient with ALS is encouraged to participate (www.alsconnection.org).

Patients from 37 different U.S. states and several patients from Canada have taken part in ALSconnection so far. Of the 228 patients who have participated, 58% receive care at large ALS centers, 17% are seen at small ALS centers, and 25% of patients are seen by other physicians in community clinics.

The data gathered and analyzed to date have shown several interesting differences in patient treatment between large clinics specializing in ALS and small community-based clinics. In general, patients with ALS who were seen in small clinics graded themselves as more limited in their abilities, less satisfied with the way they were told of their diagnosis, had less access to certain therapists, and were less satisfied with some of the therapies they were receiving. More patient data and more research is needed to validate and identify reasons for these differences.

The Internet may prove to be an important resource for patients with ALS to learn more about their disease, but conversely, it also has the potential to help ALS health care workers learn how to take better care of their patients.

## Conclusion

The ALS Patient Care Database has provided insights into a number of the aspects of ALS, particularly regarding the use and effectiveness of various therapies. Because of its large base and established protocol, the database is able to provide powerful, longitudinal determinations of treatment potential and generation of new hypotheses regarding the disease course of ALS. In addition, the development of Web-based access to the ALS CARE database (www.alscon nection.org) will provide further information about the care of patients outside of large centers, helping the field move toward optimal standardized care for all patients with ALS.

## Acknowledgments

The ALS Patient Care Database is supported by an unrestricted educational grant from Sanofi, and ALSconnection is supported by a research grant from the MDA.

## Suggested Readings

Aboussouan LS, Khan SU, Meeker DP, et al. Effect of noninvasive positive-pressure venti-lation on survival in amyotrophic lateral sclerosis. *Ann Intern Med.* 1997;127:450–453.

Arciniegas DB, Topkoff J. The neuropsychiatry of pathologic affect: an approach to evalu-ation and treatment. *Semin Clin Neuropsychiatry.* 2000;5:290–306.

Bourke SC, Tomlinson M, Williams TL, et al. Effects of non-invasive ventilation on sur-vival and quality of life in patients with amyotrophic lateral sclerosis: a randomised controlled trial. Lancet Neurol 2006;5:140–147.

Bradley WG, Anderson F, Bromberg M, et al. Current management of ALS: comparison of the ALS CARE Database and the AAN Practice Parameter. The American Academy of Neurology. *Neurology.* 2001;57:500–504.

Bradley WG, Anderson F, Gowda N, et al. Improvement in the management of ALS since 1999 publication of AAN Practice Parameter: evidence from the ALS patient CARE database. *Amyotroph Lateral Scler Other Motor Neuron Disord.* 2003;4:21-22.

Brooks BR. El Escorial World Federation of Neurology criteria for the diagnosis of amyo-trophic lateral sclerosis. Subcommittee on Motor Neuron Diseases/Amyotrophic Lat-eral Sclerosis of the World Federation of Neurology Research Group on Neuromuscular Diseases and the El Escorial "Clinical limits of amyotrophic lateral sclerosis" workshop contributors. *J Neurol Sci.* 1994;124(suppl):96–107.

Forshew DA, Bromberg MG. A survey of clinicians' practice in the symptomatic treatment of ALS. *Amyotroph Lateral Scler Other Motor Neuron Disord.* 2003;4:258–263.

Haley RW. Excess incidence of ALS in young Gulf War veterans. *Neurology.* 2003;61:750–756.

Hensley K, Mhatre M, Mou S, et al. On the relation of oxidative stress to neuroinflamma-tion: lessons learned from the G93A-SOD1 mouse model of amyotrophic lateral sclero-sis. *Antioxid Redox Signal.* 2006;8:2075–2087.

Horner RD, Kamins KG, Feussner JR, et al. Occurrence of amyotrophic lateral sclerosis among Gulf War veterans. *Neurology* 2003;61:742–749.

Jewitt K, Hughes RAC. Systematic reviews to help guide clinical practice in neuromuscular disease. *J Neurol Neurosurg Psychiatry.* 2003;74(suppl 2):43–44.

Lechtzin N, Wiener CM, Clawson L, et al. Use of noninvasive ventilation in patients with amyotrophic lateral sclerosis. *Amyotroph Lateral Scler Other Motor Neuron Disord.* 2004;5:9–15.

Miller RG, Rosenberg JA, Gelinas DF, et al. Practice parameter: the care of the patient with amyotrophic lateral sclerosis (an evidence-based review): report of the Quality Stan-dards Subcommittee of the American Academy of Neurology: ALS Practice Parameters Task Force. *Neurology.* 1999;52:1311–1323.

Miller RG, Mitchell JD, Lyon M, et al. Cochrane Neuromuscular Disease Group. Riluzole for amyotrophic lateral sclerosis (ALS)/motor neuron disease (MND). *Cochrane Data-base Syst Rev.* 2007.

Miller RG, Anderson F, Gowda N, et al. "The ALS Patient CARE Program-North American Pa-tient CARE Database. In Amyotrophic Lateral Sclerosis (eds: Mitsumoto H, Przedborski S, Gordon P). Published by Taylor & Francis Group, New York, pp. 633–648, 2006.

Yiangou Y, Facer P, Durrenberger P, et al. COX-2, CB2 and P2X7-immunoreactivities are increased in activated microglial cells/macrophages of multiple sclerosis and amyo-trophic lateral sclerosis spinal cord. *BMC Neurol.* 2006;6:12–26.

## Appendix

The ALS CARE Study Group, in addition to the authors: Walter G. Bradley, DM, FRCP, University of Miami; Mark B. Bromberg, MD, University of Utah;

Benjamin R. Brooks, MD, University of Wisconsin; Neil Cashman, MD, Montreal Neurologic Institute; Lora L. Clawson, RN, BSN, Johns Hopkins University School of Medicine; Merit Cudkowicz, MD, Massachusetts General Hospital; Maura Del Bene, RN, MSN, NP-P, Columbia University; Michael Graves, MD, UCLA School of Medicine; Yadollah Harati, MD, Baylor College of Medicine; Terry Heiman-Patterson, MD, Allegheny University; Mary Lyon, RN, ALS Association; Raul Mandler, MD, Georgetown University; Hiroshi Mitsumoto, MD, Columbia University; Dan Moore, PhD, University of California at San Francisco; Steven P. Ringel, MD, University of Colorado; Jeffrey Rosenfeld, MD, PhD, Carolinas Medical System; Mark A. Ross, MD, University of Kentucky; Michael J. Strong, MD, London Health Sciences Centre; Robert Sufit, MD, Northwestern University.

# Living With the Reality of Amyotrophic Lateral Sclerosis

# 18

# Sharing the Experience of Amyotrophic Lateral Sclerosis: Existent and Virtual Support Groups

## Marlene A. Ciechoski

Since the publication of *Sharing the Experience of ALS: Patient and Family Support Groups,* both traditional and contemporary models for support groups have addressed the concerns of people with ALS and their families and friends. The diagnosis of ALS is a profound and life-changing event. One's sense of self is threatened and one cannot help but question why this has occurred. The individual who has just received this diagnosis is anxious, fearful, depressed, and searching for comfort and affirmation. Significant needs for education about the illness, the availability of necessary resources, and, most important, the ability to connect with other people with ALS are paramount to achieving a sense of stability in the face of this illness. One cannot underestimate the torrent of thoughts and emotions that a diagnosis of ALS brings to mind.

In the challenge to gain perspective about the disease and its effects, many individuals have chosen to participate in ALS support groups. For more than 25 years these groups have provided an opportunity for people with ALS, family members, friends, and the community at large to become more aware and informed about the illness. Support groups build avenues of communication among participants. Often, it may be less stressful for a person to discuss a difficult topic in a group setting rather than in a one-on-one encounter.

Traditionally support groups have been *existent* in their structure. The group members meet in person, face to face, often with a lay or professional facilitator. Guidelines relative to location, length, and frequency of meetings; agenda; and the format for discussion are all considered and decided on by the participants.

This support group model provides unique benefits for the members. Each person with ALS has the opportunity to meet others with the illness. For many, this is the first time to actually see someone else with the disease. Family members also will likely meet other patients' family members and benefit from their experiences. The facilitator will be a resource for information, education, and community assistance. Existent support groups are developed on the basis of interests and needs of its members. Some groups are composed of patients only, others are for family members, and still others may be open to patients and families together. The structure of the support group emerges from the collective decisions of the members and is largely based on the group's perception of its purpose. Sometimes patients or family members believe that discussion is more open and frank without the other individuals present. This is often reflected when families have questions they would not want to ask in the presence of the patient. This is also true of patients who are cautious not to upset family members by their concerns. A very protective or guarded approach by participants toward others in the group is often apparent.

In the early development of support groups for people with ALS, a lay volunteer, often a family member of a patient, initiated a group's beginning. Resources for people with ALS, including support groups, were quite limited in number and location. Motivated individuals were determined to provide an opportunity for themselves and others to learn more about the disease and find ways to assist each other. With time and much effort, groups were formed in locations when people with ALS learned about each other. This was particularly true in smaller towns and cities, even though some larger metropolitan areas were just beginning to form support groups. Today, ALS groups may be conducted by a nonprofessional volunteer, although the standard now is that a health care professional (i.e., nurse, social worker, or other therapist) provides guidance to the group.

It is important that the group facilitator and participants understand the nature and scope of the group. The ALS support group is a forum for people to learn more about the disease; the local, regional, and national resources; and the research being conducted. It allows for people affected by the illness to have dialogue with each other. The group structure provides understanding and comfort to people who are living with the disease. It offers the security of shared experiences without the burden of explanation. Most significantly, ALS is an illness accompanied by great emotional and physical isolation. Support groups build bridges between people that help to transcend their greatest fears.

Participants in an existent support group also benefit from the socialization it requires. To patients it is a time to meet others. Although the idea of seeing people with the disease, who are better or worse than oneself, may be anxiety provoking, in general, patients gain ease with each other and appreciate the new relationships. Family members who participate in a group may see this as a positive change in the daily routines of life, especially if they are primary caregivers of the patient. Joining an existent group may not, however, be a choice for some patients and their families. The difficulties of distance and travel for both patient and family member may preclude attendance. Sometimes people are interested in a group experience but have incorrect ideas about what may be expected of them. With further information designed to allay any concerns, they may be willing to join.

Over the past 10 years, a new model for support groups has emerged. The *virtual group* has made its debut on the Internet. As time, tasks, and resources compete for both patients' and caregivers' attention, an existent group may not be readily accessible to them. This does not diminish the wish or need for the support provided by a shared group experience. With the Internet one needs only to search "ALS support groups" and a plethora of Web sites is made available. Virtual groups provide worldwide connections with people living with ALS, family members, and health care professionals. Internet groups may be composed of individuals with specific interests, for example, women living with ALS. Women believe that they have particular concerns that differ from those of men with ALS. Caregivers may develop a group because they may not have the privilege of a regular schedule to attend an existent support group. A full-time or part-time caregiver frequently juggles work, family needs, and the care of the patient.

The virtual support group can provide the flexibility for patients and families to garner the benefits of the group without the pressure of being physically present in an existent group. Virtual groups may lessen anxiety in the participants. A certain sense of anonymity is associated with a virtual group and often encourages fuller communication. In general, in a virtual group there is no specific facilitator, although an individual may initiate the contact among the members. Typically, the virtual group addresses issues, just as one would likely hear in an existent group. Education, research information, and community resources are all likely areas of great interest. Contrary to some thinking, virtual groups are not void of the care and comfort often very present in a face-to-face group. There is an important sense of responsibility in people who join an online support group. The participants value this special opportunity and group members contribute respectfully.

As with all Internet activities, caution and judgment are necessary to protect privacy. Many ALS Web sites are sponsored by national, regional, or local organizations whose missions are to provide care, promote education, and support/conduct research on ALS. These disease-specific Internet locales have a Web site manager, which allows for monitoring and protecting the integrity of the site and its subscribers. To access an ALS e-mail chat room or support group requires registering a valid e-mail address. Many sites specify that the site is restricted to people with ALS, family members, or health care professionals. Virtual support groups have guidelines as to appropriate communication and content that may be posted.

Questions about ALS, diagnosis, treatment, health care resources, existent support groups, clinical trials, and research are all legitimate issues to address. Significant concerns about coping and living with the disease, its effects on individuals and families, and the spectra of emotions it evokes are also discussed. Problems related to anxiety, depression, and relationships are often presented. However, an ALS online support group is not intended to allow criticism of other individuals' perspectives.

**Table 18.1** Comparison of Existent and Virtual Support Groups

| Existent support groups | Virtual support groups |
| --- | --- |
| In-person communication | Internet communication wherever available |
| Visual expression of support | Written expression of support |
| Fuller appreciation of the dynamic interaction among members | Greater physical comfort for patients |
| | Decreased stress on caregivers |

| Existent support groups require | Virtual support groups require |
| --- | --- |
| Mobility/transportation to meeting | Accessible computer, basic skills, Internet connection |
| Patients may need caregiver to attend | Patients/caregivers may participate singularly |
| Ease in speaking in a group setting | Ability to express oneself in writing |
| Comfort in seeing others with ALS | Adherence to Web site rules and policies |

Neither is it a place to post insensitive comments, jokes, or personal biases. As in a person-to-person support group, a virtual group requires considerate participation.

Understanding the similarities and differences between existent and virtual support groups helps discern which type of group best serves one's particular needs. Table 18.1 illustrates some of what each group provides as well as the requirements for participation.

Any support group in which you participate requires an appreciation of each person as an individual. No doubt, this is how you also would want to be perceived.

In identifying an existent support group, it is helpful to consider the structure of the group. Look for meeting places and times that fit your schedule. Determine whether the group is for patients or caregivers only. Find out who sponsors the group and whether there is a lay or professional facilitator. Seek information about the group's agenda. Some groups focus on open discussion with an unstructured format. Others may have discussion time and an educational component to a meeting.

If you select a virtual group, ascertain who sponsors the group. You should look at the Web site to see whether registration is required and how your privacy is protected. Is there a site manager who oversees the operation and is this person a health care professional?

Existent and virtual ALS support groups share the same philosophy. They exist to provide people affected by ALS an opportunity to connect with each other.

People have their own agenda as to why they participate in an existent or virtual support group. They may want information about ALS chapters or centers, adaptive equipment, home care, research, or clinical drug trials. People with ALS want to achieve a sense of relatedness with people in similar life circumstances. In their new and unknown world of ALS, every individual needs a reference group of people who intimately understand what an individual may be experiencing.

Not only does a person with a diagnosis of ALS have to respond to the physical, emotional, social, and economic impact of the disease, but he or she is also faced with a life-threatening diagnosis and eventually a dependent existence. These concerns and others may prompt one to seek out a support group. People often ask what is required of them to participate in such a group. Actually, the answer is courage. It takes a lot of plain old guts to present one's self in person or online to other people challenged by this devastating disease.

Both the existent and virtual models for ALS support groups are significant means for people with ALS to share their experience of living with the disease. Support groups have energy and momentum, which promote greater awareness of ALS to the members as well as to the health care community and beyond. Support groups grow hope and vision for the future of people living with ALS. There are no better advocates for the cause and cure of ALS than the collective strength of all who are touched by it.

As a group progresses, participants begin to share their personal responses to the disease. Although each person's role in the group has a somewhat different nature to it, every individual's role is valuable. Some may be creative thinkers, whereas others may use their gifts of humor, sensitivity, or spirituality to promote more meaningful communication. Each person is a knowledgeable mentor to other members.

In an existent or virtual ALS support group, themes of change and loss are constant. The absence of a member's participation, because of changes in their circumstances or because of death, has a major impact on other group members. People may be reluctant to address these issues of loss but with shared support and assistance will likely find that the group is a safe haven for discussing the most difficult topics. Support group participation allows people to speak about their own experiences. No one member dominates the conversation, but each person respects the rights of others to share their viewpoints. This is especially true when participants are family members. In the group experience people may be able to express concerns that heretofore they were reluctant to speak about. Such discussions provide a means to identify different views, problems, and, most important, strength among the members as a whole.

Participants in a support group are most comfortable when they are in agreement with the agenda and share similar views with other members. It is unrealistic, however, to think that a support group with members having like viewpoints is necessarily the best kind of group. A more realistic measure of a group's viability is the resolve of participants to tolerate conflicting ideas, allow freedom of expression, and accept that each person is a unique entity deserving of acknowledgment and courtesy.

In the existent or virtual support group setting, most members will need some additional time and help to express thoughts and feelings or to identify solutions to their problems. Other members need to be particularly aware to express acceptance of the person's current situation.

Existent and virtual support groups are therapeutic because they allow people with like concerns to benefit from others' experiences. Neither in-person nor online groups are intended to actually be psychotherapy or a substitute for it. Either group model may provide information to access professional help, but it is not the province of the support group to assume this role. As technology continues to expand we can look forward to new and exciting opportunities for communication. The ALS community has always been proactive and on the cutting edge of new and expanding horizons. It is with such determination to seek the cause and cure of ALS that innovative approaches to care and research have been made.

There are several means by which ALS support groups can be identified and located. With telephone or Internet access, easy contact is possible. As a first step, you want to ask some important questions. These include Who sponsors the group? Is there a site manager for the virtual group? Is the existent group facilitated by a health care professional? Is registration required for the online group? How is security provided for the Web site? Does the site have restrictions on participation? and What are the goals of the group?

In the United States the two major national organizations dedicated to ALS are the Muscular Dystrophy Association (MDA) and the Amyotrophic Lateral Sclerosis Association (ALSA). Throughout the country many MDA and ALSA centers sponsor existent and/or virtual groups. Further, university-affiliated centers/clinics also may conduct ALS support groups as an integral part of their programs.

Table 18.2 is a short list of contact information for some selected support groups.

Even a decade ago, one may not have thought that a support group could exist anywhere but in an actual room with people sharing their experiences together.

**Table 18.2** Support Group Contact Information

| Organization | Web address | Telephone |
|---|---|---|
| Muscular Dystrophy Association (MDA) | www.mda.org | 1-800-fight mda (1-800-344-4863) |
| Amyotropic Lateral Sclerosis Association (ALSA) | www.alsa.org | 1-800-782-4747 |
| Daily Strength, Inc. | www.dailystrength.org | |
| ALS Forums | www.alsforums.com | |
| ALS Independence | www.alsindependence.com | |
| Duke Medical | www.dukemednews.org | |

*(Continued)*

**Table 18.2** Support Group Contact Information    (*Continued*)

| Organization | Web address | Telephone |
|---|---|---|
| Yahoo! Groups | www.groups.yahoo.com | |
| HealthBoards (Health Message Boards) | www.healthboards.com | |
| NeuroTalk | http://neurotalk.psychcentral .com/ | |
| patientslikeme | www.patientslikeme.com | |
| World Federation of Neurology and Amyotrophic Lateral Sclerosis | www.wfnals.org | |
| MIT Workplace Center | http://web.mit.edu/ workplacecenter/ | |
| Inspire (together we're better) | http://www.inspire.com/ | |

Virtual support groups now allow people new opportunities to participate. The setting is a place on the Internet in worldwide locations. The unremitting needs of people with ALS to be connected at all levels of interest and awareness will continue to expand and change. Once the light of communication is seen, people will always seek it out. For all people affected by ALS the light can only grow brighter.

## Acknowledgments

This chapter is dedicated to all the people of courage who live with ALS and to all who walk the journey with them. Together you keep hope growing.

## Suggested Readings

Biegel DE, Song LI-u. Facilitators and barriers to caregiver support group participation. *J Case Manage.* 1995;4(4):164–172.

Carlson R. *Don't sweat the small stuff . . . and it's all small stuff.* New York, NY: Hyperion Press; 1997.

Feenberg AL, Licht JM, Kane KP. The online patient meeting. *J Neurol Sci.* 1996;139: 129–131.

Feigenbaum D. *Journey With ALS.* Virginia Beach, VA: DLRC Press; 1998.

Fitzpatrick J, Romano C, Chasek R. *The Nurses' Guide to Consumer Health Websites.* New York, NY: Springer; 2001.

Hsiung RC. *E-Therapy: Case Studies, Guiding Principles, and the Clinical Potential of the Internet.* New York, NY: W. W. Norton & Co.; 2002.

Hutchinson J. *May I Walk You Home?* Notre Dame, IN: Ave Maria Press; 1999.

Lynne J, Harrold J. *Handbook for Mortals.* New York, NY: Oxford University Press; 1999.

Maheu MM, Whiten P, Allen A. *E-Health, Telehealth and Telemedicine: A Guide to Startup and Success.* NewYork, NY: Jossey-Bass; 2001.

Pennix BW, van Tilburg T, Boeke AJ, et al. Effects of social support and personal coping resources on depressive symptoms—different for various chronic diseases? *Health Psychol.* 1998;17:551–558.

Ruppert RA. Psychological aspects of lay caregiving. *Rehabil Nurs.* 1996;21:315–320.

Tan J. *E-Health Care Information Systems: An Introduction for Students and Professionals.* New York, NY: Jossey-Bass; 2005.

Wolinsky H, Wolinsky J. *Healthcare Online for Dummies.* New York, NY: Hungry Minds; 2001.

# 19

# Meditation and Amyotrophic Lateral Sclerosis

**Gian Domenico Borasio**

*With all your science can you tell*
*how it is and when it is*
*that light comes into the soul?*

—Henry David Thoreau (1817–1862)

John had been a successful manager before contracting amyotrophic lateral sclerosis (ALS) at the age of 48. Yet the very first time I saw him (he had come to our ALS clinic to ask about possible enrollment in a clinical study), he struck me with a calmness and a peace of mind that was all the more remarkable because, at that time, almost 4 years into the disease, he was unable to move his arms or legs and was completely dependent on outside help. His speech, however, was still almost unaffected. I asked him about his feelings about the disease, and he said, "You know, at the beginning I was shattered. My business, my career, my life plans—I had to give it all up. It was terrible. I went into big-time depression. Suicide seemed a reasonable option, since I did not want to become a burden to my wife and family. At that point, a friend pointed out that Buddhist philosophy and meditation might help me. I was quite skeptical, but willing to try anything, and I gave it my best shot. Now I am totally dependent on others for help (the thing I dreaded most) but I would say, strange as it may seem to you, that my quality of life is actually better than before the disease started. Then, I didn't have time for anything, I was constantly rushing and stressed. Now, I have time for myself, and what is even more important, I can make use of this time and live in it."

One possible reaction to this account might be to doubt John's mental sanity. How could anybody with a clear mind say that he is happier with ALS than without? Yet John showed absolutely no signs of psychosis or delusions. He was perfectly at ease, and one could sense that he was actually trying to make everybody else in the room feel comfortable, too. On one occasion he made it clear that he was indeed not feeling "happier" in the common sense of the word. His physical disability, his breathing problems requiring noninvasive ventilation at night, and the fear of losing his speech sooner or later were all things he was painfully aware of. "But," he said "that is exactly what it is all about: awareness. At least now I am aware of what is happening to me, while before I wasn't. Therefore, now I can enjoy even little pleasures much more than before."

It should be said that John and his family were quite well off and that he could afford first-class, round-the-clock, professional nursing help. However, this was not nearly enough to explain his remarkable inner balance. I had seen plenty of other patients with equally good economic resources who were unable to come to terms with their disease. John was the first patient I knew who had turned to meditation as a way of coping. He was also one of the first patients with ALS in Germany to receive noninvasive ventilation (NIV) and had pushed for starting it even before developing signs or symptoms of chronic respiratory insufficiency, because he thought that this might delay the onset of respiratory problems. He was on NIV for almost 5 years, and during this time he helped a lot of patients with ALS overcome their fears of NIV (and of percutaneous endoscopic gastrostomy, as well) by talking to them about his own experience, either in person or on the phone.

John stopped NIV voluntarily when he was in need of ventilation for most of the day because he did not want to go on tracheostomy. We arranged for him to spend his last days on a palliative care unit to make sure that he would receive appropriate medication to relieve his terminal dyspnea. To the surprise and awe of the entire palliative care team, after having said goodbye to his wife and family, John simply slipped into sleep, from there into coma, and died peacefully a few hours later. Even through his death, John spoke to the world around him. The collaboration of our ALS clinic with that particular palliative care unit, which had been reluctant to accept patients with ALS, especially if ventilated, has been excellent ever since.

Although John's personal development was certainly exceptional, he is by no means alone. Helga, a 49-year-old patient with ALS, told us a few years ago that she had been meditating before the disease started but had actually intensified her practice since then. She had struck us before with her pragmatic, no-nonsense approach to the disease, and I had previously noticed during a patients' meeting that she had a very positive influence on other patients. Since then, Helga has led a patient support group and has offered her fellow patients some initial help with meditation techniques, which was very well received.

In the wonderful book by Mitch Albom, *Tuesdays With Morrie,* which many of you have probably read, there are no fewer than four references to meditation teachers as playing an important part in Morrie's last years of life. Again, Morrie was certainly an exceptional person with a deeply rooted love for and understanding of humanity long before he was diagnosed with ALS. However, it is notable that he thought it important to devote a considerable portion of his limited remaining life span to learning and practicing meditation. I can only assume that this was part of what led him to that remarkable serenity in the wake of his disease's progression that has inspired innumerable readers of the book and that strongly reminded me of John's attitude.

## What Is Meditation?

It may be helpful to first point out what meditation is not—it is not a relaxation technique. It is not an exotic Far Eastern ritual that can be properly practiced only by Buddhists or Zen monks (in fact, there is a new but strongly growing tradition of meditation practice within, for example, Christian communities). It is not going to change any of your symptoms of ALS, much less stop the disease from progressing, but it may change the way you look at your disease and your life.

The tradition of meditation goes back for at least 2,500 years and probably much longer. Although best known from Buddhism, where it plays a central role in religious practice, elements of meditation are present in all great religions, most evidently in their mystical currents, like the Hinduist Sadhus, the Islamic Sufis, the Jewish Hassidim, or the Christian medieval mystics.

There are innumerable definitions of meditation—some pragmatic, some poetic, some cryptic—but they all fall somewhat short of grasping its essence. One of the most compelling definitions of meditation is *just being there*. Another definition is simply *mindfulness*. James H. Austin, MD, author of *Zen and the Brain* says: "[Meditation] becomes a way of not thinking, clearly, and *then of carrying this clear awareness into everyday life*." As far as technique goes, the Zen master Dogen (1200–1253) says: "Free yourself from all attachments . . . think neither of good nor evil, and judge not right or wrong. Stop the operation of mind, of will, and of consciousness; bring to an end all desires, all concepts and judgements." The Tibetan master Jamyang Khyentse Rinpoche (1896–1959) once said: "Whenever you end a thought and before you start the next one, isn't there a little pause, a gap? Well, prolong it! This is meditation."

Meditation cannot be defined fully with words—it has to be experienced. If you try it, at first you may notice that you become more aware of what is going on, less attached to your thoughts and emotions, and more centered. Gradually, you will realize that all reasons for pain and anxiety, as well as all sources of joy and happiness, are within yourself. Ultimately, the practice of meditation may lead to the blossoming of love and compassion both for oneself and for others.

There are several different kinds of meditation practices, all of which adhere to the same basic principles: transcendental meditation, mindfulness meditation, Tibetan meditation, Zen meditation, and many others. This chapter will not teach you how to meditate. If you are interested, a number of excellent books are listed at the end of the chapter (many of which are also available as audiotapes) to which you can turn for an introduction. I would particularly recommend the book by Jon Kabat-Zinn titled *Full Catastrophe Living,* a title that can be fully appreciated by patients with ALS and their families. This book describes the Stress Reduction Program at the University of Massachusetts Medical Center and contains a working program that can serve as an initial guideline to test whether meditation may be of help for you.

Some reasons why meditation might be particularly useful in ALS are outlined in the next section—but beware of any theoretical considerations, because it is your life and it is only you who can decide what is good for you and what is not. However, there certainly is no harm in trying. Just one piece of advice: if you want to try it out, do it like John—give it your best shot. Do not feel frustrated if you do not see any immediate or short-term "results" or "improvements in well-being"—stick to it for a while. Meditation requires persistence.

## Why May It Help in ALS?

People face a radical change in their life's perspective when they are told that they have ALS. Any long-term plans or goals have to be abandoned or reshaped. Adapting to ALS often requires going through a painful phase of depression and denial before coming to an acceptance of the disease. Time is limited, and death becomes a reality that has to be dealt with. This is true for every one of us, but most people postpone confronting the issue of death and dying until it is too late. All great traditions have emphasized the importance of integrating death into our lives (a particularly beautiful example is *The Tibetan Book of Living and Dying* by Sogyal Rinpoche). Herein lies one of the chances of ALS.

Why should people with ALS invest their precious time for something as time-consuming and demanding as meditation practice? The answer is that they should not unless they really want to. At the beginning of the disease, patients are often most concerned with the quest for a cure. As the disease progresses, they find themselves having, as one person put it, both too little time and too much time. Too little time left before death, yet too much time because most of the usual activities cannot be performed anymore. The loss of physical functions and independence leads to anger and frustration. On the other hand, meditation does not require any physical ability. All it requires is an intact mind, some time, and a firm commitment.

As mentioned previously, one of the central aspects of meditation is *letting go* or "nonattachment." We are constantly in the process of clinging to certain pleasurable aspects of our lives, especially when we are in danger of losing them. Meditation can help us to release and let go and to accept things as they are. This is possibly the most difficult psychological task in ALS, but those individuals who succeed in it (whether by meditation or by other means) are rewarded with a quantum leap in their quality of life.

Meditation has no immediate goal other than making us aware of the beauty and preciousness of the present moment. This is of particular importance in a disease like ALS, in which the life span is limited but the potential for awareness is not. In a disease such as Alzheimer's dementia, for example, survival times are considerably longer than with ALS. However, patients with Alzheimer's experience a rapid deterioration of their memory and personality. Many of them are completely different people within 6 months of disease onset and have all but lost the ability to communicate with the outside world within a few years. In contrast, people with ALS retain their full intellectual, emotional, and social skills throughout the disease. However, this capacity is a two-sided sword. It may bring out constant anguish about the future course of the disease and eventually lead to the development of a nihilistic attitude ("nobody can help me") and even to requests for assistance in hastening death. On the other hand, it may also be used for the person's benefit to develop adequate coping strategies and maximize the quality of life for the remaining life span.

One remarkable example of such an adjustment and spiritual growth in the wake of ALS is the life of Philip Simmons. His book *Learning to Fall* is a must read for all patients with ALS, their families, and caregivers. Phil struggles through his disease and manages, thanks also to meditation techniques, to reach an incredible serenity and acceptance, which is exemplified in the following quote: "When we accept our impermanence, letting go of our attachment to things as they are, we open ourselves to grace. When we can stand calmly in the face of our passing away, when we have the courage to look even into the face of a child and say 'This flower, too, will fade and be no more', when we can sense the nearness of death and feel its rightness equally with birth, then we will have crossed over to that farther shore, where death can hold no fear for us, where we will know the measure of the eternal that is ours in this life."

Richard, a 55-year-old patient with ALS, and his wife had been discussing his advance directives with us for 2 hours. He had late-stage ALS, he could barely speak, and his breathing capacity was markedly impaired. He refused tracheostomy and asked that he be given morphine in the terminal phase, which he felt to be impending (he was right). At the end, I asked him if he had any further questions. He then said, quite unexpectedly, "When am I going to be cured, doc?" It took me a while before I could reply: "Medicine cannot *cure* ALS today. But when you realize that your most important qualities as a human being, your personality, your emotions, your intellect, your memory, your ability to give and receive love, are not and never will be diminished by ALS, then you will have made a big step toward *healing*." He smiled and said: "Then I am healed already, doc." He died peacefully in his sleep a few weeks later.

## A Word of Caution

What has been said so far by no means implies that meditation is the right approach for all or even most people with ALS. Which coping strategy is the right one for any particular patient (or caregiver) is all but impossible to determine in advance. You have to try it out. It is your life, and never let anyone else tell you what you should or should not do. What professionals can do is point out several alternatives that have already helped others so that you can choose which way you want to go. Meditation undoubtedly has helped some. This chapter had no other purpose but to inform you of that. If you think that it might be good for you, go ahead and try it. Later, if you could spare a few moments to tell me about your experiences (positive and negative), please do so by using the e-mail address below—your experience might help other patients in the future.

Please send any comments you might have on this chapter or accounts of your own experiences with meditation and ALS to Dr. Borasio at the following e-mail address: Borasio@med.uni-muenchen.de

## Suggested Readings

The books marked with an asterisk are also available as audiotapes.

*Albom M. *Tuesdays With Morrie: An Old Man, a Young Man, and Life's Greatest Lesson.* New York, NY: Broadway Books; 2002.

Austin JH. *Zen and the Brain.* Cambridge, MA: MIT Press; 1999.

De Mello A. *One Minute Wisdom.* New York, NY: Image Books; 1988.

De Mello A. *The Way to Love: The Last Meditations of Anthony De Mello.* New York, NY: Image Books; 1995.

Enomiya-Lassalle HM, Ropers R, Snela B. *The Practice of Zen Meditation.* London: Thorsons; 1993.

*Hanh TN. *Being Peace.* Berkeley, CA: Parallax Press; 1988.

*Hanh TN. *The Miracle of Mindfulness: A Manual on Meditation.* Rev. ed. Boston, MA: Beacon Press; 1996.

*Hanh TN. *Touching Peace: Practicing the Art of Mindful Living.* Berkeley, CA: Parallax Press, 1992.

*Kabat-Zinn J. *Full Catastrophe Living: Using the Wisdom of Your Body and Mind to Face Stress, Pain, and Illness.* New York, NY: Delta; 1990.

*Kabat-Zinn J. *Wherever You Go, There You Are.* New York, NY: Hyperion; 2005.

Longaker C. *Facing Death and Finding Hope: A Guide to the Emotional and Spiritual Care of the Dying.* New York, NY: Main Street Books; 1998.

Meister Eckhart. *Selected Writings.* New York, NY: Penguin Classics; 1995.

Rinpoche S. *Glimpse After Glimpse: Daily Reflections on Living and Dying.* London: Rider & Co; 1995.

*Rinpoche S. *The Tibetan Book of Living and Dying.* San Francisco, CA: HarperOne; 1994.

Simmons P. *Learning to Fall.* New York, NY: Bantam; 2003.

*Suzuki S. *Zen Mind, Beginner's Mind.* Boston, MA: Weatherhill; 1973.

# 20

# Family Caregivers in Amyotrophic Lateral Sclerosis

## Judith Godwin Rabkin and Steven M. Albert

### Why Caregivers Matter So Much

Facing amyotrophic lateral sclerosis (ALS) alone can be almost as difficult psychologically as it is medically, and eventually becomes virtually impossible. Having a partner who is regularly available for comfort, care, reassurance, practical assistance, and emotional support can transform ALS into a passage that is controllable and manageable, even in late-stage illness. Not only patients, but also professional care providers, rely on family (or other informal) caregivers to play central roles including information gathering, problem solving, negotiating complex medical and financial systems, communication, assistance, and companionship. Caregivers may be the first to notice patients' unmet needs or functional changes. With the patient's progressive disability, family caregivers may need to assume new roles (e.g., managing finances, meal preparation, and driving), and substantially alter their other commitments, including work, social, and recreational activities, and other family responsibilities. Emotionally, and sometimes practically, caregiving can become a total occupation, at times problematic, but also often enormously rewarding. This chapter is meant to identify potential problems and identify some strategies for their management, and to highlight factors that can contribute to caregiving effectiveness and satisfaction.

The centrality of family caregivers to patients should not be underestimated. Absence of a family caregiver usually means restriction in opportunities for quality of life and loss of autonomy. In fact, without a caregiver patients may be forced to spend the last months of life in a long-term care facility, unless they have the financial wherewithal to hire full-time caregiving support. One patient, estranged from his family, was labeled "medically unsafe to go home" after a fall and hospital admission. Because he had no family willing to step in and provide a shared, supervised residence, he was barred from discharge home. Despite strenuous effort on his part, he was forced to spend his last year of life in a nursing home.

## Job Description: Who Are the Caregivers and What Do They Do, When?

Usually but not always, the caregiver of a married patient is the spouse. Sometimes, an adult child is better able to fill this role if the spouse has medical or psychological issues of his or her own. On occasion, we have known divorced spouses to move back in and assume the role of caregivers, while in other families, the healthy spouse may seek a divorce and leave the picture. Parents, adult children, and even grandparents or siblings or networks of friends can effectively serve as caregivers. In some instances, the role is transferred among family members.

Caregivers are called on to serve in different roles as the disease progresses. Although not linear, the course of ALS illness has broadly different phases, which for simplicity's sake can be considered early, middle, and late stage. This chapter will concentrate on issues in late-stage illness, after more briefly describing the first two stages.

## Initial Stage: Learning the Diagnosis

At the point of diagnosis, it is important for the patient to be accompanied to the neurologist's visit by someone close, probably the person who is likely to become the caregiver. For married patients or those in committed relationships, this is usually the spouse but may be a parent, a child, a sibling, or good friend. During the period when the diagnosis is made, the partner may play a key role in clarifying the information provided by the neurologist, and in learning about resources for additional information. Sometimes the patient will want to get all the information he or she can; for others, there is a period when they do not wish to hear anything further. In either case, the future caregiver is likely to seek information that he or she may or may not share, about what to anticipate over time, at least in the next several months. Another consideration is who to tell about the diagnosis of ALS in this earliest stage. This also is a personal choice: some patients quickly tell everyone, whereas others feel strongly about privacy, in particular, in the workplace. The timing of information for young children is another issue that the patient and partner need to consider. It is helpful to keep in mind that there is no rush to disclose the diagnosis, and once disclosed it cannot be retracted.

Some patients and some families are not satisfied with the diagnosis and will go to extreme lengths to seek other diagnoses and treatments. A second opinion is almost always advisable, and in fact encouraged. However, some patients seek unproven, unregulated, and extremely expensive remedies (e.g., traveling to China for stem cell transfusions), which may be understandable but is seldom productive either medically or psychologically. At a certain point, denial of the ALS diagnosis may be counterproductive, depriving the patient of expertise in symptom management and access to compensatory devices.

During the first few months, one of the primary tasks is to identify and connect with medical care, if not already established at the time of diagnosis. In general, and when geographically feasible, multidisciplinary clinics can offer services that no private practitioner possibly can provide in one location, including dieticians, physical therapists, speech pathologists, occupational therapists, orthotists (specialists in fabricating braces and splints), other medical specialists, social workers, and nurses. To supplement and complement the work of the neurologist, teams can provide comprehensive care, offer expertise in matters ranging from ordering equipment to negotiating medical insurance, and help in thinking about long-term plans and advance directives.

Common questions that arise in the months after diagnosis concern work schedules, for both patient and partner, keeping in mind health insurance coverage that may be job related. If leg weakness is already present, some household modifications may warrant early consideration, such as repositioning furniture, moving electrical cords, and removing scatter rugs. Later modifications may include adding ramps, support rails, and grab bars in bathrooms. Arrangements for child care and household-cleaning assistance may be considered as well. While addressing such practical matters, it is equally important to maintain or even increase the experience of pleasant events, social or recreational activities, and church or community ties. Some families find it rewarding to become active in the ALS community, including fund-raising events and support groups, but others prefer to preserve their usual activities. In general, among both families and professionals, a great deal of attention is devoted to coping with stress and distress, with less focus on the equally important work of maintaining a positive mood for patient and partner. Research has shown that preserving positive mood, even in the presence of distress, may have important adaptive significance.

## Care Partners Become Caregivers: Roles in Symptomatic Illness

With symptom progression, partners may come to provide direct care, evolving into caregivers. This may include assistance with dressing, bathing, and cutting up food. The caregiver may suggest finding out about and arranging for assistive devices such as leg or hand braces, canes or walkers, and communication aids.

Other caregiver responsibilities may include medication management, arranging for visits to doctors, knowing who and when to call for health care or social services assistance, and calling when appropriate. Caregivers may have to learn to use and maintain more complex equipment and aids, such as feeding tubes and suctioning machines for phlegm. Once patients become dependent on either non-invasive ventilation or invasive long-term mechanical ventilation, these machines literally keep the patient alive and errors in their operation can be life threatening. Caregivers may also need to learn, along with the patient, how to use more advanced computer-assisted communication that may include a head mouse or eye-gaze cameras to track eye movements. All this means that caregivers need knowledge, skills, and professional support to feel and be competent and effective. Caregivers who experience high levels of mastery are less likely to be distressed or depressed in their roles, indicating the importance of skills training for caregivers (1).

Throughout the course of illness, caregivers need to take care of themselves as well as their patient-partner. An emotionally upset, physically exhausted person cannot be very useful to anyone else until they take time to address their own situation. Caregivers need support, encouragement, and appreciation just as patients do. Patients as well as other relatives and friends can recognize and address these needs. In fact, a friendly, appreciative patient can make a big difference in the caregiver's outlook and adjustment.

What if a spouse is unable or unwilling to take on caregiving challenges? In a series of 70 married patients, two spouses took the unusual step of divorcing and moving out of homes, forcing reallocation of caregiving responsibility to patient siblings. In both cases, patients (and spouses) were young, with small children in the home. Also, in both cases, the patient expressed a clear preference for tracheostomy and long-term mechanical ventilation (LTMV), an intervention that can lead to indefinite survival. These caregivers did not contemplate separation until late stages in the disease when they were unprepared to face the future with a spouse-patient who was kept alive indefinitely while the disease continued to progress with no end in sight. This situation clearly presents a serious test of expectations for help and support in marriage. These cases were unusual: most spouses do not dissolve marriages, although the possibility exists if the patient unilaterally decides on long-term mechanical ventilation and its caregiving challenges. These caregivers perhaps need the greatest degree of support.

## Caregiver Challenges and Burdens: Risk and Protective Factors

Months or years may pass before the patient needs assistance with everyday tasks and activities. During this time, the partner's major responsibilities may include maintaining a normal life for him- or herself and the patient, being receptive to the patient's concerns and apprehensions without making this a dominant theme in the relationship, and maintaining usual family, social, and recreational activities.

One challenge, as patients become more disabled, is allocation of time in the face of increasing demands. When problems develop with mobility, speech, or swallowing, assistance becomes needed. The partner may be the primary or only person to provide hands-on help, unless paid assistance is both financially feasible and acceptable to the patient. This can work extremely well in some settings, although costs can be significant and some patients do not like the idea of having an unfamiliar person around. If the caregiver does spend increasing time helping the patient, other roles often require readjustment. If he or she has continued to work, caregiving may require reduction in work hours if affordable and if health insurance coverage is not jeopardized. For caregivers who are homemakers or who are retired, increasing responsibilities will eventually result in less time for outside activities including social visits, recreation and hobbies, and activities with other family members. New roles and skills may be called for, such as meal preparation, social arrangements, or financial management if these were not customary activities previously. In families where the mother of young children is the patient, new or expanded child care arrangements may be necessary (e.g., preparing breakfast, driving children to after-school activities).

With advancing disease, sources of strain multiply. Family caregivers are confronted with constantly changing and increasingly demanding physical tasks, financial costs, emotional challenges, and even personal health issues. The home may be taken over by medical equipment, and hours each day are devoted to tasks such as helping the patient shower, dress, and eat, which itself may take an hour or more per meal. Days may consist of medical appointments, physical therapy, arranging transportation if wheelchairs are involved, while trying to maintain pleasant activities, social visitors, recreational outings when feasible, and whatever other current family obligations are present, such as child care, assistance to elderly parents, school, and jobs if it is possible to continue employment. Nights may be disrupted by the need to turn the patient in bed, help rearrange covers, assist with bathroom trips, and perhaps coexist with breathing equipment in bed. At this point, some caregivers may become increasingly hesitant to permit paid aides to take over such care at the same time that more care is required. Such reluctance often stems from concerns, usually unfounded, that aides may be less vigilant than they would be themselves.

Caregivers of ventilator-dependent patients with advanced illness often report substantial levels of distress. In one of the few studies of this population, they were more likely than patients to express regret about the decision for long-term mechanical ventilation (2). In another small study of 14 dyads that we conducted, caregivers reported distress after LTMV even if the patient had full-time aides (3). Their concerns ranged from regret at loss of companionship to burnout reported by one husband who was contemplating a trip to Antarctica. Nevertheless, despite burden, most caregivers of vented patients, like most caregivers of patients in general, continue to express satisfaction with caregiving.

A common risk for caregivers is isolation. Just as patients cannot really cope with ALS alone, caregivers also need both emotional and practical support. By emotional support, we mean the availability of a confidante, apart from the patient, to whom they can express negative feelings, frustrations, and fears without further burdening the patient. Practical support refers to availability of either paid or volunteer substitutes who can stay with the patient at regular intervals, once he or she is largely housebound. Often, the caregiver has to take the initiative and tell relatives, friends, and neighbors how best they can be helpful. At least a few hours, even once a week, can be a meaningful break. Otherwise, even the most devoted caregiver is likely to experience the feeling of social captivity, feeling isolated, lonely, sometimes resentful if unwilling to admit it, and separated from his or her former lives.

Professional support can make a large difference, not only for the patient but also for the caregiver (4). Professionals can help educate the family about managing progressive disability, planning ahead, and finding resources for unmet needs. When survival prognosis becomes 6 months or less, hospice can play a powerful role, not only ensuring the patient's comfort, symptom management, and sense of control, but the hospice team (including physician, nurse, social worker, chaplain, and nutritionist) may provide counseling, respite care, and emotional support for the caregiver as well. The role of hospice in the lives of terminally ill patients and their families has been clearly articulated by Lynn (5).

With illness progression and increasing use of mechanical devices accompanied by impairment of the patient's ability to communicate, both the patient and caregiver feel more secure if someone is near the patient in case of need—e.g., for help getting to the bathroom, to suction phlegm, or to adjust respiratory equipment. If family members cannot share coverage regularly, and often this is not feasible, then paid assistance can be enormously helpful, both to relieve the caregiver and also the patient's worry about caregiver burden. Some families don't like the idea of having "a stranger" around, especially if intimate care is needed, but the benefits generally outweigh such "costs" if financial resources are available. Even a good night's sleep can make a major difference for caregivers. Assistance with care of other family dependents (e.g., young children, elderly infirm parents) may also be helpful.

A common concern of both patients and caregivers concerns finances. ALS is, unfortunately, an expensive disease. Although insurance coverage varies, ranging from excellent to extremely limited, there are still many out-of-pocket costs including paid assistants, medications, household renovations, even different food and clothes as the illness progresses. For late-stage patients on long-term (invasive) mechanical ventilation, out-of-pocket expenses can exceed $200,000 a year (6). Other patients, enrolled in hospice, usually can receive only 4 hours per day of paid assistance, which is seldom sufficient at this stage of disease. Financial problems are exacerbated when working patients and caregivers must reduce their hours or end employment. There are no obvious solutions to financial problems, although some sources of assistance exist. These include "loaner closets" for equipment such as augmentative communication devices or wheelchairs that are provided by the local ALS Association or Muscular Dystrophy Association. Patients with an ALS diagnosis and medically certified disability are eligible for Medicare without waiting the usual 24 months for eligibility. Some families have community fundraisers to supplement their finances.

Illness characteristics and patient interactions influence level of caregiver adjustment. It becomes more difficult for caregivers when the patient's speech and communication become restricted or absent, in some cases weakening the bonds of intimacy and reducing the role of the patient as a companion for the caregiver. Cognitive problems and associated behavioral changes such as social disinhibition can make caregiving stressful. Patients who are consistently pessimistic, who may express envy or resentment to the caregiver over the caregiver's good health, or who are predominantly demanding and critical make it difficult to provide care with grace and good humor. All patients, like all caregivers, are cranky and upset at times; we are referring to the overall tone or tenor of the patient–caregiver relationship.

Other risk factors that may contribute to the caregiver's distress include personal characteristics such as a prior history of depression, the need to keep working despite the patient's declining condition to preserve health insurance, a troubled or conflicted relationship with the patient antedating illness onset, or having other dependents for whom he or she is responsible (e.g., young children, ailing elderly parents).

## Caregiving Rewards

There really are good things that come out of bad diseases. Caregivers often get great satisfaction through their activities, which they see as tangible evidence of their love for the patient. They may experience gratification at mastering new skills and coping with difficult challenges. Some find new meaning in their lives through caregiving and consider the time spent together with patients their most precious moments. In some cases, families are brought together in new ways in their joint commitment to the patient, while friends who remain involved can be more valuable than ever.

## Buffers That Protect Against Caregiver Stress and Distress

We have already noted some factors that support and encourage caregivers, including practical help with care, time off, support from the patient and from professionals, and continued contact with family, friends, and neighbors. Other predictors of caregiver well-being include the presence of a strong positive bond between caregiver and patient that predates illness onset, having strong spiritual beliefs or religious ties, having a generally optimistic outlook on life, and the ability to find positive meaning in caregiving.

A significant dimension of caregiver well-being concerns coping style, and the extent to which coping mechanisms match the stressor at hand. Folkman, a leader in this field, defines coping as the thoughts and behaviors that caregivers use to address practical (instrumental) problems related to the patient's illness (problem-focused coping), manage distress (emotion-focused coping), and maintain positive well-being (meaning-focused coping) (7). Ideally, instrumental kinds of problem-solving coping are used more in situations where something can be done, and emotion-focused coping to regulate distress is used more in situations that have to be accepted.

A questionnaire titled "Ways of Coping" asks about different strategies used in responding to a particular situation (8). There is almost no research regarding caregiver coping with terminal illness, but studies of caregiver coping in earlier stages of illness show that distancing (e.g., "I went on as if nothing happened") and escape-avoidant coping (e.g., "I wished the situation would go away") are associated with increased distress among caregivers. Other kinds of coping that appear to be effective in diminishing distress include positive reappraisal ("I looked for the silver lining, so to speak"), benefit-finding ("I rediscovered what is important in life"), information-seeking, and problem-solving ("I came up with a couple of different solutions to the problem").

The ability to redefine goals as circumstances change is often key to maintaining well-being. Thus, a caregiver initially may aim at helping the patient to remain at work, for instance, driving him or her to the office when limb weakness becomes prominent. When the patient no longer can manage at work, the caregiver's goal may be redirected toward maintaining a busy social life, arranging dinner with friends, and getting theatre tickets. When fatigue and loss of mobility preclude such activities, the caregiver may redirect efforts to arranging for friends and family to visit at home. It is important, however, to work collaboratively; if the patient is not prepared to stop work, for example, the caregiver may be premature in relinquishing this goal.

Another example concerns hope, a critical component of well-being, and indeed of survival. Loss of hope has been associated with thoughts or actions relating to assisted suicide in a study of patients with ALS. It helps if the patient and caregiver share hopes. At the outset, the hope may be that the diagnosis is wrong. Next, the hope may be for stability of symptoms or slow progression, or the development of a cure before the disease becomes incapacitating. Eventually, the hope may be that the patient is comfortable and pain-free, and ultimately, that death is peaceful, where the patient wishes to be, and with the important people present. Instead of seeing each change as a defeat, the redirection of goals can be sustaining for both patient and caregiver. With hope, as one doctor said, all the battles can be won except the last.

As Folkman has noted, coping theory and research have traditionally focused on the regulation of distress. However, recent research suggests that positive mood can coexist with distress and may have important adaptive functions. Coping processes that bolster positive mood are related to the individual's values, beliefs, and goals. Conversely, positive mood can predispose people to feel that life is meaningful, even in negative situations.

The line between adaptive and maladaptive coping is sometimes imprecise. For example, denial can be adaptive in some situations, malignant in others. Planning a trip for next year, even if unrealistic in terms of the patient's level of illness, can buoy spirits and provide a positive event to anticipate with pleasure. In contrast, denial or minimization of such symptoms as the patient's difficulty swallowing with progressive weight loss or inability to breathe when lying down not only fails to alleviate the patient's discomfort but can influence survival. Once respiratory capacity declines below a certain level, the risk of inserting a feeding tube outweighs the benefits, thereby excluding access to a known effective intervention.

As these examples show, coping methods do not necessarily have absolute positive or negative effects. The central issue is the appropriateness of coping strategies in relation to the stressor or situation at hand. In earlier stages of illness, information-seeking and problem-solving may be important strategies, whereas in later stages, "making time to be with other people who care about me," or "rediscovering what is important in life" may be more sustaining for caregivers. Similarly, acknowledgement of caregiver burden (e.g., "no time for myself," "my social life and friendships have suffered") may be reasonable and appropriate when the caregiver spends 12 hours per day or more assisting the patient, but burden may be offset by finding positive meaning in caregiving (e.g., endorsing statements such as, "caregiving makes me feel needed; caregiving shows my love for the patient; because of caregiving I feel I've grown as a person").

## Role of the Caregiver in Late-Stage Illness Management

As patients get sicker, the ability to communicate is often increasingly impaired and a sense of intimacy can be lost. As patients' speech become more difficult to understand, and communication is maintained by computer, the caregiver may experience a loss of companionship and exchange even though the hours spent together may increase. Some patients develop an emotional lability so they may laugh or cry easily, often, and for no apparent reason, which can be distressing to observe and awkward if occurring in public situations such as church. Infrequently, some patients may become apathetic, indifferent, and unmotivated, in contrast to their usual level of interest and activity, whereas others may become inflexible and rigid in their thinking. A minority of patients with ALS may show a decline in the soundness of their judgment, making it all the more important to clarify advance directives sooner rather than later.

Caregivers are better able to cope with such changes if they know in advance that they are part of the disease process and can do their best to maintain conversations with the patient even if there is limited response. At this time, having a confidante other than the patient can prevent the experience of increasing isolation and loneliness.

## Caregivers and End-of-Life Decision Making

Although everyone should have a designated health proxy, no matter how healthy or young they are, it becomes essential for those with a terminal illness to consider options and to communicate wishes for care while they are still able to do so. Other decisions and related paperwork include a "do not resuscitate" (DNR) order (if desired), Power of Attorney for Health Care, and wills. Neurologists may be reluctant to bring up the topic of end-of-life decision making because they fear it will take away the patient's hope, and they often wait for the patient to initiate the conversation. Talking about "terminal options" has never been easy in our society, or most others, although in recent years considerable progress has been made in terms of the public's comfort level, as seen in a 2008 column in the *New York Times* (9) and a scientific do-it-yourself suicide guide published by physicians in The Netherlands (10).

Advance directives are legal documents allowing a person to provide input into medical decisions when he or she is unable to do so at the time. These documents are variously referred to as *living wills* or *medical directives, health care proxies,* or *Durable Power of Attorney for Health Care.* Each state has its own guidelines about these documents, but the basic elements of each are similar (11). The importance of designating a decision maker, in any of these documents, is having someone who will make the decision you would have made had you been able to do so. The designee should be someone present or rapidly available to provide input should a medical crisis occur. It must be kept in mind that patients can always change their minds about these directives. As illness progresses, they may become more or less interested in extending life with medical interventions.

Some patients want to talk about such planning soon after diagnosis, whereas, at the other extreme, some patients evade the subject even as they become severely disabled. The latter situation creates extreme problems for the caregiver, who may have to make an immediate decision should the patient experience a respiratory crisis. If the caregiver knows the patient wants to have tracheostomy and LTMV, he or she would then call 911 and the patient would be taken to the emergency room and almost certainly put on a ventilator. If the patient definitely does not want LTMV, then the caregiver would not call 911 but rather provide comfort care at home, with the help of hospice if the patient has been enrolled.

An interim and reversible decision that concerns anticipation of future decision making is enrollment in hospice, discussed in more detail in Chapter 24. If a patient is certain that he or she wants to have LTMV, then hospice is not an option, because it is intended for patients with a life expectancy of 6 months or less, and patients with LTMV have an indefinite life expectancy. However, patients who do enroll in hospice, with all the benefits thus provided, can be assured that hospice personnel will alleviate suffering at the end of life and help ensure a peaceful death. Hospice is also often extremely valuable to the caregiver, who no longer feels entirely responsible for the patient's comfort and well-being. In addition, some hospice services provide support for the caregiver in an ongoing manner that offsets the stress of caring for a terminally ill, very disabled loved one. A final point about hospice is that the decision is revocable: A patient may enroll in hospice and then decide on LTMV; hospice then will be terminated.

The caregiver may realize sooner, or be more willing to acknowledge, that the patient's disability has progressed and that some clarity in advance directives is becoming necessary. Both the patient and the caregiver have to consider the quality of life the patient has at the time: Is this a life the patient enjoys? Are there meaningful activities and relationships? Are there goals (such as attending a child's wedding or graduation) that the patient is eager to reach? Other considerations include recognition that a ventilator will not improve the patient's current functioning, and in fact the disease and loss of muscle function continue to progress even when breathing is mechanically stabilized. Eventually, total paralysis is likely to develop. Although a minority of patients on ventilation retain the ability to speak, most become unable to do so even if they could before tracheostomy; communication is likely to become increasingly limited as the patient loses the ability to move his or her hands or head. Some patients retain the capacity to blink or move their eyes laterally to signal yes and no, but even these movements eventually may be lost and a *locked-in* state ensues. Patients who seek mechanical ventilation may wish to have it disconnected when this stage is reached, but when it is, they no longer can say so. That is why advance directives are essential. Otherwise, the caregivers are left with a situation in which a decision must be made, but he or she has no guidance. They may decide on aggressive care just to avoid the guilt possibly associated with the choice to let the patient die without it. However, many patients with late-stage ALS are ready to go and would not have made this choice.

When patients are indecisive about whether or not they want LTMV, it is sometimes helpful to borrow available videotapes (DVDs) about patients with tracheostomy and long-term ventilation, so the patient can actually see what the equipment looks like, and what kind of life is possible with LTMV. Web sites and chat rooms are other options for getting more direct information about LTMV. In some instances, consultation with the family lawyer may be helpful. It is extremely important for there to be some kind of documentation of the patient's wishes, so that after the event there are no recriminations from family members who were not present at the crisis.

The person who has been providing the major portion of caregiving may decide that he or she does not want the responsibility of being named as health proxy. For example, an elderly spouse caregiver may prefer to have an adult child assume this role, which is perfectly reasonable. Regardless of who is actually named as health proxy to make decisions when the patient cannot, it is important for all involved to be advised in advance of the patient's wishes regarding ventilation and LTMV. There are two components needed: whether the patient wants LTMV in the first place, and if so, whether at some future occasion there are circumstances in which he or she wants it discontinued. These wishes need to be known by family members, paid household aides and assistants, anyone else regularly in the home who may be present at the time of a respiratory crisis, and the treating neurologist, who should have this documentation in the patient's chart. If patients live in a care facility, their wishes similarly need documentation in their records. Without it, aggressive intervention is probable.

In the United States, it is legal both for patients to decline LTMV and to request its discontinuation, either in an advance directive, or at any time if they are able to communicate this decision. Advance directives may specify reasons such as permanent unconsciousness, being locked in without any capacity to communicate, having to be transferred to a nursing home, dementia, or loss of insurance. Withholding or withdrawal of treatment when it is no longer medically effective or desired by the patient is not only legal but is the norm for patients with ALS, because only a small minority choose tracheostomy and LTMV. In several studies assessing rates of elective LTMV both in the United States and Western Europe, the average rate is usually in the 5% to 10% range. In contrast, the rate in Japan is higher (27% in 2004) and increasing, perhaps related to financial considerations (the Japanese government covers many costs), social pressure from the Japanese ALS Association, and differences in cultural attitudes, such that physicians are expected to determine treatment decisions, at least until quite recently. In addition to voluntary tracheostomy, a portion of patients on LTMV have the procedure when they are brought to the emergency room during a respiratory crisis when they could not be consulted. In a German survey, 66% of patients receiving LTMV had emergency intubations, and 81% had not given informed consent for the procedure (12).

It has been observed that people with ALS who are most likely to elect LTMV "are those with gradually progressive illness that has allowed incremental accommodation, who are still able to communicate and have some independent function, who have a thorough understanding of the options and a supportive family, financial resources and who are still actively engaged in life" (6). For most patients, the decision is not an agonizing one, because at that point they are so disabled by the disease that they are ready to go.

## Hastening Death

Although ALS symptoms for the most part can be effectively managed throughout the course of illness, a small minority of late-stage patients continue to suffer profoundly. Others, facing an inevitable and impending death, may reach a decision at some point that enough is enough. These patients may ask their doctors or caregiver about assistance in ending their life. This can be done directly, for example, by asking the physician to provide the means (such as a prescription), or patients may tell their family that they no longer wish to eat or drink, with the intention of dying. Assisted suicide (e.g., providing a prescription of a lethal amount of medication) is not legal in any state except Oregon, where specific steps must be carried out. Euthanasia, where the doctor takes action intended to end life by administering medications or injections, is not legal in any state.

Thoughts of ending their lives are not unusual among patients with ALS. In a longitudinal study of late-stage patients, end-of-life decision-making and interest in hastened death were queried; quality of life and depression also were assessed (13). Among the 53 patients who eventually died during this longitudinal study, 43% had thought at some point about ending their life, and 19% expressed the wish to die to others, although only 6% did eventually hasten their death. Patients who expressed the wish to die did not differ from those who did not express this wish in terms of disease severity or duration but were far less likely to use interventions for swallowing (percutaneous endoscopic gastrostomy [PEG]) or breathing problems (BiPAP). They considered religion less important in their lives and were less optimistic about their future. Patients who acted on the wish to die felt they had more control over management of ALS and reported less suffering as death approached, compared with those who expressed the wish but did not act on it.

Ganzini (14) has studied rates of physician-assisted suicide (PAS) and wishes of patients with ALS for PAS over the past decade. In a study of 100 patients with ALS, 56% indicated that, in some circumstances, they would consider taking medicine for the sole purpose of ending their life (15). In another study, 50 caregivers of decedent patients with ALS in Oregon (16), where assisted suicide is legal, were asked about patients' wishes and attitudes about hastening death. The caregivers reported that one third of patients in the last month of life discussed wanting assisted suicide, although only one patient actually died by assisted suicide. Most recently, she reported that more than half of patients with ALS in Oregon indicate that they might consider legalized PAS, and in Oregon ALS is the disease associated with the highest likelihood of PAS (14). Staying in control, not being dependent on others, maintaining self-sufficiency, and not burdening family are reasons for this choice. Major depressive disorder did not predict interest in assisted suicide in these studies.

Overall, wishes to die and thoughts about ending life are expressed by a sizeable number of patients with ALS, and indeed among other patients with a terminal incurable illness as they approach death. Actual requests for the means to end life also are made, but it has been observed that the very fact of having control over the timing of an inevitable and impending death often enables patients to extend the duration of their willingness to live (17).

Once a person communicates such wishes, either obliquely or directly, caregivers can convey their willingness to listen and to help make choices. These may include enrollment in hospice with the assurance of excellent palliative care, relief of pain and suffering, or the discontinuation of current interventions such as respiratory equipment. Professional evaluation of clinical depression is also indicated, although, if the patient is housebound and far from a medical center, this may be challenging to arrange. Recurrent thoughts about death and wishes to die sometimes are manifestations of depression, which is a treatable disorder. If patients persist in their expression of wishing to die, or interest in hastening death, the treating physician should be involved in this conversation and may be able to offer alternatives or options that had not been considered (18).

## Resources for Caregivers

Caregivers need both knowledge and skills. Where can these be obtained? There are multiple sources. The first is the treating neurologist or the multidisciplinary ALS clinic where care is provided. Such clinics have experts in virtually all aspects of ALS management, and they are there to respond to patient needs. Most clinics encourage e-mail messages or telephone calls as needed between routine visits, which are usually quarterly. As communication becomes more difficult for patients, the caregiver may need to take the lead in contacting health care providers. Questions can be practical (e.g., help with insurance or enrollment in Medicare or hospice), or information-seeking (e.g., is it appropriate in terms of probable time left to consider remodeling the house? What are the medication side effects? What can we tell the children? What does dying look like?).

For technical assistance with equipment, the manufacturer generally has representatives who make home visits, calibrate the machine, and explain its use. Another important resource is the Internet. Patients with ALS and their families are extremely active online, with many organizations, both regional and national, providing information and advice. In most locations, support groups for patients and caregivers meet at regular intervals, providing a forum for sharing medical information and advice about local resources for transportation, adaptive equipment, and adjunctive therapies. They provide a place to discuss difficult end-of-life issues and to hear from others who are experiencing similar challenges. Support group membership may also provide a sense of community, reassurance that one is not alone in this enormous struggle for survival and quality of life. Finally, all of these resources can provide information about planned and ongoing ALS research and clinical trials, which are essential for progress to be made in understanding the cause of the disease, and to find potential ameliorative or curative treatments.

In late-stage illness, hospice can play a key role in supporting the caregiver as well as the patient. In most cases, hospice care is provided in the home, bringing services seldom available to home-bound patients. These include effective pain management; comfort care, including morphine for the respiratory distress that may occur during dying; as well as advice and encouragement for the caregiver and other family members. ALS caregivers have said that having a hospice staff member tell them exactly what to expect as death approaches dramatically reduced their anxiety and enabled them to spend final moments at peace with their loved one.

Finally, caregivers must remember that they do not have to "do it alone." The patient is a partner, as are all the health care professionals involved, as well as family and friends if they are encouraged and helped to contribute meaningfully to the patient's life and to the well-being of the caregiver.

## References

1. Yates ME, Tennstedt S, Chang BH. Contributors to and mediators of psychological well-being for informal caregivers. *J Gerontol B Psychol Sci Soc Sci*. 1999;54:12–22.
2. Gelinas DF, O'Connor P, Miller R. Quality of life for ventilator-dependent patients and their caregivers. *J Neurol Sci*. 1998;160(Suppl 1):S134–S136.
3. Rabkin JG, Albert SM, Tider T, et al. Predictors and course of elective long-term mechanical ventilation: a prospective study of ALS patients. *Amyotroph Lateral Scler*. 2006;7:86–95.
4. Rabow MW, Hauser J, Adams J. Supporting family caregivers at the end of life. *JAMA*. 2004;291:483–491.
5. Lynn J. Serving patients who may die soon and their families: the role of hospice and other services. *JAMA*. 2001;285:925–932.
6. Heiman-Patterson T, Aboussouan L. Respiratory care in amyotrophic lateral sclerosis. In: Mitsumoto H, Przedborski S, Gordon P, eds. *Amyotrophic Lateral Sclerosis*. New York, NY: Taylor & Francis; 2006:737–760.
7. Folkman S. The case for positive emotions in the stress process. *Anxiety Stress Coping*. 2008;21:3–14.

8. Folkman S, Lazarus R. *The Ways of Coping Questionnaire*. Palo Alto, CA: Consulting Psychologists Press; 1988.
9. Brody J. Terminal options for the irreversibly ill. *New York Times*. March 18, 2008: Science section.
10. Clements J. Netherlands to publish suicide guide. *New York Sun*. March 24, 2008: 7.
11. Stagno SJ. Legal and ethical issues. In: Mitsumoto H, Munsat T, eds. *Amyotrophic Lateral Sclerosis: A Guide for Patients and Families*. 2nd ed. New York, NY: Demos; 2001:307–325.
12. Mitsumoto H, Rabkin JG. Palliative care for patients with amyotrophic lateral sclerosis. *JAMA*. 2007;298:207–216.
13. Albert SM, Rabkin J, Del Bene M, et al. Wish to die in end-stage ALS. *Neurology*. 2005;65:68–74.
14. Ganzini L. Oregon Death With Dignity Act: impact on patient choice and palliative care provision. *Amyotrophic Lateral Scler*. 2007;8 (Suppl 1):36.
15. Ganzini L, Johnston W, McFarland B, et al. Attitudes of patients with amyotrophic lateral sclerosis and their care givers toward assisted suicide. *N Engl J Med*. 1998;339:967–973.
16. Ganzini L, Silveira M, Johnston W. Predictors and correlates of interest in assisted suicide in the final month of life among ALS patients in Oregon and Washington. *J Pain Symptom Manage*. 2002;24:312–317.
17. Rabkin JG, Remien R, Wilson C. *Good Doctors, Good Patients: Partners in HIV Treatment*. New York, NY: NCM; 1995.
18. Bascom PB, Tolle S. Responding to requests for physician-assisted suicide. *JAMA*. 2002;288:91–99.

# 21

# Financial Realities

## Linda I. Boynton De Sepulveda
## and Michael C. Graves

There is no predictability to life's experience, including that of amyotrophic lateral sclerosis (ALS), because the disease varies considerably from individual to individual. The changes in health status over time must be met with flexibility. ALS affects every aspect of one's being—physical, emotional, social, financial, and spiritual. However, one can acquire hope and strength through the acquisition of knowledge. This chapter will assist you to identify resources and liabilities.

Providing satisfactory medical care to everyone at a cost they can afford is a compelling issue. Many people do not receive medical care that is adequate in either quantity or quality, and the cost of that care is inequitably distributed (1,2). The economic impact of ALS may begin long before the actual diagnosis is made (3). Patients with ALS do not begin the journey with the diagnosis; it comes after a long process of evaluations and referrals. The length and extent of these evaluations are governed by 4 types of payment systems. There is the indemnity insurance payment system (IP), the managed care payment system (HMO, PPO, and EPO), the governmental payment systems called Medicare (FMC) and Medicaid (SML), and the self-payment system (Pay), also known as the noninsured.

## Financial Realities: There Is Health
## Care and There Is ALS

## Alphabet Soup: IP, HMO, PPO, EPO, FMC, SML, and Pay

### Indemnity Insurance Payment Systems (IP)

The indemnity insurance payment (IP) system pays physicians' bills on the basis of billed charges, after the deductible and coinsurance are met. The deductible and coinsurance are the patient's responsibility. The indemnity insurance approach is rapidly declining as more insurance companies are paying only up to the "usual and customary level." This change in reimbursement has inflated the out-of-pocket expenses for most people.

### Managed Health Care (HMO, PPO, EPO)

Managed care is defined as a prepayment system. The care providers are paid in advance a preset amount for all the services the client may or may not need in a given period. This form of health care service is intended to provide high-quality, cost-effective care. The most common forms of managed care are health maintenance organizations (HMOs) and preferred provider organizations (PPOs). The exclusive provider organization (EPO) is a group of fee-for-service providers operating in much the same way as a PPO but granting the beneficiary no coverage outside the network. Managed care groups work from the belief that the primary care doctor plays a key role in the management of patient care. Patients are assigned a primary care doctor, who determines the need for referrals and arranges the consultation if he or she deems it appropriate. These referrals are normally made with specialists who are salaried or have contracted with the specific managed care group. Referral to a specialist not in the group is rarely done and usually requires a petition to a medical review board.

### Disability, Medicare, Medicaid, and COBRA

Disability under Social Security is based on an individual's inability to work. The person with ALS must be unable to perform any work for which he is trained or suited, and the disability must last longer than one year or lead to death. To qualify for Social Security disability benefits, the person needs to have worked. Qualification for benefits depends on the number of years worked and the number of credits earned in that period. To apply for Social Security disability, you need to file a claim with the Social Security office either by phone, mail, e-mail (ssa.gov), or in person. Certain information is necessary to process your claim: (a) social security number; (b) names, addresses, and phone numbers of doctors, clinics, and institutions that treated you and dates of treatment; (c) a summary of where you worked in the past 15 years and what kind of work you did; (d) a copy of your W-2 form or, if self-employed, your federal tax return for the past year; (e) date of marriage

Steps in the medical evaluation of the patient with ALS are as follows:

- Initial evaluation by the primary care physician
- Referral for a second opinion
- Referral to a neuromuscular specialist
- Application of the El Escorial criteria
- Tests such as blood tests, electromyography (EMG), and magnetic resonance imaging (MRI) scans or x-rays

## Initial Evaluation

It is important for a person with the possible diagnosis of ALS to begin by consulting a general internist or family practitioner. A routine evaluation of your general health is important whether you eventually learn that you have ALS or not.

## Referral for a Second Opinion

A neurologist should be seen to diagnose ALS and to rule out the alternative neuromuscular conditions that can resemble it. What is a neurologist? Historically, the recognition of the existence of ALS and the development of the neurologist as a modern medical specialist occurred together in the mid- to late-19th century (see Chapter 3). Today's neurologist will have completed about 12 to 13 years of higher (post–high school) education before taking his or her board examinations in the specialty. After that he or she may choose to become a neuromuscular specialist by taking a 1- or 2-year neuromuscular fellowship, in which he or she concentrates on the skills of examination, EMG, and muscle biopsy needed for ALS and other neuromuscular diseases. Everyone suspected of having ALS should see a neurologist for careful examination, especially one who specializes in neuromuscular diseases including ALS.

## Cost and Benefit of the Neurologist

The cost of the first evaluation by a neurologist averages $550. This office consultation is of more value than the expensive diagnostic tests that are frequently done. The neurologic examination depends on knowledge of the structure and function of the brain, spinal cord, nerves, and muscles. The cost of seeing a competent neurologist is money well spent because no brain scan, x-ray, or other test can replace this expertise. If the correct diagnosis is not made, patients may have surgical operations for such conditions as carpal tunnel syndrome, tarsal tunnel syndrome, ulnar nerve compression, and spinal conditions. An opinion from a neurologist specializing in neuromuscular disorders is also a good idea.

## Sometimes the Diagnosis Is Difficult

For some people with ALS who have typical symptoms and are seen by a knowledgeable physician, the correct diagnosis is clear very early. When a neurologist

if your spouse is also applying. Once the person with ALS has been approved for disability benefits, he or she will receive his or her first Social Security check dating back to the sixth full month from the date the social security office decides the disability began. For more information, call the Social Security's 24-hour toll-free number: 1-800-772-1213.

In 1965 President Johnson signed the Medicare program into law. Medicare provides health benefits to people over age 65 years or to those who have been receiving Social Security disability payments for 2 years. The program has 2 complementary but distinct parts: hospital insurance (known as Part A) and supplemental medical insurance (known as Part B). After the deductible and coinsurance payment are met, Part A will pay for (a) inpatient hospitalization, (b) nursing care at a skilled nursing facility following acute hospitalization, (c) some in-home health care, and (d) hospice. All services have specific time limitations, and reimbursement is based on a specific set of criteria. In Part B recipients pay a monthly premium and must meet a yearly deductible. Part B will help pay for (a) physician services, (b) diagnostic tests, (c) durable medical equipment (limited to specific equipment), and (d) ambulance services and other health services and supplies not covered in Part A (details of the extent and type of coverage are presented throughout this chapter) (4).

On August 28, 2003, the Social Security Administration adopted new rules expediting the approval process for persons with ALS. Under the auspices of compassionate allowances, confirmation of diagnosis alone (ALS) became sufficient to receive benefits. However, the diagnosis must be supported by "a clinically appropriate medical history, neurological findings consistent with ALS, and the results of any electrophysiological and neuro-imaging testing."

If the patient with ALS disagrees with what Medicare has paid on a claim (e.g., services, durable medical equipment, deductibles, payments), he or she can appeal. The claimant has 6 months from the date of denial to file an appeal. In requesting an appeal, the claimant must be sure to include his or her Medicare number, address, and phone number and describe what portion of the denial he or she is appealing. Or, you can complete the "Request for Review of a Part B Medicare Claim" form, which is available at your local Social Security office. There is no charge for the appeal process or review. The appeal process takes 45 days. You will receive a letter detailing the decision, outlining the reason for the decision, and providing information on the next appeal decision level. If the amount is greater than $100 and your initial appeal was denied, you have 6 months to appeal for a carrier hearing. If the amount is greater than $500 and the second appeal is denied, you may request a hearing with an administrative law judge. If this appeal is denied, you can ask for the Appeals Council to review the decision within 60 days. To request an Appeals Council review, you must make your request in writing. If the amount is greater than $1,000 and the decision is not in your favor, you can bring suit in federal district court. You should have legal counsel at this stage.

Until 1965 there was no federal participation in medical care for poor people; the state provided whatever care was necessary. This changed in 1965, when Medicaid, Title XIX of the Social Security Act, was implemented. Medicaid is a joint federal and state program that provides health benefits for poor people. Eligibility for Medicaid is determined by each state and by level of income. In the early years of Medicaid, families had to "spend down" all their assets so that a family member could be cared for. Under the new guidelines, assets are divided and only those of the patient need to be spent down, thus preventing the impoverishing of the surviving spouse. There are specific legal issues and timing of the spend down that are important to know. It is important to know that the rules about what can be spent or kept vary between states. Second, the interpretation of the rules can vary between welfare offices. Third, a negotiation process is possible when the division of assets is not considered equitable. We advise anyone wishing to go through this process to seek legal assistance from a lawyer who is experienced in Medicaid law. Otherwise, a person with ALS may unnecessarily incur losses.

While people with ALS are still employed, it is important for them to determine how they can maintain insurance coverage while they go through the disability process. The Consolidated Omnibus Budget Reconciliation Act of 1985 (COBRA) is an employer group health plan that people with ALS can pay for if they must stop working because of their disability. If they worked for a company that had fewer than 20 employees and are not eligible for COBRA, they can seek legal council to determine their recourse under state laws.

## No Insurance

More than 45.8 million Americans (in 2004), including many people with ALS, do not have health insurance. Some say it is because insurance is not provided where they work, others say it is too costly, and others had believed they would never get this sick. Whatever the reason, they need to apply for disability benefits as quickly as possible. There are guidelines for working while disabled; you should check with your local Social Security office.

Financial security is something we can all relate to. Making the right choices, knowing the limitations of our insurance coverage, and knowing alternative resources can instill well-being (Table 21.1). Everyone at one time or another has been overwhelmed by insurance forms, deductibles, authorizations, justifications, and appeal processes. But knowing the system can greatly increase the chance for success in acquiring what may be necessary for survival. If people with ALS find that their insurance is inadequate, they need to know what alternatives exist.

## Medical Evaluation

This section addresses the process of diagnosing ALS, how to pay for it, and how your insurance can affect the process. The first part applies to everyone and deals with the various steps people go through in arriving at a diagnosis. The second part discusses the challenges presented to patients by the health care industry. This part should assist the patient and family in navigating through the obstacles that these systems all too often place in the way of obtaining proper medical consultation.

**Table 21.1** Know Your Insurance Policy

| General information | Insurance card | Know: 1. Name of subscriber. 2. Insurance phone number. 3. Group number of insurance plan. 4. Policy holder. Who is the subscriber (date of birth, Social Security number)? |
|---|---|---|
| | Policy | 1. Is there an annual deductible? 2. What are your annual out-of-pocket expenses? 3. Are there claim forms? 4. Is there a cap in services provided (expense limit or maximum)? 5. Can you have access to case management services? 6. What is the appeal process? |
| | Doctor visits | 1. Is there a fee for service or is it prepaid? 2. Is there a deductible? How much? 3. What is the referral process in order to see a specialist? |
| | Pharmacy plan | 1. Do you have one? 2. Is there a spending limit (cap)? 3. Does it include nutritional supplementation? |
| | Durable medical equipment (DME) | 1. Do you have DME coverage? Deductible? 2. What equipment is covered under your policy? 3. Is there a preferred provider? 4. Forms? Preauthorization? Review process? |
| | Long-term care, in-home care, hospice | 1. Do you have long-term, in-home health and/or hospice care coverage? 2. What are the limitations of these benefits (number of days, justification, preferred agency)? |

examines these patients, the typical signs of ALS are present, and alternative diagnoses are unlikely. For other patients, the diagnosis can be difficult, even by experienced physicians. Failure to establish the correct diagnosis can lead to anxiety and unnecessary medical testing, potentially harmful medical treatments, and fruitless surgery. Delays in diagnosis usually are due to one or more of the following:

1. Delay by the primary care physician in referral to a neurologist.

2. Referral for a second opinion directly to a neurosurgeon or to an orthopedic surgeon, with the assumption that the problem is one that needs surgical treatment.

3. Failure of referral to a neurologist who specializes in neuromuscular diseases and ALS.

4. Denial (the psychological kind, not the HMO kind). There is an old attitude that early diagnosis of a disease such as ALS is of no benefit to the patient because there are so few effective treatments to offer. This leads to denial by both physicians and patients and their families.

Early diagnosis will benefit the patient and also will ultimately cost less than delayed diagnosis, for both the patient and his or her insurance company (5,6). The anxiety produced by the fear of the unknown may be higher than that of facing a known and defined enemy. Other benefits of early diagnosis allow patients to do the following:

1. Choose new drugs that may slow down the disease

2. Find specialty centers to volunteer for clinical trial and to contribute to research that may help others in the future

3. Avoid unnecessary and expensive medical testing

4. Avoid expensive, fruitless, and potentially harmful treatments and surgeries

Even when examined by an expert, some people with ALS may not have enough signs and symptoms to meet the criteria for the diagnosis of ALS. These criteria are known as the El Escorial criteria (see Chapter 2). Patients may need MRI scans, muscle biopsies, and various blood tests. If even these tests are not helpful, more time is needed. These patients need to have appointments every 3 to 5 months for careful reexamination.

## Application of the El Escorial Criteria

Chapter 2 covers the details of the system developed by the World Federation of Neurology to confirm the diagnosis of ALS. These criteria are now available for neurologists to use to diagnose ALS.

## Tests and More Tests: Blood Tests, EMG, MRI Scans or X-rays, and Muscle Biopsy

### Blood Tests

Most patients with ALS seen in our clinic have had many blood tests in the hope of finding some disease that might be curable. However, no blood test can be used to confirm or rule out ALS. Diagnosis of this disease depends completely on the skills of a neurologist. If, based on his or her examination, the neurologist believes that another diagnosis is possible, appropriate blood tests are needed.

### Electromyography

The details of EMG and other tests that the neurologist may order are found in Chapter 3. The EMG alone cannot diagnose ALS. Only a physician who has done a complete neurologic history and examination can do this. EMG testing can also demonstrate a number of diseases of nerves and of muscles that can sometimes mimic ALS. All patients with suspected ALS need to have EMG testing done by a physician who is familiar with ALS and related conditions.

### MRI Scans and X-rays

Just as they have had many blood tests, many patients seen in our clinic have large packets of scans and x-rays. These are only needed in specific situations. If patients do not meet the El Escorial criteria when the neurologist first examines them, these tests are needed to rule out other conditions.

### Muscle Biopsy

Muscle biopsy is only necessary in a few patients with ALS. These biopsies should be sent to a major neuromuscular research center, because otherwise the test may not be helpful and may need to be repeated.

## The Influence of Type of Insurance on the Diagnostic Process

As outlined earlier, every patient needs to take a series of steps in the diagnostic journey, including seeing the primary doctor, the neurologist, and the ALS specialist neurologist and completing appropriate testing. Changes in how medical care is financed have begun to affect the ease of taking each of the preceding steps. However, any shortcuts that eliminate the steps outlined may lead to a wrong or delayed diagnosis. The type of insurance you have can affect the process of evaluating a diagnosis of ALS. As you compare the different kinds of insurance available, it may seem that private insurance is the best and HMOs are the worst in getting access to the experts needed to diagnose ALS. This is true if we only consider diagnosis and ignore treatment. Obviously, you need to consider more than just diagnosis in planning your budget, and that is when the various managed care plans may show their real value.

## The Conflict Between Managed
## Care and Specialists

Before 1950 there were very few medical specialists and only rarely would general practitioners send a patient with ALS to a specialist. Beginning in the 1960s many physicians became specialists and even provided the primary source of care for the diseases within their specialty. For example, neurologists gradually developed experience in the day-to-day care of conditions such as Parkinson disease and epilepsy. Additionally, patients could go directly to the specialist without any special permission. Insurance would pay the costs. However, the costs of medical care increased rapidly from 1970 through 1990. Part of this was attributed to this easy accessibility of patients to specialists.

Managed care was devised to save money, in part, by limiting access to specialists. However, this approach failed to recognize that a great deal of primary care was already being provided by the specialists. The general practitioner, or a committee, was given the responsibility to decide which patient could or could not go to a specialist or have a certain laboratory test or even a surgical operation. The primary care physician can also lose personal income for every patient sent to a specialist or diagnostic testing. On the positive side, the low monthly premiums of the managed care options are appealing for the healthy young person with limited income. For patients who do have a disease such as ALS, managed care plans may offer better coverage for drugs and in many cases lowered or eliminated copayments.

People with ALS frequently have little choice about what kind of insurance they have and/or very few options to change insurances. Therefore, patients and families must take the responsibility for requesting services outside their scope of coverage. This is known as *requesting an authorization.* If conscientious and ethical, the managed care plans should still approve all requests that are deemed medically necessary. However, the patient with ALS may need to be persistent in acquiring that authorization.

### Private Fee-for-Service Insurance

In the IP system, the primary care doctor, usually an internist or a family practitioner, can more easily make a referral to a neurologist. The average cost for the consultation is approximately $550. The neurologist may decide that testing is needed. EMG and nerve conduction velocity (NCV) testing (see Chapter 3) are almost always needed and cost up to $700. Blood tests and MRI scans are sometimes needed, adding several thousand dollars more. If you add muscle biopsies and spinal taps, the bill can come to tens of thousands of dollars. Inappropriate treatments and surgery can increase the bill to hundreds of thousands of dollars. Because patients must pay the 20% to 25% copayment, it is in their financial interest to make sure that the requested tests are really necessary. Unless one is a medical professional, it is difficult to decide what testing to get. The best guide is to seek the advice of a good neurologist before all testing and to get the advice of a neuromuscular specialist at a neuromuscular center if there is any question about what is necessary.

## Medicare

As discussed previously, private insurance generally converts to Medicare when you reach age 65. Medicare has most of the same rules as private insurance, but it may pay less. Most neurologists accept Medicare. There generally is a copayment.

## State Medical Assistance

In California the state program for low-income people is called Medi-Cal. This program pays very little to the doctor. Occasionally, depending on the locality, neurologists will see a limited number of such patients as a charitable act. Patients facing this type of situation should always try to go to an ALS–neuromuscular research center. Although Medi-Cal pays very little to doctors, it is one of the best programs in paying for drugs and durable medical equipment such as wheelchairs.

## Managed Care: HMO, PPO, EPO

HMO, PPO, and EPO are now the most popular types of insurance. In the large HMO, in general, there are few or no out-of-pocket expenses to the patient. In one large California HMO, patients can get a second opinion or even a third opinion from neurologists within the HMO. You usually can find out which neurologist in the large HMO has completed a fellowship in neuromuscular diseases or otherwise is especially interested in ALS. The large HMO will sometimes give authorization to go to a specialist outside the HMO when it is really necessary to get the correct diagnosis. In the PPO care plan, the insurance company gives you a book that lists all the doctors you are allowed to see. There usually is a wide selection of neurologists, including those at the ALS and neuromuscular research centers nearest you. Smaller managed care programs (e.g., PPOs or EPOs) often have only a few neurologists in their system. These neurologists usually are general neurologists who can take care of problems such as strokes, Parkinson disease, Alzheimer's disease, and all the more common conditions that require neurologic care. A referral to a neurologist who specializes in neuromuscular disease should be firmly requested for every patient who is in one of these smaller managed care programs.

## Role of Charitable Foundations

The Muscular Dystrophy Association (MDA) and the ALS Association (ALSA) both support a number of ALS neuromuscular research clinics around the country. The MDA clinics allow patients who have little or no ability to pay to see the experts. The MDA is able to pay for expenses that health insurance plans or HMOs should cover. These clinics frequently serve the valuable role of identifying needs. They then help patients to articulate their need in the form of a request for authorization to the HMO or other insurance company. You can find a list of these clinics on the following Web pages: World Federation of Neurology ALS (www.wfnals .org), MDA (www.MDAUSA.org), or ALSA (www.alsa.org). Or you can call your local MDA or ALSA office (see Chapter 27).

## Medical Care

### Drug Management

*Cost-Controlling Issues*

Prescription medications have been another area of great concern to the person with ALS. In addition to the rapidly escalating cost of drugs, there has been an explosion in the number of agents used to treat various associated medical problems, as discussed in other chapters. In an attempt to control costs, many states have passed legislation that allows pharmacies to fill prescriptions with a generic equivalent. Another attempt by insurance companies, HMOs, and federal programs to curtail costs is the development of formularies. A formulary is a restrictive list of available medications from which physicians can choose. In the outpatient setting, HMOs, PPOs, state Medicaid, and IPs are beginning to restrict physician prescribing practices by the use of a drug formulary. The patient with ALS can still receive drugs that are not on the approved formulary, but they probably will have to pay for them.

*Pharmacy Plans: What Are They, What Do They Offer, and How Do I Get One?*

Prescription coverage under Medicare is called *Part D*. This optional plan is run by Medicare-authorized private insurance companies. The cost (premium, deductible, copayment, off formulary, not authorized, coverage gap) will vary between drug plans and drugs used. Additional information about drug coverage under Medicare Part D can be obtained from Medicare (www.medicare.gov), State Health Insurance Assistance Program (www.shiptalk.org), and/or AARP, Medicare drug plan ratings (1-800-985-6848).

It is important to know whether persons with ALS have a prescription plan. If they do, you need to determine the amount and type of coverage. Generic drugs are less expensive than brand-name drugs, but injectable prescriptions may or may not be covered. In addition, some prescription programs may limit access to drugs. Some HMOs have a drug formulary. Drugs are dispensed from that list either free or at a reduced rate. The variety of drugs at the patient's disposal for treatment also will be limited. At present, only one drug has been approved by the Food and Drug Administration (FDA) for the treatment of the underlying disease process in ALS (see Chapter 4), but numerous medications may be needed for the management of conditions associated with the disease.

*Symptom Management*

Medications used to treat such problems as excessive saliva, spasticity, cramps, insomnia, depression, emotional lability, or difficulty breathing may or may not be listed on a drug formulary; there may not be a generic equivalent; or the drug may be in limited supply. Therefore, choices to treat a specific medical problem may be limited, restricted, or constrained by financial resources (see Chapter 4).

## Treatment of ALS (Riluzole, Vitamins, Homeopathic)

The only FDA-approved treatment for ALS at this time is Rilutek (riluzole). Over-the-counter vitamins and herbs usually are not covered by pharmacy plans. Multivitamin pills can cost as little as $5 per 100 tablets, but the annual cost could be considerably more when you add vitamin C, vitamin E, vitamin B complex, ginkgo biloba, superoxide dismutase (SOD), and/or other homeopathic-alternative remedies. This figure does not include all the other drugs that may be tried during the course of the disease. One of the most difficult decisions a person with ALS has to make is whether to pay for drugs that are only modestly effective in treating the disease (7,8), especially if they do not have a pharmacy plan. Most HMOs have approved riluzole for the treatment of ALS and pay the full cost of the medication ($650 to $1,000 per month), but pharmacy plans such as Medigap may cover the cost of the drug only for the first few months of the year.

## Recourse: Alternative Funding Sources

If the person with ALS does not have a pharmacy plan or if his or her plan has a cap, he or she needs to explore other options and develop strategies to save money. Generic drugs generally cost 30% to 50% less than brand-name medications. Prescriptions that are filled by mail tend to cost less, but you may need to shop for the best price. People with ALS should not forget to ask about the cost to fill the prescription, shipping, and any other fees (membership) that may be required. A few pharmacy programs are AARP Pharmacy Service, APP (American Preferred Prescription, Inc.), Action Mail Order, Health Care Services, and Medi-mail order. Some national and state pharmaceutical programs may assist patients in the purchase of medications. One such program is sponsored by the National Organization for Rare Disorders (NORD). Financially needy individuals can obtain prescribed medications through the NORD medication assistance program. The amount of financial compensation is determined by the applicant's financial need. NORD currently dispenses Rilutek (riluzole) tablets through the Patient Assistance Program, which provides free drugs to patients who are not eligible for public or private reimbursement. For more information, call 1-800-999-NORD. The Prescription Drug Patient Assistance Program is another national program that provides drugs at no cost to those who qualify. The physician applies to the pharmaceutical company for a 90-day supply of medication. He or she needs to reapply each time the drug is reordered. The Veterans Affairs (VA) office can also help individuals who were veterans. It may provide some drugs at a reduced rate, depending on the facility's formulary. Patients need to contact their local VA office, hospital, or outpatient facility for information. Table 21.2 provides a resource list of prescription services.

**Table 21.2** Prescription Services

| Agency | Notes | Contact Information |
|---|---|---|
| AARP Pharmacy Service | Don't need to be AARP member | 1-800-456-2226 |
| APP (American Preferred Prescription, Inc.) | No membership | 1-800-952-7779 |
| Action Mail Order | No membership required | 1-800-452-1976 |
| Health Care Services | Membership $12 if you are member of National Council of Senior Citizens. You don't have to be a senior citizen to join. | 1-800-758-0555 |
| Medi-mail order | No membership required | 1-800-331-1458 |
| NORD (National Organization for Rare Disorders) | Dependent on financial need | 1-800-999-NORD |
| Prescription Drug Patient Assistance Programs | The doctor coordinates a 90-day supply of medication with the pharmaceutical company. Restrictions are given in booklet. | 1-800-548-9034 |
| Veterans Affairs (VA) | Veterans can receive drugs at a reduced rate or sometimes for free | Local VA facility |

## Durable Medical Equipment

The term *durable medical equipment* (DME) refers to items that can withstand repeated use. The item must be prescribed by a physician, must be medically necessary (Certificate of Medical Necessity is required), must be appropriate for home use, must fill a medical need, must be something that can be used repeatedly, and must be something that would not be useful if the patient were not sick. Medicare Part B helps pay for DME and other supplies used in the home, including oxygen equipment, canes, walkers, patient lifts, wheelchairs, braces, hospital beds, and seat lift mechanisms. Medicare approves some DME items for purchase, whereas other items must be rented. Some items, such as scooters and seat lift mechanisms, require prior authorization. A prior authorization request can be submitted by the patient, doctor, or supplier. It is also important to note the order in which equipment is requested (e.g., walker or cane before wheelchair), otherwise a denial can be expected. Additional information about Medicare coverage for DME can be obtained at www.medicare.gov/Publications.

Under Medicaid guidelines, the definition of DME is similar to that of Medicare. Based on the estimated time of medical need, Medicaid will determine the need to rent or purchase DME. The physician needs to complete a medical necessity form, and the provider needs to complete a claim form. DME that has been purchased or rented by the state may be reclaimed for the use of other individuals when the original recipient no longer needs it.

Insurance companies and managed care organizations often do not cover DME or offer only limited coverage. The cost of DME can add to the overwhelming financial burden of ALS. In addition to problems with financial support, there may be delays in receiving the needed equipment or service. Various patient advocate groups have expressed concern that there is no incentive to create laws or policies to protect the consumer. "Managed care organizations and private insurers have nothing to lose and everything to gain by automatically denying or delaying coverage for DME" (9).

Adaptive devices such as grab bars, stair glides or elevators, emergency call devices, or built-up utensils are not considered DME. Therefore, these items are considered an out-of-pocket expense.

### Implication for Treatment Decisions

The person with ALS should know what his or her policy covers. He or she should know what equipment is covered and the limitations in either type or price. Table 21.3 outlines DME equipment costs and coverage.

The person with ALS also needs to know what is required to process a claim. Always ask questions, and if the supplier does not know, you should call your insurance carrier. If the claim is denied, you should know the appeal process. If all else fails, you should know where to turn for assistance. The ALSA and the MDA both have local loan equipment pools. You can contact the local service representative and ask about borrowing the needed equipment. The MDA will assist with the purchase of a wheelchair or orthotic device in some circumstances. Contact your local representative for more information. Another potential source for assistance is community programs, such as church groups or aid groups.

### Augmentative and Alternative Communication Devices

Augmentative and alternative communication (AAC) devices include but are not limited to portable computer-generated messages, either verbal or nonverbal (see Chapter 10). Medicaid funding has been established in most states, and many insurance providers offer AAC devices. Medicare-supported funding for these devices comes under the DME criteria. MDA will provide additional financial support to purchase the AAC device (www.MDAUSA.org). Denials can be appealed. The patient must first determine the device meets one of the DME criteria, such as AAC devices are durable, they are a treatment for severe expressive communication disabilities, they are not needed by persons without this disability, and/or they are portable. The patient then must follow the appeal process previously described.

**Table 21.3** DME Equipment Costs and Coverage

| DME | Cost (U.S.$) | Coverage based on insurance carrier: | | | |
|---|---|---|---|---|---|
| Type of equipment | range | FMC | SML | HMO | EPO/ PPO/IP |
| Wheelchair: standard manual | 400– 3,500 | Cap on rental | Yes | Yes | % |
| Wheelchair: standard electric | 3,500– 12,000 | 4,500 purchase | Yes | Yes | % |
| Wheelchair: full electric (tilt and recline, leg elevation, seat elevation, special trunk/ head support) | 12,000– 25,000 | No | Yes | Usually no | % |
| Cane | 9–50 | Yes with cap | Yes | Yes | % |
| Walker: standard | 70–150 | Yes | No | Yes | % |
| Walker: heavy duty, large wheels, special attachments | 275–400 | Yes | Yes | Yes | % |
| Commode | 90–1,200 | Yes with cap | Yes | Yes | % |
| Shower chair or shower bench | 50–120 | No | Yes | Yes | % |

*Note:* Yes = full coverage, with justification (HMO may have limited selection); No = no coverage, patient responsible for full cost; % = percentage of cost covered by insurance, balance patient's responsibility after deductible met; Cap = cap on rental or purchase price.

### Implication for Treatment Decisions

When all appeals have been exhausted, the person with ALS should seek additional support. Contact the ALS Association and the Muscular Dystrophy Association, both of which have local loan equipment pools. Contact your local service representative and ask about borrowing the equipment you need.

## Cough-Assist Machines (Insufflator-Exsufflator)

The CoughAssist insufflator-exsufflator is a device that helps patients who cannot cough for themselves to clear secretions from their upper airway. The noninvasive device stimulates a natural coughing process and reduces the risk of airway damage and respiratory complications associated with more invasive suctioning procedures. The CoughAssist machine assists patients in clearing secretions by gradually applying positive pressure to the airway to achieve a good inspiratory lung volume, and then cycling rapidly to negative pressure to achieve effective expiratory cough flow. Reimbursement information can be found on the Respironics Web site (www .respironics.com).

## Ventilation: Tracheostomy and Ventilator and/or Noninvasive Ventilator BiPAP

At some point the person with ALS may experience difficulty breathing. The decision to use mechanical ventilation can be difficult. Factors that affect that decision are not limited to the availability of insurance coverage but also include whether there are caregivers in the home or whether there are other funds to support private-duty nursing to assist the patient with ALS in the management of these devices.

### What Are Invasive Ventilation and Noninvasive Ventilation? Does the Policy Cover the Patient's Needs?

Invasive ventilation refers to the placement of an endotracheal tube in the nose or mouth or a tracheostomy (tube in the neck) and attachment to a mechanical breathing device. Invasive ventilation is considered a permanent method of support (see Chapter 12). A noninvasive device refers to positive pressure air delivered through a nasal mask, nasal pillows, or face mask. These methods of ventilation assist the person with ALS to breathe. Some insurance companies consider these modes of ventilation as DME rather than life support equipment. The result may be that they will not cover the cost or rental of the equipment. The person with ALS will need to examine not only the cost of the machine but all the ancillary equipment that is necessary, especially if the device is invasive (i.e., tubing, suctioning catheters, trach replacement, dressings). The financial impact could be significant.

### Implication on Treatment Decisions

We encourage the person with ALS to seek medical and financial counseling before making a decision about the use of any respiratory device. Noninvasive ventilation is simpler, less expensive, and nonsurgical (10). Invasive ventilatory support requires surgery (tracheostomy), hospital admission, and a nurse or family training. The cost of noninvasive equipment rental is not less than $6,000 per year, and invasive equipment can cost much as $20,000 per month if the cost of 16 hours of nursing care per day is included. Typically, insurance companies may pay for the rental of the equipment and some supplies, but the cost of nursing care may be limited to the first month to 6 weeks and then becomes the financial responsibility of the patient and family.

## Nutrition

What does one do to maintain proper nutrition and hydration? Dietary supplements can be used if the person with ALS has no difficulty swallowing or has some difficulty but is not aspirating (choking) foods and fluids. However, if the patient does have significant difficulty with swallowing, a surgical procedure to insert a tube (percutaneous gastrostomy tube) into the stomach can be performed (see Chapter 11). Feeding tubes are not a life-sustaining measure, but they do improve quality of life. Malnutrition and dehydration have been shown to increase (a) the rate of disease progression, (b) feelings of fatigue, and (c) the risk of further complications, such as aspiration pneumonia.

Insertion of a feeding gastrostomy tube is usually done as an outpatient procedure, although some patients with ALS may require a 1- to 2-day hospital stay. The cost of the procedure normally is covered by most insurances. However, Medicare requires that the patient have a modified barium swallow test and that the test indicate that aspiration of food and liquids is present. Otherwise, Medicare will not pay for the surgical procedure. Managed care health programs require referral to a specialist within their provider group. Other insurance programs require payment of a deductible (if applicable) and coinsurance. The cost of the procedure may be as little as $1,500 (same-day stay). Additional charges depend on overnight stay and physical condition at the time of the procedure.

Feedings consist of special formulas or prepared products. The average cost of feedings per month is $250. Feeding tubes and syringes normally cost $30 per month. However, if bolus feedings are not tolerated, slow drip feedings are recommended. The cost for the rental of a drip pump is approximately $220 per month. Medicare will cover the cost of feedings when nutrition is through a feeding tube. Other insurance programs vary in the amount that is reimbursed. The patient with ALS needs to review the specific coverage with his or her insurance company.

We are not aware of any programs that assist with the cost of surgery, supplies, or nutritional supplement.

## Nursing Care

Skilled nursing care refers to patient services that are necessary to meet specific care objectives. Registered nurses, physical therapists, occupational therapists, and speech pathologists all provide short-term skilled care. The terms *custodial care* and *in-home care* refer to those services used to maintain or support the care of an individual but not to rehabilitate him or her. Nursing homes can serve several functions, either as a skilled nursing facility, an extended care facility, or a hospice. Nursing homes at one time were the mainstay of long-term care. Over the years, however, more and more individuals have decided to remain at home through the disease and dying process. Skilled nursing facilities are used as short-term stays for the management of a specific health care problem. Extended care facilities attempt to meet the patient's long-term care needs. Hospices or hospice services are designed to provide palliative care to individuals with a terminal disease who choose not to seek curative or life-sustaining care (i.e., invasive ventilation) (see Chapter 12) (11).

## Out-of-Pocket Expense for Nursing Care

Most insurance companies cover the cost for skilled nursing services when a planned program has been developed and a letter of justification and a prescription has been provided by the attending physician. Custodial care or extended care services generally are not covered by insurance companies unless the patient has specifically selected a policy with an in-home program feature. Medicaid, on the other hand, may provide for a home health aide to assist with activities of daily living, and Medicare covers the cost of extended-care service if the patient has been discharged from an acute care facility; that coverage is limited to the first 100 days. Extended-care facilities normally are not covered by insurance companies unless the patient is on a ventilator. The cost for care in any of these facilities can be quite high, and personal resources can be spent at an alarming rate. Hospice is covered under Part A of the Medicare benefits and by most HMO and private insurance plans.

## Implication for Treatment Decisions

Whatever choice is made for assistance—short-term, long-term, or palliative—persons with ALS need to identify what coverage they have, what they need to do to get that coverage, and what their out-of-pocket expense will be. For some individuals there is no help available unless they pay for it. If this is their only option, they need to talk with their case manager, local hospital social worker, ALSA or MDA patient services coordinators, and ALS clinic coordinators about alternative resources in their community.

## Recourse: Alternative Funding Sources

The Spousal Impoverishment Program allows for the division of a patient's assets, enabling the healthy spouse to retain resources. To apply for this program, you should seek the assistance of an attorney experienced in this field.

# Voluntary Not-for-Profit Agencies and Health Care Alternatives

## Nonprofit Agencies

### Amyotrophic Lateral Sclerosis Association (ALSA)

ALSA is a nonprofit organization dedicated to the patient with ALS, family, caregivers, and health care professionals. It provides funding for research, education,

**Table 21.4** National Patient Service Resources

| | | |
|---|---|---|
| Amyotrophic Lateral Sclerosis Association (ALSA) | National nonprofit health organization. They provide several patient support services. | 1-800-782-4747 http://www .alsa.org |
| Muscular Dystrophy Association (MDA) | National nonprofit health organization. They provide several patient support services, including MDA/ ALS clinics throughout the United States. | 1-800-572-1717 http://www. mda.org |
| National Respite Locator Service | This is a national directory for respite services. | 1-800-773-5433 http://www .chtop.com |
| National Hospice Organization (NHO) | This is a national directory for hospice services. | 1-800-658-8898 http://www .nho.org |

community-based support groups, and identification of local resources, and it serves as an advocate at the local and national levels (Table 21.4).

## Muscular Dystrophy Association (MDA)

MDA is a nonprofit organization dedicated to over 40 neuromuscular diseases including ALS. It supports more than 200 hospital-affiliated clinics that specialize in neuromuscular diseases and several ALS subspecialty clinics. MDA also provides financial assistance (in the purchase of a wheelchair, braces, and communication devices), educational materials, funding for research, and community-based support groups for patients with ALS (Table 21.4).

## United Way

United Way is a national nonprofit organization that provides support to various other charitable or nonprofit organizations. Through various interface programs it can assist individuals in locating rent subsidy, utility subsidy, child care subsidy, and food programs in their area.

*The Amyotrophic Lateral Sclerosis (ALS) Patient and Caregiver Resource Guide* was developed by Rhone-Poulenc Rorer Pharmaceuticals Inc. (currently Aventis) in 1996 (12). It provides an extensive list of organizations and a description of their services.

## Health Care Alternatives

Both MDA and ALSA support clinics across the country that specialize in the care of the patient with ALS. Information about these clinics can be found on the Internet (wfnals.org, MDAUSA.org, or ALSA.org) (see also Chapter 27). The types of services and treatment costs are variable. The patient with ALS should contact the local clinic to determine what resources are available and what cost is entailed. The typical clinic supports the cost of the physical examination, limited testing procedures, and access to rehabilitation services (physical therapy, occupational therapy, and speech pathology) and some may have a social worker and nurse.

## References

1. Chio A, Bottacchi E, Buffa C, et al. Positive effects of tertiary centres for amyotrophic lateral sclerosis on outcome and use of hospital facilities. *J Neurol Neurosurg Psychiatry.* 2006;77:948–950.
2. Levvy G. The role of the amyotrophic lateral sclerosis and motor neurone disease community in health-care resourcing. *Int J Clin Pract.* 1998;94:(4)(Suppl):14–17.
3. Klein LM, Forshew, DA. The economic impact of ALS. *Neurology.* 1996;47(Suppl 2): S126–S129.
4. Mitsumoto H, Munsat T. *Amyotrophic Lateral Sclerosis. A Guide for Patients and Families.* 2nd ed. New York, NY: Demos; 2001.
5. Mitsumoto H, Rabkin J. Palliative care for patients with amyotrophic lateral sclerosis. *JAMA.* 2007;298(2):207–216.
6. Munsat T, et al. Economic Burden of Amyotrophic Lateral Sclerosis in the United States. Poster presentation at the 9th International Symposium on ALS/MND, November 16–18, 1998.
7. Ringel S. Cost effectiveness: summary. *Amyotroph Lateral Scler.* 2002;(Suppl 1): S67–S69.
8. Woolley J. Cost effectiveness: Pro. The value of economic information in medical decision-making. *Amyotroph Lateral Scler.* 2002;(Suppl 1):S63–S64.
9. Pennell F. Talking Points. Barriers to Accessing at Through Private Insurance. http:// wata.org/meeting/t-pennell-attach.htm. Accessed March 4, 1998.
10. Gruis K, Chernew M, Brown D. The cost-effectiveness of early noninvasive ventilation for ALS patients. *BMC Health Serv Res.* 2005;58:1–4.
11. Elman L, Stanley L, Gibbons P, et al. A cost comparison of hospice care in amyotrophic lateral sclerosis and lung cancer. *Am J Hosp Palliat Care.* 2006;23(3):212–216.
12. *Amyotrophic Lateral Sclerosis (ALS) Patient and Caregiver Resource Guide.* Collegeville, PA: Rhone-Poulenc Rorer Pharmaceuticals Inc.; 1996.

## Suggested Reading

Appleby C. Values. *Hospitals & Health Networks.* July 5, 1996:20–26.
Baldor, R. *Managed Care Made Simple.* Malden, MA: Blackwell Science; 1998.

Corrigan JM, Ginsburg PB. Association leaders speak out on health system change. *Health Affairs.* 1997;16(1):150–157.

Edwards JC, Donati RM. *Medical Practice in the Current Health Care Environment.* Baltimore, MD: Johns Hopkins University Press: 1995.

*Medicare & You 2008.* Medicare coverage of durable medical equipment and other devices. Centers for Medicare and Medicaid Services, official government handbooks. www.medicare.gov. Accessed December 2008.

Meslin EM. An ethics framework for assisting clinician-managers in resource allocation decision making. *Hospital Health Serv Admin.* 1997;42(1):33–48.

Orchard DW. Health policy and the quality of life. *J Palliat Care.* 1992;8(3):31–33.

Roberts CC. Keeping managed care in balance. *Health Social Work.* 1996;2(3):163–166.

Shortell SM, Gillies R, Anderson D, et al. *Remaking Health Care in America.* San Francisco, CA: Jossey-Bass: 2000.

Stroud Jackson. Financing ALS (unpublished manuscript). homepage.mac.com/DHP/page8/page10/page10.html. Accessed December 11, 2008.

Sultz HA, Young KM. *Health Care USA. Understanding Its Organization and Delivery.* 6th ed. Gaithersburg, MD: Aspen; 2008.

# 22

# Home Care Agencies

## Dallas A. Forshew and Bob Osborne

Home care is a wide range of services provided to people in their homes who need additional assistance during the course of an illness. Good supportive care in amyotrophic lateral sclerosis (ALS) can support both patients and their caregivers, anticipate what problems might occur, and assist in obtaining tools and equipment designed to maintain the patient's independence for as long as possible.

We know that the best way to get care for ALS is through a multidisciplinary care team in which each member of the team is a specialist in his or her own field and also a specialist in ALS. The ALS Association and the Muscular Dystrophy Association have both designated many clinics as ALS specialty clinics. You can find the clinic closest to you through the Web sites listed at the end of this chapter. These clinics have a wide variety of specialists to give you a full spectrum of care. Team members might include a physician, nurse, social worker, physical therapist, occupational therapist, respiratory therapist, dietitian, psychologist, rehabilitation physician, pastoral care counselor, or hospice representative. Many of these therapists are also offered by your local home care agency. You would usually go to the ALS specialty clinic about every 3 months. The clinic team members will assess you and make suggestions. They may suggest that you obtain some services from a home care agency. Services from a home care agency have to be ordered by a physician, usually the ALS clinic physician. The home care agency can send their team members into your home if needed for more frequent care.

Home care can be described in two categories: home health care and attendant home care. We will look at each category separately.

## Home Health Care

Home health care provides licensed professionals such as registered nurses; medical social workers; physical, occupational, speech or respiratory therapists; and dietician or home health aides. The team approach is very similar to the team approach in a multidisciplinary ALS clinic. In order for insurance to cover the costs of home health care, the doctor must order the care and certify that there is a skilled need for the services, and that the patient is homebound.

*Skilled need* for the services means that there is a definite problem that requires the attention of a licensed practitioner. Examples would be a registered nurse needed for wound care, or a physical or occupational therapist needed for home safety evaluation and teaching caregivers how to move you or teaching exercises or how to use medical equipment.

*Homebound* is defined as being unable to leave your home without a great deal of effort. This does not mean that you are forced to stay in your home, just that in order to go to appointments, church, and so forth requires a lot of time and work to get there.

Medicare, Medicaid, and most insurance will cover the costs of home health care. Your doctor or nurse can direct you to agencies that are experienced and reliable. The agency will receive orders for your care from your doctor and will report your progress and any other needs or problems that might occur. Your doctor will order any changes that are needed in your plan of care.

Either you or your doctor can decide whether you need home health care, but only a doctor can order home health. If you think that you need home health care, talk to your doctor, nurse, or therapist.

It is important to talk with a representative from your insurance company to find out what your particular policy offers. An excellent method of working with your insurance company is to have a case manager, who usually is a nurse. If a case manager has not already been assigned by the insurance company, call and ask to have one assigned to you. Use your case manager as your contact person whenever you need to consult the insurance company. The case manager will become familiar with you, your disease, and your needs.

## The Initial Home Visit and What to Expect
## From a Home Care Agency

As a customer, you have the right to receive quality service from the agency. You also have the responsibility to be a wise consumer.

There is a lot to do at the intake visit. The purpose of the intake visit is to introduce the agency's services to you and for the agency to ask about your needs. This visit takes place in your home. The intake clinician is usually a nurse. She or he must learn about you, your medical condition, and your social situation (family, friends, other supports you may have in the community such as religious affiliation). You also need to get to know the clinician at this visit and learn about what the agency can offer. Remember to speak up and be a partner in making the plan for your care.

There are a number of other pieces of business that usually occur at the intake visit. The agency should provide you with a copy of the Patient's Bill of Rights and Responsibilities and discuss these with you. You should be given a full description of the agency's available services. In addition, the agency should give you information about services that are available through other means such as community support and resource services. The agency should research your insurance benefits and explain what is covered and what is not. It should describe its billing procedure and how it will notify you of noncovered services. The agency is required to fully inform you before services are started.

## Skilled Nursing Care

A registered nurse (RN) will oversee your care and coordinate the activities of other people who may come into your home to provide services. You will work with the nurse to determine what services are needed. Most of the types of therapists that you see at your ALS specialty clinic are available on an as-needed basis in your home through the home care agency. The therapists (team members) at your ALS clinic provide you with recommendations that are then carried out in your home or local community. An example is the role of the physical therapist. In the ALS clinic, the physical therapist is also an expert in ALS. The clinic physical therapist may note that you have a "frozen shoulder" and he or she may recommend some exercises and also recommend that you have some sessions with a local physical therapist. If it is too difficult for you to go to a local physical therapist for multiple visits, your ALS clinic team may contact a local home care agency so that a local physical therapist will go to your home. The local physical therapist will review the information from the clinic and then work with you and your family for several weeks—until your family has learned the exercises well and your shoulder is improved. So, the clinic team members will make recommendations, but the local therapists will carry out those recommendations. The nurse from the home care agency will coordinate the activities of the local therapists from the agency.

The first duty of the registered nurse is to meet with you and your family in your home to assess your needs and to develop a plan of care. You also have some responsibilities during the intake visit. You and your family should advocate for yourselves and speak up. Let the nurse know what you need and work with him or her to develop your plan of care.

In addition to the intake assessment, the nurse is responsible for ongoing assessment of your situation as it changes. The nurse can also provide patient and family education and basic counseling and perform any medical procedures.

## Home Health Aid Care

Home health aides (HHAs) take care of basic needs such as bathing, dressing, and feeding. Depending on the agency and the level of training, aides may also help with range-of-motion or other exercises. They may do some light housekeeping.

HHAs are often in short supply. Sometimes an agency will assign a different aide to you, perhaps without letting you know ahead of time. This can be very frustrating, especially if you have developed a close relationship with a particular aide. You will want to maintain good communication with the nurse from the agency who is your case manager, the one coordinating your care. Let the nurse know your feelings and ask if you can keep a consistent aide or just a few aids. It is very upsetting when the home care agency that sends the aids changes the person from time to time without consulting patients or families. Tell the nurse, "we know that we cannot do much about it, but do you have any suggestions on how to cope?"

## Social Workers and Psychological Care

ALS changes the lives of everyone it touches. This includes patients, their families, and their friends. Some people say that ALS is harder on the family than it is on the patient. It also is a progressive disease, and it seems that every time the patient and family become accustomed to a situation and begin to manage, the situation changes and everyone has to adjust again. This is a difficult process for everyone.

Social workers are specially trained to help patients and family members cope with physical and emotional changes in their lives. Although most people affected by ALS can cope on their own, it is hard! It is much easier to have some guidance from someone who is trained in this area. Just as a HHA can help to conserve your and your caregiver's physical energy, a social worker from an agency can help to conserve your emotional energy. An agency social worker can help to guide your feelings and help your family as everyone adjusts. Social workers are an important part of the home care team and should be consulted by all patients with ALS.

The social worker helps not only the patient but the members of the family. The emotional well-being of each of us is a compilation of our life experiences, expectations, and fears. Issues of the past, the present, and loss of the future need to be discussed openly. Family members have concerns very similar to yours, not only with respect to themselves but also related to their relationship with you. Family relationships are complex, and in the face of serious illness roles within the family may change. The agency social worker can give guidance toward resolution of both old and new concerns. The services of an agency social worker may be initiated by the agency nurse or by a member of your ALS clinic team. Your ALS doctor is the one who actually writes the order for any of the agency team members to come into your home. The agency usually handles getting the doctor's order by faxing the doctor's office.

Death and dying issues are in the forefront of the minds of all people with ALS and their families as soon as the diagnosis is made. These issues remain of concern throughout the illness, whether you and your family are talking about them or not. These concerns will be easier to deal with if a social worker helps. Do not be afraid to ask a social worker, nurse, or physician what the end of the disease may be like.

It is common to have difficulty coping when you are first told that ALS has entered your life. Some depression is not unusual but it deserves full attention. If you feel blue or depressed, talk with your agency or ALS clinic social worker or nurse, who can refer you or your family member for ongoing counseling. Also, tell your ALS clinic physician because medication can sometimes be helpful.

In addition to helping with feelings, social workers are often knowledgeable about insurance matters and social agencies. Most communities have a wide range of social agencies. Some are federal or state funded and some are locally sponsored. Organizations such as the Muscular Dystrophy Association or the ALS Association are excellent resources and possible sources of financial aid. Community service clubs, good works agencies, and church groups are some of the resources available. Other sources include Centers for Independent Living, equipment loan closets, support groups, and Meals on Wheels. Social workers can sort through the maze of agencies and make appropriate referrals.

### Physical Therapy

Physical therapists provide help with mobility issues. Their services are considered skilled. Although it would be nice to have a physical therapist come to your home regularly to do exercise, this is not practical in the long run. There are specific times when a physical therapist will be of greatest use to you. These times include evaluating home safety, teaching exercises for stiff or painful joints and muscles, teaching transferring techniques, and selecting equipment.

A home safety evaluation is a good idea if you are weak and falls are a concern. The physical therapist (or occupational therapist) can come to your home and make suggestions about the rearrangement of furniture, for instance, or the placement of handrails, and the selection of equipment for the bathroom. Most of the time, your ALS clinic team recognizes that you could benefit from a home safety evaluation and they ask your ALS clinic doctor for an order. This is frequently the initial reason that a home care agency gets involved in your care. Or, the home care nurse might call your ALS clinic with this idea. The agency nurse would talk with your ALS clinic nurse who would get the order from your ALS clinic doctor.

The physical therapist can decide which exercises would be most useful to you. He or she can do the exercises and then teach them to you and your family. Exercises are necessary to keep joints and ligaments limber. Range-of-motion exercises are needed if you are no longer stretching your joints in your day-to-day activities. For example, if arm weakness prevents you from reaching for items that are on the second shelf in the cupboard, you will need exercises to keep the shoulder free from stiffness and pain and to prevent the development of a frozen shoulder. This is an area of your care in which you can really make a difference in how you feel. You often can prevent pain by starting exercises when needed and keeping up with the exercises on a daily basis.

A physical therapist can help with transfer. Transferring from a wheelchair to a car can be tricky, as can many other transfers in the home. It is important to learn how to move someone properly to prevent injury to the patient and caregiver. A physical therapist can teach techniques that keep both you and your helper safe. This teaching should be done in the home by using your bathroom, your bed, your favorite chair, and your arm. The physical therapist may need to come for several teaching sessions until you and your caregiver have practiced and feel comfortable showing the therapist your new techniques.

Equipment selection, such as deciding which type of walker or wheelchair is best, can be confusing. The physical therapist can suggest appropriate equipment for your situation and teach you how to use it. It is a good idea to get some advice before you spend a lot of money. A physical therapist can be especially helpful in measuring you for a wheelchair and helping you select it.

## Occupational Therapy

People are often confused about the difference between an occupational therapist and a physical therapist. An occupational therapist usually works with the arms and with activities of daily living. A physical therapist usually works with the legs and mobility issues. Either can perform a home safety evaluation. They both work with exercises and suggest equipment.

An occupational therapist provides expertise with issues related to activities of daily living, such as bathing, dressing, and feeding. He or she can teach you tricks that will help you remain independent for as long as possible. An occupational therapist often suggests helpful equipment or exercises. He or she may be the person to perform a home safety evaluation for you.

## Speech Therapy

Speech therapists, sometimes called speech pathologists, are trained to work with both speech and swallowing problems. Swallowing problems usually are evaluated by a speech therapist in a clinic or hospital. Communication is the main concern of a home speech therapist.

The speech therapist can help you maximize your current ability to speak and swallow by teaching you useful tricks. Examples for swallowing might include tucking your chin slightly as you swallow, taking smaller bites of food, and chewing more slowly and carefully. Examples for communication might include speaking more slowly, facing the person to whom you are speaking, and writing out words if you become frustrated.

An important role of the speech therapist is to teach you many ways to communicate if your voice cannot be understood. These methods may range from handwriting to the use of a sophisticated computer system. Substitutions for vocal communication are sometimes called *augmentative communication*. Home speech therapists should be able to teach the basics of augmentative communication, but a specialist in augmentative communication is needed for high-tech equipment such as computers. Specialists in augmentative communication often work in larger hospitals or clinics.

## Nutrition Counseling

Dietitians assess your nutritional status and help both you and your family to adjust your diet as your needs and ability to swallow change. Dietitians may suggest avoiding certain foods, offer suggestions for foods or liquids that will be easier to handle, and suggest appropriate nutritional supplements if you are losing weight.

Some people with ALS eventually have trouble swallowing and cannot maintain their weight. The main purpose of the mouth and throat is to get food and fluids down the esophagus and into the stomach. The mouth, throat, and esophagus make up a "tube." If your own tube does not work well, you can replace it with a tube that does work well—a feeding tube. A feeding tube is a good idea if you take a very long time to eat, if food or fluids are "going down the wrong pipe" and you are coughing or choking, if you get tired eating, if food no longer appeals to you, or if you are losing too much weight. A feeding tube is often called a PEG tube, which stands for percutaneous endoscopic gastrostomy. It will be much easier and better for you physically if you have a feeding tube placed earlier rather than later, especially if you wait until you have lost a lot of weight or your breathing is not good. ALS as a disease can cause weight loss, and the better that weight can be maintained, the better the chance for a longer survival. A dietitian can best suggest the formula that should be used for tube feedings and that will keep your bowels functioning properly.

## Respiratory Therapy

Respiratory therapists can help you with breathing problems. The therapist can perform tests in your home to measure your ability to breathe. These tests are called pulmonary function tests (PFTs) and might include forced vital capacity (FVC), maximum inspiratory flow (MIF), and pulse oximetry. Pulse oximetry measures the amount of oxygen in your blood by using a clip on a finger. Respiratory therapists install, monitor, and teach the use of equipment such as noninvasive bilevel positive air pressure (BiPAP) machines.

Respiratory therapists often are available, not through standard home care agencies, but through agencies that specialize in home respiratory needs. Some larger medical equipment companies employ respiratory therapists to serve patients who use their equipment. A home care agency may contract with another agency for respiratory therapy services, but frequently these services must be arranged separately from the patient's regular home care. This is easily arranged through your physician.

Invasive ventilation for the patient with ALS in the home is a complex issue and is not addressed here. However, you should know that tracheostomy and invasive ventilation (a life-support breathing machine) is an option and can be handled in your home with the help of a respiratory therapist.

## Attendant Care

After a time, your caregiver and other family members may need some help. ALS is a difficult disease for both family and patients. Your family will need both emotional energy and physical energy to give you support over the months and years. We want to keep your family caregiver(s) in good shape so they do not become overtired or burned out. We want to take care of the caregiver(s). One way to do this is to employ a HHA from a home nursing agency. The insurance company might pay for the services of a HHA if a skilled service is being provided at the same time.

Attendant care describes the services of a trained caregiver. Some agencies provide attendant care only, not as part of a home health care package. Insurance does not usually pay for attendant care, although some long-term care policies do provide this benefit.

Agencies that provide attendant care should be bonded and should be the employer so you do not have to be concerned about taxes and deductions from the attendant's wages. You may, however, chose to privately hire someone directly, and many communities have groups of people available for direct employment by the family and/or caregiver.

Attendant care is most important in families affected by ALS. Aside from the invaluable help that an attendant may provide, this type of care allows family members and caregivers to continue in their role and just "be there" for the patient without the added burdens of bathing, toileting, transfers, etc. This respite from the role of care provider is most important for allowing those close to the patient the time to be wife/husband/child/friend.

## Summary

Whether home health care or attendant care or a combination of both is the right choice for your particular needs, it is important to know that help is available, and no one can journey through this disease process without help. Your physician, nurse, or social worker can assist you in arranging for these types of care.

## Resources

AbleData Database: 800-227-0216

ACCESS Program (Advocating for Chronic Conditions, Entitlements, and Social Services): 888-700-7070. This is a toll-free number and a free service to help with insurance and disability qualifications.

Amyotrophic Lateral Sclerosis Association: 800-782-4747, www.alsa.org

Family Caregiver Alliance: 800-445-8106, www.caregiver.org

Muscular Dystrophy Association: 800-572-1717, www.mdausa.com

National Association of Area Agencies on the Aging: 800-677-1116

National Association for Home Care: 202-547-7424, www.nahc.org

National Council on the Aging: 800-424-4096, www.ncoa.org

National Hospice and Palliative Care Organization: 800-658-8898, www.nhpco.org

National Rehabilitation Information Center: 800-346-2742, www.naric.com

National Respite Locator Service: 800-773-5433, www.chtop.com

Well Spouse Foundation: 800-838-1338, www.wellspouse.org

Your Medicare Handbook is comprehensive guide from the Department of Health and Human Services. You can receive a copy by calling the Medicare Hotline at 1-800-638-6833.

# Managing Advanced Disease and End-of-Life Issues

# 23

# Palliative Care and Amyotrophic Lateral Sclerosis: An Example of the Management of Advanced Disease

## Bushra Malik and Mark J. Stillman

For the past two decades controversies surrounding end-of-life decision making in amyotrophic lateral sclerosis (ALS) have been featured prominently in both the medical literature and in the general media. In the form of legal appeals and even televised coverage of actual deaths, patients with ALS have appeared at the forefront of the debate on physician-assisted suicide (PAS) and euthanasia. Initiatives by lay organizations to pass physician-assisted suicide laws in Oregon, Washington State, and New York served to highlight past and present deficiencies in end-of-life care in the American medical system. As recently as 1998, a large survey showed that 56% of patients with ALS admitted to considering assisted suicide, and nearly 90% would reconsider it if it were legalized. Three fourths of all caregivers concurred.

Patients with ALS have limited options with respect to treatment and inevitably face decisions about accepting or forgoing life-sustaining therapies. Patient and caregiver concerns reflect fears of suffocation and pain, manifesting as both hopelessness and helplessness. Physicians caring for patients with ALS frequently fail to recognize and address patients' pain, depression, and consuming sense of loss. Because of these issues, the palliative care model, with its open style of communication among various interactive health care disciplines, is devoted to improving the quality of life for patients with incurable diseases, such as ALS.

Hospital-based palliative care programs began in the United States in the late 1980s at only a handful of institutions and now number more than 1,200. Educators in medical and nursing schools are now finally recognizing the role of palliative care, and the management of advanced disease, as a new field of medicine devoted to these patients and their families, and medical training is slowly changing.

## What Is Palliative Care?

The World Health Organization defines palliative care as the care offered by a *multidisciplinary* team of doctors, nurses, social workers, therapists, clergy, and volunteers and describes it as "the active total care of patients whose disease is not responsive to curative treatment. Control of pain, of other symptoms, and of psychological, social, and spiritual problems is paramount. The goal of palliative care is the achievement of the best quality of life for patients and their families. . . . Palliative care . . . affirms life and regards dying as a normal process, . . . neither hastens nor postpones death, . . . provides relief from distressing symptoms, . . . integrates the psychological and the spiritual aspects of care, . . . offers a support system to help the family cope during the patient's illness and in their own bereavement." Multidisciplinary refers to the continually interactive nature of care with the patients and their caregivers as the focus. Care is coordinated preferably by a scheduler or coordinator central to all of the involved services so that it is integrated and seamless, and the clinical service providers have numerous opportunities to communicate.

The components of a typical palliative care service are listed in Table 23.1. (Hospice care, as it relates to ALS, is discussed in more detail in Chapter 24.) In the United States, palliative care is predominantly a home-based system of care, and its development and refinement have been fostered by the Medicare Hospice Benefit, written into law by Congress in 1982. Regardless of which component of palliative care establishes first contact with a patient with ALS (or some other disease), the goals and principles of care are the same: to treat the patient and his or her family, using a multidisciplinary approach, for the purpose of comfort and symptom relief and to improve quality of life for as long as feasible.

Many medical practitioners and lay people equate hospice care with palliative care, failing to realize that hospice is only one component of it. At least in the United States, hospice care is a form of home-based palliative care that a

**Table 23.1** Components of a Palliative Care Service

---

1. Hospice

    (a) Home based

    (b) Inpatient or residential

2. Inpatient acute care facility for the management of acute medical or symptom control issues that cannot be managed as an outpatient

3. Inpatient palliative care consultation service for consultation of patients with palliative care issues on surgical and medical services

4. Outpatient consultation services

---

patient and family elect when life expectancy is limited to 6 months or less. On a broader basis, as it applies to cancer care, palliative care is the management of anticipated and unanticipated complications of a disease during the disease's natural trajectory.

## Palliative Approaches to Patient Care

Little has been written about palliative care of the population with ALS in comparison with a larger literature devoted to the diagnosis of ALS, its pathophysiology, and attempted cures. What has been written is derived from small studies, but the work is thoughtful and applicable to the whole. Certain principles of care—universal principles of care for any patient population—should be followed:

- Open communication between health care practitioners, patient, and family
- Good nursing care, with particular attention paid to body positioning to prevent skin breakdown in the bed-bound patient
- Awareness that most patients have a normal mental status even when they are unable to communicate
- Special attention to facilitation of communication, swallowing, and breathing
- Anticipation of consequences of immobility: constipation, pain, anxiety and depression, insomnia, fatigue, bedsores, and urinary retention

It cannot be overemphasized that the recipients of care include not only the persons with ALS but also their family and primary caregivers. Considering that the progression of ALS implies an inevitable dependence in toileting, eating, and such seemingly mundane tasks as changing position in bed or even scratching an itch, failure to recognize the physical and psychological stresses on the caregiver is a grievous oversight. The inclusion of psychiatric social workers, specially trained nurses, home health aides, volunteers, and respite time (brief hospital admissions to allow a family under stress a period of rest) in the benefit package under the Medicare Hospice Benefit indicates that the hospice–palliative care approach anticipates such problems.

## Communicating With the Patient and Family

Like any seriously ill patient, the person with ALS is in danger of sudden fatal deterioration resulting from respiratory failure or intercurrent medical complications. The family needs to be informed of this from the outset in order to make an informed decision about the level of care in such a circumstance. Involved in this decision is a consideration of cardiopulmonary resuscitation and placement of an endotracheal tube for ventilation, as well as the eventual surgical insertion of a breathing tube (tracheostomy) for long-term respiratory support. As discussed below, some people with ALS choose to have a tracheostomy to help them breathe when diaphragmatic and chest wall muscles weaken to the point that independent breathing is no longer possible. Failure to anticipate such emergencies can lead to the imposition of unwanted treatment by emergency medical staff.

## Symptom Control

Table 23.2 lists the symptoms that most commonly plague the person with ALS and that present a challenge to the palliative care or hospice team.

### Pain

Although classic neurology textbooks regard pain as an uncommon symptom of ALS, the fact is that as many as two thirds of all patients may experience pain. The pain is described as aching, cramping, or burning, and it may be attributed to either muscle cramps, abnormal stress on the musculoskeletal system from immobility (e.g., bedsores, stiff joints), or spasticity (increased muscle tone) from involvement of the upper motor neuron tracts.

Clearly, good nursing care is important, with frequent positioning and passive mobilization of joints. That may be all that is needed for some patients, but pain medications are necessary for others. The pharmacologic treatment of spasticity and stiffness is limited. Baclofen and tizanidine both work in the spinal cord to inhibit spasticity and muscle stiffness around a joint, but they do so at the expense of sedation and weakness. For those patients who rely on their spasticity to walk, the drug-induced weakness can be a problem. The dose of baclofen is between 10 and 80 mg a day in 3 or 4 divided doses, with a maximum dose of 200 mg per day. The recommended dose of tizanidine is between 6 and 24 mg per day in divided doses. Valium and other muscle relaxants may be tried for

**Table 23.2** Symptoms Common to Patients With ALS

- Pain
- Dysphagia (difficulty swallowing)
- Drooling
- Dyspnea (shortness of breath)
- Weakness
- Bedsores
- Inability to sleep
- Anxiety and depression
- Constipation

spasticity but are probably better used for muscle cramps. However, their side effects and cost make them a second choice to baclofen. Other medications such as dantrolene sodium have been used for ALS-related muscle spasms and spasticity, but they are used less frequently because of side effects.

When specific attempts to treat the pain fail, the use of pain medications should follow the guidelines established by the World Health Organization for cancer pain and acute pain. The "stepladder" approach, as it has come to be known, starts with the recognition of pain and the initiation of treatment with a drug suited to the type of pain the patient describes. Mild pain is treated with low doses of an opioid medication (narcotic) or a nonopioid analgesic. As the pain increases, either a stronger opioid replaces the initial weaker analgesic or larger doses of the opioid are added (Figure 23.1).

The successful management of pain depends on the clinician's familiarity and understanding of the mechanism of pain and the appropriate use of analgesics. The use of opioids requires the experience and skill to balance beneficial effects with side effects, and this is described, in detail, in textbooks on pain and cancer management. A brief description of the most commonly used agents follows.

The opioid analgesics are the cornerstone of therapy for cancer pain and are the most useful class of analgesics for the management of any pain that is resistant

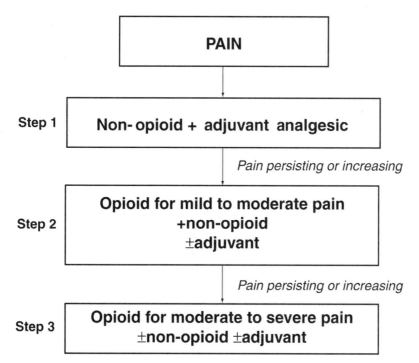

**Figure 23.1** The World Health Organization stepladder approach to the management of cancer pain.

to nonnarcotic medications. The drugs belonging to the morphine (or mu opioid) family are the most frequently used group of opioid analgesics and the ones most familiar to physicians. Weak analgesics such as hydrocodone or oxycodone are prescribed for mild or intermittent pain. Hydrocodone and oxycodone both come as combination tablets attached to either aspirin or acetaminophen. This combination is convenient, but it tends to limit the number of tablets taken in a day because of concerns about toxicity from either aspirin or acetaminophen. Fortunately, oxycodone comes in a pure preparation and is available as a liquid concentrate; it also is available in a delayed-release tablet preparation, which is ideal for patients with prolonged pain. In the delayed-release form it may be taken by mouth every 12 hours instead of every 4 hours, which is the recommended interval for the immediate-release liquid or tablet formulations. The dose depends on the severity of the pain—hence, the importance of careful assessment by the clinician—and the patient's tolerance of the medication. Doses start at 5 to 10 mg of oxycodone every 4 to 6 hours and increase as needed to control the pain, either as pure oxycodone or combined with 325 mg of acetaminophen or aspirin per tablet. Delayed-release oxycodone tablets come in 10 mg, 20 mg, 40 mg, and 80 mg.

Of all the opioid drugs, morphine sulfate remains the most versatile because it is available in short-acting liquid and tablet, long-acting tablet, and injectable formulations. It can be prescribed by mouth, under the tongue, by feeding tube, by rectum, or by injection (subcutaneously, intravenously, or intramuscularly), and charts are available that outline dosage and routes of administration. In turn, the dosage of morphine depends on the severity and persistence of the pain, whereas the route of administration is determined by the patient. One of the pill formulations can be prescribed if the patient is able to swallow. If a percutaneous endoscopic gastrostomy (PEG) is available and the patient cannot swallow, liquid immediate-release morphine can be prescribed via tube on an every-4-hours basis. For the patient who is unable to swallow and without a PEG, immediate-release morphine can be provided under the tongue as either a solid tablet or liquid formulation (10-, 15-, or 30-mg tablet, or liquid concentrate 20 mg/mL), and the dose can be repeated as needed in 2 to 4 hours. Rectal preparations of morphine come as immediate-release 15-mg suppositories or delayed-release oral tablets, which dissolve slowly and are absorbed. The delayed-release tablets are available in 15-, 30-, 60-, 100-, and 200-mg doses.

When absorption through oral or rectal mucosa is inadvisable or impossible, morphine can be infused by the intravenous or subcutaneous route. Portable pumps that infuse concentrated solutions of morphine have been in use for many years and have remedied many previously intractable pain management problems. A "rescue" button can be installed in the pump's program to permit the delivery of small doses of morphine in situations in which pain breaks through (patient-controlled analgesia).

The dose of morphine depends on the severity and duration of the pain, and careful evaluation and reassessment are necessary to adjust the dose. Oral doses as small as 5 mg every 4 to 6 hours, as needed, may be adequate for a patient with mild or intermittent pain, whereas other patients may require high subcutaneous infusion rates of morphine for comfort.

An opioid-eluting patch, the fentanyl transdermal system, which is available in 12.5-, 25-, 50-, and 100-µg patches, can be placed on the skin every 72 hours in situations in which the patient is unable or unwilling to take medications by mouth. The 25-µg patch provides approximately the same analgesia as 15 mg of oral morphine every 4 hours, but exact doses must be individualized. Fentanyl lozenges (Actiq) are also available now in a solid formulation of fentanyl citrate on a stick in the form of a lollipop that dissolves slowly in the mouth for transmucosal absorption. Fentanyl lozenges are available in 6 dosages, from 200 to 1,600 µg in 200-µg increments. These lozenges are intended for opioid-tolerant individuals and are effective in treating breakthrough pain. In December 2007, the FDA issued a warning concerning risks of opioid overdose with fentanyl patches. This was a particular concern in the following circumstances: opioid-naive individuals, defective or leaky patches, or patches exposed to high temperatures while on the patient. Since fat is the reservoir for this opioid drug, and since it takes 16 to 24 hours to reach analgesia in healthy adults, practitioners should be very familiar with the use of fentanyl before initiating therapy in the population with ALS. To make the situation worse, generic fentanyl patches made by Actavis South Atlantic LLC (formerly known as Abrika Pharmaceuticals Inc.) were recalled in early 2008 because of leakage and risks of patient overdose. Brand name Duragesic patches were not the subject of this recall, however.

New products have recently entered the market and their clinical use is governed by the same principles applied to older products: long-duration opioids for moderate to severe, prolonged or chronic pain, and rapid-acting, short-duration medications reserved for breakthrough pain episodes. Dispersible fentanyl pills (Fentora) for breakthrough pain, much like the lozenges, are tablets placed in the cheek and are absorbed through the buccal mucosa. Fentanyl is available in 100, 200, 300, 400, 600, and 800 µg, and its advantage over the lozenge is its quicker absorption into the bloodstream at lower dosage. Oxymorphone (Opana) is available as immediate-release 5- and 10-mg tablets and as an extended-release in strengths of 5, 10, 20, and 40 mg. They are, however, indicated only for patients already on a regular schedule of strong opioids for a prolonged period.

Side effects of opioids—respiratory depression, constipation, nausea and vomiting, and concerns for addiction—are widely recognized. As in the population with cancer, addiction, or psychological dependence, is virtually nonexistent, although nausea and vomiting can occur with any opioid agent, and constipation is always a constant threat. Use of antiemetics and laxatives is therefore advised. Avoiding respiratory depression requires a skilled hand, especially in the opioid-naive patient. Tolerance to the respiratory depressant effects of opioid analgesics fortunately develops rapidly in the population with non-ALS pain; in general, in the population with cancer, any patient who is awake and comfortably breathing on a stable dose of a scheduled, short-duration opioid (i.e., not methadone or levorphanol) is not in immediate danger of respiratory depression.

The use of opioids should always be attempted by clinicians who are comfortable with their application in practice, particularly in patients with compromised respiratory status. Any seasoned pain practitioner, when asked how to treat the patient with ALS suffering from pain, would unequivocally stress the importance of starting "low and slow," with frequent observations at time of peak effect for analgesia and adverse effects. If the treating physician has any concerns or doubt, it is always advisable to err on the side of patient safety and ask for help from someone who is more experienced, especially in the situation where respiratory compromise is a threat.

## Dysphagia

Dysphagia, or difficulty in swallowing, is a common symptom of ALS and occasionally is the presenting symptom. The problem extends not only to foods but also to a patient's own secretions, resulting in the embarrassment of drooling. It is not difficult to understand how dysphagia occurs if one keeps in mind that ALS is a disease of motor function. Weakness of the striated muscle—the tongue, pharyngeal muscles, and the upper esophagus—makes chewing and propulsion of food to the back of the throat and the esophagus increasingly difficult, leading to pooling of secretions and foodstuffs. Liquids, in particular, follow the quickest and most direct route directed by gravity, leading to aspiration down the trachea, and followed by reflexive coughing (choking). As a consequence, oral intake decreases and weight loss ensues because of the fear of choking or exhaustion from coughing spells. Few things are as disconcerting to the sympathetic caregiver as to see a patient suffering in this manner—wasting away from starvation despite a desire to eat.

There are several approaches to this problem. The first and simplest approach is to alter the texture of the food. If necessary, the advice of a dietitian who is familiar with swallowing disorders should be sought. Under the Medicare Hospice Benefit, a speech pathologist trained to evaluate swallowing disorders should be available on an as-needed basis. Blenderized food or food thickened with starch will enable many people to get the liquid and calories needed to maintain weight, initially.

Other options are available for those patients in whom swallowing is impaired. In the past, a procedure known as a cricopharyngotomy (the surgical sectioning of the pharyngeal muscles) was reserved for patients with spastic swallowing disorders, but technical advancements in feeding tubes have made this procedure obsolete. Until recently, the procedure of choice was a nasogastric (NG) feeding tube, a small rubber tube placed through the nose into the stomach. Pliable, silicon NG catheters are much more comfortable than the rubber nasal tubes, but they have a small diameter and tend to clog. Several procedures to deal with the problem of feeding people who cannot swallow have been developed in the past 15 years, including PEG and, less commonly, percutaneous endoscopic jejunostomy (PEJ). Feedings with clear liquids can safely commence within 24 to 48 hours of endoscopic (fiberoptic) tube placement through the abdominal wall, gradually building up to 100% supplementation of caloric needs through the use of commercial liquid diets.

The widespread use of the PEG/PEJ tube feeding has led to symptomatic improvement in the population with ALS—less choking to be certain—but has not led to prolongation of survival when compared with NG feeding. Moreover, the procedure of inserting the tube is not without complications, and there may be abdominal wall pain severe enough to warrant opioid therapy for the first 24 to 48 hours. Even in the most experienced hands, there is a 1% to 4% 24-hour postoperative mortality resulting from pulmonary complications; postprocedural pain leads to abdominal splinting and places patients at great risk for developing pneumonia, pulmonary embolus, and respiratory failure. As a result, it is recommended that patients be considered candidates for PEG tube placement *earlier* rather than later—when weight loss approaches 5% and bulbar symptoms (dysphagia, dysarthria, or aspiration of oral secretions) first develop. Patients should have preoperative pulmonary function tests to document enough reserve lung function to mount an adequate cough.

The patient's and family's reluctance to submit to a surgical procedure in favor of more natural feeding methods frequently delays this procedure. When the patient finally agrees, it often is too late to reverse the weight loss or avoid the perioperative complications. Every effort should be made to perform placement of a PEG relatively early.

## Drooling

Drooling is an embarrassing and distressing symptom that results from a patient's inability to swallow saliva often enough to prevent overflow. Beyond the obvious use of a handkerchief, control of drooling requires drying out or suppressing the salivary glands. Surgical and radiotherapeutic control of salivation has been attempted, but medicinal manipulation is usually as effective. A number of drugs may be useful.

Anticholinergic agents such as scopolamine hydrochloride and medications with anticholinergic side effects are frequently used to control drooling. A scopolamine patch used to treat motion sickness provides a convenient way to dry the mouth without the need to ingest yet another pill. This 1-mg patch is placed on the skin, usually behind the ear (but can be placed on any glabrous skin), and is left in place for 3 days. Anticholinergic antidepressants such as amitriptyline, nortriptyline, or desipramine predictably cause dry mouth as a side effect, even in doses as low as 10 mg per day. These agents have additional benefits such as pain relief, appetite stimulation, and the treatment of depression. Another medication whose side effects are useful in drying salivary secretions is the antihistamine cyproheptadine. This medication stimulates the appetite and usually is effective in a dose of 4 to 8 mg at bedtime, although higher doses sometimes are needed. A related antihistamine, diphenhydramine, in a dose of 25 to 50 mg every 6 to 8 hours, can have the same effect.

Other anticholinergic drugs that have been used to dry up saliva include benztropine (1–6 mg/day by mouth or tube in divided doses), trihexyphenidyl (6–10 mg/day by tube or mouth in divided doses), and glycopyrrolate (3–8 mg/day by mouth or tube in divided doses). The shortcoming of all these drugs, with the exception of glycopyrrolate (Rubinol), is the tendency to cause confusion and sedation. Most of them have been used to treat Parkinson disease for the very reason that they penetrate the blood–brain barrier.

Two other useful agents are propranolol and lithium. β-blockers, of which propranolol is the standard, have been used to control mucus-rich secretions when anticholinergics have failed (propranolol, 10 to 20 mg twice a day, or metoprolol, 12.5 to 25 mg twice a day). Lithium carbonate, the medication for bipolar (manic-depressive) disorder, has mucosal dryness as one of its side effects and has been used for this purpose in patients with ALS. The dose is 600 to 1,200 mg per day in divided doses.

Caregivers should be aware that saliva is essential not only for food ingestion but also for dental maintenance and health. The loss of the protective effect of salivary antibodies against bacteria increases the risk of tooth decay; good dental hygiene is therefore essential.

## Shortness of Breath (Dyspnea)

The sensation of shortness of breath is a serious and feared symptom in ALS. In general medical practice, there are numerous causes of dyspnea, including pneumonia, chronic lung disease (e.g., emphysema, chronic bronchitis), congestive heart failure, venous thromboembolism, and asthma. Although a person with ALS can have any of these, the progressive muscle weakness that accompanies the disease causes patients with ALS to develop restricted ability to breathe. Simply stated, they neither have the chest wall strength nor mobility to take deep breaths. Portions of the lung may therefore collapse and pneumonia may develop. Patients describe a force or a weight restricting their ability to take a deep breath or to fully empty their lungs. The great fear is choking or suffocating to death.

### Initial Treatment

Initial medical management should be directed at correcting any potentially treatable cause. This should include (a) controlling secretions and preventing regurgitation of tube feedings; (b) optimizing the patient's position in bed to minimize any chance of aspiration and maximize the ability of the diaphragm to function properly; (c) providing oxygen when needed; and (d) treating lung infections, bronchitis, or asthma. When these options fail or do not exist, the only therapeutic choices are to provide mechanical ventilation for the patient or to suppress the symptoms of breathlessness medicinally (i.e., palliative management).

The ultimate consequence of respiratory failure is death as a result of elevated carbon dioxide level (hypercapnea) and decreased oxygen level (hypoxia). If the symptoms accompanying dyspnea—agitation, anxiety, and air hunger—can be controlled, death can be peaceful, with the patient quietly entering a coma. Any agitation can be suppressed with sedative hypnotics. The alternative—the prolongation of life on mechanical ventilation after tracheostomy or intubation (insertion of a plastic breathing tube into the trachea)—is viewed as heroic therapy by many patients, families, and clinicians, merely forestalling the inevitable progression of the disease. It is therefore essential that families and caregivers of patients with ALS be aware of the natural history of ALS from the outset.

Symptoms indicating the approaching need of ventilatory support include disrupted sleep, orthopnea (the inability to breathe while lying flat), daytime sleepiness, dyspnea with exercise, ineffective cough, and less than 50% of the predicted ability to exhale (forced vital capacity, FVC). All too often patients and families confront impending respiratory failure without prior knowledge of treatment options. In particular, they may not be aware that the patient can receive breathing support from either a closely fitting mask, a tube placed in the trachea (endotracheal tube), or a surgically inserted hole in the trachea (tracheostomy). A patient who is mechanically ventilated for more than 2 weeks eventually will need a tracheostomy because an endotracheal tube cannot be tolerated for a longer period. One recent study found that 92% of patients who were on mechanical ventilator machines after tracheostomy had not decided in advance to undergo intubation and artificial respiration. Almost one-third were not satisfied with their quality of life as respirator-dependent patients. Sadly, many patients would not have opted for mechanical ventilation if they had known of the financial and social burdens placed on their families or if they had known they would have to go to a skilled nursing unit. The role of advance directives and living wills is apparent in such a situation, as discussed in Chapter 24.

The alternative to tracheostomy and ventilation is noninvasive ventilation (NIV) using a tight-fitting nasal mask or face mask. This is an adequate option if the patient can tolerate the mask, has no problems managing secretions, and does not aspirate. *Patients who have poor airway protection are at risk of aspiration with this ventilation technique.*

Nasal NIV is therefore indicated for willing patients who do not have brain stem dysfunction (i.e., altered swallowing mechanisms) and who do not need suction. It is covered under the Medicare Hospice Benefit and costs less and is associated with less complex care than mechanical ventilation and tracheostomy. More than 90% of patients are able to stay at home on NIV. Success with NIV can be predicted by the following:

- Absence of excess secretions
- Properly fitting face or nasal mask
- Willingness to wear mask

- A desire to live
- A good caregiver

## Symptomatic Treatment

There are well-described techniques for the relief of dyspnea, borrowed from intensive care medicine, where these approaches are routinely used for people with cardiac or pulmonary dysfunction. The benefits of opioid analgesics have been amply demonstrated for the treatment of air hunger of cardiac pulmonary edema (severe heart failure). When given in small intravenous injections, morphine reduces shortness of breath and the inflated filling pressures of a flooded heart in heart failure. Oral preparations of morphine sulfate and morphine-related narcotics have been used in a similar manner and given on a round-the-clock basis for constant shortness of breath. The few studies that confirm the utility of opioids have demonstrated improved exercise tolerance for patients suffering from chronic obstructive lung disease.

Recent interest in inhaled or nebulized opioids has led to their increased use for patients with end-stage disease and associated breathlessness. The benefit of nebulized or aerosolized drug is its direct delivery to the sites (and presumably the receptors) where it is needed. Systemic absorption and side effects are limited. Despite few data in ALS, morphine sulfate and other drugs are being used in hand-held bedside nebulizers with seemingly good results. Starting doses of morphine are 5 mg of injectable solution nebulized in normal saline every 4 to 6 hours as needed. The dose can be increased to 10 to 20 mg per treatment, as indicated. If the patient cannot tolerate morphine, a suitable alternative is fentanyl, 25 to 100 μg nebulized in normal saline every 4 to 6 hours as needed.

Even with nebulized drugs, there are concerns about side effects, especially respiratory depression in patients with impaired ventilatory function. This fear has not been borne out in chronic obstructive lung disease, although there have been anecdotal reports of respiratory depression with nebulized morphine. In cases where nebulized morphine has rarely been associated with wheezing, fentanyl has been used safely.

Other medications have been useful in treating dyspnea and associated anxiety. Sedative hypnotics have been used for years in the intensive care unit to treat agitated ventilated patients when the agitation interferes with ventilation. Benzodiazepines (diazepam, lorazepam, midazolam) and barbiturates have all been used in this situation. There has been recent interest in the phenothiazines, a class of drugs designed for the treatment of agitated psychoses. Their use has now been extended to the agitation caused by dyspnea. Chlorpromazine and methotrimeprazine have been used extensively on palliative medicine services in both the United States and Europe. Newer atypical antipsychotics, such as quetiapine and olanzapine, are being used in other fields of medicine for the purpose of sedation and anxiety reduction. These recently introduced drugs offer less tendency for serious reduction in blood pressure and are nowhere as likely to cause disturbing involuntary movements such as dystonia or akathisia.

## Bedsores

Bedsores, or decubitus ulcers, are a common complication of immobility, although they are relatively rare in patients with ALS. Frequent turning and positioning in bed is needed to prevent them from developing, and special beds using airflow or continuously moving pellets have been designed for patients with ALS, spinal cord injury, and Guillain Barré syndrome. Once a decubitus ulcer develops, however, meticulous attention must be paid to keeping pressure off the wound so that blood flow returns and airflow around the wound is maximized. Dead tissue must be removed and infection treated with dressing changes and wound cleaning; only in this way can new skin grow in and surgical grafting be avoided. There are a variety of ways to debride decubitus in the home, including wet to dry saline dressings, wet to dry iodophor dressings, specially developed adhesives, and spray granules. Severe wounds with superinfection and exposure of bone and deep tissues require surgical consultation and debridement (regular removal of damaged tissue) with or without skin grafting. It is best to prevent the development of skin breakdown by keeping the patient dry and well positioned.

## Constipation

Constipation is common in ALS, even though the disease does not affect the smooth (automatic) muscle function in the bowel wall. Immobility and drugs such as opioids induce constipation. When this problem is combined with the patient's inability to self-toilet, it can create exceedingly unpleasant and humiliating situations. As for patients without ALS, the treatment of constipation should follow a stepped approach starting with the maintenance of bowel hydration through the use of food fiber and adequate liquids as well as the institution of a set pattern of bowel elimination. A daily rectal suppository or a phosphosoda enema may help regulate the bowels, and stool softeners such as docusate should be used daily. For more severe constipation, cathartics such as magnesium compounds (milk of magnesia or magnesium citrate) or senna pills (maximum 6 pills twice daily) may be started on a regular basis. If persistent constipation is anticipated, especially with the use of opioid analgesics, the addition of other agents may be necessary. Osmotic agents that induce bowel motions, such as lactulose (30 to 60 mL 1 to 3 times a day) or 70% sorbitol (30 to 60 mL 1 to 3 times a day) can be very effective for the most resistant cases of drug-induced constipation.

## Insomnia

Many people with ALS complain of an inability to fall asleep. Table 23.3 outlines the possible causes of insomnia. The first task is to correct any reversible causes such as pain and dyspnea. Many agents are now available for the treatment of depression and anxiety. Once again, the tricyclic antidepressants are effective agents for depression, and their side effects of sedation, dry mouth, and appetite stimulation can be useful. Newer nonsedating antidepressants have been introduced in the past few years, including the selective serotonin and norepinephrine reuptake

**Table 23.3** Causes of Insomnia in the Population With ALS

- Depression/anxiety
- Inability to adjust posture
- Cramps/pain
- Dyspnea
- Reversal of sleep/wake cycle

**Table 23.4** Antidepressant Medications

|                                    | Dose (mg) | Comment |
|------------------------------------|-----------|---------|
| **Tricyclic Antidepressants**      |           |         |
| Amitriptyline                      | 10–250    | Given at night preferably |
| Nortriptyline                      | 10–250    | Given at night preferably |
| Doxepine                           | 10–250    | Given at night preferably |
| Imipramine                         | 10–250    | Given at night preferably |
| **Quartenary Antidepressants**     |           |         |
| Trazodone                          | 25–150    | Given at night to enhance sleep |
| **Selective Serotonin Reuptake Inhibitors** |  |         |
| Fluoxetine (Prozac)                | 10–60     | Tends to energize; give in AM |
| Sertraline (Zoloft)                | 25–200    | Tends to energize; give in AM |
| Paroxetine (Paxil)                 | 10–40     | Tends to energize; give in AM |

inhibitors, such as fluoxetine, sertraline, paroxetine, duloxetine, and venlafaxine. Table 23.4 lists the medications for the treatment of depression and their range of doses. The antipsychotic chlorpromazine, along with the newer atypical antipsychotic agents mentioned above, is an excellent medication for inducing sleep and at the same time is effective for treating anxiety, agitation, nausea, and vomiting. The dose pf chlorpromazine is 12.5 to 100 mg by mouth at nighttime, or given by g-tube, intramuscularly, or intravenously. For quetiapine the starting dose is 12.5 to 25 mg by mouth or per g-tube, while the dose for olanzapine to induce sleep is 1.25 to 5 mg at bedtime.

## Depression In Patients and Caregivers

It comes as no surprise that delivery of a diagnosis of ALS exacts an enormous emotional toll, affecting the psychological, somatic, and existential well-being of the patient. Recent attention has been paid to the effect of ALS on the patient's primary caregiver, with some interesting revelations. One would expect patients with ALS to bear the major brunt of receiving the diagnosis of an incurable disease, but surprisingly, one study found a relatively low level of depression among the patients. However, there was a high correlation between depression in the patients' caregivers and depression in the patients, suggesting that more attention paid to the caregivers' mental health would be rewarded in improvements in the patient with ALS. What determined the level of distress in the caregiver happened to be the appreciation of deteriorating quality of life in the patient and the perception of isolation and a loss of social support.

Recent major advances in the drug therapy for depression promise benefit to both groups. Newer antidepressants such at the serotonin reuptake inhibitors (fluoxetine, citalopram, paroxetine, and sertraline) have few side effects and work relatively quickly. A newer class of antidepressants includes venlafaxine and duloxetine, and they provide not only rapid treatment of depression but also analgesic properties. However, drugs alone are frequently not the answer, and the multidisciplinary approach of palliative medicine and hospice anticipates the impact of serious illness not only on the patient but also on the family. Built into the services provided, particularly under the Medicare Hospice Benefit, are social work, clergy, respite care, home health care while the patient is alive, and grief counseling for one year after death. As other chapters in this book discuss, the major benefit of a multidisciplinary approach, embodied in palliative medicine and hospice care, is total care, including mental health care, of the patient and his or her caregiver(s) during the trajectory of the illness.

## Special Considerations

In a large medical center, the practitioner in hospice or palliative care, along with other essential members of the team, such as the hospice nurse and the hospice's member of the clergy, can serve as an invaluable resource with the decision to withdraw a ventilator or feeding tube. Tested bioethical principles underlie the decision by hospital personnel to withdraw life support when efforts to reverse medical and personal deterioration are futile and to help deal with the personal tragedy of this decision. The practice guidelines used in intensive care units for withdrawing ventilator support for brain-dead patients can be applied to ALS. Obviously, it is easier to withdraw ventilatory support in a comatose patient, as is frequently the case in intensive care units dealing with trauma and cardiac arrests, but medications are available to sedate awake or conscious patients so that there is no perceptible respiratory distress when the ventilator is disconnected from the tracheostomy tube. It is important that the managing team be absolutely certain that the entire family agrees with the decision and documents this. This family decision often is based on an advance directive or a living will.

If the person with ALS does not have such a document, careful discussions should precede any action, and ethics consultants, clergy members, and social workers may enormously facilitate this difficult medical and social decision.

The procedure involves sedating the patient enough to prevent respiratory distress before disconnecting the ventilator. This can be done with an opioid analgesic, a sedative hypnotic (e.g., a barbiturate such as pentobarbital), a sedating phenothiazine (e.g., chlorpromazine), or a combination of these medications; extra medication should be on hand should respiratory distress develop. Depending on the family's desires, family members, friends, and clergy can be present in the room, or the withdrawal can be done in their absence.

## Conclusion

The symptomatic or palliative management of the person with ALS is a challenging problem for clinicians and caregivers alike. In addition to the emotional turmoil that accompanies this degenerative neurologic disease, progressive weakness and immobility create unique clinical problems. As with cancer, incorporation of palliative techniques early in the course of the disease, including the enlistment of hospice services if necessary, is not only advisable but warranted.

## Suggested Reading

Borasio G, Voltz R. Palliative care in amyotrophic lateral sclerosis. *J Neurol.* 1997;244 (Suppl 4):S11–S17.

Cazzolli P, Oppenheimer E. Home mechanical ventilation for amyotrophic lateral sclerosis: nasal compared to tracheostomy intermittent-positive pressure ventilation. *J Neurol Sci.* 1996;139(Suppl):123–128.

Chio A, Gauthier A, Calvo A, et al. Caregiver burden and patients' perception of being a burden in ALS. *Neurology.* 2005;64:1780–1782.

Completing the continuum of ALS care: a consensus document. Missoula, Montana: Promoting Excellence in End-of-Life Care, a national program of the Robert Wood Johnson Foundation; 2004. http://www.promotingexcellence.org/als/als_report. Accessed December 10, 2008.

Ganzini L, Johnston W. End-of-life decision making. In: Mitusmoto H, Przedborski S, Gordon P. eds. *Amyotrophic Lateral Sclerosis.* New York, NY: Taylor & Francis; 2006:811–824.

Ganzini L, Johnston W, MacFarland BH, et al. Attitudes of patients with amyotrophic lateral sclerosis and their care givers toward assisted suicide. *N Engl J Med.* 1998;339:967–973.

Goldstein L, Atkins L, Landau S, et al. Predictors of psychological distress in carers of people with amyotrophic lateral sclerosis: a longitudinal study. *Psychol Med.* 2006;36:865–875.

Mathus-Vliegen L, Louwerse L, Merkus MP, et al. Percutaneous endoscopic gastrostomy in patients with amyotrophic lateral sclerosis and impaired pulmonary function. *Gastrointest Endosc.* 1994;40:463–469.

McDonald E, Wiedenfeld S, Hillel A, et al. Survival in amyotrophic lateral sclerosis: the role of psychological factors. *Arch Neurol.* 1994;5:17–23.

Miller RG, Rosenberg JA, Gelina DF, Mitsumoto H, Newman D, et al. Practice parameter: The care of the patient with amyotrophic lateral sclerosis (an evidence-based review): Report of the Quality Standards Subcommittee of the American Academy of Neurology. *Neurology* 1999;52:1311.

Moss A, Casey P, Stocking CB, et al. Home ventilation for amyotrophic lateral sclerosis patients: outcome, costs, and patient, family, and physician attitudes. *Neurology.* 1993;43:438–443.

Newall A, Orser R, Hunt M. The control of oral secretions in bulbar ALS/MND. *J Neuro Sci.* 1996;139(Suppl):43–44.

Newrick P, Langton-Hewer R. Pain in motor neuron disease. *J Neurol Neurosurg Psychiatry.* 1985;48:838–840.

Norris F, Smith R, Denys E. Motor neurone disease: towards better care. *Br Med J.* 1985;291:259–262.

O'Brien T, Kelly M, Saunders C. Motor neurone disease: a hospice perspective. *Br Med J.* 1992;304:471–473.

Rabkin J, Wagner G, Del Bene M. Resilience and distress among amyotrophic lateral sclerosis patients and caregivers. *Psychosom Med.* 2000;62:271–279.

Rose F. The management of motor neurone disease. *Adv Exp Med Biol.* 1987;209:167–174.

# 24

# Hospice Care

**Barbara Ellen Thompson, N. Michael Murphy,
and Mary Eleanor Toms**

Amyotrophic lateral sclerosis (ALS) can cause pain, unrest, and mourning in those it touches. Hospice is dedicated to providing care and support to everyone affected with far-advanced illness when the pursuit of a cure is contributing little or nothing to the quality of life. Because curative treatment is not yet available for ALS, it is appropriate for hospice to become involved as early as possible to temper the stresses and strains in your family and help to improve your quality of life.

The modern hospice evolved within the past half century mainly as a response to the rampant technology that engulfed Western medicine. It was becoming difficult to die in peace and rare to die in the comfortable and familiar surroundings of one's home. Hospice is still considered by some as a death sentence or a place of doom and gloom. Some fear that if people are referred to hospice that they will give up or lose hope. Our experience has instead been much more optimistic; with enhanced communication among family members and the necessary support, the ever-present tension related to the fear of dying lessens, and it becomes more possible to focus on the opportunities and preciousness of each day.

More than half of people with ALS die at home, and spouses most often serve as the primary caregivers (1). Given the complex needs of people with ALS and their caregivers at the end of life, it is important to use a shared decision-making model in considering end-of-life care options that include a discussion of hospice (2,3). Hospice is not synonymous with giving up. We have seen people on hospice attend a jazz festival, rock concert, or symphony performance and even travel to distant places when they thought it was impossible; do advocacy work on behalf of other people with ALS; teach a daughter how to make a favorite pie; go to an important wedding, bar mitzvah, or graduation; create a book of photos and writings as a legacy for a newborn grandchild; reconcile with an estranged family member; write or publish poetry for the first time; learn how to use a computer or how to meditate; deepen connections with self and others; grow spiritually; and celebrate the return of the light at the beginning of the new year.

The first part of this chapter is a short history of the hospice movement together with organizational details. Consideration is then given to ALS as it affects the whole family and to how the family meeting can be a powerful catalyst to more satisfying final weeks and months of life. The chapter ends with a brief review of symptom management within a hospice framework, and considerations for caregivers.

## The History and Philosophy of Hospice

Records of ancient hospices date to the 4th century AD. They were way stations for travelers and pilgrims. Hospices proliferated in the Middle Ages. Often based in monasteries, these early hospices provided refuge for those in need. Hospices subsequently disappeared and did not reappear until the 17th century, when the Sisters of Charity in Paris opened several houses to care for people who were ill, indigent, or dying. In the 19th and 20th centuries, the Irish Sisters of Charity began to use the word "hospice" to refer to homes for persons at the end of life (4).

The hospice movement of the 20th century developed in response to unmet needs of patients dying in traditional medical environments. Dame Cicely Saunders recognized the necessity for an alternative program of care for persons with advanced illness for whom there was no hope of a cure. In 1967 she founded St. Christopher's Hospice in London, which subsequently became the model for hospice programs in the Western world (5).

The Connecticut Hospice in Branford was the first hospice in the United States, opening a home care program in 1974 and an inpatient facility in 1980. Hospice programs then spread throughout the United States through grassroots community efforts (6).

By the late 1970s there were more than 200 hospice programs in the United States, with much variation in the scope of services and organizational models. Explosive growth in the type and number of hospices led concerned providers to recognize the need to establish principles of hospice care and standards for developing programs. The National Hospice Organization (NHO) identified the basic tenets and characteristics of a hospice program, and the NHO *Standards of a Hospice Program of Care* (1979) provided the following statement on the philosophy of hospice:

> *Dying is a normal process, whether or not resulting from disease. Hospice exists neither to hasten nor to postpone death. Rather, hospice exists to affirm life by providing support and care for those in the last phases of incurable disease so that they can live as fully and comfortably as possible. Hospice promotes the formation of caring*

*communities that are sensitive to the needs of patients and families
at this time in their lives so that they may be free to obtain the degree
of mental and spiritual preparation for death that is satisfactory to
them (7).*

With the surge in the hospice movement during the 1970s, Congress mandated the Health Care Financing Administration (HCFA) to study hospice and its potential impact on the Medicare and Medicaid programs. This study showed that hospice was a cost-effective means of caring for people with terminal illnesses, and 1982 legislation provided hospice benefits to Medicare beneficiaries. Subsequent regulations established who was eligible for the benefit, reimbursement standards and procedures, the required scope of services, and the conditions for a program to qualify for payment through the Medicare hospice benefit. Additional legislation, approved in 1986, allocated federal funds for an optional state Medicaid hospice benefit. Individual states could thereby choose to amend their Medicaid plans to provide beneficiaries with coverage for hospice care. In 1990 Congress passed legislation extending coverage to eligible residents in nursing homes with hospice contracts (8).

The Department of Health and Human Services, Centers for Medicare and Medicaid Services, sets conditions for hospices to participate in Medicare and Medicaid programs in Title 42, Part 418 of the Public Health regulations. These regulations define the minimum scope of services and types of interdisciplinary care that must be delivered to patients and their families by a hospice, as well as the eligibility criteria and methods used to determine payment for services. These regulations also define hospice administrative requirements, such as evidence of a quality assurance program and regular in-service training for employees, methods used for volunteer training and supervision, and how core services are delivered and documented. For more information, please see the Electronic Code of Federal Regulations at http://ecfr.gpoaccess.gov/. Under "Browse," click "Title 42-Public Health," then click "Part 418-Hospice Care."

Currently, all federal health insurance programs and most managed-care plans offer some form of hospice benefit (9). The Medicare hospice benefit does not cover veterans receiving care in Veterans Affairs (VA) facilities. Eligible veterans are, however, able to utilize the Medicare hospice benefit if they are receiving care at home or a community nursing home (10). Although private health insurers often model their hospice coverage after the Medicare hospice benefit, it is important to check the specifics of your hospice policy. Some private health insurers and private health maintenance organizations (HMOs) require case manager preapproval for hospice services, and some policies do not cover all of the services provided under the Medicare benefit or have a lifetime cap on hospice coverage (9).

Hospice care can be provided by freestanding hospices or by hospices owned or operated by home health agencies, hospitals, and skilled nursing facilities. In 2006, the National Hospice and Palliative Care Organization (NHPCO) estimated that a hospice program cared for approximately 36% of people who died in the United States. The median length of service was approximately 3 weeks and most people (74.1%) under hospice care died at home or in a residential facility rather than an acute-care hospital setting (11). It is unknown what percentage of people with ALS seeking palliative care at the end of life are currently served by hospice programs (12). One 2001 study, based on the ALS Patient Care Database, found that 62.4% of patients died in a hospice-supported environment (13). Another study suggested that people with ALS who were affiliated with multidisciplinary ALS clinics were more likely to receive hospice services (14). The American Academy of Neurology ALS Practice Parameter recommends referral to hospice services in the last 6 months of life (1). Currently, the Medicare hospice benefit is the primary source of payment to hospice providers (11).

## The Hospice Medicare Benefit

In 2006 there were more than 4,500 hospice programs in the United States and more than 92% of these were Medicare certified (11). To choose a hospice, it is helpful to get references from family or friends who have received services from the hospice being considered. Your physician or an ALS clinic in your area may have experience in working with hospices in your community and be able to offer a recommendation. The NHPCO at http://www.nhpco.org.custom/directory/main. cfm maintains a list of 3,300 member organizations providing hospice and/or palliative care services (15). Hospices vary in their experience and knowledge of ALS so it is important to investigate whether or not a particular hospice program is a good fit with your needs.

An individual, a family member, or friend speaking on behalf of someone with ALS, a physician, or other health care provider familiar with the needs of the family can initiate referral to a hospice program. There usually is an identified staff person at hospice, often referred to as the intake or admissions coordinator, who screens referrals, answers questions about eligibility for hospice, or redirects the referral if hospice is not an option. If a referral is appropriate, a hospice nurse will visit with you and your family to discuss the option of hospice care. The following information describes general eligibility criteria and entitlements under the Medicare hospice benefit.

*To receive hospice care under Medicare, an individual must be entitled to Medicare Part A (Hospital Insurance) and be certified by their physician and the hospice medical director as having a prognosis of approximately 6 months or less to live if the disease were to run its natural course.* Eligible beneficiaries then sign a statement indicating a desire to transfer their coverage from traditional Medicare to the more comprehensive Medicare hospice benefit. Regular Medicare will continue to pay for treatment of medical conditions unrelated to the terminal illness. You may revoke the hospice benefit at any time and resume regular Medicare benefits.

*Medicare hospice beneficiaries are entitled to receive hospice care for 2 election periods of 90 days each, and an unlimited number of 60-day election periods thereafter, as long as there is evidence of disease progression and functional decline.* Following each benefit period, the hospice medical director and the attending physician must certify that the person continues to decline because of the illness (16).

*Along with the eligibility requirements defined by the Medicare hospice benefit, participating hospices usually develop additional criteria for admission to their programs.* These are discussed at the time of referral and are reviewed in more depth during the admission process. Some hospices require that an identified person, referred to as a primary careperson, be present in the home to oversee the necessary caregiving. Other hospices serve people who live alone if they can develop an alternative caregiver system through a network of friends and/or privately paid help. Certain types of care, such as ventilator care and intravenous antibiotic or fluid replacement therapy, may not be available through the hospice. Additional information on the Medicare hospice benefit may be found at http://www .medicare.gov/Publications/Pubs/pdf/02154.pdf, or call 1-800-633-4227. Users of TTY or text telephones, otherwise known as telephone devices for the deaf (TDD), should call 1-877-486-2048. Ask for the publication titled "Medicare Hospice Benefits: A Special Way of Caring for People Who Are Terminally Ill."

Most health insurance covers hospice care, though the policy specifics vary and some have deductibles and copayments that will apply. Hospice will discuss insurance issues at the time of referral and will do the billing and paperwork necessary for reimbursement of hospice services.

In order to receive reimbursement for hospice services through Medicare and Medicaid, the hospice must be Medicare certified through HCFA and provide a full complement of services in both home and inpatient settings.

## Services of a Medicare-Certified Hospice

Core services must be provided by a Medicare-certified hospice as indicated through the hospice plan of care. These include the following:

- *Home care services with inpatient backup for pain and symptom management or respite care.* "Home care" is provided in private residences, nursing homes, and residential facilities. Short-term inpatient backup for management of symptoms or caregiver respite is provided in discrete hospice units within hospitals, in designated hospice beds within hospitals, or in contracted nursing homes. Some hospices operate freestanding hospice facilities. The majority of hospice care is provided in home care settings or hospice facilities rather than hospital settings (11). Short-term, inpatient respite care is provided on an occasional basis when necessary to relieve family members or others caring for an individual at home (10). Respite care is usually provided in a number of contracted nursing facilities. Under the Medicare hospice benefit, respite care is limited to no more than 5 respite days within a 30-day period (9). If hospitalization is needed, the hospice home care nurse will coordinate the admission so that it occurs as easily and efficiently as possible.

- *Nursing care by or under the supervision of a registered nurse.* A registered nurse, who usually visits at least weekly, serves as the coordinator of services and contact person for the family.

- *24-hour on-call availability of nursing services.* If there are problems or concerns during the nighttime hours, family can use the on-call system to receive immediate consultation with a hospice nurse, who will contact other people or make a home visit as needed.

- *Continuous home care (CHC).* During a period of crisis and as an alternative to hospitalization, more intensive nursing care may be provided on a short-term basis at your place of residence to manage acute medical symptoms (10).

- *Physician services.* The hospice medical director assumes overall responsibility for the medical component of the hospice program. He or she does not, however, replace your primary care physician. The hospice medical director works in cooperation with the primary care physician and ALS experts, such as the medical director of an ALS clinic, in addressing medical needs.

- *Social work services.* While social work is considered to be a core hospice service, hospices vary in how they use social workers. Some programs provide only limited services to families considered to be at particular risk. Other programs are more generous and social workers meet routinely with families to address a variety of concerns, providing emotional support or short-term psychological intervention. Social workers can help to create an environment conducive to dialogue and decision making around end-of-life care choices, helping you and your family make plans that are consistent with your values, beliefs, and goals for the future. Another potential role of the social worker involves facilitating access to community services such as transportation, financial resources, respite care, supplemental personal care assistance, and other forms of support. By creating an environment that supports effective communication, the social worker can help you and your family respond to the changing landscape of ALS. Attention is given to the family meeting later in this chapter. When investigating a potential hospice program, it may be helpful to inquire about the role of the social worker with that program. For instance, you can ask the following questions: What types of services do social workers with your program provide? How often would the social worker assigned to my family meet with us? How would you describe the role of the social worker with your hospice? Do any of your social workers have experience working with people who have ALS?

- *Chaplaincy services.* Each hospice has a chaplain who can provide pastoral care to family members on request. Hospice chaplains are trained to work with people of diverse ethnic and religious backgrounds and faith traditions to strengthen networks of support. Their primary role is to address spiritual concerns in concert with other hospice team and community members. Spiritual care is not confined to religious beliefs and practices, but encompasses fundamental questions regarding the meaning of life and death and the experience of suffering (17). Ongoing illness-related losses can disrupt connections with sources of inspiration and can challenge prior understandings of the world. In sharing your experiences with a hospice chaplain, you and your family may discover ways of responding to the multiple challenges of ALS. Children, as well as adults, search for ways to understand and communicate their grief. Spiritual care is intended to help children articulate their questions, express their emotions, and find ways to make sense of their experiences in the company of others (18). Spiritual care is an important dimension of hospice and palliative care that supports reconciliation and reconnection with self and others and discovery of meaning, which contributes to a sense of peace, wholeness, and appreciation for life from moment to moment (19). Although this is the primary role of the hospice chaplain, other members of the hospice team are sensitized to the importance of spiritual and/or religious concerns at the end of life and you or your family may request their assistance (20).

- *Volunteer services.* Hospice volunteers come from a variety of backgrounds. Some have professional credentials and others do not. Oftentimes, hospice volunteers have had direct personal experience with hospice as a family member or friend of someone who received hospice services in the past. In all cases, volunteers are carefully screened and are required to undergo an intensive training program in preparation for volunteer work in home, hospital, or nursing home settings. Typically, hospice volunteers provide companionship, emotional support, and practical assistance, such as running errands, visiting in the home, providing respite for the caregiver, and helping with household chores. Volunteers cannot dispense medicines nor do personal care. Every attempt is made to meet the unique needs and interests of family members with assigned hospice volunteers. For instance, in our experience, one person with ALS expressed an interest in writing poetry and was paired with a poet-volunteer. Another person needed a ramp for his home, so a contractor-volunteer worked with the family to install a ramp. Hospices vary according to their resources and the backgrounds of their volunteers.

- *Bereavement follow-up.* Hospices provide support for family members and significant friends during the first year of bereavement. According to the NHPCO, support typically involves 7 contacts during the first year of bereavement, including follow-up phone calls, visits, and mailings (11). Many hospice programs offer a variety of support groups and some programs offer limited short-term one-on-one support with trained volunteers or referral to private counselors in the community at large. If there are special needs, such as those of young children, hospice can help families obtain bereavement support. Some hospices offer specialized services such as bereavement groups for children of various ages. If these are not available, hospices can facilitate referral to a community provider. There is no roadmap for bereavement and our experience of grief is shaped by factors such as our age, ethnicity, gender, social network, spiritual and/or religious beliefs, prior experiences with death and loss, as well as our relationship with the deceased (18,21). It can be helpful to meet with those who have navigated the terrain and are familiar with providing support through the physical, social, emotional, and psychological aspects of the bereavement process. Although talking with empathetic others is often helpful, there are many ways to express grief such as through the arts or physical activity (22). Some hospices employ staff or volunteers experienced in use of the expressive arts and this service may be of value for you and your family. Significant loss challenges our sense of who we are and our experience of the world. Many have found it helpful to face these challenges in the company of empathetic others, who can provide both a witness and resources for the journey of reconnecting to self and others (20).

The following services can be provided directly by hospice staff or indirectly by the hospice program through contractual arrangements with other agencies or individuals:

- *Home health aide services.* Only individuals who have successfully completed home health aide training and competency evaluation can provide (HHA) services through hospice. Under the supervision of a registered nurse, HHAs usually provide limited, intermittent coverage for personal care and household services needed to maintain a safe and sanitary environment (10). The days and times for this service are determined on the basis of availability, individual care needs, and variations among hospice providers. Families often choose to supplement this care with privately paid help. Some people have private insurance that provides for more extensive nursing and HHA services under nonhospice home care policies. Therefore, it is important to compare regular home care and hospice home care benefits before choosing hospice.

- *Occupational, physical, respiratory, and speech therapies.* When deemed necessary by the hospice team for symptom management, these therapies are included in the plan of care. Most hospices do not employ their own therapists and have contractual arrangements with local agencies to provide these services. Some hospices have knowledge and experience in the appropriate utilization of occupational, physical, respiratory, and speech therapy in end-of-life care. Unfortunately, some hospices do not understand how these therapies can be helpful and advocacy is needed to obtain services. In addition, some therapists have minimal experience in working with hospice and are more accustomed to work in rehabilitation settings, where their roles are substantially different. Therefore, it is useful to ascertain whether or not the therapists referred to you have experience in providing end-of-life care to people with ALS and their families. ALS clinics and physicians can serve as a bridge to hospice, providing education and consultation in the development of a comprehensive hospice plan of care. The overall objective in providing occupational, physical, respiratory, or speech therapy under hospice is to help manage the continually changing profile of symptoms and concerns associated with ALS so that people can experience optimal quality of life in their final weeks or months. Occupational, physical, speech, and respiratory therapists each play an important role in helping people to remain engaged in familiar, everyday activities as well as those activities involved in preparing for death (23).

• *Medical supplies and appliances, including drugs and biologicals deemed necessary by the interdisciplinary team for symptom management.* Hospice will pay for medications related to symptom management, such as medications for management of pain or respiratory distress. Certain coinsurance amounts may apply. Medications aimed primarily at extending life rather than improving the quality of life, such as riluzole, are not covered. Covered medical supplies and appliances include items such as nutritional supplements, bed pads, and catheters.

• *Durable medical equipment.* Hospital beds, walkers, wheelchairs, suction machines, and the like are covered items. Some hospices may be better able to provide more medical equipment, such as patient lifts. Hospice will arrange for the delivery of covered equipment. Neither augmentative communication equipment nor customized electric wheelchairs are covered under hospice. Some hospices cover cough assist devices and forms of noninvasive ventilation (NIV) support such as BiPAP when these are used for palliation (K. Spinelli, personal communication, March 31, 2008). Other programs do not cover such equipment, perhaps because of lack of familiarity with their palliative benefits. Therefore, it is helpful to develop the hospice plan of care in collaboration with an ALS clinic in your area.

## Hospice and ALS

The intention of hospice is to provide a comprehensive and well-coordinated range of services that can help people with ALS and their families to live as fully and comfortably as possible in the final months of life. Meticulous attention to symptom control, experience in providing care to people who are approaching death, and resources to support families through this process can ease the anxiety, fear, and worry that invariably accompany the progression of ALS. Although it would be ideal if people with ALS and their families could utilize the full range of hospice services throughout the course of ALS, there are constraints on hospice programs. Many people with ALS do not receive hospice services either soon enough or at all (24). This is due to a variety of factors, including restrictive hospice admission criteria as well as lack of knowledge on the part of Medicare, other insurers, and healthcare providers regarding the needs of people with ALS and their families at the end of life (12,25).

In l996 the NHPCO published referral and admission guidelines for use with people who had noncancer diseases such as ALS (26). These guidelines were not intended to serve as hard and fast admission criteria. Rather, they were published in an attempt to expand access to hospice. Nevertheless, HCFA codified the NHPCO guidelines for use in fiscal audits and medical review policies. As a result, many hospices now interpret NHPCO guidelines narrowly, which limits rather than expands access to hospice (27). The 1996 guidelines, currently used by many hospices, are as follows:

> The patient should have, within the past 12 months, developed extremely severe breathing disability. Examples include: l. FVC less than 30% of predicted. 2. Significant dyspnea [shortness of breath] at rest. 3. Requiring supplemental oxygen at rest. 4. Patient declines intubation or tracheotomy and mechanical ventilation. (27)

Hospices with more experience in caring for people with ALS are able to interpret the guidelines more flexibly, allowing their clinical experience to guide judgments regarding admission. Collaboration between hospices and health care professionals or ALS clinics experienced in the care of people with ALS can enhance the willingness of hospices to become more involved and effective in their provision of care. Collaboration among health care providers not only improves the quality and continuity of care from diagnosis to death but also can help to sustain the caregiving abilities of involved health care professionals through pooling of resources, experience, and support (28).

## Hospice Referral Considerations

Discussions about end-of-life care, including consideration of a hospice referral, can be initiated at the request of the patient or family, when there is distress or suffering, or when there is significant progression of the disease (29). Criteria for considering a hospice referral vary from program to program. The following are suggested considerations and criteria for a hospice referral:

1. *Approximate prognosis of 6 months or less, if the disease runs a predictable course.* The longer the family is on the program, the more closely developed will be the interpersonal relationships that improve the effectiveness of hospice care.

2. *A "do not resuscitate" (DNR) order is not required.* A DNR order is a legal document advising health care providers of an individual's wish not to be resuscitated in the event of respiratory or cardiac failure. People with ALS who have decided not to use long-term mechanical ventilation through tracheostomy will find it helpful to formalize and communicate this decision through the use of advance directives such as a DNR order. It is important to note that a DNR decision does not exclude use of noninvasive forms of ventilation support, such as BiPAP, for palliation of respiratory symptoms. Hospices previously required a DNR order before someone could be admitted, but this is no longer the case. At the time of admission to hospice, people with ALS may be undecided regarding whether they want to use any form of assisted ventilation. It is helpful for the family to meet with health care providers who are familiar with the pros and cons of assisted ventilation, in an atmosphere that is conducive to open and ongoing exploration of this issue. Under these circumstances, ambivalence usually clears over time, rendering a well-considered decision. Knowledgeable hospice personnel can be helpful in discussing this choice. No decision is irrevocable; if someone decides to use mechanical ventilation through tracheostomy after being admitted to hospice, they can do so by transitioning off of hospice and onto a program that can provide the necessary care. Noninvasive forms of assisted ventilation aimed at promoting comfort and improving symptom management are appropriate forms of care under hospice. Hospice is not appropriate if someone is firmly decided on a course of long-term mechanical ventilation because this therapy extends life beyond the approximate 6-month period covered by hospice.

3. *Progressive, life-threatening swallowing problems.* Indications of nutritional insufficiency include (a) swallowing problems that prevent the intake of nutrients and fluid necessary to maintain life; (b) evidence of dehydration such as urine that is darkened in color and has a noticeable odor, urination that is less frequent or in smaller amounts, a constant dry mouth, or dry skin; and (c) progressive weight loss (29). A weight loss greater than 10% of one's body weight is considered significant (30). If there is nutritional insufficiency and a feeding tube is declined, then a hospice referral can be considered. People with supplemental feeding support (e.g., feeding tube) may be appropriate for hospice care if they are experiencing a progressive decline in breathing capacity or aspiration pneumonia.

4. *Progressive breathing difficulty.* Some hospices follow Medicare Hospice referral criteria for people with ALS, which are too restrictive and prevent timely utilization of hospice (12,27). Other hospices use guidelines developed in conjunction with regional fiscal intermediaries. For instance, the "Admission Evaluation and Recertification Form"

from Beacon Hospice defines "critically impaired respiratory function" as an "FVC less than 40% of predicted (seated or supine) and two or more . . . symptoms and/or signs" of respiratory compromise. Based on a consensus among 20 ALS experts, however, it is important to discuss end-of-life care including the option of hospice when there is shortness of breath, symptoms of hypoventilation, or a FVC of 50% predicted or less (25). Evidence of respiratory compromise includes (a) visible use of muscles in the neck and upper chest (accessory muscles) for breathing at rest; (b) shallow breathing; (c) shortness of breath (dyspnea); (d) a reversal in the normal pattern of abdominal movement outward with inspiration, and abdominal movement inward with expiration (paradoxical breathing); (e) inability to lie supine (on one's back) because of weakness of the diaphragm; (f) abnormal arterial blood gas measurements; (g) hypoventilation during sleep—symptoms include morning headache, nightmares, daytime sleepiness, shortness of breath, restlessness during the night, and interrupted sleep; (h) inability to blow one's nose or sneeze; (i) extreme fatigue and poor endurance; (j) weakened cough; and (k) reduced speech volume (3). It should be noted that some people do not feel or perceive respiratory decline because it is so gradual that they become used to lowered oxygen levels and do not experience distress. Working collaboratively with an ALS clinic physician can educate hospice providers on the importance of early referral. Hospice programs can and do develop their own benchmarks for referral. Clinical judgment, based on experience with ALS, is critical for end-of-life discussions and hospice referral considerations.

5. *Life-threatening complications in combination with rapid progression of ALS.* One example of a life-threatening complication is aspiration pneumonia. Aspiration occurs when food or liquid, including saliva, slips into the airways and lungs. This can occur if there are swallowing problems, difficulty clearing secretions, or an ineffective cough. When coughing is ineffective or secretions increase, aspiration can cause parts of the lung to fill up, resulting in pneumonia. Pneumonia also can be caused by bacteria or viruses and may be a complication of a flu or bronchitis. A hospice referral may be indicated if there are recurrent aspiration pneumonias or if there is recurrent fever after use of antibiotics (29).

For a more extensive discussion of hospice admission criteria please see http://www.promotingexcellence.org/files/public/als_appendix_e.pdf.

## Symptom Management in Hospice

The nurse case manager will consult with members of the hospice team, the primary care physician, and ALS experts to develop and coordinate the plan of care. Physicians with clinics that are affiliated with the Muscular Dystrophy Association

(MDA) or the ALS Association (ALSA) can assist hospice with symptom management when this is needed. Occupational and physical therapists, speech-language pathologists, dietitians, and respiratory therapists can provide valuable help in promoting comfort and well-being. In addition to these traditional health care providers, hospices often have affiliations with massage therapists and practitioners of other complementary approaches such as Reiki and therapeutic touch (23).

Hospice can assist with the following common symptoms of advanced ALS:

- *Sleep problems* occur for a variety of reasons, including depression, anxiety, changes in respiratory status, muscle cramps, positioning problems, discomfort associated with immobility, or trouble swallowing with aspiration of saliva (31). Frequent position changes and use of appropriate pressure relief mattresses and cushions to improve weight distribution can help with problems related to immobility. Some people are afraid they will not be able to call for help during the night when caregivers are sleeping, so having a reliable call system is essential. Insomnia can be treated with various medications, including some antidepressants (32). Medications can be also used to address muscle cramps, spasticity, or discomfort associated with immobility, or anxiety. Stretching and massage may be helpful for muscle cramps. As weakness progresses, inadequate respiration at night can cause nightmares, poor concentration, mood changes, loss of appetite, and daytime fatigue or sleepiness. Eventually, people may experience morning headaches and increased lethargy (3). Use of NIV may provide symptomatic relief if it can be tolerated (3,29). Appropriate and careful use of sedative or antianxiety medications can also be helpful to treat insomnia due to respiratory comprise (25). Loss of sleep, from whatever cause, can contribute to a depressed mood, lowered level of alertness, poorer functioning, and a reduced capacity for coping with day-to-day concerns. Therefore, sleep deprivation should always be taken quite seriously, evaluated carefully, and treated appropriately.

- *Anxiety* may result from worries and fears related to the progression of the disease or from physiologic changes such as those resulting from impaired ability to breathe. People may not report that they are feeling "anxious." Rather, the following may be present: physical agitation or restlessness; complaints of general discomfort and frequent requests for repositioning; reports that the mind is racing or that it is difficult to think clearly; fearfulness; and increased requests for companionship, especially at nighttime. Giving attention to fears and worries, using methods to improve physical comfort and positioning, and the selective use of medications such as lorazepam (Ativan) can help with the management of anxiety. Medications such as morphine can reduce feelings of shortness of breath but not cause respiratory suppression (31). Mindfulness-based stress reduction (MBSR) approaches and various forms of relaxation training can help with management of anxiety (33,34). Other complementary approaches such as Reiki and therapeutic touch may also be beneficial (23). It is helpful for care providers to provide a calm and reassuring presence, as anxiety can be contagious, which only escalates problems.

- *Cognitive impairment* may result from organic changes in the brain. This may appear as mood or personality changes (e.g., more rigid, aggressive, or passive behavior), reduced decision-making and problem-solving ability, more distractibility, poor insight, delayed memory, or other signs of cognitive impairment. Although most people do not experience cognitive changes of this kind, it is important to distinguish them from cognitive changes due to other more treatable causes, such as clinical depression or respiratory insufficiency (3,35).

- *Depression* of one form or another can accompany the multiple, ongoing losses associated with ALS. It is important to distinguish the grief and mourning process or reactive depression from what is referred to as clinical depression. Clinically significant depression is thought to affect a small minority of people with ALS (35). When present, it can compromise a person's capacity to respond to the challenges of ALS, prepare for death, and find pleasure in one's remaining life. Symptoms of clinical depression are as follows:
  - loss of interest and enjoyment in valued activities or roles
  - changes in sleep (too much, too little, trouble falling asleep, or waking up during sleep) that are not better accounted for by respiratory changes or other causes
  - changes in appetite accompanied by weight loss due to disinterest in eating that are not the result of swallowing problems, a fear of choking, or respiratory decline
  - diminished ability to think clearly, problem solve, or concentrate during activities, which are not the result of other causes
  - significant and unexpected withdrawal from social relationships
  - a depressed mood or experience of emotional flatness most days, for most of the day, that is generally greater in the morning but improves as the day goes on
  - severely distorted and negative perceptions of self (e.g., self-reproach, feelings of worthlessness, guilt-ridden or self-accusatory ruminations) that go beyond thoughts or feelings of guilt about being sick
  - the persistence of symptoms over time with no significant change despite favorable environmental circumstances, including the presence of supportive and encouraging people in close relationship with

the person who is depressed, or symptomatic treatment aimed at other causes of depressive symptoms (36,37).

Thus, some symptoms of clinical depression, such as problems with sleep and appetite, are also symptoms of ALS progression. Thoughts of suicide are common in ALS, and are not necessarily indicative of clinical depression. People can feel hopeless regarding their expectations about the future without being clinically depressed. Feelings of hopelessness and a loss of meaning usually require nonpharmacologic approaches such as various forms of counseling and support (38). Treatment with antidepressant medication should be considered when there is a combination of symptoms that are severe and/or of long duration, when the level of distress experienced by the individual is high, and when there is a personal or family history of clinical depression. We are in no way suggesting that medications substitute for the types of support and counsel described elsewhere in this chapter. Rather, people with moderate to severe clinical depression may benefit from both psychosocial support and antidepressant medications for relief of symptoms. Some antidepressant medication may even help with appetite, drooling, sleeping, and pain either by themselves or in conjunction with other drugs (31). Many people who are clinically depressed do not recognize that they are depressed. Some may believe that their depression is somehow a deficiency of character or will rather than an actual chemical need of the brain, just as diabetes has a chemical need. The aim of treatment, whether pharmacologic and/or psychosocial, is to help people access innate coping abilities, creatively respond to problems associated with ALS, enjoy simple day-to-day pleasures, make treatment decisions, and prepare for death (35,39).

- *Muscle weakness, cramps, spasticity, and progressive immobility* can lead to pain, discomfort, and other problems. Symptoms can be managed through use of medications and therapy (31). Physical therapists can educate care providers in passive and active range of motion to prevent joint stiffness and muscle contractures and may use modalities such as ultrasound to address spasticity. Various medications can also be used to manage spasticity (32). Occupational therapists can recommend equipment for enhanced positioning and cushions or mattresses for improved weight distribution; provide transfer training and equipment or lifts if weakness and immobility are pronounced; recommend methods to increase home accessibility; and provide training to reduce the risk of injury to the caregiver. Additionally, some occupational and physical therapists have expertise in various forms of relaxation or MBSR training (23,33). As a result of immobility, lack of exercise, and the side effects of some medications, constipation can ensue. Dietary modification such as increased fiber intake, proper hydration (adequate fluid intake), and use of mild laxatives can be used to address constipation (3). As a result of muscle weakness, many people fear that they will be unable to communicate at the end of life (31). ALS clinics have extensive experience in helping people maintain some form of ability to communicate and may be able to provide access to augmentative communication devices, ranging from simple communication boards to electronic devices. Hospice programs rarely provide these forms of equipment. Speech therapy is a covered service under hospice, however, and therapists often know where to procure such equipment, if available, in the community at large. An ALS clinic in your region may have augmentative communication equipment available for loan.

- *Thick mucous secretions* can be problematic in late-stage ALS. Thick mucous secretions can result from diminished intake of fluids, chronic respiratory tract infections that impair one's ability to clear secretions, and a weakened cough. Proper positioning to enhance coughing ability is important (3). Suctioning may be beneficial for clearing the upper airways, and physical therapists can provide training in assisted-coughing techniques as progressive weakness reduces coughing effectiveness (3). Use of mechanical cough-assist devises may be beneficial (32). Moistening the air with room humidifiers and reducing substances that increase urination, such as caffeine, are recommended. Some people find that sipping thickened fruit juices, such as papaya juice, is helpful (3). Prescription medications, nebulizer treatments, and over-the-counter Robitussin are also used to manage thick mucous secretions (K. Spinelli, personal communication, March 1, 2008).

- *Dysphagia* is the impaired ability to swallow. The speech-language pathologist can provide instruction in compensatory swallowing techniques and dietary modifications as swallowing becomes impaired (31). Postural changes can also be helpful (3). A suction machine can be used to manage saliva that accumulates in the mouth because of swallowing problems (38). Although certain medications can reduce the quantity of saliva, they can have other side effects that are problematic (38). Low-dosage palliative radiation to the parotid glands to reduce drooling is effective and is covered by hospice. Use of butulinum toxin (i.e., botox injections) to the salivary glands to reduce saliva production is not covered by hospice (K. Spinelli, personal communication, March 1, 2008). Many people with ALS fear that they will "choke to death" (31). Although people with dysphagia may experience choking episodes, choking to death is not a manner of death from ALS (31). Nevertheless, these episodes can be anxiety producing for everyone. It may be helpful to remember that as long as the person is coughing and there is no evidence of food obstructing the trachea (i.e., windpipe), the coughing will eventually subside. Offering a calm presence can be beneficial. It is here that learned relaxation practices are very helpful.

the effects of respiratory compromise. These may include forms of intermittent NIV support to relieve symptoms of chronic hypoventilation; nasal oxygen during the daytime to reduce feelings of "air hunger"; medications to decrease secretions and anxiety; proper positioning to maximize breathing capacity; and relaxation training (31). Respiratory therapy is a covered benefit under hospice when it is deemed necessary for symptom management. According to Karen Spinelli, Director of the ALS Regional Center in Upstate New York, more than 50% of patients on hospice use intermittent NIV for palliation. More detailed descriptions of ways to manage respiratory problems are provided elsewhere in this book.

- A fear of suffocating to death commonly produces anxiety for both the person with ALS and family members. Gentle, yet open discussion surrounding the likely progression of the disease and manner of death can soften fear. When decline in breathing ability occurs gradually over time, people often can adapt to very low levels of respiratory reserve without evidence of distress. As carbon dioxide builds up, there is actually a feeling of greater relaxation. If the decline is more rapid, the person may be more in need of active symptom management. In ALS, toward the end of life, there may be a mixture of restlessness, agitation, aching discomfort, fear, anxiety, and sleeplessness that can respond extremely well to the use of low-dose morphine and/or antianxiety agents such as Ativan (34). Hospice has clearly demonstrated the benefits of using low-dose morphine in controlling symptoms of pain or breathlessness (3,31). Nevertheless, there still is some reluctance to use morphine in far-advanced illnesses, especially when there is respiratory compromise. The use of morphine to manage symptoms does not constitute physician-assisted suicide but rather appropriate and ethical end-of-life care (30). Reiterating the 24-hour, on-call availability of support through hospice and the possibility of hospice inpatient admission for terminal care can also be reassuring.

Providing you with knowledge of what to expect can help you and your loved ones prepare for death, prevent crises, and enhance your ability to make the most of your remaining time together. The final months of life and the manner of death can influence the bereavement process. Therefore, it is critical that support be provided to all during this important transition.

## The Family and ALS

We believe that life-threatening illness affects everyone in the family and that coming together to share experiences, concerns, and worries can lessen the additional stress of hiding fears. Giving voice to feelings and thoughts that arise in response to ALS can help each involved person feel less isolated and more informed regarding the likely course of the disease and more hopeful regarding the possibilities for mutual support and a peaceful death.

- The option of using a feeding tube usually has been discussed well i  
  vance of admission to hospice. Because insertion of a feeding tube ca  
  some risk, this procedure is not usually recommended for people with  
  FVC of 50% or less of the predicted value (29,31,40). Most people (88  
  who have FVC less than 50% choose not to have a feeding tube insertec  
  (38). Thorough exploration of this procedure needs to occur, with discus-  
  sion of its potential risks, burdens, and benefits (3). People with ALS,  
  family members, caregivers, and health care professionals may express  
  concerns about "starving to death" as the ability to take food and fluid by  
  mouth becomes more difficult. People with advanced ALS typically do  
  not complain of a gnawing hunger or pain resulting from decreased abil-  
  ity to take food by mouth. The process usually is gradual and not pain-  
  ful. Appetite wanes and fatigue increases. As the disease progresses the  
  body is less able to convert food into nutrition and body mass, therefore  
  weight loss occurs. Likewise, dehydration need not be an overwhelming  
  concern. It is important to maintain scrupulous attention to mouth care as  
  fluid intake decreases. Even for those who use a feeding tube, the amount  
  of fluids given often is decreased in the advanced stages of the disease so  
  that excess fluids do not burden the body. Likewise, intravenous fluids at  
  the end of life often create problems rather than relieve discomfort.

- Occasionally, a patient in hospice may elect to discontinue use of a feed-  
  ing tube for nutritional support. It is important for this type of decision to  
  be discussed openly with the family because caregivers can sometimes  
  interpret the decision as a failure on their part to provide adequate sup-  
  port or care or may view this as a "giving up" on the part of the patient  
  rather than a "letting go." Perceptions of the benefit or burden of a treat-  
  ment vary over time, and may be perceived differently by members in the  
  same family. It is crucial to address these issues. Hospice personnel can  
  help facilitate family meetings and provide the information and support  
  necessary to make decisions on continuation or discontinuation of treat-  
  ment such as feeding tubes.

- *Respiratory problems* are the hallmark of ALS and the usual cause of  
  death (3). Discussion of respiratory issues and management options,  
  including hospice, should take place within the context of the family sys-  
  tem so that there is agreement on how to respond as breathing problems  
  develop. Respiratory decline usually develops gradually at first; therefore,  
  there is time for discussion. Advance discussion prevents crises later. As  
  mentioned earlier, a DNR is not required for admission to hospice. If hos-  
  pice admission criteria are met and the person has not decided in favor of  
  long-term mechanical ventilation, a referral is appropriate. Knowledgable  
  hospice personnel can provide information and support that can assist the  
  decision-making process. Once a person with ALS has been admitted to  
  hospice, various forms of palliative treatment can be used to ameliorate

For many families, often despite firm protestations of their closeness, the idea of coming together as a group is terrifying. Strong feelings, with their attendant images and ideas, usually have not been openly expressed, especially in front of strangers, even when they are keenly felt. If the family has had little experience in sharing powerful everyday experiences, they will be terrified at the thought of sharing the avalanche of emotions and thoughts that can be set off by loss: fear, rage, grief, confusion, helplessness, sorrow, or a sense of unreality, to name but a few.

At a time when death is near, people are often skeptical about the usefulness of talking and fear that it will only make the situation more painful. Most of us have had little practice in finding ways to be with our own suffering and the suffering of others, even those with whom we share the most intimate ties. Far too many families remain silent, unable to bridge a sense of separateness in the face of pain that seems unbearable. The everyday complexities of living may temporarily supplant opportunities for thoughts and feelings to simply unfold in the company of others. A sense of urgency or incessant busyness can further deepen a sense of isolation and contribute to feelings of hopelessness or despair. There may be little opportunity for conversation and mutual listening without interruptions or a sense of interfering obligations. Alternatively, when there is opportunity to be lovingly heard by each other, there is the magic of soul-to-soul connection. This helps us live with the aches and pains of everyday life, even the frightening manifestations of ALS, which seem so much more powerful when we feel alone, unheard, unwitnessed, and uninformed.

Some hospices do not arrange family meetings routinely but will do so at the request of family or if there is extreme chaos. It is our belief that gatherings for every family are valuable because life-threatening illness always brings with it some degree of chaos, and there is much to say even though we might be afraid to speak.

In anticipation of a family meeting, there may be an atmosphere of tension, distrust, and doubt. Stories of old hurts and disputes may emerge along with descriptions of who is allied with whom and how the family does or does not communicate. ALS can reawaken mourning for family members who died earlier. If parents and children are present, there may be warnings not to upset "Mother" and not to say anything to "Father," because it will "only make matters worse." Skeptical, frightened, or angry family members may ask us what we could possibly hope to accomplish and why we would want to upset people "at this time." Doubt and distrust can derail a meeting before it has begun. If, however, there is someone skillful to guide the family meeting and there is willingness on the part of participants to suspend judgment for a while and let go of the expectation that the meeting will provide a fix, then there is the possibility for those present to become more fully informed and available to one another. When this occurs, we begin to notice that once-shunned feelings can be shared, hurts relinquished, and old losses mourned and let go. Feeling can then begin. Although there may be times when it seems that there is hardly any movement, quite often there is a feeling of peace, ease, and opening, as if a load had been lifted. What once seemed forbidden or intolerable has lost some of its hold, and it is now possible to breathe more easily.

## The Story of the Illness

Most people with ALS in the hospice program live and die at home. We suggest that family meetings be held in the comfort and convenience of the home environment. The gathering may be small or large. Whether there are 30 or more family members and friends or no family present, we gather with the belief that our connections with the world depend on the telling of our stories.

The family meeting may begin with the patient telling the story of the illness. The accuracy of dates and facts is of little importance. It is the images and feelings that need expression. If it is the father who has the illness, he may turn to his wife and ask her to tell the story. If she is the designated family storyteller, she may be the one who talks to the doctors, relays news to the family, and comforts them. But it is a family myth that capacity to nurture resides only in the mother and that it is her role to run interference for death. The father may be gently encouraged to speak of "the unspeakable," to acknowledge his own wounds as well as the reality of his impending death. Perhaps this is the first time those gathered have heard his story, seen his vulnerabilities, felt his fears, and been given the opportunity to offer comfort and understanding. As the father reveals his story in the supportive company of others, he is reclaiming and remembering himself.

### The Story of His Worries and Fears

"Father" may say that his principle concerns are for his wife and children. The facilitator asks him how he met his wife, what she is like, how he feels about her, and how he views their marriage. These powerful questions usually evoke jokes or nervous laughter, sometimes verging on uproar in the family, but gentle persistence can encourage him to speak. There can be surprise when disappointments, disillusionments, or resentments are voiced and let go, making room for the expression of vulnerability, tenderness, and love. These words may seldom if ever have been heard from the father, because men often hide behind their unemotional and strong facades like the Wizard of Oz, encouraged early on to armor themselves and diminish or devalue feelings.

Dark secrets can also be aired. For example, his alcoholism may have created immense pain and an unreliable emotional environment, leaving all around him in a perennial state of apprehension and distrust. For years, the silence surrounding his alcoholism may have produced torrents of anger and guilt within the family, unexpressed but palpable. Now the father may speak about his alcoholism and acknowledge the pain it has caused him and others. He may tell the untold story of his own parents' alcoholism and speak of the regret he now feels for having missed out on his children and they on him. Listening without interruption and a minimum of judgment can leave open the possibility for compassion and reconciliation.

When the father is asked to talk about each of his children, he usually starts with facts and figures—their grades, degrees, and successes. It is much more difficult for him to express feelings of love and the heartbreaking sadness of having to leave them. He may say that they know he loves them without his having to say so. He is nevertheless encouraged to relate the story of his connections with family, expressing whatever worries and concerns as well as hopes and dreams he has for each of them.

Then the father can be asked about concerns he has for himself. He may dismiss the question initially but when pressed may say that he does not wish to suffer. Then, if he permits himself to voice his concerns, he may say that he is fearful about "choking to death," "suffocating to death," "being completely paralyzed and unable to communicate," or "being a burden." At this point, it is possible for the hospice facilitator to talk about each of these fears, letting him know that they are very commonly experienced by people who have ALS, whether they are expressed or not. In an atmosphere that is open, honest, and supportive, it is possible to talk about the probable way in which his ALS will progress, along with the likely manner of death. He can be told that eventually, perhaps in his sleep, he will simply and quietly breathe out, and without emergency, he will let go. A relieved sigh and a palpable lessening of tension in the room often follow this discussion.

Death, too, can be brought from out of the shadows, and fear-laden images and ideas can be replaced with those based on more accurate accounts of death from ALS. Assurances of continued care and a commitment on the part of all to address pain and suffering can help to mitigate fears. Death from ALS is usually quite peaceful. Family and caregivers can be prepared for what lies ahead so that there is an atmosphere of greater calm and more opportunity to appreciate the beauty of life.

### Remembering the Children

It is most important that young children and grandchildren be involved in family meetings. This may be very difficult for adults who want to shield them, and they may say that the children are too young to understand. Although 3-year-olds may not understand the words, they are very much in touch with the feelings of those they love. Excluding children can convey a message that death is something to be hidden and/or forbidden.

> *Mr. Ryan, his wife, 8 children and their spouses, and several grand-children were all present for the hospice family meeting. Mr. Ryan told stories of a wonderful marriage with many struggles and offered love and encouragement to everyone in the room. In turn, they shared colorful tales of Mr. Ryan, celebrating their years together. There was much laughter and many tears. After some time, all were exhausted and the meeting was winding down. When asked if he had any questions or anything more to say, Mr. Ryan sat up on the couch and said that he wanted to speak to his 5 youngest grandchildren, who had been wandering in and out of the room but had not been directly addressed. Ranging in age from about 6 to 9 years old, they sat on the floor in a semicircle by his feet, and this is what he said to them: "Children, I am going to die and it is nobody's fault. It just happens. I won't be there to see you grow up, but I want you to know that you have each been a joy in my life, and you will always have my blessing*

*and my love." There was not a dry eye in the room for those who wit-*
*nessed this most sacred event.*

Mr. Ryan's story is a reminder of how important it is for grandparents to take leave of their grandchildren face-to-face, if at all possible. So often they are best friends and love each other unconditionally. The loss can be compounded for children when a grandparent leaves without saying goodbye, delegating the heart-breaking task to the parents. There was a sequel to this family meeting. Six years after Mr. Ryan's death, hospice staff had occasion to meet with one of Mr. Ryan's sons-in-law. During that visit, he spoke of how powerfully moved he had been by the family meeting with Mr. Ryan. The experience, he said, had given him the courage to become deeply connected with his 22-year-old daughter during her final months of life and eventual death 2 years after the family meeting. A family meeting can have far-reaching effects, and simply voiced blessings can empower and enrich the lives of others in ways that are quite unanticipated.

### Stories of Roots

The family meeting can be a chance to speak of connections with one's ancestors. It is surprising how little many people know of parents, grandparents, and beyond. Intergenerational stories provide us with an appreciation for the lives and contributions of those who have come before us, providing a sense of continuity and connection. Many will say that their parents or grandparents came from abroad and that they seldom heard them speak of their past struggles or early lives. This leaves subsequent generations without any stories to tell and pass along, with a history devoid of color, dimension, and feeling. We need to tell and hear the sad stories along with the happier ones; otherwise the picture of our roots is incomplete. Reflections about parents, siblings, and growing up often reveal continuing pain from deaths unmourned and loving words unspoken. Bringing these memories, images, and feelings into the present can allow grieving to take place, lessening the deep pain that can result from holding on to fragments of an incomplete and untold story. Unattached to the rage or grief of preceding losses and deaths, it becomes easier to die in peace.

### The Family Tells of Him

The mother may start by telling her story—how she met her husband and her view of the ups and downs of the marriage. She is always asked how the illness has affected her, and this often evokes tears and worries about present and future, together with stories of other losses and disconnections in her life. Her worries may be for the relief of his suffering, her children's grief, or her future.

Some secrets may emerge, such as a history of substance abuse. Then mother may say that the 20 years of his drinking were awful for her and the children. Family may interject that the father was wonderful when he was sober. The children are invited to say what it was like for them. They may express embarrassment, shame, anger, fear, and a sense of never having known their dad, or constant worry for their mother. In talking about this type of painful experience, the object is not to judge or to inflame guilt. Rather, the intent is to acknowledge and speak of history that had been banished into the underworld so that it does not reappear in subsequent generations, often in more disguised form. If the family is able to speak of their collective past with a willingness to listen to one another, individual members may be able to construct a new and more useful understanding of themselves in relation to others, rather than harbor unnecessary feelings of responsibility, resentment, or shame for many years to come.

Some family secrets are harder to let go of than others, so the suffering is likely to be handed on. Past experiences within the family, such as suicide, abuse, abandonment, or neglect, can be constellated and complicate the dying process and bereavement for surviving family members. Providing opportunities to speak about these can help some families heal old wounds and recreate themselves, so that future generations are not silent carriers of these painful legacies.

Most children are not plagued by such painful memories, and the family meeting is an opportunity for them to remember, laugh, cry, hug, give thanks, and take their leave. Even if their father appears to be unconscious, the children are encouraged both in the family meeting and when they have time alone with him to hold his hand and tell him whatever they wish to say. Even in the most wanting of relationships, we can express our sadness that we missed out on one another and thank our parent for giving us life. Although the task of sorting things out may seem impossible in such a short time, the power of impending loss can facilitate openings, insights, and generative change, both internally and within the family as a whole. Family meetings can provide those involved an opportunity to revisit their internalized connections through the stories that survive and can be told. These inner stories and bonds with others continue despite physical absence or the passage of time (41).

## When All Is Said and Done

Having ALS, or caring for someone with ALS, can stir feelings from the past and invite a reworking of the stories that we have constructed about our lives and relationships with others. Family or friend meetings can be an invitation to acknowledge our continuing connections with others, the suffering that is shared, as well as the beauty and brevity of life. Wayne Muller wrote the following:

> There are times in all of our lives when we are forced to reach deep into ourselves and to feel the truth of our real nature. For each of us there comes a moment when we can no longer live our lives by accident. Life throws us into questions that some of us refuse to ask until we are confronted by death or some tragedy in our lives. What do I know to be most deeply true? What do I love and have I loved well? Who do I believe myself to be and what have I placed on the center of the altar of my life? Where do I belong? What will people find in the ashes of my incarnation when it is over? How shall I live my life knowing that I will die? And what is my gift to the family of earth? (42)

## The Dying Process

Hospice staff monitor changes, discuss options for symptom management, and provide support to the person who has ALS and those involved in caregiving. During the last days or few weeks of life, the following changes may also occur, indicating that death is close:

- *Increased disengagement from the world of the living is common* (43). In the last few days or weeks, people who are dying may withdraw into themselves for increasingly long periods. People may prefer to communicate less, seem preoccupied or "elsewhere," request that visits be limited to members of the immediate family, or withdraw from even their most intimate relations. Some people will clearly communicate their wish for undisturbed time, while others will communicate this non-verbally by becoming less responsive to others and the environment. It is important to respect this process, while remaining engaged with the person and giving gentle reassurances of continued presence and concern. This can be communicated through the tone of one's voice, gentle touch, and, depending on individual history and beliefs, various forms of spiritual practice or ritual.

- *Reports of visitations from friends or relatives who have predeceased the person who is dying are not uncommon and are described in the death and dying literature.* Less common are reports of angels or religious figures (43). There may be some reluctance on the part of people to share these experiences for fear of being seen as crazy. Gentle inquiry can allow people to talk about their experiences, allay concerns, and open the possibility for further dialogue.

- *Decreased interest in taking food and fluids by mouth or feeding tube.* This usually occurs as the appetite wanes and body functions slow. At this stage, forcing foods can cause uncomfortable symptoms, including vomiting. Adequate mouth care, such as keeping the lips moist with lubricants or a wet compress, can offset the effects of decreased fluid intake.

- *Certain physiologic changes are indicative of impending death:* decreased sphincter control resulting in urinary and rectal incontinence; sluggish circulation resulting in diminished sensation, discoloration, or mottling of the extremities and cold skin (progressing from feet to hands, ears, and nose); sensory impairment resulting in blurred vision or altered taste and smell (hypersensitive or hyposensitive); changes in vital signs such as decreased blood pressure, slow and weak pulse, and shallow and irregular respirations; and decreased gastrointestinal activity resulting in nausea, flatus, distention, or constipation (43).

- *Physiologic signs of imminent death include the following:* dilated and fixed pupils; inability to move; loss of reflexes; weaker and more rapid pulse; changes in the appearance of the face such as sunken cheeks and a gray pallor to the skin; noisy breathing (death rattle); lowered blood pressure; and breathing characterized by increasingly long gaps between inspirations (gaps initially last a few seconds and can lengthen to 45–60 seconds), visible use of the neck muscles on inhalation, and mouth-breathing with the jaw relaxed in an open position (43).

- *A period of increased agitation or restlessness, symptomatic of advanced respiratory dysfunction, can precede death by a few days or weeks.* These symptoms are not always present before death, and some people experience little or no apparent distress. More often there is a transition period characterized by increased agitation, especially at night, which is associated with respiratory changes. Medications to reduce restlessness and anxiety can be helpful during this time (38). Thankfully, this period does pass, and people usually experience a time of calm lasting from a few hours to a few days before death.

- *A period of calm before the death is not uncommon.* Some describe this calm or heightened sense of well-being before death as the "shooting star" phenomenon. The transition from restlessness to calm can be quite dramatic at times. One memorable example involved a young man who had experienced a steady and rapid progression of ALS. For approximately one week, he had experienced sleeplessness, agitation, general discomfort, and other symptoms of advanced respiratory dysfunction. Then, for 24 hours before his death, there was a dramatic shift. He became not only calm but also by all appearances euphoric. Infused with a sense of well-being and initiative, he spent the day making detailed funeral plans, even composing his own light-hearted obituary. He then communicated his wishes and goodbyes to family and intimate friends with the delight of someone making final preparations before a trip. This gentleman's last day will be long remembered by those who were present, and it was later described by his family as his final gift to them.

- *Coma, or a period of unresponsiveness to sensory stimulation, can precede death by less than an hour or for several days.* Although people may not be able to respond in any way that is apparent to the observer, we always tell caregivers to assume some level of awareness on the part of the person who is dying. Hence, family can continue speaking softly to the person who is dying, providing a reassuring presence until the final breath (31).

- *Certain metaphorical themes appearing in conversation may herald that death is near.* For example, it is not uncommon for people to talk about "going home" or, in their own symbolic language, speak of preparations for travel (44). Days before she died, one woman had a series of dreams about taking care of important business and getting on a bus with a driver who knew how to take her to her beloved childhood home and early family. These dreams prompted actual discussions with her children about final legal arrangements and she was not content until she knew that her affairs were in order. Then, having made preparations alluded to in her dreams, she seemed to fully enjoy her final days with a sense of relaxed anticipation that she was going home.

We are not taught that we have a vital place in mourning with others and seldom are we taught about the possibilities for transformation at the end of life. Just as each person's life is unique, so the experience of death is unique for each person. We each bring our personality, history, sense of meaning, and magic to the process. Ultimately, when we participate in the dying process of another, we are preparing for our own death. Those who are facing death in the immediate future have much to teach us both of dying and of living. The aim of hospice is to provide an environment that can hold both the terrors and potential for transformation at the end of life.

## Care for the Caregivers

It seems fitting to close with a focus on caregivers, whose needs can be eclipsed by the day-to-day demands of caring for a loved one with ALS. It may seem that just as one settles into a manageable routine or accommodates to a loss, disease progression presents another loss, necessitating yet another accommodation. At times, the rate of physical change in ALS can seem to outpace one's capacity for adaptation and a caring response. This has been referred to as "compassion fatigue." Even the most loving, conscientious, capable, resilient, and physically fit caregiver has limits. Thus, it is imperative that the physical, emotional, and spiritual needs of caregivers assume importance. This can be difficult because the needs of people with ALS are compelling. Yet it is in everyone's best interest for caregivers to remain well and fit. Utilizing sources of support available through hospice and the types of services previously discussed can be of benefit.

It may initially feel intrusive and unsettling when ALS requires acceptance of help from strangers who enter one's home and intimate daily routines. It may be difficult for people with ALS, who have come to rely on the loving care of family members, to entrust themselves to the care of someone new. Caregivers may choose to continue providing most of the physical care for loved ones and accept help with other responsibilities such as household chores, transporting children to activities, or planning for holidays. For others, relieved of some responsibilities for providing physical care, caregivers may once again experience themselves as wife, husband, daughter, son, or friend to the person who has ALS. Providing personal care is a time of intimate connection for some people, but for others it is not. When the needs of caregivers conflict with those of the person who has ALS, it may be difficult to talk and tensions may escalate. At times, caregivers may feel that caring for themselves is selfish, or they may not recognize their own needs in the midst of caring for another. It is important to consider what some have referred to as the "ethic of self-care," meaning that caring for oneself in the midst of caring for another is ethically responsible as well as necessary on a practical level to sustain caregiving abilities (45). Hospice staff can help address these issues and help families respond creatively to the difficulties brought about by ALS. Family caregivers can benefit from access to a variety of resources and encouragement to honor their own physical, psychological, and spiritual needs.

ALS turns lives upside down, challenges the assumptions on which we base our lives, and alters our customary ways of doing things. Hospice, while not a panacea, can be of help in living and dying with ALS. Hospice also follows the family for approximately a year after the death. Hospice can provide useful information on the grieving process, along with various options for support such as small bereavement groups, intermittent contact with bereavement staff or trained volunteers, and referral to community resources including counselors who can companion and assist those who are mourning multiple losses brought about by ALS.

Ultimately, it is the aim of hospice to bear witness to both individuals with ALS and their companions, while providing tangible support and personal presence. It is our privilege to partner with people in this way. We have found that those who live with ALS, as well as their families and friends, are our most generous teachers.

## References

1. Bradley WG, Anderson F, Bromberg M, et al. Current management of ALS: comparison of the ALS CARE Database and the AAN Practice Parameter. *Neurology.* 2001;57:500–504.
2. Mackelprang RW, Mackelprang RD. Historical and contemporary issues in end-of-life decisions: implications for social work. *Social Work.* 2005;50:315–324.
3. Oliver D, Borasio GD, Walsh E, eds. *Palliative Care in Amyotrophic Lateral Sclerosis.* 2nd ed. Oxford: Oxford University Press; 2006.
4. Hadlock D. Physician roles in hospice care. In: Corr CA, Corr DM, eds. *Hospice Care: Principles and Practice.* New York, NY: Springer; 1983.
5. Thompson B, Wurth MA. The hospice movement. In: Tigges KN, Marcil WM, eds. *Terminal and Life-Threatening Illness: An Occupational Behavior Perspective.* Thorofare, NJ: Slack; 1988.
6. Corless I. The hospice movement in North America. In: Corr CA, Corr DM, eds. *Hospice Care: Principles and Practice.* New York, NY: Springer; 1983.
7. National Hospice Organization. *Standards of a Hospice Program of Care.* Alexandria, VA: National Hospice Organization; 1981.
8. Thompson B. Occupational therapy with the terminally ill. In: Kiernat JM, ed. *Occupational Therapy and the Older Adult: A Clinical Manual.* Gaithersburg, MD: Aspen; 1991.
9. Abrahm JL, Hansen-Flaschen J. Hospice care for patients with advanced lung disease. *Chest.* 2000;121:220–229.
10. Health Care Financing Administration. *Medicare Benefit Policy Manual.* Rev. 28, December 3, 2004. http://www.cms.hhs.gov/manuals/Downloads/bp102c09.pdf. Accessed February 4, 2008.
11. National Hospice and Palliative Care Organization. *NHPCO Facts and Figures: Hospice Care in America.* November 2007 edition. http://www.nhpco.org/files/public/Statistics_Research/NHPCO_facts-and-figures_Nov2007.pdf. Accessed January 15, 2008.

12. McCluskey L, Houseman G. Medicare hospice referral criteria for patients with amyotrophic lateral sclerosis: a need for improvement. *J Palliat Med.* 2004;7:47–53
13. Mandler RN, Anderson FA, Miller RG, et al. The ALS Patient Care Database: insights into end-of-life care in ALS. *Amyotroph Lateral Scler Other Motor Neuron Disord.* 2001;2:203–206.
14. Dubinsky R, Chen J, Lai SM. Trends in hospital utilization and outcome for patients with ALS: analysis of a large U.S. cohort. *Neurology.* 2006;67:777–780.
15. National Hospice and Palliative Care Organization. *The year in review.* http://www.nhpco.org/files/public/2007review.pdf. Accessed January 20, 2008.
16. Health Care Financing Administration. Hospice Care Benefit Periods. Program Memorandum no. 628. Implementation of the Balanced Budget Act of 1997.
17. Thompson B, MacNeil C. A phenomenological study exploring the meaning of a graduate seminar on spirituality for occupational therapy students. *Am J Occup Ther.* 2006;60:531–539.
18. Balk D, ed. *Handbook of Thanatology: The Essential Body of Knowledge for the Study of Death, Dying, and Bereavement.* Florence, KY: Routledge; 2007.
19. Williams AL. Perspectives on spirituality at the end of life: a meta-summary. *Palliat Support Care.* 2006;4:407–417.
20. Romanoff B, Thompson B. Meaning construction in palliative care: the use of narrative, ritual, and the expressive arts. *Am J Hosp Palliat Med.* 2006;23:309–316.
21. Neimeyer RA, Prigerson HG, Davies B. Mourning & meaning. *Am Behav Sci.* 2002;46:235–251.
22. Thompson, B. Expressive arts and the experience of loss. *Forum: Assoc Death Educ Counsel.* 2003;29:1–3.
23. Jacques ND, Thompson B. Occupational therapy. In: Zuberbueler E, ed. *Complementary Therapies in End-of-Life Care.* Arlington, VA: National Hospice and Palliative Care Organization; 2001.
24. Ganzini L, Johnston W, Silveira MJ. The final month of life in patients with ALS. *Neurology.* 2002;59:428–431.
25. Mitsumoto H, Bromberg M, Johnston W, et al. Promoting excellence in end-of-life care in ALS. *Amyotroph Lateral Scler.* 2005;6:145–154.
26. National Hospice Organization. *Medical Guidelines for Determining Prognosis in Selected Non-Cancer Diseases.* 2nd ed. Alexandria, VA: National Hospice Organization; 1996.
27. Robert Wood Johnson Foundation. *Promoting Excellence in End-of-Life Care.* Appendix E: Cost, Access and Policy, 2004. http://www.promotingexcellence.org/files/public/als_appendix_e.pdf. Accessed January 23, 2008.
28. Thompson B. Amyotrophic lateral sclerosis: integrating care for patients and their families. *Am J Hosp.* 1990;7:27–32.
29. Mitsumoto H, Rabkin JG. Palliative care of patients with amyotrophic lateral sclerosis: "prepare for the worst and hope for the best." *JAMA.* 2007;298:207–217.
30. Johnson W. *End-of-Life Decision Making in Amyotrophic Lateral Sclerosis.* http://www.alsconnection.com/Johnston,%20W%20(AAN)%208BS-006-96.pdf. Accessed January 30, 2008.
31. Borasio GD, Voltz R, Miller RG. Palliative care in amyotrophic lateral sclerosis. *Neurol Clin.* 2001;4:829–847.
32. Andersen PM, Borasio GD, Dengler R, et al. Good practice in the management of amyotrophic lateral sclerosis: clinical guidelines. An evidence-based review with good practice points. EALSC Working Group. *Amyotroph Lateral Scler.* 2007;8:195–213.
33. Kabat Zinn J. *Full Catastrophe Living: Using the Wisdom of Your Body and Mind to Face Stress, Pain, and Illness.* New York, NY: Random House; 2005.
34. Lehrer PM, Woolfolk RL, eds. *Principles and Practices of Stress Management.* 2nd ed. New York, NY: Guilford Press; 1993.

35. Averill AJ, Kasarskis EJ, Segerstrom SC. Psychological health in patients with amyotrophic lateral sclerosis. *Amyotroph Lateral Scler.* 2007;8:243–254.
36. American Psychological Association. *Diagnostic and Statistical Manual of Mental Disorders.* 4th ed., text revision, DSM-IV-TR. Washington, DC: American Psychological Association; 2000.
37. Rando TA. *Treatment of Complicated Mourning.* Champaign, IL: Research Press; 1993.
38. Simmons Z. Management strategies for patients with amyotrophic lateral sclerosis from diagnosis through death. *Neurologist.* 2005;11:257–270.
39. Rabkin JG, Albert SM, Del Bene ML, et al. Prevalence of depressive disorders and change over time in late-stage ALS. *Neurology.* 2005;65:62–67.
40. Miller RG, Rosenberg JA, Gelinas DF, et al. Practice parameter: the care of the patient with amyotrophic lateral sclerosis (an evidence-based review): report of the Quality Standards Subcommittee of the American Academy of Neurology. *Neurology.* 1999;52:1311.
41. Klass D, Silverman PR, Nickman SL, eds. *Continuing Bonds: New Understandings of Grief.* New York, NY: Taylor & Francis; 1996.
42. Muller, W. *How Then, Shall We Live: Four Simple Questions That Reveal the Beauty and Meaning of our Lives.* New York, NY: Random House; 1997.
43. Samarel N. The dying process. In: Wass H, Neimeyer RA, eds. *Dying: Facing the Facts.* Washington, DC: Taylor & Francis; 1995.
44. Callanan, M, Kelley P. *Final Gifts: Understanding the Special Awareness, Needs, and Communications of the Dying.* New York, NY: Poseidon Press; 1992.
45. Gilligan C. *In a Different Voice: Psychological Theory and Women's Development.* Cambridge, MA: Harvard University Press; 1982.

# 25

# Mourning

## N. Michael Murphy

With reasonable physical health, or even in the face of considerable sickness, we seldom contemplate or allow into full consciousness the possibility that we can die at any time. Denial of death is everyday fare for most of us, but that inner innocence or naiveté that maintains the myth of our physical immortality becomes sorely tried or even shattered by the diagnosis of any life-threatening illness. The implications of amyotrophic lateral sclerosis (ALS) are particularly hard to ignore because all the literature speaks of a fatal outcome, and the muscular decline is an ever-present reminder of finitude and death. This loss of health and innocence in ALS evokes the expression of a whole range of feelings that may be frozen by denial or given full exposure, which is the prelude to acceptance of what is happening. These responses, induced to varying degrees in patient, family, and caregivers, are the subject of the first part of this chapter. The second part focuses on some aspects of care for those who are suffering or have suffered from loss, be they the ones with ALS, their families, or their caregivers.

### Mourning and the Response to Loss

Loss transports us into a journey that ranges back and forth along a path that ends with integration and acceptance. In ALS or any other terminal illness, death may intervene at any time with the trials and tribulations imposed by the loss still unresolved. We will retain some degree of denial but most of the time will move beyond it. Most will not continue to rage incessantly against the coming of the night but may become stuck in a state of bereavement and need a kindly nudge to leave it behind. Grief is a prelude to letting go or dying and will be shunned as long as death is denied or avoided or while we are consumed by our response to bereavement.

*Denial* is a natural, self-protective response to any event that disconnects us from that which provides nurture or self-esteem. In the event of sudden death of someone close, or the sudden, unexpected diagnosis of an illness such as ALS, the immediate response is usually some variant of "Oh, no!" Taken literally, this is an exclamation denying the truth of what has just been told in an attempt to obliterate the fear and chaos inspired by the life-threatening diagnosis and to restore equilibrium. Usually the individual does not maintain the stance that the incident never happened and asks a series of questions that help to confirm the new reality. With a life-threatening illness, most will breach their denial to some degree but will often shore it up again with the aid of family members who are terrified at the prospect of loss and hide behind the possibility of doing something—anything at all—to dissipate the helplessness and fear.

Some physicians are models of sensitivity as they speak of that which is difficult to hear and still remain fully present and available. Others protect themselves by disgorging unpalatable facts over the phone or even in hospital corridors. Medical schools give scant attention to teaching students how to digest painful information and reframe it for their patients simply, clearly, and compassionately. We need to give only as many of the facts as the one with ALS needs at the moment, all within a framework of compassion and gentle hopefulness, not the false hope of the blusterer who dangles insubstantial half-truths with the justification that he does not want to take away all hope. He does not understand that real hope and optimism are always appropriate in life-threatening illness; not that the condition will be cured, but that in a loving atmosphere, with truthful communication and connectedness, we will experience the hope and preciousness of each day, and the peace that comes from having settled our technical and emotional affairs.

*Bereavement* is defined in the Oxford English dictionary as the state of being deprived, robbed, or stripped, usually of immaterial possessions. Thus, if we feel that we own someone or something that is then lost, we will believe that we have been robbed. The feelings that accompany this robbery usually include all manner of rage and outrage.

If we believe that we have a birthright to good health, and that muscular power, control, and integrity, which have been painstakingly promoted and learned from our earliest days, are "ours," we will experience bereavement with rage, outrage, and bewilderment when it is taken away by ALS. If we believe that a loved one belongs to us, then the death threat and gradual taking away of that person will cause us to go through all the pain of the bereaved. Because we are human and have been brought up to believe in ownership, we will feel bereaved many times in our lives. Those who are able to love without attachment and are not tied to goods, chattels, or the inalienable right to good health are less apt to become engulfed by anger and more ready to accept whatever comes their way.

*Rage* is a word associated with being mad, going berserk, running amok, and losing control. When we say that we are mad, we do not usually imagine that we mean it literally, that we are really insane or are out our minds. But the fact is that if we maintain rage, we are insane and incapable of responding in a healthy manner to the realities of the moment.

A well-respected physician, who had authored several books and was a wonderful teacher and observer of others, was wheeled into my office by his wife. I had no idea he was physically sick until that moment, but one look at his intense jaundice and emaciated state made it clear that he was close to death. He said that he had asked to see me because he was afraid that he was going out of his mind and wanted my opinion. His story was that carcinoma of the pancreas had been diagnosed several months earlier, and since then he had been involved in a continual technological nightmare of surgery, chemotherapy, and tests. In his words, he barely had time to catch his breath. It was as if he had been holding his breath and suspending his feelings for the past months, aided and abetted in this denial by his intellect, his family, and a horde of physicians. Now, he was beginning to experience feelings of rage, translated by this cultured man into feelings of loss of control and fear of losing his mind or going mad. With a little gentle nudging and a couple of family meetings the following week, he was able to acknowledge his rage and leave it behind. At that point, he was ready to grieve with his family, share stories, and express tender feelings, all of which had been a lifelong difficulty for this logical, controlling man. He died a few hours after the second family gathering, peacefully, with all said and done.

*Charles was a fear-filled man who raged against the diagnosis and manifestations of ALS. His rage and fear were such that he developed unremitting angina that was uncontrollable with medical treatment. This created a dilemma between the risk of surgery in one whose respiration was already affected by ALS and the prospect of pain for the rest of his life. He elected to undergo surgery, which completely relieved the angina, but then he was compelled to face his bereavement and address the rage over the perceived rape of his physical integrity. The rage and madness over his state and the outrage that this happened to him abated as he gave it voice. Years before, his teenaged son had died in a climbing accident, and at that time and subsequently he avoided his grief and dealt with bereavement by banning all thought and talk of his son. With his own life-threatening illness, he initially avoided having to deal with his feelings by almost killing himself with angina, breaking his heart rather than allowing himself to feel broken-hearted. The next year provided him with the time to experience his bereavement and grief over the loss of his son, and this in turn gave him the courage to mourn his own losses and impending death. Six weeks before he died, his younger sister was killed in a motor vehicle accident. He attended her funeral in a wheelchair and appeared to be fully aware of his outrage and sadness over her death. It seemed as though her death gave him permission to let go and die, and the last few weeks of his life were relatively comfortable and peaceful.*

*Outrage* at being the subject of life-threatening illness is rage that is more focused and controlled. The one outraged screams "Why me?" or the relative cries out against this happening to a good person like Mother when there are so many worse people out there who are perfectly free of illness. Outrage blames an unjust God or sees the illness as a punishment. It storms against a missed diagnosis or fastens blame for what is happening on anyone or anything. It is like paranoia as it projects the insanity of the situation onto an outside source, unwilling or unable to understand or accept the randomness and impersonal nature of terminal illness. It is an attempt to avoid the impotence of medicine and its regular inability to control outcomes. Rage and outrage disconnect us from each other and our world just at the time we most need connectedness and love. Its main purpose is to stave off grief, which is the necessary prelude to connectedness, acceptance, and integration.

> *Betty was in her early sixties when she came to see me following surgery for what proved to be metastatic colon cancer. She said that she had foregone chances to live independently or get married in order to take care of her chronically ill mother, who eventually died twelve years before the diagnosis of Betty's colon cancer. Her mother never said a word in gratitude and seemed to be in a perpetual state of rage, outrage, or their internalized associate, depression. The thirty years of caregiving produced little joy and a constant stewpot of anger, and Mother's death offered little emotional relief since they had never shared anything but rage and had not allowed themselves to connect through grief, which in turn leads to integration, permitting the exchange of love. The stewpot continued to simmer for the next decade, during which Betty looked after her meek and mild father until his death. The long-awaited peace and happiness, expected as a birthright, especially with the departure of her parents, never happened. Two years after her father's death, she was diagnosed with colon cancer, and I remember the spirit of her words, if not their actual form, as she raged and bubbled in my office: "It is not fair. After all I did for my parents. Now I expected to enjoy myself and travel, and look what has happened. If there is a just God in heaven, He will take this cancer away, and I am going to sit here until He does!"*

That is exactly what she did. She sat on her stewpot of rage with her spiritual arms folded and did little else for the 9 months until she died. No softness, no grief, no letting go. No kindness to herself for her service to her parents even though it was reluctantly given. No tears for the little girl within her who never felt loved. She died as she lived: a stony monument to self-righteousness and outrage, fending off the comfort and love that was within her reach.

*Bewilderment* is the state of losing one's way or being unable to grasp what is happening. It is beyond denial in that there is an understanding that all is not well. But there is a numbness or apathy that does not admit to feelings, especially rage, outrage, or grief.

*Distancing* results from not wishing to become too emotionally involved. Some family members and friends keep their distance from the one with ALS and so never accompany the dying person though grief to acceptance and a place of new intimacy born of having gone through the emotional refiner's fire together. If we keep our distance, we protect ourselves from grief but do not experience intimacy. We will not have to say goodbye, which many of us believe too painful, but this ensures that we will be forever nagged by the wish that we had made some expression of love; that we had told our loved one that he or she was important to us and would be sorely missed. It is paradoxical that such an expression is a necessary prelude to letting go, and it is only after we let go that we are free to be nourished by the everlasting images and stories that are the real essence or soul of the one who has died.

Physicians, nurses, and other caregivers frequently distance themselves from their patients. We have been taught by words or example that it is not good to become too involved. How much is too much has never been clearly defined other than the proscription related to sexual behavior with patients. Are we permitted or do we permit ourselves to love a patient or mourn his or her loss? If we grieved for each of our patients who died, there is the fear that we would burn out or go mad. Oddly enough, it is our resistance to mourning and our stubborn maintenance of distance that is a frequent cause of chronic anger and burnout among caregivers. If emotionally we will go the whole distance with patients and their families and be prepared—or unprepared—to weep and also to attend the wake or funeral, we will have done everything possible so that we can then let go and move on. Those who distance themselves emotionally and feel that their work is done as soon as they run out of technical tricks never experience completion and peacefulness with their patients who die. This, like any form of interrupted intercourse, is, by definition, incomplete and unsatisfying. It is the failure to accompany the family to the end that creates in caregivers a continuous sense of bereavement. Burnout means being consumed by the fire of rage, and this in turn precipitates fight or flight. We will fight by becoming even more angry and distanced, and we will fly by changing specialties, leaving medicine, or committing suicide.

We will go to any extreme in our attempts to avoid *grief*. We have been admonished to hold back tears and be brave. Little John Kennedy saluting the coffin of his dad. The show must go on. Keep the stiff upper lip, and be "strong."

We are uncomfortable with feelings, and being emotional in a male-ordered world is considered little short of sinful, and most certainly weak. In the face of grief, many physicians, especially the pseudomasculine, macho ones, will provide and encourage tranquilizers and sleeping pills so that its expression is muted. Others will prescribe antidepressants rather than listen to the rage and outrage and assist their patients in the delivery of their grief. There is the fear that being very emotional in grief will lead to breakdown and this inspires the fear of madness and even the fantasy of incarceration in a mental hospital. It is not always accepted that grief is the normal final expression of loss and being out of control.

The story of Dante's *Inferno* is a vivid reminder that the pain of grief cannot be avoided if we wish to emerge from mourning. The Inferno was imagined as a round pit with steep sides, and almost all of the sufferers tried to escape the flames by scrambling toward the periphery and attempting to get out by clawing their way up the steep sides. Just a few realized that the only way out was through an opening in the middle of the pit. The flames of grief will end only if we travel into their midst.

We are uncomfortable with grief because it is both the harbinger of death and the beginning of its acceptance, and in our society death is hopeless, a failure, and the greatest of all possible negatives. We may never say "die." So it is common in families for each of the members to experience grief but to do their crying alone. Over and over again I have heard variations on the theme of a daughter who was heartbroken over her mother who had advanced ALS. When I asked if she had shared her fears with mother, she was shocked, saying that she did not want to upset her and that she needed to remain strong for her. What a sad dissipation of soulful feelings. I will always remember a daughter who was the devoted caregiver for her much-loved mother: "When I am down, she holds me while I cry, and when she is sad and tearful, I am able to hold and comfort her. We are each there for the other." If we share grief and be witnesses for one another, we experience the connectedness that we crave, and it becomes the prelude to acceptance and peace. Mourning does not end while grief is in the closet.

We often wonder whether children should witness our grief and we attempt to protect them from feelings, both ours and their own. It is a real gift to share our tears and sadness with children. We are telling them by example that the loss of Grandmother to ALS is painfully heartbreaking, and that these feelings are both appropriate and very much worth sharing. Children who are protected from feelings are fundamentally deprived and are being taught that the feelings induced by loss are dangerous and not to be expressed. When feelings of loss are pushed underground, they do not disappear and may be transformed into chronic fear and anxiety to emerge in full force at the next appearance of life-threatening illness.

*Integration and acceptance* may be at hand when we have ceased fighting and raging against the coming of the night. Tears have been shed for the child within, and he or she is at peace. We have grieved with our family and have ceased to hide behind endless procedures and other doings. We have let go of family and friends and are now able to be a human being rather than a human doing, simply being with ourselves and our family for whatever time remains.

> *I remember Melba, a marvelous, energetic, humorous woman I had the privilege of knowing at different stages of ALS. In the early days she raged, but in listening to herself and being listened to, the anger seemed to evaporate in a mist of wit and wisdom. She grieved for her husband and children, and she wept for herself, and there was a wealth of healing and love between them all as they laughed, cried, and told stories. As her breathing became very shallow, talking was almost impossible, but at that point, all had been said and done. There was nothing more to say. She died quietly and peacefully, simply breathing out/expiring.*

*I had several taped interviews with Joan, a most remarkable woman who had lost the ability to speak and swallow a few months before my last interview. She had been living independently, but profound muscular weakness had made it necessary for her to leave the area and move in with family. She was able to type with one finger on a word processor and her words conjure up images of acceptance and letting go that move me beyond words: " . . . it is not easy to part from each other. That is why we should make the most of our time and be open and trusting. I'm not saying anything new. I want to say that it seems to me since I am no longer verbal, I talk a lot! It is ironic and a little sad. I don't feel sick. I keep thinking it's a big mistake and I'm waiting for someone to correct it. At least God has big shoulders, but I still think or rather I wish he had overlooked me! It is amazing. I am still struggling to hold on to life, and at the same time there are those who throw theirs away. How sad for them who have never known joy of life.*

*"Do not feel sorry for me; I have peace and love. At times I get a sense of life slipping away and it is frightening, but at the same time I know I will be fine.*

*"What is important is never to let ALS be a person instead of seeing your loved one as the person with ALS. I have seen time and time again when family members become isolated from one another. It is a gift of love that we remain connected. It is an obligation for both the person with ALS and the caregiver. It is not ALS that cuts us off. It is our fear and lack of love for one another.*

*"Finally, I want to thank you all for your generosity, friendship, and love. For being there with me, sometimes in silence, sometimes with soft suggestions, but always dealing with me as a person, as an individual. I wish I had the ability to tell you all how much you have given me. I'm not alone, traveling in uncharted waters. You have kept me safe, close to shore, and when I've drifted too far, you have gently guided me back to safety. I thank you, all my friends. You are my heroes."*

## Caring for Those Who Mourn

### Caring for the Patient

The prerequisite for caregiving is that the caregivers understand the process of mourning for the one with ALS and are also able to articulate how this process is affecting them. If we are frightened of rage, we will discourage its expression in the families to whom we are giving care. If the expression of sadness rocks our need for self-control, and we have been raised to worship the stiff upper lip and the belief that any public expression of grief is not positive or is an admission of defeat, then we will be routed by the tears of our patient and so be of little help.

Openness and connectedness among all involved are essential to good care. Family connectedness is enhanced and encouraged by the family meeting, which should be held soon after the diagnosis and repeated at the request of the family or whenever they appear to be stuck in the journey of mourning. It is important to address technical questions and any symptoms that may arise, but it is tempting to remain focused on these practical issues and not give voice to the responses to loss. Anticipation of the losses of ability to talk, swallow, and breathe, and skillful discussion of these issues over time will usually avert a crisis response, born of widespread denial, which may well lead to the patient being impelled into a course of action which, on greater reflection, he or she would not want. A peaceful death, when all has been said and done, is much more likely when all involved have given their full attention to both body and soul.

## Caring for the Family

Isadora Duncan (1), reflecting on her own grief following the death of her two small children expressed the following:

> The next morning I drove out to see Duse, who was living in a rose colored villa behind a vineyard. She came down a vine covered walk to meet me, like a glorious angel. She took me in her arms and her wonderful eyes beamed upon me such love and tenderness that I felt just as Dante must have felt when, in the "Paradiso," he encounters the Divine Beatrice.
>
> From then on I lived at Viareggio, finding courage from the radiance of Eleanora's eyes. She used to rock me in her arms, consoling my pain, but not only consoling, for she seemed to take my sorrow to her own breast, and I realized that if I had not been able to bear the society of other people, it was because they all played the comedy of trying to cheer me with forgetfulness. Whereas Eleanora said: "Tell me about Deidre and Patrick," and made me repeat to her all their little sayings and ways, and show her their photos, which she kissed and cried over. She never said, "Cease to grieve," but she grieved with me, and, for the first time since their death, I felt I was not alone.

Isadora might have said: "Don't cheer me with forgetfulness nor keep me in denial nor drug me into apathy and distance. I need to grieve. I need to be held, so that my anger and hurt flow out of me, and I need love to help me cry. Don't tell me to get on with my life and cease to grieve because at that moment we become disconnected and I am plunged deeper into loneliness."

The family will have mourned to a greater or lesser extent while the patient was alive. Few will still be in denial or in shock at the time of death. Most will have left their rage and anger behind, but some will experience bereavement after the death of their loved one even though they were the most meticulous and loving of caregivers. Mrs. B told me that the 18 months after the death of her husband from ALS were quite awful. Their marriage was intimate and unusually exciting, but the year of his illness was filled with losses that seemed to follow one another without respite. He coped with each crisis with dignity, humor, and compassion for all right up to the moment of his death, which followed removal from a respirator at his request. But Mrs. B, caught up in her husband's crises especially toward the end, never allowed herself to feel the rage and anger while he was alive, and after he died she was engulfed by overwhelming resentment at the disease and the turmoil it created in her life. She had worked alongside her husband, and that ceased. Recreationally, physically, emotionally, sexually, her life was turned upside down, and after his death some of her rage was vented toward her image of him and toward the "selfish" decision he made to disconnect the respirator. After his death, when the hubbub of family and friends quieted down, she became almost paralyzed by anger and depression. Gradually, through talking about her feelings over and over again with a handful of nonjudgmental friends, she was able to move from rage to grief. She stressed to me how important it was for her to solicit these few friends to come and share their feelings about her husband and invite them to listen to her. Without her encouragement, they would not have come and shared painful feelings, which was the necessary prelude to moving on.

Self-help groups are very good for some of those whose loved ones have died. The death can be a precious opportunity to mourn many other losses that have gone unmourned. If this happens, the individual's life may take on a new zest, freed from a dark pall of unremitting bereavement and grief from the past. I frequently advise and encourage counseling for those who have been involved with a death since many are ripe for change at that moment.

## Caring for the Caregiver

We look for and are expected to provide answers even when there are none. There is great uncertainty in medicine, and yet we are not taught how to deal with it, emotionally and interpersonally. ALS offers caregivers the perfect opportunity to confront helplessness and to go beyond it and realize we are only helpless in doing but never in being. Because of our illusions of professionalism we will be bereaved by ALS. We will be angry at the disease, the patient, or the family, or else distance ourselves behind a proclamation that there is nothing to be done. It is not a waste of valuable professional time for a physician to be with someone afflicted with ALS, although it may be one of our most difficult challenges because of our own discomfort, not the patient's. Our grief and sadness will be evoked, and we may wish to flee, especially if there have been significant others in our lives who have died and for whom we never mourned.

I believe that all caregivers who provide care for the dying, including all physicians and nurses as well as many others, need to participate in a workshop that focuses on their mourning, past, present, and future, and the workshop needs repeating at least once or twice during a career. The soul-searching workshops I have given for several years last 2 or 3 days and include time for visualizing or imagining our own death so that we can experience some of our fears and apprehensions about death and so be more in touch with what our patients are experiencing. Workshop participants also experience a simulated family meeting when they are the ones who are dying and are finishing up their business with those they love by saying what needs to be said. There is also time in the workshop to mourn other losses, and there are many opportunities to experience the art of being an impeccable listener and witness. Being a nonjudgmental, fully present witness is difficult and unfamiliar. We are so practiced in half-listening, interrupting, and dispensing advice. Experiencing the power of witnessing and being witnessed is one of the great surprises for workshop participants. They also learn a few techniques on how to nudge and encourage others to move along the route of mourning. The workshop is extremely personal, and in experiencing and processing the personal we become more empathic caregivers who are less prone to fight and flight.

Because death is still considered as failure and technology is becoming ever more insistent in medicine, it is doubtful that medical and nursing schools will take the lead by having this kind of workshop experience as an essential part of the curriculum. This should not deter smaller groups from introducing such workshops, and the collaboration, interpersonal connectedness, and skills of individuals who are members of caregiving groups for ALS and cancer will be much enhanced as a result.

Another suggestion for ALS caregiving groups is that there be an hour, every week or two, when caregivers gather together to discuss the process of their own mourning and that of the patients and families with whom they work. This is a time when personal reactions to caregiving, families, helplessness, the anger of others, and a box full of other feelings may be aired and witnessed. If we work with the dying for long, we will certainly be reminded of the past or future deaths of our own mothers, fathers, brothers, lovers, and of ourselves. We will have the opportunity to rehearse a little what it might be like when someone close to us dies, and we need a safe place where we can discuss this. Having been part of such a "process group" in St. Peter's Hospice for the past 14 years, I know of its usefulness. But I also know that these meetings can be filled with feelings, and that many caregiving groups abandon them because of discomfort with exposing their vulnerability before colleagues with whom they have to work every day. I believe the intention behind any process or support group is the key to failure or success. If the intention is confrontation and analysis, then sooner or later the group will self-destruct. If the intention is to encourage the expression of feelings that will be lovingly witnessed without judgment and without being pulled apart, the group may become a vital force in the care of the caregiver.

## Web Sites

The Love, Loss, and Forgiveness project has as its long-term goal to make film materials and interpretive guidebooks available. The project will foster an online community for those dealing with loss.

www.lovelossforgiveness.org, www.lovelossforgiveness.blogspot.com

Looking at the pdf book, you will see that we are launching an ambitious project that will impact medical professionals as well as everyone else. We have neglected the soul and spirit of people as we try to fix their mortal body. This book returns the focus to the soul and spirit.

www.lovelossforgiveness.org/PDF/LLFPbook.pdf

## Reference

1. Duncan I. *My Life*. New York, NY: Liveright; 1927.

# Where You Can Turn to For Help

# 26

# The Role of the Muscular Dystrophy Association in ALS Research and Services

**Margaret Wahl**

The Muscular Dystrophy Association (MDA), a voluntary health organization, was founded in 1950 to seek cures for a group of diseases then loosely termed *muscular dystrophy*. The association's focus was twofold: services for patients affected by neuromuscular diseases, and research to find the causes of and treatments for those diseases.

Almost from the beginning, one of MDA's goals became conquering the mysterious disease that had killed New York Yankees first baseman Lou Gehrig in 1941. In the 1950s, Gehrig's widow, Eleanor, served as the association's national campaign chairwoman.

Since the 1950s, the association has spent more than $230 million on research and services related to amyotrophic lateral sclerosis (ALS).

Today, the MDA has an ALS division dedicated exclusively to ALS-related research, services, and legislative advocacy. Updated information specific to ALS can be found at www.als-mda.org.

## Research

The MDA is the largest nongovernmental source of support for ALS research in the world.

## Academic Research

The MDA supports ALS research at laboratories throughout the world, with expenditures in 2007 of about $8 million.

Most MDA academic research projects in ALS focus on uncovering mechanisms of the disease, so that these eventually can become targets for therapy.

For example, in a ground-breaking discovery, an MDA-supported group in 1993 identified mutations in the SOD1 gene on chromosome 21 as a cause of familial ALS, and shortly thereafter, mice with SOD1 mutations were developed. Most laboratories now use these mice for their ALS studies. Prior to the SOD1 findings, there were no mice that reliably mimicked the human disease.

## Translational Research

A more recent development is the MDA's ALS Translational Research Program, which focuses on moving promising research findings out of the laboratory and into the clinic, working largely with biotechnology companies.

For example, in 2006, MDA gave a $652,000 grant to the Translational Genomics Institute (TGen) in Phoenix, Arizona, to uncover subtle differences in the DNA of people with and without nonfamilial ALS.

In 2007, the MDA pledged at least $6 million a year for 3 years to the ALS Therapy Development Institute (ALS TDI), an industrial-scale laboratory in Cambridge, Massachusetts, for identification of biochemical targets for drug development.

## Augie's Quest

In 2006, fitness industry entrepreneur Augie Nieto, whose ALS was diagnosed in 2005, and his wife, Lynne, became MDA ALS Division cochairs.

Immediately, the Nietos got to work promoting MDA's Augie's Quest, an ALS research initiative that in 2 years has raised more than $12 million for clinically relevant research in ALS. Funds from Augie's Quest are allocated through MDA's translational research program to projects with immediate treatment potential, and to helping promising laboratory research make the transition from cells and mice to clinical trials.

The TGen and ALS TDI projects both received funds generated by Augie's Quest.

## Services

MDA allocates some $10 million a year for direct services to people with ALS.

## MDA Clinics and ALS Centers

MDA established its first neuromuscular disease medical clinics in the early 1950s. In 1987, it established four centers specializing in ALS research and care.

That number has grown to 38 MDA/ALS centers throughout the United States, although people with ALS can receive state-of-the-art care at any of MDA's 225 clinics.

MDA/ALS centers deliver high-quality, multidisciplinary care to patients with ALS. To qualify as a center, an institution must show that it's providing not only a comprehensive clinical program but also conducting important research in ALS. (To see an updated database of research, click on Clinical Trials on MDA's Web site at www.mda.org.)

For instance, clinical trials of atorvastatin (Lipitor), insulin-like growth factor 1 (Myotrophin), and ceftriaxone (Rocephin) are being conducted at the MDA/ALS Center at Methodist Neurological Institute in Houston, Texas.

At the Eleanor and Lou Gehrig MDA/ALS Center at Columbia University in New York, researchers are studying whether genetic makeup and/or environmental exposures are risk factors for ALS. Among their other research studies are clinical trials of coenzyme Q10, modafinil (Provigil), and a study of nutrition and the use of noninvasive assisted ventilation in ALS.

At the MDA/ALS Center at Johns Hopkins University in Baltimore, Maryland, investigators have studied the effects of amantadine (Symmetrel), as well as the timing of assisted ventilation, quality of life with ALS, and genetics in this disease.

## Other Services

Through its nationwide network of clinics and local offices, MDA assists people with ALS with the purchase and repair of wheelchairs, braces, and communication devices. The association also offers support groups for patients and caregivers and free durable medical equipment through its loan closets.

## ALS-Specific Publications

In 1996, MDA launched the ALS Newsletter, now the monthly ALS Newsmagazine. Devoted exclusively to the concerns of those with ALS, the publication contains research developments, human interest stories, legislative news, equipment information, and help with everyday challenges.

Additional MDA publications of particular interest to people with ALS and their families are *Everyday Life With ALS: A Practical Guide*; *The ALS Caregiver's Guide*; and *Breathe Easy: Respiratory Care in Neuromuscular Disorders*. Some publications are available in Spanish.

## Web Sites

The MDA ALS Division site at www.als-mda.org contains links to services, research, active and completed clinical trials, and many other resources. The main MDA Web site is at www.mda.org. For information in Spanish, see www.mdaenespanol.org.

## Online Chats

MDA hosts frequent online chats for people with ALS and those close to them. For a calendar of chat days and times, go to www.mda.org/chat/calendar.html.

## How to Contact MDA

Registration with MDA is free. The best way to begin receiving MDA's services and information is to find your local MDA office through your phone directory, or by calling (800) 572-1717, or by entering your zip code into the search box under "MDA in Your Community" at www.mda.org.

You can reach MDA National Headquarters in Tucson, Arizona, by writing to
MDA
National Headquarters
3300 E. Sunrise Drive
Tucson, AZ 85718

or by sending e-mail to
mda@mdausa.org

or by calling
1-800-FIGHT-MD (344-4863)

## MDA/ALS Centers by State

For an updated list, click on "Clinics" on the MDA Web site at www.mda.org, or call (800) 529-2000.

### Arizona

MDA/ALS CENTER AT UPH HOSPITAL
(520) 874-2747
(520) 874-2742 (fax)
E-mail: kscherer@uph.org
Katalin Scherer, MD, Director
University Physicians Healthcare-Neurology
2800 E. Ajo Way
Tucson, AZ 85713

MDA/ALS CENTER AT THE MUCIO F. DELGADO CLINIC FOR NEUROMUSCULAR DISORDERS
(520) 626-6609
(520) 626-6925 (fax)
E-mail: lstern@u.arizona.edu
Lawrence Z. Stern, MD, Director
University of Arizona
Health Sciences Center
1501 North Campbell Ave.
Tucson, AZ 85724

## Arkansas

MDA/ALS CENTER AT THE UNIVERSITY OF ARKANSAS FOR MEDICAL SCIENCES
(501) 686-5135
(501) 686-8689 (fax)
E-mail: rudnickistacya@uams.edu
Stacy A. Rudnicki, MD, Director
4301 West Markham, Slot 500
Little Rock, AR 72205-7199

## California

JERRY LEWIS MDA/ALS CLINICAL AND RESEARCH CENTER
(213) 743-1612
(213) 743-1617 (fax)
E-mail: kengel@usc.edu
W. King Engel, MD, Director
University of Southern California
School of Medicine
637 South Lucas Avenue
Los Angeles, CA 90017

MDA/ALS CENTER AT UCLA
(310) 825-7266
(310) 825-3995 (fax)
E-mail: mcgraves@ucla.edu
Michael C. Graves, MD, Director
UCLA Neurological Services, Suite B200
300 UCLA Medical Plaza
Los Angeles, CA 90095-6975

MDA/ALS CENTER AT THE UNIVERSITY OF CALIFORNIA, IRVINE
(714) 456-2332
(714) 456-5997 (fax)
E-mail: mozaffar@uci.edu
Tahseen Mozaffar, MD, FAAN, Director
200 South Manchester Avenue, Suite 110
Orange, CA 92868

FORBES NORRIS MDA/ALS RESEARCH CENTER
(415) 923-3604
(415) 923-6567 (fax)
E-mail: rmiller@cooper.cpmc.org
Robert G. Miller, MD, Director
California Pacific Medical Center
2324 Sacramento Street, Suite 150
San Francisco, CA 94115

## Colorado

MDA/ALS CENTER AT THE UNIVERSITY OF COLORADO
(303) 315-7221
(303) 315-6796 (fax)
E-mail: hans.neville@uchsc.edu
Hans E. Neville, MD, Codirector

E-mail: steven.ringel@uchsc.edu
Steven P. Ringel, MD, Codirector
Health Sciences Center
4200 East Ninth Avenue, Box B-185
Denver, CO 80262

## Connecticut

MDA/ALS CENTER AT YALE UNIVERSITY
(203) 785-4867
(203) 785-5694 (fax)
E-mail: jonathan.goldstein@yale.edu
Jonathan M. Goldstein, MD, Director
Department of Neurology
PO Box 208018
New Haven, CT 06520-8018

## Florida

KESSENICH FAMILY MDA/ALS CENTER AT THE UNIVERSITY OF MIAMI
(800) 690-ALS1
(305) 243-7400
(305) 243-1249 (fax)
E-mail: averma@med.miami.edu
Ashok Verma, MD, Director
1150 NW 14th Street, Suite 701
Miami, FL 33136

## Georgia

MDA/ALS CENTER AT EMORY UNIVERSITY SCHOOL OF MEDICINE
(404) 778-3507
(404) 727-3728 (fax)
E-mail: jglas03@emory.edu
Jonathan Glass, MD, Director
1365 Clifton Road, NE
Atlanta, GA 30322

## Kansas

MDA/ALS CENTER AT THE UNIVERSITY OF KANSAS MEDICAL CENTER
(913) 588-5000
(913) 588-6965 (fax)
E-mail: adick1@kumc.edu
Arthur Dick, MD, Director
39th and Rainbow Boulevard
Kansas City, KS 66103

## Maryland

MDA/ALS CENTER AT JOHNS HOPKINS UNIVERSITY
(410) 614-3846
(410) 955-0672 (fax)
E-mail: jrothste@jhmi.edu
Jeffrey D. Rothstein, MD, PhD, Director
School of Medicine
600 N Wolfe Street, Meyer 5-119
Baltimore, MD 21287-7519

## Massachusetts

MDA/ALS CENTER AT MASSACHUSETTS GENERAL HOSPITAL
(617) 726-5750
(617) 726-8543 (fax)
E-mail: rhbrown@partners.org
Robert H. Brown, MD, Director
Massachusetts General Hospital
15 Parkman Street
Boston, MA 02114

MDA/ALS CENTER AT THE UNIVERSITY OF MASSACHUSETTS MEDICAL
CENTER
(508) 856-4147
(508) 856-6778 (fax)
E-mail: ChadD@ummhc.org
David Chad, MD, Director
University of Massachusetts Medical Center
55 Lake Avenue North
Worchester, MA 01655

## Michigan

THE MICHIGAN STATE UNIVERSITY MDA/ALS CENTER
(*Note: This center is located at two sites*)
(517) 353-8122
(517) 432-7390 (fax)
E-mail: wchlphysician@msn.com
David Simpson, DO, Director
Michigan State University
138 Service Road, Suite A-117
East Lansing, MI 48824

(616) 493-9583
(616) 493-9827 (fax)
E-mail: baverell1@yahoo.com
Brian Averell, DO, Director
Mary Free Bed Rehabilitation Hospital
235 Wealthy Street SE
Grand Rapids, MI 49503

## Missouri

MDA/ALS CENTER AT WASHINGTON UNIVERSITY SCHOOL OF MEDICINE
(314) 362-6981
(314) 362-2826 (fax)
E-mail: pestronk@neuro.wustl.edu
Alan Pestronk, MD, Director
660 S Euclid, Box 8111
St. Louis, MO 63110

## New Mexico

MDA/ALS CENTER AT THE UNIVERSITY OF NEW MEXICO HEALTH
SCIENCES CENTER

(505) 272-3342
(505) 272-6692 (fax)
E-mail: JChapin@salud.unm.edu
John E. Chapin, MD, Director
University of New Mexico
915 Camino de Salud, NE
Albuquerque, NM 87131

## New York

THE ELEANOR AND LOU GEHRIG MDA/ALS RESEARCH CENTER
(212) 305-1319
(212) 305-8398 (fax)
E-mail: hm264@columbia.edu
Hiroshi Mitsumoto, MD, Director
E-mail: phg8@columbia.edu
Columbia University Medical Center
Department of Neurology
Neurological Institute (N19-016)
710 West 168th Street
New York, NY 10032

MDA/ALS CENTER AT MOUNT SINAI HOSPITAL AND MEDICAL CENTER
(212) 241-7317
(212) 987-1310 (fax)
E-mail: warren.olanow@mssm.edu
C. Warren Olanow, MD, FRCP, Codirector
(212) 241-8674
(212) 987-7363 (fax)
E-mail: dale.lange@mssm.edu
Dale J. Lange, MD, Codirector
One Gustave Levy Place
Annenburg 14-94
New York, NY 10029

MDA/ALS CENTER AT THE UNIVERSITY OF ROCHESTER MEDICAL
CENTER
(585) 275-2559
(585) 273-1255 (fax)
E-mail: Charles_Thornton@urmc.rochester.edu
Charles A. Thornton, MD, Director
PO Box 673
601 Elmwood Avenue
Rochester, NY 14642-8673

MDA/ALS CENTER AT SUNY UPSTATE MEDICAL UNIVERSITY
(315) 464-2480
(315) 464-7328 (fax)
E-mail: shefnerj@upstate.edu
Jeremy M. Shefner, MD, PhD, Director
Department of Neurology
750 E Adams Street
Syracuse, NY 13210

## North Carolina

MDA/ALS CENTER AT CAROLINAS MEDICAL CENTER
(704) 446-6212
(704) 446-6255 (fax)
E-mail: benjamin.brooks@carolinashealthcare.org
Benjamin R. Brooks, MD, Director
Neuroscience and Spine Institute
1010 N Edgehill Road
Charlotte, NC 28207

## Ohio

MDA/ALS CENTER AT OHIO STATE UNIVERSITY
(614) 293-4981
(614) 293-6111 (fax)
E-mail: kissel.2@osu.edu
John T. Kissel, MD, Codirector
(614) 293-7715
(614) 293-4688 (fax)
E-mail: nash.46@osu.edu
Steven Nash, MD, Codirector
1580 Dodd Drive
Columbus, OH 43210

## Oklahoma

MDA/ALS CENTER AT INTEGRIS SOUTHWEST MEDICAL CENTER
(405) 644-5170
(405) 644-6112 (fax)
Brent Beson, MD, Director
E-mail: brent.beson@integris-health.com
4221 S Western, Suite 5010
Oklahoma City, OK 73109

## Oregon

MDA/ALS CENTER AT OREGON HEALTH & SCIENCE UNIVERSITY
(503) 494-5236
(503) 494-0966 (fax)
E-mail: Louja@ohsu.edu
Jau-Shin Lou, MD, PhD, Director
3181 SW Sam Jackson Park Road, L226
Portland, OR 97239-3098

## Pennsylvania

MDA/ALS CENTER OF HOPE AT DREXEL UNIVERSITY COLLEGE OF
MEDICINE
(215) 762-5035/5036
(215) 762-3899 (fax)
E-mail: heiman@drexel.edu
Terry D. Heiman-Patterson, MD, Director
219 N Broad Street
Philadelphia, PA 19107

MDA/ALS CENTER AT THE UNIVERSITY OF PITTSBURGH MEDICAL
CENTER (UPMC) PRESBYTERIAN
(412) 647-1706
(412) 647-8398 (fax)
E-mail: lacomis@upmc.edu
David Lacomis, MD, Director
200 Lothrop Street, F878
Pittsburgh, PA 15213

## Tennessee

MDA/ALS CENTER OF MEMPHIS MID-SOUTH
(901) 725-8920
(901) 725-8934 (fax)
E-mail: tbertorini@aol.com
Tulio Bertorini, MD, Director
8095 Club Parkway
Cordova, TN 38016

MDA/ALS CENTER AT VANDERBILT UNIVERSITY MEDICAL CENTER
(615) 936-0060
(615) 936-1263 (fax)
E-mail: peter.d.donofrio@Vanderbilt.edu
Peter D. Donofrio, MD, Codirector
(615) 343-4016
(615) 343-2939 (fax)
E-mail: jane.howard@med.va.gov
Jane Howard, MD, Codirector
1301 22nd Avenue, South #3603
Nashville, TN 37212

## Texas

MDA/ALS CENTER AT THE UNIVERSITY OF TEXAS
(214) 648-2871
(214) 648-7992 (fax)
E-mail: jeffrey.elliott@utsouthwestern.edu
Jeffrey L. Elliott, MD, Director
Southwest Medical Center at Dallas
5323 Harry Hines Boulevard
Dallas, TX 75235-8897

MDA/ALS CENTER AT METHODIST NEUROLOGICAL INSTITUTE
(713) 441-1141
E-mail: sappel@tmh.tmc.edu
Stanley H. Appel, MD, Director
The Methodist Hospital Neurological Institute
6560 Fannin Street, # 802
Houston, TX 77030

MDA/ALS CENTER AT THE UNIVERSITY OF TEXAS HEALTH SCIENCE
CENTER AT SAN ANTONIO
(210) 567-1945
(210) 567-1948 (fax)

E-mail: jacksonce@uthscsa.edu
Carlayne E. Jackson, MD, Director
University of Texas Health Science Center
HealthSouth Rehabilitation Institute of San Antonio
9119 Cinnamon Hill
San Antonio, TX 78240

## Utah

MDA/ALS CENTER AT THE UNIVERSITY OF UTAH
(801) 585-5885
(801) 585-2054 (fax)
E-mail: mbromberg@hsc.utah.edu
Mark B. Bromberg, MD, PhD, Director
Department of Neurology
School of Medicine
50 North Medical Drive
Salt Lake City, UT 84132

## Washington

MDA/ALS CENTER AT THE UNIVERSITY OF WASHINGTON MEDICAL
CENTER
(206) 598-4590
(206) 598-2813 (fax)
e-mail: gtcarter@u.washington.edu
Greg Carter, MD, Codirector
Department of Rehabilitation Medicine
(206) 598-4211
(206) 598-4102 (fax)
E-mail: mdweiss@u.washington.edu
Michael Weiss, MD, Codirector
Department of Neurology/Electromyography
1959 NE Pacific
Seattle, WA 98195-6115

## Wisconsin

MDA/ALS CLINICAL RESEARCH CENTER
(608) 263-9237
(608) 263-0412 (fax)
E-mail: lotz@neurology.wisc.edu
Barend P. Lotz, MD, Director
University of Wisconsin–Madison
University of Wisconsin Hospital & Clinics
600 Highland Avenue H4-622
Madison, WI 53792-5132

# 27

## The ALS Association: A National Voluntary Organization

### Sharon Matland, Lucie Bruijn, and Steve Gibson

### You Are Not Alone

The ALSA (Amyotrophic Lateral Sclerosis Association) and what we offer to people with amyotrophic lateral sclerosis (ALS), their family members, and their caregivers is presented in this chapter. The functions and services provided by the ALSA are described to send a strong message that people with ALS and their families are not alone. There are hundreds of volunteers and staff at this national organization standing ready to help them and provide needed services and support.

The ALSA is an organization of affiliates that exists only to benefit people with ALS, their families, and caregivers through numerous programs, services, and ALS research. Having the ALSA dedicated to fighting ALS and working to improve the lives of people struggling with this disease sends a clear message to people with ALS and their families that they are not alone.

### About the ALSA

The ALSA is a national health organization dedicated *solely* to leading the fight against ALS. The ALSA covers all the bases—research, patient services, advocacy, public education, and community services—in providing help and hope to those facing the disease.

The mission of the ALSA is to lead the fight to cure and treat ALS through global, cutting-edge research, and to empower people with Lou Gehrig's Disease (ALS) and their families to live fuller lives by providing them with compassionate care and support. Our vision states that "In the quest to create a world without ALS, our vision is to care for and support all people living with Lou Gehrig's Disease as we leave no stone unturned in our relentless search for a cure."

The people who provide leadership for the ALSA by serving as members of the national and chapter boards of trustees are volunteers whose personal lives have been touched in some way by ALS. Working diligently to make scientific discoveries and improve the lives of people living with ALS, the ALSA is committed to engaging people with ALS and families in the process of setting and achieving organizational goals. Along with the volunteers, the ALSA's national office is staffed with professionals who each focus on specific programmatic, service, and operational areas to assist people with ALS and their families and to provide support to the national affiliates.

The ALSA's affiliate network includes chapters, certified ALS centers, and freestanding support groups. We also have relationships with additional ALS clinics and ALS neurologists across the country. Our national network includes 42 chapters with an expanded geographic reach through greater than 40 satellite chapter offices; 33 certified clinical Centers of Excellence also with an expanded reach through satellite clinics; a relationship with additional ALS clinics nationally to which we refer people with ALS and, in several cases, provide varying types of support; and 2 freestanding support groups.

The ALSA has a group of physicians who serve as voluntary members of the Medical Advisory Group whose purpose is to provide the ALSA with information and advice on clinical and clinical management research issues of importance.

## What Does the ALSA Do?

The ALSA seeks to achieve the following through its programs and services guided by its national professionals and leadership: to discover the cause and cure for ALS through dedicated research while improving the lives of people with ALS by providing patient support, services and programs, advocacy for ALS research and public policy, and information/education for health care professionals and the general public. Specifically our programs include the following:

Research—discovering the cause, cure, and treatments for ALS through dedicated research

Patient services—improving the lives of people with ALS by providing information, care, support, and services to people with ALS, families, and caregivers

*Advocacy*—accomplishing changes at the local, state, and federal levels to benefit people with ALS through research and public policy

*Awareness*—increasing public knowledge about ALS to foster more research and services

## Research

The ALSA plays a leading role in ALS research and manages a diverse project portfolio through many different granting mechanisms. All grants are peer-reviewed and are of the highest scientific relevance to ALS. By leveraging novel technologies and fostering collaboration across complementary fields, the ALSA hopes to make promising new therapies available to people with ALS.

The ALSA's investigator-initiated grant program enables scientists to propose exciting new project ideas. This program has already funded studies that have led to a better understanding of the mechanisms thought to underlie the ALS disease process. Each year more than 300 abstracts are submitted for consideration.

The ALSA also proactively seeks important studies that can fill in gaps in our understanding of ALS. This granting approach has lead to several international collaborations to identify new genes linked to familial ALS, biomarker studies to diagnose ALS earlier and improve clinical trials, and the development of a rat model as a resource for the scientific community, an important tool for drug development.

To bridge the gap between academia and biotechnology and enable important lab findings to be translated into potential treatments, the research program now includes a translational effort, TREAT ALS (**T**ranslational **Re**search **A**dvancing **T**herapies for ALS). This initiative accelerates the drug discovery process by forging relationships between academia and industry. Contracts are provided to biotech and/or industry partners to support the development of novel treatments and establish preclinical data that can expedite clinical trials. TREAT ALS supports pilot clinic trials and the ALSA has established the TREAT ALS/NEALS clinical trials network to improve access to clinical trials for people with ALS throughout the United States.

Beyond the funding of research projects, the ALSA recognizes the need to encourage young investigators to work in the ALS field. The Milton Safenowitz Post-Doctoral Fellowship for ALS Research supports studies emphasizing novelty, feasibility, and innovation. Similarly, to encourage clinician scientists to become involved in ALS research, the ALSA has partnered with the American Academy of Neurology and provides a 3-year development award for clinician scientists.

- The ALSA holds scientific workshops that bring together ALS researchers and non-ALS investigators renowned in their respective specialties to explore specific ALS-relevant topics such as stem cell approaches for ALS, the biology of motor neurons and surrounding cells, and drug discovery in ALS.

The ALSA also has a Clinical Management Research Grant Program that was developed in 1998. This program aims to stimulate and support research in clinical, psychological, and/or social management of ALS to help people with the disease deal with the symptoms of ALS and improve the quality of their lives. It encourages new research to build an evidence base, the results of which demonstrate measurable, positive effects on the clinical management and lives of people with ALS.

## Patient Services

Feelings of hope, a positive mental attitude, and knowledge are powerful weapons in the battle against ALS. The ALSA materials and services are designed to offer hope, give needed information about living with ALS, and encourage people to live their lives to the fullest.

The generosity of the ALSA's donors allows people with ALS and family services and materials to be provided without charge. The specific national patient services programs are outlined below.

### Resource Connection: Information and Referral

The ALSA provides information for people with ALS and their families on what to expect and how to live with ALS. It is imperative that accurate and timely information is provided for them to be able to make informed decisions about treatment modalities and to anticipate needs with disease progression.

- *Toll-free.* Information and Referral Service can be reached by dialing 800-782-4747 people with ALS and family members are connected to informed, caring people who answer questions, mail literature about ALS, and offer hope and support.
- *E-mail.* Information and Referral Service is also available by e-mail, fax, or letter. Requests for information can be forwarded to
  - E-mail: alsinfo@alsa-national.org
  - Fax: 818.880.9006—attention Patient Services Resource Connection
  - Mail: The ALS Association
    27001 Agoura Road, Suite 150
    Patient Services Resource Connection
    Calabasas Hills, CA 91301
- *Web site.* The ALSA's web site (www.alsa.org) includes specific patient services information about the disease, resources for clinical care and second opinions, and how to obtain additional information.
- *Print and video materials.* These are the most popular source of information for people with ALS and their families. The ALSA's print materials include the following:
  - "Your Resource Guide To Living a Fuller Life with ALS." This is a comprehensive, easy-to-read overview that is designed to answer many questions that people, families, and caregivers have about the diagnosis

of ALS when newly diagnosed, and to outline the resources available through The Association.

- "Living With ALS" manuals. This is a set of 6 spiral-bound books designed to take the person with ALS through each of the stages of ALS, offering ways to cope and therapies to treat many of the symptoms of the disease.
  - *What's It All About*
  - *Coping With Change*
  - *Managing Your Symptoms and Treatment*
  - *Functioning When Your Mobility Is Affected*
  - *Adjusting To Swallowing and Speaking Difficulties*
  - *Adapting To Breathing Changes*
- "Living With ALS" videos/DVDs. A set of 5 individual programs accompanies the manuals and includes the following:
  - *Mobility, Activities of Daily Living, Home Adaptations*
  - *Adjusting to Swallowing Difficulties and Maintaining Good Nutrition*
  - *Adapting to Breathing Changes and Use of Noninvasive Ventilation*
  - *Communication Solutions and Symptom Management*
  - *Clinical Care Management Discussion Among ALS Experts*
- FYI Information Index. A series of brief flyers covers more than 35 specific topics including swallowing tips, minimizing fatigue, and speech devices.
- Brochures. A series of brochures on specific topics includes "Maintaining Good Nutrition With ALS" and "Caregiving and Basic Home Care for ALS Patients"

All ALSA print and video (videos available as DVDs) materials are provided without charge to people with ALS and their families and can be ordered by contacting the ALSA via the toll-free resource connection number or via e-mail or the Web site.

## ALSA Certified Center of Excellence<sup>sm</sup> Program

Along with medical experts, the ALSA developed standards for ALS clinics to encourage quality care that is interdisciplinary and includes a multidisciplinary team of clinicians who are knowledgeable and experienced in making the diagnosis and taking care of people with ALS.

The mission of the ALSA Center Program is to define, establish, and support a national standard of care in the management of ALS, sponsored by the ALSA. The objective of the Center Program is to encourage and provide state-of-the-art care and clinical management of ALS through the following:

- Involving all necessary health care disciplines in the care of the person with ALS and the family

- Offering care from a team of people specially trained to meet the needs of those living with ALS

- Collaborating across centers nationally to enhance ALS patient care and techniques

The ALSA selects, certifies, and supports distinguished regional institutions recognized as the best in the field with regard to knowledge of and experience with ALS; and that have neurologic diagnostics and imaging, and available on-site licensed and certified ancillary services on clinic days.

Clinics that pass the rigorous application and the peer site visit reviews are certified as ALSA centers. It is the ALSA's intent that the every-4-year recertification requirement helps to improve the quality of the certified centers. A benefit of the Center Program is the facilitation and fostering of information exchange among the medical directors and staff of the centers. Another benefit is that during one clinic visit a person with ALS and family can see all clinicians that are important to providing and planning their care, which is coordinated across the entire multidisciplinary team. At this time, there are 33 ALSA centers nationally—this program has expanded from 19 centers in 2005.

An overview of the Center Program standards and requirements includes the following:

- Active support for the ALS center from the local ALSA chapter

- An existing interdisciplinary ALS center with multidisciplinary clinical team

- A medical director with well-recognized expertise in ALS

- A full availability of neurologic diagnostic and other necessary medical services

- ALS center medical director participation in ALS research

- A number of established patients with ALS seen and a pattern of patients with newly diagnosed ALS added to those being seen sufficient to justify ALSA center status

Research study findings have shown that attending an ALS multidisciplinary clinic has a positive impact on quality of life for people with ALS.

## Someone to Talk To

Sometimes people with ALS, their families, and caregivers just need someone to talk to—someone who will listen and who understands the day-to-day challenges they are facing. The ALSA provides telephone contact with concerned, knowledgeable people from both the national office (800-782-4747) and each ALSA chapter.

## ALSA Chapters

There are 42 ALSA chapters with over 40 chapter satellite offices to connect with people with ALS and their families across the country. Patient services staff members are in place at each site providing programs and services to meet the needs of people with ALS. If a specific program is not offered by a chapter, patient services provide referrals to resources in the community to address any unmet needs.

To achieve ALSA chapter standards and guidelines, patient services staff at the chapters are to be allied health professionals and typically include registered nurses, medical and clinical social workers, physical or occupational therapists, speech language pathologists, and mental health professionals. Chapter patient services work closely with their affiliate certified centers or clinics to assist in the coordination of care and in the centers are members of the multidisciplinary care teams typically functioning as chapter liaisons.

There are several types of patient services chapter programs provided for the benefit of the people with ALS and their families they serve.

## Patient and Family Education Programs

Many ALSA chapters sponsor patient–family education programs covering general information about ALS as well as specific tips and hints that make living with this disease easier.

## Support Groups

Talking with other people who are living the same experience can help decrease the common feelings of depression and isolation. The ALSA's chapters and free-standing support groups conduct hundreds of support group meetings across the country every month. Support groups range from an informal sharing of successful ideas of how to solve problems of daily living to formal clinical presentations. There are support groups for people newly diagnosed with ALS, caregivers, and, in some areas, groups for children of people with ALS. In all cases the emphasis is on helping people maximize their physical function and maintaining quality in their lives.

## Equipment Loan Programs

The chapters provide equipment on loan to people with ALS for activities of daily living—wheelchairs, walkers, bedside commodes, and so forth. Many chapters also have a variety of augmentative communication devices that they make available to patients.

## Respite Programs

Family caregivers have demanding and often overwhelming jobs. A break from caregiving to go shopping, see a movie, or spend a day with friends can provide a needed change and rest. Many chapters offer respite care to families to help them cope with the demands and burdens of ALS.

## Transportation Programs

People with ALS requiring sophisticated wheelchairs and modified vans may need more help in getting from home to an ALS center, other medical appointments, or to support group meetings than family and friends can provide. Some chapters are able to offer transportation services to patients.

## Caregiver Support

The ALSA recognizes the needs caregivers have for information and support. Through the Information and Referral Services provided by the national office and chapters, literature, support groups, and respite programs, the ALSA is reaching out to help and support caregivers.

## Care Connection

The ALSA Care Connection program includes developing a network of caring people organized to help those living with ALS and their caregivers. The purpose of the Care Connection is to reduce caregiver burden and positively affect caregiver well-being; decrease level of worry about caregiver well-being as expressed by the person with ALS; increase social/personal hours available for the family caregiver and the person with ALS; and enhance a sense of helpfulness among family, friends, and acquaintances. Orientation and education to the program is provided by the chapters and ongoing support is provided to the participating families by the Patient Services coordinators. The network of volunteers provide assistance such as walking the dog, providing cooked meals, doing grocery shopping, or picking up dry cleaning. The person with ALS and the family define activities they would like assistance with.

## Patient Bill of Rights for People With ALS

When people are knowledgeable about their rights regarding health care they are more likely to get the services and patient care they need. The ALS Association *Patient Bill of Rights for People with ALS* is an information and advocacy tool for people with ALS and families as they negotiate the health care system.

## Advocacy—Government Relations and Public Affairs

The ALSA plays the leading role in advocacy for increased public and private support of ALS research and health care reform that responds to the demands imposed by ALS.

The ALSA's advocacy efforts in Washington, DC, have raised the profile of ALS at the White House, among members of Congress, and within federal agencies, including the National Institutes of Health (NIH), the Food and Drug Administration (FDA), the Centers for Medicare and Medicaid Services, the Centers for Disease Control and Prevention, the Social Security Administration, the Department of Defense, and the Department of Veterans Affairs. Through our advocacy efforts, the ALSA has achieved numerous victories for the ALS community.

## We've Successfully Advocated Better Patient Service

- Veterans benefits
  - Helped to secure more than $500 million in benefits for military veterans with ALS, their families, and survivors as the Department of

Veterans Affairs implemented historic new regulations in 2008 to designate ALS as a service-connected disease. Veterans with ALS and their survivors are now eligible for full health and disability benefits, regardless of where or when they served in the military and regardless of how soon after discharge they were diagnosed.

- Twenty-four-month Medicare waiver
  - Eliminated the 24-month waiting period that people disabled with ALS had to endure before they could start receiving Medicare benefits. ALS is now one of only two diseases for which the waiting period does not apply, and the waiver for ALS is the only change Congress has made to the waiting period since it was first established.

- Social Security presumptive disability, compassionate allowances, QDD
  - Orchestrated Social Security rule change under which people with ALS automatically meet the medical eligibility requirements for SSDI and SSI payments. We also helped to speed disability reviews in 2008 by advocating that ALS be included as a disease automatically eligible for the Compassionate Allowances program and Quick Disability Determination (QDD) process, which expedite reviews. These changes allow people with ALS to access their benefits months or even years sooner than before.

- Respite care
  - Passed legislation in 2006 to authorize nearly $290 million in funding for state-based respite care programs to assist family caregivers.

- Prescription drug benefit with catastrophic coverage
  - Advocated for drug benefit that provides Medicare coverage for Rilutek and other vital prescription drugs.

## We've Championed Additional Funding for ALS Research

- Generated more than $365 million for ALS research over the past 10 years
  - Increased government funding from $15 million per year in 1998 to more than $60 million in 2007.

- National ALS registry
  - Enacted the ALS Registry Act in 2008 (Public Law 110-373) to establish the first nationwide ALS patient registry, which may become the single largest ALS research project ever. The ALSA also has worked with Congress to secure nearly $5 million for registry pilot projects, including $3 million in fiscal year 2008. The registry will be administered by the Centers for Disease Control and Prevention.

- Department of Defense/Department of Veterans Affairs research funding

- Worked with Congress to appropriate $5 million in fiscal year 2009 for the ALS Research Program (ALSRP) at the Department of Defense (DOD). The ALSRP is the only ALS-specific program at DOD and is focused on translational research, leading to new treatments for the disease. The ALSRP was initially launched in 2007 when the ALSA partnered with the DOD to bring new focus to their ALS research portfolio, which, combined with the VA, has provided over $25 million in funding for ALS research in recent years.

## We've Empowered the ALS Community

- National ALS advocacy day and public policy conference
  - Directed the single largest gathering of the entire ALS community, which in the 110th Congress (2007–2008) included nearly 2,000 advocates from across the country and more than 890 meetings with members of Congress. The 3-day conference also featured educational breakout sessions on the latest ALS research and public policy issues and provided advocacy training to people with ALS, their families, ALS researchers, clinicians, and others whose lives have been touched by the disease.
- ALS advocates
  - Recruited nearly 10,000 advocates representing all 50 states, including 11 states where the ALSA does not have a chapter, a 147% increase in 2008.
- Grassroots outreach
  - Generated 22,000 e-mails and 50,000 letters to Congress over the past two years, more than 6 letters for every single person diagnosed with ALS during that time.
- Congressional hearings
  - ALS has been the sole subject of two Senate hearings, including a May 2005 hearing held by the Senate Labor-Health and Human Services Appropriations subcommittee. Additionally, the ALSA has facilitated the appearance of 3 people with ALS who testified before the 110th Congress (2007–2008).

The ALSA empowers the entire ALS community—people with ALS and families, caregivers, clinicians and researchers—with the information and tools they need to make a difference and find a treatment and cure through advocacy.

## Raising Awareness and Public Education

Through public outreach, media relations, and the Internet, the ALSA continually raises awareness about ALS and the search for a cure. On average, each month 150,000 viewers visit our Web site, a vital source of information for those battling

ALS and for people looking for the latest news and information about the disease. The ALSA's magazine, *Vision*, is distributed to approximately 100,000 people, reaching an estimated readership of 360,000. The ALSA has achieved expanded awareness and support of ALS issues through relationships with other organizations such as Major and Minor League Baseball, and through effective interaction with the nation's news media.

Raising general awareness about ALS will lead to an increase in research funding and support for clinical and support services. Everyone has a part to play in increasing ALS awareness—from talking with community friends and neighbors to writing a letter to the editor of a local newspaper. A public awareness campaign including articles, features, and public service ads in major newspapers and magazines and on radio and television is led by the ALSA's national office. Although the awareness campaign is year-long, special emphasis is given to awareness events in May—National ALS Awareness Month. The ALSA strives to involve and engage patients and families in the process of raising awareness and advocating for legislative changes. A broad base of committed people in communities across the country can create a powerful voice for increasing research funding and improving care and treatment.

## Other ALS Association Activities

- *Drug company working group meeting.* Over the past 11 years, the ALSA's Advocacy, Research, and Patient Services departments have convened the Drug Company Working Group meeting to bring together representatives of the pharmaceutical and biotech industries, government agencies, and the ALS clinical and research communities. The meetings encourage collaboration, partnerships, and new ideas to expand ALS research and speed the development of meaningful treatments for ALS.

- *Professional and scientific meetings.* Representatives of the ALSA regularly attend scientific and neurologic professional meetings to keep abreast of the most current research and treatment news and to raise awareness about ALS by presenting at the meetings and sponsoring exhibit booths.

- *ALS Association annual conference.* Annually, the ALSA conducts an ALS clinical conference for the education of health care professionals working with people with ALS and their families. Professionals from the certified center multidisciplinary clinical teams and the chapter patient services staff attend. The conference is open to all clinical and health care professionals whether from other ALS organizations or non-ALS health care environments. In conjunction with the clinical conference, a leadership conference is conducted for the education of the executive director, development staff, and volunteer leadership from the chapter affiliates.

- *International alliance of ALS/MND associations.* The ALSA is a full member of the International Alliance of ALS/MND Associations (motor neuron disease) which comprises 50 ALS/MND organizations and representatives from 40 countries worldwide. In its role as an alliance member, the ALSA actively participates on the board of directors and in the annual alliance meetings and international symposium for clinicians and researchers.

- *ALS Association medical director meetings.* Twice annually meetings of the certified center medical directors are hosted by the ALSA's Patient Services Department.

## The ALSA's Patient Bill of Rights for People Living With ALS

As a person living with ALS, you have the right to the following:

1. Receive comprehensive information about ALS, including treatment options and resources for your health care needs. This includes the right to communicate with your government representatives regarding policies and practices of the FDA, NIH, Department of Health and Human Services (DHHS), and other agencies that affect ALS.

2. Participate in decisions about your health care including the right to accept, discontinue, or refuse treatments and therapy.

3. Receive ALS specialty care in a timely manner.

4. Receive health care that is coordinated and individualized for you across the spectrum of home, hospice, hospital, nursing home, outpatient, and workplace and throughout all the phases of your illness.

5. Access health care benefit coverage and life insurance coverage without discrimination based on your ALS diagnosis or disability.

6. Obtain clear, timely information regarding your health plan including benefits, exclusions, and appeal procedures.

7. Review your medical records and have the information in your records explained to you.

8. Prepare an advance directive to state your wishes regarding emergency and end-of-life treatment choices.

9. Receive care that is considerate and respects your dignity, your cultural, psychosocial, and spiritual values, and your privacy. You have this right no matter what choices you make about treatments and therapy, what

your disabilities related to ALS might be, or what your financial circumstances are.

10. Know that information about you and your medical condition are held in confidence.

11. Receive support to maintain or enhance the quality of your life and have your family involved in all aspects of your health care.

# 28

# Resources for Patients and Their Families

## Gabriela Harrington-Moroney, Olena Jennings, and Ronit Sukenick

This chapter will familiarize you with amyotrophic lateral sclerosis (ALS) support services available to make living with this disease more comfortable for you, your family, and your friends. It is important to remember that you are not alone in your fight against ALS. These resources will help you connect with people like you and educate you about different aspects of the disease in the effort to improve your quality of life.

### MDA/ALS Research and Clinical Centers/ALS Association Certified Clinics

For ALS centers throughout the world, please see the ALS/MND association's Web site: http://www.alsmndalliance.org/

### Arizona

MDA/ALS CENTER AT ST. JOSEPH'S HOSPITAL AND MEDICAL CENTER
(602) 406-6262
(602) 406-4608 (fax)
E-mail: shafeeq.ladha@chw.edu
Shafeeq Ladha, MD, Director
St. Joseph's Hospital and Medical Center
Barrow Neurological Institute
500 West Thomas Road
Suite 710
Phoenix, AZ 85013

435

MDA/ALS CENTER AT THE MUCIO F. DELGADO CLINIC FOR NEUROMUS-
CULAR DISORDERS
(520) 626-6609
(520) 626-6925 (fax)
E-mail: lstern@u.arizona.edu
Lawrence Z. Stern, MD, Director
University of Arizona
Health Sciences Center
1501 North Campbell Avenue
Tucson, AZ 85724

## Arkansas

MDA/ALS CENTER AT THE UNIVERSITY OF ARKANSAS FOR MEDICAL
SCIENCES
(501) 686-5135
(501) 686-8689 (fax)
E-mail: rudnickistacya@uams.edu
Stacy A. Rudnicki, MD, Director
4301 West Markham, Slot 500
Little Rock, AR 72205-7199

## California

ALS CLINIC—LOMA LINDA UNIVERSITY HEALTH CARE
11370 Anderson Street
Suite 2400
Loma Linda, CA 92354
Medical Director: Laura Nist, MD
(909) 558-2128

CEDARS-SINAI CENTER FOR ALS CARE
8730 Alden Drive
Los Angeles, CA 90048
Abirami Muthukumaran, MD, Medical Director
(310) 423-6472

UC, SAN DIEGO ALS CENTER
Hillcrest Campus Outpatient Center (OPC), Neurology Suite
200 West Arbor Drive
San Diego, CA 92103
Nayan P. Desai, MD
(619) 543-5300
Department of Neurology
Outpatient Center, 3rd Floor, Suite 1
200 West Arbor Drive
San Diego, CA 92103-8674
Co-Directors: Nayan Desai, MD/Geoffrey Sheean, MD
(619) 543-5300
(619) 543-5793 (fax)

JERRY LEWIS MDA/ALS CLINICAL AND RESEARCH CENTER
(213) 743-1612
(213) 743-1617 (fax)
E-mail: kengel@usc.edu

W. King Engel, MD, Director
University of Southern California
School of Medicine
637 South Lucas Avenue
Los Angeles, CA 90017

MDA/ALS CENTER AT UCLA
(310) 825-7266
(310) 825-3995 (fax)
E-mail: mcgraves@ucla.edu
Michael C. Graves, MD, Director
UCLA Neurological Services, Suite B200
300 UCLA Medical Plaza
Los Angeles, CA 90095-6975

MDA/ALS CENTER AT THE UNIVERSITY OF CALIFORNIA, IRVINE
(714) 456-2332
(714) 456-5997 (fax)
E-mail: mozaffar@uci.edu
Tahseen Mozaffar, MD, FAAN, Director
200 South Manchester Avenue, Suite 110
Orange, CA 92868

FORBES NORRIS MDA/ALS RESEARCH CENTER
(415) 600-3604
(415) 923-6567 (fax)
E-mail: millerrx@sutterhealth.org
Robert G. Miller, MD, Codirector
E-mail: katzjs@sutterhealth.org
Jonathan Katz, MD, Codirector
California Pacific Medical Center
2324 Sacramento Street, Suite 150
San Francisco, CA 94115

## Colorado

MDA/ALS CENTER AT THE UNIVERSITY OF COLORADO
(303) 315-7885
(303) 315-7221
(303) 315-6796 (fax)
E-mail: hans.neville@uchsc.edu
Hans E. Neville, MD, Codirector
E-mail: steven.ringel@uchsc.edu
Steven P. Ringel, MD, Codirector
Health Sciences Center
4200 East Ninth Avenue, Box B-185
Denver, CO 80262

## Connecticut

MDA/ALS CENTER AT YALE UNIVERSITY
(203) 785-4085
(203) 785-1937 (fax)
E-mail: jonathan.goldstein@yale.edu
Jonathan M. Goldstein, MD, Director

Department of Neurology
PO Box 208018
New Haven, CT 06520-8018

## Florida

Suncoast ALS Clinic
Department of Neurology
601 Seventh Street, South
St. Petersburg, FL 33702
Medical Director: Steven Cohen, MD
(727) 824-7132

KESSENICH FAMILY MDA/ALS CENTER AT THE UNIVERSITY OF MIAMI
(800) 690-ALS1
(305) 243-7400
(305) 243-1249 (fax)
E-mail: averma@med.miami.edu
Ashok Verma, MD, DM, Director
E-mail: ggonzal4@med.miami.edu
Gina Gonzalez, BSN, RN, CGRN
1150 NW 14th Street, Suite 701
Miami, FL 33136

## Georgia

MDA/ALS CENTER AT EMORY UNIVERSITY SCHOOL OF MEDICINE
(404) 778-3754
(404) 778-3495 (fax)
E-mail: jglas03@emory.edu
Jonathan Glass, MD, Director
1365 Clifton Road, NE
Atlanta, GA 30322

## Illinois

University of Illinois at Chicago
Department of Neurology
912 S Wood Street
855N NPI, M/C 796
Chicago, IL 60612-7330
Director of Clinic: Julie Rowin, MD
(312) 996-9445

MDA/ALS CENTER AT THE UNIVERSITY OF CHICAGO HOSPITALS
(773) 702-9089
(773) 702-9076 (fax)
E-mail: rroos@neurology.bsd.uchicago.edu
Raymond Roos, MD, Director
Department of Neurology/MC2030
5841 South Maryland Avenue
Chicago, IL 60637

## Kansas

MDA/ALS CENTER AT THE UNIVERSITY OF KANSAS MEDICAL CENTER
(913) 859-0632

(913) 588-6965 (fax)
E-mail: adick1@kumc.edu
Arthur Dick, MD, Director
39th and Rainbow Boulevard
Kansas City, KS 66103

## Maryland

The Maryland ALS Clinic at University Specialty Hospital
601 S Charles Street
Baltimore, MD 21230
(410) 706-6689

MDA/ALS CENTER AT JOHNS HOPKINS UNIVERSITY
(410) 614-3846
(410) 955-0672 (fax)
Email: jrothste@jhmi.edu
Jeffrey D. Rothstein, MD, PhD, Director
School of Medicine
600 N Wolfe Street, Meyer 5-119
Baltimore, MD 21287-7519

## Massachusetts

Beth Israel Deaconess Medical Center
330 Brookline Avenue
Boston, MA 02215
Medical Director: Elizabeth Raynor, MD
(617) 667-8130

MDA/ALS CENTER AT MASSACHUSETTS GENERAL HOSPITAL
(617) 726-5750
(617) 726-8543 (fax)
E-mail: rhbrown@partners.org
Robert H. Brown, MD, Director
Massachusetts General Hospital
15 Parkman Street
Boston, MA 02114

MDA/ALS CENTER AT THE UNIVERSITY OF MASSACHUSETTS
MEDICAL CENTER
(508) 856-4147
(508) 856-6778 (fax)
E-mail: ChadD@ummhc.org
David Chad, MD, Director
University of Massachusetts Medical Center
55 Lake Avenue North
Worcester, MA 01655

## Minnesota

University of Minnesota Medical Center, Fairview
Box 295
420 Delaware Street SE
Minneapolis, MN 55455
(612) 626-4107

## Missouri

MDA/ALS CENTER AT WASHINGTON UNIVERSITY SCHOOL OF MEDICINE
(314) 362-6981
(314) 362-2826 (fax)
E-mail: pestronk@neuro.wustl.edu
Alan Pestronk, MD, Director
660 S Euclid, Box 8111
St. Louis, MO 63110

## New Mexico

MDA/ALS CENTER AT THE UNIVERSITY OF NEW MEXICO HEALTH
SCIENCES CENTER
(505) 272-3342
(505) 272-6692 (fax)
E-mail: JChapin@salud.unm.edu
John E. Chapin, MD, Director
University of New Mexico
915 Camino de Salud, NE
Albuquerque, NM 87131

## New York

Stony Brook Medical Center
181 Belle Meade Road
East Setauket, NY 11733
Medical Director: Rahman Pourmand, MD
(212) 720-3057

THE ELEANOR AND LOU GEHRIG MDA/ALS RESEARCH CENTER
(212) 305-1319
(212) 305-8398 (fax)
E-mail: hm264@columbia.edu
Hiroshi Mitsumoto, MD, Director
Columbia University Medical Center
Department of Neurology
Neurological Institute (N19-016)
710 West 168th Street
New York, NY 10032

MDA/ALS CENTER AT MOUNT SINAI HOSPITAL AND MEDICAL CENTER
(212) 241-8674
(212) 987-1310 (fax)
E-mail: warren.olanow@mssm.edu
C. Warren Olanow, MD, FRCP, Codirector
(212) 241-7317
(212) 987-7363 (fax)
E-mail: dale.lange@mssm.edu
Dale J. Lange, M.D., Codirector
One Gustave Levy Place
Annenburg 14–94
New York, NY 10029

MDA/ALS CENTER AT THE UNIVERSITY OF ROCHESTER MEDICAL CENTER
(585) 275-2559

(585) 273-1255 (fax)
E-mail: Charles_Thornton@urmc.rochester.edu
Charles A. Thornton, MD, Director
PO Box 673
601 Elmwood Avenue
Rochester, NY 14642-8673

MDA/ALS CENTER AT SUNY UPSTATE MEDICAL UNIVERSITY
(315) 464-2480
(315) 464-7328 (fax)
E-mail: shefnerj@upstate.edu
Jeremy M. Shefner, MD, PhD, Director
Department of Neurology
750 East Adams Street
Syracuse, NY 13210

## North Carolina

MDA/ALS CENTER AT CAROLINAS MEDICAL CENTER
(704) 446-6212
(704) 446-6255 (fax)
E-mail: Elena.Bravver@carolinashealthcare.org
Elene Bravver, MD, Director
1010 North Edgehill Road
Charlotte, NC 28207

## Ohio

MDA/ALS CENTER AT OHIO STATE UNIVERSITY
(614) 293-4981
(614) 293-6111 (fax)
E-mail: kissel.2@osu.edu
John T. Kissel, MD, Codirector
(614) 293-7715
(614) 293-4688 (fax)
E-mail: nash.46@osu.edu
Steven Nash, MD, Codirector
1580 Dodd Drive
Columbus, OH 43210

## Oklahoma

MDA/ALS CENTER AT INTEGRIS SOUTHWEST MEDICAL CENTER
(405) 644-5170
(405) 644-6112 (fax)
Brent Beson, MD, Director
E-mail: brent.beson@integris-health.com
4221 S Western, Suite 5010
Oklahoma City, OK 73109

## Oregon

MDA/ALS CENTER AT OREGON HEALTH & SCIENCE UNIVERSITY
(503) 494-5236
(503) 494-0966 (fax)

E-mail: Louja@ohsu.edu
Jau-Shin Lou, MD, PhD, Director
3181 SW Sam Jackson Park Road, L226
Portland, OR 97239-3098

## Pennsylvania

Allegheny Neurological Associates
420 E. North Avenue
Suite 206
Pittsburgh, PA 15212
Medical Director: Sandeep Rana, MD
(412) 359-8850

University of Pittsburgh ALS Clinic
Department of Neurology
Suite 810
Kaufmann Building
3471 Fifth Avenue
Pittsburgh, PA 15213
(412) 692-4920
Director: David Lacomis, MD

John P. Murtha Neuroscience and Pain Institute ALS Clinic
Suite 1000
1450 Scalp Avenue
Johnstown, PA 15904
Medical Director: Zachary Simmons, MD
(814) 269-5061

The Neuromuscular and ALS Center for
Comprehensive Care at Lehigh Valley Hospital
Lehigh Neurology
1210 S Cedar Crest Boulevard
Allentown, PA 18103
Medical Director: Glenn Mackin
(610) 402-6767

MDA/ALS CENTER OF HOPE AT DREXEL UNIVERSITY COLLEGE
OF MEDICINE
(215) 762-5035/5036
(215) 762-3899 (fax)
E-mail: heiman@drexel.edu
Terry D. Heiman-Patterson, MD, Director
219 N Broad Street
Philadelphia, PA 19107

MDA/ALS CENTER AT THE UNIVERSITY OF PITTSBURGH MEDICAL
CENTER (UPMC) PRESBYTERIAN
(412) 647-1706
(412) 647-8398 (fax)
E-mail: lacomis@upmc.edu
David Lacomis, MD, Director
200 Lothrop Street, F878
Pittsburgh, PA 15213

## Rhode Island

Rhode Island Hospital-Louise Wilcox ALS Center
Medical Office Building, Suite 555
2 Dudley Street
Providence, RI 02903
Medical Director: Dr. George Sachs
(401) 444-3032

## Tennessee

MDA/ALS CENTER AT VANDERBILT UNIVERSITY MEDICAL CENTER
(615) 936-0060
(615) 936-1263 (fax)
E-mail: peter.d.donofrio@Vanderbilt.edu
Peter D. Donofrio, MD, Codirector
(615) 343-4016
(615) 343-2939 (fax)
E-mail: jane.howard@med.va.gov
Jane Howard, MD, Codirector
1301 22nd Avenue, South #3603
Nashville, TN 37212

MDA/ALS CENTER OF MEMPHIS MID-SOUTH
(901) 725-8920
(901) 725-8934 (fax)
E-mail: tbertorini@aol.com
Tulio Bertorini, MD, Director
8095 Club Parkway
Cordova, TN 38016

## Texas

MDA/ALS CENTER AT THE UNIVERSITY OF TEXAS
(214) 648-2871
(214) 648-7992 (fax)
E-mail: jeffrey.elliott@utsouthwestern.edu
Jeffrey L. Elliott, MD, Director
Southwest Medical Center at Dallas
5323 Harry Hines Boulevard
Dallas, TX 75235-8897

MDA/ALS CENTER AT METHODIST HOSPITAL NEUROLOGICAL
INSTITUTE
(713) 441-3760
E-mail: sappel@tmhs.org
Stanley H. Appel, MD, Director
The Methodist Hospital Neurological Institute
6560 Fannin Street, #802
Houston, TX 77030

MDA/ALS CENTER AT THE UNIVERSITY OF TEXAS HEALTH SCIENCE
CENTER AT SAN ANTONIO
(210) 567-1945
(210) 567-1948 (fax)

E-mail: jacksonce@uthscsa.edu
Carlayne E. Jackson, MD, Director
University of Texas Health Science Center
HealthSouth Rehabilitation Institute of San Antonio
9119 Cinnamon Hill
San Antonio, TX 78240

## Utah

MDA/ALS CENTER AT THE UNIVERSITY OF UTAH
(801) 585-5885
(801) 585-2054 (fax)
E-mail: mbromberg@hsc.utah.edu
Mark B. Bromberg, MD, PhD, Director
Department of Neurology
School of Medicine
50 North Medical Drive
Salt Lake City, UT 84132

## Washington

MDA/ALS CENTER AT THE UNIVERSITY OF WASHINGTON MEDICAL
CENTER
(206) 598-4590
(206) 598-2813 (fax)
E-mail: gtcarter@u.washington.edu
Greg Carter, MD, Codirector
Department of Rehabilitation Medicine
(206) 598-4211
(206) 598-4102 (fax)
E-mail: mdweiss@u.washington.edu
Michael Weiss, MD, Codirector
Department of Neurology/Electromyography
1959 NE Pacific
Seattle, WA 98195-6115

## West Virginia

West Virginia University, School of Medicine
Department of Neurology
1 Stadium Drive, 3rd Floor
Morgantown, WV 26506
(304) 598-4000
Director: Laurie Gutman, MD

## Wisconsin

MDA/ALS CLINICAL RESEARCH CENTER
(608) 263-9237
(608) 263-0412 (fax)
E-mail: brooks@neurology.wisc.edu
Benjamin R. Brooks, MD, Director
University of Wisconsin–Madison
University of Wisconsin Hospital & Clinics
600 Highland Avenue CSC H6-563
Madison, WI 53792-5132

## Equipment

http://www.abledata.com/

ABLEDATA provides objective information about assistive technology products and rehabilitation equipment available from domestic and international sources. Although ABLEDATA does not sell any products, they can help you locate the companies that do.

http://www.beabletodo.com/StoreFront.bok

North Coast Medical's Functional Solutions catalog features a wide variety of products that increase independence by making everyday activities easier and safer. Products include dressing aids, household helpers, adaptive eating utensils, exercise equipment, transfer devices, and much more.

http://www.beasy.com

Beasy transfer board.

http:///www.pocketdresser.com

A tool for to aid in dressing independently.

http://www.sammonspreston.com

Rehabilitation equipment and supplies.

http://www.surehands.com/

Sure hands lift system.

http://www.ustep.com

Walking aids designed especially for neurologic conditions.

## Accessible Housing

http://www.dhcr.state.ny.us/ocd/progs/acc/ocdacc0.htm

Access to Home Program.

A New York state program that provides for financial assistance to property owners to make dwelling units accessible for low- and moderate-income persons with disabilities.

http://www.hud.gov/offices/fheo/disabilities/index.cfm

Fair Housing and Equal Opportunity.

http://www.waccess.org/

Wheelchair-accessible housing clearinghouse.

This site publishes classified advertisements for houses, townhouses, and condominiums for sale or rent that are wheelchair accessible. It also posts ads offering scooters, wheelchairs, and accessible vans.

http://www.homeaccessprogram.org/

The Home Access Program is an initiative started by Handi-Ramp, a company that has been manufacturing handicap-accessible ramps since 1958. The program helps individuals and families find realtors who can assist in the search for a handicap-accessible home or consultants who can modify a current home.

## Assistive Technology

http://www.abilityhub.com/index.htm

For people with a disability who find operating a computer difficult, maybe even impossible. This Web site will direct you to adaptive equipment and alternative methods available for accessing computers.

http://www.activeclick.com

ActiveClick automatically clicks the mouse for you.

http://www.bltt.org

Better Living Through Technology is a noncommercial Web site designed to promote the use of technology to help people with a range of disabilities.

http://www.buckandbuck.com/

Specializes in the clothing needs of the physically challenged.

http://www.catea.org/history.php

The Center for Assistive Technology and Environmental Access (CATEA) at the Georgia Institute of Technology.

Development, evaluation, and utilization of assistive technology as well as design and development of accessible environments services the state of Georgia. Also has many resources and articles on barrier-free design and accessibility.

http://www.cogain.org/about_cogain

COGAIN assistive technologies will empower the target group to communicate by using the capabilities they have and by offering compensation for capabilities that are deteriorating. The users will be able to use applications that help them to be in control of the environment, or achieve a completely new level of convenience and speed in gaze-based communication.

http://www.cre.umassd.edu/

UMass Dartmouth Center for Rehabilitation Engineering.

Engineering students from the UMass Dartmouth engineering school gain experience adapting computer systems at the Center for Rehabilitation Engineering.

http://www.etriloquist.com/

E-triloquist. A PC-based communication aid for a person with speech impairment. It serves as an electronic voice for those who cannot speak on their own.

http://www.getatstuff.com/

Assistive Technology Exchange in New England. Here you can look for a list of Assistive Technology devices for sale or for free.

http://lakefolks.org/cnt

Click-N-Type virtual keyboard. An on-screen, free-download, virtual keyboard designed for anyone with a disability that prevents him or her from typing on a physical computer keyboard.

http://march-of-faces.org/reserouces/vkt.html

Free virtual on-screen keyboard by MiloSoft. Use your mouse to type in any text environment, including chat, e-mail, and word processing programs.

http://www.onlineconferencingsystems.com/at.htm

One stop for free assistive technology.

http://www.polital.com/pnc

Point-N-Click is a free stand-alone on-screen virtual mouse designed for anyone with a disability that makes it difficult or impossible to click a physical computer mouse.

http://www.silverts.com/

Specializes in the clothing needs of the physically challenged.

http://www.usatechguide.org/

United Spinal Association TechGuide. A Web guide to wheelchair and assistive technology choices.

## Speech

http://www.asha.org

American Speech-Language-Hearing Association. A professional, scientific, credentialing association that can aid you in finding a professional speech and language pathologist.

http://www.aac-rerc.com/

The AA-RERC is a research group dedicated to the development of effective Augmentative and Alternative Communication (AAC) technology.

Assists people who rely on communication to achieve their goals by advancing and promoting AAC technologies.

http://www.asel.udel.edu/speech/clinicians.html

Model talker software. Enables a patient to record his or her voice so that it can be later used in the creation of a speech device.

http://atia.org

An organization of assistive technology companies that provides links to different speech device vendors.

http://www.asel.udel.edu/speech/

Speech Research Laboratory. A.I. DuPont Hospital for Children and the University of Delaware. For those who may be interested in the application of speech synthesis software for people who are at risk of losing their ability to speak. Includes information on voice banking.

## MDA and ALS Association Loan Closets

Many local MDA offices and ALS Association chapters have loan closets with a variety of previously owned durable medical equipment. MDA and ALS Association staff can also help you locate other local sources and funding options for daily equipment and assistive technology.

### Organizations

http://www.alsrg.org/

ALS Research Group.

Chair: Dr. Jeremy Shefner.

http://www.als.ca/resources-children.html

The ALS Society of Canada: Booklets and information for children dealing with a parent or grandparent with ALS.

http://www.als.net

ALS TDI: The ALS Therapy Development Institute is a nonprofit biotechnology company discovering treatments for patients alive today.

http://www.alsa.org

ALS Association: Dedicated to ALS patients and caregivers.

http://www.alsfamily.org/

ALS Family Charitable Foundation, Inc. A federally recognized nonprofit organization dedicated to raising funds for cutting-edge research and patient services for those with ALS.

http://www.alsmndalliance.org

Many links to personal Web sites, professional resources, and a current literature search with abstracts specific to research on ALS/MND.

http://www.lesturnerals.org/walk.htm

ALS Walk4Life. Organized by the Les Turner ALS Foundation. One of the world's largest annual ALS gatherings, the ALS Walk4Life is a 2-mile walk along Chicago's beautiful lakefront and is a demonstration of hope, courage, and community. This is a wonderful way to raise awareness and funds for ALS and show support for those individuals and families affected by the disease.

http://www.aan.com/professionals/practice/pdfs/g10058.pdf

American Academy of Neurology Practice Parameters.

http://www.build-uk.net/

A motor disease network for the United Kingdom. This forum could be used to contact others with a similar interest in MND—to decide what information and services should be provided, to tell people what you want, and to share what you know.

http://www.caregiver.org

Family Caregiver Alliance: offers updates on diseases, online support groups, excellent articles, and an opportunity to ask questions of leaders in the field of caregiving.

http://www.CAREgiverMag.com

Caregiver Chicago. Provides information on products, services, facilities, activities, treatments, providers, and community, all on a local basis.

www.cms.hhs.gov

Centers for Medicare and Medicaid Services (CMS).

(877) 267-2323

http://www.columbiaals.org/

Columbia University MDA/ALS Research Center. Links to newsletter and other informative materials.

http://www.ccals.org/home.php

Compassionate Care ALS (CCALS)'s mission is to model compassion to those affected by ALS by providing educational and legal resources, respite opportunities, instruction and guidance, subsidy of living aids and assistance, and intimate dialogue with patients and their caregivers, families, and friends.

http://dailystrength.org/

A network of people sharing advice, treatment experiences, and support.

http://www.extrahands.org/index.asp

Extra Hands for ALS is a national voluntary service charity assisting people with ALS. It was designed to help people with ALS and their families, while simultaneously building awareness of the disease through the students who volunteer to visit them.

http://www.geocities.com/freyerse

World Wide Database for PLS/HSP/ALS. This site is for the benefit of those who have a diagnosis of primary lateral sclerosis (PLS), hereditary spastic paraplegia (HSP), and amyotrophic lateral sclerosis (ALS). The intent is to provide a means for facilitating communication and information exchange for patients and caregivers impacted by these relatively rare motor neuron disorders.

http://www.healthboards.com/

Connect with others with the same health conditions.

http://www.inspire.com/

Health and wellness support groups.

http://www.lesturnerals.org

Les Turner ALS Foundation.

http://www.lesturner.org/resourceguide.htm

Les Turner ALS Foundation Resource Guide. The third edition of the Les Turner ALS Foundation Resource Guide provides information and resources for patients with ALS, family members, caregivers, and health professionals.

http://www.march-of-faces.org/newsite/home.html

The ALS March of Faces is a patient/caregiver-governed and -operated nonprofit organization, dedicated to heightening public awareness of ALS and advocating on issues that concern and/or benefit PALS (people with ALS).

http://www.mdausa.org

MDA: A branch of the MDA is dedicated to ALS. Lots of information, resources, and publications are available for patients and their caregivers.

http://web.mit.edu/workplacecenter/

The goal of this site is to build a mutually supportive relationship between the performance of firms and the well-being of employees, their families, and their communities.

http://www.mndassocation.org/full-site/home.html

The only national organization in England, Wales, and Northern Ireland dedicated to the support of people with MND and those who care for hem.

http://www.projectals.org

Project ALS is a not-for-profit organization dedicated to finding a cure for and raising awareness about ALS.

http://www.rideforlife.com

Up-to-the-minute research news, events, and resources for patients and caregivers.

www.ssa.gov/disability

Social Security Administration.

(800) 772-1213

http://www.wellspouse.org

Well Spouse Foundation: A national, not-for-profit membership organization that provides support to wives, husbands, and partners of the chronically ill and/or disabled and has support groups that meet monthly.

http://www.wfnals.org/

World Federation of Neurology Amyotrophic Lateral Sclerosis. Links researchers and clinicians worldwide to find a cause and cure for ALS.

## Forums

http://www.alsconnection.com/

ALS Connection. An ALS registry sponsored by the MDA that is used to evaluate variations in patient care, adherence to standards of care, and also to help foster ALS research. An additional focus of this Web site is to educate participating patients and visitors to this site about ongoing ALS research.

http://www.alsforums.com/

All-volunteer-driven resource providing support for those directly or indirectly affected by ALS.

http://www.alsindependence.com/

This site is dedicated to Canadians with ALS and their loved ones.

http://www.als.net/forum/

ALSTDI forum.

The purpose of this forum is to exchange information about ALS, scientific advances in ALS, and treatments for ALS.

http://brain.hastypastry.net/forums/forumdisplay.php?f=82&daysprune=-1 &order=desc&sort=lastpost

BrainTalk Communities.

Online community open to the public to participate in bulletin boards and chats on many different topics including a forum on ALS.

http://www.alsforums.com/

The ALS forum is an all-volunteer-driven resource provided free of charge to help anyone directly or indirectly affected by ALS and MND.

http://neurotalk.psychcentral.com/

Forums on a wide variety of subjects including health-related issues, pets, classifieds, social chats, and a creative corner.

http://www.patientslikeme.com

An online community that offers support and discussion for patients.

http://health.groups.yahoo.com/group/living-with-als/

Yahoo Health Group: Living With ALS.

An avenue for persons living with ALS and their caregivers to communicate with the ALS community immediately, to share information, ideas, support, and fellowship.

http://www.inspire.com/groups/als-advocacy/

The ALS Advocacy Support Community.

Connects patients, families, friends, and caregivers for support and inspiration.

## DVDs

Free to patients/family members from the ALS Association, http://www.alsa.org/

1. *Living With ALS: Mobility, Activities of Daily Living, Home Adaptations*
2. *Adjusting to Swallowing Difficulties and Maintaining Good Nutrition*
3. *Adapting to Breathing Changes and the Use of Noninvasive Ventilation*
4. *Communication Solutions and Symptom Management*
5. *Clinical Care Management Discussions Among ALS Experts*

## Videos

*Ventilation: The Decision Making Process.* The Les Turner ALS Foundation

A 20-minute video designed for patients with ALS, their family members, and health professionals. It includes interviews with 3 patients with ALS who are ventilator-dependent, family members, and the medical staff from Lois Insolia ALS Center at Northwestern University Medical School.

To order: The Les Turner Foundation
8142 N. Lawndale
Skokie, IL 60076
(847) 679-3311

## Books

*ALS: Lou Gehrig's Disease.* By: Mary Dodson Wade. Enslow Publishers, 2001

From the Diseases and People series. Wade recaps the tragic story of Lou Gehrig then addresses the historical, scientific, and medical information about ALS.—Booklist

*Amyotrophic Lateral Sclerosis.* Edited by: Hiroshi Mitsumoto, MD, Serge Przedborski, PhD, and Paul H. Gordon, MD. Informa Health Care, 2005

Cutting-edge contributions from internationally recognized experts and field pioneers. ALS is the definitive guide to the subject.—amazon.com

*Amyotrophic Lateral Sclerosis.* Second Edition. Edited by: Robert Brown, MD, Michael Swash, MD, and Piera Pasinelli, PhD. Informa Healthcare, 2006

This book is an excellent review of amyotrophic lateral sclerosis with respect to clinical features, pathologic findings, functional and psychological studies, pathogenesis, therapeutic approaches, and patient care.—Massachusetts Medical Society

*Amyotrophic Lateral Sclerosis.* By: Robert G. Miller, MD, Deborah Gelinas, MD, and Patricia O'Connor, RN. Demos Medical Publishing, 2004

You'll find answers to all [your ALS] questions and more in this highly readable book.—MDA/ALS Newsmagazine

*Caring and Coping When Your Loved One Is Seriously Ill.* By: Earl Grollman. Beacon Press, 1995

In his gentle, straightforward style, Earl Grollman shows how you can best support the person who is ill—and handle your own emotions too.—amazon.com

*Communication and Swallowing Solutions for the ALS/MND Community.* By: Marta S. Kazandjian. Singular, 1996

The professionals of communication independence for the Neurologically Impaired (CINI), have come together to create this outstanding resource manual.—amazon.com

*Easy to Swallow, Easy to Chew Cookbook: Over 150 Tasty Recipes for People Who Have Difficulty Swallowing.* By: Donna L. Weihofen, JoAnne Robbins, and Paula A. Sullivan. Wiley, 2002

Presents a collection of more than 150 nutritious recipes that make eating enjoyable and satisfying for anyone who has difficulty chewing or swallowing.—amazon.com

*Handbook of Clinical Neurology: Motor Neuron Disorders and Related Diseases.* Edited by: Andrew Eisen and Pamela Shaw. Elsevier, 2007

Deals with the remarkable advances that have occurred in recent years in the understanding of these disorders and their underlying molecular pathogenesis.—amazon.com

*How to Help Children Through a Parent's Serious Illness.* By: Kathleen McCue, MA, CCLS, with Ron Bonn. St. Martin's Press, 1996

This practical handbook prepares parents to address children's fears with absolute honest and profound empathy.—Booklist

*How Will They Know If I'm Dead? Transcending Disability and Terminal Illness.* By: Robery Horn. CRC, 1996

The book is both realistic about living with ALS and inspiring.—Quest

*The I Can't Chew Cookbook.* By: J. Randy Wilson and Mark A. Piper. Hunter House, 2003

Of special interest are the opening chapters on nutrition and tips for getting the most out of meals, including enhancing the dining experience and adapting foods for a soft-food diet when dealing with the problems of swallowing and/or chewing.—Midwest Book Review

*I Choose to Live: A Journey Through Life With ALS.* By William Sinton. Banbury Publishing Company, 2002

Uplifting and inspirational.—amazon.com

*I Remember Running: The Year I Got Everything I Ever Wanted—and ALS.* By: Darcy Wakefield and Jonathan Eig. Marlowe and Company, 2006

Darcy's story of change and loss and challenges during her first years with ALS, as she struggles to make sense of her diagnosis, redefine herself in the face of terminal illness.—amazon.com

*If They Could Only Hear Me: A Collection of Personal Stories About ALS and the Families that Have Been Affected.* By: Ed Rice. BookSurge Publishing, 2005

A collection that brings awareness to ALS.—amazon.com

*In My Dreams. . . I Do!* By: Linda Saran

A children's book describing how two sisters escape the world of their mother's physical limitations from ALS to the freedom of their dream realm where anything is possible.

*Lou Gehrig: The Luckiest Man.* By: David A. Adler and Terry Widener. Gulliver Books, Harcourt Brace, 2001

An illustrated children's book about Lou Gehrig to help explain ALS to children.

*Morrie: In His Own Words.* By: Morrie Shwartz. Walker & Co., 1999.

Holds wisdom not only for those struggling with a terminal or debilitating condition but also for families and friends who must come to grips with letting go.—Booklist

*Motor Neuron Disease: A Family Affair (Overcoming Common Problems).* By: David Oliver. Sheldon Press, 1995

Dr. David Oliver spells out what the disease is, what the doctors will do, how to cope with the difficulties, what the future holds, and the role of carers and support agencies. He shows how to treat not just the physical effects, but also the emotional ones for the whole family.

*The Motor Neuron Disease Handbook.* Edited by: Matthew C. Kiernan, PhD. Prince of Wales Clinical School, 2007

*Palliative Care in Amyotrophic Lateral Sclerosis: From Diagnosis to Bereavement.* Edited by: David Oliver, Gian Domenico Borasio, and Declan Walsh. Oxford University Press, 2006

*Share the Care: How to Organize a Group to Care for Someone Who Is Seriously Ill.* By: Cappy Capossela, Sheila Warnock, and Sukie Miller. Fireside, 2004

Aimed at use by organized groups, it may also be of great value to individuals in need of a plan of action or background information.—amazon.com

*Tomato Juice. A Tribute to My Mom: A Journey About Progressive Bulbar Palsy (ALS).* By: Diane Hamilton. Book Surge Publishing, 2006

In a loving month-by-month tribute, Hamilton offers patients and caregivers advice, suggestions, and heartwarming anecdotes.—amazon.com

*Tuesdays With Morrie.* By: Mitch Albom. Broadway, 2002

A Detroit Free Press journalist and best-selling author recounts his weekly visit with a dying teacher who years before had set him straight.—amazon.com

## Manuals

*Everyday Life With ALS: A Practical Guide* MDA, 2005
To order: ALS Division
Muscular Dystrophy Association
3300 E Sunrise Drive
Tucson, AZ 85718

## Newsletters

MDA/ALS Newsmagazine

Editor: Christina Medvescek

publications@mdausa.org

# Index